* "Like 2002's well-received V̶o̶y̶a̶g̶e̶ P9-CQG-129
this second novel in Australian author McMullen's Moonworlds Saga expertly blends fantastic melodrama and broad
farce . . . the book is especially attractive for its tricky shifts
from dark, passionate intrigue to sly but rowdy slapstick,
like a Storm Constantine plotline performed by Monty
Python. There may be a lot of story to come before the
world's balance of magical powers is restored, but the read-
ers won't mind if additional books in the series are as interesting as this one."   —*Publishers Weekly* (starred review)

"This one is much better than its predecessor, which was
pretty good itself, and suddenly McMullen is threatening to
emerge as one of the leading names in fantasy." —*Chronicle*

"Australian author McMullen depicts a world filled with intrigue and strange magic . . . His sometimes whimsical, always literate style brings a gentle touch of wry humor to a
tale of courage and cowardice, love and death, mystery and
magic."   —*Library Journal*

"A complicated and fast-moving tale of unlikely heroes . . .
fans of Terry Pratchett and Douglas Adams will appreciate
McMullen's dry wit, shifting points of view and almost
complete disregard of fantasy conventions, making for a
highly entertaining and far from typical fantasy adventure."
                                        —*Romantic Times*

"A captivating and unique blend of fantasy, comedy, cloak
and dagger, sword and sorcery, blood and thunder and almost
any other pair of linked icons you care to name . . . Such is
McMullen's expertise at action-packed scenes, so admirable
is his spare yet evocative prose, and so fecund is his sense of
invention, that you will finish this book in a gallop, eager for
a third foray into the Moonworlds realm."   —*Scifi.com*

"A boisterous entertainment, as spectacular as its memorable predecessor, *Voyage of the Shadowmoon* . . . McMullen's heady and headstrong brand of fantastic adventure is
sure to remain addictive, and I for one will follow its siren
call anywhere."   —*Locus*

PRAISE FOR
Voyage of the Shadowmoon,
Book One in the Moonworlds Saga:

* "A brilliantly inventive, marvelously plotted sea-faring fantasy." —*Kirkus Reviews* (starred review)

"*Voyage of the Shadowmoon* provides pleasures familiar from his earlier offerings: secret agents and ruthlessly ambitious adventurers in an epic-size story with a large cast and plenty of surprises in the who's-really-who department. It is a rambling and complicated tale, simultaneously busy and leisurely, woven through the several voyages of the spy vessel of the title . . . We are treated to plots, crossplots, intrigues, betrayals, reconciliations, murders, massacres, genocide, secret identities, unmaskings, rescues, and paybacks—and also to displays of loyalty, courage, romance, and chivalry. A pleasure to read." —*Locus*

"One of Australia's most inventive sf authors demonstrates his prodigious talent for fantasy in a standalone novel that belongs in most libraries. Highly recommended."
—*Library Journal*

"This novel represents world-building fantasy at its finest; complex characters and world-altering plots are interwoven to create a tapestry of great intricacy. McMullen is an expert craftsman whose stories will engage any fantasy lover, particularly those who enjoy such works are George R.R. Martin's *Game of Thrones* series . . . This fantasy novel will be popular anywhere that epic fantasy is in demand." —*VOYA*

"A marvelously unpredictable and intricate story, full of swashbuckling intrigue and adventure on a grand scale."
—*Publishers Weekly*

"With the Aussie-style rowdiness McMullen showed in his earlier Greatwinter trilogy, it's a fun read."
—*San Diego Union-Tribune*

GLASS
DRAGONS

TOR BOOKS BY SEAN MCMULLEN

THE CENTURION'S EMPIRE

SOULS IN THE GREAT MACHINE

THE MIOCENE ARROW

EYES OF THE CALCULOR

VOYAGE OF THE SHADOWMOON

GLASS DRAGONS

GLASS DRAGONS

Sean McMullen

A TOM DOHERTY ASSOCIATES BOOK
NEW YORK

NOTE: If you purchased this book without a cover, you should be aware that this book is stolen property. It was reported as "unsold and destroyed" to the publisher, and neither the author nor the publisher has received any payment for this "stripped book."

This is a work of fiction. All the characters and events portrayed in this book are either products of the author's imagination or are used fictitiously.

GLASS DRAGONS

Copyright © 2004 by Sean McMullen

All rights reserved, including the right to reproduce this book, or portions thereof, in any form.

Edited by Jack Dann
Map by Ellisa Mitchell

A Tor Book
Published by Tom Doherty Associates, LLC
175 Fifth Avenue
New York, NY 10010

www.tor.com

Tor® is a registered trademark of Tom Doherty Associates, LLC.

ISBN 0-765-34708-3
EAN 978-0765-34708-4

First edition: March 2004
First mass market edition: February 2005

Printed in the United States of America

0 9 8 7 6 5 4 3 2 1

*For my mother,
who taught me to
appreciate the
importance of good
manners, and my older
brothers, who taught
me to appreciate
good parties*

ACKNOWLEDGMENTS

Thanks to my wife, Trish, and daughter, Catherine, who drove the support car when I researched Wallas and Andry's trek.

Thanks to Alexander Albert, Mike Dyal Smith, Paul Collins, and numerous others at the Melbourne University karate and fencing clubs for workshopping the action scenes.

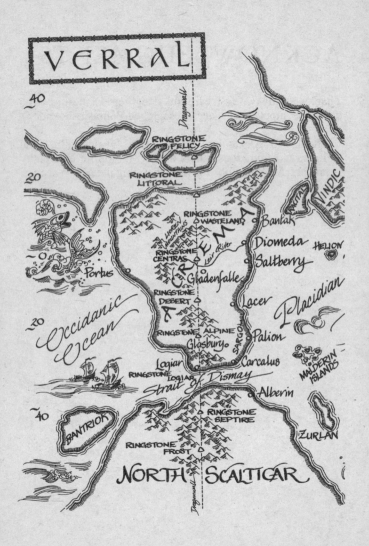

VERRAL

40

Dragonneck

RINGSTONE FELICY

RINGSTONE LITTORAL

20

Occidanic Ocean

20

Portus

LOREN MOUNTAINS

RINGSTONE WASTELAND

RINGSTONE CENTRAS

Gladenfalle

RINGSTONE DEBERT

RINGSTONE ALPINE

Glosbury

CREMA

Banlak

Lux River

Diomeda

Saltberry

Lacer

Sargo

Palion

VINDIC

VRITAL

HELION

Placidian

Logiar

RINGSTONE LOGIAR

Strait of Dismay

Carcalus

Alberin

MALDERIN ISLANDS

40

BANTRIOK

RINGSTONE SEPTIRE

RINGSTONE FROST

NORTH SCALTICAR

ZURLAN

Dragonneck

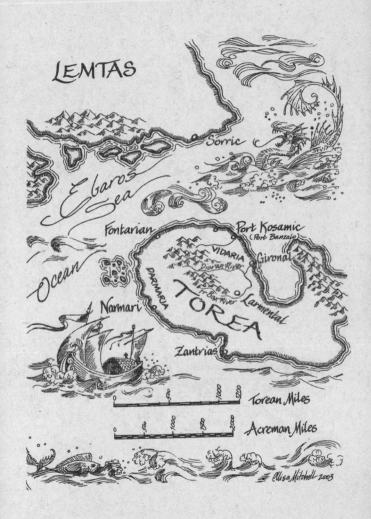

LEMTAS

Sorric

Ebaros Sea

Fontarian

Ocean

Port Kosamic
(Port Banzalo)

VIDARIA

Gironal

Dioran River

DARMARIA

Mirr Box River

TOREA

Larmental

Narmari

Zantrias

500   1000   1200
                                    Torean Miles

50   1000   1500   2000
                                    Acreman Miles

Ellisa Mitchell 2003

CONTENTS

Prologue 1

1. Dragonscheme 11
2. Dragonstrike 62
3. Dragonwall 106
4. Dragonslayer 145
5. Dragonbird 221
6. Dragonschool 262
7. Dragonfright 335
8. Dragonchick 392
9. Dragongirl 438
10. Dragonbirth 482

Epilogue 525

PROLOGUE

 Even though the streets of Alberin were being lashed by a rainstorm and the wind was so strong that one could not walk through the gusts in a straight line, the two men who emerged from the mansion were relieved to be outside again. They never once looked back as they hurried to the outer gates of the grounds, and they ignored a guard who cheerily waved a bottle at them as they walked out into the street.

"I would like to point out that recruiting *her* to our cause was *your* idea, Talberan," said the taller of the pair.

"I had heard that she is eccentric, but this was too much," admitted his companion.

"Serving men in rabbit-fur G-strings, serving maids in faun costumes, and as for what she and her guests were wearing! Had I not seen it, I would not have believed it."

"Are you sure that she is North Scalticar's most powerful sorceress, Lavolten?"

"There is no doubt of that. Lady Wensomer Callientor is also the only person in history ever to have refused a regrading to initiate thirteen. She said that 'initiate twelve' sounds elegant, and 'initiate fourteen' has grandeur, but 'initiate thirteen' has no style at all and she refused to have it after her name."

The storm had not dampened the nightlife of Alberin, it had merely moved it indoors. Music, pipe smoke, and laughter poured out of warmly lit taverns as they hurried along, and the wind flung the scent of baking bread or roasting meat past them from time to time. A drunken apprentice came staggering along the street, a bottle in one hand and a tin flute in the other. Talberan and Lavolten separated to let him past.

> "I wish I was in Alberin town,
> When'er I'm down on me luck.
> A lad's always welcome in Alberin town—"

They turned when the singing stopped abruptly, and noted that the youth had walked straight into a parked wagon and collapsed in a flooded gutter.

"He is already in Alberin, why does he sing about wishing he were here?" asked Lavolten.

"Degenerate nonsense, just like that sorceress. We offered her the chance to command the winds themselves!"

"She said she would rather command her guests to swap partners every half hour."

"To rule the world."

"She said that she had been to lots of revels staged by rulers, and they were not nearly as good as her revels."

"To be immortal."

"She said that she knew plenty of immortals, and they were all boring."

"I mean, what does the woman want?" Lavolten demanded of the rainswept darkness, throwing up his hands in exasperation.

"She told us, Lavolten. She wants the secret of weight loss without exercise or dieting."

"Did she not understand that we were offering her the chance to become a goddess?"

"She said that gods all had beautiful bodies and narrow waists, and that being made a god sounded suspiciously like she would have to diet and exercise."

They turned off into an alley. Talons that glowed faintly blue burst from the toes of their boots and the fingers of their gloves, then they began to crawl straight up a sheer brick wall.

"Who should we try next?" asked Talberan as they climbed.

"Someone old, someone who has nothing more to hope for from life, yet someone with ideals."

"Astential?"

"Yes, the initiate fourteen. He is eighty-one, and takes no interest in the delights of the flesh. He should quickly give in to temptation."

"Unlike that immoral glutton of a sorceress. Can you believe it? She flung our offer back at us because she said it was not at all interesting."

They climbed over the edge of the wall and onto the roof, and that was the last of their stay in Alberin. The next day a tiler checking a blocked downpipe found two cloaks washed into the roof's guttering. They were new, and had the stamp of a local tailor. Nearby were two purses, both containing twenty silver nobles. Being a practical and sensible man who was not inclined to bother the constables with trivia, he kept the silver, packed away the cloaks and purses to sell in the market, and charged the owner of the building for unblocking the pipe. By this time Talberan and Lavolten were on another continent, and having a very productive meeting with a wise, powerful, and temperate sorcerer who felt that he was admirably suited to wield the powers of a god.

The ringstone site was not merely old, it was exceedingly ancient. It had last been used before the first cities had been built, but now it was no more than a circular mound, one hundred yards in diameter.

The three elderly riders who halted at the site were under the escort of a dozen mercenary cavalrymen, and had half a dozen laborers trailing after them. Unlike their guards, the old men carried no weapons and wore no armor. The mercenaries watched with no particular interest as they unpacked their saddlebags, then began to trace out the dimensions of the ancient mound with pegs and strings. One supervised the laborers, who were set digging three holes in the mound. They could not have called themselves the world's first archeologists, because the word had not yet been invented, but that was what they were.

"This mound is mentioned in chronicles known to be thousands of years old," said the man with the longest beard, as he tapped a marker peg into the ground.

His companion took a scroll from a sling bag, unrolled it, and began reading.

"Devil mound . . . cursed place . . . place of death . . . said to increase virility if one lies on the summit during a solstice at dawn and—"

"All of that is folklore and hedgerow magic, Waldesar. We are concerned with its original purpose."

"Older than any kingdom or city," continued his companion. "Ah! Very significant."

Before long the sorcerer-archeologists had the circular mound mapped and measured, and were making observations of the sun's elevation, position, and movement. Two nearby goatherds also noted the sun's position, decided that it was noon, and sat down for lunch.

"They try to seem like nobles," said the shorter goatherd, inclining his head to the visitors.

"Aye," replied his companion, scratching beneath his false beard. "But nobles try to look noble, so they wear fine clothes and have a pack of hounds to chase game and bite peasants. Those three wear fine clothes, but have no weapons, hounds, or crests."

"Sorcerers, then?"

"Aye, and they study an ancient site of power."

"Very significant."

Not far away, a woodcutter and carter were loading windfall branches onto an oxcart.

"The two with the strings and pegs are Most Learned Astential and Learned Waldesar," said the woodcutter.

"And the one having the holes dug?" asked the carter.

"Hard to say, can't get a clear look at his face. He spends too much time on his knees, looking into the holes, but he's younger than the other two."

"Learned Sergal is only seventy, and practices the cold sciences as well as magic."

"But Learned Sergal hates Learned Waldesar."

"Very true, but if Sergal and Waldesar are working together . . ."

"Very significant."

Upon the ancient ringstone mound itself, two lovers were lying in each other's arms in the grass.

"Astential, Waldesar, and Sergal," whispered the girl as the boy kissed her ear.

"They keep mentioning Dragonwall," whispered the boy, who had exceptionally good hearing.

"Dragonwall was an ancient etheric engine used to turn men into gods, so that they could control the winds. Its secret was lost."

"Perhaps these folk have a mind to be gods too."

"Very significant."

On the summit of a nearby mountain, a pigeon trapper paused for a drink. Closer inspection would have revealed that the bottom of his bottle contained a lens, and that he had the neck to his eye.

"That's enough," said his companion. "You couldn't drink from a bottle for as long as that."

"They have the site mapped out," he reported as he lowered the farsight. "They have placed seventeen pegs: sixteen in an outer ring, and one at the center."

"Very significant."

Most Learned Astential and Learned Waldesar sat down beside Learned Sergal's hole at the summit of the mound. Two of them had the curiously excited yet restrained manner of people who had achieved something stunningly important, yet did not want anyone else to know.

"The news is good," announced Sergal, holding up a slate.

"How can it be good?" asked Waldesar. "We are looking for a depression lined with melted sand a foot thick. This is a mound."

"My diggings show that this is indeed a depression one hundred paces in diameter. It was deliberately filled in five thousand years ago. Look down the hole. Fifteen feet down to a layer of melted sand, and the last five feet are *below* the level of the surrounding countryside. My outer trench is only two feet deep, and there is a lip of fused sand and stones one foot higher than this floodplain."

"Then it's definitely the site of a Dragonwall ringstone!" exclaimed Astential. "It is lined with melted glass, one hundred paces across, five feet deep at the center, and surrounded by a circular lip one foot high."

"Someone hid this site!" declared Waldesar, ever anxious to agree with his master while saying something intelligent. "No wonder it was lost for so long."

"Yes, yes, and now we have located them all," continued Astential. "We shall have to empty out the soil, of course, but that needs only horses, carts, and laborers."

"Why would the builders have filled it in, most learned master?" Sergal asked Astential.

"The builders?" laughed Waldesar. "Why it might have been filled in by anyone at any time over the past five thousand years."

"I deal in proof and certainty," answered Sergal, "and I have proof of both this ringstone's age, and when it was filled in."

"Proof?" laughed Waldesar. "You cannot prove anything's age, except by records."

"Oh no?" asked Sergal, pointing to the side of his trench with a quill. "Then what do these bands tell us?"

Sergal pointed to several alternating layers of dark and light soil. Waldesar stared at the layers for a moment, then turned to Astential.

"This is beyond me, most learned one," he admitted. "Can you deduce the message?"

Sergal was not yet aware that Waldesar had neatly sidestepped his attack, and was forcing him to make a fool of Astential.

"What spell must I cast to see the meaning behind them?" asked Astential.

"Oh, only common sense is needed," began Sergal; then his voice faltered.

Sergal was known for his scholarly brilliance, but diplomacy was not his strong point. It was now a little late, but even Sergal was suddenly aware that he had just told the world's

only initiate of the fourteenth level to use common sense—
and that Astential was getting nowhere by doing so. Astential
began to allow the first signs of a frown onto his face.

"Well, actually, nothing magical is needed, nothing magical at all!" Sergal added hastily. "But, er, during my historical readings concerning this area I learned that there is a
volcano twenty miles away. It erupts every six centuries, and
is, ah, something of a curiosity, as volcanoes go. Volcanoes
are somewhat irregular, you see."

"Please come to the point, Learned Sergal," said Astential, annoyed enough to address the lower initiate formally.

"Well there are nine layers of ash in the dirt above the
river silt that someone used to fill in the depression. Nine
times six centuries is five thousand four hundred years. That
is roughly the age that the chronicles give for the Dragonwall machine."

Astential stroked his chin, which was always his reaction
when he was very excited about something but trying hard
not to show it. He took out a small book. Its covers had been
recently fashioned from ivory and gold, but the pages were of
exceedingly old parchment, and the writing was very faint.

"... and four thousand years before Logiar was built,
there was the ringstone of Dragonwall, which made wise men
as gods, so that they commanded the very winds." Astential
translated. "Logiar is known to be fifteen hundred years old,
so that makes five thousand five hundred years. That is passably close as a match. Good work, Learned Sergal."

"Ah, perhaps the sorcerers who became gods filled it in,"
said Waldesar, hastily abandoning his indefensible position. "They must not have wanted others to use their ether
machine."

"Then why were the others not filled in?" asked Sergal
with theatrical impatience.

"Because all seventeen ringstones are needed for the ether
machine to work. Hide one, and the rest are useless!"

"The sorcerer-gods removed the ringstones from every
site, that was enough to disable them," retorted Sergal.
"Why bury just one—"

"Gentlemen, please!" exclaimed Astential. "Some local
chieftain might have had the site buried out of superstitious

fear. We cannot know everything, but everything does not need to be known."

Astential seemed outwardly calm, yet he was fighting the urge to go running about in circles with his hands in the air, cheering. All the Dragonwall ringstone sites had now been located. Nothing stood between him and the reconstruction of Dragonwall, aside from commissioning the construction of two hundred and eighty-nine megaliths, eight hundred and sixteen chairs with stone seats, and the recruitment of eleven hundred and two more sorcerers.

"The soil covering this ringstone site must be removed," he said as he leaned over and peered into Sergal's excavation again.

"Oh, I could organize for that to be done," said Waldesar at once.

"And guards will be needed."

"I know the local regent, most learned sir, I could talk him around to it."

"An encampment will need to be built."

"I shall meet the cost with funds from my own estate."

It was no secret that Waldesar wanted to be regraded to initiate level thirteen, just as it was no secret that Sergal actually deserved to be regraded to that level. As the only living initiate of the fourteenth level, Astential could perform such regradings alone. The alternative was to wait for a meeting of the Board of Acreman Sorceric Examiners. Those meetings took place only once a decade, and the next meeting was eight years away. Astential needed the skills of both men. Waldesar was the better administrator, but Sergal commanded far more respect in sorceric circles. *Best to keep them both dangling*, he decided.

"Learned Sergal, there is still the matter of sorcerers to give life to Dragonwall," Astential said as he got to his feet. "Hundreds will be needed."

"Many will be reluctant," said Waldesar. "Why not just recruit those who show enthusiasm? I could have letters sent this very day."

"Because we must populate *all seventeen* ringstones, Learned Waldesar," replied Astential with a frown. Waldesar cowered. His actual movement was the merest fraction of an inch, but it was still a cower. "With four shifts of primary sorcerers and reserves, that will require nearly *every* sorcerer *anywhere*. Learned Sergal, all in the sorceric circles respect your scholarship. Could you persuade *every* sorcerer to participate in the Dragonwall?"

"I shall look upon it as a personal challenge, most learned sir," replied Sergal.

"Splendid, splendid. Learned gentlemen, when Dragonwall has been rebuilt, it will be no surprise which of you will preside as ringmaster at this ringstone round."

Both initiates were aware that the first squad of ancients to be transformed into gods were said to have destroyed Dragonwall and barred the way to all others. Astential was confident that they would race each other in order to be included among the first sorcerers to use the Dragonwall, and that their work would be done all the sooner because of it.

The goatherds continued with their lunch as they watched the sorcerers pack, then go their separate ways.

"Interesting, they split up," observed the shorter man.

"I think they found what they wanted," said his bearded companion.

"Very significant."

"We should report this to the emperor."

"Those goatherds have just abandoned their goats," observed the timber cutter.

"Spies," replied the carter.

"Very significant."

"I'll report back to the Councilium, you tell the Logiar regent."

"This double agenting will get us hanged one day."

"But in the meantime it gets us paid double."

The pair of lovers were still a tangle of intertwined limbs in the grass as they watched the timber cutter and carter hurrying on their separate ways.

"Those timber cutters have abandoned their timber," said the girl.

"Councilium spies, without a doubt," said the youth.

"Very significant. We must inform the castellan."

"Those lovers seem to have lost interest in each other rather quickly," said a pigeon trapper to his companion as they sat looking over the site from the slopes of the mountain.

"Alpennien spies, like I said," said his companion, peering through the bottle-farsight.

"They also had horses hidden, ready for a hasty departure."

"Very significant. Time for us to make a hasty departure as well."

An hour after the sun had set, an itinerant tinker lay under a tree, settling down for the night. He was wrapped in his trail cloak and using his pack as a pillow as he twisted the spigot of his wineskin and swallowed several mouthfuls.

"Ah, but it's for the cold," he told nobody in particular.

The immense, green disk of Miral shone down from nearly overhead, its rings presented almost directly side-on. Suddenly the summit of the nearby mountain moved. The tinker blinked. Amid a shower of rubble and dust, a head appeared on a long, serpentine neck. The summit now stood up and shook itself, sending yet more cascades of dried mud and dust down the mountain's slopes. The thing was glowing faintly as it spread a pair of wings whose span was greater than the length of most ships. Silently, it launched itself into the air, then swooped low over the ancient ringstone site and turned out to sea. The tinker scratched his head, then twisted the spigot of his wineskin again and allowed the remaining contents to pour out onto the grass.

Chapter One

DRAGONSCHEME

On the night of the wedding of Princess Senterri to Viscount Cosseren, there was one thought that could not have been farther from the mind of the Master of Royal Music to the Emperor of Sargol. He had heard the saying *Great elevation brings the danger of a really, really long fall*, but he was sure that it could never apply to him.

Milvarios of Tourlossen had no real political power. He merely had to look dignified and make sure that nothing went wrong with the music to be played on important occasions. Being Master of the Royal Music meant that one had to know the emperor's tastes in music, be an excellent and efficient organizer of events, know which bards, minstrels, and players were in favor or on the way up, know all the court intrigues and gossip, dress well, and be able to hold one's drink. One very seldom had to sing, compose, or play an instrument, but this suited Milvarios, because he did neither of the first two particularly well, and did not play any better than those he hired to play for the emperor. He was, however, a meticulous and efficient organizer.

The wedding music had been played without so much as a single sour note, broken string, or missed cue. The ceremony itself took place in the palace temple, and required brass bands for the processions, marches, and fanfares. The lavish reception in the throne hall featured a string consort for the feasting, and a woodwind band for the dances. None of that was as exposed as the music in the temple, so that even though the night was not quite over, Milvarios was already beginning to relax. He had spent eleven hours either posing with nobles and royalty as solemn words were chanted, or frantically scurrying about behind the scenes waving schedules, and making sure that dozens of musicians and hundreds of singers were in the right places at the appropriate times, and all with the correct music in front of them.

The career of Milvarios of Tourlossen, Master of Royal Music, had precisely nine minutes and fifty-seven seconds to go before experiencing a quite catastrophic and spectacular termination.

❊ ❊ ❊

Elsewhere in the palace, a tiny problem had emerged that had the potential to sour the occasion far worse than broken strings or missed cues. The bridal suite of the newlywed couple was in a tower that overlooked the harbor. The tower had been emptied of all servants, guards, and courtiers, and the base was heavily guarded. All of this was to guarantee privacy to Senterri and Cosserin for the night that was to be theirs and theirs alone.

Viscount Cosseren had a physique that many young women swooned over. Being from a family of considerable means, he had spent much of his life riding, hunting, and learning to excel with every weapon deemed suitable for a gentleman. Most courtiers agreed, however, that he had probably forgotten to stand in the queue when common sense was being handed out. Still, being too stupid to be ambitious or rebellious had a certain attraction about it as far as the emperor was concerned. As far as Princess Senterri was concerned, it was a very different matter. She was sitting naked on the enormous matrimonial bed, her arms wrapped around her legs while she sobbed behind the veils of brunette hair that concealed her face.

"I have never, never been so insulted!" muttered Cosseren as he laced up his shirt. "Not a virgin! I know about virgins, I've bedded dozens, there's nothing you can teach me about virgins. Why, and, and you, lost it to a common slaver, too!"

"My lord, *please listen*!" Senterri pleaded. "He was my *rescuer*, not a slaver."

"Slaver, rescuer, what difference does it make? You have been defiled by some upstart of low degree."

"He was a gentleman."

"Gentleman! A mere kavelar can be called a gentleman. What was his family's estate?"

"He was from North Scalticar—"

"A foreigner too! I am going, and I am sure that your father will be very interested to hear how you lied about your, ah, honor's status."

Cosseren strode to the door, flung it open, and slammed it shut behind him. He had taken only a dozen steps when something detached itself from the shadows of an arched brickwork vault and knocked him to the stone floor.

Viscount Cosseren awoke to find himself staring into a very pale face. The thing's eyes flickered with just the trace of a bluish glow, and its mouth was slightly open in a shallow smile. Cosseren had a vague impression that it was a girl of some description. He also wished that she were not smiling, because it exposed her two upper canine teeth. They were three times longer than they should have been, and they also glowed slightly. Although she was lightly built, she was holding Cosseren by the throat, at arm's length, with one hand. The young viscount glanced down. The drop to the courtyard was at least a hundred feet. There were guards patrolling there, but none were looking up. There was a suggestion of mildew and rotting meat on the air.

"Senterri, is upset," the apparently female daemon declared in a silky whisper. "You caused. Senterri, my friend."

"Who . . . you?" managed Cosseren.

"Myself, am very evil. Senterri nice to me, once. Grateful. Senterri, *you* hurt."

"Szzoorrgrinniy," the rapidly choking Cosseren answered as the grip on his throat tightened.

"Having any idea, how more strong, than you, am being?"

"Gnnng."

"Not drop you. Is only terror, for making. *But . . .*"

"Bnngeg?"

"But if not return Senterri, grovel, say sorry, do sexing, then . . ."

"Genng?"

"Rip throat. Suck blood. You, long time, for dying. Body never will found, be. Senterri merry widow, be. Or is joyous widow? Happy widow? Adjectives confusing."

Just around a nearby corner stood Senterri. She wore nothing but her hair and tears, and had been intending to run after Cosseren and plead with him not to dishonor her to her father. Now it had become obvious that her very strange friend was doing some rather more persuasive pleading. Cosseren was dragged back through the window and released. His wheezing gasps went on for quite a long time.

"You, to Senterri, back, go," said the menacing, silky voice with the strange and heavy accent. "If not return, I return. If Senterri sad, I return. If Senterri angry, I return. If no grovel, I return. If no sexing, I return. For you, very bad, if I return."

As he glanced at the common musicians in the string consort, Milvarios sneered in a discreet sort of way. In spite of the fine clothing they had been given, they still contrived to look just slightly scruffy. Some already looked drunk. On the other hand, Milvarios left nothing to chance, and he had selected his musicians for their ability to play well while drunk, as well as their ability to play well in the first place. One day his efficiency would see him rise to be seneschal of the imperial palace, he was sure of that.

For some reason Milvarios found himself staring at the man playing the angelwing lyre. He was tallish, with a neat black beard, curly hair, brown eyes, and long, thin fingers. He might have been the very image of Milvarios had he been about sixty pounds lighter. The man looked up and locked stares with Milvarios. There was suddenly something very alarming about him.

"My lord has had a great triumph tonight."

Milvarios turned to be confronted by a woman about ten years his senior. Other gentlemen of the court and diplomatic service had been paying her no heed, but Milvarios was motivated rather differently than the others. By paying court to women of palace society who were just a little past their prime, Milvarios generated goodwill, and had people speaking well of him when he was not there to speak well of himself.

"My lady Arrikin, you are a triumph by your very presence," responded Milvarios, bending to kiss her hand.

Widow, daughter soon to be married, spending massive amounts of gold on the wedding, wishes to impress the court, late husband made a fortune in camel-caravan speculation and bought a peerage flashed through Milvarios's mind.

"The emperor can certainly afford the best of everything," said Lady Arrikin, with a wave of her fan at the musicians.

"Ah, but I believe your most supremely lovely daughter is to be married next month. You must take care not to overshadow this lowly spectacle, you know what the penalties for treason are like."

Lady Arrikin smiled demurely. "It was on that very subject that I wished to speak with you. What would you charge to put your quill to a bridal anthem?"

"My lady!" exclaimed Milvarios softly, placing a hand across his chest. "My quill may be put to use for no other than the emperor."

"My lord Milvarios, I am sure there are certain uses for your quill that the emperor would rather not know about," replied Lady Arrikin with a discreet flutter of her eyelashes.

"Well . . . perhaps I could at least share some inspiration with you in, perhaps, one hour, once the feast has reached a stage that requires no more supervision?"

"In your chamber, then, Lord Milvarios?"

"I could not countenance the delay of a journey to some more distant tryst, most excellent lady."

As he took his leave of her, Milvarios cast a glance over the musicians. All was well, except that the angelwing lyre was leaning against a chair, and its musician was nowhere to be seen. *On the other hand, nobody seems to be paying much attention to the music by now, so there is no harm done,* thought Milvarios. *My triumph is still complete.*

Except for the music, the wedding had been plagued by tiny, annoying problems. The acrobat who had leaped out of the cake modeled after the royal palace had stumbled, but not actually fallen. The groom had answered where the bride should have spoken in several parts of the ceremony. One of the horses in the guard of honor had voided its bowels during the fifty-yard parade across the courtyard from the palace temple to the reception portico. *Only my music has been truly without flaw*, thought Milvarios over and over. The emperor had been pleased indeed, and had promised to make him Herald of the Declaration. Now Milvarios had a bedmate to impress for the rest of the night. Although she was a little older than some might prefer, her skin was flawless and she was rumored to diet—and even exercise—in order to preserve her allure.

While Milvarios could not actually sell an anthem to Lady Arrikin, he could write it, then let rumors free that he *might* be the composer. By protocol and convention, he was then free to refuse to comment rather than flatly deny those rumors, *implying* that he had composed the anthem. This also implied the emperor's favor to the woman's daughter, which was the whole point of the exercise. The irony was that the anthem did not even have to be very good, as long as he refused to deny that he wrote it. At the very worst, Milvarios would spend a very pleasant night with Lady Arrikin, then pay some starving music student to ghost-write the anthem. Glancing around one last time, he decided that everything was going smoothly. Most present were getting drunk, eating too much, and flirting with each other's partners. Milvarios managed to catch the attention of the emperor, and was beckoned over.

"My lord musician, where would I be without you?" the monarch said softly as Milvarios bowed before him. "Such a myriad of petty annoyances with the wedding. Does it portend a similar clutch of vexing little problems with the marriage itself?"

"I cannot say, Your Majesty. I am a musician, not a seer."

"Only your music was without flaw. Now, surely you could read a meaning into that?"

"Perhaps . . ." began Milvarios, thinking very quickly. "Perhaps it means that the marriage will indeed be plagued by vexing little problems, but the couple will live in *harmony* in spite of it all."

The emperor smiled, then chuckled. It was his first sign of mirth for all of that day.

"Tell me, most harmonious friend, what is your experience of seneschal work?" he asked, smiling up at Milvarios.

"A music master must also be a seneschal, Your Majesty, but a seneschal need not be a musician."

"Oh clever, Milvarios, very clever. Now then, why did you want to see me?"

"I hoped to be granted leave to retire for the night, sire."

"Certainly, go to your bed at once and sleep deeply. I shall have some extra duties for you tomorrow, attend me at the hour before noon. Perchance you can bring some of your harmony to the running of the palace."

Milvarious felt that he was walking on air as he slipped away to prepare his quarters for his visitor. This would involve scattering important-looking scrolls and declarations about, for her to chance upon and find impressive, but soon his mere name would be vastly more impressive. The emperor was to appoint him as palace seneschal in a mere twelve hours.

He was not to know that the emperor had a mere three minutes and fifty-seven seconds to live.

Senterri hurried silently back to the matrimonial bedchamber, climbed onto the bed, and sat waiting for her husband to return. Presently she heard the cautious tread of leather-soled riding boots outside. The footsteps slowed. They stopped. A hand reached around and tapped on the open door.

"Yes?" said Senterri in a clear, sharp voice.

"Er, dearest petal, I, er, thought it over," said Cosseren, sidling into view.

"So I see," responded Senterri sternly.

Cosseren had thought that she would be almost hysterical with relief that he had returned. Senterri was not, in fact, sounding at all hysterical. This did not bode well.

"And I decided, that, well, you are so lovely that I could not dishonor you, so I have decided to forgive you and return to your bed."

Senterri turned her head to one side.

"That is a very sweet story," said Senterri, "but the finger marks on your throat tell me a rather different tale. *I* think that you have met a friend of mine, a friend who can climb sheer walls, is stronger than you and your horse combined, and has some awfully unsettling eating habits."

Cosseren put a hand to his throat and glanced hastily over his shoulder.

"Look, I, er, really am sorry," he replied. "Very sorry. Desperately sorry."

"Oh, but you will soon be sorrier, much, much sorrier," rasped Senterri. "You may not have had the chance to dishonor me in front of anyone else, Viscount Cosseren, but dishonor me you certainly did. Bedded dozens of virgins, have you? Well, if you so much as *smile* at another woman's *portrait* from now on, I shall be very angry. Do you know who will return if that happens?"

"Ya-ya-yes."

"And what is more, you will—as my daemon friend put it so charmingly—'do sexing' with me six times a night—"

"Six times? I say—"

"—until I become pregnant. Now take off your clothes and get into bed."

"Yes, my petal bowl, at once," babbled the viscount, kicking off his boots and literally tearing off his shirt. "But, but, *six times!*"

"Think of someone else if it helps, I shall certainly do so."

"Whatever you say, delight of my eyes."

"And Cosseren!"

"Yes, my petal storm?"

"That first time did not count for tonight."

Milvarios turned the ornate, three-tumbler key in the lock, then pushed the door open. It was as well never to rush through any palace door, especially one that had been locked. One might disturb someone in the process of making off with the silverware, and people of that kind tended to be armed. Milvarios glanced to the gold coin that he always left on the table. Were that missing, he would have pulled the door shut, locked it, and screamed for the guards. The coin was still there, however, and all that was moving within his suite of rooms were the flames in the fireplace and the shadows they cast on the walls. He entered, glanced about, closed the door, and turned the key in the lock.

Halfway across the room, he suddenly realized that the gold coin was no longer on the table.

"*Oh dear, I forgot to order a jar of expensive wine for my beloved and I to share tonight!*" exclaimed Milvarios in a voice that bordered on a shout, had suddenly become highly pitched, and was on the very edge of hysteria.

He turned, and was confronted by a rather thin, bearded mirror image of himself. The image slammed a fist into his plexus. The wheeze that Milvarios gave as he doubled over was barely audible. With the skill of one who did that sort of thing for a living, the intruder guided Milvarios down to lie in front of the hearth, then tied his wrists after looping his arms through the heavy iron bars that stopped burning logs from rolling out onto the floor. Next he gagged him, then tied his ankles.

"You came back a little early, Milvarios," said the intruder as he peeled off his beard. "I had expected you to spend at least another half hour brown-nosing with the emperor, but no matter."

Milvarios watched as the intruder lifted his robes and began to insert a framework of cane slats beneath. In a very short time the slats took the form of about sixty pounds of good living, and with the man's robes back in place and smoothed down, there was nothing to distinguish him from the Master of Royal Music in either form or face.

"You are probably wondering who I am," said the intruder in a soft, casual voice. "I cannot tell you that, but I can tell you about my identity. Actually, I stole my identity. It belonged to a peasant, but he was not making very good use of it."

The intruder walked out to another room, then returned with a small crossbow and a basket of flowers. Milvarios watched him cock the string, pour something from a phial onto a bolt, then load the weapon. He was a little puzzled when the intruder started clipping flowers onto the weapon, but suddenly he understood his purpose all too clearly.

"Who I am is of no importance, however," said the man who was not a peasant. "The peasant who provided my identity is working hard for the first time in his life, feeding the fish about half a mile out to sea, and may he have a good story for the gods to explain his transgressions in life. But enough of him. I used a very powerful casting to make my flesh as dough; then I fashioned my face to pass for yours. Now I shall *become* you for a minute or two, kill your monarch, then become the dead peasant again. You see, Milvarios, I do not exist."

He inspected the crossbow, which now resembled a bouquet.

"As I return, I shall accidentally lose my hood and cloak, and be recognized as you. Before I unbind you and remove that tiresome gag, I shall then pour a particularly subtle poison into your ear. The poison will soon have you crazed with pain, and you will go thrashing about and screaming as if in a rage. The guards will think you are fighting them, and they will kill you. Alas, Milvarios, I would like to leave you alive to face the wrath of the soon-to-be crown prince, but I cannot have you telling people to search for a peasant with your face, can I? You know, I do look forward to this part of each assassination. My reluctant doubles are the only people that I can ever tell about my skills and methods, and I do enjoy performing to an audience. No, please don't bother attempting to applaud."

He left. Milvarios looked about frantically, but saw nothing nearby that could aid him. He strained against his bonds, but his captor had done his work well, and they were as tight as a harp string. He could barely move; in fact, the early stages of cramp were taking hold of his left calf. He stretched his legs. This had the effect of pushing his hands closer to the flames. He quickly drew his legs back . . . then he stretched them out again, and extended his hands to the fire. Some blind scrabbling soon had a partly burned log extracted. He turned it so that its hot coals were facing him, then pressed the cords binding his wrists against the coals.

Milvarios was not used to discomfort, and he flinched away from the sharp, bright pain of the red-hot coals; then he reminded himself that the alternative to a little burned skin was death. He pressed his bonds against the coals again, and again, and again. The cords binding Milvarios's wrists began to char. So did his wrists. He squealed with pain through his gag, but such was the noise from the nearby revel that nobody could have heard him. There was the scent of burning cloth, burning hair, and burning meat. Suddenly he felt the bonds give a little. They snapped. As he sat up, Milvarios saw that quite large areas of both wrists were blistered and even charred. *Not nearly so much of me as will be charred if I wear the blame for the emperor's death*, he thought as he pulled the gag from his mouth.

"Murder!" he shouted. "The emperor's to be murdered! Warn the emperor!"

There was no response. Too much noise from the feasting and music, he knew. He undid the bindings on his ankles and stood up, then fell down again because his legs had lost circulation. The distant music and singing became screams. *He's done it*, thought Milvarios. *He's done it, and as me!*

For a moment the Master of Royal Music lay rigid with despair; then despair became outrage. The assassin was going to make sure he was seen running about with a crossbow, and then he would come back to the room, grab his disguise, and be gone. It was not fair! Milvarios picked up a poker from the fireplace.

He is a master assassin with any number of deadly weapons, thought Milvarios. *I am a musician with a poker. I have about as much chance of taking him by surprise and hitting him over the head as I have of winning the Dockside Topless Hoyden of the Month competition. So what to do?*

He dropped the poker. The assassin would have a way to escape from the room, having led the guards back there. How? Where? Milvarios suddenly remembered that there was a lover's hide behind a secret panel, but he knew that it led nowhere.

Somewhere in the distance he heard a female voice shriek "Milvarios!," then another crying "Milvarios, what have you done?"

Even though it led nowhere, the lover's hide had the advantage of being the only hiding place that was unlikely to be searched within the first quarter minute of the guards arriving. Milvarios crawled across the floor, and was through the secret sliding panel and sitting silently in the darkness within the time it took to draw five breaths. He heard the door's outer latch rattle; then there was a slam as it was shut. The inner latch rattled as the assassin bolted it from the inside.

"Now, Milvarios of Tourlossen is about to go free, but not for long—" began the assassin.

He had noticed that the Master of Royal Music was no longer there. Milvarios heard a brief and enthusiastic clatter as the assassin made a frantic search of the bedchamber and other rooms. Fists began pounding on the door, gruff voices called upon Milvarios to surrender. The assassin finally thought to abandon the search for his scapegoat and merely escape. Fingers scrabbled against the filigree fretwork of the sliding panel and pressed a hidden release. The release did not release, however, and the panel certainly did not slide. Milvarios was holding the mechanism very, very tightly from the inside. There were soft but intense curses from the other side of the panel, curses in some foreign language.

A loud crash reverberated as the door burst in, followed by the sounds of blades clashing and furniture being smashed. Screams and groans were mixed in with the sounds of the fight, and from the general tenor of the cries, it was apparent that the assassin was winning.

"Stand clear!" someone called, then added, "Shoot!"

There was a patter of loud snaps as the guardsmen's crossbows spat their bolts at the assassin. For some moments Milvarios heard little more than boots tramping on the shattered remains of his expensive crockery; then a voice announced, "The traitor is dead." Milvarios sat listening to the guards talking while they waited for someone to persuade their senior officers that the assassin really was dead.

"Who would have thought it, a fopsie like him."

"Killed five of us."

"Game bastard, fought like a daemon."

"We're lucky we killed him."

"Lucky for him, you mean, penalties for regicide being what they are."

"Would've been hung by his toes over a slow fire."

"Aye, while his ballads was read to him."

"So, you had to stand guard at his readings too?"

"Ye know, it makes sense. Such a terrible balladeer turns out to be a master assassin."

"Aye, a man can't be bad at everything."

Milvarios slowly released the mechanism and lowered his hand. His fingers found clothing—and the string of some instrument! The soft note was as loud as a thunderclap to Milvarios, but was not heard by the guards. Very carefully he examined the thing that had very nearly betrayed him. It was a board lyre, a commoner bard's instrument. He decided to stay hidden for a few more moments, at least until the officers arrived. Guards tended to do hasty things in the heat of the moment, and he was not convinced that the moment was sufficiently cool for him to emerge. There were sounds of feet approaching, and someone shouted "Attention!" Boot heels clicked, and there was a brief silence.

I'll make sure that every man in this room stands guard at my readings until his dying day, thought Milvarios as he sat shivering in the narrow, drafty space.

"He looks dead," said a cultured voice.

"Crossbow bolt through the forehead is always hard to argue with, my lord."

"Is he safe to approach?"

"I'd bet a month's wages on it, my lord."

"Look at this! Cane hoops and frames under his clothes. A thin man disguised as a fat man!"

"Amazing. With all the food he scoffed down, you'd think he'd be fat without any help."

There was another pause.

"Prince Stavez is furious. He ordered the Tourlossen mansion and warehouse burned."

The moment is still hot, thought Milvarios.

"Surely the elder Tourlossen would protest."

"The elder Tourlossen would require a head for that, and likewise his wife. Their other two sons are abroad, and I doubt they will ever be back."

"Give me your crossbow, I must report the assassin's death to the prince."

The sound of receding footsteps reached Milvarios.

"Bastard's thinking to take credit for the kill himself."

"Aye, and he will."

The moment is being lowered into a volcano, Milvarios decided. Surely someone knew he was genuinely fat—of course! The wife of the Clerk of Provisioning, who was his secret lover. *Secret*, that was the tricky word. Not only would she be unenthusiastic about her husband finding out about the liaison, she would be even less happy about being associated with a man accused of murdering the emperor. No, being fat would not help Milvarios.

One movable panel of wood was separating him from the attention of the guards. Should he slide the panel aside, they would want to know. Know what? What was the worst thing that they could ask? Why had he hidden quietly in his room while the emperor was being murdered? Why—no, that first why was sufficient.

Milvarios took stock in the light leaking past tiny cracks in the woodwork. Aside from the robes he was wearing, he had on hand one pair of grimy, roughweave trousers, a pair of reeking boots, a tunic stained with red wine, a woolen cloak, a half-empty wineskin, and a board lyre. He reached forward for the boots—and something batted softly at his face. Milvarios nearly screamed with terror, then realized that it was only a dangling rope. He groped above his head, and discovered a circular hole cut in the hide's roof. *This was how the bastard entered my locked suite*, Milvarios realized. *It is also the way he intended to flee.*

The presence of an escape route changed everything. Milvarios also had the knowledge that Milvarios of Tourlossen was safely dead, and that nobody was currently looking for Milvarios of Tourlossen. He examined the assassin's disguise in more detail. A grimy drawstring purse contained a few coppers, and a city gate pass scrawled out to Wallas Gandier, goatherd. Very slowly, and in complete silence, Milvarios began to ease himself out of his own robes and into the dead goatherd's clothing. The trousers were a tight fit, and that of the tunic was not much better.

"Will ye look at this?" exclaimed someone on the other side of the panel.

"Gold!"

"Lots of gold."

"It's the assassin's fee, that's for sure."

"And a right generous fee. Feel the weight."

"Surely a coin each would not be missed."

"Among five of us?"

"Still not much amid all this."

"Two for me, I killed the assassin."

By the time Milvarios of Tourlosscn had become Wallas Gandier, each of the guards had seventeen gold coins and the leather pouch was burning in the bedchamber's grate. One of the more literate of them had written "Death to the emperor who seduced my beloved" on a sheet of reedpaper and left it in the chest where the gold had been found.

"What I can't think is why he fled here, where he's been trapped."

"There's a secret panel somewhere, what slides aside. Bet he meant to hide there."

"How d'ye know?"

"All the palace bedchambers have 'em. They're to hide lovers in, like when husbands of wives show up at the door unexpected."

"But how d'ye know of 'em?"

"Well, I've had occasion to make use of a couple."

Time to move, thought the former Master of Royal Music. He slowly straightened. The space was small; in fact, it appeared to be an old built-in cupboard that had been converted into a hide. There was a roughly cut hole above his head, however, and through it dangled the knotted rope.

While the guards poked and pressed at the filigree work on the panels, the man who was now Wallas hauled himself up the rope left by the assassin. The space was narrow, and he was both broader than the assassin and unused to climbing. The rope was tied to a beam, but above the beam were boards. He pushed, and found that the boards were not nailed down. He climbed out into a portico that led out onto the battlements. Wallas replaced the boards and stepped outside, just as the sound of tramping feet sounded from around a corner.

Thinking faster than he ever had in his life, the former Master of Royal Music sat down on the edge of the outer wall and strummed the board lyre. It was badly out of tune, which did not surprise him at all.

"The great emperor, wise and old,
Struck dead by an assassin bold.
The deadly Milvarios, full of stealth,
Betrayed his emperor for golden—"

"Hey! You! Halt!" barked the squad's leader.

Because he had not been moving, the newest bard in all of the Sargolan Empire stopped playing instead.

"What are you doing here?" the marshal of the squad continued.

"I'm composing a lament for the dead emperor," replied the grubby intruder.

"I mean how did you get up here?"

"By the stairs."

"The stairs were guarded."

"No, my lord, you ordered all men to the Master of Royal Music's chambers," said his corporal, who was holding the squad's torch.

Wallas gestured to the overcast sky without looking upward, then strummed the board lyre.

"I came here to compose between the mighty strength of the battlements and the frail beauty of the stars," he declared. "While the horror of the assassination's moment was fresh in my mind, I sought to call upon the muse of my art to—"

The marshal placed a boot on Wallas's chest and pushed. Wallas tumbled from the battlements, and screamed for the entire sixty feet to the dark and rank waters of the moat.

"Some people just don't appreciate art," said the marshal as he looked over the edge with his hands on his hips. Then he strode away with his men.

✱ ✱ ✱

Still clutching his board lyre, the new Wallas crawled out onto the mud at the edge of the moat. He then vomited up his dinner, some very expensive mulled mead, at least three pints of reeking moatwater, and half a dozen tadpoles. The perimeter guards now came running up. He was frog-marched to a servants' gate in the outer promenade wall of the palace grounds, then sent on his way into the city beyond with a hefty kick. He hurried away into the dark and forbidding streets, but by now it was raining again and the more dangerous urban predators had retired to the taverns.

By just walking aimlessly Wallas eventually came to the river, and one of the three stone bridges that spanned it. The bridge appeared to be burning, but only because a couple of dozen beggars had a driftwood fire on the bank beneath.

"Hie, bard, join us!" someone called, and Wallas needed no more persuasion than that.

"Thee be wet," observed a beggar as he joined the circle on the mud.

"Jumped in t'moat of palace," he replied economically, aware that his educated speech was the single flaw in his disguise.

"And why was that?" asked a streetlord, who was wearing a crown made from scraps of rubbish held together with string.

"Were set on fire," Wallas said, holding up his wrists to display his burns.

"And why was that?"

"Some bugger said me music were not bright enough," replied Wallas ruefully, and they all laughed at what may or may not have been a joke.

"Now what would ye have for us?" asked the streetlord. "What say a tune?"

Wallas thought fast. A bard who could not play his own board lyre would be the occasion for comment. On the other hand his wrists were badly burned and his lyre was wet.

"The catgut got soaked as I swam, so there's no tune in me strings," he replied. "And me wrists are roasted."

There was silence. The silence lengthened. Clearly Wallas was meant to contribute something. He thought of the purse on his belt, which contained a few grubby coins.

"What's the skin, then?" asked a beggar beside him.

"Wine from the emperor's table," said Wallas at once.

It had probably been wine from the musicians' servery, but nobody present was in a position to know that. He offered it to the beggar streetlord, who accepted it with undisguised delight. Wallas was now guaranteed a refuge for the night. A beggar who claimed to have once been an herbalist rubbed a reeking paste onto Wallas's burns, then bandaged them with strips of sacking. While he sat steaming his clothes dry by the fire, Wallas entertained the company with descriptions of the royal wedding—and subsequent assassination—as they sat passing the wineskin around. In turn, Wallas learned how to gut, skewer, and roast a rat, along with several songs about beggars, lamplight women, sailors, and getting drunk on very cheap wine. Wallas was relieved to discover that the soaking in the moat had allowed his trousers and tunic to stretch to accommodate his size a little better.

Dawn saw the rain at an end, and a heavy mist on the river. Even though Wallas's clothes were now dry, they were cheap and coarse, and they stank. His woolen cloak did double as quite a reasonable blanket, however, and the beggars had kept the fire alight all night. He again took stock. He had the clothes that he was wearing, a purse containing four copper demis, a small knife, and a board lyre. Some twelve hours after acquiring the instrument, he finally looked at it more carefully.

As its name implied, it was a board that had been cut into a lyre. It had no sound box, only four gut strings, three bone frets, and the wooden pegs. It was designed to put out just enough sound to be heard within a few feet. It was also designed to be virtually worthless but practically unbreakable. Were it ever to be stolen, one could always build another as long as some scrap wood and a slow cat were within reach. The problem for Wallas was that he could not play it. The former Wallas could probably do something with it, but the former Master of Royal Music was not even sure how the thing was meant to be tuned.

As he sat pondering the lyre, several lamplight girls and women came out of the mist and joined the group.

"Aye, more news from the palace," one of them told the streetlord as he hailed them. "Seems that the music master may be livin'."

"What's yer meanin'?" asked the streetlord.

"I 'eard it from a militiaman, what 'eard it from a guard. The dead man were skinny, like, but a chambermaid the master 'ad rogered said she'd noticed that 'e were definitely fat. Seems the master let a warrior in to do the killing."

"Makes sense. Court fopsie like that would lose a duel 'gainst a roast chicken," said the streetlord.

Chambermaid? wondered Wallas. *Must have been after that terrible night at the Musicians' Guild banquet.*

"She expected a reward, yet they beheaded 'er for just knowin' 'im."

Wallas stayed silent as they laughed. What they were saying was largely true. He knew that one grasped a fighting ax by the end without the sharp metal bit, and he owned several ceremonial axes, but he had never actually swung one in anger—or even in training, if it came to that. As for crossbows, he had not so much as picked one up since the day he was born. Horses and riding? Horses were a long way up, and a lot more unsteady than a carriage. Wallas was definitely no warrior.

"Breffas, squire?" asked the former herbalist, holding up an oblong of charred meat by its tail.

"What is it?" asked Wallas, accepting the offering for fear of not fitting in.

"Roast battered rat."

"I see no batter."

"Nay, it's rat wot's been battered to death, then roasted."

Wallas gingerly removed a little meat with his teeth, smiled and nodded at the old man, then spat it out as soon as he turned away. His parents were dead. The thought took a while to make an impression on Wallas. In his time at court he had tried to live them down, because they were mere merchants. His father had actually been a pastry cook, and his mother distributed the produce. That made them technically merchants, rather than artisan-class. More or less. Actually from a strictly legal point of view his father was an artisan, while his mother was an artisan's wife. On the other hand, she did sell his loaves, buns, and pastries to five shops, making her a type of merchant. Now they were both dead, and because of him. More or less. *I try to rouse grief within myself, but grief is apparently still in bed,* he thought as he nibbled absently at his battered rat again. The odds on his own head being mounted on a pike and joining those of his parents above some gate were strengthening by the hour.

"Five hundred gold crowns is the reward for 'is 'ead, attached or otherwise," one of the lamplight women announced.

Wallas shivered with fear. Five hundred gold crowns was more than three generations of millers could earn in their combined lifetimes. He knew all about millers, because his father had employed one after he had become more prosperous. Wallas left the bridge, taking the empty wineskin with him. Through his father's associates he knew that wineskins were worth two copper demis.

By noon Wallas had indeed sold his wineskin for two copper demis, and exchanged one for a loaf of bread and a cut of cheese. He had eaten while watching his effigy being shot full of arrows and pelted with rotten fruit and vegetables. It was then burned at the stake. He tossed a stone at his burning straw form for the sake of blending in with the crowd. One of the militiamen who had brought the effigy and brushwood to the marketplace got up on the back of a cart and rang a bell for attention.

"Hark one and hark all!" he shouted. "Be it known here and throughout the city that this very afternoon there will be a gathering of bards within the palace grounds. At this gathering there will be free beer for one and all, and without limit."

The militiaman paused until the cheering and shouting died down. The vendors of assorted used musical instruments would soon be doing uncommonly good business, but the court-wise Wallas had already guessed the agenda. He had his lyre hidden under his stained and ragged cloak, and was already edging away.

"At the end of the afternoon, Prince Stavez will bestow a prize for the best loyal toast to the dead emperor, in verse."

It was all too clear to Wallas. Someone had collated the accounts of all the palace guards who had been on duty the night before. That someone soon realized that only minutes after the assassin had been killed, a bard had been discovered within mere yards of the exit to the secret escape route from the Master of Royal Music's bedchamber. The master was thus known to be alive, and to be hiding in the guise of a bard. There could be only one reason for the prince to stage a gathering of bards, and Wallas was fairly sure that everyone was liable to get a very unpleasant prize.

As far as stormy nights went, Alberin was hard to beat. Near-freezing rain lashed the port city, driven along by winds from the chill heart of the continent of Scalticar. Alberin was so often in the path of bad weather that the streets were all fringed with awnings, covered walkways, over-hangs, and public shelters. Keeping loiterers out of small, dark alleyways was easy: the alleyways were merely left open to the sky, and the rain kept them free of shadowy fig-ures with suspicious intentions.

The three shadowy figures of suspicious intent who were on the streets on the fortieth day of Threemonth, 3141, were not loitering, however. They were purposefully scanning what was visible of those streets by the light of one of the very few public lanterns that were still burning. So far their quarry had proved elusive, but they persisted with the pa-tience of professionals. The lamplight girl that they now ap-proached was distinguishable from the trio only by her strident perfume. The main occupational hazard for street-walkers in Alberin was pneumonia, so that when they dis-ported themselves in public they were even more heavily robed than members of some celibate religious orders on other continents. The girl turned as the men splashed over to her. They surrounded her. One held up a sack and a length of cord. Another waved a cudgel. The third offered, five silver coins on the palm of his hand.

"You have to be joking!" she exclaimed, not quite laugh-ing.

"No joke," said the man with the silver coins. "Can you help?"

"Add another silver one to those in your palm, and you can have an experienced sailor with a Carpenters' Guild plate."

"Oh aye, and which house do we have to break into, and how many guards do we have to fight our way past?"

"None."

"None?"

"Well?"

"If he's what you say he is, three down and three on pickup."

A pale hand emerged from the folds of the girl's clothing, accepted three chilly silver coins, and withdrew again. She sauntered off, and the three men followed. Around a corner and halfway down the next street she stopped at a doorway, where what appeared to be a pile of dark, sodden rags lay in one corner. The press-gang's leader hunkered down.

"Gah! Peed his trousers!" he exclaimed.

"Not so," said the girl, nudging a piece of broken crockery with the toe of her shoe, then pointing to the shutter above the door. "I saw it all. He bunked down in the doorway, then got out his fife and started playing. The madam of the house emptied a chamber pot over him, then dropped the pot on his head when he didn't go away."

The press-gang's leader fingered a lump on the unconscious man's head, then looked up at a window. "Good shot. Aye, and there's a guild plate on the chain around his neck. Hammer shape, he's a carpenter all right. You say he's a sailor too?"

"I heard him playin' a river-barge jig before the pot hit him," replied the girl.

"A riverman, the only kind left, I suppose. Very well, me boys, truss him up and get him into the sack." He dropped two coins into the girl's outstretched hand. "I ought to deduct one for the smell."

"Skinny bugger, too," said the man with the rope.

"It comes out of your fee for the next one," the girl pointed out. "Could you have found him by yourselves?"

Another coin dropped into her hand. The largest of the men heaved the sack onto his shoulder.

"Don' tell Mother," mumbled the youth from within the sack, without really waking up.

"His name's Andry," the girl remarked.

"D'ye know him, then?" asked the leader.

"Not so, I got standards!" said the girl indignantly. "I

heard the madam shouting 'Piss off!' and he shouted 'Andry Tennoner pisses off for nobody!' "

"True? Well, that saves them flogging it out of him later. Are ye calling it an early night, then?"

"Nay, I'm for a tavern and a mulled wine first. Who's he for?"

"The *Stormbird*."

"Oh aye, the last big coaster? Is she bound south again?"

"Nay. This is a special, a charter voyage to Palion, in the Sargolan Empire."

"Palion!" the girl exclaimed.

"Aye."

"Palion, as in across the Strait of Dismay?"

"Aye."

"But, but, you might as well set the ship afire and drown the crew at the end of the pier. Drooling Gerric was aboard the last ship to cross the Strait of Dismay. He's the one who drinks his ale under a table in the Lost Anchor, and crawls about on all fours."

"And that ship was the *Stormbird*," said the press-gang leader, with the calm of one who was not to be going on the voyage. "The cargo made everyone aboard rich."

"Oh aye, and the voyage left Gerric raving mad."

The press-gang moved off, reached the end of the covered walkway, and walked straight out into the rain and darkness. The girl stood looking after them, a hand to her mouth.

"He seemed a nice young fella, even if he were a slobby drunk," she said softly and with genuine remorse. "Like, I never knew . . ."

The crashing of unseen waves thundered from the direction of the harbor, foretelling what was sure to be Andry Tennoner's fate.

The megaliths of ringstone circles and other magical places often stand undisturbed for thousands of years, but all of them begin their existence as work that pays money to masons. In societies where money has not yet been invented, the payment might be a number of sheep, fish, or chickens in proportion to the size of the megalith, but there is always payment. Golgravor's Significant Stones never accepted any work from charities, least of all religious charities, but although the yard's current commission was definitely religious, it was paying large amounts of real money.

Golgravor Lassen's commission stated that seventeen megaliths were to be made, and the overall dimensions and design were specified quite precisely. Decoration was optional. Golgravor was particularly fond of the Grattorial school of floral embroidery of the twenty-seventh century, and he had directed his apprentices and assistants to cover every square inch of the stone megaliths in his workyard with entwined and flowering primroses, and bluebell vines.

"Not the seat area, however," Golgravor explained to a new freelance mason who was having his first tour of the workyard. "The dimensions of the seat area are absolutely precise, and are to be plain, unadorned rock."

"Looks to me like a man would recline with his arms held open above his head," replied Costerpetros.

"That is the general shape of it, yes."

"So, this is intended for some temple, to hold some priest in a position of prayer?"

"I cannot say. What I can say is that I'm paid in plain gold bars, and the gold is of a very high grade of purity."

"Oh. Well, er, who takes delivery of the stones?"

"The stones vanish, and someone drops a bar of gold payment where they stood."

"Just like that?"

"Yes."

"About ten tons of rock?"

"Five tons, actually. There's a bit hollowed out in the base, like it's going to sit on a rounded surface."

"And gold is left behind?"

"A bar of the very purest of gold."

"What does your client look like? Surely someone has seen him?"

"No, not a one. We were told never to spy on the collection. At dusk everyone withdraws, and at dawn we return. The megalith is gone, and there is one gold bar in its place."

"How many have you been commissioned to carve?"

"Seventeen, at five tons each. Now to work. That one goes out tonight, and there's one more to go after that. You're to work on number seventeen, doing the primrose decorations. It must be finished by the end of this week, and we've been falling behind schedule. That's why you've been hired. There's a big bonus if we finish on time."

"But who are the buyers? Don't you have any clue?"

"No. Be they people, dragons, spirits, or gods, they pay in large bars of pure gold. That's all we need to know, and that's all I want to know."

Costerpetros made sure that he was in place before dusk. He had worked hard for a week, even doing double shifts, and he had proved to be a popular recruit. He told good jokes, always shared his jar of wine, and was particularly interested in what even the most boring of artisans and apprentices had to say about the routines of the yard. At one stage he even ran a competition to see who could come up with the best theory of how the completed megaliths were being carried away, and by whom. Everyone pooled their knowledge and gossip, and the winner's theory was that a god reached down out of the clouds and took the megaliths away to be pieces in some enormous board game.

Now Costerpetros was lying flat-out in the long grass, with a green cloak draped over himself. The bar of gold that would pay for the megalith was reputed to weigh one hundred pounds. Costerpetros had a heavy-duty sling sewn with pack straps to carry the bar. A hundred pounds would be a strain, but he was strong. There would be a walk of a mile through woodland to where his brother was waiting with a horse and cart. Costerpetros knew he could manage that. He had even practiced walking that distance with twice the weight, for he left nothing to chance. On his feet was a pair of great taloned bird's feet, half a yard in length. They were made from leather, with claws of ivory, and would leave quite alarming impressions in the circle of white sand where the megalith had been left.

The megalith was on a wooden pallet, securely tied down, and with four thick ropes running from the edges and woven into a loop of braids that could support ten times the weight. It had been lifted from the working platform by a wooden pulley crane, and placed at the center of a circle of pure white sand that had been raked and brushed smooth.

The light faded in the west, and the sky was lit by two moonworlds and the stars. After all the chipping, hammering, cursing, work shanteys, and foremen's shouts of the daylight hours, the workyard now had a quite unsettling quality. By day it had been bright, hot, and noisy, but now it was dark, cool, and silent. Costerpetros lay absolutely still, apart from his breathing. Something would come by, something would appear. He thought about all the theories that had been suggested by his workmates. Perhaps a rent really would appear in the air above the megalith, and a huge, taloned hand would descend, draw the megalith up, then leave a gold bar. Daemons could open holes in the air itself; his brother had studied the magical arts to the seventh level of initiation, and he knew those things. Daemons also had good hearing, however, so it was important not to cry out with astonishment or fear if one appeared.

There was a swish in the darkness, and something briefly eclipsed the stars and moonworlds. Great wings beat above the workspace; then a shape like an enormous bat descended slowly and straddled the megalith. *A daemon, not a god*, thought Costerpetros. The thing's wings had a span greater than the workyard was wide, and its eyes glowed a faint bluish violet. There was a very large hook in its jaws, and from this hook a rope ran up into the sky. The daemon neatly attached the hook to the loop of rope—and Costerpetros saw no more. Neither did his brother, because another vast, winged shape swooped over the part of the woods where he sat waiting in his cart, spat a streamer of white-hot fire, then ascended back into the night sky.

✳ ✳ ✳

Golgravor Lassen looked down at the body in the long grass, his hands on his hips and his head shaking. The hundred-pound gold bar had obviously been dropped from a great height, as it had obliterated the man's head. There was a lot of mess splattered about, but he had clearly been taken by surprise, because there was no sign of a struggle. A dark green cloak covered most of the body, but two large, clawed feet protruded. Golgravor lifted the cloak and determined that the body was that of a man. A search of the clothing produced a seal and guild scroll identifying him as Costerpetros. At this point a foreman came running over from the direction of the burned-out woodland.

"We found some metal fittings and powdery bits of bone that might have once been a cart, horse, and driver," he called.

"And I think I've found an accomplice," replied Golgravor, indicating the body.

The foreman took in the body, the bird feet, and the gold bar. He thought long and hard before trying to reply.

"When I was a lad, my mother said that if I did not finish all my dinner, then Chicken God would come and peck my gronnic off for wasting the flesh of his worshipers. I used to think it was just a story, but now . . ."

"According to the scroll in his pouch, this was Costerpetros, the new contract mason. Or maybe Costerpetros is really Chicken God in disguise."

The foreman tugged at a clawed foot. It came away. He let out a loud sigh of relief.

"I cannot tell you how cheered I am that the feet are false," he declared.

Golgravor waved a hand over the gold bar.

"Have a couple of apprentices collect it in a tool cart, then wash the blood and brains off."

"And the body?"

"Have it scraped up and disposed of after the constables see it."

The foreman tossed the false bird foot onto the body. "What are we to tell the men?" he asked.

They stood in silence for a moment, contemplating the body.

"The gold bar looks to have been dropped a full mile, from the way his head's splashed," said Golgravor. "The cart appears to have been turned to ash by something that can breathe fire as hot as the inside of a forge, and the megaliths are being lifted into the air when they are removed. All that points to very large things that can fly and breathe fire—and are very bad-tempered about being spied upon."

"Dragons?"

"Dragons don't exist."

"Then what?"

"Very large and rich birds wearing dragon costumes."

"Birds can't breathe fire."

"Then we are definitely narrowing the field to dragons."

"But you said dragons don't exist."

"Of course not, but if they did exist and they learned that you knew they existed, they might drop a gold bar on your head, too."

"So why do the dragons that don't exist want five-ton megaliths?"

"I neither know nor care."

"Er, you have not yet told me what we tell the men."

"Tell them that spying on our customers is a very dangerous idea, and show them the proof. Now get people moving! We've already wasted enough time this morning."

✳ ✳ ✳

The fact that the *Stormbird* arrived at all was an occasion for wonder in Palion. The maze of shoals and rocks that lay across the approach to the harbor was now acting as a natural breakwater to mountainous waves raised by the latest Torean Storm, and no pilot had been willing to row out to the ship and guide it in. This proved to be no problem for the *Stormbird*, however. A particularly large wave had caught the ship, lifted it high, then flung it safely over the rocks in a seething, thundering maelstrom of foam. Within the harbor the waves were a mere five feet or so in height, and those of the crew who were capable of movement had no trouble guiding the ship past the inner breakwater and to the wharf.

It was now that a few dockers braved the screaming wind and stinging rain to help the crew tie up. What was left of the embarkation flag declared the ship to be from Alberin on the continent of Scalticar, a mere four hundred miles to the south. Normally the voyage would have taken little more than a week, but this crossing had been dragged out to thirty-two days by a continuous storm. Cold, hard rain was lashing the city, driven by a wind that howled like a mortally wounded dragon.

A gangplank was brought up and its grapples dropped onto the side of the ship. An ashen-faced, haggard woman of about thirty appeared and shuffled cautiously down to the wharf. She had a large sling bag over her shoulder, and her robes were soaked with water that had burst over the ship as it was carried over the rocks. Having stepped off the gangplank, she dropped to her knees and began to kiss the wet timbers of the pier. The rain beat down without mercy, and the wind flung spray, rain, and occasional hailstones at her.

A heavily robed official hurried along the pier, stopped, and extended a hand to the woman.

"Welcome to Palion, gateway to the tropics," he said as he helped her to her feet. "Are you willing to make a declaration before whatever gods you worship that you are not under sentence for any civil or felonious crime within the Empire of Sargol or its allies, or do you carry goods in excess of the value of five gold crowns?"

The woman reached into her robes, fished about for a moment, then drew out a gold crown. She pressed it into the official's hand.

"No," she croaked, with the energy of someone who has been vomiting almost continuously for thirty-two days.

"Ah, I see," responded the official, holding out a small scroll. "Just write your name at the bottom of that at your leisure. Bear in mind that it's from a batch declared stolen, so try to stay out of trouble. Any other passengers aboard the ship?"

"None that can move."

"Ah good, I'll pay them a visit right away."

As the official hurried aboard the ship, the woman began walking unsteadily down the pier. A youth now hurried down the steps of the wharf wall and ran out onto the pier.

"Learned Elder?" he ventured. "Learned Elder Terikel of the Metrologans?"

The woman looked up and focused her red-rimmed, bloodshot eyes on the youth.

"Yes," she wheezed.

"Learned Rector Feodorean sent me to greet you," he explained. "She regrets that she cannot be here in her personal persona, so to speak, ha ha."

The attempt at a joke was either ignored, misunderstood as bad grammar, or missed completely.

"Not nearly so much as I regret having made the voyage to be here in person," rasped the Elder.

"The emperor was assassinated recently, so Rector Feodorean's services are required at court."

"Lucky emperor," muttered the Elder.

"My lady!" exclaimed the youth. "Our emperor's death is not to be made light of."

"Young man, for over thirty days I would cheerfully have died to escape the waves, wind, spray, damp, tossing, pitching, rolling, vomiting, and cries of 'Pump, ye buggers, pump!' Even now I am not sure why I did not kill myself on the first day out."

"But that is all part of life at sea, my lady. Why, I have been to sea as well—"

"And was your ship ever airborne, due to the severity of the waves and wind?" rasped Terikel.

The youth gulped. "Surely not," he managed.

"Surely so. I lost count after our tenth flight." She stopped and leaned against a bollard, comforting herself with its solidity. "I never believed in love at first sight until I saw the timbers of this pier."

"But why did you leave Scalticar?"

"For a start, to see your mistress. What is your name?"

"Oh! My most abject apologies for not introducing myself. The shock of seeing your distress rendered me—"

"What is your *name*?" Terikel insisted.

"Brynar, Brynar! Brynar Bulsaros, acting head prefect of the Palion Academy of Aetheric Arts. We call it the A-three when—"

"I know, I know, the A-three when you are trying to impress tavern wenches, the Arrr when you are drunk, and the Aaah when you are falling asleep in boring lectures. Now take me to the academy's bathhouse, and kindly carry my pack. While I am cleaning up, you are going to burn my clothes."

"Burn them, my lady?" gasped Brynar.

"By the time even a diligent washerwoman gets the stench of vomit out of them, I am liable to be dead from old age. Check my pack, I have a change of clothing sealed in wax paper and leather."

Behind them, on the deck of the *Stormbird*, the official waved his arms crosswise three times. One for *examine her disembarcation scroll*, two for *arrest her*, and three for *confiscate whatever she is carrying*. As the Elder and Brynar reached the end of the pier a second official and two guards emerged from a building whose sign declared CUSTOMS, EXCISE, AND ALIEN MOVEMENTS. They barred the way.

"In the name of the crown prince, halt and declare—" began the official.

He got no further. Terikel breathed a tangle of fiery threads into her cupped hand and flung it down at the official's feet, where it exploded with quite an impressive blast. The man flew several yards through the air, along with some fragments of flagstone. The guards fell to their knees and scrambled to hide behind each other. The official began to get up, but having reached a kneeling position he decided that it might be sensible to rise no farther.

"The Most Learned Elder Terikel Arimer of the Metrologans," growled the *Stormbird*'s only passenger who was still capable of walking. "Late of Alberin, capital of North Scalticar."

"I, I, I, er, charmed," the official responded.

"That clown who met me at the ship took a gold crown for my disembarkation fee and said you would give me a *legal* scroll, write my name in the arrivals register, and give me forty-seven silver vassals in change."

"He did?"

"It might be a very good idea to do it," warned Brynar.

Two minutes later Elder Arimer emerged from the CUSTOMS, EXCISE, AND ALIEN MOVEMENTS office with a legal scroll, a small bag of silver, and the satisfaction of knowing that her name was legally in the port's register. She had also claimed a reward of ten more silver vassals for handing in a blank scroll that she said she had found on the pier.

"If there is one thing that I cannot stand, it is a corrupt official who does not provide value for money," she muttered as they began climbing the steps of the wharf wall.

"Yes, it breaches the principles of this new merchant economy that everyone keeps talking about," said Brynar.

They were soon over the wall and amid the buildings of the wharfside. The few people who passed them were on their way to see the only large ship to have arrived in the past month.

"So, an exciting voyage, you say?" asked Brynar as they walked, sharing his rain cloak.

"If you call three-hundred-foot waves exciting, yes," Terikel replied.

"Surely not!" exclaimed the student, suspecting that the Elder was joking, but wise enough not to laugh.

"Prefect Brynar of the A-three, the sea swells from the Occidanic Ocean are funneled between Scalticar and Acrema by the Strait of Dismay, and after a year of the near-continuous Torean Storms they have become very, very big sea swells. Three days after we passed across the mouth of the strait, I saw one particularly large wave break over Seadragon Pinnacle, and send spray over the top. That rock is definitely over three hundred feet high. In the fourteen days it took to clear the strait I doubt that I saw a single wave rearing less than a hundred feet. We were driven so far west into the Placidian Ocean that we passed the Malderin Islands. I would have given anything to have stopped there, but the shipmaster said that he could never have persuaded his sailors to come back aboard had we paused to do any more than take on provisions. There was only one member of the ship's company not reduced to a gibbering wreck by the time we tied up here, and he was killed by a falling spar on the fifth day out."

"But at least you survived."

"Are you trying to tell me that I'm not a gibbering wreck?"

When they reached the academy's temple complex Terikel went straight to the kitchens, took a half-baked loaf

of bread from an oven, and began to eat it, explaining between mouthfuls that she had been fantasizing all the way
from Alberin about warm, dry food that did not taste of salt.
Next she had a hot bath, with a tray of cakes and hot tea
floating on the soapy water.

Brynar unpacked the Elder's sodden sling bag while she
watched from the tub. He sorted through the contents, and
set the sealed pack of dry clothing aside. There was also a
sealed wax-paper cylinder with Feodorean's name on it.

"My spare clothes and those parchments were probably
the only dry objects aboard the *Stormbird*," said Terikel.
"Take the parchments to Learned Feodorean. Now. I need to
rest. . . . Let me know . . . when she has read them."

Outside the bath chamber, Brynar told a maid to make
sure that the Elder's head did not slip below the surface of
the bathwater if she fell asleep.

"The parchments must be important if she went through
such a nightmare to get them here," the girl commented.

"I cannot understand why she did not send a hired agent-
at-arms, or even an auton carrier bird," he replied, then
added, "Unless there is more to the message than just the
text."

✷ ✷ ✷

An hour later Feodorean returned from the palace, to find
Brynar waiting with the parchments.

"And how was the Most Learned Terikel?" asked the head
of the academy.

"Haggard, wrung out, exhausted, and chilled to the bone,"
replied Brynar. "She spoke of three-hundred-foot waves, the
Torean Storms, and winds that flung the *Stormbird* bodily
through the air."

"Ah, poor woman. Sea voyages never agreed with her.
Now, what was so important that she had to bring the news
here herself?"

Brynar handed the parchments to her. After a few lines
Feodorean let them flop to her lap and began massaging her
temples.

"Bad news, my lady?" asked the youth.

"Young man, this missive defines whole new frontiers for the term *bad news*. The Elder of the Metrologans is here to halt the building of the ether machine, Dragonwall."

Ringstone Logiar was the last of the seventeen ringstones to be completed. There was a very simple reason for this: wind. The ringstone site was on a floodplain, barely a mile from the coast, and although it was in the lee of a mountain that sheltered it from the prevailing westerly winds, the turbulence in the vicinity was quite severe. Those who delivered the megaliths were airborne, and turbulence is of great concern to everything that flies.

Waldesar always supervised when the megaliths were delivered. The deliveries were made in a field thirty miles inland from Ringstone Logiar, and this was in a sheltered valley whose permanent inhabitants had been forcibly evacuated. The elderly but very powerful sorcerer waited beside a massively built cart that weighed twelve tons, and had to be drawn by a hundred oxen with fifty drivers. They were currently five miles away, awaiting his signal.

So far Waldesar had met all the deadlines set by Astential, but Sergal was behind on his quotas of sorceric recruits. Waldesar had a feeling that whichever of them finished first would be given the position of ringmaster of Ringstone Logiar, and Astential had already specified that only someone with the thirteenth level of initiation could hold that position. The ringmaster would preside, sitting on the seventeenth megalith when Dragonwall was brought to life. Waldesar was very concerned with history—or legend, at any rate. The legend of the original Dragonwall was that the presiding ringmaster sorcerers who established it somehow destroyed the megaliths rather than let others join them as gods. That was a very good reason to be presiding when Dragonwall was established.

The night was overcast, but that was good, because the delivery crew was sensitive about being seen. The sorcerer did another tour of inspection of the wagon, checking that the massive strut brakes were all locked in place at each wheel. It was while he was checking the front right-hand wheel that there was a heavy gust of wind over the wagon, followed by a soft thud nearby.

Waldesar looked up. The darkness in front of the wagon was now just a little lighter, and the shape of this vague glow was that of something huge that was practically all wings, but that also had quite a long neck. The shape was in the process of folding its wings as Waldesar walked in front of the wagon and bowed deeply.

"The last of our gifts to you mortal sorcerers," rumbled a voice from some distance above Waldesar.

There was a series of creaks from the wagon as a very heavy weight was gently lowered onto its tray. Waldesar knew better than to try to watch. It was too dark to see very much, but if he did happen to see something that he was not supposed to see, then his life would be ended so quickly that it would probably not even get a chance to flash before his eyes.

"On behalf of all sorcerers, in Acrema, Lemtas, and Scalticar, my heartfelt thanks!" the sorcerer replied in a shrill, nervous voice, even though he was trying to make the words sound like a grand pronouncement on behalf of all the sorcerers of three continents.

"Release the hook," commanded the dark shape.

Turning to the wagon, Waldesar climbed the steps onto the tray, then slowly clambered up the rope and netting that enmeshed the megalith. He was eighty-two years of age, and quite stiff in the joints, but although he was happy to delegate some work to sorcerers of lesser levels of initiation, he never shared tasks that involved glory. Nobody else was sure who came to meet him on these delivery nights, and even Waldesar was unsure of the true nature of his benefactors, but if everyone else knew even less than he did, then it raised his status with everyone else.

For the seventeenth time he freed the hook attached to a rope that hung down from the sky, supported by things that were so vast that their wingbeats were more like booms than flaps. It was evident that the things above him could also see in the dark, for the hook was drawn upward the moment that it was released. There was a *whoosh, whoosh, whoosh* of huge wings fading into the distance, then silence.

"May I thank all the other . . ." Waldesar caught himself about to say *dragons*. "The other entities for carving the megaliths and bringing them here?"

It was a delicate moment. As a very senior sorcerer he was acutely aware of how touchy glass dragons could be, and he was sure that they were glass dragons.

"The other entities do not require thanks," rumbled the shape in a voice that resonated right through the sorcerer's body. "Neither do I."

"I see. Well, er . . . we shall not fail you."

"I should hope not. We have gone to a lot of trouble to provide you with the foundations of this ether machine. It is your responsibility now."

"Ringstone Logiar's sorcerers are highly disciplined. It is the other ringstones whose crews may fail. Ringstone Alpine has not got the—"

"Typical of you mortals. You prefer to see your rivals humiliated rather than have the main task succeed."

"Oh no, lordship, we are just friendly rivals of the Alpennien sorcerers, not enemies. We hope that they will perform well enough, it is just that we have little faith in them."

"Should one fail, all will fail, and Dragonwall will not become established. Should that happen, all of you will lose, and so will we. Should we lose, we shall be exceedingly angry, because these Torean Storms are troubling us greatly. I warn you, *do not* try to cause the other ringstones to fail, just to make fools of those you dislike. Be ready when the transit of Lupan, across the face of Miral, provides a signal to all sorcerers at all ringstones. It is then that Dragonwall must be brought to life, across half the world, from pole to pole."

The great wings began to unfold in the darkness, and Waldesar held tightly to the rope netting that covered the megalith. The downdraft from the first beat of the huge wings was a mighty gust of wind that lashed Waldesar with dust and pebbles, and all but tore him from the megalith, but by the second beat it was already some distance away.

Now that he was alone with his megalith, Waldesar slowly climbed down to the ground. He spoke a minor fire casting onto his fingertips, and it hovered as he checked the pyre in its light. The first pyre had been a disaster. One beat of the huge wings had scattered the brushwood so widely that it had taken Waldesar an hour to gather enough together to make a proper signal fire. All the pyres since had been tied down with ropes secured to tent pegs. The sorcerer flicked his casting into a bundle of kindling at the base. It blossomed into a nest of flames, then became a bright blaze.

Several miles away, a lookout noticed the bright gleam of the pyre, and he blew three sharp blasts on his whistle. The ox drivers had their huge team in motion almost immediately, but the riggers rode ahead to tie the megalith down to the cart. Between the riggers and the ox team were the floral decoration and lighting crews. It was over three hours before the oxen reached the cart, but it took only minutes to hitch them up for the thirty-mile journey to the ringstone. By then, the megalith had been securely tied down to the cart by the riggers, and there were dozens of escort riders waiting in orderly ranks, all carrying torches. The cart had been garlanded with freshly cut vines and seasonal flowers, and yet more burning torches had been tied along its front, back, and sides. All of the oxen were garlanded as well, and their drivers each carried a torch.

"I cannot see what all the fuss is about," said Garko, one of the level-twelve initiates, as he sat with the other level-twelves around the megalith. "For the first twenty miles there is nobody to see us, apart from the occasional shepherd."

"Waldesar likes a parade," said Sergal sourly. "We proper sorcerers lurk about in the shadows, back rooms, towers, and wild, isolated places doing arcane things. Learned Waldesar likes people to know that he is important. He is no true sorcerer."

"Could be that we're late as well," added Landeer, who was the most senior sorceress in any of the ringstones, and who specialized in hidden agendas. "Ringstone Logiar is the last ringstone to be completed, and that makes us look late. This way Waldesar makes it look like we are saving the best and most important until last."

"But we *are* late," said Garko. "There were tons of dirt that had to be dug away at the site. That took a lot of time and labor."

"But it sounds like a mere excuse," said Landeer.

"It is a valid excuse," said Garko, "and the high winds and Torean Storms also delayed our, ah, deliveries of the megaliths."

"Waldesar does not want excuses, so he turns them into triumphs. This parade will tell people that we were *meant* to be last because we are so important. Did you know that thousands of people are to be sitting on the walls of Logiar to watch us drag this thing past?"

"Free ale and a butternut pastry for everyone who has a basket of flowers to fling at us as we rumble past," said Sergal.

"Paid for out of Waldesar's own purse," Landeer added.

"Learned folk, may I ask a difficult question?" asked Sergal.

His two companions nodded.

"Why is Dragonwall being built?"

"To blunt the force of the Torean Storms," said Landeer.

"Yes, Astential approached me a month after the first of the Torean superstorms began. Now tell me, how could have Astential surveyed the sites of sixteen out of seventeen ringstones stretching halfway around the world in such a short time? Remember, Ringstone Logiar was the last site to be explored, and that was just a month after the storms began."

"Obviously the glass dragons helped," said Landeer, dropping her voice to a whisper. "They could fly to the sites within days."

"So the glass dragons do most of the survey, carve and deliver the megaliths, and quite possibly even suggest the idea to Astential. This implies that the Dragonwall machine was being prepared long before the Torean Storms began."

"If that is the case, then the glass dragons have an agenda that has nothing to do with taming the storms," concluded Landeer.

"That is my thought, and it worries me," agreed Sergal.

The procession escorting the last megalith moved very, very slowly. By the time the overcast sky began to lighten with dawn, it had traveled ten miles. At that point the procession was halted to refresh the torches, repair and water the garlands of flowers and vines, provide the escort with breakfast, and feed the horses and oxen. Because the chief initiate of Ringstone Logiar wanted to preserve the appearance of dignity and avoid any semblance of haste, nose bags for the horses and oxen were forbidden. Thus they had to stop to be fed, and this gave everyone a short rest. The short rest lasted until noon, which suited everyone, including Waldesar. This way they would be at their closest point to the city of Logiar about two hours after sunset. The torches would be ablaze, and all attention would be focused on the procession.

The afternoon was a foretaste of what was to come. Villagers who had seen sixteen other megaliths pass through and barely paused to give them a glance now suspended their routines as the great chunk of carved rock slowly rumbled through on its enormous decorated wagon. People cheered, and flung flowers and green leaves. Members of the escort managed to stop at the taverns in the general confusion, and even Waldesar flung the occasional pyrotechnic casting into the air to impress and amuse the villagers. At sunset the torches were lit again, but this time the break was kept down to a mere hour.

Two hours into the night, they reached the part of the road where it passed the city walls. It was halted at the city gate, where the acting regent of the Principality of Capefang rode out on a white horse. He gave his compliments to Waldesar, then rode to the head of the team of oxen and gestured the procession into motion again. Like Waldesar, the acting regent was convinced of the importance of being seen on grand occasions, and so he always chose a white horse and white surcoat for night parades. His alchemist had even mixed a fuel for his torch to make it burn with a brilliant blue-green flame.

At one level Waldesar was flattered that the acting regent

would honor the procession with his presence, but at another he was annoyed that someone was stealing the glory of his parade. Nevertheless, Waldesar smiled and waved, acknowledging the cheers of people who understood no more about the ether machine than that this was the last bit, and that the parade was less boring than sitting at home and wondering whether or not to go to bed early. Most of the petals flung from the walls were going in the direction of the acting regent, and this rankled with the elderly sorcerer as he glared at the distant white figure.

"Damn you to the lowest level of the deepest of all hells," muttered Waldesar.

Abruptly a hundred yards of road collapsed into a vast hole that belched fire. The first two-thirds of the hundred oxen vanished into it, dragging the others and the wagon after them. The acting regent of Capefang and his horse also plunged into the gaping conflagration. Now the city walls began to collapse, tumbling over into the hole, and bringing thousands of onlookers with them as they smashed down into the pit.

Waldesar was jerked off his feet, and he recovered to see his initiate twelves leaping from the accelerating wagon with all possible haste.

"I didn't mean it!" the sorcerer shouted in horror; then he recovered his wits.

Only ten yards from the edge of the pit, Waldesar grasped a small and inconspicuous wooden lever and wrenched it back with all his strength. The lever tripped a hair-trigger release. The release popped open an iron joint. The iron joint was all that attached the wagon to the oxen, but its release also triggered four iron shafts to drop and jam the wagon's wheels. The wagon stopped a single yard from the edge of the pit, just as a section of the city's wall crashed down on the last of the oxen.

Later investigations revealed that there had been a large, deep siege tunnel beneath the road, the product of a siege some three hundred years earlier. The siege had ended early, when the hungry citizens had rioted, defeated their own militia, killed their well-fed rulers, then flung open the city gates to the enemy. Faced with the cost of refilling the enormous siege tunnel, Logiar's conquerors decided to merely fill in the entrance. After all, the roof was held up by strong beams and pillars. True, they were designed to collapse if anyone pulled at a rope attached to a keystone, but if the entrance was blocked off, then that would never happen. The conquerors not only blocked off the entrance, they built a memorial over it to commemorate their glorious victory.

Folk memories are not easy to erase, however. Several ballads had managed to survive three centuries in the taverns of Logiar, all telling how a mighty cavern had been excavated under the road beside the west wall of the city. Someone had listened to the ballads, then rented a house near the city walls and dug a shaft all the way to the ancient siege tunnel. Whoever had rented the house had had the sense to vanish as soon as the collapse had been triggered, so the city officials contented themselves with executing the owner. Traders and vendors in the Logiar markets revealed, in some cases under torture, that enough hellbreath oil to conduct a small war had been purchased recently by foreign-looking merchants. Several minor intermediaries were caught and tortured, but those behind the plot had covered their trail too well, and they went free.

In the meantime, the megalith was transported along a detour that went through the streets of Logiar itself, then out the south gate of the city and along the coastal road to the ringstone site. This time people stayed as far as possible from the procession. The wagon was pulled by a thousand laborers who had been rounded up at spearpoint, and these men were made to wear garlands of flowers and vine leaves, even though there was nobody to see them but the city militiamen who were escorting them at what they hoped was a safe distance. The deputy acting regent watched from the distant battlements of the palace, surrounded by courtiers who were sipping spiced mead and hoping to witness another spectacular attack on the wagon. No such attack took place. Although a little late, the megalith arrived undamaged at the ringstone site, and was lifted into place by a spindly but effective wooden crane.

Waldesar had been severely shaken by the spectacular attack, yet once he had returned to his operations tent, called for a goblet of wine, and checked over the damage and casualty lists, he realized that Goddess Fortune must have had a strong liking for megaliths. None of the senior initiates had been killed, the megalith was undamaged, and there was every prospect of having Ringstone Logiar operational with an hour to spare before the transit of Lupan. What disturbed Waldesar was that the seventeenth megalith was definitely the target of the attack. It was too big and heavy to steal, too tough to damage easily, yet too small to hit easily with a stone shot from a siege engine. Dropping it into a deep pit and collapsing a section of Logiar's walls onto it would definitely have left it in poor condition, however. The two thousand people who had been killed when the walls collapsed did not even enter Waldesar's thoughts. They were merely bystanders, and he was only concerned with being seen to save the world.

Without any warning, Astential entered his tent. Waldesar bounded to his feet as fast as a man of eighty-two could manage. He had not been aware that the level-fourteen initiate was within a thousand miles of the place.

"Most learned sir!" exclaimed Waldesar slowly, gathering his thoughts as he spoke. "I was not told of your arrival."

"Neither was anyone else," replied Astential. "Gather the level-twelve initiates, Learned Waldesar. Four of you are to be regraded to the thirteenth level, and of those four, you are to be declared ringmaster of Ringstone Logiar."

Andry Tennoner left the *Stormbird* and strode down the pier with a roll pack slung over his shoulder and forty-seven silver nobles in the pouch under his tunic. There was the small detail that he was meant to remain in irons until the following morning, but he had picked the lock with a quite precisely bent length of stiff wire, and freed himself. He then wrote his own release in the penalties register, took it up on deck, and showed it to the duty watchman. Not only could the man not read, but he assumed that Andry could not write. Further, he wanted Andry to believe that he actually could read, so he pretended to read what Andry said was there.

As sailors go, Andry did not stand out. Skinny, a little taller than average, and with shoulder-length, straggly hair and thirty-two days of beard growth, he was bulked out by his leather knee-length jacket and sea boots. In his belt was a light ax that had a sea serpent with its tongue poking out carved into the handle. He stopped at the customs checkpoint.

"What's to declare?" asked an official with a bandage around his forehead.

"Three ship's blankets, a ship's ax, a ship's backsaw, a chisel, a caulking iron, a ship's-issue spare tunic and trousers, and a knife ground from a broken deckbrace."

"So, press-ganged, were you?"

"Aye, so they tell me."

"Currency?"

"Fourteen silver nobles."

"What? All the others had five *gold* crowns."

"Aye, but I had a few expenses."

"Such as?"

"A fine for spending a night in the shipmaster's liquor store, a fine for pissing from the rigging, a fine for being sick over the deckswain, a fine for—"

"Try to behave in Palion," said the official. "Any floggings?"

"Aye, for insubordination, and attempted desertion."

"Insubordination? Desertion?"

"Aye, I, er, annoyed the prime mate. Then at the Malderin Islands I punched the deckswain and tried to jump overboard to swim ashore."

"The penalty for punching a ship's officer is death within twenty-four hours of the offense."

"Aye, but I was the only carpenter aboard."

The official pressed the fingertips of both hands together, and pursed his lips against his thumbs. It was his impression that the sailor had helped to make the voyage from Scalticar just that little bit more unbearable for everyone aboard, possibly including the sorceress who had blasted a large hole in the flagstones, and an even larger hole in his self-confidence. He tossed Andry a copper.

"Welcome to Palion, and have a drink with the compliments of the Sargolian Customs, Excise, and Alien Movements Service," he said as he began to write out a seaman's visa for Andry. "Now take this visa and piss off."

Andry found his way to a nearby tavern, where part of the crew of the *Stormbird* was already a good way along the path to becoming blind drunk. There was a newly lit fire in the taproom grate, and about two dozen young women had already arrived to help the sailors spend their money. He was surprised to see the ship's deckswain over in a corner near the fire, smoking a long-stemmed pipe and oblivious to the noise around him. Andry went over to the serving board and leaned on it.

"Hie champion, could I get a pint of amber?" he said in passable Diomedan, the trade language of the Placidian Ocean's ports.

"Amber?" asked the somewhat harried Sargolan tapman.

"Aye, amber. Comes in barrels, people drink it."

"You mean sandy? That's beer."

"Oh aye. Give a pint here, I'll try it."

Andry made short work of his first pint of sandy, and was midway through his second when he found the deckswain beside him, leaning on the serving board.

"Pint of sandy," he called, and was given a tankard of beer.

"Nothing like travel to broaden the education, know that?" said Andry when the deckswain showed no sign of returning to the fire. "Like I've been here just five minutes and I've learned amber is sandy."

"Thought you were in irons," said the deckswain with no real interest in his voice.

"Well, you know. Asked for the punishments register to be checked, and Sonning found I was overdue for release."

"But the register is only filled out when punishment is complete."

"Is it then?" exclaimed Andry. "Why then Sonning must have mistook someone else's punishment for mine."

"Lad, you're quick as a rat up a drainpipe," laughed the deckswain. "Still, you did well to keep the *Stormbird* in one piece. Without you, we'd not be here."

"Hie, that's fine," laughed Andry, elbowing him in the ribs. "Without *you, I'd* not be here!"

"You're going to have to get us back again."

"Now that assumes I *want* to go back," said Andry with a wink. "Miles from mother, no brothers closing me, no sisters shouting at me, money to spend—Hie champion, another two pints of sandy!"

"But don't you have a girl back in Alberin?"

"What Alberin girls look at Andry Tennoner? Think I like it here, that I do."

"Well, I call Alberin home, and the *Stormbird*'s the only way back," sighed the deckswain. "She's almost the only large ship left *anywhere*. Too many shipmasters tried to sail during the first of the Torean Storms. The profits were fantastic, because so many ships had been lost in the wars. The more ships were lost, the greater the profits became. Gold tempted the crews to sail again."

"But we were tempted too."

"Well, yes and no. We carried a load of furs and oils that could ransom the crown prince of Alberin—were anyone to take him prisoner, that is. But we also carried the Most Learned Elder of the Metrologans over here."

"Why, and who's she anyway?"

"You heard of the Torean Storms?"

"Oh aye man, I've just spent thirty-two days in 'em."

"I mean how they started. Andry, could you imagine storms like this being normal weather, all the time? You must have heard of Torea."

"Oh aye, a big island, long ways off. Some sorcerer set fire to it."

"Torea was a continent the size of Scalticar. An enchanted weapon called Silverdeath got out of control and melted the place down to the bedrock. It was like . . . well, come and see."

The deckswain led Andry across the taproom to the fire,

then took Andry's tankard and set it down on the edge of the hearth. He scraped out a large, glowing coal with his knife. Very carefully, he balanced it on the blade, then tipped it into the tankard of sandy. Brownish foam erupted from the tankard with much hissing and bubbling. A few of the nearby drinkers clapped and whistled.

"The magical heat that melted Torea was dispersed on the winds, and it's made them right buggers for sailing. A large number of sorcerers are trying to do something to stop the Torean Storms with a thing called Dragonwall. I'm no sorcerer, but I try to help. I volunteered for the voyage. The Elder is something to do with Dragonwall, so we sailed the *Stormbird* here."

"Hie, deckswain, that's a brave cause," said Andry, genuinely impressed.

"So let's drink to it. Hie, tappy, two more pints."

"You're being bold, telling me the likes of this, dekky. I could be a spy."

"Hah, I'm in need of someone to talk at, ye know, and I'm fairly sure that you'll soon be drunk, and liable to remember little of what I've said."

"You talk like you're more than a deckswain."

"We all are."

"Er, say again?"

"We're the tools of many factions, most of 'em with different aims and agendas. Some radicals like the idea of the storms continuing, to cause chaos and destroy the status quo. Most want the storms to stop, but some inland kingdoms want their seafaring neighbors to be ruined first, and so they prefer the storms to continue for a little longer. The seagoing folk want less wind but more rain, so the inland kingdoms' pastures and crops will rot. That means the demand for fish goes up."

They drank on, the deckswain and Andry matching each other pint for pint. The deckswain bought drinks all round, then again, and yet again. All the while, he talked.

"Then there's the sorcerers. They've got to, to, ah, do something . . . magical, to make this Dragonwall work. Thousands of sorcerers, getting together at places called ringstones. Become gods, control the winds."

"Oh aye, gods control winds," agreed Andry. "Everybody knows that."

"They'll control Dragonwall, and it . . . controls the winds. Stop the Torean Storms."

"Oh aye, and that sorceress Elder, she's one of them, then?"

"Strange one, she is. Born in Torea."

"Torea? The melted continent? Hie there, champion, two more pints—No, hands off your pouch, deckswain, this round's mine. Another round for the house, tappy."

The vintner and serving girls began filling the order as eager drinkers gathered around. Andry turned back to the deckswain.

"Big problem, Torean Storms."

"We're so small, and the problem's so big, Andry," said the deckswain. "Why do we bother?"

"Er . . . tell me."

"No, I mean, like, *I don't know* why we bother."

"Then don't."

"Should find some bawdy wenches and get drunk."

"Bawdy wenches?" echoed Andry, instantly thinking about the consequences if his mother found out.

"Aye, bawdy wenches. They drink with ye, ye spend money on them, then they take off their clothes and get into bed with ye."

"Oh aye. Then what?"

"You play making babies."

"Er . . . aye? And then?"

"Once you're asleep, they sneak away, takin' what's left in your pouch!"

The deckswain roared with laughter, then flung half a dozen silver nobles into the air. Several girls and drinkers dived for the coins. The deckswain put an arm across Andry's shoulders.

"You need a bawdy wench," he declared. "Thas an order."

Andry swallowed. A girl. A girl to sleep with. He had never been in bed with a girl. He was not even entirely sure of what to do, but had gleaned a lot of what was involved from countless conversations in shipyards, taverns, barges, ships, and late-night drinking sessions on curbstones. More to the point, his mother was a long way away. Almost as important, if he made a real fool of himself he was so far from Alberin that his friends were unlikely to find out.

By now several girls had converged on the deckswain, on the theory that if he had silver to fling into the air, then he probably had more silver available to spend on them. Andry fumbled for his pouch. He found nothing. He looked back to the deckswain, who was taking a silver noble from a suspiciously familiar pouch and pressing it into the cleavage of the giggling girl on his knee. Suddenly realizing what was going to come next, Andry drained the pint that he was holding.

"I'll be troublin' ye for the price of that round for the house," declared the vintner.

Being unable to produce any money, Andry was promptly set upon, beaten, and ejected by the vintner and barrelkeep. Moments later, his rollpack and ax were flung out after him. His pack of tools remained within the tavern.

"Ye can 'ave 'em back when ye return wi' the price of the round!" shouted the vintner, before slamming the door.

"Stolen anyway!" bawled Andry at the closed door.

It was only now that Andry realized some of his silver nobles had leaked down his trousers and into his sea boots when he had been fumbling for money earlier. He picked himself out of the gutter, wiped off some of the scum and slime, then set off in search of another tavern. After all, his mother really was very, very far away.

In a rather more genteel part of Palion, Rector Feodorean and Elder Terikel were sipping Angelhair 3129 frostwine from crystal tumblers, and lying on silk and goose-down cushions before a fire in a blackstone grate carved in the shape of a sea dragon's mouth. Terikel was drinking rather more than the rector.

"The Dragonwall Council did ask me to journey to Ringstone Alpine," the rector was explaining. "Learned Sergal himself came to convince me. I said I'm too old for raw power castings. Three weeks in a coach on muddy roads, then strenuous etheric castings? Not for me."

"Compared to a voyage from Scalticar, it sounds luxurious," said Terikel.

"You are game, crossing the Strait of Dismay," said the old woman. "I would rather enter myself in the Dockside Topless Hoyden of the Month competition than do that. And speaking of futile quests, why do you wish to stop Dragonwall?"

"I have done calculations, based on observations of my Metrologans. Dragonwall is not necessary, and it is very dangerous."

"The Dockside Topless Hoyden of the Month competition is not really necessary either, but trying to stop it could also make you very unpopular."

"Dragonwall *is* dangerous. The Torean Storms have already peaked, and are slowly declining. All that Dragonwall can do is bleed energy from the winds and change it into etheric potential. Such energy must be stored somewhere, and it can then be used for great evil. Look, imagine your basement is flooded, and a clever sorcerer comes along. He says he will change the water into beer, then you can put a *free beer* sign at the cellar door and all the neighborhood layabouts will come rushing along and drink the place dry. What would you do?"

"Oh, charge admission, I suppose."

"Precisely! You could not bear to waste it. Now imagine huge amounts of magical etheric energy, stored in a mighty casting stretching across the sky! Would you waste that?"

The rector waved the decanter of wine in the air, then poured Terikel another measure.

"Just say you are right, what can we do? We are both initiate eleven, Astential has a thousand times our etheric potential."

"So the enemy is strong. That is no reason to surrender without a fight."

"Terikel, Terikel, you are starting to sound like young Wilbar of the Clovesser Academy of Applied Sorceric Arts. He founded a little group of radical students called the Sorceric Conspiracies and Occult Plots Exposure Collective, and they are the laughingstock of the empire's academies. His theory is that the Dragonwall is a plot by the sorcerers of another moonworld to control the minds of our own sorcerers."

"Then this Wilbar admits the possibility of conspiracy in the first place, which is more than you are doing. I know there are conspiracies, Rector, and I know far more than I am willing to discuss. Dragonwall will store titanic energies. The last time a mortal got control of such energies, Torea was melted down to the bedrock."

"Suppose you are right. What power do I have? I am not even a member of the council."

"You don't need to be captain of a ship to sink it," replied Terikel. "You have connections in the royal palace. Four of the ringstones are in the Sargolan Empire, or lands controlled by its allies. The late emperor had a lot of doubts about Dragonwall. He even insisted that an audit be made of Dragonwall's powers, capacities, and controls. When that is completed the truth will emerge."

"The audit has been completed, and the crown prince has seen it," said Feodorean impatiently. "He is satisfied that Dragonwall is no threat."

Feodorean expected an outburst from Terikel, but the Metrologan went strangely quiet instead. She stood up, put her glass on the sideboard, and folded her arms.

"The emperor opposed Dragonwall, now he is dead," she said slowly. "Now the crown prince just happens to be 'satisfied,' as you put it. Very significant."

"The emperor was due to be shown the results on the day after his assassination, so that he could veto the commencement if anything dangerous was found."

"Suddenly everything makes sense," said Terikel, shaking her head, but not looking as agitated as the rector expected.

"Terikel, you cannot be suggesting that the crown prince of Sargol is involved in some conspiracy to murder his father."

"Of course not, it would get me arrested. I should go now, Rector. Thank you for your hospitality."

"What will you do now?"

"The *Stormbird* sails for Diomeda in a day or two, to buy tropical produce for sale in Alberin. I shall be on it."

"Why Diomeda?"

"According to a, ah, consultant of mine, Dragonwall has a weakness. I can travel up the River Leir to Ringstone Centras. What I do there is between me and my conscience, but I certainly can collapse Dragonwall even *after* it has been initiated."

Once Terikel had left, the rector spoke a small casting, then shaped it. It took the form of a small image of herself, but with a few cosmetic improvements. Holding it in her cupped hands, she spoke to it for several minutes, then bound it to an amulet. As the figure was dissolving into the polished stone, Rector Feodorean rang a small bell. Brynar appeared a half minute later.

"Take this to the palace and give it to the usual person," said the rector, handing the amulet to him between her thumb and forefinger.

"The Metrologan Elder looked grim as she left," observed Brynar.

"The Metrologan Elder is a very dangerous person, Brynar. Now go."

Brynar took his leave, pulled the door to the rector's room shut behind him, and hurried away down the corridor.

"Yes, a very dangerous person," said Feodorean as the prefect's footsteps died away in the distance. "And something must be done about her."

Chapter Two

DRAGONSTRIKE

Wallas contemplated his worldly possessions: three copper demis, a length of fermented sausage, a crust of black bread, and a small, chipped jar filled with rainwater. He was sheltering from the rain under a wagon, and while he would not have considered it even as transport only a few days earlier, he now had to admit that it kept the rain off and was cleaner than most doorways.

That same day, twenty of the city's bards had been executed on suspicion of being him, and all the others who had attended the royal bardic competition had been jammed into the palace dungeons while investigations continued. Although cold, frightened, and tired of stale bread and cheap salt sausage, Wallas was strangely cheered. For a start, he was alive, at liberty, and surviving. Further, several days after their soaking the strings of his board lyre were finally dry. He had finally worked out that they tuned as DGBE, and was able to play a suite of foredeck jigs that he had heard a beggar whistling.

Wallas knew that he should flee Palion, but the question of where to flee kept defeating him. He only had to reach a border, but geography was not on his side. The nearest border was five hundred miles away. The mountains to the west were closer, but they were wild and lawless. On the other hand, while wild and lawless mountains were not Wallas's favored environment, they were vastly preferable to being executed for regicide in an orderly and legal manner.

In the meantime, he needed to live. Living required money. Money required work, and while he knew enough cooking to get employment, he would have to clean himself up before meeting any prospective employer. That would make him recognizable as Milvarios, and that would in turn get his head separated from his body very quickly. On the other hand, there were so few bards and minstrels in the city now that just about anyone could earn money by playing. Wallas could put his suite of six tunes together in various combinations of two and three to make dance brackets, so a career as a street musician beckoned.

Wallas shivered with the cold, and folded his arms as tightly as he could. The drawback with the wagon was that its spoked wheels did not stop the wind. He crawled out from under it, straightened slowly, stretched, and set off for a nearby tavern. As he entered, the usual comments greeted him.

"Hie, brave man, carryin' a board lyre."

"Fetch the guards, it's the Master o' Music."

Wallas sat on the floor not far from the fire, tuned the board lyre, and began to play his bracket of dance tunes. It was music to drink by, there was no doubt of that. The landlord brought him a tankard of beer every hour or so, patrons tossed copper coins, and even an occasional silver vassal. Suddenly a voice bawled out in Diomedan:

"Come all yer brave seamen, attend to me tale,
Steer clear of the lamp girls, from dockin' ter sail,
When lookin' fer pleasure just stick ter the ale,
An' ye might keep yer silver till mornin'."

The singer was Scalticarian by his accent, and was singing a foredeck song to the tune of the three-step that Wallas was playing. Wallas was annoyed at being upstaged, but was in no position to start a dispute and call attention to himself. He kept playing. After seven verses, the song ended. The drinkers threw a scatter of coins. Wallas gathered them. They were roughly a half night's takings.

"Hie, d'ye know 'Flash Girls of Diomeda'?" cried the singer, obviously a dozen or so ales ahead of Wallas.

"Er, not personally," replied Wallas.

Those nearby laughed.

"He means 'Melissen's Jump,' " called another drinker.

Wallas knew only the opening bars of the jig, but after

that the singer drowned out his playing quite effectively. By the end of the song Wallas had added another tune to his repertoire. The singer bought him an ale.

"Name's Andry, just came over the strait on the *Stormbird*."

"I'm Wallas. I just play here a bit."

"Been to sea?"

"Er, just on the coasters to Lacer. The storms sank my last ship, but we were close to shore, so here I am. Alive, but short of a copper."

"Well, if you're alive, let's have a tune."

Andry took a tin flute from his belt and began to play a jig, Wallas did not know the tune, but he knew the key, so it was not really hard to strum an accompaniment. Wallas was pleased with himself. He knew that he was fitting in, and that he looked and sounded like a street musician.

Within three hours Andry and Wallas had been thrown out of five taverns. Andry had managed to steal a jar as they were being dragged out of the second establishment, but it had turned out to be Mother Antwurzel's Creme of Garlic Medicinal Wine. Andry drank most of it as they made their way to the third tavern. Here Wallas had finished the last mouthful before they entered. When they came to be thrown out of this place, the barrelkeep had gagged at the smell of Andry's breath, and they had to be prodded and shepherded out by men with quarterstaffs.

The evening degenerated somewhat after that. Andry had lost two stolen blankets, traded the third for two pints of sandy, and lent two silver nobles to Wallas, who had in turn given them to a lamplight girl. She had then climbed out of a privy window and fled into the night rather than face the prospect of a night trying to breathe in the immediate vicinity of Wallas and his friend. Their needs were eventually reduced to finding a sheltered doorway with a nice, soft pile of rubbish to nestle down in. Andry was teaching Wallas his first Alberinese drinking song as they meandered along, leaning against each other for support.

"I wish I was in Alberin town,
When'er I'm down on me luck.
A lad's always welcome in Alberin town,
A lad never wants for a—"

A black shadow dropped out of the darkness beneath an awning, knocking Andry to the cobblestones. A knee to his midriff winded him, and inhumanly strong, ice-cold hands pinned him down. There was the smell of blood, decay, mildew, and sharp, stale sweat on the air. All that the folk in the nearby houses had heard was the welcome end to some rather annoying, drunken singing in Alberinese. Wallas cowered against a wall, frozen witless with terror.

Suddenly Andry was released, and the weight of the cold shadow surged up and off him.

"Gah! I cannot feeding on that!" hissed a female voice in Diomedan, but with a totally unfamiliar accent.

"Why not?" asked someone nearby in a youthful-sounding voice, but with no accent at all.

"Dirty, greasy, hairy, smelly."

"I am too," said Wallas hopefully.

"Then *you* feed on him!" snapped the fearsome spectre.

"Maybe if I wiped his neck?" suggested the youth in the shadows.

"No! Smelling like turd from garlic farmer in tar bucket, and, and—what is word, soaking in wine, cooking, for purpose of?"

"Marinating," said Wallas, before he could help himself.

"And being marinating!"

"Now jus' a moment," wheezed Andry.

"You shutting up!" snapped the woman, kicking him in the ribs.

"What about the fat one?" asked the youth.

She turned to Wallas, her hands on her hips. Eyes and fangs gleamed faintly blue; then she slowly shook her head.

"Gah! If friend of his, too dirty!"

"You're sparing them *both*?" exclaimed the youth, surprise evident in his voice.

"To drink his blood, thought is, ah, revolting."

She turned away from Wallas to glare at Andry again.

"So, er, esteemed fiend—er, ladyship, may we, er, go?" asked Wallas, not even sure what he was talking to. "Seeing as like you're not thirsty."

Wallas was aware of the gleaming eyes being turned in his direction. He put both hands to his throat, but she shook her head again.

"Lost appetite after smelling *that*!"

By the time Andry had recovered his breath and managed to sit up, his attacker and her companion had melted silently into the shadows of the ill-lit streets. Wallas had the feeling of one who had just had such a close encounter with a crossbow bolt that a dozen or so hairs had been torn from the crown of his scalp.

"Andry, are you . . . living?" managed Wallas, who had crawled over to him on all fours.

"Aye, I think so."

"What was *that*?"

"Ah, I be open to suggestions."

With the help of a nearby wall they got to their feet, then staggered a few hundred yards farther and turned in to an alley. It turned out to be a blind alley. They staggered out again, then Andry turned, staggered back in, and dropped to his knees.

"It's sailcloth," he announced. "Rotten sailcloth."

"Havn't got a ship," replied Wallas.

"I mean it's fine for sleepin' in, like."

"But the rain?"

"Look up, there's stars."

Wallas looked up, lost his balance, and collapsed. Having collapsed, he decided to have a short rest before crawling for the sailcloth. Andry crawled over to him.

"Wake up, ye'll get a chill."

"Piss off," mumbled Wallas.

Andry attempted to drag Wallas over to the pile of discarded sailcloth, but he was too heavy. Instead, he took the bard's board lyre and crawled back to the sailcloth.

"Hie, I got your lyre," he called. "Come get it."

"Mind me lyre," replied Wallas, not entirely awake.

After playing a few notes on the lyre, Andry tried to re-member the words to "Alberin Town," then remembered that his last attempt to sing "Alberin Town" had attracted some-thing with inhuman strength that drank blood. He rubbed at the place whcre he had been kicked in the ribs, then settled down into the sailcloth.

"Ye know, Wallas, for a sailor you're a two-pint scream-er," observed Andry.

"Mind me lyre," Wallas replied.

"Now there's a thought. D'ye have lodgings?"

"Mind me lyre," seemed to Wallas to again be a neutral sort of thing to say.

"I mean, we could go to yer lodgings an' sleep under a roof."

"Mind me lyre," mumbled Wallas, sidestepping the sub-ject.

"Ye know, Wallas, yer a piss-awful bard, but ye know how ter pick out a tune or two on this thing."

After ninety silver vassals on angelwing-lyre lessons, so I bloody well ought to, thought Wallas, but he just responded, "Mind me lyre."

Someone screamed nearby, and there was the sound of running feet. Whoever it was, they were getting closer.

"Woman," said Andry in an urgent slur.

"Mind me lyre," said Wallas, who was nearly asleep.

Someone darted past the entrance to the alley, then turned back and ran in, stumbling over Wallas and scambling past Andry and the pile-of sailcloth. Andry caught the slightest suggestion of perfumed soap, and heard the ragged, whim-pering breath of a woman so exhausted that hiding was the only option left to her.

Unfortunately, her pursuers had been sufficiently close that they had seen her make for the alley. Now they closed in. More feet trampled Wallas, then scrambled over Andry and his sailcloth bedding. By now the woman had found that she was in a blind alley, and was cornered. She turned to fight, speaking a fire casting into her hands, then flinging it at her pursuers. She missed. Her casting hit the pile of sailcloth.

Andry bounded to his feet, primarily because the sailcloth had burst into flames all around him. The firelight showed that five burly-looking men had cornered a woman and pinned her to the ground. Behind him, Wallas had raised himself to his knees. Andry heard cloth ripping, and saw the gleam of pale legs and the glint of knives.

"Hie, thas pathetic, warraye thinyer doin' there?" demanded Andry, in what was meant to be Diomedan but which came out as nothing particularly comprehensible to anyone.

He waved Wallas's board lyre for emphasis. The five men looked up in surprise. So did their victim. There was a moment of absolute silence.

"Mind me lyre," quavered Wallas from behind Andry.

"Thas pathetic, ye know, thas terrible," insisted Andry. "If yer mindin' ter jump a woman, ye pay her like rest of us."

"Take 'em," rumbled out from the end of the alley. Two hulking shadows charged.

In a fleeting moment of clear thought, Andry snatched his ax from the pile of burning sailcloth and whirled it for effect. Unfortunately, the handle had been struck by the woman's fire casting when it had burst to ignite the sailcloth. The ax head and stump of handle broke off and whirled past the leading thug, but in dodging it he blundered into his companion. They fell together. Andry kicked the head nearest to him, then struck the other with Wallas's board lyre, breaking it over his head. The Alberinese was left holding two pieces of board lyre and the remains of an ax handle.

"Come *on*, come *on*!" bawled Andry. "Hav'ne got a pair of balls between ye, I'll wager!"

The hair, beard, and clothing of the man straddling the woman now burst into flames, and he rolled off her with a shriek. Another charged Andry, or at least he charged in Andry's direction. He was, in fact, fleeing for his life by now, but Andry was not to know that. He lashed out with his pieces of board lyre and charred ax handle, sending the thug staggering past him and into the still kneeling Wallas. Andry leaped onto the pile of flailing limbs and punched at what he hoped was not Wallas. A fist thudded into Andry's left eye; a bright blue star flashed in the Alberinese's head. Moments later he awoke on the ground, watching Wallas clinging onto the thug's arm and being lifted into the air as he raised a knife. Andry's foot lashed out and caught the man's knee. He and Wallas came crashing down on top of Andry.

Suddenly nobody was moving. More to the point for Andry, nobody was trying to kill or even hit him, but at least one body was lying across his. He heaved himself up. The thug rolled over. Wallas's hand was still grasping the handle of the knife that was protruding from the center of his attacker's chest.

Andry stood up. The woman was on her feet by now, leaning against a wall for support, her clothing torn away in places. The sailcloth was still burning. So was one of the thugs, but he was no longer moving. Beside him lay the fifth thug, his head struck by a chance encounter with the back of Andry's broken ax. He still had a grin on his face. One of the two unconscious thugs groaned. Andry kicked him in the head.

"Mind me lyre," whimpered Wallas.

"He's dead," said Andry. "Ye must have hit a heart."

They both turned to the woman, and the nearby human torch.

"He's burning," said Andry.

"I set him on fire," the woman wheezed.

"Look, er, it could be a really good idea to leave," said Andry, slowly and deliberately, as he picked up the remains of the lyre and handed it to Wallas.

"Me lyre's broken," said Wallas.

The woman collapsed.

Andry kicked at the base of the door to Madame Jilli's Recreational Rooming until a bolt rattled back and the door was flung open. Three women in minimal although expensive-looking clothing stood, crouched, and knelt before him. Each had a tiny crossbow pointed at his chest. The weapons looked like toys, but Andry knew that if these were the type that the Alberinese lamplight girls wore strapped beneath their skirts, then the bolts would be poisoned. A moment later the fact that Andry had a woman slung over his shoulders registered with someone farther back in the gloom.

At the words "Admit them," the women lowered their weapons and moved aside. Andry entered, carrying the woman he had rescued. He was followed by Wallas, who was carrying an ax head with a charred stump of handle, the other bit of handle, a bloodied dagger, four purses, and the shattered remains of a board lyre. The sleeve of his left arm was soaked in blood.

"We, er, like rescued a lamplight girl, like from some men," explained Andry.

"They were very bad men," added Wallas.

"They were, like, tryin' to take a free one, but we stopped them," Andry continued.

"I stabbed one," admitted Wallas. "But with his own knife."

"That makes it better?" asked Madame Jilli.

"Aye, like it wasn't Wallas's fault," added Andry.

Wallas was not the sort of person who liked to admit that he would own something as offensive as a dagger, a lewd sketch, or a sheepgut condom. He held up the charred pieces of ax.

"Well, admittedly, but it wasn't Andry's fault either."

Andry lowered the unconscious woman to a couch. "There were three others. I, like, reasoned with them."

"Andry kicked them in the head," explained Wallas. "He kicked them very hard, so that, well, they were not inclined to get up quickly."

"The woman, like, set the other on fire," added Andry.

"But we're not sure if it was her fault," added Wallas.

Madame Jilli stood with her arms folded, looking calm, yet frantically trying to arrange the mess of facts and stories before her into some sort of coherent picture. Finally she hit on a detail.

"She set someone on fire?"

"Oh aye," said Andry.

"Only a powerful initiate of the eleventh level can set a man burning," said Madame Jilli as she examined the woman. "Are you sure she's a lamplight girl?"

"Oh aye, because I . . . er—Wallas, you tell her."

"Er, well, she . . . was out at night."

"Oh aye, you don't get any other women out at night, alone."

"Her escort might have been killed," Madame Jilli pointed out, loosening the woman's clothing.

"Oh, er, maybe we're not so sure, then," admitted Andry, feeling embarrassed but trying to get a better view.

"Why did you bring her here?" Madame Jilli asked, taking something from the woman's pouch.

"We saw your sign, and we thought, like, lamplight girls help each other."

"This is a Metrologan Order priestess!" exclaimed Madame Jilli, looking at some sort of seal.

"Er, aye?" asked Andry.

"They are a scholarly order, dedicated to the measurement of all things," explained Wallas. "They also have a ministry to the harlots, orphans, and cripples in the cities where they have temples."

Madame Jilli stood up and faced Andry, "Lamplight girl she is not, but as a Metrologan she is welcome here. Why did you rescue her?"

"Well, because," said Andry. "Like those arseholes had her down, for a free one, like, and like, that's terrible."

"Well yes," agreed Wallas. "They seemed awfully lowerclass, and she was screaming in a quite educated voice. Naturally we people of refinement must support each other, so we intervened."

"Let me get this clear. You rescued what you thought was a lamplight woman from five of the Throne Guards because it seemed like the decent thing to do?"

"What?" laughed Andry. "Throne Guards? Oh no, they were just heavies, like."

Madame Jilli took the serviceable but ornate dagger from Wallas and held it up between her thumb and forefinger.

"The crest on this is of the Imperial Throne Guards. Only Throne Guards can carry them. The penalty for others using the Throne Guards' crest on their weapons is death—by whatever weapon happens to bear the crest."

"I killed an Imperial Throne Guard?" whimpered Wallas,

who then dropped everything that he was carrying, swooned, and fell really heavily.

"Poor man," said Madame Jilli. "So brave, yet so well spoken. Andry, is it?"

"Aye."

"Go with Ellisen, she will attend your needs. Roselle, Melier, help me with Wallas and the priestess."

Ellisen did not let Andry near a bed until he had surrendered his clothes, taken a bath, and washed his hair in thornbush oil to kill the lice. Ellisen was taller than Andry, broader across the shoulders, and obviously not accustomed to taking any nonsense from any man. She did, in fact, remind Andry of his mother, and once he had realized this he found her a lot easier to get along with. Soon she was scrubbing his back with a scouring brush and sand soap, and they were exchanging stories about great tavern fights they had been in.

Andry climbed between the scented coverings of the first double bed he had ever slept in. For a while he lay there, listening to the noises coming from the next room—and suddenly it was morning. His clothes were laid out neatly on a chest by the wall. They did not smell, and they seemed to have changed color. Andry puzzled over this for a moment, then realized that they had been washed. He dressed hurriedly, then pulled on his sea boots—which had been cleaned and polished. He got dressed in the clothes that were no longer entirely familiar, then noticed a mirror. It had been placed so that it could only be used if one was lying on the bed.

"No use to anybody," muttered the puzzled Andry as he picked it up, rotated it, and placed it on the floor. The image in the mirror seemed a lot more respectable than Andry thought himself to be. "But if I really look that good, why can't I get a girl?" he wondered doubtfully. "Maybe you're one of those magical mirrors what only shows what you want to see?" he asked the mirror. It remained silent.

He opened the door, to find Ellisen curled up against the

opposite wall under a blanket. Her crossbow was beside her. Not entirely sure whether she was there to keep him in or others out, Andry announced that he was awake. Ellisen stood up, stretched, then escorted Andry to Madame Jilli, who was having breakfast with Wallas in a room that was too small to be a refectory, but too large to be a dining room. Wallas was looking very pleased with himself.

"Apparently a large squad of assassins and five foreign sorcerers killed two Imperial Throne Guards last night," Madame Jilli reported.

"Us?" Andry replied.

"Oh no," laughed Madame Jilli. "No, it could not possibly have been you. Come now, your most tireless companion and I have been awaiting your company."

Andry ate his breakfast largely in silence. They had little company in the dining room, as most girls who worked in the house were by now asleep for the day. A serving maid stood at a nearby bench, folding napkins, and Madame Jilli was having a cup of tea and reading scrolls of reedpaper.

"I never, like, fought to kill," confessed Andry between mouthfuls of smoked ham.

"Of course you did," said Wallas. "Last night. So did I."

"No, like I mean before that I never did. Kicked a few heads and all, but never tried to kill anyone."

"But you *didn't* kill anyone."

"Oh aye, it's true."

"Awfully good throw with the ax," said Wallas, with a sidelong glance to Madame Jilli. "I would have thrown my knife, but you seemed to be on top of the situation, as it were."

"Accident," said Andry with a shrug. "Couldn't do it again to save my life."

"Well, it helped save the Metrologan's life last night."

"But *you* killed someone, Wallas. How do you stand the feeling? The guilt, like, and thinkin' that here I am havin' breakfast and there he is, no more breakfasts. Ever."

"I don't know, but yes, I do feel bad. I've never killed before last night."

"Is that true?" asked Madame Jilli.

Wallas suddenly remembered some of the boasts he had made in her bed during the night just past.

"Well, it is just that when you are as savvy with fighting as I am, you can afford to be merciful except in the most extreme of circumstances."

"So that cut across his right heart and transverse artery was your first?" asked Andry.

"You actually know what the transverse artery is?" asked Wallas, hurriedly changing the subject.

"Oh aye. The big one, it connects our two hearts. It's part of the reciprocation system."

"How do *you* know all that?"

"I used to steal bodies from the graveyards for the Medicars' Guild, like, on my days off. They cut them up, for their students to learn what's in bodies. I'd hang around, like, then help clean up for another twenty coppers. Never thought of the bodies as ever being alive, but last night there were five alive, and then there were two not alive. Both of them were on the way to the Dark Places."

"You know that feeling of guilt you mentioned?" asked Wallas, lowering his voice to a whisper.

"Yes?" replied Andry.

"What do I do about it?"

Andry put a hand to his face, unable to answer, then shrugged. He ate in silence for a few minutes.

"First time I've slept in a bawdyhouse," said Andry.

"Recreational rooming establishment," said Ellisen, who was standing by the door with her arms folded.

"Men do not come here to sleep," said Wallas suavely.

"Should have heard them in the room next to me. Sounded like they were rowing the bed around the room."

The serving maid giggled, Madame Jilli put both hands to her mouth, and even Ellisen smiled.

"That was Madame Jilli's room," explained Wallas with a sneer, vaguely proud of being responsible for the noises, yet somehow annoyed by the analogy. "So what were *you* doing?"

"Trying to get to sleep!"

"You mean you had no company?" said Wallas with a sly glance in Ellisen's direction.

"Aye, true."

"Must have been the first time that bed had a man in it without a woman."

"Aye, I mean nobody would come in here for just a wank."

By now Madame Jilli had her face buried in her hands, the serving maid was wiping tears from her eyes, and Ellisen was staring intently at something on the ceiling.

"Well, now what?" asked Wallas.

"Find a tavern, have a pint," replied Andry.

"Andry, we're wanted men. We killed a couple of the emperor's elite guards."

"Aye, but we saved that lady."

"Andry, the other guards lived. Whatever lies are on the bulletin boards, they are going to be telling one and all to watch out for some loon in sailor gear, carrying a carpenter's ax, and with a heavy Alberinese accent on his Diomedan."

"Oh aye, and a fat friend with a board lyre."

"We need to leave Palion, and in haste!" insisted Wallas.

By the time Andry and Wallas were ready to leave, there had been some changes to their appearance. Andry had shaved his cheeks and tied his hair back. This gave his head the appearance of a mop wearing a girdle. Wallas glued some of Andry's beard onto his upper lip and the point of his chin, and burned the remains of his board lyre.

Madame Jilli took the Throne Guard's knife and dropped it into the river. Soon she was back at her establishment, where her unexpected guests were getting ready to leave.

Andry and Wallas were getting their first look at the woman they had saved. She looked to be about thirty, and she seemed frail and exhausted.

"Gentlemen, again let me thank you," Terikel said in Diomedan, but with an odd, unfamiliar accent.

"Hie, think nothing of it," replied Andry.

"But if you happen to know a cheap, discreet way to leave the city, we would be very grateful," added Wallas.

"Why?" she asked simply.

"We're not really wanted here," said Wallas.

"Well, like, we're wanted in every guardhouse in the city," Andry added. "That's the problem, like."

There was a short silence. Andry scratched his head.

"Why did you help me?" asked Terikel, as if it were the last thing she would have expected a stranger to do.

"You needed help, like," Andry managed.

"And that is all of it? I needed help?"

"Aye."

"And for no other reason?"

"Aye, why not? I mean, you Metrologan priestesses help sick and beaten lamplight girls. D'ye ask *them* how they got to be that way?"

The priestess frowned as she thought for some moments. Only now did Andry notice that she was wearing clothes borrowed from the communal lockers of Madame Jilli's girls. Somehow her face did not say *lamplight girl*, however. A hawk with a rather bad headache might have looked like that, but not a woman of the streets by night.

"I need to leave Palion too," she announced, "but I need to see some people first, and to arrange a few things. I am a merchant's agent, you see."

"Madame Jilli said you were a priestess," blurted Andry.

"Every guardsman and mercenary in the city is looking for a priestess," she said pointedly. "Better for me to be a merchant's agent."

"Oh aye, so you're a merchant's agent," said Andry.

"Very good. Now listen carefully. My employer's rivals wish to ruin a very important venture that I am negotiating. Understand?"

"Aye," said Andry and Wallas together.

"If you want to leave the city, you can come with me, working as my guards. What do you say?"

"He says yes!" Wallas snapped, with a sidelong glance at Andry. "We both say yes."

✳ ✳ ✳

Ringstone Centras was to be the first of the ringstones to test the basic form of the Dragonwall casting. Astential surveyed the ringstone site from the lip, checking that all of the sixteen sorcerers were at their ringstones and ready to perform their castings. His own megalith was in the center, at the bottom of the circular depression.

Just does not seem right, Astential thought as he began walking down into the bowl of fused sand. *All the sixteen outer megaliths proudly standing tall for everyone to see, yet my megalith hidden away in the depression.* It did not take Astential long to climb his megalith and seat himself, and he wasted no time with grand gestures and theatrical pauses. After all, this was only a test.

"Learned colleagues, speak your castings," called Astential, and his sixteen sorcerers spoke the powerful but unstable castings into their cupped hands. "Extend!" added Astential. Sixteen sorcerers separated their balls of glowing, writhing tendrils of raw etheric energies into two, then raised them into the megaliths' armrests. "Cast!" Thirty-two streamers of blue fire spiraled upward, a pair from the extended arms of each sorcerer at the rim of the ringstone. Now Astential spoke the special controller casting, pulled the writhing ball into two handfuls of energies, then cast a pair of streamers skyward.

Roughly a third of Astential was eventually recovered for burial, and there was not a person or animal within a quarter of a mile of the ringstone which was not splattered by fragments of him.

"It's the central megalith," said Lavolten as he and Talberan inspected the site later that day. "It should be the same height as the rim megaliths or you get resonances. We all know what resonances can do," he added with a gesture.

"We know now," responded Talberan. "Why build this place in the depression shape, then?"

"Because it is not part of the original design! Something very hot exploded here five millennia ago, leaving a crater

lined with melted glass. To get the ringstone's original configuration, we must build a stone platform to raise each central megalith to the level of those on the rim."

"More delays for a tight schedule," sighed Talberan.

"Better delays than disasters," said Lavolten, nudging a
fragment of ear with the toe of his boot.

Terikel, Andry, and Wallas set off into the midmorning
crowds of Palion, and to the casual observer, the priestess
could have been a rich man's mistress being escorted home by
two contract guards. Terikel went straight to a market street,
where there were shops instead of stalls. Andry had not been
in a shop in the whole of his life, and was so edgy that the
shopkeepers suspected him of planning a robbery. Terikel selected an ankle-length, dark grey coat. While she haggled to
keep up appearances, Andry and Wallas wandered in the direction of one of the other stone shops, farther along the
street.

"That Madame Jilli, you would not believe what she was
like!" said Wallas, at last free to be indiscreet about his night
with the manager of their sanctuary.

"Would she want you passing details to me?" asked
Andry, looking uneasy.

"Soft and charming, yet she never tired—well, not at first,
anyway, because I—"

"It's not for my ears, Wallas!" hissed Andry, with a finger
to his lips; then he turned away sharply through a doorway.
Wallas followed, and found himself in a music shop. Andry
reached for a bamboo flute about the length of his forearm.

"You already have a flute," said Wallas.

"That I do," said Andry, who then played a few notes of a
reel. "But this is for you."

"Me? But I can't play one. It's lower—" Wallas caught
himself beginning to say "lower-class." "It's, ah, lower-
pitched than I like."

"Oh no, this one's in D, it's very versatile," said Andry,
producing his own rather battered tin flute.

"But how shall I sing?"

"Wallas, your singing's terrible, especially when there's a few wines in you. Do us all a favor, and learn the flute."

Wallas was speechless with shock and anger. Being Master of Royal Music meant that only the former emperor had been able to criticize his playing. Because the former emperor had been tone-deaf, this meant that he had had no criticism for some time. The shopkeeper now came over, smiling and rubbing his hands.

"Ah, it is a very fine instrument, sir, but do you play the board lyre as well? We have a special rate, three-quarters off the price."

"Well, I just happen to require a board lyre," Wallas declared.

Andry looked away, through the door and into the street. He noticed that several people outside appeared to be watching the shop. Two of them were on their feet and stretching. He turned back and saw Wallas playing the lyre.

"Oh no, that's a bard's instrument and you're no bard," said Andry pointedly, indicating the watchers by winking and rolling his eyes in the direction of the street.

The shopkeeper rubbed the top of his head in a circular motion. The people trying hard to look casual and not obviously watch the shop exchanged words to each other. Terikel entered the shop, transformed by her newly acquired grey coat.

"Ah, very good, my man," she said in Diomedan that was suddenly flawless. "Now, I shall need an instrument as a present for my husband, and it must be something that he will be able to learn quickly."

"You can learn a tune on a board lyre in mere days," Wallas assured her.

Andry had not a clue what was going on, but cast a glance at the shopkeeper—who was tapping the top of his head with his thumb. A glance to the watchers outside confirmed that several had suddenly become agitated, and were making discreet, coded signals. Andry looked back to the shopkeeper. He was scratching the top of his head with his little finger. A quick scan of the street outside revealed that the rest of the watchers were now making signals to people unseen.

"We have a special sale of board lyres just now," the shopkeeper was telling Terikel.

"Ah splendid, so what price are you asking?" she said, taking the instrument that Wallas held out to her. "I want something to remember Palion by. I am here from Diomeda, and I asked my contract guards to choose a simple instrument. I am so unmusical, you know."

"And I shall negotiate the price of that quite inferior instrument," said Wallas.

The shopkeeper seemed anxious to haggle extensively with Wallas. Andry took Terikel aside.

"There's people watching the shop, ladyship," he whispered.

Terikel looked across into the street. The watchers were not particularly competent, and could not hide their excitement.

"So, they found me at last," she whispered back.

"They? Who's they?"

"The people who are meant to find me."

Somewhere in the distance a whistle sounded, and someone began to beat a gong.

"On second thought, perhaps the wrong people have found me."

Andry went over to the door and looked out into the street. To the north, a group of guardsmen was advancing purposefully. He looked in the other direction. A group of at least two dozen warriors in skirmishing armor was approaching. Opposite the shop, the spies were signaling in both directions while glancing uneasily at each other. There appeared to be no other people in the street, because the local people had somehow learned that guardsmen were on the way and had removed themselves to safer places. Andry walked over to the shopkeeper, seized him by the tunic, and punched him in the face. The man fell to the floor, stunned.

"What do you think you're doing?" demanded the horrified Wallas. "I had him down to three silver—"

"Now it's on the house. Quickly, out through the back door."

"There is no back door!" shouted Terikel from the back of the shop. "No window either."

Suddenly there was a commotion from outside. The swish of arrows and sound of running feet mingled with screams of pain and battle cries. The watchers in the street were staggering and falling, caught in the crossfire between the City Guard—in search of Wallas—and a detachment of Throne Guards—in search of Terikel. The two squads of warriors charged each other.

Terikel, Wallas, and Andry watched in fascination as the battle raged in the street outside. There were several times more City Guards than Throne Guards, but the Throne Guards were an elite and deadly force. A hand-to-hand engagement now began. The City Guards surged past the shop; then the Throne Guards stopped them and began to force them back. The front line passed the shop again. By now the leader of the Throne Guards had decided that the other force had rescued Terikel from the shop and was leading his men in a frantic scramble to capture or kill the Metrologans' Elder. Andry took a three-stringed rebec and bow down from a rack on the wall.

"Andry, that's stealing!" exclaimed Terikel.

"Oh aye, is that so?" responded Andry. "Then he can take it out of the reward for turning us over to those heavies out there!"

Andry selected a few spare strings, then stepped out into the street and stared at the battle, which was by now seventy yards to the north.

"Er, I think we'd best be on our way," he said, beckoning to the others.

Terikel and Wallas joined him, and they began to walk away briskly. They were within a few feet of a crossroad when the shopkeeper staggered out of the music shop, waving his hands and shouting.

"There he goes, stop him, he bought a board lyre!"

A Throne Guard glanced back at exactly the wrong moment—at least as far as Terikel, Andry, and Wallas were concerned.

"Behind us, the Elder!" he shouted.

The Throne Guards turned, and nine of them flung light throwing axes. One of them embedded its blade in the shopkeeper's skull, but Terikel, Andry, and Wallas were beyond

the range of even axes flung by Throne Guards. The City
Guardsmen now set upon the Throne Guards, thinking that
they were retreating. The Throne Guards turned back and
reengaged the City Guards. Terikel, Andry, and Wallas vanished around a corner.

"Might I ask what all that was about?" Wallas asked as they
sat in a tavern a mile from the music shop, gathering their
wits and recovering their breath.

"The shop was being watched!" said Andry.

"They were watching for *me*," explained Terikel.

"But the shopkeeper was shouting about a board lyre,"
Andry pointed out.

"That was because of when you rescued me," said Terikel.
"The three surviving throne guards would have reported that
one of my rescuers had a board lyre which was broken in the
fighting. When Wallas asked about the lyre, the shopkeep
must have made a signal to someone outside the shop."

"But there were two groups fighting each other."

"There must be a very large reward for me. They must
have been fighting over the right to claim it by killing me."

Andry turned to Wallas. "Keep that damn stupid lyre out
of sight!" he snapped.

"What do we do now?" asked Wallas, wrapping a ragged
blanket around his board lyre.

"Well, the shopkeeper is dead, along with all the watchers
in the street," Terikel pointed out, "and the guards only saw
us at a distance. With some minor changes in our grooming
and clothes we can look quite different. I have white pilgrim
headbands for each of us. Playing pilgrims will allow us to
wander the city as strangers, going to odd places without
seeming odd."

"What sorts of places?" asked Andry with genuine curiosity.

"How odd?" asked Wallas suspiciously.

That afternoon they did indeed tour the temples, shrines, holy monuments, and places where holy people had been put to death for one reason or another over the past couple of thousand years.

"Your accent, it sounds Alberinese Scalticarian," Terikel commented to Andry as they walked.

"Oh aye, that's well placed."

"Have you been here long?"

"Got here yesterday."

"Ah yes . . ." began Terikel, then she caught herself.

"Your pardon, ladyship?"

"Yes, a deepwater trader arrived yesterday, the *Stormbird*."

"Oh aye, I was on it. Carpenter's mate, that's what I am. Except there was no carpenter."

"Are you not a little young to be a carpenter's mate?"

"Oh aye, I'm nineteen, I think. But I got articles of apprenticeship."

Terikel had seen little of the *Stormbird*, aside from her cabin, the master cabin, and whatever happened to be outside the spray shutter whenever she happened to be throwing up. That was generally waves, although once she had looked up from the water to the sight of a monstrous wave breaking over the mighty Seadragon Pinnacle. She had managed to attend six meals at the captain's table in thirty-two days, but amid the talk of cold, misery, and trying to keep the ship afloat and moving vaguely north while being swept west, she also remembered them complaining of "that young bastard," the carpenter's mate. He had been press-ganged just before they sailed from Alberin, and had been punished nearly every day, for everything from fighting to drunken singing during night watch to general annoying behavior.

"You also got a twenty-five lashes for emptying the prime mate's rum flask and refilling it in a manner that caused him considerable distress, and another twenty-five for striking an officer and trying to desert at the Malderin Islands."

"I—you—how—I . . ." stammered the astounded Andry.

"Striking an officer is a hanging offense normally, so they must have really valued your services to let you off with a flogging."

"But, but . . . how?"

"There are five dozen seamen from the *Stormbird* in port, and they have been spreading the story of the voyage, Andry," she continued. "It has been the only ship from Scalticar for quite some time, so every scrap of news from the south and every detail of the voyage has been bawled out all over the city, mostly by drunken voices with Scalticarian accents."

"Oh—ah, aye."

"But mind this well, Andry and Wallas. I listen, I remember, and I connect facts that other people don't bother with. *Never*, *ever* lie to me. If I don't already know the truth, I shall soon hear the truth. Then I shall be very disappointed in you."

The memory of the greatly weakened sorceress setting one of the Throne Guards on fire flashed across the minds of Wallas and Andry simultaneously. Both found that memory seriously upsetting.

"Now Wallas, *you* are only pretending to be a sailor."

By now Wallas was feeling so intimidated that he did not even contemplate denial.

"Er, aye."

"Then what are you?"

"On the run."

"From what crime?"

"I didn't do it."

"That was not the question."

"Murder."

"Shyte me!" exclaimed Andry.

"See how easy that was?" said Terikel brightly, apparently not in the least concerned about what Wallas swore he had not done. "Every so often I ask a question when I already know the answer. You did indeed save me from a very unpleasant fate, and quite probably death, but then all of that might have been a big act on your part."

"An act?" exclaimed Wallas and Andry together.

"Oh yes. Consider this plan. I get chased, beaten, and thrown down with my robes all but ripped off. Then you two come along and wipe the cobbles with the most elite warriors on the continent. I then trust you, and share all my secrets, secrets that the late emperor's finest torturers could not otherwise have extracted from me. Gentlefolk, if you are genuine I owe you my life, and my thanks will be genuine and generous. But if you are deceiving me, your fate does not even bear contemplation."

Andry and Wallas dropped a little behind, then stopped as Terikel stared at the statue of Barbaroon, the storm god. The area around its base was strewn with offerings, in view of the Torean Storms, which were far more violent and frequent than what was considered normal.

"Hie, what's 'contemplation'?" whispered Andry to Wallas.

"That's when you think about something really, really carefully," replied Wallas.

"Like thinking about Marielle Stoker taking off her clothes and having a bath?"

"Aye, but think instead about that thing that dropped on you last night, and very nearly tore your throat out to drink your blood."

"I'd rather not."

"Ah-ha! Now you're seeing what the sorceress meant by 'not bearing contemplation.' "

Terikel rejoined them, and they set off for the next place of interest.

"Ladyship, do you worship Barbaroon, then?" asked Andry as they walked.

"Barbaroon and I have shared interests," Terikel replied. "Dragonwall is designed to drain his strength, but my mission to Dragonwall is to . . ." She gave Andry a sidelong glance. "My mission is to take detailed notes."

Early in the evening Terikel returned to Madame Jilli's establishment, talked with her for a few minutes, then spoke with one of the lamplight girls for rather longer. They went into a bedchamber together, and emerged soon after with the girl wearing Terikel's clothing and Terikel dressed as a merchant. Her coat had been padded and her breasts bound with cloth, giving the effect of a man with large, broad shoulders and a deep chest.

"This is Melier," Terikel announced, gesturing to the girl now disguised as herself. "Melier, these are Andry and Wallas. They are your escort. Melier is a Diomedan who came south to Palion in search of her fortune. In return for traveling aboard the *Stormbird* disguised as me, I have given her a small purse of gold coins, along with free passage home to Diomeda. You will travel on the *Stormbird* as her escort. Diomeda is outside the Sargolan Empire, so you should be as safe as anyone can be in this world. And now, ladies and gentlemen, I really must go. You will never see me again."

Terikel left without scene or ceremony, just a bow and the closing of the door behind her. Melier returned upstairs, and Andry and Wallas sat tuning their instruments while they waited for her.

"Odd wench, the Elder," said Andry softly. "You'd think she was just popping out to buy a jar at the market, not leaving forever."

"Probably can't wait to be away from you," replied Wallas. "Fancy that, pissing in the prime mate's rum."

"Not so! His flask was empty."

"Oh ho, so you drank his rum first!"

"Bastard threw my fife overboard, had to steal another from the bosun. So where's this Melier wench?"

"Oh, packing her bags, I suspect."

"For a quarter hour? When I used to travel upriver in the barges, I'd have a blanket and the clothes that I stood in."

"No wonder people cross the street to pass you."

"What's that supposed to mean?"

It was now that Madame Jilli sauntered over, waving her hand in little circles. She pointed upward.

"Wallas, be pleased to advise Melier on what it will be like during the voyage," she ordered.

"But, but I don't even know how to swim!" exclaimed Wallas.

"Then advise her on what to pack. Ellisen, go with them."

Madame Jilli watched them climbing the stairs, then turned away and beckoned to Andry over her shoulder.

"Attend me, Andry, there are a few details I need to discuss with you."

The closest Andry had ever been to a bawdyhouse before his arrival in Palion had been on his last night in Alberin, when he had collapsed in the doorway of one. Now he was in the private room of a woman who ran such an establishment. Andry put his bag down in a corner, cringing with the anticipation of what might come next, and of how he was likely to make a fool of himself. The place smelled faintly of lavender, and contained a large bed with a brightly colored quilt and a pair of pink pillows sewn in the shape of two pairs of breasts. There were several trunks, a table with a mirror, another table with a writing kit, and several register books. *She just lives here*, thought Andry, and all of a sudden the place seemed far less threatening. Madame Jilli opened one of the larger trunks and rummaged in it.

"You are probably wondering why I brought you in here," said Madame Jilli as she straightened, swinging a small pouch.

"Oh aye," replied Andry uneasily.

"Well, what were your thoughts?"

"Begging your pardon, ladyship, but they're all passable rude."

"Only to be expected, but giving you that sort of thing is not what I have in mind. What I am going to give you is this pouch."

Andry put out his hand, and she placed it on his palm. He stared at it for some moments.

"Er, does it have something magical?"

"In a way, yes. It contains a demikin needle, a ball of black thread, a cake of soap, a toothscour, a washcloth, and a nail file. Make sure that you use each of these items every day for the next week and you will find that girls do not treat you as a joke. Use them for a month, and you might well get a declaration of love. Use them until you decide to journey back from Diomeda to Scalticar, and . . . well, remember to pay me a visit."

"You're saying I should just wash my face, clean my teeth, patch my clothes, and clean my nails?" said Andry doubtfully.

"You could try combing your hair too, but you do have a pleasingly rugged look with it unkempt," Madame Jilli said as she opened the door.

Andry hurried through the door, but once out of her room he managed to muster his courage. He placed the pouch on a hallside table.

"My thanks, ladyship, but no," he said.

Madame Jilli blinked in surprise.

"I meant it when I said call past if ever you travel here again," she insisted.

"Why?" asked Andry, his voice almost a whisper.

"Oh Andry, to see how you turned out, silly."

"But I'd look like I am now: washed and dressed clean."

Madame Jilli smiled at him, her head inclined to one side.

"I might fancy you," she conceded coyly.

"Begging your pardon, ladyship, but you fancied Wallas when he were scruffy. What's wrong with me will not be set right by cleaning."

"You're jealous!" laughed Madame Jilli, her eyes wide.

"Not jealous, ladyship, just a wee bit hurt. Wallas gets a tumble, I gets a sewing kit. It's like in Alberin taverns. Serving maids give me a free beer for a song well done, then sit on another's knee. Can you tell me why it's so?"

It was a surprisingly perceptive question, and Madame Jilli was certainly taken by surprise. She put her fingertips to her lips as she tried to think of a credible answer.

"Some men present well on first sight, I suppose," she managed.

"Aye, and some don't," said Andry miserably.

A door slammed above them, and Wallas, Ellisen, and Melier came clattering down the stairs. Ellisen was carrying Melier's five bags. They stopped before Madame Jilli, and Ellisen presented Andry with the five bags.

"My dear Madame Jilli, I fear it is time to take leave of your charming house and even more charming self," declared Wallas, spreading his arms wide and bowing.

Madame Jilli backed away a pace, unsmiling. Wallas immediately dropped his arms and gave a small, formal bow. She lifted her skirts until the entire length of her left leg was visible. Four pairs of eyes had her undivided attention as she took a dagger in a lace sheath from the garter on her thigh.

"This once cut the tongue from a man who boasted about

what was done between us in our single night together," she said, flourishing the little weapon.

Wallas turned chalk white, Melier looked puzzled, and Ellisen gave a slight grin. Andry tore his gaze from the direction of Madame Jilli's exposed leg with considerable difficulty— to see that she was holding out the dagger to him, handle first.

"Lordship, I regret most sorely that I was too shy to offer a place in my bed to you last night," she said softly, staring straight at Andry. "Please accept this, the most intimate of the things that I own, to remind you of me. Should you ever return to Palion, my heart will break if you choose to sleep in any bed other than mine."

Andry's hand was shaking somewhat as he accepted the dagger in its lace sheath; then Madame Jilli put her arms around his neck and kissed him very firmly on the lips. After more words of farewell had been exchanged, Ellisen held the front door open. Wallas was so anxious to leave that he stumbled on the step and fell headlong into the street. Melier followed, a puzzled expression still on her face, then Andry walked out sideways, with the bags hanging from a pole across his shoulders.

Madame Jilli and Ellisen stood together, watching the trio walk away down Naughtingly Street.

"I think I understand Andry now," Madame Jilli declared.

"How so, madame?" asked Ellisen.

"He has been raised rough, yet he is decent, brave, good-hearted, and very, very intelligent. His trouble is that he does not fit among his own folk, they know not what to make of him."

"True, madame," said Ellisen, who was quite familiar with problems of fitting in.

"Yet he has no place among noble folk, where he could be better than the greatest of them. I hurt him, Ellisen, but I tried to make it up to him."

"Your esteem for him is now in no doubt, madame."

"I failed."

"Failed is a very strong word."

"Do you think I humiliated Wallas sufficiently?"

"Without doubt, madame."

"Good."

✳ ✳ ✳

Suddenly aware that Andry might be a serious contender for Melier's affections, Wallas combed his hair, straightened his clothes, and began speaking in his very best courtly Sargolan as they walked away from Madame Jilli's. Before long he realized that this excluded not only Andry from the conversation, but Melier as well. He switched to educated Diomedan.

"Of course, agents of the emperor such as myself have a need to be masters of disguise," he was saying before they had even left the street in which Madame Jilli's establishment was located.

"And what is the nature of your mission?" she asked, her eyes quite wide with a mixture of suspicion and admiration above the veil that she now wore to obscure most of her face.

"Oh, the protection of the Elder Terikel, of course."

"But were not the late emperor's own Throne Guards chasing her?"

"Ah no, they were mere contract assassins, disguised as Throne Guards. I could tell, of course, they were so much easier to dispose of than real Throne Guards."

"And you, Lord Andry," she said, turning away from Wallas to Andry, who had four of her bags on a pole across his shoulders and another strapped across his back. "I feel so bad that a great noble such as yourself should carry my bags."

Not half as bad as I feel, thought Andry, but he said, "All part of the guise, miss."

"What is your story, Andry? Madame Jilli let slip that you are a peer with Lord Wallas."

"I'm just a lad," said Andry, staring at the road ahead.

"Hie, but you could make no other reply, could you? I think I'll spend the voyage trying to work out who you really are. The weather seems much better than yesterday, so we should have good sailing."

"Weather turns sour from fair faster than the reverse," replied Andry. "A bit like folk, the weather."

Had Andry wished to make a play for Melier, Wallas would indeed have found himself on the losing side of a very one-sided battle. Melier, however, took Andry's restraint and manner as that of a nobleman so great that a mere lamplight girl such as herself had no chance with him. Wallas was soon able to steer the conversation back to the subject of himself, and he went on to entertain her with accounts of scandals from the palace.

"Of course, nobody was able to get near Viscount Cosseren and Princess Senterri when they came to their matrimonial bed, but I had words with Lady Cormendiel, whose fourth daughter has been known to exchange her favors about the palace in return for royal favors."

"No!" breathed Melier, who had heard of neither Lady Cormendiel nor her daughter.

"Yes, and after entertaining Viscount Cosseren for a night, and the next morning, well! She said that he was uncouth and ill mannered, and had no idea of what pleased a lady. Why she even said that all the conquests that he boasts about must have been sheep."

They both broke into ill-controlled laughter, clinging to each other for support.

"And lower-class sheep at that," Wallas managed after some moments, finally able to deliver the punch line to a story that, for all its embroidery, did contain a surprising amount of truth.

Andry stopped until they were able to compose themselves and walk after him again.

"What sorts of, ah, skill does it take to please a courtly lady then, Lord Wallas?" Melier asked with studied innocence, although even Andry recognized it for the leading question that it was.

"Oh, it is hard to put into words," responded Wallas with a throne-room flourish that no beggar should have known or could have executed so well. "Small gestures, winks, bows, courtesies, caresses, they are refinements that are best demonstrated, not sullied by words."

"It would please me much to know something of courtly refinements for when I return to Diomeda."

"Well then, after this voyage you might even say that you have had a liaison with a courtier."

I could never be a great seducer, my dignity would get in

the way, thought Andry as he trudged along, carrying more than his own body weight in luggage. *Did I just think what I thought I thought? Me, dignified? Andry Tennoner of Barge-yards? Fourteenth of seventeen children. At least Madame Jilli had style. Style? Did I just think style? Having my hair washed must have done something to my brain. Or maybe it was from killing the lice. But how could Melier be taken in by such daft banter from Wallas? If the woman had half a wit, she'd be a half-wit!*

Andry was still deep in thought as they reached the *Storm-bird*. Melier had her hand on Wallas's arm as they went aboard, followed by Andry with the bags. They were met by the shipmaster, who made a long and elaborate show of examining Melier's papers.

Wallas then addressed her as Terikel, having become confused by the woman's triple persona. The shipmaster then leaned closer and whispered something to her. She slapped his face. *Interesting voyage coming along*, thought Andry as he turned Melier's bags over to the purser, who was standing near the passenger hatch and trying to stifle his laughter. Nobody paid Andry much attention at first, because the ship was being prepared to sail with the evening tide.

"Hie, but swab me with bilge if it's not young Tennoner!" exclaimed the deckswain, suddenly catching sight of Andry.

"It's myself," replied Andry simply.

"But there's no place for ye aboard. We signed up both carpenter and carpenter's mate today."

"But it's as a passenger I come aboard this time," replied Andry. "I work for the Diomedan lady there, who has passage to her home city. I'm a contract guard."

"You, a contract guard?" the deckswain laughed.

"I have special skills as suit me for the work. We've good weather for sailing, I see."

"Aye, but how long will it last?"

At that point Wallas strode over, selected one of Melier's bags, then returned to her side and vanished into the passenger hatch with her. Andry noticed the shipmaster scowling after them. He was also rubbing his face. He called to the deckswain, and they spoke together for some moments, then shared a joke and laughed. Andry knew what could be done to a person on a long voyage. Wallas was in for an interesting time, he decided. He would probably be given a dose of some purgative in his first meal, and that would have him confined to the sick bay in agony—while the shipmaster introduced Melier to the delights of being in the favor of the master of a large vessel. On the other hand, once they hit the large waves beyond the harbor and out to sea, perhaps Wallas would not need a philtre to make him ill. Perhaps Melier would not be very good company, either.

Why am I such a rough slob in rough company, yet I show signs of being like my betters when I mix with them? Andry wondered. *Am I a nobleman, brought up in Bargeyards, after being orphaned or abandoned?* He certainly looked like his father, tall and scrawny, but fairly tough. It would have been noticed if his mother had not been his mother, and besides, he had her talent for remembering things and learning fast. When he had been with Madame Jilli, though—His stolen rebec! Andry now remembered that it was back at Madame Jilli's Recreational Rooming, in her bedchamber.

At first Andry thought of jumping onto the pier and dashing back to Madame Jilli's, but the hawsers were already being cast off, and a scoreboat was waiting to tow the *Stormbird* out into clear water. *No, it's a good reason to call back there next time, in all innocence*, he decided; then he suddenly slammed his fist down on the ship's railing. *Damn innocence, I really want to get back into Madame Jilli's room and do what Wallas is doing with Melier down in her cabin.* The daylight was almost gone, but the weather was as calm as it ever got with the Torean Storms about. *When will I see Madame Jilli again*, thought Andry—and then he thought nothing at all.

Lavolten and Talberan slowly walked the circumference of Ringstone Centras, which was now not only deserted, but under guard. Beyond the ringstone, an additional three rings were being surveyed and installed.

"I am still not entirely sure about the wisdom of the extra rings," said Talberan as they walked. "I mean, how can you call those things ringstone rounds when the megaliths are just wooden chairs with high backs?"

"Oh, but the seats are of stone, all hollowed out to buttock shape. Besides, they are sited on stone slabs."

"It is not the same. The ancients—"

"The ancients built the smallest configuration that would work. We are building the largest configuration that mortals can sustain."

"What about the central megalith?"

"Oh, I think we know what went wrong, it all makes sense now. All the etheric energies have to be channeled through the central megalith, and it has to be in perfect balance with the other sixteen. Our megalith was too low because of being in a crater, so boom!"

Lavolten raised his arms to the sky in exasperation.

"Boom, as you so crudely put it, has cost us the confidence of every sorcerer in the camp. What I really meant was that nobody will volunteer for it now."

"We should have tried to keep the problem a secret."

"A secret?" laughed Lavolten. "How? Everyone within four hundred yards was hit by bits of Astential."

"Well, we can still preserve a modicum of secrecy. Sergal is at Ringstone Logiar. He is easily powerful and skilled enough to replace Astential. I shall leave tonight and order him here. Meantime, you must begin building the stone platform in the center of the crater to bring the central megalith to the height of the others."

"It was a traumatic way to learn that this thing is a crater, and why."

"But at least we have solved an ancient mystery."

Andry found himself standing in near-darkness, confronted by a lean and very fit-looking girl. At first glance she seemed quite naked, but closer inspection revealed that she was wearing a tightly fitting white garment that left only her hands, feet, and head exposed. There was a dark and slow-flowing river behind her, and pulled up onto the bank beside her was the most sleek, streamlined boat that Andry had ever

seen. Even the oars were so long and thin as to be almost
spidery. She was holding a very large book open.

"Got a bad feeling about this," said Andry.

"You know who I am?" she asked.

"You're the ferrygirl, but I don't know your name."

"And why are you here?"

"I'm dead, I expect."

"In theory, yes . . . but there seems to be a problem."

"You're not what I expected. You're supposed to be in
rags, with a pole and black punt."

"There are many instances of the ferrygirl, including me.
I'm on contract from another world. There were too many
deaths when Torea was burned, so the regulars are still
working on the backlog."

She stared at the book, then frowned. Andry could not
help but notice that her ears were rounded, and that the
pupils of her eyes were circular.

"Now what?" asked Andry.

"I ought to row you over to the afterlife, but . . . there is a
death written in here, but no name."

"Oh. So that's all of my life?"

"Umm? Just a moment, I shall check Abstracts for your
name. Goodness, there's plenty in here. Apprenticeship articles, sailor, fifty lashes, voted Bargeside Drunken Brawler
of the Year 3140, petty theft, brave, know three languages,
very intelligent . . . For sheer misuse of talent, you ought to
get a prize."

"Is that bad?" asked Andry.

"Disappointing, rather than bad. Have you a coin?"

"Coin?"

"Coin, as in payment for being rowed across this river, to
that afterlife," said the ferrygirl, pointing into the blackness
beyond the water.

Andry checked his clothing. He appeared to have no
money at all. The ferrygirl looked back to her book.

"No coin," Andry admitted.

"I see," the ferrygirl said without looking up from her
book. "You're a musician. What about a tune?"

"Love to, but my rebec's at Madame Jilli's."

"Something odd about this entry. Wallas is drowning because he cannot swim, yet he is still alive at the moment, and you are definitely dead. Very, very messy."

"What happened? Did the *Stormbird* sink?"

"No. The shipmaster was jealous of Wallas and Melier. He had you struck over the head and heaved overboard, thinking you were their guard. Then he had Wallas flung overboard too . . . look, I think we can help each other."

"Me? Help Death?"

"I'm the ferrygirl, not Death. You rescue Wallas, I'll fetch your rebec. What do you say?"

"I'm game."

Andry was suddenly in the cold waters of Palion's harbor. Beside him was a floundering mass of thrashing limbs and foam that he assumed to be Wallas.

Terikel was alone as she entered a hillside plaza that overlooked Palion's harbor. Half of the plaza was edged by a stone wall; the other side featured the houses of those sufficiently wealthy to pay for a view of the sea. Evening was quite advanced as the Elder walked the fifty yards to the center of the wall and leaned on it, gazing out at the view but occasionally glancing behind her. She was dressed as a wayfarer merchant, implying that she was male, strong, but not at all rich—and thus more trouble than it was worth to rob.

After less than a minute had passed, a pair of figures appeared on the other side of the plaza. They stopped, conferred, then looked across at her. Finally one strode over to join Terikel while the other vanished between two houses. Terikel heard feet approach, then stop. She became aware of the smell of mildew, and of something rotten. For a time they stood together, resting their elbows on the weathered marble capping of the wall. Finally Terikel turned, but could see little more than that her new companion was dressed in black.

"Velander?" asked Terikel.

"Yes, Learned Elder," came a voice which was soft, silky, yet definitely menacing. "Best not to come too close, I am very dangerous."

The voice was speaking in a dead language from a dead continent, but it was also Terikel's language.

"I thought I would never see you again," she replied.

"But it is not so, Learned Elder. I am pleased. We were apart for too long."

"We were not on the best of terms when we last saw each other."

"True. There was hatred between us. I betrayed you, Learned Elder, I tried to ruin you. That was unforgivable."

Terikel straightened, folded her arms, unfolded them, rubbed her chin, waved a hand in the air while preparing to say something forgiving that would also sound convincing, failed to find any words that would convince even herself, let alone Velander, then folded her arms even more tightly and stared down at the capping of the wall. She shifted her weight from foot to foot, both embarrassed and uneasy.

"You must have felt so hurt and betrayed when I—" Terikel began.

"I did, but that is no excuse for what I did. I cannot be forgiven."

"But Fortune punished you," Terikel pointed out. "Why should I punish you further? I want to be your friend again."

There was a sound like a strangled sob. "Your friend? Look at me now. I am a dead thing that walks. I prey upon the living, and I am *always* hungry."

Velander's eyes gleamed as she turned to regard Terikel, and her tongue flickered over her lips. Terikel fought down an urge to back away. By now she had identified the stench on the air as that of stale blood. There was a sense of danger, as one might get standing beneath a very heavy crate suspended by a very thin and frayed rope.

"Velander, there is much I want to make up between us."

Terikel stepped forward and put her arms out, but Velander glided back along the wall, and out of reach.

"No touching please!" she exclaimed. "It would be like a sheep embracing a wolf: a very bad idea."

Terikel considered this. Together with the smell of stale blood and mildew on the air, there was also the sharp reek of sweat. The sweat of seriously terrified people. *All of them now dead, no doubt*, she concluded. Her old soulmate had become a fiend.

"Was that Laron who arrived with you?" asked Terikel.

"Yes, we can see him later, but just now he has to attend problems in the palace," said Velander, gesturing in the direction of the royal palace.

"I have heard that he is no longer like you."

"You mean dead, and a dangerous wraith?"

"Ah, well, yes."

"That is true, he is feeling better now. Why are you here? Can I help you?"

"Officially, I am actually not here, I am booked on that ship down there, the *Stormbird*."

"But it has left the wharf, and is under sail."

"Yes. It will sail up the east coast of Acrema, and on to the northern kingdoms. My enemies know that, and what my friends think hardly matters."

"Yet you are still here, Learned Elder."

"Yes. I must travel to the Capefang Mountains. I have business there concerning Dragonwall."

Velander stared at the departing *Stormbird*. The shape of the big ship was picked out by its running lamps, and it was making good progress. For a change, the weather was fine, and there was a light, steady wind.

"Dragonwall is not what it seems," began Velander.

Suddenly fire boiled up around the *Stormbird*, great streamers of flame that set the sails and rigging ablaze, swept along the decks, and leaked out through the scuppers. Long, sinuous necks swayed in the light of the burning ship, necks tipped with large, flattish heads that occasionally swooped down to the surface of the water to pluck out and swallow small, dark struggling things.

"Andry!" exclaimed Terikel in horror, her hands to her face. "Melier! Wallas!"

"Are those the decoys you sent aboard?" asked Velander, without taking her eyes from the scene.

"Decoys, but friends," cried Terikel.

The burning oil sprayed by the sea serpents was sticky, so that some of it would cling to their prey and disable it quickly. The *Stormbird* was a floating bonfire within the first minute. The serpents continued to feast on the sailors who had dived overboard.

"There is no recorded case of such pack behavior by arcereon sea dragons," said Terikel.

"I trust someone will write up this instance," replied Velander.

"They are deepwater creatures, yet here they are, within sight of the shore. They are surely being controlled."

"Someone is trying to kill you," Velander concluded.

"I had noticed," said Terikel, shaking her head.

"What now?" asked Velander. "Your pursuers must think you are dead."

Part of me is indeed dead, thought Terikel. *I thought I was doing my friends a favor.*

"I need somewhere to stay, somewhere secure. Then I need safe passage to the Capefang Mountains. Airwalking is out of the question. I am too weak, after the voyage and . . . other experiences."

"Then I can help," said Velander, gesturing to one of the streets that led out of the plaza. "Come, you do not need to see that any longer."

They walked across the darkened plaza, which was no longer so deserted. People were leaning out of windows or leaving their houses to run to the low wall and stare. Suddenly a bright flash from behind them lit up the taller buildings. Terikel was aware of some of the onlookers screaming.

"Sometimes, just sometimes, I feel that there is no warmth left in the world for me," Terikel whispered as she walked.

"I am sorry for your friends," said Velander. "I know how you must feel."

"Then you must know guilt beyond endurance, Vel. In a way I am so glad that they are dead. I could never, never explain that I did not intend this fate for them."

Soaked, filthy, and crouched on a mudbank beneath the pier, Andry and Wallas gaped at the burning ship and the nightmares that were attacking it.

"Shyte me!" exclaimed Andry.

"Not today thank you," wheezed Wallas.

"Mistress Melier was on that!" cried Andry, pointing at the floating fireball and the feasting sea serpents.

"*We* were very nearly on that!" Wallas pointed out.

"They thought Mistress Terikel was aboard," replied Andry.

"Who is *they*?" demanded Wallas.

"*They* are one mean gang of drinkers," said Andry.

There was a sudden flash of lurid red streaked with yellow as the *Stormbird* exploded.

"Oh shyte," whimpered Wallas.

A wave of flames lashed out over the feasting sea dragons. Even though they were capable of breathing fire, their skins were certainly not flameproof. They dived out of sight with shrill squeals, and did not reappear.

"What was that?" gasped the badly shaken Wallas.

"Cargo of lamp oil," said Andry. "High value, low storage space. Just the thing for the last big vessel left afloat. It would have fetched a fortune in Diomeda."

"You mean—the *Stormbird* was *intended* to explode like a thunderbolt?"

This had not occurred to Andry.

"The Elder," he said slowly. "She arranged for Melier to dress like her to go aboard."

"Melier, aye."

"And her enemies would search the vessel at the first port it visited, discover that the Elder herself was not aboard . . . but now nobody's to know she's not dead. Could she have summoned those things?"

"You mean to fake her own death?" said Wallas in disbelief, pointing at the remains of the conflagration.

"Aye."

"The murdering bitch!"

"Aye."

"Think anyone survived?" asked Wallas, thinking of Melier and feeling vaguely guilty for still being alive while she had perished.

"Only you," replied Andry, staring at the patch of smoky flames in the middle of the harbor. "What have you got?"

"Sodden clothes, three silver nobles, and a few coppers," replied Wallas. "What little else I had was in a bag on the *Stormbird*."

"But your board lyre was in my bag."

"So what? That was on the *Stormbird* too."

"Not so. I forgot my bag, it's in Madame Jilli's place."

Wallas glanced out across the harbor again, where the burning lamp oil was illuminating the agonized thrashings of a burned sea dragon that had just surfaced. He wondered how Melier might have died, and he hoped her death had been quick.

"I've got my life, too, for what it's worth," he sighed.

"Well you're ahead of me," replied Andry, who then fell down dead.

Madame Jilli was lying fully clothed on her bed with her arm across her face when the knock came. There were three taps at her door. She ignored them. After a half minute there were another three taps.

"I said I want to be alone!" she shouted without removing her arm from her eyes.

"I am afraid I must insist," said a soft contralto voice.

Madame Jilli sat up at once, furious. "How dare you enter my room!" she rasped, glaring at the girl standing before her. "Nobody may enter . . ."

Her voice trailed away. She was in her bedchamber, but she was also in some very dark place beside a river that appeared to be flowing with black ink. Not far away, a figure was sitting next to a sleek, exceedingly narrow boat.

"Oh no," whispered Madame Jilli.

"A lot of people say that when they see me," said the girl, reaching down through the fabric of Andry's bag and drawing out his rebec and bow.

"But how? I was lying on my bed, the door was locked."

"Dangerous places, beds. More people die there than anywhere else. Actually, you're not dead, but Andry is. I need your permission to take his rebec to him."

"My permission?"

"He left it with you, so I must ask. Well?"

Madame Jilli slipped from her bed—then turned to stare at her body, which was still lying on the bed.

"I should not do that for too long," said the ferrygirl. "Not unless you want a rather more serious visit from me."

"A visit . . . from Death?"

The girl laughed. "Oh, Death doesn't exist, that's just an anthropomorphism created by neomodernist sorcery theoreticians and metaphysical philosophers. There's only me, and a few associates."

"What did all that mean?"

"Death is a process, not a person."

"I still don't understand."

"Look, may I just take Andry's rebec for him? The real-world original will remain in his bag, and he will have real trouble crossing the river without playing me a tune."

"If Andry needs it, take it," said Madame Jilli. "But wait!"

"I cannot do conditions," warned the girl. "May I take it or not?"

"Please, just listen. I wanted to change Andry, I wanted to give him something that would last. Gah, I suppose I dangled the promise of my company on some future night . . . well, perhaps it was but a poor prospect, but I meant well. Now he's dead, and I wish I had treated him more, well, honorably."

"It happens a lot," said the ferrygirl.

Madame Jilli noticed that the bedroom was fading slowly, and the gloom of the riverbank was replacing it.

"You are actually close to death," said the ferrygirl. "Stay with me too long and you will not be able to return."

"Do I have long enough to hear Andry play?"

※ ※ ※

Andry was alone on the riverbank when the ferrygirl returned with his rebec and bow.

"What tune would you like, miss?" he asked as she handed them to him.

"Oh, I don't know any tunes from your world," she said

with a little wave of her hand. "Something nautical, perhaps. I am a type of sailor, after all."

Andry played a jig, then a slip jig, then a reel, and finally he sang "The Press-ganged Barge Lad." The ferrygirl sat listening, obviously enjoying the music. Figures began to gather behind her, vague, ghostly figures. *Ghosts should be no surprise here*, thought Andry. He paused in his playing as the ferrygirl held up a hand.

"That was very pleasant, Andry," she declared. "I am satisfied, you may enter the boat."

"No, wait!" called one of the figures behind her.

A couple with impossibly attractive and physically perfect bodies came forward, and the ferrygirl introduced them as Fortune and Chance.

"We were wondering if you would play 'The Heel-Toe Galloppe,' " asked Fortune.

"Oh aye, that I can," replied Andry.

"You don't have to, Andry," said the ferrygirl. "You are beyond their power here."

"Maybe so, but I'd like to."

Fate strode out of the shadows, bowed to the ferrygirl, and held out his hand. By the time Andry had played several brackets, there were dozens of gods, demigods, and lost souls dancing on the riverbank. He noted that one figure stood well back, however, and did not join in. At last the ferrygirl called for a rest.

"So how did you die, Andry?" asked Fortune. "I had been favoring you."

"Act of Fate," said Chance.

"Blind Chance," retorted Fate.

"I am not blind," Chance pointed out.

"All that time you spend in taverns, with drunken gamblers, I would say you were blind drunk," replied Fate. "Anyway, people never say Fortune is blind, and she spends as much time as me in taverns. They curse *me*, but pray to *her*."

"If you count taverns, then Chance and I have more temples built to us than any other gods," said Fortune, elbowing Andry in the ribs.

"So who killed Andry?" asked the ferrygirl.

The gods looked to each other.

"It was not by Chance, it was deliberate," said Chance.

"It was not Fated, I was visiting Destiny at the time," Fate pointed out.

"Well he was in my favor," Fortune pointed out, putting an arm around Andry's shoulders. "I like you, Andry."

"Did he really die?" Chance asked the ferrygirl.

"He was Fated to live," said Fate.

"I would wager that it was one of those random fluctuations that Probability leaves lying around," said Chance.

"Are they legal on this world?" asked the ferrygirl.

"There was a Probability that he might be struck too hard upon the head," Probability admitted. "That would reduce the Probability of the cold water reviving him, so that he would breathe that same water and drown."

"So it was you?" asked the ferrygirl.

"No, he has a tough head, and has been in many fights, it was just by Chance that—"

"No it was not!" shouted Chance. "I'm tired of my name being taken in vain."

The ferrygirl stood up and beckoned Andry to come with her. They walked over to her boat and stood watching the otherworldly entities bickering.

"It happens from time to time," she explained. "Ask the soul to play a tune, a few of them come over to listen, and before long they are trading insults. I like sailors, that's why I ask the nicer ones for a tune instead of money."

"I don't understand," said Andry.

"A combination of Fate, Chance, and various others often kills people. They get annoyed when that happens. Demarcation, you see. Add to this the fact that Fortune favors you, and things are looking very promising."

"I still don't understand," said Andry.

"Just watch," said the ferrygirl, taking a register book, quill, and bottle of ink from her long, lean boat. "Ladies, gentlemen, Andry has played his tune for me, so now I just need a signature beside his name so that I can row him over to—"

"I am signing nothing!" snapped Chance.

"The Probability of me putting my name against any involvement in his death is vanishingly low," declared Probability.

"His death was not Fated, so it was nothing to do with me," said Fate.

"I favored him, so don't look at me!" said Fortune firmly.

"I just collect them," said the ferrygirl, "I am not authorized to sign the register."

Andry's life hung in the balance as the ferrygirl and several quite significant gods paused to consider the situation. Chance cleared his throat. The others turned to him.

"There is a small Chance that the cold water slowed his bodily processes, so that he did not need as much air as usual."

"There is a small Probability that the waves from the sea dragons revived him and washed him onto a mudbank beneath the pier," said Probability.

"He had been Fated to live a lot longer," declared Fate.

Fortune vanished without warning. Fate bowed to Andry and walked away into the shadows. Probability said good bye, and flickered out of existence. It was now that the figure that had been watching in silence walked forward, stepped into the ferrygirl's boat, and sat down. Chance flipped a coin into the air, caught it, slapped it onto the back of his hand, looked at the result, shrugged, then bowed to the figure that had been watching.

"By Chance, your transverse artery could rupture, madame," he warned.

"Madame, this is a very bad idea," said the ferrygirl, approaching the boat.

The figure's head shook beneath its cowl. Chance wrote something in the large book, then closed it. He placed the book upon a table that had not been there a moment before. Andry blinked. The table vanished. He got to his feet and walked over to Chance.

"Am I dead?" he asked.

Chance looked at him with expressionless eyes.

"There was a Chance of that," the god replied. "Do you want to go on living?"

"Oh aye, I got some great thoughts together since arriving in Palion. It's, like, stepping outside of my life in Alberin, and seeing that I was just pissing all my talents against a wall, you know?"

"Well you certainly have stepped out of your life."

"I want to find out what I ought to be, like, and become that person. Better myself, like, learn things, study."

The god nodded, but his face remained expressionless.

"I am sending you back, Andry, mainly because you appear to have been touched by Change. He may have touched you a little too hard, but then it's difficult to get some people's attention. I warn you, however, spurn the gift of Change and you will be in deep trouble."

"Er, how so, sir?"

"His next gift might be interesting times. Go now, and live—oh, and great playing!"

Chapter Three

DRAGONWALL

Wallas pounded on the front door of Madame Jilli's Recreational Rooming, expecting to be confronted by a squad of exotically dressed women holding crossbows. Instead, the door opened, Ellisen punched him in the face, and the door was slammed shut again. Wallas came to his senses lying on his back in the street. His jaw clicked every time he moved it, and some of his teeth felt loose. He sat up, wondering what to do next. Andry's bag had contained money, some clothing, and a rebec, in addition to the board lyre. With the bag, he had the resources to flee Palion at once. Without it, he was stuck in the city and back to begging for coppers.

The door opened again and Ellisen emerged. She stepped out and stood over him, her arms folded.

"Why are you still alive?" she asked firmly. "The word is that all aboard the *Stormbird* were lost."

"Andry and I were flung into the water," explained Wallas

breathlessly. "I dragged him ashore but he died there. Look, I need his—"

"You said you can't swim."

"Oh all right, yes, *he* dragged *me* ashore, but before he died he said that he left his bag in Madame Jilli's room."

"Andry is dead?"

"Yes, yes, he was hurt when those sea dragons smashed the ship. Ellisen, please, my board lyre is in his bag—along with my money. That is, half of the money in his bag is mine. The rest you can keep—but if you felt disposed to be charitable, I am in sore need of it to flee the city."

Wallas smiled up at her, hoping that he looked pathetic yet deserving.

"Come in," she said, then turned and stepped back inside.

The door to Madame Jilli's room was open, and at least a dozen girls and women were gathered around her bed. She was lying on it, fully clothed, surrounded by flowers of various degrees of freshness that had been scavenged from elsewhere in the building. A constable with a medicar's band on his arm was leaning over her and holding one eyelid open.

"You say she gave a single scream?" he asked Ellisen as she returned.

"I heard a single scream, lordship. When she did not answer my knock or calls, I shouldered the door open."

"She died from a rupture of her transverse artery. There would have been a single stab of pain, then the end would have followed in moments. I'll write a declaration that no felony took place here."

Wallas kept Ellisen between himself and the medicar constable until the man had left. Ellisen looked about until she saw Andry's bag.

"You may have the board lyre and half of the silver, Wallas, but nothing more," declared Ellisen as she picked up the bag. "But first you must take me to Andry's body."

"What? But, but I would be in danger!"

"From who?"

"The constables, the people who had the ship sunk, the sea dragons, and from—"

"How would you like to add *me* to that list?" asked Ellisen, her hands on her hips.

"I . . . I would rather not," said Wallas reluctantly.

"Splendid. Lead the way."

Pulling the sodden cowl over his head, Wallas walked to the front door, opened it—then shrieked and leaped up into Ellisen's arms. Ellisen promptly dropped him to the floor. Before them stood Andry, his fist raised to knock on the door. Like Wallas, he was still dripping water, and covered in mud.

"Er, could I have my bag?" he asked. "It's in Madame Jilli's room,"

Ellisen delivered a heavy kick to Wallas's backside.

"*That* is for trying to rob Andry," she barked like a drill marshal.

Over the next hour Andry explained that he had in fact passed out after dragging Wallas ashore. Given that Wallas had assessed him in near-darkness, and in cold, wet mud, under a pier, it was hardly surprising that he had seemed dead. They were yet again given baths while Ellisen rummaged through a chest of clothing abandoned or forgotten by various patrons over the years. She found enough to clothe both Andry and Wallas with a reasonable fit.

Andry sat beside Madame Jilli's bed with the women on the death vigil. Ellisen stood behind him, combing out his hair.

"I sent Wallas away to the night market with Roselle, our newest lamplight girl," Ellisen explained. "She had a list of things to buy, and after that they will wait for us at a particular tavern."

"Er, why is that, ladyship?"

"Terikel knows you to have friends here."

"She thinks we're dead."

"Best keep it that way."

A half hour of Ellisen's combing resulted in a considerable amount of loose and matted hair being freed from Andry's head. Ellisen pulled his clean, dry, and untangled hair back and tied it with a leather thong, then held a mirror before him.

"Recognize yourself?" she asked.

"My head looks to have shrunk."

"Folk will have to look hard to recognize you, and the folk who could hurt you will not be expecting you to be alive. Say your good-byes to Madame Jilli now, we must be going."

"But how? She's dead."

"Oh . . . do something romantic, Andry! She did take a curiously strong liking to you."

"I'd not be sure of that. She said nice words to me, but she slept with Wallas. That's real liking."

"That's a stupid mistake, and we all make them. She gave you her star dagger. It's a very special weapon, made from star iron collected by women, forged by women, tempered and honed by women, and touched by men only when it slashes them open. There are more fingers on my hand than men who have been given one. She was trying to tell you she was sorry, Andry. Sorry to have been swept along by Wallas's banter, and sorry to have hurt your feelings."

Andry sat with his fist against his lips, contemplating Madame Jilli's body. At last he took his pile of loose hair, lifted one of her hands, and laid it on the tangle of curls.

"Now, like, she can run her fingers through my hair forever," he said, with his hand still on Madame Jilli's. "I've seen serving maids do that all evening when with lads they really fancy."

One of the women beside the bed sniffled. Ellisen put her hand on Andry's shoulder.

"It really is time to go now," she said.

"I have never been so embarrassed in all my life," said Madame Jilli as the ferrygirl's boat returned to the bank at the edge of life itself and grounded in the pebbles.

"Except that you are dead now," said the ferrygirl, who also looked as if she was not having a very good day.

"Turned back from Arcadia for not dying properly. The very nerve of that immigration cherub."

"The case is a precedent, even for me."

"They would not even let us land at hell."

"I warned you. All the most officious clerks go there."

"So now what? Do I just stay here?"

"Not forever. Your death process is linked to Andry's, so when he dies, you can share the boat with him. Very romantic."

"But he could live for decades!"

"Well that's not forever."

"What am I to do? I like having people around, and I like meeting new people. This place is depressing."

"I have to get back to my own world, my contract has nearly expired . . . but I tell you what. I shall show you how to enter the library, where the books of precedent and procedure are kept. They have lots of romantic stories, seductions, betrayals, and all. Use the Abstracts to find the nice, juicy ones."

"Oh, I like a nice romance."

"Splendid, I'm sure you will be very happy."

✳ ✳ ✳

After having resigned himself to being merely deputy ringmaster of Ringstone Logiar, Sergal was very surprised to find himself the object of an unannounced visit from Talberan. The meeting took place on horseback, in the rain, on the road to Logiar.

"So I am to leave for Ringstone Centras *today*?" asked Sergal for the third time, still not quite able to believe his ears.

"If you agree, learned brother, then you have already left. A coach will be waiting at Logiar, and will take you north along the coastal road. The horses will be changed in relays, it has all been arranged. You will eat, sleep, and study some very important castings in the coach."

Sergal turned to look back at Ringstone Logiar; then he looked to the north.

"Ringmaster of Ringstone Centras, you say?" he asked for the fifth time.

"Well, actually you will be ringmaster of the whole of

Dragonwall," replied Talberan, raising the incentive's value a little more. "All other ringmasters would be subordinate to you."

"And you are sure you know how it happened? Astential's death, that is?"

"Oh yes, and he did not die in vain, either, he solved the mystery of why the original Dragonwall was destroyed. You see, the sorcerers doing the Dragonwall casting must be at precisely the same level within the ringstone, and the level of the central megalith is particularly critical. In that ancient etheric engine, some central megalith was but poorly erected. At some stage, after Dragonwall was cast, the megalith toppled. This disrupted not only the ringstone, but all ringstones generating Dragonwall. All its energies were instantly liberated through the central megaliths, blasting out craters where the ringtones had been sited."

"So the craters are not part of the ringstone design?" concluded Sergal, nodding and stroking his beard.

"No, they are just evidence of an ancient accident," responded Talberan cheerily.

"It does confirm what I have suspected for some time," said Sergal, turning to look back at Ringstone Logiar again. "I have had many arguments with Waldesar on the subject."

"Oh and he is wrong, that is now known to be a fact. He will be ordered to build a stone platform and raise the central megalith of Ringstone Logiar to the correct height."

There was something in the slightly malicious tone of Talberan's voice that appealed to Sergal, something suggesting that he despised unimaginative, political sorcerers like Waldesar, and that he was happy to trample on their petty ambitions when they were no longer useful. Even though his rain cloak was leaking, and he was facing a road journey of nearly two thousand miles with not so much as a single night in a proper bed, it was an offer that Sergal could not refuse.

"You have a new supreme ringmaster, Learned Talberan," he declared, turning away from Ringstone Logiar for the last time.

✳ ✳ ✳

Ellisen took Andry through a maze of alleys, lanes, and dark places until she was satisfied that nobody was following them; then she made for the Wayward Wayfarer. It was not far from Palion's west gate, and was known for staying open all night. Roselle and Wallas were there, sitting together beside a bulging pack. They were not entirely sober, and were getting along very well indeed. At the sight of Ellisen, Wallas sat up straight and assumed a solemn expression.

"We were having a wake for Madame Jilli," he explained.

"Wallas says, got to celebrate life after death's happened," added Roselle, who then got up and swayed off in the direction of the serving board.

"Got to bribe the ferryman with drink," continued Wallas.

"The ferry's rowed by a girl, and she's only about twelve," said Andry, sitting down and rubbing at a tender spot on the back of his head.

"How would you know?" laughed Wallas. "Ever met her?"

"Yes."

Wallas looked from Andry to Ellisen, then back to Andry. Neither was smiling at what should have been a joke.

"Is everyone here mad?" asked Wallas, still trying to maintain a smile.

"No, merely alive," said Andry, who now felt that this status was taken for granted by far too many live people.

Wallas lost color and stared at Andry, remembering that his companion had showed signs of neither breath nor pulse beneath the pier. Ellisen stared too, then looked down at the table, clasped her hands together, cracked her knuckles, and nodded to herself. Wallas decided not to pursue the matter further.

"You'd not have my board lyre there, would you?" he asked.

Andry took the instrument from his pack and handed it to Wallas, who strummed it.

"It's out of tune!" exclaimed Wallas.

"Fortune favors me," responded Andry.

"But not by much."

"Fortune's deserted me."

"What do we do now?" asked Wallas as he turned a peg and plucked at its string.

"You can have another drink," said Andry, pinching the skin of his wrist to make sure that he could still feel pain.

"What of you?"

"After drinking half the harbor, I'm not in the mood."

"So when do we go back to Madame Jilli's?" Wallas asked Ellisen.

"It's Madame Ellisen's now, and you do not go back there," said Ellisen. "We stay here until dawn, then you and Andry leave the city."

"But where do we sleep?" protested Wallas, with a glance to Roselle, who was returning with four tankards.

"Tonight, we do not," said Ellisen, in a tone that made it clear that she resented the fact that Wallas even existed. "The city gates are locked until a half hour before sunrise— unless you would like to climb the city walls."

"Well then, there are any number of diversions to pass the night hours," said Wallas as Roselle sat down opposite him.

He reached under the table and ran a hand along a thigh. It turned out to be Ellisen's, instead of Roselle's. Ellisen seized Wallas's little finger and twisted sharply. There was a snap, and Wallas shrieked with pain.

"Well, who fancies a tune?" said the embarrassed Andry, hurriedly unpacking his rebec.

"What I really fancy is a drink at the serving board," muttered Wallas, cradling his injured finger as he stood up.

"What I fancy is a dance!" cried the rather severely tipsy Roselle, bounding up and taking Wallas by the arm.

Andry played several dance sets, which Wallas and Roselle danced in a clear space before the fire. The serving girls and some of the drinkers joined in, and the owner of the Wayward Wayfarer looked on approvingly. All of this helped to establish the tavern as a place where one might find entertainment at odd hours, as well as unadulterated ale at competitive prices. What was more, these musicians were playing for free.

At the first break, Wallas approached the table, gave Ellisen a wide berth, then sat down beside Andry, panting heavily. He drained a tankard that happened to be in front of him, and rubbed at his injured finger. Andry rummaged in his bag for a strip of cloth and bound Wallas's finger to the one next to it.

"You know Andry, all this dancing is rare good practice for the open road," he said convivially.

"Is that a fact?" asked Andry.

"Oh yes, but I would not expect you to know that, being a sailor. The pure, cool, bracing air of the countryside, the sun on your face, sleeping in warm, clean haystacks, the honest, friendly peasants, and the security of knowing that you depend on nobody but yourself."

"Aye, well, that's true enough," agreed Andry. "On a ship the air is foul below deck and freezing above. The crew has to work together or die, and the officers are not too friendly."

Wallas took a deep breath and began singing.

"Tramp, tramp, tramp the road, walking to the sky,
Tramp, tramp, tramp the road, only you and I."

Andry recognized the marching tune, which he had heard on his first night in Palion. He picked up his rebec and began playing along.

The rest of the night took the form of a slightly subdued revel. Andry and Wallas played rebec and board lyre while the Wayward Wayfarer's other patrons danced and sang. Some time after midnight two of the night watch came in, informed the tapman that regulation closing hours had been observed, then sat down and called for an ale each. Presently they were dancing with Ellisen and a serving maid, while Andry played. By then Wallas and Roselle were nowhere to be seen.

The sun was already up when Andry led the way from the Wayward Wayfarer to the city gate. Ellisen was carrying Wallas over one shoulder, and had Roselle by the collar and was trying to steer her in a straight line. The two guardsmen of the night watch had decided to tag along, just to be sociable. Andry was carrying both packs, an unopened jar of wine, and his rebec. The smaller of the guardsmen was carrying a wineskin that had been presented to Andry by the patrons of the tavern, while his very tall offsider was telling Ellisen what a grand coincidence it was that they were both guards and worked the night shift, and would she be interested in breakfast?

"So what did you have Wallas and Roselle buy for the road?" said Andry as they stopped within sight of the city gate.

"A blanket each, some bread and fermented sausage, and a waterskin," said Ellisen. "I was once in the militia, pretending to be a man. I know the needs of the road."

"So you're for a trek, lad?" asked the tall guardsman, who then presented Andry with a silver noble. "Grand night of playing."

The gesture was intended more to impress Ellisen than thank Andry, but it had the desired effect. She dumped Wallas to the ground, released Roselle, then stepped back, squeezed the guard's arm and whispered that it had been very sweet of him. Andry uncorked the jar, drank two mouthfuls, then poured some down the front of his tunic. He poured the rest over Wallas's head, causing him to sit up, spluttering and cursing.

"On your feet, wayfarer, time for the joys of the open road," he laughed.

"Andry, this is for you," said Ellisen, holding out a blackwood comb, carved to resemble a set of long teeth in a demonic face. She glanced to one side, then lashed out with her foot and kicked Wallas. "And that is for you, Wallas. Go now, Andry, and may Fortune be kind to you."

By now the shorter of the night guardsmen was away with Roselle, who was draped over a hitching rail, being sick. Andry spent some time getting Wallas on his feet, and with the pack on his shoulder. Ellisen began talking quite earnestly with the taller of the guards about interesting armlocks and strangleholds. Andry slipped his arms into his pack's straps, then hoisted the wineskin from the Wayward Wayfarer.

"Now make like you're drunk as we approach the gate," said Andry as they set off.

"Whadder you mean, 'make like'?" responded Wallas.

They staggered in the general direction of the city gates,

and with their free arms they clung to each other for support. The traffic at the gate was light, which was bad. The guards would have little to do, and from sheer boredom would more carefully scrutinize those few travelers who were passing through. A guard stepped into their path. Andry and Wallas made a point of saying nothing coherent. After some rummaging Wallas managed to produce a few copper coins for a bribe, but the guard shook his head.

"I'll be needin' passage papers for the both of ye," he said firmly.

Andry had expected that papers might be needed to enter a city, but not to leave. In Alberin it was an occasion for celebration when people looking like Wallas and himself left the place.

"Havne papers t'hand, maybe inner pack," Andry mumbled hopefully.

"I'll be askin' ye to turn out those packs, or stay within the walls," the guard began. Then the taller of the night-watch guards stepped between them.

"Undesirables, bein' expelled by the Dockways magistrate," he explained.

"Bein' expelled, ye say?" asked the gate guard.

"I'se ordered to march 'em to the gates and see 'em off within the hour of dawn. If any tries to assist them stayin' within the walls, I'm to take their names and report to the magistrate."

"Aye, aye, thanks for the warnin'!" exclaimed the guard, who then stood aside and pointed through the gate to the road beyond. "You two, out!"

※ ※ ※

Andry and Wallas were four hundred yards beyond the west gate of Palion when the first signs of trouble appeared.

"These pack straps are digging into my shoulders," grumbled Wallas.

"You carried it around the city without complaint," said Andry.

"Yes, but . . . it was not so heavily loaded, and I could sit myself down to rest when it became a problem."

"Well put up with it. We need to be out of sight of the guards on the gate before someone decides that we need to be checked again."

They managed to trudge another quarter mile.

"My left foot hurts," complained Wallas.

"You're walking on it, what do you expect?" replied Andry.

"Can we stop to rest?"

"No! We're not even half a mile from the gates."

"Half a mile? Feels like five! You're a sailor, how can you judge it's only a half mile?"

"That whitewashed stone up ahead there, with PALION ½ MILE carved into it."

They continued for yet another quarter mile.

"I cannot believe we have not reached the first milestone as yet," complained Wallas. "Time seems to have slowed down. Some evil sorcerer has put a curse on us—or maybe someone stole the milestone."

"Talk sense, Wallas, they weigh half a ton!"

"Perhaps someone really strong stole the milestone."

"I bet you one copper we pass it within a few minutes."

"You're on!"

Andry pointed to a white stone in the distance, then asked for his copper.

"Damn surveyor must have got the distance wrong," muttered Wallas.

"I've been counting footsteps, the distance seemed about right at the half mile."

At the milestone Wallas was in considerable distress.

"The heels of my feet feel like there's needles in the leather of my boots," he moaned.

"They're called blisters, I have 'em too."

"And I have a cramp in my left calf."

"Walking does that to you."

"But it hurts!"

"Did you know that Torean miles are twice as long as our Acreman miles?"

"Shut up!"

"You should do more walking."

At the two-mile post they were actually obscured by a grove of roadside trees, so Andry allowed a stop. Wallas greedily gulped gown a substantial amount of wine. Andry drank some water, then borrowed Wallas's ax and chopped a long, straight branch from one of the trees, then trimmed the leaves and twigs from it.

"Hah, you need a staff for support," snorted Wallas. "Your sailor's feet are not up to the walking."

"I need a weapon," explained Andry. "This will make a passable quarterstaff."

"Commoner's weapon!" laughed Wallas. "Gentlemen carry axes."

"Do you know how to use an ax?"

"I . . . ah, now that you mention it . . ."

"I can give you lessons—"

"No! Nothing that involves standing up, if you please."

"I'm afraid that you must be standing anyway. We have to move on."

Wallas took a few more gulps from the wineskin. "Just making it lighter," he explained.

✳ ✳ ✳

At five miles Wallas was quite literally in tears, and begging that they stop and make camp for the night. Andry pointed out that from the position of the sun it was barely nine o'-clock in the morning. It was at this point that Wallas stumbled in a rut in the road and fell heavily. He then writhed about on the ground, screaming with the pain of the cramps that had gripped both of his legs. After massaging Wallas's legs until he could stand again, Andry relented and allowed them to take a break. Wallas hobbled over to a sheltered haystack, lay down without removing his pack, and was asleep in moments.

Andry inspected a few of the items that Ellisen had added to his pack. There was a pink, frilly blanket with *Madame Jilli's Recreational Rooming* embroidered in red at each corner, a small rug, sundry items of food, and a small book.

"*Wayfarer's Almanac for the Sargolan Empire*," Andry read aloud; then he ate a little bread and began to read. After a time he repacked everything and dozed. Around noon they were awakened by a farmer, who had arrived to discover that Wallas had been throwing up in his hay. He chased them back to the road with a cudgel.

"Oh, my head," groaned Wallas, once the farmer had turned back.

"Mine hurts too, and it's not even from a hangover," said Andry.

"Wanner die," croaked Wallas.

"Five miles," said Andry. "Look back there, you can only see a sort of smoky haze. We're clear of the city."

"I was in a tavern . . ." ventured Wallas, but he was not entirely sure what had happened there.

"You know, we do a good dance tune, with the rebec and lyre. I'll wager that once we started playing we didn't have to buy a single drink for all four of us."

"That's right, a lot of dancing, in a tavern. Singing. Roselle, dancing on our table. Serving maid took me out the back, to find a good barrel to breach."

"And left me playing by myself for a half hour."

"Broached the best barrel of all," laughed Wallas. Then he winced in pain.

Andry picked some of the straw out of his clothing.

"What about Roselle?" asked Andry.

"What about her?"

"She seemed to fancy you."

"Pah, just a hoyden. Anyway, tumbled her out in the stables."

Andry considered this for a hundred steps. He reached a startling conclusion, because it was an opinion that everybody else had always reserved for him.

"Wallas, did you know you're an arsehole?"

"What? You should talk! I've a mind to go it alone."

"Do so—"

"No! I, er, cannot leave you, a foreigner, alone in the Sargolan countryside. You need a guide and translator."

He squirmed with the pain of the straps on his shoulders, then found that he could gain a little relief by easing them out onto his deltoid muscles.

"How far to Logiar, I wonder?" said Wallas, thinking aloud.

"Five hundred miles."

"Five hundred! Why, that's a hundred times further than we have tramped all day."

"It's barely afternoon."

"How do you know it's five hundred?"

"Ellisen gave me an almanac."

"Hah! No doubt in memory of what you gave—Argh!"

Andry had casually put his staff between Wallas's legs. Wallas fell heavily.

"Oops, mind the road," said Andry without stopping to help.

It was half a mile before Wallas managed to catch up with Andry. They walked in silence until the six-mile marker.

"Think I'll only go as far as Glasbury," Wallas decided.

"Fine, big city. How far is it, I wonder?"

"Two hundred miles," replied Andry with malicious satisfaction.

Wallas frowned, and considered this unwelcome fact for a time.

"Well there's a big provincial town called Clovesser."

"One hundred and eighty miles."

"Dammitall, then which is the nearest village?"

"Harrgh, at seventy miles. You can do it in two days with a forced march."

"You mean what we're doing is *not* a forced march?"

"A forced march is eighteen hours of march per day, stopping only to sleep and piss. Eat on the march, drink on the march, and no stopping for rain, snow, or hangovers."

"There must be an inn somewhere on this accursed road!" wailed Wallas.

"Oh aye, it's called the Score of Miles Rest."

"Stupid name for an inn."

"It's because it is at the twenty-mile marker."

"Twenty miles!" cried Wallas. "That's four times further than we have already walked."

It began to rain.

✳ ✳ ✳

It was the hour of the day when travelers tended to be in the taproom, having lunch or just drinking. Thus the guests' parlor of the Wayward Wayfarer was empty as Terikel entered. She went over to the fireplace and rubbed her hands before the bright flames. When she turned to warm her back, she found that Laron and Velander were standing before her.

"Learned Elder," they said together, giving an identical bow and flourish.

"Laron," began Terikel, stepping forward, then stopping. This was the first time she had seen him for almost a hundred and sixty days, and he had changed considerably since then. "You look, er—" she began tentatively.

"Alive, Learned Elder?" suggested Laron.

"I was going to say . . . very well. Wonderful, in fact. Handsome, dashing, and awfully gallant."

"Thank you, Learned Elder, but I am still only a youth of fifteen," replied Laron.

"But one who has lived for seven hundred years."

Velander stepped off to one side as Terikel and Laron embraced. Terikel noticed that he was indeed warm-blooded again, and his face was clear of the pimples and acne that had marred it for seven centuries. They sat before the fire while Velander prowled the shadows at the other end of the taproom—alert, aware, and hungry.

"But, but how did Velander become the way that you once were?" Terikel asked. "I mean, was she not dead? When I was in Diomeda I talked to those who had seen her body. It was definitely lifeless."

"True, but I know something of enchantments and energies at the very edges of life's borderlands. I found her shade lingering there, stripped of nearly everything that could anchor her to this world. Any other sorcerer would have been able to do no more than bid her farewell, but I had existed in those borderlands for seven hundred years. She was terribly weak, and it was too late to save her life, but it was possible to do . . . dangerous things."

"And they worked?"

"Oh yes. Now Velander is dead, but not gone. The blood of others nourishes her cold body, while their etheric vitality provides her strength. When Miral is below the horizon she must lie as one dead, but at other times she can walk and speak as the rest of us."

"You turned Velander into what you once were?"

"Yes, but I meant well," said Laron, squirming a little.

"So, she kills people?"

"Well, yes, but only those who spread misery to those around them."

"Another vampyre social reformer," sighed Terikel, putting a hand to her forehead, then rubbing her left temple.

"Laron tutored me in the way of chivalry," Velander explained from the other side of the room. "I feed only upon those who, ah . . ."

"They leave something to be desired as good citizens?" ventured Terikel.

"Ah, yes."

"And there is no shortage of them," added Laron.

"Oh Vel!" cried Terikel, standing up and spreading her arms.

"No embraces, if you please," said Velander, already backing away. "My control is merely adequate, not perfect."

Terikel sat down again, relieved at the support of the chair. Her head was spinning. Velander had become a thing with cold flesh, the strength of five men, and a taste for blood. She was also incapable of movement when the great ringed disk of Miral was below the horizon. Still, of all the people on the continent of Acrema, Velander and Laron were probably the two she could trust most.

"What is to be done now?" asked Laron, when the silence that followed began to seem embarrassingly long.

"I must reach the Capefang Mountains," replied Terikel, resting her head against a hand.

"Easily arranged, as it happens," said Laron. "A squad of lancers that I am associated with is going there. Can you ride?"

"No," said Terikel.

"Oh. What about ax fencing?"

"I've chopped firewood."

"Use of the lance?"

"Never touched one."

"Ah, do not take this as an insult, Elder, but is there anything that you can do that is also required of militia lancers—apart from wear their uniform and chain mail?"

"I know medicar skills."

"That provides possibilities," Laron decided. "You *will* need to learn to ride, however. Perhaps we should visit the stables later today, go over a few basics, then put you through some intensive riding lessons. The, ah, expedition to the Capefang Mountains leaves in a week, so we should have more than enough time to have you riding like an old hand by then. Why do you want to go there?"

"There are, er, people living there, very learned people. I must speak to them about Dragonwall, so that . . . Perhaps it would be best if I did not tell you, everything is very complicated and difficult. Dragonwall is to be initiated in two days. I wanted to stop that happening—"

"Stop Dragonwall?" exclaimed Laron. "The biggest magical venture in the history of this world?"

"As I said, it is all quite difficult, and certainly very dangerous. You saw what happened to the ship last night, and before that I was attacked in the streets of Palion by the Throne Guards."

"But I heard that your own contract guards saved you," said Laron.

"No, I was alone. I killed two sorcerers, then ran. By the time the five Throne Guards cornered me, I was too drained to fight them. Then two drunks rescued me. Alberinese sailors, or at least one of them was, anyway."

"Alberinese?" exclaimed Laron. "Sailors?"

"Yes. One had a very strong accent."

"Gods of moonworlds, they must have rough sailors in Alberin," said Laron, running his fingers through his hair, and staring intently at her with his alarmingly green eyes. "They actually killed Throne Guards?"

"Well, one of them killed a Throne Guard, and I burned another alive. The effort took me so close to the edge that I nearly died as well."

"And the other three?"

"The skinny sailor just beat them up."

"But, but, to become a Throne Guard, one must beat ten

armed, condemned criminals. At once. Starting out unarmed and naked."

"Good fortune may have been involved, although perhaps they used up the city's quota of good fortune for the next decade," explained Terikel.

"Where are they now?" asked Laron.

"They were on the *Stormbird*. I had a lamplight girl disguised as myself go aboard with them as escorts. They are all dead now."

Aware that once she got up, it would be the start of a journey that would take weeks and cover many hundreds of miles, Terikel cast about for any excuse to enjoy a little more of the chair and fireside. She stared across the room at Velander, who looked almost disappointingly familiar, although a little thinner, and very pale.

"Vel, you have not changed at all," Terikel said pleasantly.

"I never change, Learned Elder. I shall be like this forever, or until someone manages to strike off my head, burn it to ash, cut out my hearts and bury them at a crossroad, then—"

"All right, all right, please, I'm sorry I raised a sensitive subject!" exclaimed the seriously overextended priestess.

"Learned Elder, only I should be apologizing. I was merely telling you how I may be destroyed in order to put myself in your power."

"But Velander, I am not worthy of this."

"Learned Elder, it will be a long time before *I* may be worthy to be your soulmate again after hurting you so much. In the meantime, I do what little I can."

"But Vel, I forgive anything you ever did to me—"

"Learned Elder, you do not understand. Forgiveness, you can give, but *I* must be worthy of your forgiveness. I must do . . . substantial things. I was very cruel to you, and there is much to heal."

While Terikel was developing the foundations of her first saddle sores at riding practice, Andry and Wallas were counting off the milestones to the Score of Miles Rest. The country around the inn was all flat, open pasture with very few trees, so that they could see the whitewashed walls of the inn for three miles before they actually reached it.

"There is a saying among the Vindician people," said Wallas, who was putting most of his concentration into thrusting one foot in front of another, and not really worrying about what his tongue was doing. "It goes *His face looked as if he had just finished a long journey*. I'll wager my face looks like that now."

"It does," replied Andry, "but seventeen miles is not long. Most inns on the road are about twenty miles apart, according to the almanac. It's considered a day's walk for a fit, strong peasant."

"I'm not a fit, strong peasant!"

"Wallas, just what are you?"

"Footsore, sick, miserable, tired, and—Oh shyte! It's starting to rain again."

"Well, we can always run the remaining three miles to the Score of Miles Rest."

"Your father is a nearsighted sewer rat, and your mother is a small, green, warty thing that eats flies."

"So you're not up to a run?"

"The sun was only out for two hours, and in that time my face got sunburned. Now it feels as if it's been scored with a wire brush."

The rain got heavier. Andry unrolled the rug from Madame Jilli's bedroom and used it at a rain cape. Wallas did not even attempt to keep the rain off. He shifted his straps again, but by now every square inch of his shoulders was bright with pain.

It was an hour past evening as they reached the Score of Miles Rest. The rain eased away, then ceased just as they reached the door, but Wallas did not even stop to cast a curse skyward. Instead he went straight for the taproom, made for the hearth without even noticing the crowd of travelers and drinkers from the nearby farms, and dropped to the floor. He removed his boots very, very slowly. His socks were soaked in a mixture of muddy water and blood. The drinkers nearby whistled. He removed his socks, to reveal large and raw blisters on the backs of his heels and the balls of his feet; then he shook tatters of bloody skin out of his socks. Again the onlookers whistled and pointed. Wallas dropped his socks on the hearthstones, where they began to steam. The smell reminded him of goulash that had been heated up after having become just slightly rancid.

Andry arrived with a pair of tankards, and it was only now that Wallas realized he was still wearing his pack. He shrugged it off and let it drop to the floor, then drained his ale in a single swallow.

"Had a big day on the road, then?" asked a very old man who was sitting on a stool beside the fireplace.

"Seems so," grunted Wallas.

"Should try ox fat and oil of eldenbush," he said, offering Wallas a little jar.

"Nay, tiger fat and lanolin oil," said the owner of a hand offering him another jar.

"Need hay, t'pad thy boots," advised someone behind Wallas.

"Nay, fresh grass, nothin' like it."

"Only use serrated bloom grass, it has restorative properties, medicars advise it."

"You only have a single pair o' socks. I allus wear two."

"I wears three."

"Should wipe thy feet in spirits of honeywine. Stings, but it's just the thing. Wait here, I'll get a thimbleworth."

Andry's impression was that for people who did not sail, ride, drift along on rivers in barges, or roll along in carriages, there was nothing in all of the world as important as their feet, and the care and comfort thereof. Wallas screamed hoarsely as the spirits of honeywine was poured over the raw flesh of his blisters; then it was all soothing oils and bandages, with a lot of talk about boot design.

It was at this point that one of the local merchants entered, secured a tankard of mulled wine, then joined the crowd in the taproom.

"Well now, what a cheerful room of hale fellows this is!" he declared in a loud and unsympathetically cheerful voice. He ignored the ominous mutters that floated about but that seemed to come from nobody in particular. "I have just had the most bracing walk here from my storehouse across the field," he continued. "Ah, I would not trade this for life in the city for a bag of gold."

"I'd trade it for a forged copper," said Wallas softly, but only Andry heard.

"Yes, the cool, refreshing air of the country evening, it's simply magical," continued the merchant. "No smells or smoke, just your own two feet beneath you on a road that ends all too soon, but at a friendly inn. No churlish city outlaws, just honest, friendly peasant faces, eager to share a pint and a song."

Wallas eased himself to his bandaged feet. The pain was considerable, but he forced himself to endure it. He willed his right foot in front of his left foot. His calves felt as if they were filled with hot needles. He forced his left foot forward. The merchant drank from his tankard, then took a deep breath.

> "Tramp, tramp, tramp the road, walking to the sky,
> Tramp, tramp, tramp the road, only you and—"

Wallas's left hand seized the merchant by the green lacework front of his tunic, then his right fist smashed into his face, connecting with his left eye, cheek, and nose.

"Take a bloody proper walk sometime, wanker," bawled Wallas, standing over him with his fists held out to either side. "*Then* see if you're inclined for a stupid, frigging tramp, tramp, tramp song!"

Wallas was cheered lustily as he hobbled back to the hearth, and a traveling cobbler even offered to modify some of the design defects in his boots for free. Andry took out his rebec and began a slow air from Scalticar as the drinkers returned to their talk and drinks.

"I say, there's some rough types about these days, tappy," said a voice from the direction of the serving board.

"Think I'd like to get home to Alberin," said Andry as he played.

"As in North Scalticar?" asked Wallas, easing a sock over his bandaged feet.

"There's only one Alberin," said Andry wistfully.

"Have you forgotten the Strait of Dismay? Waves bigger than mountains? Anyway, the only ship capable of making the voyage across the Strait of Dismay was reduced to a cloud of smoke, along with some warmish bits of charcoal floating on the harbor."

"My plan is to get to Logiar first. There I'll wait until the storms die away. When that happens, I'll work my way over the strait."

"But there's no ships left."

"The strait is only a hundred miles wide at its narrowest. There's lots of fishing boats laid up, and when the storms are over, they'll be all that's left to haul cargo. There's lots of cargo in need of moving."

"Me, I'll settle for Glasbury," said Wallas, beginning to ease his second sock on. "It's the old capital of Sargol, like before the empire. One hundred and eighty miles more! That's nine days at today's pace. Actually, I'd settle for anywhere I'm not known."

"But people think we're dead," Andry reminded him.

"People will only think we're dead until they see us alive again. When they find out that we're not, they are going to be seriously annoyed."

"Oh aye. We've just seen what they can do when they're annoyed," Andry admitted. "I can scarcely give this credit. Folk all over Palion trying to kill Elder Terikel, then Elder Terikel tries to kill us to pretend she's been killed."

"Aye, and she did kill Melier," said Wallas. "So sad, she was a pleasant tumble."

"Melier too?" exclaimed Andry. "That's three women in one night."

"Yes—I mean, aye," replied Wallas.

"*That* really is disgusting."

"*You* are just a lower-class prude," said Wallas dismissively. "Women want flattery and charm, and they are willing to pay for it in very pleasant currency."

Andry had never thought about the whole business of dalliance in such unemotional terms. He stared into the fire, pondering relations between the sexes, and hoping that they were not really so lacking in romance as Wallas said. His thoughts returned to the *Stormbird*.

"All my shipmates, gone," he said to the flames rather than Wallas. "I get such a pang, thinking of them as drowned, burned, or swallowed by monsters."

"But they flogged, robbed, fined, and beat you," Wallas reminded him.

"Oh aye, but that's what shipmates do. Here's to them, and to Melier."

Andry and Wallas drank the toast.

"At least we're still alive," said Wallas.

"Oh aye, even though certain folk want to do terrible things to my body—like roasting it to a little bit of char, or tearing its head off for a few pints of liquid refreshment."

"Oh, there I agree. That daemon girl was reason enough to leave Palion without any of the others."

❊ ❊ ❊

The transit of Lupan was an astronomical event, and was therefore fixed in time. That time was day thirty-six of Fourmonth, 3141, at six minutes past the ninth hour. It could not be avoided, missed, moved, or reasoned with, but it could be seen from half of the world. It was thus a marker for the sorcerers of Lemtas, Acrema, and Scalticar, sorcerers spread out over seventeen ringstone sites along a line nearly thirteen thousand Acreman miles from Ringstone Glacien to Ringstone Terminus. Communication between the sites was difficult, because the sites were eight hundred miles apart, but Most Learned Astential had chosen a marker in time that could not be mistaken or misinterpreted.

Most Learned Astential was, of course, dead, but by now his Dragonwall scheme had a momentum of its own. Dragonwall did indeed promise to drain the violence from the Torean Storms. Most participating sorcerers also realized that the ether machine promised the participants some control of titanic energies, and even the prospect of immortality. Everyone wanted to participate in that.

The seventeen ringstones were all on land, with four on Lemtas, five on Scalticar, six on Acrema, and two on islands. Scalticar's ringstone sites had been cleared and provided with megalith seats before the Acreman sites had all been surveyed, so the Sargolan emperor had hurriedly decided to order his own sorcerers to take Astential seriously. Three ringstone rounds were within the boundaries of the Sargolan Empire and its allies, and deserts contained the other two Acreman sites. These areas were ruled by mere nomad warlords, and so were easily invaded, conquered, and annexed. The northern kingdom whose coast featured the only other ringstone round on Acrema had a ruler who was quite pragmatic about powerful and eccentric neighbors. He decided that after what had happened in the desert, the Sargolans were not to be toyed with. He agreed not only to clear Ringstone Littoral, but to supply the most senior and learned sorcerers in the northern kingdoms to operate it.

The island to the north was no problem. The Diomedan navy mounted an invasion of the island of Felicy, conquered the area where Ringstone Felicy was located, and thus gained a stake in Dragonwall even though Diomeda was nowhere near the ringstone line. As it happened, the Diomedans had acted just in time. The Torean Storms were making sea travel increasingly dangerous, and particularly severe weather sank the Diomedan invasion fleet at anchor soon after their victory. The Lemtas sites were no problem. Realizing that they had a chance to control four ringstone sites, and that Acreman rulers were willing to go to war in order to rebuild the ringstone rounds, the Lemtas rulers decided to set up the ringstones with their own sorcerers before someone else did it for them.

Building Dragonwall was rather like building a stone arch bridge. It was somewhat unstable until complete, but after that it held itself together. The key words were, of course, "until" and "complete." Sergal had likened establishing Dragonwall to navigating a raft down a particularly dangerous stretch of rapids in some mountain river. It would be fast, dangerous, and terrifying, and stupendous forces would be involved. Unlike with a river, however, one did not have the option of getting off and walking around the dangerous bit.

All four shifts of the Ringstone Logiar sorcerers formed into a line, and they walked out of the support camp in a procession that encircled the ringstone round. Waldesar led the procession, making the most of the fact that he was still the ringmaster. He was very fond of processions and public spectacle, and as a young man had aspired to joining the Journey Guard and escorting the emperor himself in parades. Instead, his scholarly and etheric talents had been recognized early, and he had been sent to the local temple for a proper education. He had gone on to the Sargolan Academy of the Arcane to train as a sorcerer, and there he had displayed a flair for magical castings. By the time his father died and his brothers had started killing each other over who was going to get the inheritance, Waldesar was the court sorcerer to a provincial governor, and wealthier than his father had been.

Now Waldesar had the authority to stage parades, and as far as he was concerned, the initiation of Dragonwall was the occasion for a parade. Merely walking from one's tent to the ringstone and sitting in the bench carved into one's assigned megalith was simply not good enough. Waldesar decreed that the procession would circle the ringstone complex seventeen times, which actually worked out to a distance of several miles. For the vast majority of sorcerers, this was farther than they had walked in decades, and in a few cases, ever. By the time they reached the seventeenth time around the ringstone, most were discovering facts about walking that Wallas had known since his first day on the road west from Palion.

At the sound of a trumpet fanfare, the sorcerers of the fourth shift left the circular parade and spiraled in to a ring of sixteen small marker stones with wooden chairs outside the main round. At a second fanfare, the third-shift sorcerers spiraled in until they reached a smaller ring of chairs and stones. The second shift took its cue correctly, and paraded inward to be seated at the innermost ring of small marker stones; then the first shift turned inward for the primary megaliths. They threaded their way between the sorcerers sitting in the three outer rings, then climbed into the carved seats in the megaliths. It was now that the music from the band changed to a grand march, and Waldesar began his trek to the central megalith.

First he circled behind the outermost ring, inspecting each of the fourth-shift sorcerers from behind; then he dropped inside the ring·and inspected all sixteen of them again, from in front. He repeated the process for the other two concentric rings, then moved on to the innermost ring. Waldesar circled each megalith in turn, and finally moved on to his central megalith.

Just a simple shout of "Are we all ready?" would have done, thought Landeer.

Waldesar finally climbed into his megalith seat. The marching tune being played by the band was brought to an elaborate climax, and then a most emphatic plagal cadence announced total silence.

"Learned gentlemen, speak your castings!" called Waldesar.

What about us learned ladies? thought Landeer as she spoke casting words that formed a tangle of blue-white fire in her cupped hands.

"Transit of Lupan in two minutes at the third gong!" a herald shouted from outside the circle, and three beats of a deep-noted gong echoed out. Most of the onlookers glanced to Miral, which was low in the western sky but had not yet set. The tiny, gleaming disk that was Lupan was very close to the enormous ringed planet.

For the initiation of Dragonwall, all four shifts were to be used at once. This would generate a vastly bigger ether machine than that of five thousand years earlier, but the consensus was that one shift of sorcerers could maintain it once it was cast.

"Shift Four, extend!" ordered Waldesar.

Landeer, who was in the fourth and outermost circle, moved her hands apart slowly, and her tangles of etheric energy split into two, one in each hand.

"Shift Four, cast!"

Landeer raised her arms, with the palms of her hands facing upward. As they reached an angle of forty-five degrees, the tangles of etheric energy streaked upward in a pair of streamers that met a few feet above her head, then circled a vast cylinder with its base on the fourth ring of stones, met again high above the opposite side, and continued on up into the dark sky. The effect of all sixteen sorcerers executing the casting was a quite impressive sight, and nearly every pair of eyes in nearby Logiar was on the faint column of interlaced spiral streamers of light that had appeared in the southwest.

"Transit of Lupan in one minute at the third gong!" warned the herald.

Waldesar suddenly realized that in his quest for splendor, pomp, and ceremony, he had left very little leeway to keep up with Dragonwall's initiation schedule.

"Shift Three, extend!" cried Waldesar above the beating of the gong; then he counted to ten and added, "Shift Three, cast!"

A second column wove itself into the sky within the outer column, but this one was less coordinated, as several of the older sorcerers were not used to being hurried, and so had not been quite ready. The column wobbled, flickered from blue to bright red several times, but then steadied.

"Shift Two, extend!" called Waldesar with a slight note of despair in his voice, and this time he stood up and clambered to the top of his megalith.

"Transit of Lupan in a half minute at the third gong!"

Hurriedly looking around to assure himself that all second-shift sorcerers were ready, Waldesar cried "Shift Two, cast!" then added almost immediately "Shift one, extend!"

The third woven cylinder flashed into the sky far more steadily than its predecessor. Waldesar glanced upward only long enough to be sure that it had been established before checking that the primary sorcerers were ready. Two of the sorcerers were still extending, Waldesar realized.

"Transit of Lupan in a quarter minute at the third gong!"

Precious seconds flew by, but for every second there were three beats of Waldesar's pulse. *Well, if the second shift managed to recover from an uncoordinated cast, the first shift should be able to as well,* he decided.

"Shift One, cast!" shouted Waldesar. Then he slid back into his megalith's seat while speaking a casting into his own hands and extending it with almost comical haste.

"Transit of Lupan at the third gong!" the herald announced as Waldesar raised his arms to rest in the grooves carved into the megalith. He cast as the beat of the gong sounded.

Two orange streamers speared straight up into the sky from the palms of his hands. At the second beat Waldesar realized that he actually had a moment's grace; then he tilted his hands north and south. The two orange streamers began to topple in opposite directions, bringing down two separate cylinders of woven blue with them. They began to bend; then suddenly they steadied, as two immense tubes of woven light that converged and met on the ringstone. The castings from Ringstone Logiar had met and merged with those from Ringstone Alpine, to the north, and Ringstone Septire, which lay south, in Scalticar.

Very slowly, Waldesar removed his arms from the grooves and brought his hands together above his head. The bases of the orange streamers merged as the heels of his palms touched; then they detached from Waldesar, brightening as they ascended into the sky. Waldesar waited until there was an even streamer of orange stretching from horizon to horizon before he sat forward. He nearly fell from the megalith, so draining had been his role in the enormous joint casting, not to mention the five-mile procession.

"Shift Four, merge castings!" he croaked, and the sorcerers of the outermost circle brought their hands together above their heads. The streamers of blue rose from their palms, merged, and rose into the sky. The orange band that was Dragonwall now brightened considerably. Waldesar stood down the next two circles, again with the same brightening of Dragonwall.

"Shift One contract!"

The twin tubes of woven blue streamers began to remerge, forming a single column whose divergence was soon lost to the watchers in the sheer distance above them. The streak of light across the sky that was the Dragonwall flowed and separated into rainbow colors. Waldesar glanced about, then cleared his throat.

Learned gentlemen, I declare the ether engine, Dragonwall, to be initiated! Waldesar rehearsed in his mind. It would be the signal for cheers from the audience of nobles, guards, servants, and assorted lackeys . . . and Waldesar discovered that he was paralyzed. Control filaments sparkled and flickered within the central ringstone. The sorcerers in the nonoperational shifts tried to move, but found that they too were paralyzed. Every sorcerer was held rigid in the ringstone complex, whether sitting on one of the chairs with stone seats or reclining in the seat of a primary megalith.

Streamers of orange were cascading down from the mighty rainbow band high above them. They slammed into the ground, hissed as the rocks and soil melted around them, then began spinning along an axis that stretched all the way to the band in the sky. Two horses, a guard, and a baron were impaled by the etheric spikes, and died instantly. Everyone nearby screamed, panicked, and ran.

You would think Waldesar would have made an announcement about that, thought Garko. On the other hand, an announcement about a barrier of etheric spikes crashing down out of the sky and permanently dividing the continent would have generated a lot of protests.

The baron's son now recovered his nerve sufficiently to sidle over and inspect his father's body more closely. He was twenty-six, and had considerable experience of the carnage on battlefields, but the sight of what his father had been reduced to quickly had the warrior down on his hands and knees, and retching. Presently he felt well enough to go back and examine the mighty fence that had dropped out of the sky. Just above each ground-anchoring spike, the etheric material curved along the axis in an S shape to form a vertical rotor blade. Each was effectively a wind tower, about six inches wide. They were already beginning to spin.

"A windmill, half a world in length," he said to a kavelar who had gathered the courage to join him.

A bat was foolish enough to try to fly through the pale orange curtain of spinning castings. Fur, blood, and diced flesh and bone rained down on the two men.

"I can see problems for migrating birds," said the kavelar, wiping at his surcoat and chain mail.

"Well then, I shall put in a protest on behalf of the migrating birds, and everyone else in Acrema," said the newest baron on the continent.

It was later found that the rotors were not just anchored

at the surface. The anchor castings had burrowed down into the ground, six inches apart, and they were hard, unyielding, and very, very long. In one of the Alpennien mine shafts they were found to have penetrated more than a mile underground. Out in the Strait of Dismay, they ran from the tops of the waves to the seafloor. If anything solid, such as a driftwood log or large fish, was pressed against them, they became white-hot and sliced it into six-inch-wide chunks.

Because nobody had explained that this would be a byproduct of the Dragonwall, quite a large number of people were drastically inconvenienced. The young baron gathered his escort of ninety kavelars together, mounted his horse, and approached the ringstone's herald. He demanded to see Waldesar, and declared that if he was not given satisfaction within two minutes, he and his men would slaughter every sorcerer who had participated in the Dragonwall casting.

To everyone's surprise, the image of Waldesar appeared, floating in front of the baron, and just a little higher.

"That is no way to pray to a god," said the image. Then there was an intense flash of light and a blast that was heard as far away as Logiar.

Where the young baron and his kavelars had been was now a glowing circle of ground dotted by lumps of partly melted metal and charred meat. Waldesar's image looked down at the black, smoking thing that had been his loyal herald only moments before. *Well, he was probably guilty of something*, thought Waldesar. *We demigods are always right.*

It was the third night on the road for Andry and Wallas. The sky was clear, and Miral was low in the western sky. By now Wallas had achieved a balance between the agony of his feet, the pain in his legs, and a fatigue that was nevertheless granting him the most sound sleep of his entire life. They had decided that the inns were far too expensive as accommodation, and so were only drinking in them at the end of the day's walk, then sleeping in the fields. The Five-Dozen Milestone was quite a large inn, with a large, covered balcony that looked out to the west, so that the drinkers could enjoy the very last of the sunset—and the innkeeper did not have to light his oil lamps until quite late in the evening.

"Transit o' Lupan soon," said a tinker who was sharing the same table as Andry and Wallas.

"Aye, it's in the almanac," replied Andry.

"Make a wish on the transit o' Lupan, Fortune's said ter favor wishes on the transit o' Lupan."

"I wish my feet would stop hurting," said Wallas.

"I wish you'd stop whining about your feet," said Andry.

"Don't your feet ever hurt?" asked Wallas resentfully.

"Aye. I got blisters of the feet and cramps of the calves."

"You'd not think so, to see you walk. Why don't you slow the pace?"

"I'm used to being uncomfortable, it's like that aboard ships," laughed Andry. "You're not, so you carry on about it."

"One hundred and forty miles to Glasbury," said Wallas wistfully.

"Four hundred and forty miles to Logiar," said Andry.

"You can have 'em," muttered Wallas.

"Logiar, you say?" interjected the tinker.

"Aye, and what's the road like?" asked Andry. "The usual bandits that rob folk, and beasts that eat them?"

"Hah! More than that, they's got one o' them ringstones there. Ain't natural. I's there a while back, when they started buildin' it. More sorcerers that ye'd ever wave a wand at, and peasants by the thousand, chippin' away at, well, complicated things. They had ten mega-thing stones up when I was passin'. Huge things, like big chairs."

"Go on with you," said Andry.

"Aye, laugh if ye like, but I saw what I saw. They's to be turnin' on magic with a huge castin'. Not natural. Shouldn't be tried."

"True," responded Wallas. "Just like walking twenty miles every day."

"So what are you fellas on the road for?"

"Quest," said Andry without really thinking.

"Quest, eh? What sort? Magic? Woman? Honor?"

"Bit of all three, really," said Wallas. "My tireless companion here, who does not feel pain, rescued a woman through some sense of misguided honor, then she repaid us by nearly getting us eaten by magical creatures."

"So, you're on a quest to hunt her down?" asked the tinker.

"We're on a quest to get as far away from her as possible," replied Wallas.

The tinker laughed. Andry and Wallas did not.

"I'm on a quest to see the Dragonwall, too," said Andry, now improvising his story. "It's the biggest magical venture ever. How could I tell my grandchildren that I was alive during the greatest casting in history, but didn't bother to go take a look?"

"Bit young fer grandchildren, ain't ye?" cackled the tinker, elbowing Wallas in the ribs.

"He's not even tried making children yet!" Wallas responded with a knowing leer, banging his mug on the table.

A blue spike of light flickered into existence to the northwest. The entire company of drinkers progressively fell silent and gaped at the horizon as those in the groups pointed it out to each other.

"That's Ringstone Alpine's direction," said Wallas. "To be visible from . . . er . . ."

"Three hundred miles," said Andry.

"Oh, yes, from three hundred miles, well, that thing must be simply enormous."

As they watched, the distant blue spike split into two, and these fell away to either side. The split now began to heal from the base upward, while the upper part became orange. The drinkers at the Five-Dozen Milestone saw it stabilize into a line of orange across the western sky, supported by a spike of blue; then the orange line spread out into a band of rainbow colors. Orange cascaded downward from the rainbow band of Dragonwall, until there was a curtain of orange hanging from an enormous rainbow. In just one place there was still a line of blue spearing up through the orange curtain, marking Ringstone Alpine.

"Shyte me," breathed Wallas.

"Quest over," whispered the tinker.

✦ ✦ ✦

Andry and Wallas slept under a tree that night, and had a breakfast that was late even for lunch. For Wallas it consisted of half a loaf of bread and about a pint of wine. Andry ate a few slices of sausage and what Wallas had left of the bread, all washed down by a mouthful of water.

"Notice you're not drinking like before," observed Wallas.

"Aye, the thirst is not in me since we left Palion."

"Your thirst seems to have moved over to me and made an alliance with mine. And you're combing your hair!"

"Aye."

"That's not like you."

"Aye, so folk trying to find me and slice my body up won't know it's me."

"Next you'll be cleaning your teeth."

"Done that already."

Now feeling a lot more cheerful, they set off down the road. Wallas greeted everyone that they passed, and refreshed himself from the wineskin as they trudged. He had discovered that alcohol took the edge off his misery, but it was an expensive fuel for his trekking. Within three hours they had gone two miles. Normally there would be very few travelers that a herd of goats would manage to overtake, and Andry and Wallas noticed the herd approaching when it was a hundred yards behind them. Evening was beginning to color the sky.

"Feet hurt, need medicine," said Wallas, pausing to take another drink.

"Goats after us," observed Andry.

"Do they have lances and axes, and are they shouting 'Death to Andry and Wallas'?" asked Wallas.

"Something more along the lines of 'Baaaa.' "

"Then let 'em catch us."

"If we follow goats, we'll be walking in goat shyte."

"Splendid idea, it will make the road seem softer," concluded the footsore Wallas.

They moved to the edge of the road to let the herd pass, paying it no particular attention. Wallas took the opportunity to have another drink.

"Hie there, Wallas!"

The greeting struck Wallas like an arrow. He whirled

around, spluttering a spray of wine, looking for the circle of
bowmen or the ax blade poised to swing down. Instead he
saw a goatherd waving.

"Aye there, thought it was you, even though you've gained
weight."

*The original Wallas, the one that the assassin killed, his
clothes smelled like goats*, flashed through Wallas's mind.
These people know him, but I don't know them! On the other
hand, his entire career in the imperial court had been built
on bluffing his way through conversations with people that
he was supposed to know but had either forgotten or had
never met in the first place.

"I'll handle this," he said softly to Andry, then made his
way across to the goatherd. The man had spoken in Sargol
Common, which Wallas knew better than most courtiers because of having been born a commoner.

"Hie, keep thy voice down, brother," he said quietly, trying to match the man's accent.

"Oh aye, would ye be in trouble, brother?"

"Oh nay, there's employ for me with that lad there."

"Employ?"

"We're players, a band for fairs and festivals."

"Aye? You? A player?"

So, the original Wallas could not play music, the new Wallas concluded. He decided to build on that inference. Reaching over his shoulder, he patted the pack on his back.

"The lad thinks I has a hundred tunes on the board lyre in
this, but I only has a dozen, like. Bluffed me way into playing aside him, said I've played for years. I just know a very
few tunes passable well. The lad's a young Scalticarian bard,
a-travelin' Acrema in search of heroic tales to sing about.
I'm lookin' after him, and he's teachin' me a tune or two."

"I'd not known ye could play at all."

"Been learning. Now then, if ye'd keep me secret, we can
speak up again," Wallas concluded with a conspiratorial wink.

Over the next few minutes, Wallas found out that he was
talking to his cousin Raffin, and that they lived in a village
called Harrgh. Harrgh was about a week away, traveling at
the herd's speed. This was an admirable pace as far as the
footsore Wallas was concerned. The single problem was that

he and Andry would be expected to play dance tunes together. He communicated all of this to Andry as he and
Andry ambled along with the herd.

"Well, we really can play a few tunes together," said
Andry.

"Maybe so, but I don't know how long I can keep up the
act. I—"

The words froze on Wallas's lips as he heard the sound of
approaching hoofbeats behind them. A squad of cavalry was
cantering along from the east. The herders hurried to clear the
goats from the road to let them through, but the noble in charge
of the lancers stopped his men and called for whoever was the
herders' leader. Raffin walked forward. He was questioned
about any suspicious strangers that he might have seen on the
road. Raffin denied seeing any strangers pass them that day.
That was, in a sense, true. Wallas was not a stranger to Raffin,
while Andry was not a stranger to Wallas. The squad rode on.

"Maybe we should stay with the herd," suggested Wallas
as they stood staring after the departing cavalry.

"Oh aye, it gives us local color," agreed Andry. "Mind,
we'll be expected to help with guarding."

"What does guarding involve?" asked Wallas.

"Remember that ax you're wearing? Swing the sharp bit
at anyone who tries to steal a goat."

That night Andry and Wallas emptied both skins of wine
with the four goatherders, then played dance tunes while
their hosts pattered out jigs and reels around the campfire.
Wallas could not help feeling that the herders seemed oddly
respectful of him, but that meant that he had less scope for
being discovered not to be his namesake, so he was happy.
He and Andry laid out their bedding apart from the others
when they finally retired for the night.

"How are they taking to you?" asked Andry.

"No problem, so far. I'm good at getting people talking
about themselves while forgetting to ask about me. All part
of being a courtier."

"A what?"

"A—er, a courier," said Wallas, quickly.

"Not sure I see how that follows," said Andry.

"Couriers are, er, like spies, sort of."

"So you're a spy."

"Er, used to be. I made too many enemies, had to become a beggar. Couriers travel far, deliver things, then just listen as folk talk, and throw in questions to keep their tongues moving. We learn much and say little, then report back to our masters."

"So where are we going?"

"Their village is on the main road west, about a week's walk from here. I say we stay with them until the village, then set out for Glasbury on our own."

"Sounds sensible."

Andry looked to the west, where orangish lights were flickering beneath the rainbow that was Dragonwall.

"Resembles a distant storm," he said, shaking his head.

"No storm, that's Dragonwall," said Wallas.

"I mean it's *like* a storm. You can see it coming a long way off, but it's so big you can't escape it."

"Who cares? For us, er, commoners, it's no matter. Just a streak of magical fire across the sky. Some grand scheme by the greatest of sorcerers."

"Sorcerers? Now, *there* are folk to worry about."

"Oh yes—er, aye. That Elder Terikel was a sorceress."

"Aye. She's one I worry about a lot."

A thousand miles to the north, in the coastal city of Diomeda, Rector Yvendel of Madame Yvendel's Academy of Applied Castings stood on one of the few roofs of the academy that rose high enough above those of the neighboring buildings to give a view of the western horizon. Unlike her daughter, a certain Alberinese sorceress named Wensomer, Yvendel was tall, elegant, svelte, in her early fifties, and dressed in brightly colored silks. In spite of being well into middle age, she still had a face and figure that allured a good many men. Beside her was Lavenci, the albino academician, who was almost as tall as Yvendel. Both women had their hair brushed out, in preparation for bed. Glowing against the night sky was the beautiful Dragonwall, and almost directly west was the blue spike from Ringstone Centras.

"So, the ether machine seems to be stable," said Yvendel.

"Not only stable, Rector. From what I can see of the patterns and colors, it seems to be strengthening," observed Lavenci.

"I warned people," said Yvendel.

"Some of us listened," Lavenci reminded her.

"Agreed, and I thank you. How is the packing coming along?"

"Practically done. All the books are in crates with waterproof linings of wax cloth, and the personal belongings of staff and senior students have been selected on the rule that whatever they cannot carry two miles unaided, stays."

"Everything that stays behind must be sold in the markets. A property speculator has already made a fair offer for the academy's buildings, and I have explained that the king has granted us new premises—but that he should not say anything until the public announcement, unless he wants to attract the king's displeasure."

"How many know?"

"Just the five of us in the Academy Senate, and those who are going. I will send the juniors home for a holiday tomorrow. None will ask questions about an unexpected holiday."

Yvendel and Lavenci fell silent, again contemplating the beauty of the distant Dragonwall.

"May I ask yet again, mother, how did you find out?" asked Lavenci presently. "Was it from the spy, Pellien?"

Yvendel took some moments to decide about her reply, but then decided that nothing was to be gained from secrecy.

"I did not find out from anyone, if the truth be known," she admitted without taking her eyes off Dragonwall. "I merely put myself in the place of the etheric engineers who fabricated that thing. They are not true sorcerers, they are just planners of plans and builders of buildings. Their initiation levels merely indicate skill with sheer power."

"Surely it counts for something?" asked Lavenci, who had hopes of attaining the initiation level of twelve within a decade.

"If a man can lift very heavy weights and is skilled with an ax, would that make him a good king? The etheric engineers have no soul, no compassion. They have sight without vision, and cunning without intelligence. They also have a very simplistic view of the world. It is not hard to think as they might, although after doing so I really feel like giving my mind a bath."

"All this trouble. Surely it might be wise to secure some form of definite proof before imposing further disruption on the academy?"

"Proof we shall have, academician, but by then it will be too late to do what we are doing currently. Just now we must make do with paranoia. We sail tomorrow night, on the small deepwater trader *Pangelon*. It will journey to the island of Helion, then to the Malderin Islands, then the Zurlan trade protectorate, and finally Alberin. The voyage will take us so far into the Placidian Ocean that the enormous waves in the Strait of Dismay will have died away to being merely large waves. We shall be at sea for months, but that means we shall be invisible for months."

"Alberin," murmured Lavenci, running her fingers through her hair. "Does not our Wensomer live there?"

"Yes."

"Wensomer, who dislikes you intensely, and has a potential initiation level higher than yours?"

"The same."

"Wensomer, who caught me in rather awkward circumstances with one of her gentleman friends last year, and now hates me even more than she hates you?"

"Serves her right."

"Wensomer Callientor, the most senior sorceress on the continent of Scalticar, who lists her profession as belly dancer and reveler, her passions as fine food, expensive wine, and interesting men, and her hobby as sorcery?"

"That's my little girl."

"Bury-me-in-a-waterproof-coffin-filled-with-expensive-3129-frostwine Wensomer?"

"It would not surprise me at all."

"Is there no city other than Alberin where we may take refuge?"

"Academician Lavenci, we are going to Alberin because a dark and terrible age is about to descend upon our world. Armies will be smashed, mighty cities will be razed, and fortresses will be blasted to slag. Alberin is a joke, however. Its kavelar list is smaller than this academy's staff list, and there's only fourteen of us. As for its ruler! The man is such a degenerate, he might almost be suitable as a husband for Wensomer. No, when the young, stupid gods of Dragonwall begin to rain fire down on the cities of the world, they may not bother with Alberin. After that, Wensomer, you and I may be the only sorceresses not dead, or merged with Dragonwall. Should that come to pass, we shall be the only ones left who can destroy it."

Chapter Four

DRAGONSLAYER

The herd of goats took four days to cover the ten miles to Harrgh, and even that was considered to be good progress. This did not upset Wallas, however, as he had been reduced to a bare shuffle by cramps, blisters, falls, and an occasional butt from a goat. On three occasions squads of lancers with plumed helmets and gold cloaks passed them, and each time they were asked if they had encountered anyone unfamiliar on the road. In particular, the lancers were asking about a woman who spoke only Diomedan. All that the goatherds replied was nay, and all that they gave was blank stares.

The musical duo that was Wallas and Andry was beginning to sound like a band, in an unsophisticated sort of way. They had played at every roadside tavern they had passed, and been given occasional free drinks. In turn Wallas bought more wineskins for the road, and the trip was generally a quite convivial time for all concerned. They arrived at Harrgh on the evening of the eighth day after leaving Palion. It was a fortified village, with a wooden stockade surrounded by a scatter of farmlets. The produce of the area was goats and goat products, along with a few vegetables for the closer markets. The sky overhead was by now flickering with purplish light, shot through with streaks of green and curtain-like shimmers of orange. Over in the west, the rainbow and orange wind curtain that was Dragonwall also glowed, but more steadily.

"Ain'ne natural, those lights," said Raffin as they trudged after the goats.

"That's 'cause it's not," replied Wallas. "All that's our betters, doin' castin's against the bad weather."

"Git aht!"

"All true." Wallas pointed a thumb at his chest. "Ye learn things in the city."

In the distance a bell began to ring, and then the people of Harrgh streamed out with torches to greet the herders and inspect the new breeding stock they had bought. None of this was unexpected. What took Wallas by surprise was the buxom woman with red cheeks and auburn hair who greeted him nervously and addressed him as "husband."

"Aye Wallas, lucky devil wi' a wife like Jelene an' all," said Raffin.

✵ ✵ ✵

It would be wrong to say that a great feast was laid on for the herders' homecoming to Harrgh. After all, they had been gone only two weeks. Nevertheless, the road was not entirely safe, and with news of the emperor's assassination coming through in their absence there was anxiety about civil war. The goat stew that had been mellowing since the middle of the day was supplemented by three freshly roasted goats, and along with the village beer the herders were presented with was a type of mash spirits and rainwater mixed with berry juice.

Andry and Wallas got the music under way as soon as they could, because it removed them from conversations that were sure to feature questions for which Wallas had no answers. People were soon too busy eating and drinking to ask questions, however, and Andry and Wallas made plans to make a dash in the direction of Glasbury early the following morning. Andry was brought beakers of village beer by a succession of girls, but he discreetly poured most of it into the grass.

"Why am I doing this?" Andry asked himself as he emptied most of his sixth beaker behind his seat. "This is good beer, and I like beer."

The woman Jelene, who was married to someone—alive or dead—named Wallas, arrived with Andry's seventh beaker. He had a feeling that something might be about to go seriously wrong, and that feeling was soon confirmed.

"I heard you speaking Diomedan," she said as she took his beaker and offered him the full one. "That means we can talk."

Oh shyte, she speaks Diomedan, thought Andry, who had been feigning a weak grasp of Sargolan Common in order to keep himself out of trouble.

"Oh aye, all we sailors all speak it in Alberin."

"A Scalticarian sailor?" she said, sitting down beside him.

"Aye, came over on the *Stormbird*. My first voyage, and all."

"My parents sold me to Wallas," said Jelene. " 'Twas a hard year when they did it. Their hard year ended, but mine continued for three, so here I am."

Andry drained what was left in his beaker. Jelene shifted her weight and nudged Andry with her hip, smiling. *Aye, but she'd not do that unless she was trying to catch me off guard*, he thought.

"So, er, you're married to Wallas?" he asked.

"Wallas, aye, married we are. Are you knowin' him well?"

"Er, ah, not very. What about you?"

The sheer idiocy of asking a man's wife of three years' standing if she knew him suddenly hit Andry like a punch to the plexus, but Jelene seemed to take it as a subtle play on words.

"I thought I did. Wallas the drinker, Wallas the adulterer, Wallas the wife beater, Wallas the killer of goat poachers. Now here he be, well spoken, polite, gracious. He speaks Diomedan, even. I just don't—"

"Uh, uh, just hold back a moment," said Andry. "Could I hear more of one of those Wallases?"

"Wallas the adulterer?"

"No, no, it involved goats."

"I'd not think he ever—oh, you mean with the goat poachers and all. Aye, he's killed five. Fierce, surly piece, is our Wallas. Now he's changed. It might be imagining of mine, but he seems taller, stouter, and all. His hair be thicker and darker, there's wrinkles and sunspots missin', too. Where did you meet up with him?"

"In a tavern, on my first night ashore. We got to singing along with his board lyre, then drinking. We got into a fight with . . . nay, you'd not believe it. Then we came upon . . . nay, you'd not believe that either."

"Wallas can't sing," said Jelene.

"Oh aye, now there we agree. Never ask for him to sing one of his ballads. It can clear a taproom faster than shouting 'Fire!' "

"You don't understand. Wallas *never* sings."

She's almost got me, thought Andry. *Stand by to repel boarders*.

"Aye, well, people change when away from home a long time," he replied innocently, as if the problem with Wallas was not his problem.

"He's been only three months gone," insisted Jelene.

"Oh. Ah, well, maybe . . ."

Andry was aware that words were about to fail him, but then Jelene started talking again.

"He'd not change so much in three months. Oh, maybe he might have learned a grace or two, and a dozen words of Diomedan, but somewhere within should be Wallas of old. That Wallas who only ever said to me *Beer! Dinner!* and *Bed!* He's had me in terror of him three years now, always trying to please him for fear of a beating. I thought he was not coming back, but now that he's returned . . . well, fancy another beer, would ye?"

Once she was gone Andry suddenly became aware of someone standing in the shadows of the house just behind him.

"You, the Scalticarian," came a gravelly female voice in Diomedan.

"Me?" asked Andry,

"You, the friend of Wallas. Wallas is in danger."

"What? How do you know? Who are you?"

"I'm the village herbalist. Jelene got a phial of daemon-glare juice from me, not an hour ago. She said it was for killing a rat. Now I know who the rat is."

Daemonglare grew in Scalticar as well as Acrema. The berries were bright red, with a black streak. Against the dark green leaves of the bush, they looked like red eyes with slit pupils. It was one of the most poisonous plants known to herbal lore.

"He—I—but what do I do?" gasped Andry. "He's my friend."

Friend? After eleven days? thought Andry. *Well, maybe it's true*, he decided. They had already been through a lot together.

"Get into her house and steal the poison."

"Why don't you do it?"

"She has a wolfhound."

"A wolfhound! But it can bite me as easily as you."

"You miss my meaning. Seduce her. She will tie up the wolfhound. Once she is asleep, steal the poison."

"But Wallas—"

"Get him drunk first. Hush! She comes!"

Jelene sat down with Andry again, and they drank a toast to the goddess of the goats. In the distance Wallas was play-ing a dance tune on his board lyre, along with a couple of villagers who were playing tin flutes. Some villagers danced to the music, and the rest were drinking.

"Well, I'm for a dance," announced Andry, hoping for an opportunity to put off decisions that he had no wish to make. "What of yourself?"

"I just might at that," said Jelene.

Andry had not had a great history of having dance invita-tions accepted, and this fact had driven him into playing in bands for most of his short social life. Thus Jelene's reply came as a surprise. He had actually intended to merely walk in the direction of the musicians after Jelene declined his in-

vitation, then warn Wallas somehow. Harrgh's dances were
similar to some of the pierside dances that Andry had
learned with his sisters in Alberin, and they danced two
brackets together before the players took a break. While Jelene went back to help with the serving, Andry made for
Wallas.

"Andry, what do I do about that woman?" Wallas whispered before Andry could open his mouth.

"What do you mean?"

"I'm not her husband! Oh, I've gotten away with it so far
because I've only spoken a few words to her, but soon we'll
be off home, and, well, what am I to do?"

"I'd have thought that was fairly obvious."

"Not that! I won't know anything about her, I, I, oh what
am I to—"

"Stop there, don't worry. Look, she said her man's a big
drinker, so drink up big. Get yourself legless, then you won't
be expected to talk. Next morning we're away to Glasbury,
and you only have to tell her that you'll be back in a month."

"Drink big, you say?"

"Never fails!"

What he doesn't know can't hurt him, thought Andry.
What it will do to me is anyone's guess, though.

Wallas downed five pints in as many minutes, but Andry
decided that he had better stay relatively sober in order to
watch over him. The dancing did not resume again, and only
drinkers and singers were left near the fire. Wallas reached a
state where he was not capable of walking, and to Andry's
horror some men offered to carry him home. Andry went
with them, and insisted that they leave Wallas with him at
the door.

"He'll be needing a piss outside, he's not up to aiming at a
pot when he's like this," Andry explained.

Once they had gone, Andry guided Wallas around to the
wood shelter. Having persuaded him to lie down, Andry returned to the cottage door. Jelene was still away with the
other women, cleaning up after the feasting. He pushed the
door open. Coals glowed red in the grate, illuminating a
huge shape that was padding over to him. To his surprise, it
just sniffed him, then wagged its tail and licked his hand.

"Oh aye, I've been dancing with your mistress!" exclaimed Andry softly, and with considerable relief.

He did a quick search of the cottage, which was a single room that contained everything but the firewood. The poison would be kept in a small phial, and daemonglare always had a large daemon's eye painted on the container. Andry lit a tallow candle from a coal, which burned smokily but gave more light than the grate. *Where would she hide it*, he wondered. *Where would a man like Wallas never look? The herb pantry!*

The phial of daemonglare was behind some jars of dried leaves on the pantry's top shelf. Andry emptied it into a corner of the fireplace, rinsed the phial with rainwater, then filled it with more rainwater before putting it back where he had found it and pinching the candle's wick. He straightened, turned—and found himself face-to-face with Jelene. She was carrying an armload of firewood, and a pottery lamp.

"Andry!" she exclaimed. "What is it you're doin' here?"

I keep wondering that myself, he thought, but he said, "I helped bring Wallas home."

"So I noticed. He's in the wood shelter, with his arms around the chopping block—and he's been sick into the kindling box."

"Er, yes, I, er, thought he would be better in there. Like, for the night."

"For the night?"

"Er, aye."

"So what is it you might be doing in here?"

That question again, except that the extra "in" makes it a lot harder to answer. Why would he be in a woman's cottage, late at night, while her husband was lying outside in the wood shelter? Apart from emptying a phial of poison into the fireplace, there was only one possible reason. Andry's jaw worked soundlessly for a moment. *Go ahead, you know what it's like to get your face slapped and be kicked out,* said one voice within him. Another said, *Go ahead, it has to happen sometime.*

"I, like, thought I'd better explain," he began, hoping that this would be enough.

Jelene said nothing, but she did put the firewood and lamp down.

"About Wallas dead drunk outside and all," he continued. Andry saw her features relax. *That's it, I'm here to explain about Wallas.* Andry then made the mistake of not leaving, and the worse mistake of continuing to talk. "I thought . . ."

"Go on."

"Well, er, that he was drunk, so now you know and . . ."

And what? She was standing before the doorway with her hands on her hips. There was no way that he could get past her. In a moment she would have him flung down on the bed and then . . .

"Mistress Jelene, he's not Wallas!" exclaimed Andry.

Jelene's jaw dropped open, but only for a moment. She nodded slowly, folding her arms.

"I suspected as much," she said.

"The real Wallas . . . is dead."

Jelene's features did not so much as twitch.

"This man is a noble, and a very rich man," Andry improvised. After all, Wallas lied so much about his past, surely he could add a few lies of his own. "He had an evil wife who wanted his money. She . . . er, must have met your Wallas in the street, and realized that he was identical to her husband. Maybe she took him home and tumbled him, we could never glean the truth. All the, er, Wallas outside knows is that he arrived home and entered his bedchamber, carrying a lamp. His wife flung back the blankets to reveal someone looking like him in the bed, and dead—with a knife in his chest. His own servants seized him, and all the while she was screaming about how he'd killed her husband and was trying to pretend he was someone else."

"It's all too strange to be true," whispered Jelene.

"Well, Wallas realized that it looked bad for him, and the magistrate was, er, his wife's father, so the case would surely go against him. He fought his way free and fled. In the days that followed, there were proclamations put up about Wallas, so he realized who the man had been."

"So who are you?"

"I'm a close friend of, well, the man who now calls himself Wallas. I can't clear his name, but I can help him to flee."

"Are you another noble?"

"That I can't say, Mistress Jelene. He decided to get drunk, rather than sharing your bed and dishonoring you."

"But he could have just pretended . . ." Jelene's voice trailed away as the full meaning of what Andry had said hit her. She put her hands to her cheeks. "He feared for my *honor*?"

"Oh aye—I mean, yes! Yes, that's it."

"Nobody's ever given a thought for my honor in all of my life! A nobleman, in my woodshed! Quickly, help me get him inside—er, if you please—lordship!"

Wallas was carried inside by Jelene before Andry had a chance to help. She dropped him backward onto the bed, then enlisted Andry's help in removing his rather vile-smelling clothes. Wallas awoke to the touch of a damp cloth, which was also shockingly cold.

"It's all right, my lord," Andry explained. "Mistress Jelene knows you're not her husband, and she's very concerned for your welfare."

"Everything spinning," mumbled Wallas.

"Oh lordship, you got so drunk, and all for me!" wailed Jelene, her quite considerable cleavage looming above Wallas as she stroked his forehead. "You must lie in my bed for the night. Oh, and Lord Andry! You are welcome to stay beneath this roof, too."

"Me?" gasped Andry. "Ah, perhaps not. I should keep watch outside. You never know when his enemies might be upon him."

Not to mention his admirers, Andry added to himself, and then he hurried outside, found his pack, and made himself as comfortable as possible in Jelene's wood shelter. After about a half hour of listening to the giggles, gasps, and creaks coming from within the cottage, however, he moved beside the remains of the feasting bonfire and finally managed to get to sleep—for an hour, at any rate. It began to rain. This time Andry sheltered under a wagon, where he managed to spend the rest of the night more or less dry, if not in comfort.

The things we do for our friends, thought Andry as he lay trying to doze. *And the randy clown is not even my friend.* "You fool," Andry said aloud as he drifted to the edge of sleep, and then wondered why he had said it.

Andry was awakened at dawn by the villagers as they set up stalls and tables for a market. The sky was now clear, although the ground was muddy from the overnight rain. He decided to stay where he was, and after not sleeping particularly well all night, he now dropped into quite a deep sleep in spite of all the commotion. The morning was quite advanced when the owner of the wagon woke Andry and apologetically explained that he had to move it.

The market was filled with herders and other peasants from outlying farms and hamlets, along with a sprinkling of lancers in clean, expensive-looking surcoats and gleaming chain mail. By now Andry was less nervous about armed people in authority being nearby. Nobody had chased him or tried to kill him for over a week, probably because the Andry that people in Palion had been trying to kill was thought to be dead.

Andry felt the urge to wash his hair, shave, and generally clean up. It felt like something he always did, and that his morning routine would be incomplete unless he did it. That was quite odd, because the number of times he had ever done all that was less than the number of fingers on one hand. He was washing his face at the horse trough when Wallas emerged from Jelene's cottage and began to buy eggs, cured meat, and herbs. Andry shouldered his rerolled pack, and joined Wallas.

"So you'd be doing breakfast?" he asked Wallas, who was buying a jar of oil.

"Oh no, I did breakfast hours ago, Jelene and I had it in bed. This will be lunch—and you're invited."

"Not if it's to be in bed."

"Oh no, at table, laid out like a courtier's," laughed Wallas. "Jelene thinks you're a noble like me, she's so anxious to have you as a guest."

"But Wallas, neither of us are courtiers."

"She *thinks* we're courtiers pretending to be commoners. Just act like you always do, but try to look a bit nervous. Oh, but shave your cheeks, and try to look neat, like a noble disguised as a commoner."

"Wallas, I'm a *commoner* disguised as a commoner."

"Andry, maybe you should learn a few graces. Then you could be a commoner disguised as a noble. *Nobody* would suspect it's you."

Although meant as sarcasm, the gibe made some sense to Andry. He returned to the trough, took out his knife, and began to shave his cheeks. He checked his reflection in the water, then rinsed his hair. Some minutes of pulled hairs and cursing with Ellisen's comb had his hair and beard looking passably neat. He had just tied his hair back when there was a shout of anger, followed by a scream. Andry looked up and quickly realized that Wallas had seized a lancer and had both the man's arms pinned behind his back. Andry hurried over, and abruptly realized that the lancer was Terikel.

"Fetch a magistrate, I've caught the sorceress, there's a reward!" Wallas was shouting.

They fell to the mud, Wallas pinning the Elder of the Metrologans down. Another lancer raced for the struggling pair, drawing his cavalry ax.

"Laron, help!" cried Terikel.

Laron's blow was aimed between Wallas's shoulders, but Andry's staff parried it. Laron danced back as Andry backhanded a blow at him, then threw a cut that Andry caught on his handle. Andry kicked at Laron, who caught his foot in one hand and twisted. Andry kept on twisting, however, dropping to the ground and rolling, then striking for Laron's knee with his staff. It was a glancing blow, but Laron went down for a moment. Andry tried for a backhand at Laron's head, but Laron parried upward, sending the staff spinning out of Andry's hands. Laron chopped down at Andry, but the sailor swept his arm in a circle before him, snared the ax handle, seized the shaft just above Laron's hand, and, using the ax handle like a lever, drove the butt into Laron's jaw. Laron collapsed. Andry glanced about. Wallas was being held by two other lancers, while a third was helping Terikel to her feet. At least two dozen more lancers ringed Andry, holding either cavalry axes or lances.

"Drop your ax, fellow, I'll not say it again!" called an educated voice in Sargolan Common.

Andry dropped his ax.

"Ladyship, are you all right?" the officer asked Terikel.

The officer was now speaking Diomedan, and he walked over to Terikel, went down on one knee, and bowed.

"I am not hurt, I just want to leave," she said quickly and softly.

The officer wore the helmet of a captain, and a dark blue surcoat over chain mail. His cloak was also dark blue, and trimmed with scarlet braid. The royal crest was on the clasp pin, but a different crest was on his helmet. A straggle of village militiamen now came hurrying up to see what the disturbance was about.

"I am Captain Gilvray, of the Royal Journey Guards," the captain announced to them, switching back to Sargolan Common. "My authority exceeds that of your local magistrates."

Nobody had any dispute with that. Andry was now seized by two lancers, and a lancer marshal punched him in the stomach. He doubled over, and was then punched in the face. He raised his legs, still held by the other two lancers, and kicked the marshal in the face with both feet. The marshal went down, stunned. A dozen lancers converged on Andry, but by now Terikel was screaming for them to stop. Andry head-butted one of the lancers who had been holding him, drew the man's ax, and backhanded the other lancer in the stomach. He was quickly encircled by lancers with their cavalry axes and lances at the ready.

"Stop, release these men, I know them," cried Terikel, wiping the mud from her face.

"But they attacked you," said Captain Gilvray.

"There was a misunderstanding."

"Misunderstanding!" exclaimed Andry. "She tried to kill us, she sunk my ship."

"Andry, please!" pleaded Terikel. "We can talk about this somewhere else, quietly."

"Why? Afraid of the truth?"

Terikel began to walk in the direction of Andry. Having seen the Elder set a Throne Guard afire, Andry prepared to dodge whatever casting she flung at him. Instead, she went down on both knees and hung her head. This caused a great deal of surprise among the lancers.

"Andry Tennoner, I apologize for your sufferings, and those of Wallas," she said clearly in Diomedan, "but I did not sink the *Stormbird*. I was just as horrified and surprised as everyone clsc when those creatures set upon it."

"You say you didn't know?" said Wallas.

"I had no idea. Please, will you two come away from the market with me and just hear me out?"

Andry shook his head. "You want us quietly out of the way, so you can have us quietly killed."

"Again," added Wallas.

"So you don't believe me?" asked Terikel.

Laron was now conscious again, and he got to his feet. "I shall vouch for the Elder with my life," he said, unsteady on his feet but staring straight at Andry.

"Oh aye, but it's *my* life that concerns me," Andry replied.

It was at this point that Terikel made what Andry immediately realized was a difficult decision.

"Captain Gilvray, I shall not require further protection from you," she declared to the nobleman.

The surprise was evident on Gilvray's face. "Do you mean to stay at this village?" he asked.

"No, I shall travel on to Glasbury, alone. If these two gentlemen, Andry and Wallas, would consent to travel with me, perhaps my chances of survival will be improved."

"My lady, you cannot!" exclaimed Gilvray. "This is madness."

"It is my decision, Captain Gilvray, and my safety is not your first concern. Thank you for your hospitality thus far, and my compliments to your mistress."

There was no arguing with Terikel, and it was not long before the lancers withdrew from Harrgh to the main part of their force outside the stockade. The squad set off, escorting several wagons and a coach, but Laron returned.

✳ ✳ ✳

"You managed to command an escort fit for an emperor," said Wallas as he, Terikel, Andry, and Laron sat in Jelene's cottage. "They were the Journey Guard."

"It was his daughter's escort," said Terikel.

"Princess Senterri?" exclaimed Wallas.

"Yes. She happened to be traveling to Port Logiar with her husband, Viscount Cosseren. She is to become the regent by way of command, and the queen by way of law. I was allowed to travel with her. A highly placed friend arranged it, after I seemed to perish aboard the *Stormbird*."

"Why did you send us off on the *Stormbird*?" asked Andry, again flushing with anger at the mere thought of the vessel's fate.

"You wanted to leave Palion, and I wanted to *seem* to leave Palion for Diomeda. I had no idea that my—my enemies would destroy an entire ship and all its company."

"Just what is going on with the palace?" demanded Wallas, his educated Sargolan accent breaking through. "First the Throne Guards and city watch try to kill you, then the Journey Guards arrive as your escort."

"Nobody is quite in charge anymore," explained Laron. "With the emperor dead, all of his sons are grasping for power. Should that come as a surprise?"

"Who is your highly placed friend, who has so much influence with the princess?" asked Andry.

"I am," said Laron.

"What? You're just a boy."

"I'm fifteen!" said Laron indignantly.

"Oh aye, that makes all the difference!" Andry laughed.

"I am a confidant of the princess. I am also a guard, when needed. Technically, I am an unattached lancer with the rank of captain in the Imperial Highways Militia. I answer directly to the princess."

"Yet here you are, allowed to leave her for guarding the Elder?"

"That, my most suspicious of commoners, is a measure of the Elder's importance."

Terikel clasped her hands together and hung her head. "Laron and I being here is also a measure of my remorse at what nearly happened to you two. I hold you in great esteem, so it was a matter of honor."

"Esteem, honor, that's all for foppy nobles with money!" exclaimed Andry, who felt that the exchange was all words and little substance. "What can you give us that's more than words?"

"The benefit of the doubt!" exclaimed Laron, exasperated. "Take it from the other side, lad. The Elder is meant to be aboard the *Stormbird*, with you two. You jump off. Why? Because *you two* know the ship is to be set upon by sea dragons?"

"Not so, and we two knew the Elder was not aboard!" Andry shouted back. "The veiled woman who went aboard was a decoy dressed as the Elder. She died."

"Then why were you not aboard?" demanded Laron.

Andry glanced uneasily at Wallas. Wallas squirmed.

"I . . . I believe I was struck over the head and put overboard as we sailed," said Andry. "There is a cut on the back of my head, and the remains of a lump."

"Indeed? And why might that have been?"

Wallas cleared his throat. "Because of the, er, decoy."

"Could you clarify that?"

"Because we were guards for the decoy woman," said Andry.

"I still don't follow," said Laron.

"The, ah, lady that the Elder chose to . . . to represent herself on the *Stormbird* had an eye for my charms," declared Wallas. "The shipmaster took offense, and so Andry and I were thrown overboard."

"You rogered her as soon as you got to her cabin, yet you can't remember her name!" exclaimed Andry.

"Roselle, it was Roselle."

"No, you mounted *Roselle* about four hours later in the Wayward Wayfarer's stables, you filthy slime pail. By then the poor decoy lady was dead and in some sea dragon's belly."

"Will you say her name, then!" demanded Wallas.

"Melier," responded Andry.

"Melier, that's it, I knew it all along," cried Wallas. "Yes, well, er, Melier found me attractive, and we, ah, thought to get to know each other better as soon as we reached her cabin. After a half hour or so, as we were sailing, an officer rapped at the door and said I was urgently needed on deck. Something to do with the Sargolan Customs, Excise, and Alien Movements Service. Naturally I popped on a tunic, trews, and boots and hurried out at once, but as I emerged onto the deck I was seized and bundled overboard so fast that I scarcely had time to cry out before I hit the water. I then called out that I was overboard, but nobody heeded me."

"So, saved by the jealousy of the shipmaster," said Laron.

"And myself," said Andry. "The clown couldn't swim, it was I who dragged him ashore."

"Then the sea dragons attacked the ship," concluded Wallas, with a quick sneer at Andry.

"Why would the shipmaster feel so passionate about her so quickly?" asked Laron.

There was a sudden silence. Everyone glanced from one to the other. Terikel closed her eyes and hunched over.

"Because I had been the shipmaster's mistress on the voyage to Palion!" she snapped. "When I was not throwing up, anyway. How else do you think he was persuaded to risk his vessel on such a dangerous voyage? I had the endorsement of the crown prince of Alberin, but it still took nearly everything in the Metrologan Order's coffers to pay for the voyage. Once we were at sea the shipmaster told me he was going to take my money, sail to Zurlan, and dump me there, and . . . I am not proud of what I did to persuade him to sail here—but there's an end of it."

Nobody was quite sure about how to respond to that.

Laron's face betrayed no emotion, Andry was clearly shocked, and Wallas gave Terikel a sly, appraising look. Looking like a magistrate about to give his verdict, Laron stood up and spread his arms.

"Elder Terikel, Andry, Wallas, who has the most unlikely story?" he asked.

Andry muttered that he probably had a point. Terikel conceded that her own actions probably looked bad from the viewpoint of Andry and Wallas. Wallas wagered that if he told his own complete story, nobody would believe him anyway.

"So what do you want to do, then?" demanded Laron, staring Andry in the face.

"Why should you give a stale turd for what I want to do?" asked Andry defiantly.

"You beat me in fair combat while I was trying to kill you. Then you spared me, so I owe you my life. Tell me what you want to do and I shall make sure that it is done."

"I want you to look after her Ladyship, understand? She put herself in my protection, but I didn't accept. Now bugger off, take her with you, and catch up with the Journey Guards."

"But what do *you* want to do?"

"Me? What does that matter?"

"Tell me."

"I want to go to Logiar. Now you know."

"Elder, and what is your wish?"

"The same as before. To go to the Capefang Mountains, a place called Skymirror, near Port Logiar."

"And Wallas?"

"Well, I was going to Glasbury," he began, flicking a glance at Terikel, "but Port Logiar has certain attractions."

"Like being a long way from Palion," added Andry.

"Quite. So if I don't have to walk, I'm all for going there."

"And finally there is me," said Laron, placing a hand across his chest. "Actually, I seem to live for other people, so I don't much care about what I do." He clapped his hands together. "I shall make sure that you all reach Logiar."

"Take the others," said Andry sullenly. "I'll go where I will."

"Well, I have a horse, but all of us would be a bit of a strain for him, so it seems that we need a cart as well. I shall take steps to secure one. Elder, be so good as to secure provisions for us at the village market."

"And me?" asked Wallas.

"Do what you will, Wallas, just be ready to leave tomorrow morning. And Andry, you have until then to change your mind. There will be room for you in a cart."

"I'll be gone by then," replied Andry.

"As you will. Oh and Wallas, I have something to say to you," said Laron, turning back to Wallas.

"Yes, Captain Laron?" said Wallas, clasping his hands, smiling broadly, and bowing slightly.

Laron rammed his knee into Wallas's groin. Wallas doubled over, with surprise, shock, and agony all struggling for a place on his face.

"Unchivalrous bastard!" snarled Laron, who then turned to Andry and said, "Well?"

"Think I may come with you after all," said Andry, smiling for the first time since they had met.

Once Laron and Terikel had left, Jelene returned. She sat on the edge of the bed, while her two guests remained on their stools.

"I, er, need a drink," said Andry, standing up. "Just a small one."

"There's jars of wine above the pantry, lordship," said Jelene. who bounded to her feet and fetched a small jar for him before he could take a step.

"Not 'lordship,' I'm just a scabby sailor," said Andry. "Not sure about Wallas."

"Whoever you be, it's not my husband," Jelene said to Wallas.

"Er, no."

"But you're better. Be he dead?"

"I didn't kill him!" exclaimed Wallas.

"But he killed the man who did," added Andry.

There was still not a trace of grief on the woman's face. She pondered the news for some moments.

"Different story to last night," said Jelene. "So where is my husband?"

"Dead," said Wallas.

"So it's a widow I am, then?"

"Yes," said Wallas and Andry together.

Jelene thought about this for a while. "It would have been easier to just pretend to be Wallas," she concluded.

"Oh aye, but there was your honor to worry about," said Andry diplomatically.

"But who worries about my honor?" sniffled Jelene.

"Er, I do," said Wallas, going across to the bed and putting an arm around her. After the bad feeling generated earlier on the subject of his relationships with various women, he was anxious to show that he had a caring and compassionate side to anyone who could be bothered to look. In particular, he was worried about Andry's opinion, because Andry was providing protection on the trek.

"But I still bedded you," said Jelene.

"Aye, but you knew I was not Wallas, as in husband. You were not deceived."

As they embraced each other. Andry stood up, walked over to the door, and held up the small jar that he had been given.

"It's been a trying morning," he said. "I think I need time in the fresh air to clear my head and settle my nerves. I'll be back this evening."

✳ ✳ ✳

At a farmstead two miles from the village, a freehold farmer awoke to the sound of growls and yelps from his five wolfhounds. He emerged with a loaded crossbow, accompanied by his son, who was holding a burning torch in one hand and an ax in the other. One of the wolfhounds lay dead, and three others were looking down anxiously from the top of the cow shed. The fifth lay on the ground, still struggling, and something black and human shaped appeared to be feeding on it. The farmer raised his crossbow and fired at the predator. It looked up, growled, plucked the bolt from its side, and flung it away.

"Were I you, I would not load that thing again," said a voice beside them.

The boy whirled, tossed the torch to his father, and swung his ax. There was a flurry of limbs that lasted about as long as an indrawn breath. The ax was blocked by a pair of crossed arms, then twisted around before the boy even had a chance to let go. The butt slammed into his jaw. The boy dropped, stunned. What appeared to be quite a handsome youth of about his own age tossed the ax into the darkness and gave a little bow to the farmer.

"Forgive the lateness of the hour, but we are here about the cart you have for sale," he declared in Diomedan.

"But my cart is not for sale," said the retreating farmer with a pronounced quaver in his voice.

"Oh, but I'm afraid it is, and so are two of your wolfhounds—but I am offering a very good price. Your discretion had better be for sale as well."

"Er, what's discretion?"

"Discretion is forgetting all about us, especially if anyone comes asking. Otherwise, you may get a visit from my friend here. She prefers humans, and she is always hungry."

✷ ✷ ✷

While Laron was returning with the cart, Jelene was sitting up in bed watching Andry, who was beside the fire playing "Waves of Bantriok" on the rebec while Wallas played accompaniment on his board lyre. Every so often Wallas, who was wearing Jelene's nightsmock, would stop to stir the stew, turn the roast, and prod the baking tubers. *This is even more pleasant than playing at court*, thought Wallas. There was a knock at the door, and he danced across and opened it. Terikel stood before him, framed against the blackness outside.

"Ah, just in time for dinner," said Wallas, giving a wink followed by an exaggerated bow and standing back for her to enter.

"Er, gentlefolk, Laron is outside, and he needs to introduce you to a friend of ours," Terikel announced. "She will be traveling with us."

"Enter, enter, one and all. There is food for ten, the mighty Wallas has been cooking."

Laron entered next. The pale, hawkish-looking youth was still dressed in a surcoat over chain mail, although he had his helmet under his arm. Velander entered. She was wearing a cloak that concealed everything except her head and boots.

"Thanking for offer, but have eaten—Them!"

Andry and Wallas had already recognized Velander's voice from the darkened alleyway in Palion, and had bounded up and collided with each other. Velander could see in the dark, and so remembered their faces. Andry seriously contemplated an escape up the chimney, fire or no fire. He decided to make for the window instead. He again collided with Wallas, who had also decided to flee that way. Wallas frantically scrabbled at the latch of the shutters while Andry snatched up a bottle and held it before him.

"Why are you waving that beer bottle at my friend?" asked Laron, who actually had a fairly good idea what the answer was going to be.

"That thing drinks blood!" shouted Andry.

"It will do you no good to run, Velander is three times faster than mortals," Laron began to explain.

"Bugger that, I just have to run faster than Wallas!" exclaimed Andry.

"Dirty, filthy, revolting, smelly drunkard!" hissed Velander, but she did not move.

"Oh aye, but I'm worse!" babbled Wallas, who had just got the shutters open.

"Never could do a fart when I needed to," said Andry.

Through a veil of blind panic, Andry suddenly remembered Jelene. He dragged her out of bed and pushed in the direction of the window—in which Wallas was by now jammed.

"Run, run in opposite directions, she can only go after one of you!" shouted Andry without turning.

Jelene threw her weight against Wallas's feet, and the window frame and shutters came free of the wall and crashed out into the darkness, along with Wallas. Jelene scrambled out after him. Andry slowly backed in the direction of the hole that had once been the window; then Jelene appeared at the door with her wolfhound and shouted, "Take her, Fang!" Fang took one look at Velander, turned in a blur of flailing legs, and fled into the night with his tail between his legs, dragging Jelene with him.

"So, you have already met Velander?" asked Laron, who had not actually seen their faces during the encounter back in Palion.

"Only man I ever catch, but could not stomach," growled Velander.

Strange, thought Andry. *She sways like a drunk.* Andry had seen a great many drunks in his time, and considered himself an expert at picking them.

"*They* saved you, Learned Elder?" asked Laron. "I mean, are you truly sure?"

"Use your eyes, Laron," said Terikel, gesturing at Andry. "For all his terror, he stood his ground in defense of Jelene against Velander. He once did that for me against Throne Guards."

Alcohol on the air, Andry noticed. *Rot, mold, and blood too, but someone has been drinking heavily. Terikel and Laron are steady on their feet, leaving . . . the daemon.*

Jelene returned presently with some of the braver members of the village militia, but they were soon informed that all was well, and sent off in search of Wallas. Wallas was found some distance down the highway, with the window frame still jammed around his body. A full hour after Velander had first entered, the entire company was again in Jelene's cottage. A blanket had been draped over the hole in the wall, and Wallas had been freed from the frame.

"I should like to try the introductions again," began Terikel. "Laron is Velander's contract guard."

"He must have a busy time, guarding folk from her," said Andry.

"Aye, er, so he's the one who *doesn't* eat people?" asked Wallas.

"I would not be caught dead doing a thing like that," said Laron, with the slightest trace of a sneer.

"Of course there are still some very bad men trying to kill me," Terikel continued.

"You mean they're worse than *her*?" said Andry, pointing at Velander.

"For a time I was thought to have perished aboard the *Stormbird*, but my escape was discovered. There are traitors and spies everywhere, even in the palace."

"Especially in the palace," added Wallas.

"And Velander has promised to do something about them," concluded Terikel, with a puzzled glance at Wallas.

"Whoever they are, they have my sympathy," said Andry.

"Velander is not well, however," said Laron.

"Am dead," explained Velander.

"So she needs a lot of sleep. We three men must provide the defense when Velander is indisposed."

"She sleeps a lot?" asked Andry hopefully.

"Twelve hours or so each day, when Miral is down," said Laron.

"*You* will be safe from Velander, of course," Terikel said soothingly, looking to Andry.

"Would not feeding him upon, if he was—were—last man in world," muttered Velander.

"Hie, hear what she said?" exclaimed Andry with relief.

"Bugger that, what about me?" cried Wallas.

"Velander and I have secured a cart, and I already have a horse," concluded Laron. "I suggest that we get a full and proper night's rest, then set off for Glasbury soon after dawn."

✳ ✳ ✳

Velander retired to the cart, but everyone else slept in Jelene's cottage. Wallas was made to sleep on the floor, as Jelene had been less than impressed with his lack of heroics when Velander had entered. At dawn Terikel paid Jelene for the damaged window while the others loaded the cart. With Laron and Terikel standing behind him, Wallas made a sacred declaration to the regional magistrate's representative in the village that he was not in fact the Wallas who was Jelene's husband, and that to the best of his knowledge the other Wallas was dead. Jelene was noted to be a widow in the village register.

Andry was washing his face at the horse trough when Jelene called to him. He walked over to her cottage, and entered to find her filling Wallas's wineskin from one of several large jars. The other wineskin lay beside her, already full.

"With my husband dead an' all, I'll not be needin' these," she explained. "They're for your journey. You can also take any spare jars as will fit after the skins are full."

"For us?" exclaimed Andry.

"All you can carry. I'll be sellin' the rest. Sit down, lord-ship, rest a moment and talk."

"What will become of you now?" asked Andry, presuming that this was what she meant by talk.

"I've got coin saved and hidden. Raffin makes excuses to come over and borrow things, then visits again to give them back. Some night soon I'll be sayin' that his trews need mendin', even if they don't."

"Well then, that's all right," said a very relieved Andry. "I'd better get this skin out to the cart, then."

"I'd like you to have this, too," said Jelene. "It's a way-farer's sewing kit, to keep you smart on the road. Got it for Wallas, my Wallas, but he'd not use it."

"Women keep trying to give me these things," said Andry with a sharp pang of distress. "It's beyond me why you want me to sew instead of . . . but all right, give here, and my thanks."

He tucked the little cloth roll under his belt.

"Andry, like, I feel bad!"

"Sick, you mean?"

"No, but . . . well, should you have acted, like, with a bit of interest, on that first night, like, I might have been in-clined to be . . . to be friendlier with you."

"Oh," managed Andry, suddenly alarmed that his unspo-ken complaint was now under discussion. "Well that's flat-tering, I suppose."

"Like I don't want to seem to presume. Like me steppin' out of my station, an' you bein' a gentleman in disguise an' all."

"I'm not a gentleman, Jelene. Wallas and Laron are the only gentlemen hereabouts."

"Not so, you're a true gentleman, Andry, and cannot be hidin' it," she said as she gave his hand a squeeze. "You changed my life."

Andry blushed, then stood up with the wineskin. He turned to the doorway—in which Wallas was standing. Wal-las scowled, then strode away in the direction of the cart.

"What do you think he heard?" asked Jelene, who had suddenly gone pale.

"If it was only the part about changing your life, he may be assuming the worst," replied Andry.

✳ ✳ ✳

Andry had much to think about as the cart rumbled out of the village with Laron driving. Andry had been mistaken for a gentleman, and Wallas was under the mistaken impression that he had spent time in Jelene's bed. Andry was not sure which thought gave him more satisfaction.

A gentleman. Andry Tennoner of 5 Pokewossit Lane, Bargeyards, Alberin. *A gentleman, like . . . well . . .* Andry realized that he did not know any gentlemen. There was Laron, of course, and possibly Wallas, but then Wallas was not actually acting like a gentleman. Laron had a refined voice, and he appeared to even know the dead emperor's daughter. Nevertheless, he traveled with a predatory fiend who smelled like a pile of offal and rubbish behind a tavern. Did gentlemen do that?

Andry wondered about Velander, too. Laron had explained that she was sleeping under a pile of blankets in the tray of the cart, and would not stir until Miral rose again. Andry took a sip of wine from one of the jars, found it had turned sour, and flung it into a nearby field.

"That's from my wine pile," grumbled Wallas.

"Well your wine's rotten," replied Andry, reaching for another jar.

"Drunken slob," muttered Wallas, who was nevertheless nursing his own jar of wine.

"Just lightening the load for the horse," replied Andry cheerfully.

"You'd lighten it more were you to throw yourself off."

"Oh aye, but you weigh more."

"Stop it, both of you," called Laron without turning.

Andry uncorked the jar, took a sip, then picked up Wallas's board lyre and began to play "Jik the Carter Lad."

"Uses my woman, then uses my lyre," said Wallas sullenly.

"You didn't stay to defend your woman against the fiend—er, I mean Lady Velander."

"The only reason *you* stayed to defend her was that I was stuck in the window."

In an odd sort of way Velander is a gentleman too, said a voice within Andry's head. He thought about this. There was indeed a type of nobility about her, and in a sense she was almost tragic. Perhaps Laron saw something about her that others did not. Perhaps that was part of being a gentleman, they could see things that others missed. A group of peasants waved and clapped Andry's playing as the cart passed them. Wallas threw them a full jar of wine.

"That's from my wine pile," said Andry.

"The wine's from *my* woman, so it's *my* wine."

"She wasn't your woman anymore when she gave us the wine, so it's wine for all of us."

"Then consider it from *my* share, and let it go at that," said Laron without turning around.

"You don't have a share," said Wallas.

"If you two don't stop bickering I'll take a selection of jars from both of your stacks, call it my share, and heave them onto the road!"

By now the five of them had distanced themselves from each other as far as was possible within a small cart. Andry and Laron were on the driver's bench, with Andry playing and Laron concentrating on driving. Terikel was lying in the tray, under a blanket, concentrating on staying out of sight. Wallas was sitting on the tailboard with his legs dangling, gazing along the road they had traveled. Velander was somewhere deep beneath their food, luggage, and wine in the tray. The thought of what Jelene had said returned to Andry. *A gentleman. Andry Tennoner, gentleman.* It was like someone else speaking in his head.

"Er, lordship?" said Andry without ceasing his playing.

"Just Laron," replied Laron.

"Oh aye, Laron, then. All those lancers, were they gentlemen?"

"All are gentlemen, and some are even gentlemanly as well."

"Oh aye. So, er, how's that? Is being gentlemanly sort of, like, on the road to becoming a gentleman?"

"For some, yes. You can *buy* the title of gentleman, but you have to *be* gentlemanly—and you can do that for free."

Suddenly something clicked into place within Andry's mind. Wallas was a gentleman, but Wallas could act—as Laron had put it—like an unchivalrous bastard. Andry was not sure what "unchivalrous" meant, but it sounded like Wallas.

"Is 'chivalrous' sort of, er, gentlemanly?" Andry asked.

"Oh yes."

"Ah, well that makes sense then. And, er, what does a lad have to do to be gentlemanly?"

"Well . . . first there are manners."

"Oh aye, manners, you say?"

"Yes."

"What are they?"

The idea of manners took a little time for Laron to explain. He began to provide specific examples. Andry asked a sprinkling of questions that actually made sense. Laron extended his lesson to etiquette and social refinements. Over the next ten miles Andry learned the basic forms of address for a guardsman to use with commoners, peers, officers, nobles, kavelars, royalty, foreign royalty, the clergy, and prisoners of war. The etiquette of eating at table caused him more problems, as Andry had never eaten at a table on a regular basis. Laron had reached the subject of bows and flourishes when Andry enthusiastically stood up on the footboard, attempted a formal bow, and fell from the cart.

Andry spent the next five miles lying in the tray of the cart, nursing his bruises. Then Velander woke up, surfaced amid the clutter, and snarled at him. Andry hastily clambered back onto the driver's bench. Laron handed him the reins.

"When about to fight someone, it is very important to salute in the right way," said Laron, drawing his ax.

"Salute?" said Andry.

"Yes, salute. What do *you* do before entering a fight?"

"Oh I yells 'Come on, come on, why's the wait? Cat got yer balls?' "

"Er, the salute is a little more formal than that," said

Laron, a slightly pained expression on his face. "You draw your ax with your left hand, grip the base of the handle with your right, hold it vertical with your left arm at your side and your right fist at your left shoulder, then bring it up to the ready position for your particular school of ax fencing."

"Er, I never learned ax at school," volunteered Andry.

"I—Oh! So, you actually went to school?"

"Oh aye, I can read and write in Alberinese and Diomedan. Not too well, mind. Can count and add up, too. I learned Sargolan in taverns, like, from sailors."

"This gives me an idea," said Laron. "The Elder is about the same size as you, and she wears the uniform of a Journey Guard."

"Aye."

"Yet *you* would be a more convincing guard. You know ax fencing, after all, while she is more likely to injure herself than an enemy if given a weapon. If she fought with magical castings, people would know she was a sorceress at once, and we can't have that. If we dress her as you, though, and you as a guardsman, we look more like what we wish to seem."

"What's that?"

"A support cart, hurrying after the main squad of Journey Guards. There are always two guards for every cart."

Evening saw Andry dressed as a guardsman and Terikel dressed as Andry. Terikel was looking thoroughly demoralized as Laron tried to explain to her that it was all for the best. Andry was trying to put his newly learned table manners into practice, even though there was no table. They were eating Wallas's meal of beans and meat strips from tin bowls, using small, wooden Sargolan eating spades and their utility knives. Andry carved something that looked to be the right shape for a spade, then began to eat with it. It was a little more tricky than pushing food out of a bowl and into his mouth with a crust of bread. His piece of meat shot out of the bowl and fell to the dirt. He rinsed it in wine and popped it into his mouth. Laron shook his head.

As Andry was helping Wallas clean up the cooking gear, he noticed a familiar smell of damp carpet, mildew, and alcohol on the air. It did not take long to identify which shadow Velander was lurking within. By now Andry had begun to regard her rather like a large and ill-tempered guard dog. As long as someone was holding the leash, one merely had to stay out of its reach.

"You rogered my wife," Wallas muttered, as they knelt at the side of a muddy stream, scouring the pots with handfuls of grass. Terikel was wiping them dry and packing them back onto the cart.

"She wasn't your wife," Andry replied, happy to continue the myth of the seduction that never was.

"*She* thought she was."

"*She* was also going to poison you."

"So you go to bed with her. How was that meant to save me? Talk sense."

"But she really was going to poison you."

"Then why didn't you warn me?"

"We didn't want any fuss —"

"Oh that's charming. My life on the scales and *you* don't want any fuss."

"—so I told you to get drunk."

"How might that help? She might have prised my lips open and poured the poison down my throat."

"I . . . distracted her for a short time," said Andry.

"What is a short time?"

"Oh, a quarter hour."

"What? You filthy wretch, you rogered my wife! You really did."

"Will you two ever stop fighting?" asked Terikel, who was waiting for the utensils that were no longer being washed.

"He was not married to her, he swore at the magistrate—" began Andry.

"I think you mean he made a sworn statement," said Terikel.

"Anyway, people *thought* I was married to her," continued Wallas. "He humiliated me, I was cuckolded in front of all those people."

"You'll never see those people again," laughed Andry.

"What do you mean? There's three of them here—four, if we count you as a person."

"Give it a week or two, Wallas, then you'll be on your way to somewhere where nobody knows you."

"You have never been near Harrgh in your life, have you Wallas?" asked Terikel.

"Well, obviously not," he admitted.

"Wallas really is dead, is he not?"

"I didn't kill him. I never killed anyone—apart from that guard."

"So! You are someone else who looks like Wallas."

"Well, after a fashion, one might say."

"You are someone passably talented and very refined, who can draw conversations out of people easily, like a courtier from the palace. Someone who can play a couple of dozen instruments, but specializes in the lyre."

"Someone who makes up ballads so awful that they're funny," interjected Andry.

"Someone accused of murder, but who has not so far said who he is accused of killing," concluded Terikel pointedly.

Suddenly Andry backed away from Wallas, dropping a tin dish.

"Tell me you didn't kill the emperor," he cried.

"I didn't—"

"You're lying!"

"Well you told me to say—"

"You're a master assassin—You bastard! You let me fight all those Throne Guards, alone!"

"I killed one."

"Aye, and I had to drop three, and even her Ladyship here had to take one. You're a master assassin, you could have dropped all five—probably by boring them to death with one of those awful ballads."

"Would anyone like to hear my side?" cried Wallas.

"It had better be the truth," warned Andry. "So who are you?"

"I'm . . . Oh, you would not believe it."

"Try me!" snapped Andry.

"I am Milvarios of Tourlossen," he declared grandly, "Master of Royal Music—"

He got no further. Andry collapsed to the muddy bank, in a fit of near-hysterical laughter. Somewhere in the nearby shadows, even Velander giggled.

"I said you wouldn't believe me," said Wallas sullenly.

"Tell me more," gasped Andry, getting up again.

"He—the real assassin—came through a secret passage into my chambers. He had my face! He bound me, but I burned off the ropes." Wallas displayed the burns on his wrists. "He said he had used a magical casting to mold his face to be mine."

"Was Torean assassin guild," said Velander. "Shape-shifters, was name. Making use of powerful castings, ah, for to change shape of face."

"Yes, yes, that is what he said!" said Wallas eagerly.

"All died when Torea melted, but . . . one overseas, maybe. On contract. Big contract. But is trouble. Shapeshifters were joke. After killing, easily caught. Faces . . . Damn, what is word? Wanted? Desired? Sought?"

"Needed?" asked Andry.

"Yes. Needed year for recovering, enough, for molding again. Caught, killed, very often, while waiting. Wallas, perhaps right."

"You can't believe him!" exclaimed Andry. "His ballads are terrible."

"Why you—" snarled Wallas.

"Hah! Master musician, disguised, not performing well for part of disguises?" asked Velander with a sneer at Wallas this time. "Princess Senterri saying, to me, talk in Palion court, now is, er, 'Hurrah, Milvarios gone, no more boring ballads.' "

"By Miral's ring's, so it *is* true!" exclaimed Andry.

"I resent that too!" cried Wallas.

"Did assassin, ah, leaving you for guards, for to find?" asked Velander.

"Yes, but I hid in the secret passage and jammed the entrance hatch closed. He was trapped in my chambers and was killed by the Throne Guards. As I crouched there in the secret passage, I discovered that the assassin had left a disguise for himself. Perhaps I should have emerged and told my story, but would I have been believed?"

"No!" exclaimed Andry.

"You see? You see? You would have had me killed too. I had the assassin's face—or he had mine, that is."

"Perhaps shapeshifter . . . sensible. Killing Wallas. Real Wallas. Live as Wallas. Having Wallas face."

"But Jelene's Wallas had a chance resemblance to me!" exclaimed the former musician of the late emperor. "Perhaps all shapeshifters did their killings this way. No shapeshifters may *ever* have died. Dozens of innocent courtiers and guards may have been killed while the assassins fled, but there were no suspicious strangers fleeing the area. The assassins had another identity waiting, with friends, family, masters, and servants, all unaware that the person they knew was dead, and that they were living with a stranger."

Wallas paused, impressed by his own line of reasoning.

"Congratulations, Wallas," said Terikel.

"Oh, er, what do you mean?" he asked, giving her a broad smile.

"Perhaps have undressed, er, exposed, best secret in Torea," said Velander. "Before was melted, anyway. Shapeshifter escape method."

"So you really were the Master of Royal Music?" said Andry.

"I did have that honor."

"But even I could be Master of Royal Music if that's the sort of talent that is needed. I've heard dogs throw up in the street more melodiously than those ballads you sing."

"And so do *you*, all the time!" shouted Wallas. "All right, then why are *you* not master of some monarch's music?"

"Lack of bath," suggested Velander, but Andry ignored her.

"I've seen his ballads empty taverns in a dozen breaths," cried Andry. "Even drunks lying asleep on the floor got up and crawled out."

"Pearls before swine, what do you expect?"

"Those swine were my friends!"

"They were still swine!" shouted Wallas, flinging a pot at Andry and knocking him into the stream.

Wallas splashed into the water after Andry, and they began trading blows. Wallas was stronger and bigger, but

Andry had been in a lot of drunken brawls. Wallas soon had a bleeding nose and a split ear, and he dropped to his knees in the water with his hands before his face, surrendering. Andry waded to the bank in triumph, with his arms folded. Velander stood, and looked Andry up and down. He was suddenly very conscious of being covered in mud and dripping wet.

"Dirty, smelly, stupid," she said. Then she glided away into the shadows.

Madame Jilli looked up from her book at the sound of a polite cough. An image about the size and shape of a person was standing before her, slowly changing from a warrior's form into that of a ragged peasant.

"Madame Jilli, I believe?" said a small girl holding a bunch of flowers.

"Er, aye."

"I am Change," explained a guardsman resting on his spear.

"As in the god?" she gasped, standing and giving a curtsy.

"Yes, yes, that one," replied an elderly sorcerer. "Where is that contract ferrygirl?"

"She said her contract had run out."

"Damnation!" exclaimed a priestess in snowy white robes. "My clerk must have funded her out of minor capital instead of the salaries vote."

"I'm sorry to hear that," said Madame Jilli, clasping her hands to keep them from shaking.

"Again!" said a skeleton wearing rags. "I'll have you know there's a queue building up out there."

"I wish I could help," said Madame Jilli, with the glimmerings of an idea. "Limbo is a bit of a bore to be in."

"I agree," said a naked toddler clutching a toy bear. "I say, do you like meeting new people?"

"I spent my life meeting new people," said Madame Jilli.

"Providing services?" asked a belly dancer.

"Serviced more souls than I can remember," admitted Madame Jilli.

"You don't get seasick, do you?" asked an elderly man whose beard reached his knees.

"Been around sailors since I was a girl."

"And why are you here?" asked a laborer with a pickax over his shoulder.

"I did not die properly."

"Splendid!" exclaimed an innkeeper. "How would you like to earn a few coins and meet a lot of people? A lot of Change is due soon for your world, and I am very short of ferrygirls."

Madame Jilli's first customer was a farmer, and he had his coins ready. Horvessol was not expecting to see a snow white punt crewed by a woman in a red gown split all the way up to her waist. From what Horvessol could see, the seamstress had run out of cloth for the breast area, and had attempted to finish the job with a short length of red silk lacing.

"Well, according to the Register of Movements, it's Arcadia for you, Horvessol," she said cheerily, pushing the punt off with a pole as white as snow. "And how did you die?"

"*You* don't know?" asked the astonished spirit of the farmer.

"Er, no, afraid not. I was taking delivery of a new boat and did not get time to read the Abstracts."

"Oh? Ah yes, very nice boat, too."

"So how did you die?"

"A bloodsucking fiend tore my throat out as I was walking home from the tavern."

"Really? A lot of that going around these days."

Andry carefully washed the mud from his trousers and surcoat, shame burning hot on his face. He had shouted like a fishwife and brawled like a costermonger. *There was no nobility in that brawl* kept echoing through his head. To add a crowning insult to all his other woes, he could not even blame his behavior on being drunk. Velander had been there, and had heard everything. Andry did not mind looking like a fool in front of his friends, but he was a little sensitive about how he looked to people he did not like. He had been striding proudly about as a royal lancer . . . *no, dressed as a royal lancer*, he reminded himself. What had Jelene said about her real husband, only the night before? He'd not change so much in three months. It all seemed so hard. A commoner could not change to resemble even Wallas in three months.

His surcoat and trousers were steaming on sticks above a bed of coals as he cleaned the mud from his boots, and finally Andry washed his hair and naked body in the chilly water of the stream. With the point of his knife, he dug thick mud from beneath his fingernails, then sat shivering, watching his clothes steam. Velvety footsteps approached from behind him, and then his old trousers and tunic were dropped beside him. He looked up to see Velander standing over him.

"Laron worried," she said in a tone that made it quite evident that *she* was not worried at all. "Says you catch chill."

Andry riffled through memories of his afternoon's lesson in manners, looking for the words that a cold, wet, naked man might use by way of response to a dead, dangerous, and supernaturally strong woman who had just brought a change of clothes to him.

"Aye, thanks," he said after a moment.

"Suit you better, old clothes," said Velander huffily.

Andry picked up his old trousers and tunic. Velander was right, he decided, the clothes showed him for what he was— Andry Tennoner from Bargeyards. A voice within his head said *Don't go back*. The words had been so clear that Andry glanced about to see if anyone else had joined them. Don't go back. Andry was all too aware what the words meant, and with very little hesitation, he dropped his old clothes onto the coals. They smoked at first, then burned. He looked up at Velander, who was looking surprised, and swaying visibly. Even from several feet away, he could smell that her breath was freshly charged with alcohol.

"So what is Elder Terikel wearing, then?" Andry asked.

"Caught drunken farmer, leaving inn, two miles away. Ripped out throat, drank blood. Took clothes, Elder Terikel, for to wear."

Andry felt his head spinning for a moment. Reckless indignation rather than courage boiled up in him.

"You killed a man for his clothes?" he exclaimed.

"Was hungry. Prey, he was."

"Hungry? Bollix! For you he were a wine jar on legs."

"Was drunk! Drunks evil. Laron, has teaching me, been. Improve world, when feeding."

"Laron?"

"Laron cares! Guide me, teach me. Laron understands. Must kill, for feeding, so kill evil, feed on evil."

"Evil? You're just a sot, looking for cheap wine."

"Can only drink blood!"

"But you're athirst for drunks' blood."

"*You* are drunk!" snarled Velander, a rather more dangerous expression than usual on her face.

"Wrong! For ten days I've rolled back to just enough wine to keep the shakes and jitters away. Soon it's to be a swallow, then a sip, then it's a drink as and when I *like*, and not when I *need*. You're a drunk yourself, aye, and you're evil. No passing on that one."

"Not drunk!"

"Think I can't spot a drunk? Besides, what was evil about a farmer rolling home from the inn after a few ales?"

"Go home, beat wife, perhaps."

"You don't even know he was married!" cried Andry.

With quite astonishing speed Velander's hand shot down and seized Andry's throat. She dragged him to his feet and drew his face very close to hers. Etheric fangs gleamed in her open mouth, the reek of blood, rot, and drink poured out into Andry's face, her eyes were huge and wild as they stared into his—and then her hand trembled.

"Help me!" whispered Velander; then she flung Andry aside and fled into the darkness.

✳ ✳ ✳

The following day they stopped at another village, where Laron bought a rather more placid horse than his own stallion to pull the cart, and a horse for Andry as well. They also bought several items of carefully chosen clothing at the market. By the time they left, Wallas and Terikel were wearing red scarves and red armbands, signifying that they were new recruits to the Imperial Highways Militia, and had the status of unattached militiamen. Wallas was also concentrating hard on learning to drive the cart in general, and in particular on persuading the horse not to stop beside the road and graze every hundred yards. Andry and Laron were mounted, and in the uniform, armor, and colors of the Journey Guards.

"I fear I'll always be just a brawling scruffy, even though I want to be, like, above that sort of thing," Andry confided to Laron as they rode together, some distance ahead of the cart.

"Now, about what 'chivalry' means."

"Er, aye?"

"It is a little like honor."

"Oh aye, I know honor. That's like when some skirt-lifter get your sister with a bun in her oven then won't marry her, so you strop up your ax and go after him. Did that to Branny Caulker when my sister Kellen—"

"Well, that is a narrow but intense instance, but would you like to hear a little of the *way* of chivalry, Andry? It will take some time."

"What good's it to do, sir? I'd still be a churl, with no prospects."

"The Imperial Militia gives prospects. With your carpenter's articles, good manners, and brave fighting you could be militia engineer one day."

"But I'm not even in the militia," Andry pointed out.

Laron rode on in thought for a minute or so, then held up his hand. They halted. Andry peered about, but saw nothing suspicious or threatening. Laron dismounted. Andry followed his example, and Wallas got out of the cart to ask what was happening.

"Do you, Andry Tennoner, wish to join the Imperial Highways Militia of His Highness, the heir apparent of the Sargolan Empire?" asked Laron. "You would be a lancer basic, which is the lowest rank of cavalry."

"Doubt they'd have me, sir," said Andry with a shrug.

"Besides, I'm a citizen of the Alberin principality in the North Scalticar Empire."

"Mercenaries can be recruited, as long as their homelands are not at war with the Sargolan Empire."

"Are you serious, sir?"

"Perfectly serious."

To Andry, this was a similar commitment to burning his old clothes. It was like being forced down the road to change at spearpoint. He was not sure who was holding the spear, but on the other hand he liked what lay ahead.

"Aye, then."

Wallas had also been thinking quickly about the advantages of being a militiaman. For a start, it would give him papers and a place in the world. If he could wrangle five years of being a cook with the baggage wagons, he would return to civilian life with a reasonably legal identity. The key word was "wagons." They meant he would no longer have to walk.

"Hie, what about me?" asked Wallas, raising his hand. "I fancy myself in a surcoat and wearing a crest. I say the militia needs clever cooks to keep morale high."

Laron stroked his chin for a moment, then smiled.

"Very well, then, why not? Wallas, what do you say to being a wagoner third class in the Imperial Highways Militia?"

"Need my background be checked?" asked Wallas at once.

"If every militiaman needed his background checked, there would be no militiamen at all—and quite a few would end up hanged. And while the recruiting stall is open, would you like to witness the oath, Learned Elder?"

"Certainly," said Terikel, getting down from the wagon.

"How long are we in?" asked Wallas.

"Five years, and I can arrange for you to be attached to the Logiar garrison when we get there."

Andry scratched his head. Wallas rubbed his chin.

"Could I really be a cook?" asked Wallas.

"You do as you're told, but if you cook with skill then I expect you will end up doing little else."

Terikel witnessed Andry and Wallas accepting a Sargolan silver vassal each; then the two recruits knelt in the dust by the roadside to take the oath.

"Names and homelands?" asked Laron.

"Andry Tennoner of Alberin."

"Wallas, er, Baker, of, er, Sargol."

"Can you be more specific?"

"Palion, then."

"Andry Tennoner of Alberin, and Wallas Baker of Palion, do you swear loyalty to the throne of the Empire of Sargol, while you serve in the Imperial Highways Militia, by the gods that you serve and worship, as witnessed by Elder Terikel Arimer of the Metrologan Order?"

"Aye, sir," responded Andry.

"That I do, sir," declared Wallas.

"Then arise, you have been inducted. The penalty for a first desertion is one hundred lashes, while a second brings death by hanging. Let us be on our way, then, Learned Elder. Now that your differences with these two fine militiamen have been sorted out, I suggest that we rejoin the Journey Guards."

"I am agreeable to that," replied Terikel. "Honor has been satisfied."

✦ ✦ ✦

Laron began to force the pace now, in order to catch up with Senterri and her escort. After just one more night in the open and two days of quite hard traveling, they reached the town of Clovesser. Wallas was dismayed to find that he was confined to a quarter pint of wine per day while on escort duty, but Andry looked upon it as no challenge.

Andry was rather nervous about Velander, however, who appeared not to have fed recently, and seemed to spend a lot of her waking hours staring at him, and licking her lips. Andry took to wrapping a strip of cloth soaked in garlic around his neck before he lay down to sleep. Velander was predictably sarcastic about Andry and Wallas being in the Imperial Highways Militia, but they saw little of her because she was awake during most of the night with Miral in the sky, and she spent her active hours away from their camp.

Clovesser was quite a large town about a day's hard ride east of the city of Glasbury, and as they reached the customs gate, they saw that the imperial family standard was hanging on the town wall. A member of the imperial family was in the town, and that person could only be Princess Senterri. It was early evening as they entered Clovesser.

Once they had left Terikel and Velander in a hostelry, Laron rode with Andry and Wallas to the town garrison. There he registered his two new recruits, and had standard surcoats, tunics, trousers, caps, and boots issued to them. Andry was dismayed to find that recruits had to pay for their clothing. Wallas was assigned to provisioning duties at once, while Andry learned that he would be a reconnoitering lancer, or reccon. Laron left him with the Journey Guards marshal.

"And who are you sir?" the marshal bellowed in Andry's face.

"Lancer Basic Tennoner, at service, sir," Andry replied slowly, and in Sargolan.

"Well, Lancer Basic Tennoner, Captain Laron informs me that you are to be a reccon attached to the Journey Guard. That does *not* make you a member of the Journey Guard, or entitle you to say that you have served with the Journey Guard. Do I make myself clear?"

"Yes sir," replied Andry, who had not understood much of what had been said, except that he was being asked a question to which the answer was supposed to be yes.

"Well don't just stand there! Get out of that Journey Guardsman's mail and uniform and into your reccon's trail tunic!"

A solid hour of being shouted at followed, during which Andry brushed down his horse, cleaned and polished his saddle, bridle, and saddlebags, then cleaned, sharpened, and polished his ax. He was then taken through the basics of parade drill and marching until the sun reached the horizon. At last he was dismissed, but ordered to wash for a formal dinner.

"After all your misbehaviors on the *Stormbird*, how can you now stand for all this being thrown at you?" asked Wallas as he collected Andry's tunic for washing.

"The *Stormbird* was like Bargeyards, Wallas. I could rise no higher than carpenter, even were I to try. Here it's different. I could rise to be militia engineer."

"Engineer is an officer ranking. It's equal to that of lieu-tenant, if I recall my heraldry-school lessons correctly."

"Aye Wallas, so I must work hard and learn to mind my manners. It's a long road to being a gentleman, but at least I'm on it."

"You may be disappointed when you get there," warned Wallas.

Terikel decided to keep Velander close by, for the welfare of the citizens of Clovesser as much as protection for herself. Clovesser was actually large enough to support a small sor-ceric academy, and it was here that Terikel went with Ve-lander as her escort. The vampyre was wearing a black cloak over a black tunic, and her hair was tied back sharply so that she would be taken for a contract guard by the others in the darkened streets.

"I need to meet some very odd people," Terikel explained in a dead Torean language as they left the hostelry.

"Bad people?" asked Velander hopefully.

"No! And please, try to behave. They are rather peculiar, focused people, but they are not bad."

"Afterwards, perhaps we could visit a tavern?" suggested Velander.

"So that you can look for drunks to prey upon? Velander, I am becoming really worried about you."

"Nobody is worried if Andry drinks too much," said Ve-lander smoothly.

"He does not get his wine from other people's blood. Be-sides, I do worry about Andry, just as I worry about you."

"Who are these peculiar people?" muttered Velander, not particularly interested in the subject under discussion.

"I was told about them in Palion. They call themselves the Sorceric Conspiracies and Occult Plots Exposure Collective."

"They do indeed sound peculiar."

"They are a group of radical students who wish to over-throw the establishment."

"They sound earnest, and earnest people are often evil,"

said Velander, licking her lips and again hopeful. "Are any of them heavy drinkers?"

"No! Remember, leave them alone! I . . . Oh Vel, it saddens me to see you in such a state. Can't anything be done to help you?"

Velander shrugged, then clasped her hands behind her to stop them shaking.

"No," she said simply. "One day I shall be led to a sad end, then I hope you will scribe up my story as a warning to others."

"Vel, if I could help I would, but what can I do?"

"If Laron cannot help, then there is nothing anyone can do for me. But we are digressing, Learned Elder. What may I do to help you tonight?"

"As I said, these odd people are dedicated to the exposure of the establishment, and currently I am almost alone in my own struggle with the establishment."

"What establishment?"

"I wish I knew. I must accept allies where I can find them, so if you mean me well, Velander, do not molest them."

Dinner was in the garrison refectory, and Andry was sent to a table at the very back of the hall. There were six other reccons attached to the Journey Guard, all of them from the Empire of North Scalticar. The group had been appointed on the theory that foreign mercenary commoners would be less likely to become involved in local plots against the royal family than local militiamen. So far that theory had proved sound. The surest way known to secure the loyalty from foreign commoners was to make them feel just slightly superior to local commoners. The problem for Andry was that the marshal had not introduced him to the other reccons, and they were feeling very superior indeed.

Following correct protocols, Andry marched up to the reccons' table, located the reccon who was wearing the red delegate's star, bowed, presented him with a small metal plate, and said "Tennoner, reporting, sir!" in Sargolan.

The delegate reccon tossed the plate to a vacant space at

the table and said, "Sit." The delegate reccon was the unit's liaison with the Journey Guard marshal, and thus its leader as far as the guardsmen were concerned. The reccons did in fact have no leader, but asked the delegate his opinion when orders needed interpretation. To actually obey an order from the delegate was a joke.

Andry sat, then observed what the other reccons were doing with great attention while he waited to be served. The first thing that he noticed was that they spoke Alberinese among themselves. They were also on unranked name terms with each other. He noticed that they had bowls of stew, while he had nothing. Andry sat patiently. Presently the reccon that the others called Essen got up, walked over to a small serving table, and served himself with another helping. Suddenly realizing that he was expecting to be treated according to codes that did not apply to him, Andry blushed, then excused himself and went across to do his own serving. He also noted that the others had small mugs of wine. The wine was being served at another small table, but Andry decided that he could do without another mistake in protocol, so he did without wine. Thus in correcting one mistake, he compounded another.

Thus far Andry had broken five unwritten rules that the reccons observed, plus one that the marshal had neglected to tell him in advance. Reccons were meant to reconnoiter, and this included researching any new group before one presented to serve with it. One breach was almost expected. Two was unpromising but forgivable. Six was quite beyond the pale.

"Some folk say reccons are too low-born to drink with," said the one named Danol.

"What folk are they?" asked Porter, the delegate.

"Foppy toffs, none as be important," replied Danol.

Go to all this trouble to learn manners, and they call you a foppy toff, fumed Andry as he got up, excused himself, and strode off to serve himself a mug of wine. He returned and sat down. By now he had decided that he was going to eat and drink, and worry about not offending people later.

Although he had exceedingly common Alberinese origins, Andry was not quite so disadvantaged as an absolutely raw recruit. He had been forced to learn something of shipboard discipline on the *Stormbird*, he had learned fighting in the Bargeyards taverns and work yards, and he already knew how to ride, thanks to tending the barge horses for years. He also had the elements of social manners and deference from Laron, and table manners from Wallas. When combined with the fact that he could count, he could read and write Alberinese, and he knew Diomedan Trade and Sargolan Common, this put Andry not far below the requirements for submarshal in a squad of commoners. Andry was, in fact, a genius who had been brought up in less than ideal circumstances, and now it was beginning to really show. He only had to be told something once, and thereafter he would not only remember it perfectly, he would put it into practice. All that he lacked was experience, but he reminded himself that experience was just what he was getting at the reccons' table.

It was becoming increasingly clear, however, that the other reccons felt Andry's appointment as a Journey Guard support reccon was a mistake on the part of whoever had been responsible. As reccons went, they were the elite.

"They say us reccons are more highly thought of, lately," said Porter.

"Not think it, considerin' our pay," said the rather large and chunky Costiger.

"Oh aye. Young foppies wanting to buy into the unit, like they buy into commissions in the regular militias."

"Say then, do we get a share of the buy-in?" asked Sander.

"Well trained they are, too, even though some think they're superior, with their foppy manners," said Porter.

"They go to dog school, like nobles have for hounds," added Danol, the youngest reccon. "Tell 'em 'sit,' and they sit."

Andry was beginning to catch on. Years of drinking and fighting in Bargeyards began to rally in his defense.

"Thought the dogs were supposed to beg bones on the floor," remarked Hartman, who had a shaven head to hide the fact that his hair was greying.

"If a dog can obey orders, a dog can be on the squad," replied Delegate Porter.

"Dog's got the advantage over us, he can lick his arse to get the taste of trail rations out of his mouth," suggested Danol.

"Keep it clean, Danol. All recruits to be made welcome."

Andry steadied a shank bone with a spoon and carefully cut off the meat with his knife before delicately placing it in his mouth with the point. Danol and the others merely gnawed at their own bones. Inevitably, Danol noticed Andry.

"Oh hie, nobody's told doggy that fingers is right for reccon table," he said as he lifted another bone to his mouth.

"Very good manners for a dog," said Sander.

"Must have run away from a foppy noble," said Danol.

Andry's knife left his hand in a flicker of movement and struck the bone that Danol was gnawing, driving it back between his teeth. There was an eternity of absolute stillness at the reccons' table that in fact lasted only about ten seconds.

"I do apologize," said Andry with a big smile, slowly reaching over and taking hold of the handle of his knife. "My knife slipped."

He removed the knife and bone from Danol's mouth, detached the bone from the point, and placed it delicately in the seriously rattled reccon's bowl. He held the knife up for a moment, displaying to the reccons that the hilt was two breasts in outline and facing in opposite directions, while the pommel appeared to be a pair of buttocks.

"Not regulation, I know," explained Andry, "but it is a token of esteem from the late Madame Jilli, of Madame Jilli's Recreational Rooming, in Palion, so I am rather fond of it."

Andry's accent had been a fairly good imitation of Laron's Alberinese, that is, educated without being affected. He picked up his mug of wine.

"Reccon Tennoner!"

The marshal's voice resonated through the hall, and everyone, from Princess Senterri to Andry, fell silent. Most even stopped moving. The marshal strode across to the reccons' table.

"Reccon Tennoner, Delegate Reccon Porter, to attention!" shouted the marshal.

Both reccons got to their feet hurriedly, saluted the marshal, then stood to attention together, facing the front of the hall, where Senterri was sitting.

"Delegate Reccon Porter, allow me to introduce the new recruit Reccon Andry Tennoner. Tennoner is to be allowed to have no wine at meals, as he is a reformed drunkard—so he says—and the drink puts daemons from the lowest level of all hells into him."

"Sir!" responded Porter.

"Secondly, Tennoner put three of the late emperor's finest Throne Guards in the palace infirmary—where they remain—and then gave the gallant Captain Laron a rather severe thrashing and beat up several Journey Guards in a separate incident. You are to make sure that from now on Tennoner's talents are employed upon the enemies of the princess, and not in thrashing her own warriors."

"Sir."

"Thirdly, Tennoner is something of an animal—as you may have gathered by now—and is in no need of toughening or basic martial instruction. He is, however, being forced to study a course in *manners* and *protocols*, in order to try to make him somewhat less of a danger to those who are meant to be on his own side. Kindly make sure that his efforts to observe the practices of civilized behavior are encouraged, by both yourself and your men."

"Sir."

"That is all. Stand down, and return to your table."

"Sir!" barked Andry and Porter together.

Andry returned to his seat, pushed his mug of wine away, and began slicing another chunk of meat from the bone in his bowl. Very slowly, the other reccons began to eat again, and the rest of the meal was passed largely in silence at the reccons' table.

Across the hall, the marshal resumed his place at the high table, next to Laron.

"Splendid suggestion for introducing young Tennoner to the squad and reccon unit, Captain Laron," he said as he picked up his goblet of wine.

"I like people to know where they stand without a lot of silly misunderstandings," replied Laron.

"You are very perceptive and sensible for one so young.

Why, I would say that even young Tennoner has at least five years on you."

"On the contrary, Marshal, I am a lot older than I look."

Terikel met with Wilbar, Riellen, and Maeben in a rooming house where Wilbur and Maeben shared an attic. Through the window they could see the great swath of lights that was Dragonwall, splashed along the western horizon. Wilbar wore spectacles with tinted lenses, even at night, and always had a hand to his mouth when he spoke. Maeben explained that Wilbar did this to seem inconspicuous, because of his status as a secret revolutionary. Terikel and Velander glanced at each other, but did not think that any possible reply could be diplomatic.

"What we have here is an auger ringstone," Wilbar was explaining as he held up a device that was actually five lumps of darkish glass stuck to the top of a circular stool. "You know, like when you drill through a wall and get a look into the room where the masters are drawing up the examination castings."

"We're called augers," said Riellen proudly, peering at Terikel over the top of her very thick pair of reading half-spectacles. "We drill into the castings of important ventures."

"And we look at the control tendrils," said Maeben, anxious not to be left out.

"It was designed by me, and by rights it ought to be called the Wilbar Inclined Ringstone, except that for security reasons we can't have our names associated with equipment—at least until the establishment is exposed for what it is and overthrown, and it's safe for honest, enquiring people to be credited in full fairness for their innovative—"

"What does it do?" asked Terikel impatiently.

"We use it to listen to the command words of the sorcerers managing Dragonwall," said Riellen.

By now Terikel was getting a feeling for the personalities present in the Sorceric Conspiracies and Occult Plots Exposure Collective. Maeben was less than four feet tall and very sensitive about not being noticed, Riellen was an Alberinese girl with very thick spectacles and fewer social graces than Andry, and Wilbar was two feet taller than Maeben but probably weighed about the same. Wilbar fancied himself as a revolutionary reformer who was going to expose the sorceric establishment for what it really was, but was currently having trouble determining just exactly what it was he was trying to expose.

"But any auger ringstone needs to be pointed directly at the Dragonwall to achieve any sort of contact with it," said Terikel. "This tends to confine them to locations directly beneath the Ringstone Machine."

"Ah, but that's where you are wrong!" declared Wilbar in triumph, waving his stool in the air.

"Yet you are still right," added Riellen, who liked to support women, being the only female student in a student population of five dozen.

"It's just that you are not right enough," explained Maeben, hopping on the spot and waving his arm for attention.

"The glass is from the melted continent of Torea," said Wilbar proudly. "We all had to work in our spare time for a month to buy the original chunk."

"I have to know a lot about glass cutting and lenses, on account of needing special lenses myself," said Riellen. "I cut the chunk into five pieces."

"I stuck it to the stool," called Maeben.

"But you need five people who can do castings," said Terikel. "There are only three of you."

"Oh, Holbok is serving beer at the King's Arms tonight," said Wilbar.

"And Allaine is scrubbing floors at the Queen's Legs," called Maeben.

"But *you* are another caster," said Riellen. "If you can wait an hour for Allaine to finish work, that will be five, and we can demonstrate it for you."

"We cannot wait as long as that," said Terikel, "but Velander can do castings."

Velander nodded as the three students turned to regard her. They bowed, assuming that she was some senior sorceress in disguise.

Setting up the auger ringstone involved tying the stool to a

table with the face pointed through the window at Dragonwall. Wilbur was very fussy about the angles, and about
the importance of not bumping or otherwise moving what
was possibly the smallest ringstone in the world.

"Hie, but we need the book of casting codes," Riellen suddenly pointed out. "The books are all in my room."

Books were valuable, and Ricllen lived in the dormitory
of the Clovesser School for Grooming, Deportment, and Etiquette, because it was the only establishment that provided
accommodation for young female students. It was also
guarded, so most of the books on sorcery that the five augers
had liberated from their own academy's library were stored
there.

"I think I can do a suitable casting from memory," said
Terikel. "Let us start now."

In a full-sized ringstone, the sorcerers would actually sit on
the stones, but this was not particularly practical when the
stones were four-inch-high slices of sand fused into glass.
Each of the five conjured auton images of themselves about an
inch tall, and sat these on the glass slices. The little autons then
spread their arms out and generated fine filaments of etheric
force that intertwined and vanished through the window in the
direction of Dragonwall. Wilbar spoke castings for his little
image, and presently a glowing ball of etheric energy appeared
at the center of the tilted stool. The energies resolved themselves into a tiny head, which spoke in a faint voice.

"Ringstone Alpine reports a windstorm thirty miles north.
Please acknowledge, Ringstone Centras."

The ball of unformed etheric energies replaced the head
again, and did not resolve itself into anything else. Several
minutes passed. Terikel broke the circle.

"They stopped," she said. "Do they know about us?"

"No, they just need to be close by for us to pick up anything at all. Nobody in Ringstone Alpine was speaking after
that first message, so we heard nothing from the distant
ringstones."

"I'd like to hear more of that," said Terikel, straining to
hide her excitement.

"Ringstone Alpine is all that we can listen to—" began
Maeben.

"Auger into!" interjected Wilbar.

"—with this particular device," Maeben concluded.

"But we have another!" said Riellen tentatively.

"Riellen!" cried Wilbar and Maeben together.

"Why hide it?" Riellen said with her fists on her hips. "These ladies are not of the sorceric establishment."

"Am I to understand that you have a bigger tilted ringstone?" asked Terikel.

"We admit nothing," said Wilbar firmly, and this time the others remained silent.

"Well, thank you for all that you have shown me," said Terikel as she stood up. "It is interesting, but of no special promise."

"Many thanks," added Velander, now standing also.

The students bounded to their feet, but then realized that they were not sure what they should do. Velander flicked her tongue across her lips. The three students shrank back. Terikel reached for the door's bolt.

"Wait! Please wait," said Wilbar. "We, ah, have such a ringstone already, and we have performed, er, certain tests. It might be, ah, to the advantage of us all for you to be at a stone when we operate it. I—we—noticed that when you helped us with the very small ringstone, we had a more clearly defined image at the center than we ever get with the big one."

"It's because you're so much stronger at castings than us," said Riellen with undisguised admiration.

"So imagine what you could do with the big one!" cried Maeben, jumping up and down and waving his hand.

Terikel folded her arms and regarded them steadily.

"Where is this 'big one'?" she asked.

"On the roof of the academy," said Wilbur.

"But not at the moment," said Riellen.

"But we can have it up there in an hour," explained Maeben.

* * *

Sergal was by now a desperate, frightened, and trapped man. In this he was not alone, for all the sorcerers of all the ringstones were certainly trapped, and quite anxious about their fate. The fact was that there was no way to leave the Dragonwall casting. That was where the name came from, as they now realized. Glass dragons were sorcerers who lived permanently inside an auton casting, one built up carefully over decades, and enhanced for centuries or even longer. Their bodies were preserved in a magical stasis: they did not age, or require food, drink, or air. Dragonwall was similar, and the participants had quickly realized that in order for them to leave, the entire casting had to be collapsed. All the plans to activate the outer rings as required were suddenly about as relevant to the sorcerers as a lamplight woman was to a eunuch, as were the plans to rotate the megalith sorcerers in eight-hour shifts. Their predicament did have allure, however, because their bodies were effectively immortal, and Dragonwall allowed all of the participating sorcerers to look down on the world from a height of several hundred miles and communicate with mortals using auton castings. Many elderly, frail, arthritic sorcerers viewed all of that as a definite improvement in lifestyle. It was like becoming a glass dragon without the centuries of hard work and development.

However, there was an immense amount of energy built up in Dragonwall, and if the structure collapsed, it had to go somewhere. There was a thing called Windfire mentioned in the texts that Sergal had been given, and that was said to store etheric energies generated by Dragonwall's spinning wind machines. The problem was that he had only the casting to launch Windfire, and the knowledge that it stored energies. He had not a clue what else it did.

Now unauthorized, inclined ringstones were attaching themselves to Dragonwall, like suckerfish on a shark. Even sorcerers of indifferent power and initiation could set one up with a suitably inclined hillside or roof. Five had already connected to Dragonwall from the continent of Acrema alone, and more were being tested along its entire length. Worse, there was something even more menacing about Dragonwall, a secret so terrible that he would have devoted his life to destroying it had he learned it earlier. So far none of the others had realized who was actually in control, but sooner or later one of the newcomers from an inclined ring-stone would discover the truth and tell everyone. When that happened, it would indeed be the end of the world as they knew it.

Meantime, Sergal knew that he could at least discourage some new members from attaching. It was too dangerous to attack full-sized inclined ringstones once they were fully attached, because of the risk of destabilizing Dragonwall itself. On the other hand, not all inclined ringstones were full-sized.

* * *

Andry, his fellow reccons, and the unattached militiamen with the Journey Guard were granted leave from the end of the dinner until midnight. Once they had left the hall, Andry located Wallas and suggested that they find a tavern.

"How are you finding it with the cooking?" asked Andry as they walked.

"I'm welcome. More than welcome, I suppose. I can cook much better than anyone who gets assigned to field duties. Even the Journey Guards get quite inferior meals while on the road and on duty."

"You do have talent to conjure wondrous tastes from base supplies," said Andry. "Where did you learn all that?"

"From parents who made base and limited ingredients transmute into wondrous meals, and thus transmute into a lot of money."

"Your parents were cooks?"

"That they were. They made a lot of money, and they decided that my brothers and I would be educated as courtiers. I learned rhetoric, flattery, heraldry, etiquette, and all the other little graces and tricks that the noble, idle, and exceedingly bored rich cultivate. I also learned music, and turned out to be very good at it."

"Well . . ."

"All right, sneer if you will. I do admit that my original compositions were seldom appreciated for their true worth, but in playing the work of others I excelled. Even the trashy rubbish written by the empress would sound halfway good when I played it. Other men could flatter her, but *I* could make her creations seem better than they were. This gained me advancement. Runs in the family, you see: making the most of base materials."

"Wallas, the thought of you as the top musician in the Sargolan Empire never ceases to worry me—Ah, this looks promising, The Dragon's Breath."

They entered a small but crowded tavern, whose customers were mainly foot soldiers, militiamen, and lancers from the nearby garrison barracks. Andry bought two pints of the local ale, then stood with Wallas by a window, watching the night traffic outside.

"Wallas, have you ever noticed how those who most hate to see a poor boy advanced by reason of talent are always those who are just above him, or those of his own station?"

"Trouble with the reccons?" asked Wallas.

"Lots, and during the meal. I'm not entirely sure what happened, but the reccons were complaining that my manners are too good. Then the marshal came over and shouted at me for being an animal, then the reccons stopped talking to me. They even stopped talking to each other. Am I really stepping up over my station?"

"In a way, yes. You could fit right in with those reccon commoners if you wished it. Nobody's more common than you, yet you try to learn manners and graces that aren't yours. What do you really want, Andry?"

"What do I want? Just now I want a rowdy tavern, a full purse, and a good rebec."

"You have all that. This place is full of soldiers, we have money, and there's a rebec in your pack."

"True. The problem is that when I put on that surcoat I wanted to become an officer."

"Uh-uh. You'd have to be a real gentleman first."

"I could advance through the ranks."

"Impossible. You need to be known to the princess to rise as far as that, and to be known to the princess you need to already be a gentleman."

"The princess heard the marshal shouting at me. That means she knows of me."

"Trust me, Andry, that is not the same."

They were interrupted by a rotund man with a pint in one

hand and what appeared to be a wooden flute attached to a cow's horn in the other. He was swaying alarmingly as he stood before Andry and Wallas.

"Buy a courterly musical instrument, what's been played fer the royal court of Palion?" he asked.

"That, sir, is a common hornpipe," said Wallas. "A very, *very* common hornpipe."

"It's a family treasure. Me old mother used to play it."

"It's not a woman's instrument," said Wallas. "You got it from someone who stole it, and if anyone buys, you will drink the money."

"Give here," said Andry, holding out his hand.

There was a double reed at one end, and Andry checked it as if he knew the instrument well. He put the reed to his mouth and played "Kavelar's Jig." Some of the other drinkers clapped. Andry bowed.

"I'll take it," said Andry. "If the price is right, anyway."

Some haggling reduced the price to what Andry considered to be reasonable.

"What need have you of a hornpipe?" asked Wallas as Andry counted out the price of the stolen instrument. "You have a fife and the rebec—*and* you keep borrowing my board lyre to practice singing drinking songs."

"It's loud, and the sound carries, that's good for dancing. Besides, I did do a love song last night. Gentlemen sing love songs."

" 'Five Pints Afore She Tumbled Him' is hardly a love song. Anyway, you encouraged the criminal economy by buying that hornpipe."

Andry handed over the hornpipe's price.

"There you go, lad. Wallas, even criminals like a good dance tune. Why, I actually know a cold-blooded assassin who plays—"

"All right, fine, enough, I'm convinced, you win."

"What's your name, lad?" Andry asked as the hornpipe's vendor double-checked his handful of copper and silver coins.

"Transer's the name I go by."

"Odd name," said Wallas. "I did not encounter it in Heraldry Lists Two-A."

"It's a trade-based name, lardship."

"*Lordship!*" exclaimed Wallas, who was quite proud of his recent loss of weight, even though it had not been voluntary.

"I's a transer of properties from people who has, to people who wants."

"You don't look like a tax official," said Wallas.

"Ha ha, sir, you're a laugh. I'm really in a helping situation, as it were. Folk help me, and I help folk. We're all folk what needs help, helping each other. Tax foppies help nobody."

Andry tossed a coin on the table.

"Cheer up, Wallas, buy us a drink while I try this out," Andry began, but for some reason two words surfaced from a conversation that seemed to have taken place a very long time ago. *Help me.* It crossed Andry's mind that he had drunk little that was alcoholic since then. It was not as if he had any fondness for Velander, but doing something about her very peculiar condition would certainly save the lives of enough drunk men to form a large, if not very effective, battalion. "Hie, but it's just water for me," said Andry as Wallas stood.

Andry began to play "The Willow by the Water," and Transer got up and danced an unsteady jig while the rest of the drinkers joined in by clapping or stamping their feet. As hornpipes went, it turned out to be a bargain. Andry decided that he was happy, even if the original owner was not.

The Clovesser Academy of Applied Sorceric Arts was actually an old hostelry with some of the walls between rooms knocked out to form a lecture hall and a library. It consisted of five dozen students, five teaching sorcerers, and a clerk. Unlike the academies of the big cities, where everyone lived in campus hostelries and dormitories, the Clovesser staff and students had lodgings scattered throughout the town. This meant that the academy was deserted during the night.

Getting inside was no problem. Wilbar had borrowed some keys and made wax impressions, and then Riellen had used the impressions to make copies. The trick was to move about inside the academy without setting off the guard castings left by the warden.

"There are no castings on the roof, Elder, it's just getting to the roof that's the problem," Riellen explained as they waited in a laneway over the street from the academy building.

"The roof?" asked Terikel.

"The roof is where we set up the ringstone," said Wilbar.

"We know where the castings are, and we've been in there lots of times," said Maeben. "Trouble is, we do it by, er, sort of without thinking. We'll have to talk you through, really slowly."

"On roof, is rope?" asked Velander.

"Aye, it's actually a double roof," said Wilbar. "We hide the ropes, beams, and things for the tilted ringstone in the gutter between the roofs."

"Waiting," said Velander.

After crossing the street, Velander climbed straight up the brick wall of the academy with the claws on her fingers. Moments later a rope was lowered. Terikel grasped the rope and was drawn up. Before Terikel could catch her breath, Velander was away down the side of the building again. She rejoined the three students.

"On roof, is Elder," she said. "There, too, you go."

"But, but we need you there too," said Riellen.

"In hour, be back."

Velander padded away into the darkness, leaving the students exchanging puzzled glances amid the shadows.

Andry had seen plenty of corpses in his life, having been brought up in Bargeyards, but the corpse that was lying a few streets from the tavern where he had been playing was different in two important ways. Andry had bought something from it when it had been alive, and that had been less than an hour earlier. Transer's throat had been torn out, and the formerly florid little vendor of stolen property was now as pale as chalk in the lamplight.

Andry and Wallas paused to stare as a watchman and crier

examined the corpse. Wallas shook his head as the crier felt for a pulse at what was left of Transer's neck. A scatter of drinkers, idlers, and lamplight girls had gathered. Andry touched the hornpipe under his coat and shivered.

"Velander," Andry whispered to himself so softly that even Wallas did not hear.

"I seem to remember your very self nearly having much the same end," said Wallas fearfully. "And myself besides. I wonder if Mother Antwurzel's Creme of Garlic Medicinal Wine is distributed as far as Clovesser?"

"What a way to go out into the Dark Places," said Andry aloud. "How can gentlefolk such as Lord Laron and Lady Terikel allow such a fiend to go loose?"

"Perchance they can't interest Velander in the health benefits of vegetarianism," suggested Wallas. "If it comes to that, nobody's been able to convince me, either. No vegetarian I've ever met has seemed an inspiring mentor."

"She says she feeds only on evil men," said Andry, hardly hearing. "So what was evil about Transer? He sold goods stolen from others, then drank the profits."

"He could have saved his money, bettered himself," suggested Wallas.

"Plenty of folk are as better themselves and save money, yet are evil."

The watchman picked up a jar from beside the corpse, removed the cork, sniffed the contents, then drank what remained.

"Disgusting," said Wallas. "He didn't even use a cup."

"Mentor," said Andry, turning away and setting off down the darkened street. "You said 'mentor,' Wallas. What's a mentor? Is it like an apprentice's master?"

"Not really, more like when an old and experienced artisan befriends one who's just finished articles of competency. Someone to provide a good example, rather than teach."

"A mentor," said Andry, tapping his new hornpipe in the palm of his hand. "Velander asked for help, yet I did nothing."

"Help? I should think she can pull down a drunk without help from anyone."

"I'm going back to the barracks, Wallas. Coming?"

"Oh yes. I have a proper bed to stretch out in for the first time since I fled the palace in Palion."

"And Madame Jilli's."

"Uh, well, yes."

"And Melier's bunk on the *Stormbird*."

"Well, briefly, yes."

"And Jelene's bed in Harrgh."

"Admittedly."

"And—"

"Oh shut up!"

The larger inclined ringstone was a series of markings on a very steep tiled roof on the academy. The building had a north-south alignment, so it was already parallel with Dragonwall. By tying some very precisely measured beams of wood in place over precisely measured marks on certain tiles, and by placing the lowest slice of Torean glass in the gutter, a ringstone pointing at the band of light on the horizon was assembled after an hour of furtive work. The positions of the five initiates involved in the casting were precarious, but the arrangement was workable.

"How much more is involved?" asked Terikel, once she noticed that the students were merely double- and triple-checking the alignments.

"Begging your pardon, ladyship, but your friend is not back, and we need five initiates," said Riellen.

"Damn her," said Terikel.

"Ladyship?"

"Nothing. You mentioned others in your group."

"Holbok and Allaine. Allaine should be finished at the Queen's Legs by now. I could fetch him, as his room is close by, but Lady Velander could well return—"

"Lady Velander can do as she will. Fetch Allaine."

It was another half hour before Riellen returned with Allaine, who resembled nothing more than a brunette broomstick on legs, wearing a tunic. Riellen had left a note under the door of Holbok, who also lived in Allaine's house.

"Holbok is very earnest and good-hearted, but a little

slow," said Riellen to Terikel while Wilbur briefed Allaine. "He excels at arguing things out, but it takes days for him to reach the conclusions."

"I cannot believe he is in a group dedicated to exposing conspiracies," Terikel commented.

"Oh, his conclusions are very good. The trouble is that he does not like to be hurried."

"That can be a problem when acting outside rules, regulations, and laws that have dangerous people to back them up."

Andry contemplated the cart standing in the darkened stables for nearly a minute before he spoke. The truth was that nobody had ever asked him for help before. He had occasionally been able to surprise people by actually being able to help when they were in trouble, but being approached for help was definitely a new experience.

"Well, Velander?" he began without approaching the cart.

Velander flung back the cover, sat up, then flowed out like black, shadowy quicksilver and stood beside the cart.

"Well, you saying?" she asked.

"You asked for help, and I helped."

"Helped? How?"

"I tried to be your mentor," he replied, embroidering the truth somewhat. "I have not been drunk since I started."

Andry was not really sure why he was drinking so much less. Gentlemen drank as much as anyone, after all, but they were just less rowdy about it.

"I—You are not drunk, becoming?" Velander asked, suddenly sounding uncertain.

"No."

Velander looked away. That was also a first for Andry. Velander always stared people down.

"Just drinking . . . one," she said reluctantly.

"That one drink was named Transer. He was forty-one years old, and he danced a jig while I played my new hornpipe at the Dragon's Breath. He had a wild rat named Kryl living in his room, he fed it cheese rinds. Once he was a costermonger in the market, but the heavies kept smashing his cart and stealing his stock, so he moved into stolen goods. Not much choice, really. His spirit was broken by all, yet he remained cheery enough. He harmed others less than he had been harmed."

"No more!" said Velander, holding her hands up, but not raising her eyes to meet Andry's. "To do, what is?"

"Honor our agreement."

"Was no agreement."

"You asked for help."

"You not say agreement!" shouted Velander, stamping her foot so hard that the flagstone beneath it cracked.

Andry flinched with surprise and fear, but stood his ground.

"Well I'll say it now. I'll give up the drink completely if you steer away from innocent drunks."

"You give up?" gasped Velander.

"Aye. Very hard, that, when all my friends hang about in taverns, and I play in them."

"Hard? Very hard?"

"Aye. Have we a pact?"

Velander turned her face to meet Andry's gaze, but she was not trying to stare him down this time.

"Yes, then we agree this: I kill, you have night on taverns, getting drunk. Am sad, er, about . . . Transfer. Now."

Velander's effort to remember her latest meal's name impressed Andry so much that he did not have the heart to correct her.

"Laron says you can feed on dogs and wolves," he mentioned.

"Is true. But, ah, is like wine turned to vinegar. Not nice as wine."

With one initiate for each stone, Terikel and the students again spoke their castings and formed their autons. The little figures perched precariously on the slices of glass, then raised their arms and cast tendrils of etheric fire in woven spirals that reached out across the city to the rainbow above the distant smear of orange light in the western sky.

This time Terikel was leading the group, so the castings

were a lot tighter and better defined. A head formed from the tangle of etheric energies at the center.

"Ringstone Centras reports another ripple in the control filaments. Other ringstones, report."

The voice was loud and clear. Perhaps too loud. Terikel wondered what a passing watchman would make of the strange lights and voices on the academy roof. A succession of heads morphed into being and spoke their status in Diomedan.

"Ringstone Septire: All well."

"Ringstone Logiar: Noted the ripple, but did not cause it."

"Ringstone Centras: All normal."

"Ringstone Wasteland: Very quiet here."

"Ringstone Alpine: Observed the ripple, and noted that it was self-damping."

"Ringstone Centras: Declare again, Ringstone Alpine?"

"Ringstone Alpine: The ripple seemed a strong pulse that damped slowly. There may be waves in the background ether that could not be observed until Dragonwall was built."

"Ringstone Centras: You are saying that these ripples are natural, Ringstone Alpine?"

"Ringstone Alpine: It is our theory."

Ripples, thought Terikel. *Drop a stone into a pond, and you get ripples. Slam an unauthorized casting into Dragonwall and it might ripple too*. It seemed odd that such a small and weak ringstone could have an effect on the mighty Dragonwall, yet the water in a pond would ripple when struck by a stone millions of times lighter.

Images of filaments of control flickered past Terikel's eyes as the line of ringstones stretching halfway around the world reported their status to each other. There was something odd about Dragonwall to Terikel's way of thinking, however, because the filaments were all within reach of her control, should she wish to reach for them. That would draw attention to herself, of course, but with control of some filaments she could defend herself with Dragonwall's own resources. It was all too easy to control, it was almost like a trap. *Anyone can do anything,* she thought. *This is like a huge battle galley powered by a thousand rowers, yet every one of them can steer.* Terikel spoke a command to her casting, and it accessed an aqua filament stacked above the others. This time the head was of an elderly man, and he looked very frightened.

"Mel'si dar, tik-le trras asgir."

The language was familiar to Terikel. It was a Torean scholarly language, Larmentian. The lectures at the University of Larmental were all delivered in Larmentian, and she had studied there ten years earlier. *Trras.* "Strike," or perhaps "Strike at." *Asgir.* "Intruders" . . .

"Break off, flee!" she shouted, abandoning her auton and glass fragment. "They see us."

Terikel slid down the steep roof, hit the gutter, and tumbled over it, but landed in one of the bushes flanking the front entrance. Looking up, she saw Riellen sliding down the rope tied by Velander, followed by Wilbar. Allaine hit the gutter and grasped it. The gutter tore away, swinging the emaciated student down into the street as gently as might be expected. There was a shower of slate tiles around Terikel; then Maeben crashed down into the bush beside her.

"Hurry, make for the lane!" shouted Terikel, struggling free of the branches.

Considering that they had made an extremely rapid departure from the roof of a fairly large building, there were found to be surprisingly few injuries, and not one was serious.

"What is it?" panted Wilbar as they cowered together in the shadows.

"A . . . thing, in Dragonwall," replied Terikel. "A mass of control filaments," she whispered in his ear. "Dragonwall must be destroyed!"

"What? Why?" Wilbar hissed back.

"*Everybody* can have total control of the energies!" whispered Terikel, grasping him by the collar. "It's far worse than I thought. Now I know that I have to destroy it, and soon I shall know how."

"Hie!" warned Riellen. "Who is that?"

All they could see in the gloom was someone in a cloak, with a long, ragged feather in his hat. As they watched he took out a key and walked to the academy door.

"Holbok!" called Maeben. "Over here, hide!"

"Brothers, where are you?" replied Holbok, looking about. "The note said that the time for hiding was past."

"Holbok, don't argue!" shouted Wilbur. "Come here, hide."

"But brothers, the note said this was the night we would smash the academy establishment by—"

A blinding flash annihilated the roof and ringstone in an interval of time too short to be measured by the cold sciences of that world. The explosion was so loud that none of those in the lane actually remembered hearing it. Dust swirled on the air like a thick fog, and fragments of hot slate and brick rained down around Terikel and the students.

Terikel looked up, then got to her knees. Through the dust she could see fires in what was left of the academy, which was not very much. The roof appeared to have been blasted by something like a year's supply of lightning strikes, and the four walls of the academy had fallen outward. Terikel picked her way across the rubble in the street. A pair of legs protruded from beneath a section of the wall that had come down largely intact. She returned to the others.

"You need to gather your belongings and flee!" she said firmly to the cowering students.

"But we must look for Holbok first!" cried Wilbar.

"From the knees up Holbok is now about the thickness of a sheet of parchment."

"My house, it's afire!" exclaimed Allaine, looking down the street.

That was indeed true; in fact, several other houses were also on fire and the occupants were running into the street, or leaping through windows and hoping for the best.

"Well, that's one less place we have to visit," said Terikel. "Now move!"

The town was rapidly coming to life as they ran through the streets. Bells and gongs were ringing, alarm trumpets were being blown, and people were running about with pails of water and ladders.

"I suspect that the royal coach will be leaving very soon because of that," said Terikel, pointing back the way they had come. "And if it's not I shall soon convince the princess to leave anyway. I'd like to offer you a place on it, but I suspect that even I shall have trouble getting a ride."

"You?" exclaimed Wilbar. "The royal coach?"

"Long story. Even parts of the establishment don't like the establishment. Or maybe the baron could shelter us."

Moments later a scatter of faint, golden butterflies burst up into the night sky around them.

"What are you doing?" demanded Terikel, rounding on Wilbar.

"Why, just sending out autons announcing that the establishment is to blame for this atrocity."

"Wilbar, the time for revolutionary movements is over, and the time for trying to survive is well and truly here. Do no castings, in fact do *nothing* unless I say so. Is that clear?"

"Well yes, revolutionary sister."

"We'll need a cart to take all of our things," panted Riellen, who was not used to exertion.

"You will take money, one blanket, one weapon, a pack, and one change of clothes," explained Terikel firmly as they approached the large but shabby hostelry. "Also whatever food is in—"

A disk of pure, dazzling whiteness turned the area around Wilbar's third-floor window to very, very hot vapor. Because vapor takes up considerably more space than wood, brick, and plaster, Wilbar's room exploded. The explosion demolished the rest of the hostelry in a dusty fireball that rained burning fragments down on the neighborhood.

"Correction, you take the clothes that you stand in, and your lives," said Terikel.

"They must have decided our small ringstone was worth bothering with after all!" exclaimed Wilbar.

"I would have thought that obvious," replied Riellen.

No meetings or experiments involving the Sorceric Conspiracies and Occult Plots Exposure Collective had ever been held in Riellen's room, because the dormitory of the Clovesser School for Grooming, Deportment, and Etiquette was off limits to men. Terikel and Riellen entered, stuffed a pack with the books Riellen had spirited out of the academy library, then bundled a blanket roll with handwritten pages of spells, castings, and conspiracy theories, spare spectacles, a small farsight, and a crossbow about as big as Terikel's hand.

"Personal security device, to allow mobility in a violence-oriented male society," muttered the embarrassed girl.

"Don't you have any clothes?" asked Terikel, picking up the crossbow.

"The pillow."

The pillow on the bed was stuffed with Riellen's spare clothing and underwear, and this was because she could not be bothered buying a pillow. They fled out into the street, where Wilbar, Maeben, and Allaine were waiting.

"What now?" cried Wilbar as they hurried away.

"We flee the town and try to stay alive," replied Terikel.

"I say, could we flee more slowly?" gasped Allaine, who was in exceedingly poor condition.

"I know where there is a cart and a horse," said Terikel. "Can any of you drive a cart?"

No hands were raised.

"Looks like the princess will have to flee without my company," muttered Terikel.

The principal shortcoming of the Clovesser Sorceric Conspiracies and Occult Plots Exposure Collective was that they had not been sufficiently paranoid. Currently in the town were members of no less than thirty different groups and organizations with secret and dangerous intentions. The Ringstone Security Brotherhood did not know that Dragonwall had been responsible for the two explosions, so it reacted by attacking the Clovesser Academy's staff in their homes. The consequent castings of fireballs and warrior autons very quickly had a lot more of the town afire, then the militia arrived and joined in the fight, disrupting the castings with their iron-tipped weapons. The Journey Guards were instantly on the alert, and Princess Senterri was bundled into her coach while the guardsmen prepared to leave the town. Seeing the guardsmen forming up in their armor and with their weapons ready, the local baron assumed that he had fallen foul of the late emperor's heirs, so he sent his personal guardsmen into the streets to engage anyone moving in the general direction of his small palace. Those from Palion who were hunting Terikel assumed that the Journey Guards were attacking, and so rallied several other factions in the town for a showdown.

Andry and Wallas reached the garrison staging ground in time to see the Journey Guard streaming out with the royal coach under escort.

"They're leaving without us!" wailed Wallas as Andry pulled him off the road.

"If you were a princess I'm sure they'd stay. Now do as I say. Take my pack, go to the barracks, get our gear together, then meet me at the stables."

Andry had his horse saddled and was hitching the cart horse into its straps by the time Wallas returned. Wallas heaved the packs into the tray. An unsteady Velander appeared, hissed at Wallas, then pulled the tray cover back over herself. A flight of fire arrows streaked high above them and hit the garrison's barracks.

"Can't we leave her behind?" called Wallas as Andry mounted his horse and drew his ax.

It was at this moment that Terikel and the surviving members of the Sorceric Conspiracies and Occult Plots Exposure Collective came staggering into the stable yard, close to collapse from the exertion of running.

"Andry! Is that you?"

"Terikel?"

"Can you take us?" she gasped. "All of us? The royal coach has already left and we all need transport."

"By the ferrygirl's oars, who are these people?"

"Can you take us?"

"Aye. Climb in, mind Velander."

Out in the streets there was heavy fighting, but nobody was entirely sure who they were meant to be attacking. The cart had negotiated several streets when someone in a mob that was a mixture of town militia and town thugs called that it should be stopped. Hands grasped at the walls of the tray, and then Velander appeared, seized a man by the hair, and slashed his throat with the claws of her other hand. The man beside him hesitated just a little too long in his decision to let go. Velander seized his arm and drew him up into the tray. His shrieks did not last long, but they were more than enough incentive for the mob to flee the cart.

An enormous shape sailed overhead, heading in the direction of the local palace. Moments later a stream of white-hot plasma and etheric castings poured into Clovesser's largest building.

"Now dragons!" shouted Wallas. "What is this? Clovessen seemed like such a nice little town when we first arrived."

They emerged into a small plaza that was quite well lit by the burning buildings that bordered it, but what caught Andry's attention was a dragon rearing about twenty feet above six horsemen who were drawn up around an overturned coach. They were dressed identically to Andry.

Several thoughts went through Andry's mind, none of them particularly logical. He drew back to the tray of the cart. Terikel and the students were all crowded together at the driver's end, while Velander fed on the rioter that she had seized a few streets back. Reversing his ax, Andry struck Velander across the buttocks with the handle.

"Leave him!" shouted Andry. "That's a night on the wine you owe me!" Velander did not react, so he struck her across the head. She looked up with a squeal like tearing metal. "Greedy, drunken baggage!" shouted Andry. "Leave him, and stand with me!"

Andry turned his horse for the dragon and spurred it. The horse proved reluctant to charge. In the meantime three reccons charged the dragon. A streamer of brilliant white washed over the leading rider; then the dragon strode to the coach, ignoring the other reccons. Its jaws tore part of the cabin away, and then it looked inside. Evidently it did not like what it saw, for it poured another streamer of fire down upon the coach, reducing it to char and ash, and turning the cobblestones beneath into a pool of molten rock.

It is a fact that dragons take a few seconds to recast their fires after such an attack. A great many things happened in the next ten seconds. Andry charged from behind. The dragon swung its head and knocked over Danol and his horse. Velander left her victim and sprang from the cart. Andry reached the dragon and chopped into its back. His blade thudded onto something that had an oddly hollow sound, and energies blazed up around the steel blade of the ax. Two more blows had the blade through the strange, fibrous material that Terikel later explained was interwoven filaments of castings. Metal weapons disrupted them, but only after repeated blows to the same spot. Andry's blade encountered intensely concentrated etheric energies at the third blow. Etheric energies and iron do not mingle at all well, and there was a flash of energies that blasted the ax out of his hand. The dragon roared more with outrage than pain, turned, and breathed a streamer of fire. Andry ducked, and the blast passed over his head and slashed across several houses, setting fire to those which were not already burning.

The jaws of the great head opened above Andry—and then something dark scrambled up the dragon's neck, clung on just behind the head, slashed at the skin until blue light shone through, then bit. The dragon howled, staggered, then spread its wings. Its wingspan was greater than the width of the plaza. Wallas drove the cart away into a side street. The dragon lifted off into the air, flapped its wings three times, stalled, then crashed amid some buildings. A plume of smoke and sparks marked the general direction of the impact's site.

The cart reappeared. Terikel had Riellen's hand crossbow pressed against Wallas's ear. A reccon that turned out to be Danol limped across the square holding an ax with a partly melted blade. Andry shepherded the cart over to him, and the students helped him into the tray. There was a shriek of revulsion as Danol tumbled onto the remains of Velander's last meal.

"Toss the body out!" cried Andry in Sargolan Common, having been shouted at by the marshal that it was always used as the battle language. Danol heaved the corpse out of the tray. "Wallas, take the road west!" Andry added in Diomedan, as the fact that the marshal was probably not within earshot asserted itself in his mind. "Delegate Porter, where is he?" he called, switching back to Sargolan Common, not being sure whether the reccons would report him for using the wrong language.

"He's that pile of char on the pool of molten rock!" called one of the four mounted reccons.

"Who are you?"

"Essen, sir."

"You all, go, with the cart!" shouted Andry.

"What of you sir?" asked Essen.

"I'm going to find a, ah, er . . ." began Andry, who then found himself unable to think of any Sargolan word that approximated "demon," "monster," or "homicidal, blood-drinking fiend." "Lady! To find my, er, lady friend!" he shouted. Then he turned his horse and rode for the column of smoke and sparks that marked where Velander had come down with the dragon.

By now the horse that Andry was riding had concluded that in spite of the terrors of the past few minutes, it was alive and more or less unharmed, so there was a good chance that its current master knew what he was doing. It was, however, greatly relieved when Andry reined in before the burning warehouse where the dragon had crashed. He dismounted, tied the reins to a wrecked fence, and climbed over the rubble to where the immense outline of the dragon lay amid the burning ruins. "Outline" was the key word, however, because there was no body.

"Velander!"

There was no reply. Andry tried to work out in which direction the head of the dragon lay, because its tail and neck imprints were passably similar if you could not see what bit was at the end. Something set off a small slide of rubble, and because nothing else was moving, Andry set off in that direction. He found Velander emerging from beneath a pile of smashed boards. Her clothes were shredded and her skin was bruised, scratched, and dusty. Her eyes glowed with white light, and she was dragging what appeared to be a body wearing armor.

"Velander!" Andry shouted.

"Andry. Not seeing," she called, and more glow came out of her mouth.

"I'm coming, wait there."

Andry saw that the body's armour had been torn open at the neck, and that there was bloody flesh beneath.

"Please tell, is sorcerer alive?" asked Velander.

"I'd say not, the head is only held in place by a few shreds of armor. Who is he?"

"Glass dragon."

Only now did Velander let go of her victim. Andry took off his surcoat and helped the dazed and battered vampyre into it as they scrambled clear of the rubble.

"This is hopeless, we'll have to fight our way out of the town, and there's only me to do the fighting," said Andry, and he led her to his horse.

Lined up behind his horse were four reccons and the cart. By now Terikel had Wallas in a headlock and the little crossbow was pointed up his nose.

"Hurry up, damn you, the wagon's double-parked!" Wallas shrieked as Andry stood staring in astonishment.

Madame Jilli looked at the queue in dismay, then hurriedly leafed through her Register of Movements, memorized several names, then put the register down beside her and opened Abstracts of Lives.

"Falzer Rikel, D'brz-Thrth—also known as Lavolten—Holbok Harz, Transer, you are going to have to share the boat," she called. "Any objections?"

The spirits of the dead looked to each other and shrugged.

"No? Good. Please enter the boat, and be seated on the floor. Lucky you, Mr. Transer, you get the seat at the end."

Madame Jilli read the Abstracts of Lives as she pushed the punt along with one hand.

"So, crushed to death by falling masonry, Holbok? What's the world coming to when you just can't walk the streets in safety? Transer, oh dear, throat ripped out by a bloodsucking fiend. I bet you wish it had been quick and clean like for young Holbok? D'brz-Thrth—my goodness, a sorcerer turned glass dragon, and six hundred years old! We ferry-girls don't see many like you, can't wait till I get back to tell them in the tearoom in the Library of Souls. And Falzer, my word, it's that bloodsucking fiend again."

They traveled through gloom that was suffused by mists, and presently a red glow appeared through the murk. Distant screams became audible to those on the boat; then a dim shoreline with grotesque, gesticulating figures became visible. All four men were staring at the scene with dread when there was a swoosh, and the ferrygirl's pole struck Falzer on the head, knocking him into the water. As his head broke the surface of the black waves, Madame Jilli rammed the end of the pole into his back.

"Rape lamplight girls, did you?" she screamed. "Well this is what it feels like to be held down and poked against your will!"

In spite of facing damnation, the three spirits remaining in the punt began to laugh. Madame Jilli finally drew the pole back and swung it around behind the boat. D'brz-Thrth did not realize that anything else was wrong until the pole completed its circle and struck him as well. He tumbled into the water.

"Try to kill my beloved, you did, murdering bastard glass dragon!" she shouted, smashing the pole down squarely on his head as he struggled to get to his feet in the inky shallows. "And you flamed his commander! Get over to the shore now, the pair of you!"

The daemons on the shore cheered heartily, and Madame Jilli waved and blew them a kiss.

"Any time ye want a job here, luv, yer welcome!" cried a daemon who was waving a set of manacles in one hand and a white-hot pitchfork in the other.

Madame Jilli began pushing back into the darkness as her two passengers waded ashore. Holbok and Transer were now huddled together at the other end of the boat and not laughing at all.

"Er, are we not supposed to go there too?" asked Holbok.

"No, you're for Arcadia. Now try to sit still, this thing is not very stable. Sorry, I hate rapists. As for Andry's safety, well, I get a little emotional about that."

Presently Madame Jilli returned to where the other spirits of the departed were waiting their turn.

"Porter," she called. "Just you this time, step into the boat and sit at the center of the seat." She pushed away from the shore. "Now then, I believe you commanded my sweetheart, Andry Tennoner."

"Andry?" exclaimed the startled spirit, suddenly hugging his knees. "He never said his lass was Death."

"Oh, I'm only a ferrygirl, and I was alive when Andry knew me. It's a long story, we can go to Arcadia via Hell-wharf if you really want to hear it. How is Andry these days?"

"I only had command of him for a short time. A very short time. Only hours, really."

"Oh that's not a problem, most of the men in my life only stayed an hour or two. Tell me, has he a sweetheart yet?"

"Er, ah, no, but he had this little knife, like. A special, sort of, er, special lady's knife."

"Oh no, he's still pining for me!"

It was much later in the night that the reccons stopped to rest the horses and take stock. Although now five miles behind them, the glow of the burning town was still quite distinct in the east. Andry stood with his arms around his horse's neck for some time, thanking it for its loyalty during the fighting. When the animal made it clear that it preferred to graze rather than accept further thanks, Andry sat down with his head in his hands.

"Delegate Tennoner, sir!"

Andry looked up to see Essen standing a respectful distance away. He got to his feet and saluted.

"I'm not the delegate," replied Andry.

"Yes you are, sir, beg pardon for contradicting your word, though. The men await your orders."

"Orders?" asked Andry, unsure of whether he had the Sargolan word right.

"Your orders, sir. Porter was our delegate to the Journey Guard officers, but he is dead. We elected you to replace him."

It took some time for Essen to explain what had happened. The reccons had the right to elect their own spokesman, who was called the delegate. They had elected

Andry as they rode. It seemed that anyone who attacked a dragon with an ax to save a reccon was probably to be trusted as their liaison. He also filled in some details of what had happened before Andry arrived.

"So as the Journey Guard was fleeing the city, the dragon was noticed overhead," Essen concluded.

"Not easy to miss it," said Andry.

"Captain Gilvray decided to put Princess Senterri on a horse and overturn her coach. On Delegate Porter's own initiative, we stayed to defend the wreck, as if the princess was still inside. When you went off after the dragon to save your lady, me and the lads got together and took a little vote."

"What? You would be led by someone who takes such stupid risks?"

"Aye sir."

"Oh. Well then, who is the most senior officer in this group?"

"You sir."

"Me?"

"You sir."

"We're doomed," muttered Andry softly, but he rallied himself nevertheless. "Right then, tend those with wounds and get under way. Glasbury is not far, and is sure to be safer."

"Aye sir, but permission to ask one question?"

"Ask."

"How did you know your lady friend was where the dragon crashed?"

"Because she was on the dragon."

"Begging your pardon, sir, but there was only a daemon wrapped around the dragon's throat, slashing it open. There was no lady held in its claws or suchlike."

"That daemon is my lady friend, Reccon Essen, and I'll thank you not to refer to her as a daemon."

She has a sufficiently poor self-image as it is, added the voice in Andry's head.

Once everyone had been checked by Terikel, it became clear that there were a great many injuries being ignored. Almost an hour passed before Terikel had treated everyone as best she could, given that she had nothing more at hand than some wine and strips of cloth. Velander lay wrapped in a blanket, and did not want anything to do with anyone. Andry decided that if he was in charge of the entire group, he had the right to be treated last.

The others were getting ready to leave as Terikel bound up the last of Andry's cuts, burns, and scratches. Andry gazed at the flickering lights of Dragonwall on the western horizon to take his mind off the sting of cheap wine on his burns.

"Andry, what do you understand of the Dragonwall?" Terikel asked as she tied the last of his bandages.

"It's, er, a magical casting to drain strength from the Torean Storms that have sunk our ships and brought so much rain, ladyship."

"Yes, that is what is involved, roughly speaking," replied Terikel, surprised at the simple accuracy of his reply. "Those terrible storms have developed since the continent of Torea was burned last year."

"Oh aye, even I've heard that," said Andry, now standing up. "You're said to be Torean, ladyship. What happened, like? Were you there?"

"Oh I was there, make no mistake, and I escaped by the barest of margins. There was a war being fought, and the opposing sides were evenly matched. One leader used an ancient, enchanted weapon called Silverdeath, thinking that it was no more than an improved siege engine. He did not know that its powers were many millions of times greater than those of the biggest catapult ever built. The weapon got out of control. Everything that it could not burn was melted. Some very brave people destroyed Silverdeath before further harm was done, but the heat that destroyed Torea had already upset the climate. The sorcerers of Lemtas, Acrema, and Scalticar have set up seventeen ringstone circles. A thousand of their number are powering them with mighty magical castings. They are spread out along a line running from north to south, and it stretches halfway around our world. Their combined powers have set up that beautiful yet dangerous splash of lights in the western sky, and it is meant to draw off some of the force from the Torean Storms, just as a mill wheel slows the flow of a stream by just a little."

"Seems a worthy venture," said Andry, scratching his head. "But why are you here?"

"Nobody has ever assembled the combined etheric control of a thousand of the most powerful sorcerers on three continents before. Well, not for five thousand years, anyway. Figures concern me, Andry. There were odd, raggy bits at the edges of Dragonwall's figures, and questions that got answered only with hand-waving and promises. I am a Metrologan, I measure things and ask questions. Things that others do not bother with, and questions that people prefer to be left unspoken."

"Like what?" asked Andry.

"Like where all the energies go that are drained out of the storms."

"Into the sky?"

"Officially, no, but in truth, yes. There they can be stored, aimed, then spat down like hellfire at people who are not in favor. It happened tonight, and they were aiming at me."

"Back in Clovesser?" exclaimed Andry. "No, it was rioters, sorcerers, and dragons as set the town burning."

"Those fools, incompetents, and bungling idiots helped to spread the fires, but they were started by Dragonwall. Those directing it know that someone has their measure, and soon they will have reports that they failed to kill me."

"Can't believe that, ladyship. What harm can come of light in the sky?"

"Andry, I was standing beside the town academy when it exploded like a melon struck by a mallet. I was walking to a hostelry when that went the same way. They were trying to kill me, and they were willing to kill hundreds of others to do it, too. I am very concerned about that."

"Oh aye, sign me up for some o' that concern too," said Andry, suddenly quite alarmed.

"I know how to stop it, but the trouble is that I do not know how to stop a thousand of my fellow initiate sorcerers starting it up again. It gets worse . . . but enough of my problems. Can we reach Glasbury tomorrow?"

"The horses are tired and hungry, but they could be urged on. The reccons say that it is five miles away, but I'd not take the direct road if there's folk out to spy on you, or worse. We

can rec out the back roads, and loop around to Glasbury
from the north. Thirty, forty miles, maybe. If we take no
sleep, leave now, and risk killing the horses, perhaps we
could get there late tomorrow. I'll order the reccons and
Wallas to fall in as soon as I'm bandaged."

"Good, good, it is a relief to be in trusted hands."

The compliment from Terikel stopped Andry's breath almost as effectively as a punch to the stomach. Fighting his
way out of a morass of pride, he remembered an important
issue.

"Before we set off, though, may I have a question?"

"I owe you that, and a lot more."

"I've heard tales and ballads about fiends, daemons,
wraiths, and flesh-eating monsters, but I've never heard tell
of one with a drinking problem. What's Velander's trouble?"

Terikel looked surprised in the dim light from their small
fire.

"Velander is dead, but sustains herself on the blood and
etheric essence of others. People by preference, animals
when there is no choice."

"Not that. I heard that Laron tried to school her to prey
only on evil people, but now she hunts down drunks—for the
wine in their blood."

"Andry, you astonish me. You deduce secrets that the
whole of the Imperial Secret Constabulary would be hard
put to discover."

"I like to listen, ladyship, and folk like to talk. Especially
folk as is stressed."

"Andry, Velander is a monster, and she has all the restraint
of a starving wolfhound. The trouble is that a fragment of
the former Velander is still in there, and it is horrified to see
what she is doing. She hunts drunks for the oblivion in their
blood, because she cannot stand what she is, or what she
does. Laron and Princess Senterri watched over her for a
while, and tried to teach her something of restraint. Laron
and the princess were sleeping together at that time and—
Andry! How do you do it? I shouldn't be telling you all
this!"

"Then don't, ladyship."

"Oh . . . all right, I'll tie up some loose threads, but no

more! Laron rescued Senterri after she had been abducted by slavers, so Senterri was understandably grateful to him."

"I have your meaning."

"Now Laron and the princess have fallen out somewhat, because Senterri married Cosseren for power, political convenience, and the title of Queen of Logiar."

"Oh aye, folk do that. Did Velander, like, ever go skirts-up with Laron?"

"If you really want to learn refinement, Andry, the term is 'intimate.' And the answer is no. When she was alive, Velander was a little . . . difficult to deal with. Laron took her into his protection because she was alone and helpless. Now she is no longer helpless, and he has problems of his own."

Chapter Five

DRAGONBIRD

One did not enter Glasbury suddenly, one passed increasingly frequent villages that merged into a patchwork of houses, vegetable gardens, markets, taverns, and temples. As the traffic increased, the roads narrowed, and it was not until the sixth hour past noon that the reccons and the cart reached the old city walls. The palace dominated the skyline of the city, and it was in its direction that Andry took his charges. At the palace barracks Andry's men made a declaration that he had been elected their delegate, and he was issued with a pair of red stars to sew onto his surcoat.

"One for the front, for the enemy to shoot at, one for back, for us to shoot at," said Essen. "Can ye sew, sir?"

"Aye, I learned aboard the *Stormbird*," said Andry slowly. "The sails needed a lot of sewing, what with the Torean Storms."

The reccons gathered in the hayloft above their horses in the stable, and ate pies bought in a tavern not far away. By the light of a pottery lamp Andry sewed on the badges of the second-lowest rank in the Sargolan military. He then began to sew up the cuts, burns, and tatters in his clothes from the battle in Clovesser. There was a creak as someone below began to climb the ladder. Moments later Captain Gilvray's head appeared, and by the time he had climbed into the hayloft, the reccons were on their feet and standing at attention.

"Gentlemen, take your ease," said Gilvray in Sargolan Common, with a gesture to the straw.

They sat down again, but the general feeling of relaxation was no longer present. Gilvray sat at the edge, with his back against a support beam.

"Delegate Tennoner, I read your report of the fight with the dragon, in defense of an empty coach."

"Aye sir," replied Andry.

"You realize that your men had not been given permission to sacrifice themselves as decoys for the princess?"

"Aye sir."

"It says in this report that the delegate had been killed by rioters by the time you encountered the squad, and that they elected you delegate on the spot. You then found the overturned coach of the princess just as the dragon landed, and decided to defend it as if the princess was within it—to allow the princess to escape. The dragon charged past you and burned the coach to cinders, then flew off, thinking it had killed the princess."

"Aye sir."

"You are a damn liar, Delegate Tennoner."

"Aye sir."

The reccons shifted awkwardly, their eyes everywhere but upon Andry or Gilvray.

"Testimony from Militiaman Wallas of the Imperial Highways Militia indicates that you came across the late delegate defending the overturned coach against the dragon, saw him killed, attacked the dragon, then led the reccons to safety when the dragon began fighting with another enchanted creature."

"Were this the case, the delegate's widow would get no pension, for he died in breach of orders, sir," explained Essen.

"Did I give you permission to speak, Reccon Essen?" demanded Captain Gilvray.

"No sir."

Gilvray turned back to Andry.

"Are you calling Wallas a damn liar, sir?"

"He's a recruit, sir. A new recruit, who's signed on because he's good with a ladle rather than an ax."

"Ah, so you are saying that Wallas is a mere cook, too inexperienced to have appreciated what was really happening?"

"Yes sir."

Gilvray considered the situation for some moments.

"I do believe that Militiaman Wallas should be given a little incentive to follow events more sharply in the future. Perhaps ten lashes?"

"I'm thinking five, sir."

"Then five it shall be, and within the hour. Meantime, you are now in breach of orders regarding the defense of the coach."

"Yes sir."

"You are fined one silver vassal. Pay me at your leisure."

Andry's reccons leaned forward almost instantly, each offering a silver vassal to Captain Gilvray. Andry held up a coin of his own.

"Perhaps you could send those other vassals to Delegate Porter's widow," said Gilvray, taking Andry's coin. "Meantime, I have here orders for Tennoner, Essen, Costiger, Danolarian, Hartman, and Sander. Good night to you all, gentlemen—oh, and Delegate Tennoner, be sure to wear the ax that you used to strike the dragon when you, ah, carry out your orders."

It was not until Captain Gilvray was out of the stables that Andry broke the seal on his little folder and discovered the invitation to a ball in honor of Princess Senterri the following night.

"By his hand, Haraldean, King of Glasbury City and Midlands Principality, and client monarch in the Glorious Sargolan Empire," read Andry aloud.

"Shyte me, a king knows I exist!" exclaimed Costiger.

It turned out that all troops who had fought in defense of the princess in Clovesser were invited. By the time the crack of whiplashes and Wallas's shrieks rang out across the darkened barracks, the reccons were down at a horse trough, stripped naked and frantically washing their uniforms.

Costiger whistled at the sight of Andry's back.

"You been flogged, sir!" he exclaimed.

Andry shrugged. "Aye."

"Were ye, like guilty?"

Andry thought quickly. A suggestion of injustice in his background would do no harm, he decided.

"I say I was guilty, so I was guilty."

"Takin' blame for some friend, were ye then?" rumbled Costiger.

"I said I was guilty."

"Now listen good, sir. You take the blame fer one of us again, I'll punch yer face. Understand?"

"Ah, that's not regulations."

"Never you mind regulations. Just you remember."

Costiger held up his coat, which by now was no longer black.

"Ere, somethin's wrong with me coat," he said.

"Same as with the rest of us," said Essen. "The real color's olive green."

Costiger tipped the murky water from the trough and began to work the handle of the pump again.

"Sir, how many lashes?" he asked Andry.

"Fifty."

"I got two hundred," said Costiger, proudly turning his own back to Andry.

"Take blame for another?" asked Andry, choosing the words with care.

"Nah, I pissed on an officer's bedroll, sir."

"They say you don't feel it after a hundred."

"You do, sir, you just feel it different, and it's worse."

It was past midnight before they left off their patching, cleaning, and polishing and offered themselves to be claimed by sleep.

"Hie, Essen," Andry heard somewhere in the darkness.

"Aye, Costi?"

"I feels like I'm ter face a savage and bloody battle tomorrow night."

"So do I."

"What do I say if the king talks to me?"

"Laugh at his jokes and call him king."

"The form of address is 'Your Majesty,' " called Andry. "Now give it a rest, lads. We're two days without sleep. It's just a dance we're going to, except the entry's free and all but us are very rich."

✦ ✦ ✦

The following morning saw Wallas putting the reccons through a very, very hasty course in ballroom etiquette. Wallas was in considerable pain, because while he had received only five lashes, the flogger was particularly good at his work, and had broken the skin with every stroke.

"But I just reported what I saw!" Wallas kept insisting.

"Someone else saw it differently," said Essen. "That someone else was who the captain believed."

"If I ever find out who that someone is, he'll get burned cutlets and lumpy soup for the rest of his enlistment. Now then, if a man with a red glove was to come up to you, bow, and take you by the arm, Costiger, what do you do?"

"I punches 'is face, sir. My mum warned me about—"

"No, no, no! That man is the envoy of a lady of greater rank than yourself who wishes to dance with you. You must allow him to lead you across the floor, and when he presents you to his mistress, you must ask her for the pleasure of the next dance."

"Oh. And what if she says yes?" asked Costiger, looking uneasy.

"You take out your program and check what dance is next, and whether you know the steps. This is to be a military ball, however, because military heroes are being honored, so the dances are all common enough."

"Oh aye, and who would the heroes be?"

"*Us*, you boneheaded, hairy-arsed muck-raker! So, it's military dance sets. The musicians will be playing galloppes, reels, chases, and jumps, the sorts of dances that soldiers and their wenches are wont to do."

"I knows all them."

"Well then, that's one problem out of a hundred taken

care of. The other ninety-nine are beginning to worry me, though."

By midafternoon the reccons were looking a lot better. They could do most of the dances on the program that came with the invitations, and were used to parade-ground etiquette, so it came down to teaching them to eat and drink with passably good manners. Andry decided to put them through a heavy fencing session, correctly deciding that if they were weary they would be a lot less nervous. By the fifth hour past noon they were washing each other down at the horse trough and comparing old scars and floggings. Sander mixed laundry soap with ground-up incense to make a scented wash for their hair. Costiger then discovered that his hair was brown, not black, and Essen found that once the grease was washed from his hair it was actually wavy.

Velander awoke, or more accurately, she became aware rather than conscious. Etheric energies hummed and danced in the blackness around her, boiling, writhing tendrils of blue and orange. She was at their center, in a small sphere of void. Tendrils floated within reach, hundreds, thousands, millions. A handful of tendrils trailed from Velander to the writhing mass of energy, all that was left of her grasp on life. There was feeling too. Velander's impression was of stepping out of a warm bath into a very cold room, with heat pouring from her skin. *Stand naked too long, and I die of the chill*, she thought. Now the heat had become the life force of her latest victim, sustaining her, yet pouring out into the darkness, sponged away by the cold.

Still the tendrils of energy danced and sparkled. Velander did not like to think of what she looked like. A mass of stumps, of tendrils torn away and consumed by predators so strange that they had no names, even in the sorceric texts. Predators, like she had become. A man was staggering along an alleyway, swaying alarmingly and apologizing to every wall or doorway that he collided with. Closer, closer. There was nobody else on the street, and she was watching from beneath the shadowed struts of an upper bay window. Closer, closer. Thirst smothered the thought that she did not know this man. Raw, animal thirst. Laron had taught her something. Could not remember what. Important, but . . . but only thirst was important. A shameful thirst. Thirst for the sweet reek of alcohol mixed with blood and etheric energies.

A single hand tipped with retractable, inch-long claws flashed down, seizing a neck, drawing the drunk up into the shadows beneath the bay window. Warm flesh against cold lips, etheric fangs plunging into the sweetness of blood and alcohol, tingling with the etheric fires of life. The crunch of bones and gristle, the sensual thrill of weak struggles against her grip, as if she were a sea serpent holding a sailor under the water to drown, or a cat straddling a doomed pigeon.

Velander writhed at the memory, jerking at the few tendrils connected to the core of her life force. This sent her crashing into the wall of etheric fires. Pain blazed up everywhere, the pain of falling into molten lead, pain to blot out the thought of being a fiend, pain to punish herself for losing her grip on the last fraying threads that connected her with mortal people and all of their feelings and values. The remains of the living Velander had pulled herself into the wall of energies, but the vampyre now fought to escape. Torn stumps blazed with pain, bright blue and violet pain.

There was no time where Velander was floating. She felt exquisitely sensitive and vulnerable. The sphere of fire was still there . . . but now at least three dozen more tendrils trailed through the space to where she floated. They tingled where they were joined to her. Joined to her! There had been eleven tendrils left of her former life. Now there were nearly forty.

"Where's the daemon?" asked a voice nearby. It was Essen, one of the reccons.

"She lies in the tray of the cart," replied someone, who might have been Wallas. "Likes to sleep while Miral is down."

"It's when Miral's up as worries me. I saw what she did to that dragon."

"So she'll not be hungry for a while. Dragons are very filling."

"How do you know? Ever eaten one?"

"I'm a cook. We know these things. Now then, I'm a pretty young girl of a lower social class than you. How do you ask me to dance?"

"Er . . . Hie, well by Goddess Fortune, you're a pretty one. Fancy a pint?"

Wallas gave a rather lengthy sigh.

"*Your pardon, most charming and winsome ladyship, but may I have the honor?*"

"Honor of what?"

"Don't argue! Think of these as skirmishing orders from your commanding officer."

"Look, I, er, don't know the galloppe."

"You know the tune, you dolt! I heard you playing it on Andry's rebec this morning."

"Aye, but I've never danced it."

"Ach, it's just like the Waves of Bantriok, only you change hands midway. Pretend I'm a girl, take my right hand in your left and put your right around my back— Ow! Mind my lashes, you dolt!"

"This is very embarrassing."

"Shut up and concentrate. A dozen hop-steps this way, turn and change hands— Argh! Remember my lashes! Then back the other way, break off, hold my left in your right at head height and hop-step around the wall until the next repeat."

"Think I got that. Much in your debt, Wallas. Where'd ye learn all this?"

"Oh, I cooked for some important people, so I saw a lot of balls and dances."

Velander heard their voices fading as they walked away. *I should not have been able to hear any of that,* she thought. This was something to do with killing the dragon, she decided. It had flown with her clinging to its neck, her fangs buried in a soft spot amid the glassy armor of woven etheric tendrils. Then it had crashed. Etheric energies had deluged her, yet they were not energies that she could feed upon, they were not the energies of life. If not, then what? The dragon

seemed almost like an immense puppet, with these tendrils
as the strings. She had found and killed the sorcerer at its
core when its structure had collapsed . . . but everything else
had not been alive, so it was not fading like the life force of
her normal victims.

Dragons. What were they? An outer shell of etheric hide,
etheric wings, enormous amounts of etheric energies within,
and within those energies, what? Velander had almost
blacked out while absorbing the sheer volume of energies
from the glass dragon. Andry had been calling to her . . . and
she had emerged blind. Was she still blind? When Miral
rose, she would find out. No! She was aware, so Miral had to
be up. That meant she was blind and paralyzed. She could
not move. All around her was . . . there was no word for it.
Being, identity, an empty house, a trunk full of clothes, border papers, examinations passed, the experience of love, humiliation, greed, hate, longing, curiosity, ambition . . .
Velander was alone in the life of a dead man.

*Take my memories away, leave me in a city on a far conti-
nent, and will Velander still exist, and be alive?* It was the
opposite to what she was. Velander the vampyre was consciousness without the ability to sustain life force. This was
life force without consciousness. An inferno of empty life
force, enough life force for a city, yet not something that she
could feast upon. It was more like . . . *clothing?*

Sounds came to her from far away. The clang of a blacksmith shaping something, cries of vendors at their stalls, the
shouting of a marshal as he trained recruits at ax fencing.

"Afternoon's compliments to you, Wallas, Andry!" came
Laron's youthful voice in the distance.

"Afternoon's compliments," Wallas called back.

"And how are you this fine day?"

"In great pain, from my flogging," replied Wallas.

"From five lashes? Academy students get worse for not
doing their applied sorceric homework."

Afternoon, thought Velander. *Miral is still down. Then
what am I doing awake, or even aware?* She drew herself
over to the surrounding sphere of tendrils again, hesitated,
then gently brushed it. Thunderflashes of pain obliterated

everything, she screamed soundlessly. Gradually Velander's perceptions of her surroundings returned. She counted the attached tendrils. Fifty-seven. There had been less than fifty at last count. There was the vaguely moldy smell of something nearby. *Probably me*, she thought. *How many tendrils make a life? Tens of thousands? Millions? Each and every one of them a blaze of agony like white-hot needles under the fingernails.* Velander cowered away from the prospect.

"So, Velander is still in the cart?" asked Laron.

"Yes," replied Andry. "She is not well."

"I am sorry about all this," said Laron. "Once, I thought that I could have put her on the same path as me."

"As you? But you are alive, your blood is warm."

"It was not always the case. I spent a very long time as a vampyre, like Velander. The Metrologans did some experiments, seven hundred years ago. They reached out to another world with an etheric device, and they copied an image of a monster. That was me. They put it into a dead body. I escaped them, and have roamed your world ever since as an undead thing that feeds on blood and life-force ether. I was fourteen for seven centuries, I did not age, I did not change. I had a name for every pimple on my face: the one on my chin was Pustella, and another on my left cheek was called Pultic."

He tapped at what seemed to be clear air before his forehead, and a silvery circlet with a starburst of rays faded into view. Andry exclaimed with amazement. At the center of the starburst was a green, spherical jewel. Andry stared for a moment, trying to work out what seemed odd about it.

"Before you ask, the back part of the green gem extends into my brain, yet it does not quite exist, so it is no problem or discomfort. My . . . my soul, essence, spirit resides within the green gemstone. Take the circlet off, and my body becomes dead. Last year I got entangled in a—a very advanced sorceric machine. It had incredible powers. Power to destroy Torea—"

"Miral's rings!" exclaimed Andry.

"—and power to restore my body to life. Here I am now, alive."

"Were you like Velander while you were not alive? Sort of miserab' like, and preying on drunks like the rest of us drinks a pint?"

"Not entirely, although I was not entirely happy, either. While I was dead I followed the way of chivalry, and it kept me from becoming a complete fiend. The temptation to treat people as cattle was almost overwhelming, yet I fought it. Velander is . . . not so strong. Oh I managed to keep her preying upon churls that most towns and cities would be better off without, but she began to waver after a time. She is desperately unhappy as a vampyre, Andry, more so than I was."

"Should I be surprised?"

"In a way she may be nicer than me, perhaps, but that makes it harder for her to be a monster. The machine that restored me to life is smashed, however, so that is her fate. Now Velander has discovered that the blood of drunks renders her insensible for a time, and reduces the sharpness of her sorrow and misery."

"I noticed."

"She is slipping, Andry. She tells me that she still selects her victims among the criminals and bullies, but I know better, as you do. One day I shall be forced to end her existence."

"When will that be?"

"When all the Velander has faded, and there is only daemon left. That will probably be soon, I fear."

"Lordship, I'm trying to help. I've sworn not to drink as long as she keeps from killing folk."

"You? A pact with Velander?"

"Aye."

"You stopped drinking to give her moral support?"

"Aye, and I don't feel so flash either, I can tell you that. I'd give anything for a jar. But sir . . . this may sound sort of odd, but . . . she's my lass."

Laron swallowed, then smiled broadly.

"Amazing. Andry, you were a filthy, drunken sailor when I first saw you, yet now! Now you drink nothing, have a rank in the Sargolan Empire's forces, command five reccons, have manners that I could never have thought possible, and have an invitation to tonight's ball for the princess. That is a vast transformation in only . . . By the lordworld! Only eighteen days!"

"Oh aye," said Andry bashfully.

"It's impossible."

"Not so, Lord Laron. How many drunks with their throats torn out might have also fought their way out of the wine jar if given a chance? You gave me a chance, now I try to give Velander a chance too. You know the only thing that once stopped me heaving her onto a fire while Miral was down and she slept?"

"Tell me."

"The fact that she is as I was, and that she may find herself clear to fight her way back."

"Easier for you than her, Andry, I swear it."

"Think so? I've drunk no wine since Clovesser, and at this moment the longing for the drink makes my head ache and my tongue burn, while visions dance before my eyes. I can understand—"

In the distance someone called Andry's name, and asked about mustache wax.

"Best be going," said Andry.

"Your men are taking this ball very seriously."

"Just as I am. Will you be there, lordship?"

"No. Terikel wants an escort to visit some dangerous place. It is as good an excuse as any not to attend."

"Does not Velander always attend Terikel?"

"As you know, Velander is proving less than reliable. Back in Clovesser it cost a student his life."

"With all the other lives lost in Clovesser, I'm surprised anyone noticed."

There was an even more urgent call for Andry, by someone who wanted to know if he knew how to use a comb.

"I must be off, lordship, have to shave my beard right down to a mustache for the ball. May the dark hours smile upon you."

✦ ✦ ✦

Velander was no longer cowering by now. Bracing herself against her existing tendrils, she flung herself against the en circling, writhing mass as hard as she could. There was the pain of a thousand lashes, all delivered at once, the pain of being rolled in salt after a thousand lashes, and the pain of another thousand lashes. Velander's senses drifted back together long enough to count over a hundred tendrils attached, and then she flung herself against the etheric encirclement again.

By sunset the reccons were done repairing the cuts, gashes, frays, and tears in their uniforms, which were now clean and dry, but after cleaning their boots they discovered that they had to clean their fingernails again. At last clean, dressed, and groomed, they set out across the inner city for the palace, talking excitedly and speculating about whether anyone would want to dance with them. After a quarter mile, they turned and dashed back to the barracks for their invitations.

Terikel and Laron were having a less fortunate time of it. The Glasbury Etheric Arts and Sciences Academy was being administered by a junior prefect of initiate level nine, all the other senior students and academics having left months earlier to participate in Ringstone Alpine's contingent of sorcerers. Most of the younger students had been sent home, and even the cleaning and cooking staff had been laid off.

"There is something profoundly disturbing about a seven-hundred-year-old organization suddenly falling apart like that," said Laron as he and Terikel walked back to the guest wing of the Glasbury palace. "For seven centuries it was functioning, just like me, but now it is like a terminally sick grandfather."

"I agree," replied Terikel. "It feels like the end of the world."

"Learned Terikel?"

"Yes?"

"Do you think it really is the end of the world? Dragonwall, and all that goes with it?"

"The works of people are puny, and the world is big. It takes a lot to destroy everything."

"Yet an etheric machine fashioned by the sciences and arts of the very distant past melted Torea only a short time ago."

"Yes, the legendary Silverdeath. Thanks to you and Wensomer, it is gone."

"But now our sorcerers have built a different but very dangerous etheric machine. It may be less powerful than Silverdeath, but it is on a vastly bigger scale. Do you not think that our sorceries have become too powerful for our poor little world to endure?"

"Yes I do, Laron, and so do a few other people."

"So what do we do?"

"Take exceedingly drastic action."

"That being?"

"I'll not speak for myself. Others have plans that involve them controlling Dragonwall, on the theory that they are trustworthy and nobody else is. My little faction wants to see it destroyed."

"Who are they?"

"I do not have the slightest idea. I play my part, and hope that those above me know what they are doing."

In tavern dances, a drinker or two starts playing, a few more drinkers do jigs or reels with the lamplight girls and serving wenches, and the owner rubs his hands in satisfaction because a lot of people are in his taproom and are making themselves thirsty. In fairs, a sponsor sets up a table with a barrel and a bench with three or four musicians, and the whole show is more or less self-maintaining from then on. In hall dances it is the same as with fair dances, except there is someone at the door to charge admission. Musicians play, and get paid in drink and occasionally a few coppers as well. The couples dance, and the unattached saunter about and try to make their interest in each other clear by a series of very obscure and subtle glances, winks, smiles, and gestures. The gestures can range from bowing and extending a hand to one's prospective partner, to accidentally spilling a drink over her in order to at least get a conversation started. Everybody knows their roles, and the rules are minimal. Balls are an entirely different matter, however, and to a novice, utterly terrifying.

Andry and the reccons were escorted through a series of very grand archways and corridors by a series of grandly dressed lackeys and servants. They were almost continually asked their names, then checked off against lists. Armed guards shadowed them, wearing gilded chain mail and carrying highly ornate weapons.

"I'd say they're to make sure we don't try to grab a jar of the hard stuff and run," said Andry to Essen, but just then Essen was led away to yet another door by a man who seemed to be dressed entirely in gold braid. The man returned for Andry.

"Stand with your eyes up while you are being announced, then allow the delegate of the hostess to lead you away," he said as he guided Andry through the door where Essen had gone without returning.

"And who are you, then?" asked Andry.

"The entrance herald, or course!" exclaimed the man in the genuine surprise at the question.

They stopped at a huge double-door archway, flanked by the most elaborately and expensively dressed guards that Andry had ever seen. Beyond this was a room filled with more nobles than Andry had thought existed in all the world. The entrance herald at the door banged his staff three times, and the crowd's chatter diminished a little.

"The king's pleasure to present ... Delegate Reccon Andry Tennoner, unattached, of the Imperial Highways Militia, subject of the crown prince of Alberin, and currently sworn to the service of the imperial regent."

There was polite but studiously enthusiastic applause, then Andry found himself being led into the hall by a woman whose strength and grip stated that she had never taken any nonsense from any man, whether warrior, sorcerer, or king. He also noticed that the women and girls were staring at him quite intently, and he now rather wished that he had combed his hair one extra time, and perhaps used a newer leather thong to tie it back.

For all their nervousness about the conventions and protocols of grand balls, the reccons soon found out that while they were indeed elaborate and complex social gatherings, they were planned and programmed with an astonishing degree of attention to detail. Their invitations were checked at the door, and they were assigned to a floor warden who shepherded them over to a table where they were served drinks. Andry asked for an empty goblet, so he was given one. Next they were taken to a group of militiamen, which included Wallas. They were introduced to each other, even though they already knew each other, and left to talk. A few minutes later, facilitators came over with invitations to speak with various men and women of middle to upper Glasbury society, most of whom had never spoken to soldiers below the rank of lieutenant. The facilitators were highly skilled at keeping awkward conversations going, however, so everyone had the impression of things being quite friendly and chatty.

The dances began. Women who had never come closer to a militiaman than to step over drunk ones lying in the street now had their facilitators convey invitations to dance, and the reccons' feeling that the night was going to be a complete and absolute disaster was quickly forgotten. The women realized that the lower-class soldiers were strong, fit, and surprisingly shy men with slightly quaint accents, while the reccons and militiamen learned that noblewomen were very skilled at putting men at their ease.

"Laron tells me that it's all they ever do, so they're good at it," Andry explained to Costiger during one of the breaks in the programming.

"What about the washin' and all?" Costiger asked skeptically. "Whose ter cook, scrub floors, go ter market, and keep tykes in line?"

"There's servants as do that, Costi."

"What's servants?" asked Costiger, who heard the word occasionally, but never thought to ask what it meant.

The herald at the door banged his staff three times, and the crowd's chatter diminished a little.

"The king's pleasure to present . . . Captain Laron Aliasar, unattached, of the Imperial Highways Militia, and hero of the flight from Clovessen. Apologies from Captain Aliasar for his lateness, as caused by needing to escort a lady of rank on business of the imperial court."

There was a murmur as quite a number of the girls and women present noticed that Laron was obviously important, brave, romantically handsome, from some good family, and very, very young. At least a dozen envoys of ladies converged on him as a facilitator took him in the direction of the drinks table.

"Andry, how are you enjoying yourself?" asked an all-too-familiar voice, and Andry began his salute to Captain Gilvray even before he had finished turning.

"Enjoyable evening, sir!" he replied crisply.

"Take case, Andry, we are all meant to act as peers once we walk through the doors."

"Oh. Yes sir."

"Young Laron certainly made a grand entrance just now. The daughters and mothers of the highborn are after him like hounds after a fox."

"Fortune smiles upon him, sir."

"Yes, but we know little of him. I had a check done of the peerage registers, and there is only a single mention of Laron Aliasar. That one was made last month, and it says that he is on leave from the service of the emperor of North Scalticar. Strange, though, that there are other Aliasars in the peerage in earlier times. About every fifty years an Aliasar arrives from North Scalticar, spends a year of two distinguishing himself in various ways, then travels on, always to 'the north.'"

"Perhaps a family tradition, sir?"

"Perhaps. I like to learn about those I serve with, you see. Take you, for example, Andry. I do not even know your age, but I wager you're only seventeen."

"I'm nineteen, sir. I think."

"Ah, and on what day were you born?"

"Don't know, sir, but five years ago the old man wanted the excuse for a drink on the last day of Threemonth, so he called it my birthday and the family had a bit of a revel."

"Oh so," said Gilvray, taking the quite unusual assignment of a birthday in his stride. "Is it your first time away from home?"

"Oh not so, I've been upriver from Alberin, with dry barges."

"Dry barges?"

"When timber barges are towed back upriver, any needing repairs are carried on two others. A bargemaster and his team travel with them, repairing as they travel. That way the barge is not laid up in dock. That's unprofitable, like. Mechant Economy says so, whoever he is. I've been riding the tow horses since I was nine. Three days upriver, sleeping on board, repairin' barge, a day in Ahrag, helping load timber, then two days back, dressing timber and carving rigging pins."

"Ah, a carpenter's mate."

"Aye, like without the storms smashing all the big ships I'd maybe get a position like that. Then I got press-ganged, and . . . well, I was really made a carpenter's mate."

"So you can ride quite well?"

"Oh aye, been riding barge horses for nine years, I said that. Riding them along as they pull, and exercising them at the end of the day."

"And you can use an ax to great effect."

"Aye, sort of. I'm better with yardstick, and I'm best with ax held just below the head and used as a yardstick. Improves the balance, sir."

"Obviously. I saw you standing your ground against Laron and two dozen lancers in a village market, and that very mangled ax at your belt tells me that you even went up against a glass dragon. Martial prowess can be taught, Andry. Courage cannot."

"Thank you, sir."

"How many men have you killed?"

"None, sir."

"None?" exclaimed Gilvray in quite obvious surprise, his eyes widening.

"None, sir. Nor women, either."

"But if you found yourself against someone who deserved to die, what then?"

"Thus far I've not met a man who deserves to die, but if I had to kill, I'd do it."

"Astounding. Most warriors boast about how many lives they have taken. You're as good a skirmishing fighter as ever

I have seen, yet you're proud to have killed nobody. Your reccons seem to like you."

"If you say so, sir."

"You do not agree?" asked Gilvray, picking up the trace of doubt in Andry's voice at once.

"No sir, but . . . it's nothing."

"Tell me."

"Sir, I've been seven days in the service and less in the reccons. Not another man has been there less than a year. I've little experience, so I'll get us all killed if I stay delegate."

"But many enlistees come into service as officers when their parents buy them commissions."

"Just speaking my mind, sir."

"Indeed? I don't hear that often—but I've no problem with it. People with high rank hear too few honest opinions from people of lower rank looking for advancement. Your reccons are behaving very well tonight."

"They are all, er, gentlemanly in their own ways, sir."

"Indeed? Were you to vote for delegate, who might your choice be?"

"Reccon Essen, sir. He's respected, experienced, and all like him. He makes good decisions, and he's a damn fine musician."

"But delegate is not a command rank, one merely passes on orders from the Journey Guard's captain."

"Begging your pardon, sir, but most times you are not there, and the reccons ask the delegate what you meant by the orders."

"Ah yes, interpretation, you may have a point. So, you're Alberinese. Is there any conflict of loyalty possible?"

"North Scalticar and the Sargolan Empire are not at war, sir, but should that ever happen, I expect to be stood down from Sargolan service."

Gilvray nodded, then smiled and looked around.

"A pleasure to speak with you, Andry, but now I must be off. Do enjoy the rest of the ball."

Laron came up to Andry once he was alone again, and behind him was an entourage of envoys, with the girls and women that they served not too far distant.

"Please, gentlemen, give me some space. I need to speak with Delegate Tennoner on the protection of the princess," said Laron, waving them back; then he turned to Andry and rolled his eyes. "I don't really need to speak to you, I just want breathing space."

"You're in luck, it's only the mothers as ask me for a dance," confessed Andry.

"Ah, that's because you're seen as being of low birth. They are checking your manners before they allow their daughters to send their envoys after you. Nobody gets to the rank of captain without being of a noble family, however, so I have been quarry from the start. Give it another half hour, and you will be in as much trouble as me. How are the reccons doing?"

Andry looked around. The others were clustered nearby, being talked to by a variety of women, and all looking as intimidated as Andry felt by the sheer volume of finery, rank, and wealth around them.

"They are . . . there's a proper word—*acquitting* themselves well in this, ah, skirmish," managed Andry. "Captain Gilvray seemed to think so, anyway."

"A fine man, that Captain Gilvray," agreed Laron. "His father was Master of the Imperial Chase. Not a noble, mind, but a gentleman of Alpennien descent, with skills in the hunt as well as etiquette and manners to put a herald to shame. Mark me, the princess likes him. Give it ten years, he'll get a castellany."

"He seems more deserving of good fortune than most, sir," said Andry.

"Give that 'sir' business a rest, Andry, it's only me. Getting back to Gilvray, he's already a captain, so once he gets land he'll become a noble. The thing about nobles is, however, the bathhouse test."

"You mean they take baths, like, even when they don't need them?" asked Andry, not sure if he was hearing correctly.

"That too, but put them in a bathhouse with just a towel to wear, and folk like Captain Gilvray sound and act like nobles. Put commoners beside them, and anyone can soon tell who is noble or commoner."

"Wallas is meant to be a gentleman, and he may even be a noble—" began Andry.

"Exceptions, there are always exceptions. Terikel told me that she had learned from people—not named—that Wallas was the previous Master of Royal Music."

"Ridiculous notion, sir—er—lad—that is, Laron."

"But if true, well, consider this. The master's parents were bakers who bettered themselves through hard work and rat cunning. They spent a small fortune on their son's education, and Wallas rewarded them by getting all the way to the imperial court. There he managed to get his father granted a family crest and have it presented by the emperor himself . . . but he would still fail the bathhouse test. Where is he, anyway?"

"Over there with, er, some rich-looking lady."

"Countess Bellesarion!" exclaimed Laron at once.

"You know her?"

"She is a local associate of Prince Valios, who is third in line for the imperial throne."

"Oh so? The wretch is doing well, then—you mean as in the Palion court?" gasped Andry.

"No, she keeps her ears and eyes open here, and writes long and informative letters back to the prince."

"But Wallas is sure to ply her with his usual garbage about being an imperial agent or whatever."

"Oh, now that might be serious. Countess Bellesarion knows, or knows of, every courtly spy in the empire, and quite a few of the merchant-class and commoner spies as well. If she thinks Wallas is some new agent in Princess Senterri's pay, there will be a very detailed letter being couriered back to Palion tomorrow morning—or even carried by auton bird if Wallas impresses her sufficiently."

"Shyte and damnation, Wallas!" muttered Andry, noticing Countess Bellesarion's eyes widen as Wallas earnestly explained something to her.

"That should have been 'Oh bother, Wallas, you are a real silly!' " suggested Laron.

Suddenly Wallas bowed and took his leave of the countess. She made for a well-dressed and much older man, paused to say something, then waved in the direction of a curtained door. He escorted her to the door, disappeared inside for a moment, then emerged again. Across the room, Wallas stopped to speak with a serving maid, and then they went into a servants' entrance together.

"The sublime and the ridiculous in the same room," said Laron, who had also been watching. "That was Count Igon Bellesarion, by the way. He is a very jealous type, so the countess goes over to reassure him after speaking to any stranger. I doubt that the peerage registers have a mention of the wench that Wallas—"

"Wallas, your body has a groin instead of a brain as its commanding officer," snarled Andry softly. "That assignation with the wench must have taken all of a quarter minute to complete."

Laron laughed. The next dance was announced by the floor herald.

"Brace yourself, the girls' envoys are closing in."

Andry quickly found himself paired with one of the girls, and she explained that her mother had vetted him in an earlier dance. Her name was Murellis, and she had a pretty face featuring a turned-up nose, and framed by golden curls held back by silver combs.

"I hardly ever speak Sargolan Common!" giggled the girl. "This is so exciting, dancing with a hero of the ranks. This is almost like being swept out of my coach by a bold highwayman."

"My place is to hunt down highwaymen, ladyship," replied Andry softly, trying to keep the conversation neutral.

"Oh yes, but then you would come to my rescue and chop him with your ax, like you did with the dragon, and you would put me on your horse and bear me away to safety in your arms."

"Your dreams are, er, very intense, young ladyship," said Andry awkwardly.

Andry suddenly realized that the countess was not back on the floor. Neither were Wallas and his serving wench. Two more dances passed, and both were quite long and slow.

"What is that door there, behind the red curtains?" Andry asked his partner.

"Oh, so bold, you are," giggled Murellis.

"What do you mean?"

"You do not know?"

"I have never set foot in a real palace before tonight," Andry assured her.

"The respite rooms are through there. It is where ladies go to rest, and get away from the noise and heat of the dance floor when they feel fatigued. It's considered very fashionable to feel fatigued easily."

"Rest?" gasped Andry, a suspicion at the back of his mind suddenly hurrying forward.

"Well, not every time. Come, let me show you, it goes like this: Oh, dear, I feel so faint, will you see me to the respite rooms, Reccon Andry?"

Andry walked from the dance floor with Murellis, and straight through the red curtains and the door behind them. Beyond was a wide passageway, and from it ran a dozen identical doors. All but one stood open, and Murellis guided Andry to the nearest, closed the door behind them, and bolted it. Before Andry could comprehend much more than the fact that a couch was among the furnishings, Murellis set a little clock in motion, then flung her arms around his neck and jammed her lips against his. Then, with skill that could not possibly have been developed without extensive practice, she dragged him down on top of her on the couch, kissing him again and again and wriggling beneath him.

"This is so exciting!" she squeaked. "I am in the respites with a commoner hero between my legs."

Aye, and about twenty layers of dress and cloth and ruffles separating us, thought Andry.

"But surely folk will talk," he warned.

"Oh no, you are only meant to stay for a short period, not enough time for us to become too ardent. Besides, my mother has vetted you, so unless she has misjudged you, it is all quite proper. If not, well, this is where you pull down your trews, pull up my skirts, and give me a baby, but of course you are a gentleman commoner so you would never do that."

"Oh yes, that I am," Andry assured her, rolling off to sit on the edge of the couch.

"Mind, you might seek to please me honorably by just doing this."

Murellis took his hand and ran it up beneath her skirts and between her thighs. Andry realized that he was trembling uncontrollably, and beginning to sweat. *What would Velander think?* he wondered, then thought *What do I care what Velander thinks?*

"And then I could say in truth that I have been intimate with you, for this is indeed intimate. You did indeed lie between my legs, you did do that, yet my mother's medicar can swear that I am still a virgin—but go now, you must not stay *too* long. I shall stay here and enjoy the feel of you that lingers with me."

Andry got up, but Murellis pointed to a little beam-action clock on the wall that appeared to mark out an interval of only five minutes on the dial. Barely a minute had passed.

"Stay, it's not an honorable time yet," whispered Murellis.

As he stood there, Andry noticed a bell rope with a tassel on the end and a plate engraved with KITCHEN on the wall behind it. At two minutes Murellis hissed "Go!" and Andry unbolted the door and stepped outside. Murellis bolted the door behind him immediately. Andry leaned against the door for a moment, thinking, *At least there was more to her promises than those of Jelene or Madame Jilli.* Suddenly the door at the end of the corridor opened, and the maid who had been with Wallas entered. She glared at Andry, looked into the open respite room nearest to her, seemed puzzled, then hurried back through the door.

Andry had Madame Jilli's dagger out at once. He walked along to the other closed door. It was a type with a solid frame around thin panels. He found a crack, inserted the dagger's point, pushed it in a little, then withdrew it. He looked in. A pair of bone white legs were waving in the air, and between them was a pair of hairy buttocks. Andry also registered that the back of the man who was entertaining the woman—who could only have been the countess—was scored by five lashes. Andry marched straight out into the ballroom—to be confronted by Murellis's mother.

"Two minutes and a half, young man," she declared, smiling broadly and squeezing his arm. "That was indeed both honorable and flattering of you."

"I—ah—then what time was expected of me?" stammered Andry.

"You do not know? Well, a quarter minute is considered a snub, one minute merely polite, two minutes is honorable, three is a little naughty, four is the limit of proper behavior, and five is a scandal."

"Oh. Ah, well, Murellis is quite an honorable but alluring girl," Andry managed, floundering for appropriate but neutral words.

"Oh yes, many young men pay court to her, she is very popular."

Hardly a surprise, thought Andry. *So, this is how nobles do it. It's seriously different from wenches who sit on a lad's knee while sharing a pint in the Alberin taverns.* At this point the last dance in the bracket ended. Andry went straight to the first reccon he could see, who happened to be Essen. The other reccons quickly gathered around, some with partners still on their arms.

"I want something done about Wallas!" he managed to hiss in Essen's ear, but that was as far as he got.

"Gentlemen, may I have a word with you?" someone called.

Neither Andry nor his men turned around, none of them being used to being addressed as a gentleman. A uniformed envoy with several loops of gold rope pinned to one shoulder came up to Andry and gave a shallow bow.

"You, sir, are Delegate Andry Tennoner?" he asked.

"Aye," replied Andry guardedly, aware that he was not obliged to show undue deference to civilians below a certain rank.

"Her Royal Highness Princess Senterri wishes to be introduced to you. Kindly stand ready, and have the men you speak for standing ready behind you."

Andry snapped to attention instantly, and there was some shuffling of boots as Andry's reccons positioned themselves. The princess approached through the crowd on the arm of Viscount Cosseren, and they were escorted by Captain

Gilvray. Everyone turned to see what was happening, and the conversations died away.

"Delegate Tennoner, also known as 'the animal,' I have been looking forward to meeting you," said the princess, who had suddenly filled Andry's entire universe and stopped time absolutely dead. He managed to notice that she had brunette hair that had been very tightly braided and looped, and that she was beautiful in a sensual rather than pretty way.

"Your Highness is kind—er, gracious," Andry answered, suddenly terrified that his bladder might fail him.

"I have read a report, about how you defended my empty coach to deceive a glass dragon into thinking I was cowering within it. Delegate Tennoner, you are a very brave animal. It seems that you actually cut through the dragon's scales, and lived to tell of it. Your ax blade was partly melted, the handle charred. May I see your ax?"

Andry drew his ax and presented it to the princess on his palms. She took it by the base and unconsciously dropped into guard position for a moment. *Knows ax fencing*, thought Andry.

"Remarkable," said Princess Senterri. "I should like to have this ax on the wall of my new throne hall in Logiar. May I keep it?"

"Yes, Your Highness, I'm honored."

"But you will need a new ax," she said, passing Andry's ax to the lackey. "I can't have you fighting for my honor with a beer bottle. Captain Gilvray?"

Gilvray handed his own ax to her. The coat of arms of the Journey Guard was stippled into the blade.

"May I respectfully remind Your Highness that only members of the Journey Guard may carry a weapon with its coat of arms," said Gilvray.

"Ah, quite so, and only kavelars may be appointed to the Journey Guard. But is Delegate Tennoner a gentleman, Captain Gilvray?"

"He has the qualities of one, Your Highness. He can play a tune, sing, dance, read, write, discuss both cold and magical sciences, and deport himself with proper etiquette and good manners. He also speaks three languages."

"The qualities of a gentleman make a gentleman, Captain Gilvray, even if people think him an animal. Delegate Tennoner, kindly kneel."

Andry went down on both knees. The ax descended, its blade facing upward. It touched his right shoulder, then his left.

"Delegate Tennoner, you will rise with the right to declare a crest. Arise, Reccon Kavelar Andry Tennoner," She now turned to Essen. "Reccon Essen Essaren, kneel. It has come to my notice that my loyal reccons need an experienced leader to interpret the orders brought back to the reccons by their delegate, who is inexperienced although brave. I hereby grant the post of marshal commoner to the Journey Guard's reccons, and appoint you as the first incumbent. Arise, Marshal Essen Essaren."

The assembly was clapping as Essen got to his feet; then he and Andry seemed to stand together and receive the applause for a very long time. The princess turned away, walked a few paces, then suddenly turned back.

"Oh and Kavelar Tennoner, this is yours," she said, tossing Gilvray's ax to Andry, who caught it with a single brisk movement.

Essen was bowing to Andry the moment that Senterri was gone.

"Sir, thank you, thank you so much," he whispered, grasping Andry's arm. "I'll try to live up to your good opinion of me."

"Me? I didn't say anything to anyone," replied Andry softly, the room spinning before his eyes. "Someone just noticed your skills and talents, that's all and— Wait a moment! You're *my* superior now."

"Sir, she's made us part of the squad!" Sander pointed out. "We're attached to the Journey Guard itself, technical, like!"

"Uh, aye," said Andry and Essen together.

"Sir, permission to get blind drunk?" Danol asked Essen.

"Granted—er, after the ball," replied Essen.

After that, the rest of the evening seemed to fly past very quickly. Wallas appeared on the dance floor again, and Andry noticed that the countess was also back amid the company and chatting to her husband. *If only he knew,* thought Andry. *If only Murellis's mother knew, too.*

"Andry!"

Andry's knees nearly buckled at the sound of Murellis's voice behind him. He turned and bowed, all in the same motion.

"I must apologize, I missed your being granted a crest," she said softly, taking his arm.

"Oh, it was not much to see," replied Andry.

"Mother said that had she known, she would have told me to give you three minutes and a half."

A list of things that might have been practical in three and a half minutes scrolled through Andry's mind, but he said nothing.

"I must go to Lord Coriat's estate with Mother tomorrow, for the betrothal of my sister, but in three days I shall be back. Mother says you must come over for afternoon tea, and we may have *twenty minutes* together, alone. You know what that means?"

"I, er, have a fair idea," said Andry, "but we have orders to leave in just two days."

"You do? Oh bother. Well when will you be back this way next?"

"I can't say. I will be assigned to the Logiar palace garrison for five years."

"Five years, oh dear. But perhaps by then I shall have been married to some rich old dotard, and you can climb into my bedchamber window and give me the baby that he cannot, and the boy will be brought up as a lord, but he will be your son, and he will be strong and handsome, and very, very brave. Oh Andry, I can hardly wait."

"Oh aye, neither can I."

✦ ✦ ✦

It was the third hour past midnight when Andry finally left the palace with the reccons. Oddly enough, none of them had got drunk. The reccons were so proud of being attached to the Journey Guard that they wanted to prove that they were gentlemen who conducted themselves with grace and dignity.

"So this fopsie comes up an' says please not ter hit 'im, but he 'as ter take me arm," laughed Costiger as they entered the gate. "An' I says ter him, that's all right sir, I knows that yer lady wishes for me ter ask for a dance, an' can't do it herself fer reasons of class distinction. By Fortune's smile, yer should have seen 'is face!"

"Very good," commented Andry.

"So what's class distinction, then?" asked Costiger.

"This old tart felt me bum," said Hartman. "Jolly piece, she was."

"What did you say?" asked Essen.

"I says ladyship, was yer tryin' fer my attention?"

"That old tart is worth three hundred gold crowns a year, according to the wench I was dancing with," said Danol. "Besides, she didn't look much older than you."

"Three hundred gold crowns?" exclaimed Hartman.

"Her late husband was in brewing," said Danol.

"You should have felt *her* bum," laughed Costiger. "Might have got an invitation ter her mansion."

"For tea," added Danol.

"In her bunk," suggested Costiger.

"She gave me this favor to remember her," said Hartman, waving a card.

"That is not a favor, it's an invitation," said Andry.

"What? Quickly, over to that lamp. Who can read?"

"Give it here," sighed Andry. " 'Lady Polkinghans-Clunes of Swallow Ale Mansion . . . requests the pleasure . . . Reccon Hartman of the Journey Guard . . . for tea . . . cakes . . . third hour past noon . . . or maybe it's 'dawn'?"

"Noon? Dawn? What's the word, damn ye—sir!"

"Dawn," said Danol, looking over Andry's shoulder.

"Find the soap and fill up the horse trough," cried Sander.

The soap had all been used before the ball, so Hartman led the others on a raid to break into the laundry. Andry went into the stables with a pottery lamp and began to pump water into the horse trough, muttering, "This is a night such as bards may well write about."

"Andry?"

He turned slowly at the sound of Velander's voice. She was leaning against the cart, and did not look well. She was dressed in a spare surcoat, tunic, and trews from the cart.

"Andry, is you?"

"Aye, it's me. Can't you see?"

"No. Am blind."

She opened her eyes, and intense, blue-white light streamed out of them. She closed them again.

"Velander, what has happened to you?" Andry exclaimed.

"Dragon's ether, poisoned me. Can't see. Hardly move. Got up, washed, got clean. Found clothings in cart. Wanted to be clean. Oh! On you, is, ah, girl scent."

"Oh aye, I danced with a few. It happens at balls. But what about you?"

"Pah. Forgetting that, if please. What happen? Girls nice?"

"Nice but, not . . . interesting." Andry was not sure where the word had surfaced from, but it seemed appropriate. "Oh, and the princess gave me the right to have a crest, and made Essen a marshal. The reccons are—damn, what was the word? Attached. That's it, attached to the Journey Guard. It was all a great triumph."

"Ah, am pleased. Take congratulations, of mine."

"Oh aye, my thanks."

"Just wash, I was doing. Cleaned teeth, fangs, all that. Wash hair."

"You could have gone to the ball, had it been earlier," laughed Andry. "You could have come as my partner, it was on my invitation that I could bring one."

"Me?" gasped Velander, opening her glowing eyes, then hastily shutting them again.

"Why not? There were none as looked better than you."

Andry's problem was not so much that he was not good at small talk with girls, but that he did not even know what it was . . . or know when he was speaking it. Velander was silent as she stood leaning against the cart in the gloom. She was wringing her hands together, and her shoulders were hunched over. She did look sick, but she looked anxious as well.

"Andry, make a pact. Yes? Remember?"

"Oh aye, and I only drank water mixed with lime juice at the ball."

"You hardly drinking, I hunt no more . . . people."

"That's the bones of it. Why?"

"You, I . . . respect. Is all."

"And I respect you for trying, too. I know how hard it must be . . . I of all folk."

"You are brave, am knowing this. Will do something, ah, I need much? Need to know?"

"If I can."

"Come closer."

Although the look on his face contained nothing but the purest of horror, Andry walked forward. Velander slowly raised her hands. She slid them around Andry's chest; then her arms tightened about him with alarmingly firm pressure. He forced himself to put his arms around her, and she was indeed cold, hard, and quivering with the conflict of blind feeding instinct fighting iron restraint. Her embrace tightened. Joints popped and crackled in Andry's back. Her cheek pressed against Andry's, as cold and hard as an Alberin gutter outside a tavern, at midnight, in winter . . . yet she smelled only of soap, and there was the scent of mint leaves on her breath.

Before Andry realized it Velander was drawing back.

"Thanking, ah, so much," she whispered.

With the ordeal over, Andry was even more relieved than when he had managed to cope with getting the right to a crest from the princess without doing something stupid. Then it happened. He never consciously decided to raise his hand, or put it to Velander's neck.

"In Clovesser, when you were in the cart and feeding . . . I struck you and, er, you looked up."

"True."

"The look on your face . . . it was, er, pretty bad."

"Interrupt my feeding. Dangerous."

"Still, you did not attack me, yet you did attack the glass dragon. Why?"

Velander tensed, pressed her lips together, then suddenly relaxed so much that Andry thought she was going to collapse. She drew breath for a long moment, as if she was also trying to draw courage out of the air as well.

"Because I love you," she finally whispered.

Andry was aware of a door opening, and feet tramping on straw, then suddenly becoming very, very still. *Audience or not, I cannot escape this moment*, he thought as he tried to draw Velander closer. It was suddenly like trying to move a bronze statue that had been bolted to the floor. His fingers stroked her hair, which was wet and cold.

"Am hearing other reccons," she whispered.

"What of them?" Andry whispered back.

No stink, thought Andry. *Soap, scent, chewed mint leaves on her breath . . .* His lips pressed against hers, and her lips were not just cold, they absorbed heat. He felt the hardness of etheric fangs beneath the flesh; thin tendrils of his life force were being drawn off from his lips into hers. He drew back, but slowly, so as not to humiliate Velander in front of the reccons. The tendrils stretched taut, flickered, then snapped. His lips stung, then quickly became numb.

Velander turned in the direction of Andry's astonished reccons.

"Can never know how much is brave, fine man," she said softly.

"Begging pardon, ladyship, but I think we do," said Essen.

"Now especially," added Costiger.

Velander turned back to Andry, drew him so close that her fangs brushed his ear, then whispered.

"Going now. Going to hell fires. Think on me."

"Love you," Andry heard himself say.

She turned, groped at the cart, then tried to climb into it. She failed.

"Please Andry, help," she said softly.

Andry clasped his hands beneath one of her feet, then hoisted her up. Velander slithered into the cart and under the tarpaulin covering the tray without another sound. Andry collapsed. His reccons dashed forward.

"Andry, sir, are you alive?" demanded Danol.

"Feel drained," managed Andry.

"Girls do that to a fella," said Costiger.

"Need sleep," said Andry, who then fell soundly asleep against the cart's wheel, and had to be carried to his bunk.

Half an hour after they had all gone, Terikel slipped from the shadows not far from the cart and left the stables as silently as years of practice might allow. She did not allow her sobs to escape until she was well away, but there had been tears on her face for quite some time.

Laron entered the King's Pleasure, called for a tankard of wine, and drank a third of it, having flipped the payment through the air and into the serving maid's cleavage. She gave a squeal of surprise, drew back, then stopped. He was a captain in the Imperial Highways Militia, after all, and he looked very young. The maid knew that there had been a ball that night, and suspected that some assignation might not have gone quite to plan.

"Unlucky in love, lordship?" she asked, advancing to stand by the table.

"Not at all, young lady," replied Laron, who then drained another third of the tankard.

"Then what is your sorrow?"

"My sorrow?" laughed Laron, balancing the now empty tankard on his head. "My sorrow is that my best and only friend in all the world is lost to me."

"Dead?"

"Oh yes."

"Ah, I am so sorry. Lost in battle?"

"One might say so."

"Poor young warrior," she said as she ran her fingers through his hair.

Captain Gilvray did not allow himself the luxury of retiring to his rooms until all of the company that he rode with were not only out of the ballroom, but back in their rooms, suites, and barracks on the other side of the palace complex. The Registers of Movement had the complete story, and they took a quarter hour to check. The entry next to Laron was annotated by / ACCOMPANIED / WOMAN / SERVANT / EXTERNAL/. Gilvray smiled grimly. *At least someone is getting over Senterri*, he thought. At last he opened the door to his suite, entered cautiously with his candle, glanced about for intruders, then closed the door and bolted it. He turned to see Terikel standing before him.

"How did you get in here!" exclaimed Gilvray. "Where were you?"

"I'm a bloody sorceress," said Terikel with something like impatience, letting that stand as her explanation.

"If the princess finds out, I shall lose all honor in her eyes."

"Unlikely. There are castings in the corridor, castings configured to let you through, but to cause unease and foreboding in anyone else."

There was a lengthy pause during which neither of them moved. "Well?" asked Terikel.

"Well?" echoed Gilvray.

"Should you not ask why I am here?"

"All right, why?"

"I want safe passage to Alpenfast. Safe passage *anywhere* has been somewhat hard to come by lately, especially for me."

Gilvray walked to the bed, set his candle in the stand, and began removing his boots.

"Why come to me? I have been hard-pressed to provide even Princess Senterri with safe passage of late, and that has been with the entire Journey Guard at my call."

"You are also of Alpennien descent, and Alpenfast is just over the Alpennien border, near Karunsel. Senterri is to spend three days in Karunsel, because it is the first large city she will visit in her new territories. Three days, Captain Gilvray. You can ride to Alpenfast with me, see me safe within the walls, and be back in Karunsel in time to lead Senterri and the Journey Guard out on schedule."

"Riding day and night, not sleeping, changing to fresh mounts at every town . . . it can be done. But why just me?"

"Do not play the innocent with me, Captain. I research everyone that I deal with, and I researched you in considerable detail. I am a Metrologan priestess, remember? We like to know things. You are descended from an Alpennien noble, captured three generations ago, taken to Palion, but never ransomed. Another faction of your family took the estates and castellany, but your line kept the title. The Sargolan Empire actually recognizes your title, but the usurpers of the family lands swore fealty to the empire, so the empire is content to leave everyone with what they have."

"True," said Gilvray, leaning back against the bedhead. "If one side steps out of line, the other gets the empire's backing. I broke the cycle, I am making a new name for myself, and will get lands of my own granted in Capefang. I formally renounced my ancestral lands last month."

"And that caused great goodwill to flourish in the Alpennien castellanies. You have an invitation to visit whenever you will, so you could visit with me. You could pass me as your lover, and say you are showing me your former ancestral lands."

"That would be a difficult story to hawk about, ladyship. There is little privacy in the Journey Guard, and everyone is bored senseless and on the lookout for anything to gossip about. Were we lovers, it would have been noticed quickly."

Terikel sat down on the opposite end of the bed, raised a leg, and draped it over Gilvray's legs. His eyes widened, but he did not move otherwise.

"It would not be hard to give them something to gossip about, Captain, in fact it would be very agreeable for both of us."

"My lady . . . you are alluring and beautiful, but my heart is elsewhere—"

"And the princess knows it!" said Terikel firmly. "So does Viscount Cosseren, and so does Captain Laron. I have spoken with her, and she is agreeable to granting you a small castellany near Logiar *if* you are seen to be out of love with her. You have your title, you will soon have new lands. All that you need is a lover."

"She—the princess wants my heart to be elsewhere?" he whispered.

"Needs, not wants."

Gilvray put out a hand, lifted Terikel's foot, hesitated, then let it rest across his legs again. Terikel smiled, and it was a soft, broad, and genuinely inviting smile. She snapped her fingers, and the candle flame died.

"Your guard castings will make it hard for servants, gossips, and other busybodies to discover us," Gilvray pointed out as they ran their hands over each other in the darkness.

In reply Terikel breathed etheric tendrils into her hands, then began to fashion them into an auton. It took the form of a small, glowing dragon that lit up her face with blue light as she held it up and spoke a few words to it in a Torean language. At a word that might have been "Go!" it flapped up from her hands, flew to the door, clung to the wood for a moment, then dissolved through it. Darkness returned to the room with the auton gone. Gilvray began to remove the shoe from Terikel's foot.

"I feel like such a traitor," he said, idly running his fingers over her toes. "Senterri is the lordworld about which my life circles."

"But your liaison with me makes her life easier, Captain. You really are doing this for her."

"I still feel like a traitor. I have never, never betrayed my devotion to the princess."

"Good, a little guilt makes dalliance all the more intense, my dashing captain. Trust my word upon it."

The following morning Essen signed a ticket of leave for Hartman. Andry reported to the armorer, and was given a mail shirt, green trousers and jacket, a green surcoat with the royal crest, greaves, and a helmet with a very large dent. He dressed while the dent was being hammered out by the armorer's weaponsmith. To his relief, he was allowed to keep the gelding that he had been riding, rather than have to cope with a war stallion. Essen sewed the triple red stars of a marshal onto his jacket's shoulders.

"It's not right, just me having one of these, sir," said Andry to Essen, holding up his mail shirt. "All reccons should have one."

"Not worth a pinch of shyte, Andry. Ax blades and arrows go right through. Mail shirts only stop odd cuts."

"It's still wrong, sir."

"We need to ride fast. Heavy mail might well get a man killed."

Andry slid the mail shirt on, picked up an ax, and practiced a few blows against a pell.

"Heavy on the shoulders, but not a real burden."

"Like the cares of the world, Andry. How is your, er, girl?"

"Not well, sir."

"Love each other?"

"Aye."

"Then she's lucky, and so are you. Princess Senterri and Viscount Cosseren? No love there. I'm told she makes him roger her six times a night, then orders him out to sleep on the floor outside her room."

"Surely not, sir."

"Well, sometimes it's the ground outside her tent."

"On the ground outside is where I always sleep. I've no tent."

"During the ball, Andry, with that curly-haired one. Did you, like . . . ?"

"Nothing substantial, sir. I do have a sweetheart to be faithful to."

"Aye, so you do. She's ice cold, drinks blood, and is dead."

"But she needs me. She's blind, sick, and must sleep all day and night in the spare mess cart. They say that love is blind, Marshal Essen."

"Then a certain countess must also be in need of spectacles, Andry. Wallas is boasting to all who will listen how he bundled into a kitchen maid, in the respite rooms, but that it was all a trick to later slip into the next room where the countess was waiting."

"The only reason that nobody's yet ripped his hearts out is that they're too small to find, sir," muttered Andry. "So what's to do if all love is so hopeless?"

"Oh, not all love is hopeless. Captain Gilvray and the Elder have apparently shared a bed for the night past."

Andry gasped, swallowed, then clamped his teeth together until he thought he could speak with steady voice.

"Oh aye?" he replied. "Now there's a good and loving match. Both lacking sweethearts, yet fine and winsome people. May Fortune smile on them."

"Fancy a tune, lad?"

"Oh aye. Like to try the hornpipe? I'll do the rebec. 'The Flash Green Marshal,' sir?"

"I'm not so flash, lad. Say what, let's put a new tune together to honor the captain and his lady."

"Oh aye, we can call it 'Captain Gilvray's Fancy.' "

✶ ✶ ✶

When the squad set off the next day, Velander's body had been carefully concealed in the supplies cart that Wallas was still driving. There were five other supply wagons supporting the Journey Guards, and Senterri was in a new coach supplied by the local king. Wallas was becoming popular with the squad, because he was better at cooking a tasty meal with minimal ingredients and utensils than practically any other cook in the imperial service. Now that he had been flogged, he was also popular with the reccons and irregulars.

At each break to rest the horses, Andry was put through ax and lance practice, and when he was actually resting, both the marshal and Laron continued his education in protocols and etiquettes. Wallas helped with Andry's education as well, and in turn Andry began to teach Wallas the basics of riding. Wallas also spent a great deal of his time complaining, however, which tended to hinder the lessons.

"Got five lashes, I did," Wallas said as Andry led a horse that Wallas was riding in a circle around the Journey Guards' perimeter. They had paused while Senterri met with some provincial official who had a petition for her.

"If you had five lashes for every time you've talked about it, you'd have had five thousand lashes by now," said Andry.

"It *feels* like five thousand."

"Wallas, will you let it rest? I've had fifty lashes, but I don't whine."

"Yes, but I was innocent!"

"That makes it hurt more?"

"Yes!"

"Cheer up, women will admire you for being tough."

"Tough? With five measly lashes?"

"I can arrange—"

"No!"

"Wallas, just what did you tell the countess about us?"

"Ah, the countess, I thought you'd never ask. The gates of paradise were open beneath her skirts, she wore no undergarments at all—it's all the fashion in Glasbury at the moment."

I too had occasion to find that out, thought Andry, but he merely nodded and smiled.

"Ah Andry, her husband is past it, she said, and the thought of lying with a hero of the flight from Clovessen filled her with such a head of passion that she—"

"I said what did you tell her, not what was she like!"

"Oh, just sweet nothings, and mere embroideries around the edges of the rather plain truths."

"Perhaps that you are a courtier in disguise, and that this trip is not what it seems, and that the Dragonwall and ringstones are involved, and that you are on a mission to avenge the emperor's murder, and that Senterri is going to do far more than merely assume the regency of Logiar, and that the empire will be shaken to its very foundations because she will establish Logiar as the new hub of power in the south, and—"

"You were listening!"

"I'd not bother, you're as predictable as the sunrise, but not nearly as pretty. Wallas, do you realize that if she believes even a tenth of the rubbish that you plied her with, it could touch off a moderately large war?"

"What! Never! Who would take her seriously?"

"Prince Valios, the third in line to the imperial throne of Sargol, to begin with! The countess is one of his most trusted spies."

Wallas opened his mouth to reply, then left it open as his mind began to process a very large number of possible consequences from his banter of two nights earlier. The horse plodded on, led by Andry. The reins were limp in Wallas's hands. His mouth remained open. A fly cruised in. Wallas closed his mouth, spluttered, then spat out the fly.

"If you are lucky, the countess may have merely wanted a quick tumble with a pretentious dolt," said Andry presently.

"I say, if she is so well known as a spy, she might have thought I was trying to slip her false information," Wallas suggested hopefully. "Why, she probably ignored everything I said."

"And if she believed it, then—as the Elder Terikel once said to us—the consequences do not bear contemplation."

The squad traveled the seventy miles to the border of Fertellian and Capefang in a single day of truly arduous riding, then the pace became quite relaxed. Senterri was making a point of meeting with as many of the local nobles as possible, and of being seen by everybody. Capefang was the southernmost region of the empire. The eastern half was fertile plains and forests, crammed with towns, farms, and castles, and scrawled over with roads. The west was mountains, and very little else. Logiar was the capital, and was on the southwestern corner of the continent. Logiar was also so remote that it had never fallen to an invader. The journey there was far too difficult and depressing for most armies, and the locals could be very unpleasant if one got on their bad side. Senterri was going out of her way to win her new province over with charm, but the task was not difficult. A member of the royal family had not traveled that road in over a century, and that particular prince had been at the head of an army, and had left fifty thousand dead in his wake. He had then led his men into the mountains to attack some minor warlord . . . and was never heard of again.

The Dragonwall was only a hundred miles away now, an orange swath in the blue of the day's sky, and an unending glow of unnatural sunset by night. Velander spent all of her time in the cart, but people were so relieved to have her quiet and out of sight that nobody checked her closely. Besides, investigating Velander was a good way to become dinner. Some said that she was ill, and starving. Most hoped that it was true.

Some reports did have to be investigated, however. The followers of a bandit chief were found trying to cram themselves into the lockup of the local garrison. Senterri and her nobles were told that a giant dragon a hundred feet high had swallowed the bandit whole. Terikel was sent to investigate,

under the escort of the reccons, and she found that the terrified outlaws had been exaggerating.

"The five-foot-long tracks and broken branches on some
trees indicated that the dragon was only twenty-nine feet
high," she reported to Senterri, Laron, and Gilvray.

"Twenty-nine feet," said Laron, to fix the figure in his
mind.

"Ah, yes. And sketches made from descriptions by those
who saw it indicate that it had a seven-foot beak, small stubby
wings, and a long neck. I have them here, on reedpaper."

The sketches were passed around. As Terikel expected,
the princess and her two captains looked more bewildered
than terrified as they examined the sketches.

"It looks like something drawn by a person who was
never very good at doing dragons at school," said Gilvray.

Five Journey Guards and Essen were sent to follow its
trail, but they proceeded no farther than a pile of droppings.
What they at first assumed to be giant turds turned out to be
three mummified bodies that crumbled when touched. At this
point the reccon refused to track it any farther. It was not as
if the trail was particularly hard to follow, but Essen's refusal
to continue seemed as good a reason as any to turn back.

"You never saw bodies like those," said the badly shaken
Essen to Andry and the other reccons after he had delivered
his account to Gilvray. "They had the look of absolute horror
on their faces."

"Suppose I'd look a bit upset if I was forced to look at a
giant bird's arse from the inside," said Danol.

"They say creatures like that are being driven out of the
mountains by Dragonwall," said Sander. "Tavern wench I
chatted up last night said animals with etheric talents don't
like it."

"Why not?" asked Andry.

"She said it make 'em release all their etheric energies at
once, sir. They goes pop, just like when hit by lightning."

"Did she see it happen?"

"Well no, but she's also professionally involved with the
entertainment of lonely male travelers, and one of 'em was a
sorcerer's level-six assistant last week. He said his master
stood almost directly beneath the curtain of castings from

the sky. He cast an auton around a rat and tossed it through Dragonwall. It exploded."

"A casting did that?"

"More like the casting and the rat together. Everyone watching got spatters of muck on 'em."

"An exploding rat? What about the sorcerer?"

"No problem, he said. It's only active castings as go pop. A sorcerer can walk through the curtain of ether with no effect. Try to fly a bird through with an auton casting controlling it, and you get charred feathers and roast bird spread over a very wide area. An uncast bird could fly right through, he said. Then he walked into it himself."

"Don't tell me," said Andry. "The assistant, level six in initiate rating, got an even larger laundry bill?"

"Er, the sorcerer's assistant was standing at quite a distance for the second demonstration. Apparently the annual goblin migration through the mountains got called off after that. They had an envoy there, watching."

Chapter Six

DRAGONSCHOOL

On the fifth day after leaving Glasbury, the Journey Guards came in sight of the Capefang Mountains. They were a young and jagged range, all pointed peaks and sharp ridges, and with practically no gentle, rounded slopes. There was a lot of snow visible, and the wind from the west had a sharp chill on it. Behind the mountains was the orange immensity of the Dragonwall wind curtain, crowned by the mighty rainbow.

They had been traveling on the main road southwest when they encountered a local militia unit gathered around five dark brown, vaguely cylindrical things beside the road. Two of them were a cow and her calf, but three of them looked as if they were wearing clothes. Gilvray stopped his horse and leaned over to speak with the militiamen's leader while Essen, Andry, and Terikel inspected the bodies. Essen began to sing softly.

> "There were an old lady,
> She swallered a cow,
> I don't know how
> She swallered a cow . . ."

"A seven-foot beak might have made the job easier," said Terikel, prodding at a crumbling body with a stick.

Gilvray came over with the elderly leader of the militia, and the man waved his ax in the direction of one of the bodies.

"That there's Blondarian the Ravisher," he explained. "Ye can tell by the blond hair. 'Cept it's sort of brownish now. Wanted in these parts for robbery and ravishin', was he. Earn'd a crust by highway robbery, like, but preferred ravishin'."

"So these two others are his men?" asked Captain Gilvray.

"Ah, er, not easy ter say, but it's likely. There was a fourth, but we caught 'im last month, and the magistrate had 'im taken out and 'anged fer, er, ravishin'."

"This dragon bird is bigger than the one further north," said Terikel, checking some figures that she had written on reedpaper. "The tracks are over six feet long."

"How many of them are there, I wonder?"

"At least three, by my measurements. They seem to hunt by night, and eat only what is out in the open. That includes cows, calves, sheep, shepherds, bandit warlords on nocturnal raids, and highwaymen in search of late-night travelers."

❋ ❋ ❋

Andry got to see a lot of the three commanding nobles of the Journey Guard, because of being the liaison with the reccons. He noted definite tensions between Senterri and Cosseren, but also between Captain Gilvray and Laron. The two captains always rode flanking Princess Senterri's coach, but they never spoke to each other if they could help it. *Jealous of Terikel*, Andry surmised. Laron had apparently never had any dalliance with Terikel, but it was now obvious that he had probably indulged in fantasies that featured her. Cosseren always rode in front of the coach, yet the princess spent most of her time gazing through the little rear window. Cosseren liked to lead, and to be seen to lead, so that he generally looked happy until they had to stop. Senterri just looked unhappy all the time.

On the eighth evening out of Glasbury, Andry had retired soon after sunset, and was lying on his groundsheet, beneath a blanket that had once covered a bed in Madame Jilli's Recreational Rooming. Velander slipped from the tray of the cart, and her groping hands found Andry lying on his blanket between the wheels.

"Frilly edging?" she remarked. "For soldier's blanket, odd."

"A present from Madame Jilli of Palion, for saving Terikel," laughed Andry sleepily. "It's very warm."

"Andry, are alone?"

"Nobody is nearby," replied Andry.

"Good. Now, telling you, er . . . not much lover, I am. Cold blood, sick, dead, blind. Every day, weaker. Look, in mouth. Fangs fading, almost gone. Claws too. One day, be dust pile. In dust pile, circlet, with green stone. If you are being near, take out stone, smash with back of ax."

"I've been speaking with Laron, he also wears such a circlet. He said—"

"Contains soul. If smashed, soul gone."

"Velander!"

"Promise?"

"So you truly want it to all end."

"Yes. By your hand."

Velander without sarcasm was not quite Velander, but Andry liked the change. The trouble was that she seemed constantly in pain, and was definitely weakening. There had been no stories of horrifying murders in Glasbury, no throats torn out, no bloodless bodies sprawled in the streets. The evidence all pointed to starvation as Velander's affliction.

"Is more," declared Velander, putting out a hand to him. He took it in his, and it was both icy cold and limp. "Love you, but . . . if nice girl says, er, fancy you, be saying yes."

"Velander! No—"

"Listen! Like am saying already, not much lover, I am. But love you. Sexing nice, is, am led to believe."

"Oh aye, folk have told me as much, too."

"Then doing it with girl, for me! Am not jealous. Hate jealous."

"I think you mean jealousy, you're confusing things that Terikel calls nouns and adjectives."

"Jealousy, being, ruin of life, mine, was."

Even Andry knew that no reply was appropriate under the circumstances.

"Velander?"

"Yes?"

"Lie out beside me."

"But—Andry, what doing?"

"Covering us with the blanket."

"No! No sexings. Er, am losing control, I am, if doing. Kill you."

"I suspected so, but lying in each other's arms with our clothes on and just sleeping may be safe."

"Oh, er . . . am having no words," Velander admitted, very moved.

They lay quietly for a time, Velander with her head on Andry's chest, listening to the syncopated double echo of his hearts beating. Presently she unlaced her tunic, took his hand, and guided it onto a soft, smooth, but extremely cold breast.

"Not much, but all to offer, safely," she explained. "Problems, problems, always damn problems!"

"Everyone has problems," replied Andry. "We have love, too."

"True. Others, many problems, but no love."

"I notice that Laron and the other captain do not speak to each other," remarked Andry.

"Captains adoring princess. Viscount sexing with princess. Sometimes. Captains have hurt feelings."

"Er, how does Princess Senterri feel about them?" asked Andry, who was suddenly so far out of his depth that he felt like a mouse dropped into a well.

"Seduced Laron, she did. Rescued her, when she was, ah, captive—no, slave. Was grateful, she was."

"Understandable."

"Tried to love Laron, did princess. Myself also, did try but . . . not happen."

"But—but he seems to have everything! Good looks, manners, money, rank!"

"Laron is . . . damn! What is word for old man, annoyed all the time?"

"Crotchety."

"Yes!"

"But Laron is only fifteen."

"Laron is seven hundred years old."

"He told me that story too, and I don't believe it."

"Is true. Senterri, nice girl, young, pretty. But . . . no sense."

"Truly? I thought princesses were all very wise."

"Hah! Good-hearted, but out of depth in birdbath, is expression. Few men notice. Less care. Laron, been everywhere, done everything. Of world, very tired. With her, with me, not patient. World-weary. Like old, old man."

"I suppose it makes sense," said Andry after considering this. "It's hard to tell Laron anything, he is always right."

"Only young people, can believe in love, Andry. You, me, are being young. Laron, is not. Andry, wish saying personal thing. Ask you, being discreet. Please."

"I promise."

"First despise you. Then tolerate you. Then admire you. In thirty days, you are going from smelly, drunk sailor to crest from princess, kavelar. Drinking, hardly do. For me. Andry, your example, do I follow. Look into soul, of mine, see evil. See weak fool. Ashamed, of me, I am. Laron, has give up, with me. Senterri thinking, Velander weak, stupid, not to bother with. Letting myself, er, what is expression? Go down slippery slope. Not wash, dirty clothes, hunting drunks. Now, with you doing something."

"But you're starving yourself."

"Can feed on animals. But even that, no. Now question. Coach burned, only reccons left, and cornered. You attacking glass dragon, for to save reccons, commoners. Then you come for me, dirty, drunk fiend."

"It was my duty—"

"Testicles!"

"I think you mean *balls*."

"Yes, *balls*! Real reason?"

Andry paused to think. He had his reasons, it was just that he had never paused to think upon them before. As he slowly assembled his story in his mind, he noticed that Velander's right breast was making his hand numb with cold.

"Well . . . I was in Alberin's riverside bargeyards, once, working on a crane scaffold. Down below I saw a docker turn his bullhound loose on a mother cat that was cornered with her kittens. By the time I'd got down, the cat and kittens were all dead. She could have escaped, being a cat, like, but she stood her ground. I killed the hound with a finishing hatchet, then I fought the docker. I smashed his elbow, so he could never work again as a docker. Then I made him eat his hound. Raw. All at one sitting. Now he mops floors at the Ship's Worm, and looks nobody in the face. When I squared up with the glass dragon, I became that mother cat, if you get my meaning."

"Ah. So you are cat person?"

"I—uh, yes, now that you mention it."

"Am also."

"So, we have lots in common," laughed Andry. "I'd ask you to marry me, but you'd have to promise not to bring up the children as daemons."

"Promise, I do," said Velander simply.

There was silence that stretched to cover many minutes. *Even someone good with words would be thinking hard to reply to that*, thought Andry.

"Andry, have everything. Handsome man, lying with me, asks marriage. Am loved, and love. Is all can want. Now want stopping. Evil. Ashamed. Still killer, in dreams. Every day, getting worse."

"Velander, if there is something I can do, tell me."

"All that can do, are doing."

Gilvray and Terikel vanished almost as soon as the Journey Guard arrived in Karunsel. This was not good diplomacy, as there was going to be a ball on the second night to celebrate Senterri arriving in her new domain. Senterri appointed Laron to command the Journey Guard in Gilvray's absence, which was calculated to annoy Gilvray when he returned. This it certainly did, but Gilvray took it as punishment for his affair with Terikel, and made no outburst. Because they had not recently done anything heroic, neither the guardsmen, reccons, nor militiamen were invited to the ball. Laron was the exception, being the most senior officer present, but he merely attended without a partner, spoke politely to whoever spoke to him, declined all offers to dance, and left early.

The morning after the ball, Andry and Wallas took the cart to one of the Karunsel markets to buy supplies for the last leg of the trip. By now Wallas's skills as a cook had been recognized all the way up the chain of command to Senterri, and he had quite a long list of supplies to purchase, plus the silver to pay.

"Good oil, you can never have enough Karunsel oil," Wallas said as he loaded the sixth large jar aboard the cart.

"Especially if you're going to be boiled in it for unloading secrets to a notorious spy," responded Andry.

"Will you shut up about that? What else? Lamp oil, mixed with essence of crushed minderic."

"Lamp oil and minderic?"

"It keeps the mosquitos away when burned at open air dinners, and it has a very pleasant scent. The princess asked for it especially."

Wallas vanished back into the market's crowds, leaving Andry to watch over the cart. Several suspicious-looking characters were lurking nearby, and Andry noticed how they looked away when he glanced in the direction of any of them. He found himself glancing about almost continually,

and began to regret not bringing Costiger to keep watch
back-to-back with him.

"Brother Tennoner!"

Andry had been glancing about so much in search of
suspicious characters trying to look innocent that he had
failed to notice the approach of four genuinely innocent
characters—even though one was wearing heavily tinted
spectacles and had a hand over his mouth almost constantly.

"Wilbar, just the lad I want to see!" he exclaimed. "Hurry,
up into the cart, sit back-to-back with me, and watch for
riffraff."

Wilbar climbed up, and those who had been circling the
cart discreetly now became genuinely uninterested in it.

"Brother, we heard the princess was coming, and we were
hoping you would be with her," explained Wilbar.

"And Elder Terikel," called Maeber, hopping on the spot
and waving his arm as if he were seeking permission to dash
off and find a privy.

"We're out of money," said Riellen bluntly, and Andry
glanced down to see that she was dressed as a boy, and had
even cut her hair to shoulder length. "We were wondering if
the Elder could get us permission to travel to Logiar with the
Journey Guards."

"What?" exclaimed Andry. "A student revolutionary
group travel in the entourage of the fifth in line to the empire's throne?"

"It's not royalty we oppose, it's the sorceric establishment," explained Allaine.

"Well, we oppose that more than we oppose royalty,"
added Riellen.

"We would defend her!" cried Maeber, waving a knife
that was about a third of his height.

"Are you sure you're not of a mind to do something weird
with the ringstone near Logiar?" asked Andry suspiciously.

"We want to enroll in the academy in Logiar," said
Wilbar. "Brother Maeber says we can all stay with his parents. They live there."

"Look here, I have no power to let you do anything, and
Lady Terikel rode out with Captain Gilvray two nights ago. I

can speak to the acting captain, but if he says no, there's an end of it."

Three hours later the marketing had been done, with the enthusiastic help of the students. Wallas was delighted to again have people to order about, and was all in favor of having the students travel with them, but then Wallas was as low on the chain of command as it was possible to be. Andry led Wallas and the students up to the room in the palace guest wing where Laron was staying.

"Opulent luxury that is wrought by the oppression of the toiling peasantry," muttered Wilbar as they ascended a polished wood staircase that spiraled up around an exquisitely tiled floor depicting the mythical casting of the first glass dragon.

"And gross distortions of historical fact," hissed Riellen.

"Enough of that!" snapped Andry with a finger to his lips. "If you want royal favor, you behave politely to royals."

They turned off into a wide, carpeted corridor, then stopped at the door with Laron's crest plate hanging on a gold hook. With his hand poised to knock, Andry heard angry voices from within.

"I shall still be within the Guard!" insisted an angry female voice in Diomedan.

"We travel by the rules, and we maximize security!" Laron shouted back. "In matters of security, the judgment of the Journey Guard's commander prevails."

"I can appoint a new commander!"

"Do so—Your Highness."

There was a pause so pregnant that a midwife should have been in attendance. Andry's hand seemed to knock of its own volition.

"Enter!" called Laron at once, obviously eager for a distraction. Andry depressed the brass latch and pushed the door wide open. Laron, the princess, and one of her servants were standing in a line, spaced evenly, and all facing him. "Come in, come in, we don't stand on ceremony here, we just stand all in line," said Laron a trifle loudly. "Andry, you have met Her Royal Highness the princess, but perhaps not her lady-in-waiting. May I present the most excellent Dolvienne, holder of the title Defender of the Royal Chamber, and quite probably the next commander of the Journey Guard. How can I help you?"

Andry found himself wringing his hands in an overtly servile fashion. He gripped his hands together very tightly as he bowed to the princess, offered a prayer to the god of the River Alber that the students behind him had had the sense to bow as well, then straightened.

"Sir, pleased to report that volunteers have been located to assist Militiaman Third Class Wallas Baker with the preparation of royal food on the journey, sir!"

"Students?" said Laron softly.

"Aye, sir! That is, yes. Sir."

"Not militia?"

"No, sir."

"The Journey Guard is a military squad, Reccon Tennoner. Only escortees and enlisted warriors of the emperor may travel with it."

Andry noticed that Princess Senterri was staring intently in his direction, but not directly at him. *Oh no, she's recognized Wallas,* thought Andry. *I wonder how long we'll take to die in boiling olive oil?*

"Sir!" barked Andry. "I explained this to Wallas, Third Class Baker—that is, er, in the militia, sir!"

"The answer is no. You are dismissed."

"Wait!" called Senterri, who was still peering past Andry. "You four, were you the students who helped my reccons flee Clovessen?"

"Oh yes, Your Most Gracious and Wise Highness," said Wilbar behind Andry.

"Oh well then, my apologies, I have not yet seen my way clear to reward you. What is it that you desire? A gold crown each, my written recommendation to the court of the duke of Karunsel? Perhaps something else?"

"Er, leave to work our way to Logiar with your entourage, Most Just and Enlightened Highness," responded Wilbar.

"Is that all? Of course you may travel with me, and as my guest escortees. Should you wish to assist my most skilled militiaman cook, I am sure you will also be rewarded by learning some wonderful cookery techniques. Is all of that in order, Captain Aliasar?"

"Perfectly so, Your Highness," responded Laron without a trace of emotion.

Once they were outside Laron's suite, Senterri silently beckoned the group to follow her. She led them to the royal visitors' suite, ushered them in, and closed the door. Taking Allaine by the arm, she walked over to the floor-length mirror. Andry noticed that the youth was almost identical to her in height, although adding her breasts and hips to his skeletal frame would have doubled his weight. His hair was indistinguishable from her own vividly brunette tresses, except that it came down only as far as his shoulders, and had not been washed since before he had fled Clovessen.

"I am thinking of having you cut my hair, Dolvienne," she said slowly. "Young man, your name is?"

"Allaine Allec—"

"Highness, permission to be dismissed with Third Class Man, er, Militia Wallas Baker," Andry babbled, desperate to get what was probably the empire's most notorious gossip and security risk out of her room. "The fourth supplies cart needs to be packed for tomorrow's departure."

"Baker, go. Tennoner, you stay."

With Wallas gone, Senterri addressed the group, her arm linked in Dolvienne's.

"Allaine, you will bathe yourself thoroughly, then Dolvienne will wash your hair as if it were mine, and will brush and perfume it until it is in no wise different to mine. You will then dress in some of my less flattering, voluminous robes, and Dolvienne will school you in walking with my gait and gestures. I am in a sour mood with every noble in my entourage, Dolvienne excepted, and I have a wish to spend time amid better company on the supplies wagons. Some of the finest people I have met have been commoners. Sometimes I wonder whether being of the nobility poisons the soul. . . . But enough philosophy. Allaine, be as me, and you can earn the right of all your friends to travel under my protection. Are you agreeable?"

"Yes, Your Highness," replied Allaine at once.

"Splendid. In return you will have a pleasant fortnight chattering to the most lovely Dolvienne of this and that in the luxury of the new royal coach. Now all of you go, except for Allaine."

Nobody spoke until they were again on the great spiral staircase.

"Most Wise and Gracious Highness?" said Riellen as they descended.

"She is a princess of the people!" insisted Wilbar. "She said it herself, she returns to the people to renew the purity of her—"

"Most Just and Enlightened Highness?" interjected Riellen.

"Stop it, both of you!" hissed Andry. "Your fare to Logiar is Princess Senterri's whim. If her whim is to exchange name, clothes, and, and, and—"

"Gender?" prompted Maeben, waving his hand.

"Aye, gender with Allaine, then that is her use for you until you are within the city walls of Logiar. Until then, no bickering—and shut up unless spoken to!"

* * *

Karunsel was on the edge of the low but steep foothills of the Capefang Mountains, and the views were spectacular as the Journey Guard rode through the city gates to the genuinely heartfelt cheers of the local people. Senterri was, as usual, wearing a scarf that kept the sun off her sensitive skin, but her distinctive brunette hair was visible. She waved graciously all the way to the hovels that were spread out beyond the city walls.

Gilvray had arrived back that morning, and although he looked very tired, he reassumed command of the Journey Guard. Terikel had decided to stay with the sorcerers and priests of Alpenfast, he announced curtly, and Laron put a hand to his mouth to hide his smile. The reccons were sent ahead as usual, with the tent wagon and what Wallas had termed the gourmet cart. When the princess was to camp in the open, they were to travel a half mile ahead of the Journey Guard and royal coach, set up camp at a prearranged place, and have tents, field bunks, canopies, and a meal waiting by the time the royal coach caught up. Within the coach, Allaine was waving to Senterri's subjects while conducting a conversation with Dolvienne.

"And then Riellen and I split from the Clovesser Sorcerers' Liberation Collective and formed the Popularist Movement for the Liberation of Sorceric Knowledge, but after a month we had recruited no new followers, so we amalgamated with the New Student Alliance for Applied Popularist Theory—which had three members—and formed the Clovesser Sorceric Conspiracies and Occult Plots Exposure Collective."

"You must be very clever, remembering all those complicated names," observed Dolvienne.

"Er, I—that is—you're flattering me!" said Allaine indignantly.

"That is considered to be courteous convention in courtly circles. Someone of my station must—"

"No, no, no, your station is a fabrication of the establishment."

"It is what?"

"You should speak your true opinion to me."

"*My* opinion? Who cares for my opinion?"

"Your opinion is as important as mine, that of the princess, the Elder, or the reccon delegate, and, er . . . who is the lowest in class status—that is, class as defined by the establishment?"

"Militiaman Wallas Baker."

"Oh, yes, his opinion, too. And what is your opinion, Lady Dolvienne?"

"My opinion? About what?"

"Oh, er, what were we talking about—oh, yes, your opinion of me when you're not trying to flatter me?"

"I think you are indeed clever, and very well intentioned."

"Er . . . oh. Thank you."

"And very naive. Your talk is pure treason, and has the intent of destroying the imperial monarchy. I could report you and have you hanged—"

"No, no, no, no, the royal house has a place, as a symbol of the empire, but true power should reside with popularist opinion."

"What opinion?"

"Popularist opinion. The opinion of those elected by the people."

"Which people?"

"All people!"

"Even peasants?"

"Oh yes."

"Madness! Peasants are ignorant."

"So are all nobles and rulers wise?"

Dolvienne thought briefly of the princess before answering. "Some more than others. But *all* peasants are ignorant."

"Am I ignorant?"

"Oh no," said Dolvienne earnestly. "You could be a gentleman. Maybe a kavelar, if you learn to fight."

"My father was a blacksmith, my mother did laundry at the riverside."

"Indeed? Then you are half an artisan and half a peasant. Perhaps you could only be a marshal, shouting at peasants. Marshal Allaine, it has a fine sound to it."

"No! Anyone can be anything! Merit and popularist opinion should decide. Ladyship, you could be a—a princess."

"Preposterous! I have no talent for rule."

"Less talent than your princess?"

Dolvienne stopped to consider this. Nobody had ever credited her with talent to lead, yet the princess nearly always asked her opinion—and when she did not follow Dolvienne's advice, embarrassment, misfortune, disaster, and even catastrophe had followed.

"Tell me more," said Dolvienne.

"I have some pamphlets, here, under my skirts, all written by my own hand," said Allaine as he drew up the layers of cloth, frills, and flounces and fumbled for his selected pamphlets.

"Oh, interesting."

"You haven't read them yet."

"I mean you have nice legs."

✳ ✳ ✳

"This is the edge of the secure territory," said Gilvray as he rode through the gates of Karunsel with Cosseren and Laron flanking him. "Before us is the floodplain of the Racewater River, and sixty miles away is Fort Misery."

"It's actually quite a pleasant place," said Viscount Cosseren, "but travelers are so depressed by the time they reach it that they named it . . ."

His voice trailed away under the influence of the unsmiling faces trained on him.

"For sixty miles we are totally in the open, with no cover at all," Gilvray went on. "The Racewater River borders the west, with steep foothills hard by it. There is a bridge over the Racewater. The river marks the border of the Alpennien protectorate, which is the least stable of the empire's lands. Ignore that turning, and go straight, and we end up in Logiar. My thought is to get to the fort tomorrow night, and to stay there to rest for a day. The road is hard and cold from here to Fort Misery, and we must spend one night camped beside it."

"My wife's written wish is . . ." Cosseren unfolded a square of reedpaper and squinted at at it. "To pay compliments at the fort and take tea with the commander, then ride on to the city of Olvermay and meet with the earl of, er, Olvermay. I approve of this."

"*Intelligence* reports from the garrison commander at Karunsel suggest that three or four Alpennien brigades are in the area," said Laron.

"Are you questioning my intelligence, sir?" demanded Cosseren indignantly.

"The level of your intelligence is beyond question, my lord," replied Laron.

Cosseren frowned, trying to determine whether he had been insulted or not. Gilvray cleared his throat.

"My mission to take Elder Terikel to Alpenfast prevented me from reading the disposition and intelligence reports, Captain Laron," said Gilvray. "I must rely on your judgment to determine whether the way ahead is safe for the princess.

Otherwise we should call a halt and return to the gates of Karunsel while they are only yards behind us, rather than miles."

"For that I must rely upon you, sir," replied Laron.

"Me, Captain Laron?"

"You, Captain Gilvray. You traveled fifty miles into Alpennien territory, along the main road to their United Castellanies heartland. Were three or four brigades in the area, you would have seen them. Did you see any signs of large numbers of highly trained cavalry with warlike intentions, moving in this direction?"

"I did not, sir."

"In that case, sir, we may proceed in safety. Despatch riders from Logiar report nothing unusual, so the road ahead is clear. You report that there are no Alpennien brigades lurking, ready to dash across the Racewater Bridge and effect an abduction once we are too far from Karunsel to get back without being cut off."

". . . the level of my intelligence is beyond question," muttered Cosseren, who had not been listening. "I say, Captain Aliasar, were you referring to the level of my intelligence or those who might question it?"

"Honor and humiliation mean a lot to the mountain people," said Laron to Gilvray, ignoring the viscount. "Humiliate a member of the Sargolan ruling family, and one gains honor. Gain honor, and the mountain provinces may unite behind one. United, they could block off every mountain road from Baalder to Logiar, and charge tolls. That would either trigger a war, or split the empire."

"Which of those would you like, Viscount?" asked Gilvray.

"Er, none, actually," said Cosseren at once.

"Senterri was abducted and made a slave, once," Laron continued. "For that, some warlords think her weak. Should she be taken again, they would *know* her to be weak."

"That will not happen, of course," said Gilvray firmly.

✦ ✦ ✦

Far ahead, in the gourmet cart, Senterri and Riellen were sitting together on the supplies in the tray, while Maeben and

Wilbar sat with Wallas. Wallas was listening to everything that was being said while keeping his face averted from the view of the princess. Unfortunately for Wallas, most of the talking was not being done by the princess.

"So although I am only rated as an initiate of the eighth level, in truth my skills go as high as the ninth," Riellen was saying to the princess. "Have you ever heard of the glass roof, Highness?"

"No, but I imagine the first big hailstorm would shatter it."

"The term is just an analogy, Highness. It means that there is an invisible barrier that stops women of talent rising too high in areas of venture dominated by men."

"It sounds like the Palion royal court," sighed Senterri, but another thought quickly distracted her. "Ah, but I wish I could rise like a bird, high above roofs of glass or tile. I want to look down on my new dominions."

"Your eyes can soar, Highness, even though your feet remain on the ground."

"Oh! How is that."

Riellen took off her thick spectacles and rubbed them on her sleeve.

"An auton bird casting, with an ocular binding."

"Er, what are those?"

The student sighed. Explaining anything complex to Senterri would take a long time, but a demonstration was worth several thousand words. She put her glasses back on and looked about for Andry, then called for him to ride over to the gourmet cart.

"Brother Tennoner, sir, the prin—that is, my revolutionary sister—"

"Brother!" prompted Senterri.

"My revolutionary brother wants me to cast a glamour over a bird, so that we can see through its eyes. Can you present me with a living bird?"

"I dare say that a reccon could do it. I'll speak with the marshal."

Andry rode over to the reccons and saluted Essen.

"Those crows that circle above us," said Andry, waving a hand at the sky. "Can one of the reccons bring one down alive for the, er, student in the gourmet cart? She wishes to do some tests with auton castings."

Essen took his cavalry crossbow from its sling, worked the lever to cock it, then took a padded bolt with spiral flights from his saddle's arming pouch and pressed it into the weapon's loading braces. He then brought it up to his shoulder and fired, seemingly without aiming. A stunned crow tumbled out of the sky.

"Fetch bird for the princess, lad, I'll get my birding bolt back," said Essen.

"Sir! How did you know about her?" exclaimed Andry.

"Reccon's vocation is to reconnoiter. That's folk as well as countryside."

Andry presented the stunned bird to Riellen, who spoke a casting that enmeshed the crow in what seemed to Andry to be a fine net of blue glow that sank beneath its feathers and vanished. She then attached casting tendrils to Senterri's closed eyes. Riellen did yet more castings that Andry did not really understand, then launched the bird into the air. It flapped vigorously, gaining height as it flew upward in a spiral. Neither Riellen nor Senterri moved. The crow became a dot, barely visible.

"I see the Journey Guards, spread out along the trail," squealed Senterri, delighted. "What a view! I see sheep grazing, some shepherd huts, and there is the city—my city! Wonderful! Oh but this plain flood thing is very plain and utterly boring. Fly my eyes over the Alpennien Mountrains, I want to see snow."

Riellen had to concentrate harder as the distance increased. There was silence for a time. All of Riellen's control other than speech and hearing was guiding the distant, englamoured crow.

"There's a bridge over a river, with lots of men riding over it," said Senterri. "It is a very fast-flowing river, and it's a long way down to it. What a big bridge! Three, no four riders can ride over abreast."

Riellen flew farther afield, noting that hundreds of cavalrymen were queued up and ready to cross the Racewater Bridge. She also noted that the cavalrymen were splitting into two columns, one going northeast to Karunsel, the other southeast to nowhere in particular.

"Something odd here," said Riellen, beginning to make the englamoured crow circle.

"Something boring here," retorted Senterri. "All those boring Alpenniens in their boring uniforms."

"Alpennien uniforms?" gasped Riellen.

"Oh yes, even I know about surcoat uniforms. The Karunsel warriors wear brilliant red, the Journey Guard has dark blue trimmed with red braid, and—"

"There must be hundreds, thousands!" exclaimed Riellen, flying the crow upward in search of a better overall view.

"They cannot threaten a hundred Journey Guards, girl," Wallas called back from the driver's seat. "They don't have the authority."

"But should they be there at all?"

"This is all too much!" exclaimed Wallas. "I'm not a soldier."

"Your pardon, your pardon!" cried Maeben, waving his arm in the air. "You're paid as a soldier, you're wearing a uniform, you took the oath of enlistment, so thus you must be—"

"Reccon Tennoner, you are needed here!" called Wallas.

Andry rode over to the gourmet cart, and was given a rather confused briefing by Wallas, Senterri, and the three students, all generally speaking at once. He called a halt and asked everyone but Riellen to remain silent while she described the scene at Racewater Bridge.

"Beyond the bridge, dozens and dozens of lancers!" she reported, her eyes still closed. "All drawn up along the road, four abreast. Hundreds have already crossed, and are still splitting into two groups. There's a building starting to burn."

"Are you sure they're lancers?" asked Andry.

"They're riding horses, wearing uniform surcoats and chain mail, and carrying long poles with pointy bits on the top. I estimate that hundreds have already passed over the Racewater, into Capefang territory. Perhaps five or six hundred in each of the two groups."

"But that's two *brigades*!" exclaimed Andry.

"I shall send a very serious complaint to the Alpennien castellans!" said Senterri firmly.

Senterri then made the mistake of opening her eyes. This broke her connection with the auton bird, and causing a small but intense flash before her own eyes which left her dazzled. Riellen maintained contact, her eyes firmly closed and her fingers to her forehead.

"There is a hawk, some distance below me, flying in quite a straight line for the Journey Guard and royal coach," said Riellen. "It may be a spy auton, like mine."

"How do I get the view back?" asked Senterri, but Riellen ignored her.

"By the look of it, the Alpenniens will soon have the royal coach cut off from Karunsel," Riellen reported.

"Bugger the royal coach, what about us?" cried Wallas.

"I'll have you know that your words amount to treason!" cried Senterri, still dazzled and not sure who had spoken.

"We are already lost," said Riellen. "We are too far ahead, we could never return in time. Er . . . the bridge is clear now, all the lancers are riding to outflank us to the north and south."

"*All* the lancers, miss?" asked Essen, who had ridden over, and had been quietly listening to everything.

"There's not a one left. They seem to have attacked the guardhouse near the bridge. It's on fire, and I see bodies on the ground."

"Where is the Alpenniens' auton hawk?"

"Just a moment . . . still flying north, in the direction of the Journey Guard and royal coach."

"Has it seen yours?"

"Hard to tell, probably not."

"Could you kill it?"

"Kill it?" gasped Riellen. "I don't even know how to fight as a person, let along a bird."

"Besides, hawks eat crows," said Maeben, waving his hand in the air.

"What would happen if you dived the crow very fast, and just smashed it into the hawk?" asked Essen.

"Er, much the same as if I were dropped onto you from a

great height. I'm not a warrior, you are, but neither of us would escape without broken bones, at best."

"Then dive your auton onto the hawk, now!"

"But sir, we'll lose our view of the Alpenniens," protested Andry.

"Aye, but we've already seen enough."

Gilvray, Laron, and Cosseren had already seen the approaching lancers by the time two dots in the sky above them collided in a bright flash, which then became a cloud of smoky feathers out of which two bodies dropped. The Journey Guard and royal coach had been halted a minute earlier, when the distant riders had first been noticed.

"There, dust to the south!" cried Gilvray. "Dust to the north and south. We can't run and we can't return to the city."

"I can see a brigade pennon," said Laron, holding a farsight to his eye.

"Very fast decision called for," Cosseren pointed out.

"Two brigades, then," said Gilvray. "Five hundred each, but only one coming in our direction. Viscount Cosseren, would you say that one Journey Guardsman is worth five lancers from anywhere else?"

"Oh indeed, Captain."

"Two to one, but only maybe!" interjected Laron.

"Then we turn and run for the city, riding as a wedge around the coach," Captain Gilvray decided. "The enemy will be thinly spread out, so we can smash through if they get in front of us, and get the princess safely to the gates." He turned his horse to face the squad and raised his ax. "Journey Guard, form a wedge, shield the royal coach. Paced by the coach, make for the city gates. Coachman, turn for the city and proceed at a gallop. Guardsman Calliar, sound the signal bugle. Form up!"

There was a brief flurry of intense activity, but the highly trained men and horses were rearranged and facing the city before Calliar had finished blowing the coded notes.

"Pacing up to the gallop, at my order, forward!" shouted Gilvray.

"What in all hell's levels is going on?" cried Dolvienne as she leaned out of the coach window. "We've turned back to the city!"

"Perchance someone forgot something?" suggested Allaine.

"This is a wedge formation!" cried Dolvienne, turning back to him.

"How can you tell? Just looks like a lot of horses to me."

"They think the princess is in this coach! But she's back behind us, half a mile or more. If we are running from danger, then Princess Senterri is in the thick if it!"

Allaine leaned out of the opposite window and looked back. He could see only dust.

"Nobody's chasing us, er, that I can see," he ventured.

"What are we running from?" Dolvienne called to nobody in particular. "Guardsmen! Guardsmen! Attend me!"

Nobody paid Dolvienne any attention. She began to climb out of the coach window.

"My lady, is that allowed?" called Allaine, but he thought the better of trying to stop her.

Dolvienne climbed the foot loops at the side of the coach, then hauled herself up into driver's bench.

"Coacher! What is the word?" she demanded.

"Orders to gallop for the city, my lady!" he cried.

"Why?"

"I don't question orders, ladyship."

"Surely you saw *something*! You ride higher than a mounted guardsman on this bench."

"Just dust to the west, ladyship."

"Dust? Just dust? Raised by what?"

"Couldn't see, ladyship."

Dolvienne considered the facts for a few moments. Dust, but nobody visible. So much dust raised by very distant riders could be raised only by a large number of distant horses.

Whoever they were, Senterri was half a mile behind and definitely not under the protection of the Journey Guard.

"Coacher, we must turn back, the princess is not in the coach!" Dolvienne shouted.

"Saw her get in, ladyship."

"Not so, she's in the gourmet cart."

"Ladyship, it's no time for girl's games. Now just you stay quiet and hold on."

Again Dolvienne considered the situation. Senterri was notorious for playing tricks on her guards, especially when she was bored. The trip had not been boring, but the guardsmen had gone out of their way to shield their princess from any disturbing but nevertheless interesting incidents that came their way. They had done their work well, and Senterri was indeed bored. What they had not realized was that while Senterri might have been a little silly, she was quite cunning. She could cover her escapes so well that the guardsmen would not believe that she was gone.

Dolvienne seized the reins and leaped from the driver's bench.

The horses immediately found themselves being hauled sharply into a turn. Too sharply. The horses lost their footing, the coach swung around, skidded, then overturned, tore away from the harnesses and horses, and began to disintegrate as it tumbled.

In spite of the spectacular way in which the coach wrecked itself, it was almost half a minute before the wedge of guardsmen could be stopped, ordered, and turned back. The coacher had tumbled, balled up, after being thrown from the wreck, and so was almost unhurt. Dolvienne was bruised and bloodied from being dragged through the dust and gravel, but was not so badly injured that she could not stand up by herself. The coacher was limping slightly, but quite coherent, and very angry.

"It was her, Captain, she grabbed me reins—" he began to shout, gesticulating at Dolvienne across four horses that were either dead or in their death agonies. Dolvienne soon silenced him.

"Princess Senterri is in the gourmet cart!" she shrieked at Gilvray.

"What? Are you serious?" Gilvray demanded, while look-ing away at the approaching Alpenniens.

"Look in the coach!"

The marshal dismounted and hurried over to the coach. He quickly hauled Allaine's body out of the splintered woodwork and paneling. The skirts and red hair were con-vincing, but the face was not that of Senterri.

"The boy student, sir, and he's away with a broken neck."

Gilvray thought very, very quickly. Senterri would be in the gourmet cart, and the reccons would naturally be escort-ing it back to the city as fast as the horses could draw it. They would never make it, of course, but if the Alpennien brigade was to be delayed, there was a chance that a supplies cart might escape in the confusion—especially if a red-headed body in skirts was not inspected too closely by any of the enemy lancers who reached the wreck of the coach.

"Viscount Cosseren, you will stay here and escort the gourmet cart and your wife to the city gates once it gets here," Gilvray shouted.

"Yes, but what—"

"Captain Laron, we shall form a line and charge the flank of the enemy brigade. Journey Guards, form up in a line, facing west!" shouted Laron, indicating west by waving his battle-ax in the direction. "Guardsman Calliar, sound your bugle."

"You're going to charge?" cried Cosseren. "Without me?"

"At my word, charge for the brigade's flank!" ordered Gilvray.

"I'm leading the charge!" shouted Cosseren, riding in front of Gilvray.

Gilvray seemed to have anticipated this, for his cavalry crossbow was already cocked and loaded as he raised it.

"Marshal, mount up, take the viscount's reins, and keep him here until the gourmet cart arrives," ordered Gilvray. "Pace the squad up to a gallop, Captain Laron. At my order, proceed!"

The Journey Guard raised a cloud of dust as they set off, and the marshal looked first to the furious but impotent Cosseren, then to the south for the gourmet cart. Cosseren drew a dagger and flung it at the marshal, just as he was turning back. He flung it badly, for the point was actually facing away from the marshal as it struck. The butt hit him squarely in the right eye, however. The marshal released Cosseren's reins and fell from his horse. Cosseren rode off without so much as a glance in the direction of the gourmet cart.

Left alone, Dolvienne limped over to the marshal's horse, then led it back to the marshal, stripping off her skirts as she walked.

"What in all hell's levels—" began the coacher.

"Hand over your trews or I'll have you charged with aiding the abduction of the princess!" Dolvienne screamed.

The coacher considered. Disobey an order involving the princess and be charged with treason, or take off his trousers. The coacher decided upon the latter alternative. After taking the stunned marshal's ax and stripping off his surcoat, Dolvienne pulled on the clothing that she hoped would disguise her as a guardsman at a distance, then stiffly climbed up into the saddle and looked south. What she saw surprised her a great deal. After some seconds of frantic thought, she cocked the marshal's cavalry crossbow with its step-lever and pressed a bolt into the groove's braces. Dolvienne then set off after the Journey Guard.

Gilvray and Laron brought the squad up to a canter, and when Gilvray judged the distance correct by the apparent size of the enemy lancers, he ordered a full gallop. The gap between the two groups narrowed—and then a rider streaked past Gilvray, shouting "Journey Guards, to me! Charge!" in a shrill voice.

"Viscount Cosseren," began Laron, but the words "fall back" died on his lips. In the heat of battle, they might be interpreted as a general order to retreat. Gilvray raised his ax to herald an order. "Royal Journey Guard, charge!" he shouted, with his ax pointed at the Alpenniens.

Cosseren actually outpaced the line of the charging Journey Guard, but as far as he was concerned, *he* was leading them, so that did not matter. Ahead of them, the nobles and officers of the enemy brigade slowed in confusion. The guardsmen were not making a desperate dash for sanctuary in the city, they were actually attacking! Laron realized that his ax was still held at the front, while the riders to either side of him   l theirs held high for the clash. Feeling oddly embarrasse. .e raised the weapon. The enemy brigade was a dark mass ahead of them, looming larger all the time, raising dust, and with weapons glinting in the sunlight. The royal guardsmen now raised their cavalry crossbows in their left hands as Gilvray raised his ax again, then fired as he brought it down. Bolts poured into the enemy brigade, horses fell, bringing down other horses; then the gap narrowed further and the surviving Alpennien mounted longbowmen fired back. The arrows pouring out from the charging Alpenniens punched gaps in the Journey Guard's line. Cosseren swayed in the saddle as arrows struck him, but he did not fall. Moments later he ploughed into the enemy's flank, and then the Journey Guard slammed into it after him.

It is a fact that horses are not silly enough to collide with each other at full gallop; rather, they aim for the gaps in the enemy ranks. The Journey Guard's horses did this, and so the guardsmen buried themselves in the flank of the thinly spread brigade, striking out with their axes and lances at the Alpenniens as they passed among them. Some even rode all the way through the enemy's ranks; then they turned to reengage. Laron blocked an overhead ax blow from an Alpennien, and backhanded his ax into the other's helmet. Again Laron engaged, parrying a vastly stronger warrior's blow in a wide arc that drove the blade into the man's own horse. The animal bucked and plunged. Laron had already turned on another Alpennien, who had just impaled a journey guardsman with his lance, and his blade bit into the chain mail at the base of the man's neck.

The Journey Guard more or less achieved its goal within the first minute of the clash. No more than a dozen Alpenniens managed to fight their way clear of the battle and ride on to the wreck of the coach. There they found the coacher and marshal defending the wreck with spare cavalry crossbows from the armory box of the coach. There was another minute of fighting, during which the two defenders were joined by ten cavalrymen from the city. Together, they successfully defended the wreckage of the coach, and the dead body of one male student of sorcery disguised as a princess.

✦ ✦ ✦

In the middle of the floodplain, a small group of riders and two vehicles were drawn up, and were not engaging anyone, but they were far from idle. Essen had ordered Costiger off the tent wagon and back onto his own horse. The tent wagon's horses were then sent galloping south along the main road with it, as if someone were trying to dash past the second Alpennien brigade and make a run for it into open country.

"Miss, are you sure the Racewater Bridge was free of Alpennien lancers?" Essen asked Riellen.

"If there are any Alpenniens left there, it could not be more than a half dozen."

"Then attend, everyone. We will make for the bridge at a gallop, paced by the cart. Once across the bridge, we tear up enough decking planks to prevent the Alpenniens pursuing us too quickly, then leave the road and climb up into the hills where cavalry can't follow us."

"But what about the cart?" called Wallas.

"What about the cart *sir*," said Andry.

"We abandon the cart and horses," said Essen.

"You mean I have to walk again—sir?" cried Wallas.

"Militiaman Baker, you may have the option of staying with the cart and being slaughtered," shouted Essen. "Now at my word, to the bridge. Move out!"

✦ ✦ ✦

It is a very curious fact that people who criticize tactics and strategies used in battles usually have the luxury of looking down on the scenario in the form of a map in a history chronicle, and the even greater luxury of having time to carefully consider what the best course of action might have been. In real battles, auton spy birds get attacked by other auton birds, or get shot full of arrows, and everything hap-

pens distressingly quickly. There is dust everywhere, people
do things that rational people would not do in calmer circumstances, and people in key roles get killed.

Thanks to the marshal, the coacher, and the ten riders
from the city, the road back to the city gates was actually
clear by the time Essen set off with the reccons and the
gourmet cart for the bridge over the Racewater. Essen was
not to know that, however, but what he did know was that the
road beyond the bridge was clear. Nobody expected that
Princess Senterri might flee for the very lands of those who
were in pursuit of her. The Alpennien brigade that was racing to block the southern part of the road had expected that
someone might make a break in that direction, so those
Alpenniens positioned themselves to intercept the driverless
wagon. All the while, those in the other brigade and the Journey Guard were hacking each other into the afterlife.

Dolvienne was a very sensible young woman, but even she
became confused by the disposition of the various groups on
the floodplain of the Racewater River that morning. Confronted by a distant wagon racing south, and a cart escorted
by the reccons going west as fast as the horses could be
urged, she correctly concluded that Senterri was in the cart,
not the wagon. She incorrectly concluded that the reccons
were taking the cart to the battle, where the Journey Guard
could provide at least some protection. Thus Dolvienne rode
to skirt the long, thin line of the battle, but there was only
one Journey Guardsman for every five Alpenniens. The
Royal Sargolan Journey Guard was thus being annihilated,
so there were Alpenniens to spare from the fighting.

Four Alpenniens broke off to intercept Dolvienne, correctly deciding from the long hair that she had forgotten to
tie up that she was a woman in disguise—quite possibly the
princess, with her hair dyed. Capturing her was the whole
point of them being there, so they made for her. Captain
Gilvray broke off too, and went after them. One of the
Alpenniens fired an arrow at Dolvienne's horse, but instead
hit Dolvienne in the right thigh. They closed. The Alpen-

niens were trying to take a princess alive, but Dolvienne had
no such agenda.

Seeing that she was cut off, she slowed and waited until a
lancer was about to seize her horse's reins, then shot him
with the marshal's cavalry crossbow. The bolt burst through
his chain-mail shirt, then passed through his shoulder. He
cried out and rode off, trying to pull the bolt free. Dolvienne
dropped the weapon into its saddle rack and drew the marshal's ax. One of the Alpenniens raised his bow; then
Gilvray engaged the other two Alpenniens. The bowman
turned in Gilvray's direction, Dolvienne urged her horse forward, the bowman turned back to her—and her ax swung
around in a flat arc. The blade hit the bowman's hand and the
bow, and the arrow went wild. With his right hand split and
his bow snapped, the man rode off before Dolvienne could
swing the ax again.

Dolvienne looked back to Gilvray, in time to see an
Alpennien topple from his horse and Gilvray trying to free
his ax head from the man's chest and chainmail. The other
Alpennien closed, Gilvray released his ax and brought his
arms up in a cross-block as the Alpennien's ax descended,
but the blade still cut through the metal of his helmet and
found flesh. The Alpennien raised his ax for another blow—
and Dolvienne's ax hit his helmet, knocking him from his
horse and stunning him. Gilvray had fallen from his horse by
now, and was staggering about, his helmet gone, blinded by
his own blood and clutching his head. Dolvienne rode over
to him.

"Captain, to me!" she shouted. "It's Dolvienne."

"Can't see!" cried Gilvray, raising one bloodied hand.

"Get up with me, Captain."

"Can't see. Miral's rings, I'm hit."

"Here's my hand, get onto my horse."

After an eternity of desperate scrambling, slipping, and a
feat of strength that Dolvienne had not known she was capable of, Gilvray managed to crawl up behind her, then hold
on with one hand as he pressed the other against his bleeding
head. In the distance, she saw that the brigade was disengag-
ing from the remains of the Journey Guard and was making
for the wreck of the coach. Laron rallied the eight surviving

guardsmen with a bugle call from Calliar as Dolvienne approached. She rode past Cosseren's body, which had been struck by at least half a dozen arrows. The one protruding from his right eye seemed to have a passably good claim on having actually killed him.

"Journey Guard rallied, sir!" Laron called, but Gilvray could see nothing, and was starting to feel giddy.

"He's wounded," Dolvienne explained, somewhat redundantly.

"I am assuming command!" called Laron, raising his ax.

"The princess is in that cart, Captain," called Dolvienne, pointing in the direction of the bridge.

Suddenly Laron realized what Essen had decided to do. The way was clear to the bridge, the cart was almost there, and there was a slender hope that not too many Alpenniens had been left behind to defend the bridge.

"Journey Guard, to the bridge," cried Laron.

Wallas was aware of only one thing as those around him urged their horses along and cursed him for not driving his cart horse faster. Of all the people on the floodplain, his life was of least worth to anyone. He was also undergoing a crisis of personal worth.

"I am a fat wanker and indifferent musician," he said aloud as he flicked the reins almost continuously. "I can toss together a gourmet meal out of a garbage barrel with no more than a tin pan and an open fire, but who wants a gourmet meal with two brigades of mountains lancers closing in?"

"Well I don't!" Wilbar called out over the rumble of wheels and thudding of the horses' hooves.

"Not hungry!" cried Maeben, waving his hand in the air.

Back in the tray, Senterri and Riellen were heaving sacks of flour and vegetables out over the backboard to lighten the load.

"Only this cart and horse stand between us and a thousand rebellious Alpenniens!" cried Wallas, as if he had to remind himself of what was going on around them.

"Alpennien revolutionaries!" called Riellen.

"They might torture us hideously, then kill us," said Wallas.

"Worse, they might torture us hideously and *not* kill us," Maeben pointed out.

"They only want to capture me," shouted Senterri. "I am worth a lot as ransom."

Wallas considered this, which seemed to be the single positive aspect of the situation. They might all merely be ransomed back to the Palionese faction of the Sargolan royal house . . . where he might be given a shave, then recognized as the former Master of Royal Music, then . . . *On the other hand, maybe torture and death at the hands of the mountain barbarians is the positive side after all*, Wallas decided.

"Must try to escape, preserve your honor, Your Highness," Wilbar shouted to Senterri. "Isn't that right, Wallas, sir?"

"You're officer material!" Wallas called back.

The horse was not used to any sort of pace while harnessed to a cart, but was managing something approximating a gallop. Off to his right, Wallas could see a cavalry battle, which he assumed to be the Journey Guard engaging one of the brigades of mountain lancers. To his left, there was dust rising into the air where the other brigade was now advancing, having intercepted the tent wagon and found nobody to be aboard. The reccons were pulling ahead, and for a moment Wallas thought they were being abandoned. Then he saw that the bridge was not far off, and that a few riders were drawn up in front of it. Wallas cursed himself for not unloading the cart first. After all, who would be wanting meals now? The heavy jars of cooking oil, lamp oil, and fortified medicinal spirits were securely tied down, and neither Senterri nor Riellen were very good with knots, judging by the sound of the curses and cries coming from the tray.

Reaching the bridge, the reccons engaged about ten mountain lancers, who had been left behind to hold the Alpenniers' line of retreat. Wallas steered to skirt the skirmish. A lancer that looked like Hartman was engaged in an ax-fencing exchange with one lancer when another thrust his lance at him from behind. Wallas saw the reccon go limp and fall, but his killer's head then flew free, struck off by a reccon who was so burly that he could only have been Costiger.

"By the moonworlds, but people can die damn quickly," muttered Wallas to himself as he wondered how long *he* might take to die. Now another group of cavalry closed in, and for a moment Wallas actually did give up.

"We're doomed!" he cried, letting the reins go limp.

"Journey Guardsmen!" shrieked Senterri.

Wallas immediately developed a renewed interest in escaping, and steered the cart for a stone customs house whose roof was on fire. As he passed the building, he saw the bodies of the garrison guards and clerks, but the gate to the west road had been left wide open, although the wooden arch above it was trailing smoke and flames into the clear sky while dropping burning fragments onto the road. Wallas drove the cart through. Glancing back over the floodplain, he noticed that lancers seemed to be converging from everywhere. Wallas also noticed that his wagon was on fire, and that Riellen and Senterri were batting at the flames with empty sacks. Essen rode past, pointing at the bridge with his ax.

"Wallas, stop in the middle of the bridge!" he shouted, then rode on.

The road narrowed and became the bridge. Wallas found himself high above the seething, thundering rapids that were the Racewater River at this place. Ahead of him, Essen had stopped, turned his horse, and raised his ax. The gesture might have meant *Stop here!* but it could also have meant *I'll kill you if you don't stop here!* Wallas reined in.

The cart only half blocked the bridge, but Wallas realized that they could block the entire bridge in only moments, then hold off all comers, by turning it sideways and fighting from behind it. He locked the brakes and ordered everyone out.

"What are you doing?" asked Wilbar.

"Essen's plan to save us!" cried Wallas. "Turn the cart."

"No, take a vote!" said Wilbar.

"Treason!" shrieked Senterri. "I *command* you all to do what Essen says."

Several blows of an ax had the horse free of the straps and harness, and Senterri and Riellen led it away to the west side. Essen raised a whistle to his lips and blew three short blasts. Wallas tried to remember if that meant *rally to me*, *charge*, *retreat*, or *stop for lunch*, but the reccons and guards now broke away from the Alpenniens and rode for the bridge.

"Students, can you fight?" asked Essen.

"We prefer to negotiate," explained Wilbar. "In fact it may not be too late to call a meeting and—"

"Go to the women, and if anyone threatens them, try to get in the way."

The reccons reached the bridge, and Essen waved them past the cart. They were followed by Dolvienne, who had an arrow in one thigh, and Captain Gilvray mounted behind her. Wallas recognized the captain by his surcoat, his face being covered in blood. Last of all came the guardsmen, and there were only eight of them left. As soon as they were past the cart, he and Essen unlocked the wheels and began to turn the cart. By now the reccons had dismounted and were firing their cavalry crossbows over the burning cart at the Alpenniens.

"Burning." The word was to Wallas a flash of inspiration like a bright meteor in a sky devoid of both Miral and the moonworlds.

"Your ax!" demanded Wallas, who then slashed through the bindings of the jars of cooking and lamp oil with Essen's weapon.

"You can't be thinking to save your damn olive oil—" began Essen, but Wallas smashed the jar beneath the cart. He took out another jar and did the same. Now Essen caught on, and he began to smash jars on the planks just east of the cart. Wallas heard an Alpennien horn, and he noticed that several dozen lancers were gathering at the east end of the bridge.

"That's enough, now run!" shouted Essen, flinging a scrap of burning tarpaulin onto the spilled oil. Flames blazed up around the cart and spread along the bridge, and then Andry was pushing past Wallas. Essen tried to stop him, but Andry hit him in the face and ran on. Leaping through the flames and into the cart's tray, he hauled a body out from under the jumble of cloths and stores. Wallas realized that he and Essen had forgotten Velander. Andry and the girl were on fire as he staggered back, but the others quickly gathered around, rolled them on the decking to put out the flames.

They fell back from the wagon, to the west side of the bridge. Back in the middle, several mountain lancers had dismounted. Two were chopping at a railing while others were beating at the flames or pushing at the cart with their lances. One had wrapped his hands in his trail cloak and was unlocking the wagon's brakes.

"We need to stop them!" cried Laron, dismounting. "There are two brigades behind them! All dismount, and at my word—"

A large jar of lamp oil that Wallas had overlooked exploded within the burning cart, scouring the mountain lancers from the bridge and blasting away the railings on both sides. The bridge continued to burn.

"Can you do those fireball castings, sir?" asked Essen, hurrying up to Laron.

"I could do a small one, but I would not be good for much else after it," replied Laron.

"Sir, look under the bridge!" shouted Andry to anyone more senior than him who happened to be listening.

Everyone looked, except for Gilvray, who had passed out and fallen from Dolvienne's horse, and for Velander, who had been unconscious for the entire battle. The understructure of the bridge was on fire, and was blazing really fiercely.

"Soaked in pitch to stop rot from the spray," said Essen. "Drips of burning oil must have set it alight."

"Everyone with a crossbow, load up and fire at the Alpenniens!" shouted Laron. "Stop them charging over the bridge before the wood burns through."

The reccons and guardsmen began to fire across the bridge as fast as they could load. Even the bugler Calliar joined in, taking the crossbow from Dolvienne's horse. A few arrows were fired back, but the enemy archers were scattered among the lancers, and not well coordinated. A nobleman arrived, followed by a pennant bearer, and he began to shout orders and organize the riders. It took two minutes, and by then the supply of crossbow bolts was running low. The Alpenniens charged.

About two decades earlier, a contractor had been paid to replace some rotting beams of the bridge's understructure with ashwood. The contractor had, however, used much cheaper pinewood, and covered it with pitch to hide the substitution—then charged extra for special waterproofing. By the time the Alpennien lancers charged across the bridge, the pinewood had not burned through, but it was sufficiently weak that sixty horses and their armored riders were just a little more than it could cope with. The center of the bridge collapsed, followed by two large sections of decking that were crowded with horsemen. The reccons and guardsmen cheered, then trained their cavalry crossbows on the Alpennien brigade commander, his pennant bearer, and a squad captain—who were now stranded on the west side. They stared at the huge gap where the center of the bridge had been, then the struggling men and horses being borne away by the rapids, then the reccons and guardsmen who had their weapons trained on them.

"Commander, tell your men to drop their weapons and dismount, then surrender your ax!" Laron called in Sargolan Courtly.

"To whom do I have the honor of surrendering?" asked the Alpennien commander.

"Captain Aliasar, for Princess Senterri, the new regent of Logiar and all Capefang."

"Are you a gentleman, sir?"

"Would I be a captain were I not, sir?"

The commander gave the order, then dismounted and surrendered to Laron. As Laron collected the brigade's pennant, however, arrows began to patter down around him from the enraged Alpenniens on the other side of the bridge.

"Everybody, back to the bend in the road," he ordered, and they moved away with the horses.

First the wounded were attended to, but the wounded accounted for nearly everyone. A sewing kit that Andry had been given by Jelene contained the only needle in the group, so it was used to sew up all the wounds. There was a very large number of wounds. The only ointment was a jar of triple-fortified wine that Costiger had in his saddle pack, and the bandages were cut from clothing.

Wallas discovered a small lance wound to his leg that he could not remember receiving, and he promptly fainted. Andry had two broken ribs as well as a gash that ran from beside his right eye to his jawline. Priority was given to sewing up the wound to Gilvray's head, however, and removing the arrow from Dolvienne's thigh was scheduled next. Laron had medicar training, and Essen knew some hedgerow and campaign medicine, so they did most of the work. Senterri sat on the ground with Andry, dabbing at his wound with a wine-soaked cloth as he waited his turn for treatment. Dolvienne sat on the other side of Andry, holding her thigh tightly, and trying not to look at the arrow.

"I was told that the guardsmen here are the only survivors from the Journey Guard," Senterri said in a flat voice, as if she could not comprehend what she was saying.

"Can't say, Your Highness," replied Andry. "There could be prisoners, or some lying wounded."

"Did anyone see Viscount Cosseren?" Senterri asked.

"I did," replied Dolvienne. "He looked dead."

"Dead!" exclaimed Senterri, dabbing Andry's eye instead of his wound. "How can you be so sure?"

"He had an arrow through one eye, and was not moving."

Senterri put a hand to her face, smearing it with Andry's blood. Essen walked over from where Gilvray was being treated.

"Highness, 'twould be a help if you could tend the captain," he said, bowing.

"Tend him? How?"

"Wash his face, keep the flies off, give him water, just . . . be there, like."

She left for Gilvray as Essen examined the arrow in Dolvienne's thigh.

"Horse arrow, meant to stick in and stay there. Captain Laron, sir?"

Laron held Dolvienne's arms and Andry lay across her legs, holding them down as Essen cut away the cloth around the wound. He then eased the barbed arrow out, but it was a long and messy operation, and torment for Dolvienne. To Andry it seemed to take forever, and he could only imagine how it must have felt for her. At last Essen gave the arrow to Andry, poured fortified wine over the wound, and sewed it up.

"Save the arrowhead," she whispered as Laron wiped at the perspiration on her forehead.

Andry snapped the arrow and put the head in her hand. Then it was his turn for the needle's attention. He lost track of time, then realized that it was all over, and that he was lying beside Dolvienne and Gilvray.

"Does getting cut across the face hurt?" Dolvienne asked Andry, Gilvray being unconscious.

"Not half as much as having it treated," replied Andry.

"I'd thought arrow wounds looked so small and neat," she said, still panting from the pain of having the arrow removed. "But not anymore."

"Are you in need of anything more, ladyship?" said Andry, heaving himself up. "I have an inventory to take."

"Reccon, you are not fit to stand, let alone work."

"Neither is anyone else," Andry pointed out.

"What about Militiaman Wallas?"

"He only revives long enough to look around at all the wounded folk, throw up, then faint again. Your leave, ladyship."

Andry reported back to Laron after the last of the wounded had been treated. There were twenty-three people and eighteen horses. Eight guardsmen and four reccons were well enough to be considered on duty, and five others would have to ride with the more badly wounded behind, tied in place. Bedding, money, and field rations were all in short supply. Laron reported this to Senterri, and she in turn called a meeting. They were already in place to be addressed, owing to being laid out on the ground and recovering from their wounds.

"I may not be much use to you, but as your monarch I can still do a few things," declared Senterri. "I thus declare the Regency Guard of Capefang to be formed. This will consist of the Journey Guard from Palion, the Palace Guard of Logiar, and the reccons who protected me this day. All three units will remain distinct and separate, and retain their names within the Regency Guard."

"So we're not actually guardsmen, but we're officially in the Queen's Guard," whispered Essen to Andry.

Andry shrugged, which seemed to say it all.

"Guardsmen, I know that you are not going to be pleased that commoners share your elite status, but without those commoners I would already be an Alpennien trophy. Now, you may wonder what we are to do next. Captain Laron?"

People glanced at each other. Nobody had in fact been doing any heavy-duty thinking at all, but clearly the question "What now?" required an answer rather quickly.

"The Alpenniens will have a rope bridge across the rapids before the day is out," warned Laron.

"But sir, a bridge strong enough to support a horse will take at least several days," a guardsman pointed out

"But then they will put only fit, strong, unwounded men across, and they will be fully armed. Most of our weapons are damaged, and we have only two dozen crossbow bolts between us. We are short on supplies, and shorter still on money to buy more with. The longer we take to reach Logiar, the more likely it is we shall be caught, or lose some of our number to their wounds."

"When may we move out, Captain Laron?" asked Senterri.

"A half hour from now. It should take as long as that to get everything together. Is there anything else?"

There was. Senterri had made the transition from fear to anger.

"First of all, we shall speak Sargolan Common," she said, as she turned on the three prisoners. "Some of my men are commoners, and I want all of them to hear what you have to say for yourself. Now, then: Precisely what caused you to break a treaty generations old, and rebel?"

The princess was in an ugly mood, and there was blood on the blade of the cavalry ax that she was carrying. She had several bruises, and a cut on one arm that had begun bleeding again.

"I claim my heritage, the fertile valleys stolen from me in the unjust treaty of—"

"Not good enough, try again," shouted Senterri.

The Alpennien commander blinked.

"My people have outgrown their poor and barren mountain pastures, we were forced to—"

"Captain Aliasar, what do you think the chances of survival are like for a man in armor, with his hands bound, were he to be marched off the end of the bridge and into the rapids?"

"Vanishingly small, Your Highness. He would drown within moments."

"I should like to try an experiment."

"Indeed, Your Highness?"

"Yes. I think that he might be, say, battered to death on the rocks, or chilled to death by the cold water long before he had a chance to drown. Use the commander as a subject."

"We are probably about to violate some awfully important treaty on the treatment of prisoners," Laron pointed out.

"Oh dear, do you think he might complain to the regent of Logiar?" replied Senterri.

"I suspect she may be willing to overlook it, just this once," said Laron.

The commander shuddered, then seemed to make a hurried decision.

"I have no loyalty to either side in Palion's power struggles," he said in as steady a voice as he could manage.

"Then I should like the truth, even if it is limited," said Senterri. "And remember that I know something of the intrigues in the imperial palace, being a princess and all that. If you say something that I know to be false, well—"

"Ask your questions," said the commander, sounding almost impatient to get on with the interrogation.

"Who are you?"

"Carasern, the castellan of Mountfort."

"And who did you plan your rebellion with?"

"A royal envoy, from Palion. I was promised to be made baron of the lower plains if I was to capture you. I was also to kill a sorceress with black, curly hair and a strange accent.

Her age is about three decades, and her name is Terikel Arimer."

"Kill a sorceress? Why?"

"I was told that a faction is using her to take over Dragonwall, and that she would use it to burn our castles and towns. The Dragonwall passes right over my lands."

Senterri and Laron exchanged glances.

"This envoy," said Laron. "Describe him for me."

"I saw him only in poor light."

"Describe him," said Gilvray more firmly.

"Ah, he was, ah, tall, and had a paunch, but was broad of shoulder."

"What was the manner of his dressing?" asked Senterri.

"A russet cloak, with brown riding boots. He wore a hood. I saw little of his face."

"Think hard," warned Senterri, with a gesture in the direction of the ruined bridge.

"His chin! I saw his chin! It was shaven clean."

"Describe the manner of his salute," ordered Senterri.

"His salute? I, ah . . ."

"Think very, very carefully," added Laron.

"Er, a bit foppish. He brought both hands up to his face, back to back, then spread the left out wide while repeating the first flourish with just his right hand. Then he bowed."

Senterri thought for a while, then took Laron by the arm.

"The salute of a prince's envoy, but it means nothing," she said as she led him away to talk privately.

"Quite possibly it means everything," said Laron. "Two hands spread wide is that of the envoy of the emperor or the crown prince. That could narrow it from four princes and a princess to three princes. The envoy could be anyone, though. The palace is full of tall, clean-shaven, middle-aged warriors with paunches."

"Probably why he was chosen to be the envoy," said Senterri. "On the other hand, it might have been some other group, trying to make it seem as if a prince had organized this."

"I doubt it," said Laron. "The castellan was in Palion four months ago, and he visited the royal palace. I think that the

envoy was known to him; in fact, they were probably introduced in the company of a prince. Remember, he must have
had some very good reason to send two brigades against the
Journey Guard. We had our pennons flying, after all, and
those in the city would have seen the whole thing. It would
have been an act of armed rebellion, in fact war. The castellan has nothing to gain from a war with the entire Sargolan
Empire."

"Unless he was sure that the empire would not retaliate!"
concluded Senterri.

"Yes. So you think your own people are behind this, Your
Highness?"

Senterri led Laron back to the commander of the mountain lancers.

"Thank you, your information was exceedingly helpful,"
she said pleasantly. "Now then, you are my prisoner, and
when I arrive in Logiar you will be given the choice of swear-
ing fealty to me or raising a ransom. Captain Laron, I should
like to have the Regency Guards made ready to set off."

Hartman looked past the long line of warriors to the approaching white punt. *Even in the journey to the Dark
Places, the nobility goes first*, he thought.

"Is Reccon Hartman here yet?" called the woman in red
who was guiding the boat.

"Oh aye," said Hartman's spirit, raising a hand.

"Would you have met my sweetheart, Andry Tennoner?"

"I—what?" exclaimed Hartman, shambling forward past
the astonished spirits of the dead nobility. "But you're
Death."

"How is he?" asked Madame Jilli as she helped Hartman
into the punt. "Does he have a new sweetheart yet?"

"Well, sort of. She's got supernatural strength and cold
blood, but she gave up ripping people's throats out and
drinking their blood for love of him."

"She did?" squealed Madame Jilli, pushing away from the
bank. "Wonderful! Oh by the way, please don't call me
Death, people get the wrong idea."

✦ ✦ ✦

Wallas had an enforced lesson in prolonged riding, and rapidly developed saddle sores. The wounded were not happy with the hard pace that Laron set, but there was no alternative. Essen estimated that given perhaps three days, the mountain lancers would have completed makeshift repairs to the bridge, and begun to move men and horses back over the Racewater River. As soon as these lancers caught up to them, it would be all over very quickly, because the Journey Guard was no longer much of a fighting force. However, Essen's estimate did not take account of the fact that the mounted militia in the nearby city might charge through the gates and attack the stranded Alpenniens. This was in fact what happened, so that had Senterri and her escort stayed near the bridge, they could have been rescued just as soon as a temporary rope bridge could have been set up by her own loyal subjects.

They stopped to graze the horses as the last of twilight faded behind the Dragonwall's glow. They were near a small, fortified tavern, but those inside were Alpennien loyalists, and would not admit them. There was a cart abandoned in the field where they hobbled their horses and set them grazing, and Andry quickly determined that it only had a broken axle. He got to work making a new axle by the firelight.

Laron ordered that the others sleep only until dawn, when they would set off again. The innkeeper was a subject of the castellan, after all, and would tell their pursuers everything that he knew. Andry had the axle finished after several hours, in spite of being both wounded and exhausted. A glow behind the mountains indicated that Miral was rising, so he knew it was past midnight.

"You should sleep, there will be little enough chance," came Gilvray's voice from nearby.

"Too many thoughts, sir," replied Andry, looking around in the gloom for his commanding officer.

"Your first battle?" asked Gilvray, standing up carefully, then walking over very slowly.

"Battle, oh aye, my first, sir."

"Yet you fought well. Guardsman Palver said you broke up a pair of Alpenniens that had him bracketed, and I caught sight of you fighting."

"I've been in a lot of brawls."

"I have been in eleven real battles. A few were bigger than yesterday, but none were so close."

Andry did not reply. The silence began to stretch.

"I left Palion with nearly a hundred guardsmen, but only nine of us are left."

"And us five reccons sir, and Captain Laron—and Militia-man Wallas."

"Well then, that makes it sixteen, but only nine are guards-men. We lost nine out of ten killed yesterday, Andry. Even one out of ten would have been considered to be terrible ca-sualties in my other battles. I can name every man killed. Every one of them was brave, whether they lived or died."

"The protection of the princess must be very important to you, sir."

"Oh yes, and not just to me, but to all of the guardsmen, living and dead. It is a matter of honor. Last year Princess Senterri was abducted, and we were powerless to do any-thing about it. The Chamber Guards guarded empty rooms, and we Journey Guards rode the deserts finding nothing but false rumors. All while the princess was in the hands of slavers. When it was discovered that she was still alive, it was one of her brothers and his regular lancers who brought the news. When she escaped, it was without our help. She then chose not to return to the palace, but to stay in another country, helping other escaped slaves and people in need. Then she returned. . . . This time we *were* present when she was in danger, and this time we preserved her honor. She will be a good regent, when we get to Logiar. With Cosseren dead she is no longer queen, though."

"What is a regent, sir?"

"Regents rule when there is no suitable monarch: too young, too stupid, too lazy. In the case of Capefang, the rul-ing family allied itself with the Alpennien warlords, some eighty years ago. The rebellion was crushed, and the Cape-fang monarchy disinherited, but there was a pretender to the throne. That was Viscount Cosseren. When she married him,

Senterri was declared queen of Capefang on a fine point of
Sargolan law."

"He seemed a good-natured man, sir, and skilled with
horse and ax."

"So he should have been. He spent most of his twenty-
four years riding and fencing under the instruction of the
greatest masters of the empire—courtesy of his court al-
lowance. He was the best ax fencer in the Journey Guard, he
was far better than me. Out of sixty duels, he lost none. Two
were against Laron, and one against me."

"Might I be so bold as to ask who challenged, sir?"

"Oh Cosseren, every time. If you had a reputation for ax
fencing he would be sure to find fault with you on some fine
point of honor and force a duel."

"He never challenged me, sir, and I beat Lord Laron at ax."

"But you, sir, are a foreign mercenary, and one of very du-
bious origins. You might even be . . ." Gilvray put a finger to
his lips and winked. "Lower-class. Just say you put a cut on
his face, then actually beat him. He would have faced going
through the rest of his life explaining how some hairy-arsed
muck shoveler from Alberin got the better of him. A scar
from me would have been from the captain of the Journey
Guard, and something to boast about."

"Was he, like, much good in a real fight, sir?"

"There was no question that he was brave, he was just exceedingly thick. A drunk lying in the gutter during a rainstorm had more common sense than Cosseren."

"Surely not, sir. Princess Senterri favored him."

"The princess did not favor him, she just signed some
scrolls, made a vow, and lay in the royal bed while he . . .
Actually, he apparently did something in the royal bedchamber that annoyed the princess a great deal! Well, perhaps
Fortune does not always torment those in love."

Andry caught the agenda behind Gilvray's words almost
instantaneously. He hesitated for some moments, then decided that perhaps normal protocols were being suspended,
and that perhaps Captain Gilvray even expected him to ask a
very obvious question.

"Permission to ask if you love the princess, sir?" asked
Andry.

"Oh yes. I adore her, and have for the two years I have served her. But I understand her reasons for marrying Viscount Cosseren. She gained a kingdom within the empire. Others have sent many thousands into battle to die, just to gain much smaller kingdoms. Now he is dead . . . but I have no kingdom to offer her."

✳ ✳ ✳

"Wallas!" hissed Andry.

Wallas grunted, then rolled over.

"Wallas, are you asleep?" asked Andry, pulling his blanket away.

"Of all questions that might be asked, that one must rank as—"

"I'll take that as no. I need help getting the wheels onto my new axle."

"Pox take your wheels."

"That cart is what you can ride in tomorrow, if the wheels are on. Captain Gilvray spoke with me for a while, just now. He said that if the cart is not ready for use when we leave at dawn, then we abandon it."

"Pah, damn you, Andry. All right then."

For all his pretensions and complaints, Wallas was actually quite a strong man, and unlike most of the others in the group, he was practically uninjured. They soon had the right wheel attached and pinned. The left wheel was no more difficult, and within twenty minutes of Wallas being roused, the cart was off its rock supports and standing on its wheels.

"All that agony learning to ride, and now I have a cart again," sighed Wallas, sitting down and staring at the cart in Miral's green light.

"Doesn't matter how good the news, Wallas, you always have something to complain about," Andry pointed out as he sat down beside him. "What do you know of Captain Gilvray?"

"You mean the captain of the Journey Guards?"

"Gods of the moonworlds, Wallas! There's only one Gilvray here. He's the only one with a bigger gash in his head than mine."

"Oh, he's the great-grandson of an Alpennien warlord, who was dragged to Palion in chains eighty years ago after the great rebellion of 3061. His family has been in the service of the Sargolan emperor for three generations."

"I noticed friction between him and Cosseren," began Andry.

"Well, don't mention it, unless you wish to overstep about thirty levels of rank and class with just seven words."

I've already done that, thought Andry. "And now there is friction between him and Laron."

"Ah yes, Laron. The rather pretty young boy who fights like a wildcat, and has the wisdom and manner of a very old man. His is an odd story. He played a part in the escape of the princess from the slavers; then he was her companion while she spent some time living as a commoner, in search of her true self. There are those who say that she took Laron as her lover."

"Was it true?"

"Probably not. Viscount Cosseren would have been stupid enough to complain, had his bride not been a virgin—even though she was the emperor's daughter."

"I can scarcely believe she married the like of Cosseren," said Andry, shaking his head.

"Hah! The man made even you look intelligent, but it was all the emperor's doing. Senterri wanted to be independent, but her father played upon that to bring her into line. The regency of Logiar and title of queen promised her considerable independence, and the temptation was too much for her. She returned to court life in Palion, and was crowned queen and declared regent by the emperor himself after she had wed Viscount Cosseren—who is the pretender to Capefang and—"

"I know all that."

"The emperor was assassinated an hour later, and I—"

"I know that too. So what is the princess's place with Cosseren dead—like with Captain Laron?"

"Laron is her personal sorcerer, even though his initiation level is but nine. The boy has an initiate's scroll from some Diomedan academy, but nothing else. No rank, no past, no family. He says he lost them when Torea burned. Very convenient, Torea burning. All sorts of things and people got burned there, and most of them were not even in Torea at the time. By his manners, speech, and bearing, he probably is a noble of some description, though."

By his manners, speech, and bearing, thought Andry. *By my own manners, speech, and bearing, what could I become?*

"What will become of us, do you think, Wallas?" Andry asked, suddenly feeling very fatigued.

"Our prospects are actually good. If you do not retire with less than a thousand acres and a small castle, I should be very surprised."

"And you, Wallas?"

"Oh, I'd like to become your squire, attach myself to your household. Can't get too well known with a record like mine, can I? We can be a great force in the Logiar court, with your bravery and my grasp of intrigue, passion, and politics. I—"

"Intrigue, passion, and politics!" exclaimed Andry softly.

"There's a lot of it about, and I've learned that commoners do the like too. It's just that courtiers don't gossip about commoners, and bards don't sing about them."

Andry did not reply. Wallas thought at first that he was pondering a suitable response; then he realized that the reccon was asleep.

"Typical," muttered Wallas. "Wakes me up, then goes to sleep. Now I can't get to sleep. Still, at least I have a cart now."

The following morning they broke camp with the sun still below the horizon. Gilvray called them together before they set off. He looked very weak, and needed to be supported by Costiger, but he wanted the group to know that standards were being preserved.

"I wish to announce that early this morning Her Royal Highness appointed Captain Laron to the Regency Guard until we reach Logiar," Gilvray began. "This was done in order to have the most able-bodied officer in charge for the duration of this most perilous journey. Captain Laron will now address you."

Laron now stood. He spoke rapidly, as if anxious to be under way.

"Our numbers are down, but after what we did in yesterday's battle, I doubt the Alpenniens will come after us unless they have at least a hundred lancers and their horses over the rapids. That will take time, but count on it that they *will* be after us. When they arrive here, the people in that fortified inn will tell them when we left, how many of us there are, and in what condition we appeared to be. For that reason, hide your bandages, sit straight in the saddle, and look as if you are ready for another battle. That will make our pursuers more cautious, and cautious people are slow people. I should also add that I shall be consulting Captain Gilvray in all major decisions, and that should anything happen to me, he is next in command."

Essen took Laron aside while the others were mounting. He inclined his head in the direction of the fortified inn.

"All dead, sir," he said softly.

There was no smoke from the chimney, Laron observed.

"I don't understand," Laron said with a shiver, although he had a fairly good idea that he did understand.

"Come, you should see for yourself."

The side of the inn's roof facing away from their camp was torn out, and several thick beams were splintered, as if by an enormous beak.

"I was on watch, two hours before dawn," explained Essen as they walked. "A dragon bird came. It was very quiet, even though it was as high as a tower. It leaned right over the inn's wall, and put its head through thatch roof. I saw it pull out five, and swallow. Then it left."

"Why didn't you raise the alarm?" demanded Laron.

"We had quenched our fires, and our people were lying silent and still. I thought it best to leave them like that, sir, rather than start a panic and attract the dragon bird."

Laron took a moment to visualize the consequences of a panic involving a couple of dozen sick and wounded people, and a bird big enough to swallow a cow.

"Good decision, Marshal Essen," he conceded.

They entered the inn through the hole in the roof. The

enormous predator had merely taken the people, and had left everything else intact.

"Have Wallas bring the cart over, but tell him that the people from the inn fled during the night," said Laron after looking around. "Load up whatever supplies the cart can carry. It may see us through a week of travel."

"The birds seem to go where we go," said Essen.

"So I have noticed. Perhaps they are being guided into our path, perhaps someone hopes that they will attack us too, but perhaps they are no more intelligent than the late viscount. This one attacked the inn, where people were likely to be staying. Perhaps we should avoid inns. Perhaps, perhaps, it is always perhaps."

Laron made sure that they made very good progress along the winding mountain roads that day, although in terms of moving between points on a map they moved but slowly. Essen knew the roads very well, as a result of serving in the area five years earlier. The initial plan was to follow the main road and pass through the heartland of the southern Alpennien castellanies, then go south to Logiar. There was always enough pasture for the horses, and the people in the farmsteads and villages thought that the group was just some Alpennien warlord, his escort, and prisoners. None of the outlaws thought to attack such a big and well-armed group, but Laron began to worry that things were going too well. He wondered if someone was trying to give them a false sense of security.

"We only need a single churl to recognize our prisoners, and the local Alpennien militias will be straight onto us," said Laron as he and Essen rode together at the head of the group. "Could we hide them in the cart?"

"There are at least five customs forts on the roads we must travel, sir. The cart would be searched at every one."

"I will not allow them to be killed, and we cannot let them go, so we need some different route to Logiar. Is there one?"

"There is, sir, through Alpenfast. That's where the Skymirror temples are."

"Alpenfast. That is an independent Alpennien castellany, as I recall."

"That it is, sir. They would make us release the prisoners before passing through their lands, but they would not attack us. Alpenfast is deep in the mountains, though, so by the time the prisoners got back to the nearest large town and raised the alarm, we would be safely away."

"Is there any other way to Logiar?"

"Not unless you can fly, sir."

"Then Alpenfast it is—but tell nobody before we actually turn off this road."

On the third day, Essen directed them to turn southwest onto a very small track. This generated much comment in the group, and most thought it was not a good choice in terms of the road's surface.

"Were this road a ship, the rats would be leaving it," said Andry as they picked their way around boulders, washaways, and bushes growing in the middle of their path.

"Looks to be a road that nobody's traveled in a thousand years," commented Wallas. "Why would people stop using a road?"

"Perhaps some clown burned a bridge."

"Now you just take that back! Had I not set that bridge afire we'd all be providing the main course at some lower-class dinner party for mountain vultures."

"Come to think of it, I've not seen many vultures or eagles for some time."

"Little to eat, perhaps," grumbled Wallas. "Nothing for us to hunt, either, when supplies run low. Makes it hard for a cook."

Laron had them halt while the reccons went back and swept away the tracks and horse droppings from near where they turned off. The road resembled a track to a farmstead, so there was a good chance that any pursuers would miss or ignore it. There proved to be less fodder for the horses, but that which there was had not been grazed recently. From time to time they would see a cottage with smoke issuing from its chimney, but nobody ever came out to greet them.

"Just imagine living here," said Andry. "The nearest tavern's days away."

"And the nearest decent market's in Karunsel," added Wallas.

The strangely derelict trail took them high into an area where even the occasional cottages had become just occasional ruined cottages. At night the mighty shimmering curtain of light that was Dragonwall towered above them so close that the rainbow edging was almost overhead, and it was as bright as Miral. By now Miral was rising at about eight in the morning and setting a couple of hours after sunset. At noon on the twenty-eighth day of Fivemonth, they came to a neat but massive wall. It was at least sixty feet high, and had been built across the ravine that the trail followed. At the base was a double door of ironwood, and carved into the rock above it was the word ALPENFAST.

Even before they reached the wall, the left door opened. A guard in a polished steel helm and gleaming chain mail emerged and held up his hand. Laron dismounted and walked forward to him.

"Who approaches?" the guard asked formally in Sargolan Courtly.

"My name is Captain Aliasar, and on behalf of Princess Senterri of the Sargolan royal house, I claim respite from the attacks of Alpennien rebels."

"It is not usual for travelers to approach this way," replied the guard. "Only raiders and bandits ever come from within the mountains. That is why we built this wall."

"We used this track to escape our pursuers, we had no choice. Please, what is your word? Most of our company have serious wounds."

"I see that you have three prisoners."

"Yes, they were from the brigades that attacked our party."

The guard returned to the open door, but it was not closed after him. Some minutes passed, and then he returned.

"Captain Aliasar, I can offer your party respite on behalf of my lord, but Alpenfast is a place of truce and peace. Your prisoners will have to be set free."

"Princess Senterri is aware of your community, and its rules. She is willing to let the Alpenniens go free here."

"In that case, enter with our most sincere welcome."

By evening they had reached Alpenfast itself. Less than a town, but more than a monastery, it was more like a collection of temples scattered through a sprawling university, and some of the buildings extended out into a lake. Skymirror Lake was a broad expanse of placid water bordered by mountains. They arrived on an unusually calm evening, and the peaks and slopes were reflected almost perfectly in its waters.

"These are the Etheorens," explained Laron as they approached the buildings, skirting Skymirror on a path paved with red granite bricks. "They are priests dedicated to the study of etheric forces and the firmament. They have been here over four thousand years."

"Their waterside temples and palaces are works of art in themselves," said Dolvienne.

"Ah yes, and are they not beautiful? They represent eleven important architectural styles and schools, each from an Acreman civilization that has risen and fallen while the Etheorens quietly got on with their routines and researches.

"There's a Sargolan-style palace being built," Wallas said from the cart, pointing to a building that was all curves, domes, and huge, arched windows.

"Someday the empire will be gone, and that palace will still be in use," said Laron.

"It's good living," said Andry. "Where can I sign on?"

"They are total abstainers, and observe a lifetime celibacy rule."

"Oh. So it's only good for a visit, then."

"I thought you had given up the drink, Andry?"

"Very nearly, but I still like the company of drinkers. Besides, I have a sweetheart."

"*That* is just about the most extreme use to which that word has ever been put," called Wallas.

"You don't know the meaning of the word," replied Andry.

"She's starved herself until she's become incapable of even moving."

"Aye, but I respect her for it. She's doing it for me."

"I would never starve myself for any woman."

"Wallas, would you prefer her to break her fast on you?"

"Oh. Er . . . well, I am always charmed by the silly little things that lovers do to prove their devotion, of course. Give her a kiss for me, Andry."

"If the path leads back to you, Wallas, I doubt that she would accept it."

Everyone was attended by the medicar priests when they reached the hospitality palace that the Etheorens had built five hundred years earlier for their guests. Many of the wounded had fevers, and their injuries had become infected in spite of Laron and Essen's best efforts. Oddly enough, despite having the most serious of the wounds, Gilvray was recovering well. Over dinner Laron formally handed command of the Regency Guard back to him. The priests insisted that the Alpenniens not leave before the princess and her party were about to leave as well, just so nobody could take advantage of anyone else.

After the meal Senterri, Dolvienne, Laron, and Gilvray were served spiced mead on a stone balcony that dropped sheer to the water on its lakeside edge.

"The water is so tranquil, you can see the stars reflected," said Gilvray.

"It looks like a hole in the land, where another sky is showing through," said Dolvienne.

"The priests say that we are lucky," Laron explained as he walked over to lean on the marble railing and look down into the water. "The Torean Storms usually render the surface choppy. Perhaps Dragonwall really is taming them."

"Was it not meant to do just that?" asked Senterri.

"Yes, Your Highness, but many designs do far less than the designers intended."

They were silent for a time, luxuriating in not having to

travel, and being able to sit down on something more comfortable than saddles, rocks, grass, and the seat of Wallas's cart. The air cooled rapidly, now that evening had become night. When Dolvienne wrapped her arms about herself and shivered, Gilvray gave her his cloak.

"I was wondering how many guardsmen and mountain lancers died in the battle," said Senterri to nobody in particular.

"Captain Laron estimates that some ninety guardsmen, one reccon, and a student are either dead or unaccounted for," said Gilvray. "Perhaps three hundred Alpenniens were killed, or were injured so badly that they fell from their mounts. I estimate that sixty more died when the Racewater Bridge collapsed."

"So very many," responded Senterri, who had never seen a real battle before.

"In all of history, a squad has never put a brigade to flight," said Gilvray. "The guardsmen who died will be sung of by the bards and militiamen for centuries."

"Yet it was a terrible price to pay, merely to preserve my honor."

"We were all honored to pay the price, Your Highness. It made up in part for our disgrace while you were in slavery."

"Yet am I really free? These are *Alpennien* mountains, and the Alpenniens appear to be in revolt."

"You are still under the protection of the guardsmen, even though they are but a tenth of their former strength."

"True," sighed Senterri, lying back in her seat. "I would rather have you and your eight guardsmen with me than nine brigades of militia lancers, Captain. Will you see us to our chambers?"

"Certainly, Your Highness. Lady Dolvienne?"

Gilvray gave his hand to Senterri as she got to her feet; then he helped Dolvienne to stand. Dolvienne limped along between Senterri and Gilvray, with her arms around their necks. Laron watched them go, then turned back to the lake. *Not once did they mention Viscount Cosseren*, thought Laron, *and only once was I mentioned. Still, one mention is an advance on no mention at all.*

✦ ✦ ✦

Velander had been taken to the infirmary, where she was bathed by the nurses and put into a bed. The nurses were very concerned that she was icy cold, and that her hearts were not beating, but Andry told them that this was normal for her. Her etheric fangs and claws had faded to nothing, which saved him the trouble of some very awkward additional explanations. When a medicar priest lifted one of her eyelids, brilliant blue-white light shone out.

"I am Selveris, the medicar," said the priest who showed Andry into Velander's room. "She was conscious for a short time while I examined her, but now? Well, all I can say is that she does not respond."

"Her condition is a bit, er, worrying," said Andry guardedly.

"Worrying?" said the priest said as they stood beside the bed. "Do you realize that she is dead, according to several quite reasonable tests for life, yet she can speak and move her hands a little? As for the light from her eyes, well!"

"What can you recommend?" asked Andry. "Tomorrow we must leave."

"There is no question that Velander is better off here. She is welcome to stay as long as she, ah . . ."

"Lives?"

"I was going to say *wishes*. Andry, I can do no more for now but I suspect that it would be good for her if you stayed here for the night. The night nurse can fetch a recliner so that you can sleep by the bed."

"Sir, I could not impose—"

"Captain Laron said that you are very dear to her."

"I—I—I—" gasped Andry, his face burning.

"I am sorry, Andry, did I cause offense?"

"I—er, no, but . . . Velander means a lot to the captain as well, and it's, er . . ."

"Another very unfortunate situation?"

"Er, yes! Yes. Er . . . another?"

"People often say things to their medicars that they would not even say to a lover—especially if that medicar is unlikely to ever see them again. Andry, for sheer quantities of frustrated emotional entanglements, this group of people has problems that might have made my hair curl—had I any hair to curl, of course. Stay with your girl, my lad. I shall have a recliner sent in."

The medicar bowed and left. Andry sat on Velander's bed and held her hand. Her skin was cold but dry.

"Andry," she whispered.

"Vel, you're awake!"

"Heard all. Were wounded, Andry?"

"Just my face."

"I may feel?"

Andry put her fingers to the stitches in his right cheek.

"Impressive. Must look . . . rakish. Impress girls."

Andry gently pressed his lips against her forehead, then her lips. Thin, violet filaments of ether trailed out and snapped as he drew back.

"I only want to impress *you*."

The nurse brought in a cane recliner and placed it beside the bed, but Andry lay with his head on Velander's chest. There was no sound from her hearts.

"Was bad, the battle?" Velander asked when the nurse had gone.

"Aye."

"Kill someone?"

"No. Hartman and I fought as a team. I engaged, he came around behind, he did the killing. Until he was killed, that is."

"You killed none?"

"Oh aye, that is true."

"Was by chance, Andry?"

"I hit with the blunt of my ax whenever I could."

"Why?"

"Well, because they were alive."

"They were trying, for to kill you!"

"Oh aye, but you know. They all had girls and families and friends, and they liked a pint and probably had thoughts of bettering themselves. What I mean is, they all had a life, and a place in the lives of others. I couldn't really end all that."

"Andry, Andry . . . amazing. You want learning of manners and refinement, for to better yourself . . . yet already, you are better. Better than rest. Than me."

"You're being silly, Vel."

"No Andry, listen. Some you will meet, must kill. To leave alive, is evil."

"Are you saying that I should have killed people in the battle?"

"Am saying, you think, er, all people like yourself. Good. Am saying, wrong. Most worse."

"Before you died, Vel, did you ever kill anyone?"

"Yes. Was war."

"Oh. Then you probably think I'm weak and foolish."

"No. Think are being, finest man in world, all of. Admire you. Adore you. Killing dragon, ah, changed me, but . . . meeting you changed me more."

Andry sat up, caressed her tapering ears, and stroked her hair. For a while they just sat quietly, enjoying each other's company in silence.

"Laron says you are a Metrologan priestess. Fine people. They study the stars, yet they help people in the gutter."

"Very pretty way, ah, for to describe."

He put his hand over hers.

"Velander, if you pull through, do you think we might get along, like?"

With obvious effort, Velander curled her fingers around his.

"If would be nice . . . but if will not be. Andry, liking Terikel, are you?"

"Oh aye, she's a grand and wise lady," replied Andry guardedly.

"No! Liking her as, how you saying . . . your lass?"

"What? She's Elder of the entire Metrologan Order, and she's one of the greatest sorceresses in the world, I wouldn't dare dream of even holding her hand."

"Terikel, is troubled, Deeply. Gives orders, works hard, suffers, endures horrible things, all for greater good. Sometimes, endures horrible people, for greater good. Be near her, Andry. If is holding she needs, hold her. If you are doing, is possible for me, er, go walk into Dark Places, more easily."

"No, Velander! *You're* my lass, it's not honorable."

"Honor?" laughed Velander softly. "Silly boy. Sounding like Laron."

At the sixth hour past midnight Andry was shaken awake as he lay in an exhausted sleep beside Velander's bed. In the light of the night-lamp, he saw Laron standing before him with a finger to his lips.

"Come with me," he said quietly, then led him outside.

"It's not even dawn, Captain," said Andry as they walked along cloisters lined with pillars smothered in vines. "What's been happening?"

"You are invited to breakfast. It will be a very nice breakfast, held on the great stone balcony beside the lake, with the sun streaming over the peaks from the east, and the waters of Skymirror dusted with mist and as blue as the sky. I believe crustbread and clover honey is to be served, washed down with chilled mintmilk. Unfortunately some of the people who are going to be there are rather anxious to beat each other to a pulp, then heave that pulp over the balcony's railing and into the lake—the drop is currently ninety feet, by the way. People have been comparing stories, you see, and the details of some of those stories have been fitting together very badly."

"Oh. And who are these people?"

"Me, Captain Gilvray, Princess Senterri, Lady Dolvienne, to name but a few. The observer-general of Alpenfast has agreed to adjudicate, and his inquisitor will ask the questions."

"Ad, er, adjuri—"

"Adjudicate. It is something like a magistrate does when people are suing each other. Now then, reliable sources lead me to believe that you have never killed any person, and that you are a virgin."

"Wallas!" muttered Andry, looking as if he might now wish to spoil his record concerning homicide.

"Is it true?"

"I get little enough privacy as a reccon, Captain, can't I at least keep people guessing on these matters?"

"Andry, you are about to be asked to be part of a very dangerous etheric casting. If you have killed, or had a tumble with someone, it will hurt about as much as white-hot needles being poked into every part of your body that is capable of feeling pain. If not, you will feel no pain at all. Again I ask, have you ever killed or had a dalliance?"

"Will Wallas ever find out?"

"No."

"Then the answer is no and no."

They walked on for another hundred feet before Andry took Laron's arm and stopped him.

"Can I ask a very sensitive question?" asked Andry.

"You may get an insensitive answer, but ask if you wish."

"Just say a lad loves a great lady, but a lass loves him. The lass really needs him, and he gives her what love he can but keeps his deepest feelings secret—like to protect the feelings of the lass, and to keep things uncomplicated for the great lady. Er, is he doing the right thing?"

Laron folded his arms and regarded Andry for a moment, his green eyes gleaming in the lamplight.

"Now let me guess. You are the lad, Velander is the lass, and Senterri is the lady?"

"I'd rather not answer that, lordship, but could you answer me?"

"Yes, Andry, he is. The lad sacrifices his full happiness for the girl, he would even die for her. That is truly noble. If all the while, he secretly loves a great lady, that is even more noble. It is called courtly love, and was devised on another world a long time ago. I introduced the idea here, so in a sense you could not have asked a better person for advice on the subject."

"So it's a gentlemanly thing to do?"

"Oh yes, very much so—and thank you for being what you are to Vel."

"Oh lordship—"

"Not another word! Even I cared for her but loved another in secret, you have no monopoly on being noble, Andry. Now, let us walk on, there are important and angry people in need of us in a quite lovely setting."

As Laron had promised, the surroundings were breathtakingly beautiful, the food and drink were simple yet delicious beyond description, and the atmosphere as poisonous as a barrel brimming with large, hairy, and extremely bad-tempered spiders. Terikel was present, Andry noticed at once, and she seemed very unhappy about it. For some time nobody said anything, as if they were not anxious for the hostilities to begin until they had finished eating. The sun cleared the peaks, the trays were cleared away from the stone table, and everyone took a quite extended look at the exquisitely beautiful buildings, lake, countryside, and surrounding mountains. At last the observer-general and inquisitor arrived, and Andry was surprised to learn that the medicar, Selveris, was also the observer-general—and thus master of all Alpenfast. On the other hand, everyone in Alpenfast wore only a brown, cowled robe and sandals, so appearance was a poor guide to seniority. The inquisitor was a redheaded but balding man who wore wire-rim spectacles.

"It has been brought to my attention that considerable animosity exists among you, my guests," Selveris began, standing at the head of the table. "There has been shouting, fighting, and exchanges of castings. In one case a guest's silk robes were turned to powder, to the outrage of the guest and the consternation of some of my priests."

"Who had never seen a naked woman before," added the inquisitor.

"While we seldom interfere in the affairs of our guests, in this case you guests are heads of state, very powerful commanders, and the head of another scholarly order. Some of you may be spying on us, perhaps even planning an attack. Thus it may be in the interests of a great many people if the truth were discovered. Are you all willing to have the truth imposed upon you? None may leave here unless we are given the truth."

The reluctant mutterings that passed around the table were along the lines of "yes." Selveris took a pace back, allowing his colleague to speak.

"I am Malecniar, the inquisitor for Alpenfast," said Malecniar, giving a little bow and rubbing his hands together. "For my work, I require two people, one male and one female, who have never killed, and whose virginity is still, er, uncompromised, as it were. The volunteers are Dolvienne and Andry, I believe?"

Dolvienne and Andry came forward at Malecniar's gesture.

"Ah, splendid. Now then, are there any questions, before we proceed?"

"There must be hundreds of male virgins who never killed within your temples," said Andry. "Why do you need me?"

"You have no initiate training, and that makes you more effective than any of the Skymirror priests. Strong initiates can control the casting, and even bend the truth, sometimes. Have you no questions, my dear?" he asked Dolvienne.

"I have never knowingly killed, Learned Inquisitor, but if anyone I have fought later died of their wounds, what would that mean?"

"Intent and knowledge are all that are required. Anything else? Splendid, then we should begin. Would you two just hold hands and stand at the head of the table while I do the verity casting, please?"

After having little to do with any woman other than Velander since Glasbury, Andry was almost surprised to find that Dolvienne's hand was warm and moist. Malecniar spoke a series of casting words into his cupped hands, then began to fashion the etheric energies. They grew into a violet sphere, about the size of a person's head.

"Please place your free hands against the verity casting," he said, holding the sphere up before them.

As Andry and Dolvienne touched the sphere, it spread up their arms and across the skin beneath their clothing until they were covered in fine, violet meshwork. Andry felt nothing, other than a slight tingling sensation.

"Well now, this is promising. The casting is complete and neither of the speakers died in unspeakable agony, so we may proceed. As it stands, neither Andry nor Dolvienne can speak a lie. Further, Andry can sense when a man is knowingly telling a lie, and Dolvienne can say the same for a woman. For example, Andry, what do you really think of me, the inquisitor?"

"You seem too nice to be an inquisitor, sir," Andry said without being able to help himself.

"Oh well, thank you. Because the verity casting is so very effective we do not need horrid people who torture and frighten people into telling the truth."

"More often, we need someone kind and sympathetic, like Malecniar, because the truth is so upsetting," added Selveris.

"Dolvienne, tell us what you really think of your mistress, Princess Senterri."

"She is a self-indulgent, empty-headed, faithless little brat, whose best decisions have been my own advice, and whose whims and fancies have led to the deaths of countless thousands of men and—"

"I think that will do," interjected the inquisitor, who then turned to Senterri. "Ah, Your Highness, by the look of intense shock on your face I see that the true feelings of your loyal servant have come as something of a surprise. That is almost always the case. Perhaps you should be first into the verity casting, right of reply and all that. You will not be able to stop yourself speaking. Although a powerful initiate can even speak lies, the casting hosts will tell us if that happens."

Senterri walked unsteadily around the table, and the inquisitor guided her between Dolvienne and Andry. At his word, they clasped their free hands to encircle Senterri.

"Well now, Your Highness, perhaps we could hear what you should really think of Dolvienne?"

"Self-righteous, overachieving bitch, I'm not surprised she is still a virgin, she is so tight and controlled in everything she does that you could not breach her virginity with a mason's chisel and sledgehammer—"

"That's enough on that subject!" said the inquisitor with a wave of his hand. "My, my, there certainly are some nasty feelings being bottled up among you all. Your Highness, may I ask what your real feelings for Captain Gilvray might be?"

Senterri managed to resist for some moments, but the compulsion to speak was rather like the last moments before a sneeze: very uncomfortable, unless one gave in.

"He is so serious, I just can't help but tease him. I know he is in love with me, men have to be in love with me before they can join the Journey Guard. I disguised myself and traveled in the gourmet cart just to tease Captain Gilvray. Yet now I learn that he betrayed me to the Alpenniens. How could someone in love with me do that?"

"That is enough, Your Highness, you may stand down," said the inquisitor. "Commander Emtellian, perhaps you could be next."

"I cannot believe I said all that," muttered the trembling and perspiring Senterri as she sat down.

"Commander, tell us who you are," said the inquisitor.

"I am Castellan Emtellian of Windover, and a brigade commander appointed by myself."

Stunned silence greeted this announcement. The inquisitor recovered first.

"And what were your dealings with Captain Gilvray?" he asked.

"I offered him the abandoned castle of Cloudfall, with one hundred square miles of land containing three hamlets and good grazing land, if he would deliver Princess Senterri into my hands. He said yes, and together we formed the plan to seize her just after the Journey Guard escorted her out of Karunsel."

"You vile basted," hissed Senterri slowly, glaring at Gilvray, but he sat with his eyes closed and remained silent.

"Oh, I see. You wanted to hold her for ransom?" asked the inquisitor.

"No, I wanted to marry her, and unite all the Alpennien lands with Capefang."

Laron's mouth dropped open.

"Impressive. That would give you over half of the empire's lands and a third of its population. But Senterri was already married."

"The highest priority was to be given to providing Viscount Cosseren with a glorious death."

"Castellan Emtellian, you may return to your seat. Captain Gilvray, please come here and stand within the verity casting."

Gilvray walked as if he were on the way to his own beheading, and he stood with his eyes closed rather than face the stares of those sitting at the table.

"Captain Gilvray, tell us your history of service?"

"I served in the Palion court as a page for three years, then spent seven years in the militia, starting as a kavelar ensign. I have been in the Journey Guard two years."

"And what are your feelings toward the princess?"

"I adored her from the moment I first set eyes on her. I thought there was feeling in her hearts for me, and when she married Viscount Cosseren I was ready to die of grief."

"Yet you planned to betray her?"

"No, I had intended to send Cosseren against the Alpenniens with the Journey Guard, while escorting the princess safely back to Karunsel in her coach. She would be widowed, and I would be left by her side, and that vile, ignorant pig Cosseren would no longer be defiling her. She might even develop favor toward me."

"You?" laughed Senterri. "A landless career officer?"

"I lived in hope. Hope is all that warriors have. Hope that a stray arrow does not find us on the battlefield, hope of advancement, hope to catch the eye of a rich woman."

"And what were you doing behind the borders of the most volatile and rebellious province of the entire empire?" asked the inquisitor.

"Elder Terikel asked me to escort her here. We had been sleeping together since Glasbury, and I felt that I owed her something."

"You vile betrayer!" shouted Senterri. "You adore me yet you, you . . ."

"I have had many dozens of lovers since you appointed me to the Journey Guard. I would close my eyes and pretend that each of them was you. Terikel—"

"He said I was the first one!" exclaimed Terikel, rising to her feet, then dropping back into her chair.

Laron put his hand to his eyes and shook his head. Senterri smirked for a moment, then stared out over the lake.

"Terikel asked me to escort her here, to Alpenfast, while the princess was spending time in Karunsel. I came here with her, alone; then I was approached by Castellan Emtellian as I rode back."

"Thank you, Captain, please sit down," said the inquisitor. "Gentlefolk, by now you can probably see why the verity casting is only for very brave people—or those who have no choice. The truth hurts, and you are not able to lie. Everyone sees you for what you are, and it is not a pretty sight. We priests subject ourselves to it once a week, and it does provide a great degree of serenity to us in spite of the trauma. Terikel, it is now your turn."

Terikel squirmed, and seemed almost to shrink before their eyes.

"I—I am not sure I can face it," she admitted in a small voice.

"Elder, once you have seen the inner thoughts of others laid bare, you must do the same. You have no choice in this matter."

"No! There are things that—"

"Elder, look to the upper balconies surrounding this one. Those figures on the railings are not gargoyles, they are warrior priests with contest crossbows. Each and every one of them can put a bolt through an apple on a string, at a hundred yards, on a windy day. Should I point at you, there will be three dozen bolts in your chest within the time it takes to draw breath. All must be equal within the verity machine, and even I shall step into it at the end and face your questions if you like. Come, Elder Terikel, yield. The experience may change your life."

Terikel took longer to walk to the verity casting than any of the others, and as Andry and Dolvienne clasped their hands to complete the circle around her, she kept her eyes tightly shut.

"Elder Terikel, what can I say?" said the inquisitor. "I know what you must be going through, my dear, and trust my word that I shall try to be as sympathetic as possible. Now then, why did you seduce Captain Gilvray? Was it only to get safe passage through Alpennien lands, to get here?"

"No—No, I . . . I had . . . private reasons."

"Amazing, my lady, amazing," said the inquisitor in awe. "You are resisting, even though you are only an initiate eleven. I have only ever seen an initiate thirteen do as well. Perhaps you should look to having your initiation level reexamined soon, but that is not our concern here. What was your other reason?"

Beads of perspiration glistened on Terikel's forehead, and

she began to shake with the strain. Her mouth opened, her jaw worked silently.

"The truth would be easier," said the inquisitor.

"Like . . . him—"

"That is a lie!" said Dolvienne at once.

"This will not stop until we have the truth," prompted the inquisitor.

Tears began to flow down Terikel's face, but they were pinkish tears. Their color began to darken, then her nose began to bleed.

"To betray, I wanted to betray, I long to betray!" Terikel suddenly burst out.

"Tell us who was being betrayed and the nature of the betrayal."

Terikel suddenly seemed more relaxed, as if she had decided to surrender to what was inevitable.

"Just betrayal, betrayal for its own sake. Betrayal is for me like a very strong and sharp spice, believe it, it is true. I betrayed Roval, a man who was so, so dear to me, when I seduced . . . other men to get over here. With my very fine, affectionate and gallant Roval, the dalliances were serene, enchanting, and beautiful, soaked with affection, trust, and mutual tenderness. But . . . No . . . Stop this."

"Continue," said the inquisitor.

"But with . . . my sponsor . . . astride me . . . and later the shipmaster—it was intense, brilliant, blazing bright with evil and guilty ecstasy, oh yes, and as I dressed in the morning I was awash with remorse, but there was always the allure of the next night. By the time I reached Glasbury the shipmaster was sea-dragon turds, but Gilvray was there, ah and I knew that he was a gallant man and would have escorted me here as an act of kindness if I but asked, but the need to go to Alpenfast was an excuse to seduce him, to do a thing that would make Roval curse my memory if he ever found out, but the intense pleasure from guilt and risk was—"

"Enough, Terikel, this was not what—"

"Trust my word on it, I first surrendered myself to my sponsor in the Metrologan temple in Alberin, the night before we sailed. My priestess Justiva turned Roval away when he came looking for me, I heard his voice in the distance. He asked where I had gone and why I had not told him I was going away, they were the last words of his that I ever heard. Justiva replied that I had gone to the nearest ringstone, he set off for Ringstone Septire, not realizing that Ringstone Logiar is slightly closer to Alberin, although across the Strait of Dismay. All the while my arms were around another man. Captain Gilvray adored the princess, and it is so much better when the betrayal is mutual. It was after the ball, he—"

"Andry and Dolvienne, release her!" shouted the inquisitor, and Terikel fell into the priest's arms. "Good, thank you, and I apologize," he said as he carried her back to her seat. "I made a mistake, I should have remembered that you said the reason was personal. I could have defined its boundaries without humiliating you thus, but it is done now. I have heard far worse, take comfort at least from that. Learned Selveris, what is your opinion?"

"You did make a severe blunder, Learned Inquisitor. When the verity casting has been collapsed, the triangle and a whip will be brought in, and you will be given one hundred and one lashes."

"No need," panted Terikel. "It is I who deserves the flogging."

"It is my duty not to make such mistakes, ladyship. When I do, I have to be given a little incentive not to reoffend. I should be trying to find the truth as it relates to matters of state, not trying to destroy you." Malecniar turned on the others. "Think upon your deepest and most vile secrets, and think that I can hunt them down. Should any of you so much as breathe a cruel or sarcastic word to the most lovely and dedicated Terikel, I shall look upon another one hundred and one lashes as but a small price to pay for avenging her honor."

"I have seen him do it," said Selveris.

The inquisitor turned back to Terikel. "My lady, can you face the verity casting again?"

"Yes," whispered Terikel, and she returned to Andry and Dolvienne unaided.

"Why did you come to Alpenfast?" asked the inquisitor.

"To learn by what means the Dragonwall may be destroyed," replied Terikel, her voice hoarse and ragged.

"Why do you want it destroyed?"

"Because too much power is finding its way into hands of stupid, cruel, greedy, or ambitious people."

"Stupid, ambitious, greedy, cruel, I think that accounts for nearly everyone who walks upon this world. Personally, I think that Dragonwall is the biggest disaster to befall us since Torea was burned by another type of ether machine, Silverdeath. The trouble is that Silverdeath was a weapon left over from some ancient and very skilled race, and once destroyed it could not be rebuilt. Dragonwall can be rebuilt, for we know the general principals now. What is the point of destroying it, Most Learned Terikel?"

"When a soldier meets an enemy on a battlefield, he fights even though he knows he may have to fight dozens of others. He fights, hoping that his side will eventually win. There are but few on my side, but I hope that we can eventually win."

"And what are your interests in the politics of the Sargolan Empire?"

"None whatsoever. I hate the place and want to go home."

"What do you want from us at Alpenfast?"

"An introduction to one of the oldest of the glass dragons: Teacher, Examiner, or Judge."

"Nothing more?"

"Nothing more."

"Thank you, ladyship, you may sit down now. When it comes time for me to be flogged, you will of course be allowed to deliver as many lashes as you think appropriate."

Terikel paused before the inquisitor, then slid her arms around him and pressed her cheek against his.

"There is no need for you to be punished for what I am," she said as she drew back.

"That is not why I am being punished," replied Malecniar. "Castellan Emtellian, please return to the verity casting. Trust me when I say that nothing personal will be asked that is not relevant to the matters of politics before us. I am not anxious to receive any more lashes than I am already facing. Oh, and Terikal, you shall have your introduction to the elder glass dragons."

Emtellian was looking quite relaxed as he stepped between Andry and Dolvienne again.

"Castellan, how long have you and Senterri been plotting to elope?"

"Since this time last year," said the castellan before he even had a chance to panic. There were several gasps of surprise from around the table.

"Tell us of the plot."

"Don't you dare!" shouted Senterri, rising to her feet.

"Sit down, Your Highness," said the inquisitor, staring calmly at Senterri. "I shall not ask a second time."

"Do it," said Gilvray.

Senterri tried to stare the inquisitor down, then collapsed more than sat.

"Senterri and I met quite some time ago, when I was attending the Palion court to renew my vows of fealty to the emperor. We took a fancy to each other, but there was no way that the emperor would approve any liaison between us. She traveled to the city of Diomeda in disguise, supposedly to take belly-dancing lessons. I was to travel there too, disguised as a slaver. I would seem to abduct her, then take her across the desert to my homeland mountains. I would seem to rescue her from slavers. Senterri would claim to have been ravished by the slavers, and I would claim to have avenged her by killing them. By the protocols of honor and obligation, I could restore her honor by marrying her, because I had killed those who ravished her."

"But real slavers abducted her before you could?"

"Yes. I failed, and you all know what happened to her. I was devastated when she married Cosseren. I had been planning to challenge him to a duel over some imagined slight, I hoped to kill him, I love her, I—"

"Thank you, that is enough, stand down. Senterri, please enter the verity casting again."

Senterri was defiant but frightened as she stepped into the casting for the second time.

"What are your feelings for the castellan?" asked Malecniar.

"When he failed to arrive at Diomeda as part of our plot, I thought . . ."

"She is not answering strictly correctly!" exclaimed Dolvienne.

"Please try that answer again, Your Highness," said the inquisitor.

"I am sorry, Emtellian. I never bothered to think longingly about you, I am silly, spoiled, and self-centered. Fate decreed that I was truly abducted before you were due to arrive in Diomeda. When Laron and his daemon rescued me . . . you were a long, long way away. It is true what Elder Terikel says, there is intense sweetness in the act of betrayal. I took Laron as my lover, and gave my maidenhead to him. After that . . . I could not go back to you. When Father proposed that I marry that idiot Cosseren, I did it to punish myself. Then Countess Bellesarion approached me at the Glasbury ball, and gave me your message. I dared to hope that once more there could be a future for us."

"Thank you, please stand down, Your Highness. Gentlefolk, you will be relieved to know that I have finished. Before facing my punishment for what I did to Terikel, I shall give all of you an opportunity to make a statement in the verity casting."

"Learned sir, why was I not called?" asked Laron.

"Because I can spot an innocent bystander when I see one. Innocent within these matters, anyway. You may, however, make a statement if you wish, but not yet. Dolvienne, speak first."

"I never want to set eyes on Princess Senterri again as long as I live," said Dolvienne. "Captain Gilvray, I despise her for what she did to you."

"Thank you. Reccon Tennoner, what do you wish us to know?"

"I want Velander to get better. If anyone can help her, please do so. And I wish that my true love can live down the shame of what happened here today."

"Your true love is not Velander?" exclaimed Laron.

"No, she is—"

"Stop!" cried the inquisitor. "Andry, keep her name secret; it is no business of ours. Terikel, step here and speak, if you will."

"My only wish is to destroy Dragonwall," said Terikel, now with her arms folded and her voice steady. "Damn the rest of you, and damn your petty plots and intrigues. The world is going straight to hell's lowest circle on a runaway wagon, and none of you cares!"

"Very good, Terikel, please step down. Captain Gilvray?"

Gilvray walked slowly to where Dolvienne and Andry hosted the verity casting, as if thinking over something important.

"Lady Dolvienne, a week ago you saved my life on the battlefield. You are brave, gracious, intelligent, resourceful, and very, very beautiful. You have my hearts forever, whether or not you fancy me, and I curse myself for not recognizing your worth long, long ago."

"Ah!" exclaimed the inquisitor. "You may reply, my lady."

"Captain, you have been my only fancy since the day you joined the Journey Guard," said Dolvienne softly.

"Castellan, do you wish to speak?" asked Malecniar.

"I do, learned sir," said the castellan as he got up and walked to Andry and Dolvienne. "Laron, for sleeping with my beloved, I shall kill you. For rescuing my beloved from the slavers, I shall give you a day before I come after you. Senterri, you have my love, should you want it. Inquisitor, you have my thanks. Captain Gilvray, you are the finest commander I have ever fought against. That is all."

"Laron?" asked the inquisitor.

Laron bowed within the verity casting before speaking.

"Learned Terikel, for a long time your former lover Roval has been my best friend, and often my only friend. I . . . I hope to return to Alberin, because I think he will need a friend nearby when he finds out what you did. That is all, Learned Inquisitor."

"Your Highness, you are all that stands between me and a flogging," said the inquisitor. "Speak as long as you like."

"My regrets, Learned Inquisitor, but I have little to say. Accept my gratitude, you forced me to grow up within a mere half hour. Dolvienne, Gilvray, I sentence you to death for treason. You have a day to flee before I send my guardsmen after you. Castellan Emtellian, my love is yours. Whether you want it or not is your decision. I have no more to say."

"The verity casting has a strange allure," concluded the

inquisitor. "People are so anxious to learn the secrets of others that they blind themselves to their own secrets. The first experience of the casting is usually voluntary. The second . . . is very rare."

With the inquisition over, Malecniar stood at the head of the table again, his hands clasped in front of him. Nobody was particularly interested in having him step into the verity casting, as he had earlier offered to.

"Before I collapse the verity casting, I have a favor to ask of you," he said. "Last night, two of your party were found in our library, after they very clumsily set off an alarm auton. I should like to subject them to the verity casting, with your permission."

All those present agreed. They were in fact looking forward to some light relief at the expense of someone else after what they had been through. Wilbar and Riellen were brought out from a doorway by two priests. After some very basic explanations of what the verity casting could do, Riellen was made to stand within it.

"Why were you spying on us?" demanded the inquisitor, with a lot less patience in his tone than he had shown to those now seated at the table.

"We were liberating knowledge from this oligarchical order of scholars with the intention of presenting it to the common people," replied Riellen.

"Who are you working for?"

"The Sorceric Conspiracies and Occult Plots Exposure Collective."

"And who else is in this, ah, collective?"

"Wilbar and Maeben."

"Why was Maeben not with you?"

"He said his mother taught him never to abuse the hospitality of a host, so he stayed in his room. I told him that he should not entertain such upper-middle-class and lower-upper-class notions of honor when the common people's right to knowledge was at stake, but he said to piss off and he hoped we got caught."

"The common people are too stupid to even come in out of the rain," said Emtellian.

Wilbar was pushed toward the casting, but he fell to his knees.

"I need no verity casting, I live for Princess Senterri, and I would die for her!" exclaimed the student, raising his clasped hands in the direction of Senterri. "Setting eyes on her changed my life, I renounce revolutionary intrigues forever, I had no courage to tell Riellen and Maeben, but now I shall speak nothing but the truth and I declare that I adore the very dust that Princess Senterri walks upon—"

"Enough, please, go away!" cried the inquisitor, putting a hand over his face.

"Your organization sounds subversive," observed Senterri, glaring at Riellen, who glared defiantly back. "If ever I catch you outside Alpenfast's boundaries, you will be hanged for treason. Wilbar, you are, as of this moment, under my protection and patronage."

The inquisitor collapsed the verity casting, and Dolvienne immediately released Andry's hand and limped to Captain Gilvray. By now Senterri was already in the arms of Emtellian, and Terikel was wiping the blood from her face with a napkin and mintmilk. Laron walked over to Andry.

"Time we were gone, lad, unless you enjoy watching floggings," said Laron, gesturing to the main doorway.

"So this is what our betters do at court?" muttered Andry, his face held studiously blank.

"Our taxes at work, Andry. I forgot to ask, how is Vel?"

"Slipping away, but we've said our goodbyes."

"Do you think she would like a word with me, before I flee yet again?"

"I think she would insist on it."

Laron fled with Riellen, Dolvienne, and Gilvray later that morning. Maeben decided that he had a vocation to the priesthood, and came to Andry's room to present him with his worldly goods before taking his vows as a novice. These consisted of some clothing that did not fit anybody less than two feet shorter than Andry, a few stolen books on magical castings, some silver and copper coins, a blanket, and a knife.

"I heard that the reccons are to be sent after Captain Gilvray and Lady Dolvienne," said Maeben.

"That we are," replied Andry. "We are to keep them in sight until a day is past, then direct the Regency Guard and the castellan's men to them. Seems that they took a wild but direct track for Logiar, so it is there we are going."

"But I thought you liked the captains."

"True, but I am a soldier, and Senterri is my supreme commander."

"Andry, I heard that Learned Terikel is to travel with the reccons."

"Oh aye, and Wallas is, too. Senterri filled him in on what happened with the inquisitor, then promised to make him a cook in the palace in Logiar. He's anxious to get there and have a feast ready for when she arrives. And now, Maeben, I must fall in with the reccons, because we are leaving at noon. Look after Velander, while she lingers."

"I'll do that, and you look after yourself, Andry."

Chapter Seven

DRAGONFRIGHT

 On the second day after leaving Alpenfast, the reccons began to encounter strange, circular, glassy patches in the trail, generally with a few bones scattered about nearby.

"Glass dragons hereabout," reported Essen, dismounting to remove a fine, expensive ax from the skeleton of an arm that ended at the edge of the glassy patch.

"It's not as if I hadn't noticed, sir," replied Andry, accepting the ax from him.

They forded a broad but shallow river, then rode alongside

it for a while. The trail turned out into a flat, grassy field amid the mountains.

Essen rode with Andry for most of the time now, slowly having the story of the verity casting explained to him. Andry also explained something of the manners that he had been learning from Laron and Wallas.

"Do not mistake stiffness for dignity when you meet a person for the first time," Andry said, within earshot of Wallas, who was driving the cart. "Stiffness can be put on by anyone. Dignity must be learned."

"Since when have I been stiff?" called Wallas.

"Since the last woman who didn't slap your face as soon as you leered at her," laughed Essen.

Everyone except Terikel and Wallas laughed too, and then Andry continued with the lesson.

"The truly dignified people have nothing to prove, and so are very easy in their manner."

"Like, dignified folk don't boast?" asked Essen.

"Aye, that seems to be it. Laron said boasting won't get you anything of value. Confidence and ease of manner tells folk more than an hour of talk about yourself."

"But, like, what's to talk about?"

"Everything about the person you are talking to. Makes them feel important."

In the distance a deep-noted bell began to toll. It was a steady, rolling sound, mixed into echoes by the mountains.

"What's that sound?" asked Andry.

"Big bell," replied Essen.

"No, I mean whose is it?"

"It is the Alpenfast death bell," called Terikel forlornly from the cart.

"But ladyship, Velander has hovered close to death for a long time," said Andry. "How can they be sure she is truly gone?"

"They are better qualified to judge such things than we are, Andry. Let her go, now, but love her memory."

✦ ✦ ✦

Terikel asked that they stop late in the afternoon. They were in a small, grassy patch, and the road ahead narrowed to barely the width of the cart's wheels as it skirted the mountain that towered over them. Terikel said that its name was Taloncrag. On the other side of the road was a sheer drop that Essen estimated to be at least half a mile.

"Costiger, Danol, go up that mountainside and check that no outlaws are lurking there to attack us while we pass along the narrowing," said Essen. "Stay there until we're through, and we'll wait with your horses on the other side. Ladyship, how long will you need?"

"Perhaps two days, Marshal Essen."

"Two days? We can't wait more than this night."

"I can make my own way back to Alpenfast, but I do have one request. Can you spare Andry to play a little music? It's very important."

Essen frowned and shook his head.

"There's Andry, Danol, and me as play, but we're reccons and we're bound by orders to trail the captain and his lady."

"Did I hear someone say music?" asked Wallas, hurrying over. "I just happen to have a board lyre with me, and I am not a reccon."

"Aye, but gag his lips so he can't sing his bloody awful ballads," laughed Essen. "Aye then, ladyship, but the cart goes on with us, as outlaws would think it a tempting target. I'll leave two horses for you and Wallas. Wallas, I'll write a note to fall out, but when ladyship's done with you, ride after us."

"Oh understood, sir," said Wallas, bowing.

They tethered the two horses out of sight; then the reccons continued along the narrowing road and around the mountain. The light began to fade, and Terikel asked Wallas to light a fire and wait with her. They were above the tree line, so there was little to burn except brushwood and twigs.

"Ah now, would you like a tune or a song, Learned Elder?" asked Wallas with a flourish of his board lyre.

"Not just now," replied Terikel, feeding twigs to the fire. "When the time is right, I shall know. Then you may play."

"Ah, the right time for a tune! Now *there* is an art, that of choosing the time to perfection. Take us, as we sit here, alone in the wilderness. Why, what better time or place for a romantic song of dalliance?"

"Wallas, when I need a tune, I shall tell you. There is an end to it."

"But, but—"

"When I need the tune, I shall tell you!"

"But what about payment?"

"Payment?"

"I have gone to some trouble to provide your tune. Why, I shall have to ride alone to catch up with my comrades when you are done with me. We all know what that means, of course."

"Means? Of course?"

"Why, I volunteered for this perilous venture because I assumed you wanted to lie with me, and again feel the intense pleasures of betrayal. I quite understand, I am very broad-minded and—"

"Wallas, I need a tune as part of a—a signal. *I* cannot play music. Without you I am lost."

"Oh, ladyship, then you do have a problem. Out of gallantry I shall stay until morning to see you through the night's perils, but I shall need payment for a tune—bard's fee, and all that."

Wallas laughed knowingly. Terikel put a hand to her forehead, closed her eyes, and shook her head. She contemplated her situation for some time.

"Very well then, Wallas, but this is nothing to do with the pleasures of betrayal. I merely need a tune, the very fate of the world depends on a tune, and I *shall have* a tune. All I feel for you is mild—no, considerable revulsion, but I revolt myself as well, so does anything really matter? Come on then, let's be about it and have your filthy little chore done."

"Ladyship, ladyship," said Wallas, flourishing his board lyre. "Never a chore, I promise you—"

A crossbow bolt removed the board lyre from his grasp with a sharp thud. Wallas screamed and raised his hands high. Terikel had drawn her tunic up and had reached for the lacing of her riding trousers, and in this position she froze.

"Thought you might need a *man* to stand guard, ladyship," called Andry from not far away. "It's not a skill Wallas is known for. Neither is music, either, so I've brought my rebec, and I play for free."

"Andry?" quavered Wallas, slowly lowering his hands.

"That's me."

"You can't be here!"

"But I am."

"You're a reccon. You're ordered to pursue Gilvray and Dolvienne."

"I deserted."

"You what? You—you're jealous!"

"Ladyship, I'm here to play tunes, and to guard you," said Andry. "Should you wish to make merry with Wallas, I shall make sure that you have privacy."

"I would rather kiss a slug!" snapped Terikel, pulling her tunic down again.

"I, ah, only sought fair payment, and, ah, I understood that the Elder was seeking, that is . . ."

He stopped speaking as a vast shape glided overhead. It banked, then came around, inspecting them with keen, glowing eyes, even though it was at least a thousand feet above them.

"Dragon," squeaked Wallas.

"Tell me something I don't know," replied Andry, also with quite a distinct trace of unease on his voice.

"I'll need a tune, now!" said Terikel.

"He ruined my lyre!" cried Wallas.

"Lucky shot," said Andry, taking out his rebec. "I think I'll start with 'The Dragons of Alberin.' "

"There aren't any dragons in Alberin," said Wallas, still looking skyward.

"Stone ones, on the city gates," explained Andry, looking around for any human intruders that might be approaching.

"They say their breath is hotter than white-hot steel," said Wallas. "They say their wings are two hundred feet across."

"They say they can speak," said Andry. "They say they're smarter than us."

"Whoever *they* are, they are well informed," said Terikel. "All of that is true."

After circling several times, the dragon flew for a ledge on the mountain they were skirting. It perched there for some moments, then withdrew from sight.

"I request that you begin your tune, Andry," said Terikel, gazing up at the place where the dragon had perched briefly. "It reassures them that we are friendly."

"I'll play too," said Wallas, scrambling after the lyre and snatching it out of the grass. "Look at this! Ruined! Your bolt split the frame."

"Fortune guided my hand," said Andry, beginning to play a reel on his rebec.

"You are playing well, Andry," said Terikel. "If the dragon does not flame us to char and smoke, you may become known as Andry Dragoncharmer."

"Dragoncharmer?" gasped Wallas. "You mean if I had an instrument to play, I too could be called Dragon-charmer!"

"Touch my rebec and I'll cut your balls off and feed 'em to the dragon," said Andry, without stopping his playing.

Terikel pointed upward, and Andry and Wallas followed her gesture. The dragon was back.

"It has invited us up to talk," said Terikel. "That is the code, circling, sitting on a ledge, then staring down at us as the tune is played."

"Big bastard," said Andry. "That ledge must be a thousand feet above us."

"Dragons never make it easy for people," said Terikel.

"You mean we have to climb?" gasped Wallas.

"Yes," said Terikel. "We have a dragon above us that wishes to talk. We must climb up to meet it."

"Would the dragon be offended if the rest of us rode on?" asked Wallas.

"It has heard playing, and knows that someone is climbing up for an audience. If anyone is seen leaving, that will be taken as a slight."

"I'm still riding!"

Wallas had to be dragged off his horse by Andry and left tied up on the ground while Terikel packed for the climb.

Wallas screamed curses and begged to be cut loose. Andry picked up his rebec and began to play again.

"The dragon likes your playing," said Terikel as she hoisted her pack.

"How can you tell?"

"We are still alive, in spite of Wallas's disrespect. Come, time to begin climbing. Every few minutes, we stop for a tune."

Andry cut Wallas loose, then set off after Terikel, who had found a trail up the mountain. It took Wallas only moments to decide that being alone was not a good option in this place, but just where to find company remained his problem. Terikel seemed to know how to stay on the right side of the glass dragons, but the reccons had the virtue of being farther away.

"Terikel told me she put castings on the horse tethers," Andry called back. "Touch one, and it will burn your hand off."

It was some time after sunset that Terikel allowed them to rest. Wallas quizzed Andry on their prospects of escape should something go wrong, but concluded that a dragon could definitely fly faster than he could ride. Terikel sat some distance away, meditating and generating a complex etheric field around her head.

"Ghastly muck," grumbled Wallas as he ate his dinner of crushed nuts, dried fruit, and water with a wooden foraging spoon.

"Pity it's not hot," replied Andry. "When I was at sea—"

"I know, I know, the food was all soaked in cold salt water. I wouldn't mind a little salt, actually."

They sat eating out of the tin for a while. Terikel sat unmoving in the distance. Andry picked up his rebec and began to play.

"Will you just look at that?" said Andry, lying back and looking up, but continuing to play the rebec.

"Aye, it's Dragonwall."

"But just look at it! Half the sky is lights."

Wallas lay back and stared as well. Dragonwall was not quite overhead, but slightly to the west.

"So what?" he asked.

"So it's something we've never seen the like of before. What's it really for, I wonder?"

"If I knew that, I'd be an important sorcerer."

"But Wallas, doesn't it, er, sort of fill you with wonder?"

"You know Andry, sometimes I think you just talk to hear the sound of your own voice."

Wallas wrapped himself in his blanket, walked to an overhang that formed a shallow cave, lay down, and turned over. Andry sat up, retuned the rebec, then played several tunes to reassure the dragon that they were indeed still there, and friendly. Terikel ended her meditations, then came over and sat beside Andry. She toyed with her hair for some moments, weaving it into little braids; then she cleared her throat.

"I know this is not a good time, Andry, but about Wallas," she began.

"Aye?"

"I—I owe you my thanks," she said softly. "I also owe you an explanation."

"None needed, ladyship."

"Please! Play on, but listen, I'd not have Wallas overhear me if he be awake. Once, a decade ago, I was a beautiful young priestess, newly ordained. I had the highest marks ever obtained in the Metrologans' castings theory and applications examinations. The Elder of the time wanted to gain the confidence of a certain count, however. He was a man of no great charm or attraction, but he was one who had been entrusted with a great many secrets. I was ordered to . . . be nice to him, ordered by the Elder herself."

Andry sighed, looking distracted and seeming as if he would prefer not to hear what she was saying.

"I prefer a good, clean fight, ladyship."

"Fight pigs, and one smells of pigshyte, Andry. I was successful in my sordid little combat. The Elder was so pleased that she sent me to storm the bed of yet another important minion of some faction that was unimportant, but whose secrets were very important. A dozen or two seductions later, and I had taught myself to be allured by horrible men, and excited by betrayal. Then I became friends with an idealistic and earnest young student named Velander. She even asked me to be her soulmate, and there is no higher personal honor you can have in the Metrologan order. On the night that Velander was to complete her ordination ritual, and when I should have kept soulmate vigil for her, the Elder ordered me to seduce a man. Well, more of a monster than a man, but I did it. In a sense it was easy. Guilt and pleasure flung me about like a leaf in rapids."

Andry was now playing a tune that was crammed with runs and trills, one that would best mask words from nearby ears.

"Senterri told Wallas what you had said while in the grasp of the verity casting," he said. "Wallas boasted of it to me. I had a feeling that he would try what he suggested to you tonight."

"The man is a toad, but I did lift my tunic for him before you appeared. He got the surrender from me, Andry. That rankles."

"Hah, not so!" laughed Andry. "I know Wallas, he'd take nothing less than, er, consumption—"

"The word is 'consummation.' "

"Er, oh. What I mean is, anything less than that is defeat, for him. You're no victory."

Terikel undid a tangle in her hair, then hugged her knees.

"Andry, Velander hated me for what I did to her, but after learning for herself that the world can be very cruel, she forgave me. I am very grateful to you, Andry, but I cannot hurt you by—"

"Not another word, ladyship," said Andry tersely. "I've had too many women say they want to protect me from the evils of dalliance, or whatever. You'd roll Wallas for a tune, but not me, even if the music is free. I'm without much educating, ladyship, but I'm not stupid. Women think I'm a joke, and they hold their kind words until I'm on my way and going. I loved Velander because she asked me for help. She asked me, scruffy young Andry with the wineskin in one hand and the stolen rebec in the other. All the while I loved

another because she . . . But no, can't speak on that. Now off
to sleep with you, I think tomorrow's to be rough going."

Terikel hugged her knees even more tightly, and dark
tears began to run down her cheeks. Andry suddenly
stopped playing.

"Ladyship! Your tears, they're blood again."

Terikel put a fingertip to one, then held it before her.

"The verity casting sliced me up a little inside when I re-
sisted it, that's all. Andry, I was about to tell you to leave.
Now. I mean to pay Wallas's filthy price and have him as my
musician tomorrow."

Andry shrugged. "As you will, ladyship. Like I said, Velander asked me to look after you, but if you've other plans,
I'll be away. Remember, though, I play for free."

"You are also a virgin, Andry. The glass dragon will de-
vour you for some subtle quality in your life force. Wallas
would be safe. *That* is what I tried to tell you some moments ago."

"Oh aye, is that all?" laughed Andry. "Then leave the
filthy wretch where he is, ladyship. I'll play you up to the
dragon, then fight it off when it turns on me."

"You will die!" exclaimed Terikel.

"Perhaps, but who cares? I've met the ferrygirl already.
Nice lass."

Terikel sat hugging her legs for some time, and Andry began playing again. Dark tears ran down her chin and stained
the cloth at her knees. Slowly she straightened and sat up,
stretched, then whispered a casting and began forming it in
her cupped hands. To Andry, it had an angry, jagged, dangerous look to it, and he fancied that the energies looked almost
hungry. She stood, then looked down at Andry with the casting held in one hand.

"I must go to Wallas for a short time," she announced.

How does the man do it, Andry asked himself. *She hates
Wallas, yet she would rather lie with him than even give me a
kiss on the cheek.* Terikel delivered a sickeningly hard kick
in the buttocks to Wallas. He squealed and tried to sit up, but
hit his head on the rock overhang.

"I wish you to watch this," Terikel declared as she began
taking tendrils from the casting and pressing them onto the

rocks of the overhang above and around Wallas with her free hand. They began to take on a pattern that resembled a very large spider's web.

"What are you doing?" asked Wallas, who had the perfectly reasonable feeling that whatever she was doing was not in his best interests.

"As soon as I am finished here," she whispered, "I sincerely hope that Andry and I are going to be making use of each other's primary sexual features, hopefully paying some attention to the secondary ones as well. I do not want an audience. Take my advice, Wallas, and do not touch the web."

Terikel released the casting, and it spread out along the filaments right up to the rocks that formed the mouth to the little cave where Wallas was now imprisoned. The casting wove itself finer and finer, until it formed a continuous and opaque fabric of glow. Terikel returned to Andry, who had stopped playing when she had kicked Wallas.

"What did you do to him?" Andry asked.

"That casting is normally to keep nasty things out when one is camping," explained Terikel. "In this case, it is keeping something nasty in."

"Oh. I hope he has no need for a piss."

Terikel knelt down, reached out, and took Andry's bow and rebec. She laid them carefully on the sparse mountain grass beside them.

"Andry, I have just hurt and humiliated a very horrible man who desires me greatly," she said. "Be my musician tomorrow, please?"

Andry smiled, drew his knees up, and hugged his legs, just as Terikel had done a few minutes earlier.

"Aye, I'd be honored."

Suddenly there was a scream of anguish from over where Wallas was sealed in his cave.

"Somebody touched the casting!" called Terikel; then she turned back to Andry and stared at him for what seemed like a substantial portion of the night. "Andry, I do not want you to die tomorrow," she whispered. "Think on what that means we must do."

Terikel was smiling winsomely and giving Andry her undivided attention.

"This is very embarrassing," said Andry. "Fate is definitely playing tricks with me."

Suddenly Terikel slumped against her knees and turned away.

"I forgot, you saw a very, very ugly side of me in Alpenfast. You must be revolted by me, I understand now."

"No, not so—"

"Pity, because . . . well, when you reappeared in my life in the village of Harrgh, I was happier than I have been for years. I was so proud of the way you had changed, and the way you met challenges, and progressed so far and fast. You are like Laron, only, well, you are genuinely young and fresh. I . . . I resolved to sleep with you. You are nineteen. I was nineteen when the Elder first ordered me to defile myself. With you, I thought I could pretend to be young and unspoiled again, but I was too slow. When you grew close to Velander, I knew Fate was punishing me for my past. Innocence was not to be mine."

"Me—you?" exclaimed Andry.

"Oh yes, you are truly wonderful, and your innocence cannot be killed. My bedmates have all been horrible, older men. Well, Roval was not horrible, but he was too much of a mother hen for me to love. I was too shy to approach you, being ten years your senior and all. You would not laugh, but you might pity me. That would have been worse. Do you understand?"

Andry slowly extended his hand to Terikel, palm up. Terikel's eyes widened; then she reached out to him and her fingers enfolded his hand.

"Aye, that I do. I love a great lady, but I'd always worried that she would be like all the others, and send me on my way with really kind and, er, diplomatic words. I preferred to live in hope and have nothing, than have her hurry me along and away if I told her. When I was in the verity casting, remember I nearly spoke the name of my true love? Her name was Terikel."

"Andry Tennoner, are you trying to say that we just traveled halfway across Acrema together, pining for each other the whole time, and with *nothing* to prevent us doing anything about it until Glasbury?" cried Terikel.

"Er, aye."

Terikel released his hand and began massaging her temples. "Someday I would like to become a god," she declared.

"Why is that, ladyship?"

"Because I want to wring Fate's neck for what he just did to us!"

Terikel put her arm around Andry's shoulders, and they sat with their heads resting together for a time in the orange light, then got down to the practicalities of laying out bedding and getting undressed. From nearby came another muffled scream as Wallas touched the casting again.

Andry awoke to the last of several important lessons from Terikel. He had just realized that people who sleep together keep each other a lot warmer than if they had been sleeping apart. He lay there with his arms around her until she stirred and awoke.

"So now you know," she whispered to him.

"It will make going without all the worse," he sighed, knowing that the pleasant interlude was probably soon to end.

"A subtle but powerful compliment, Andry. Thank you. For what it is worth . . . you delighted me. You gave me the strength to face some very difficult decisions, and I shall face them for the sake of people like you: good people, caring people. Come now, let's get into our clothes, then kick Wallas."

Once they were dressed, Andry watched as Terikel walked over to the overhang where Wallas was sealed. She reached down, and dug her fingers into the casting that still imprisoned him. It collapsed with a soft pop. A kick in the backside woke Wallas.

"Up with you, sluggard, time to climb."

"Yes, Mother, whatever you—I, where, what—It's morning!" exclaimed Wallas.

"Yes, I have just spent the night making Andry distasteful to dragons. Just as well I sealed you in here, or you would have felt truly inadequate."

"She's very considerate that way," added Andry.

Wallas tried to look contemptuous, but merely seemed nervous and somewhat crushed.

"Mist soon," announced Terikel, as she picked up her pack. "The dragons make it with a casting. We need to get moving again."

"What about breakfast?" protested Wallas.

"Forget breakfast," advised Andry. "Women prefer lean men, trust me on that."

Only minutes after they began climbing again, a thick mist materialized around them. With the sun gone, it quickly became very cold, and visibility could be measured in just inches.

"Stop here, give the glass dragon a tune," said Terikel.

Andry played a reel, then Terikel decided that they should continue climbing again. Soon the mist was so thick that Wallas could barely see his hand in front of his face.

"The air is freezing," said Wallas, hoping for a reply that would prove the others had not left him.

"Aye, and I'm not breathing all that well" was Andry's comment.

"Me neither. Gets that way in very high mountains. Thin air, not so much to breathe."

"Well, I'll be a monkey's uncle."

"As long as you're not its father."

"No, I mean, dive in water and you can't breathe. Go too high and you can't breathe. That's interesting. Wait till I tell the boys at Bargeyards."

"You know something else?"

"Tell me."

"There's an echo, like a cave."

"Cave?" said Andry. "It must be a very big cave."

"We are indeed in a cave," said Terikel. "Please keep the chatter to a minimum."

The mist around them began to darken; then a bright, bluish light cut through the gloom. Terikel had spoken a casting that had fashioned a small globe of brightness that floated along just above her head. The mist thinned as they walked farther in. On a wall nearby was a drawing of a serpentlike beast with very large wings.

"Dragon," breathed Wallas.

"Aye, draggin' its tail!" said Andry, poking Wallas in the stomach with his rebec's bow. "Get it?"

"No, a dragon! Magical animal, breathes fire, eats people, don't they teach you anything in Alberin schools—Gah! Was that meant to be a pun?"

"Will you two keep up?" called Terikel, "Andry, walk slowly and play as you go."

They followed Terikel, with Andry playing a slow step-march as they walked deep into the great cavern. The floor was straight and level, and it was evident that it had once been a place of worship. There were colorful pavings underfoot, but evidence of neglect as well. The remains of ancient, broken columns and statues had been pushed aside to the walls. Eyes watched from the rubble, but nothing made any sort of threat. The only statues still intact were those of three enormous lizards with wings, sitting up on their haunches. They were fashioned from light blue glass, except for their eyes, which were dark and hollow-looking. A slight glow outlined the dragons against the darkness, and Andry saw that the edge of every joint and scale was traced out in a line of white so intense that it seemed to glow. They were similar to the blackstone statues that flanked one of the city gates in Alberin, but those were no larger than a horse. The heads of these were halfway to the cavern roof, and the clawed points of the folded wings were within easy reach of the rock overhead. There was an inscription on the wall behind them, and Andry realized that he could see some of the ancient lettering right through their bodies.

"Now, *they* are dragons," said Wallas. "Statues, anyway. Real dragons are not nearly as big as that, and they don't glow."

"Wallas, a word?" said Andry.

"What?"

"That statue on the left just twitched its tail."

Ahead of them, Terikel had stopped, and was activating a casting. The head and shoulders of an Alpenfast priest materialized in midair, then began speaking a message to the dragons on Terikel's behalf. Having reached the end of the introduction, the casting of the priest's image winked out. The Elder of the Metrologans bowed deeply to each of the three huge figures in turn. The eyes of the central dragon flickered into blue-white life, then blinked slowly.

"Alive," managed Wallas, in a tiny, strangled voice at least two octaves higher than before.

Andry's concern was not so much that the glass dragons would notice them, but that they would not notice them— especially if one decided to take a walk or belch a fireball. The central dragon opened its mouth, and silvery light with a bluish sheen began to spill between its fangs as it cleared its throat with a rumble like that of an approaching thunderstorm.

"This is it, I'm betting he had a curry last night," said Andry in a voice so highly pitched that it seemed like someone else talking.

"And I am honored to meet you, Teacher," said Terikel in Diomedan, bowing to the central dragon. Then she bowed to the other two. "And Judge, and Examiner."

The dragon's jaws moved again, and again the rumble filled the cave.

"The two men behind me are also mortals," explained Terikel.

Andry now realized that the enormous dragon of blue nothingness had been speaking. He resolved to pay closer attention next time it opened its mouth.

"The lean one is my musician and warrior," said Terikel. "The other is my cook. They both have good manners."

"Musician *and* warrior?" asked a voice like a thunderstorm speaking.

"Yes. He is a loyal and trustworthy man."

The dragon bent slowly, and stared at Andry and Wallas.

"I'm not a virgin!" cried Wallas.

"Oh aye, neither am I, either, like, as of last night," babbled Andry, indescribably relieved that it was true.

"Filthy little boy," snapped Wallas, suddenly remembering the torments of the previous night, forgetting the dragon, and turning on Andry. "But *I've* done it more often."

"Oh aye, and sometimes even in company," replied Andry, annoyance with Wallas suddenly swamping his fear of the dragons.

"Now, *that* was cheap and crude! I happen to know you've only done it once."

"It was five times, and—Oh! Er, ah, my apologies, lady-ship."

Ter... l was standing with a hand over her eyes and shaking her head. The dragon turned away from them and looked back to Terikel. It rumbled some brief words that were not quite comprehensible to Andry.

"It does not seem likely," Terikel replied.

The dragon said something else, too quickly for Andry to follow.

"I have not noticed, but then I am only three decades old."

There was a rumble that sounded distinctly like a question to Andry.

"I mean that you have been studying the sciences of the ether for many thousands of years, and have developed skills that I cannot even guess at."

The following rumble again had the note of a question.

"Dragons share some of the interests of Metrologans. I am Terikel, the Elder of the Metrologans."

"There are no more Metrologans."

Andry was developing the knack of teasing words out of the rumbles from the enormous creature. Wallas continued to merely look terrified.

"A few of us were clear of Torea when it was destroyed," replied Terikel. "We are rebuilding our order in Alberin, and we have missions in Sargol."

"Many of us died in Torea," said Examiner. "That disaster was caused by humans. Again humans are meddling with forces that they barely understand. If Dragonwall were a workable venture to mold the winds and direct the rains, glass dragons would have constructed it long ago."

"That is why I am here," replied Terikel.

"We shall give you no secrets of etheric machineries."

"I want no secrets, I want just your observations of the winds. You are creatures of the winds, you know them better than any mortal ever could. Tell me, are the winds changing? Is Dragonwall making a difference?"

"Does a mill wheel slow a raging torrent?"

Terikel thought for a moment.

"It does, but by a very small amount."

"In just the same way, Dragonwall does slow the winds, but it is of as much use against the Torean Storms as a mill wheel would be in slowing the rush of a flood."

"But do the sorcerers realize this?"

"Only a fool could miss it, but then they are fools for re-building Dragonwall in the first place."

Terikel hurriedly consulted a mental checklist. "Will the Torean Storms grow worse?" she asked.

"They are passing their peak," replied Teacher. "In five years the climate will again be as it was before Torea burned."

"Can you give me measurements?" Terikel asked immediately.

"Dragons do not make measurements. We know the strengths of winds that we fly upon. We view clouds from far above, and we sense both heat and the lack of it more finely than you mortals. We remember everything, and we can read trends that extend into the future. The storms *are* diminishing, Elder Terikel, but they were diminishing before Dragonwall was initiated. The machine's effect is less than one part in fifty."

"One part in fifty? That is not worth bothering with."

"Correct."

"So Dragonwall is of no use," Terikel stated rather than asked.

"Dragonwall is very useful, but that use does not involve controlling storms."

"A weapon, then?" asked Terikel, moving further down the list in her mind.

"Mortal, you *know* that it is a weapon. Dragonwall was used to strike at you as you traveled here. Why did you come to us?"

"To expose Dragonwall as a weapon. To ask how to destroy it forever."

"All those participating know that it is a weapon already. More inclined ringstones tap into it every day, people are frightened of not being part of it. There is also a conspiracy to use it as a weapon."

"There are dozens of such conspiracies, soon there will be hundreds."

"Hundreds?" asked Examiner. "Can you name one?"

"The High Circle of Scalticarian Initiates wishes to use it to destroy the temples of the Skepticals, the Independent Order of Dissenters, and the Popularist Sorceric Front, as well as to weaken its own ally, the Sargolan Governance of Initiates. The Sargolan Governance of Initiates wishes to use it to wipe out the leadership of the High Circle, after which it will take over the leaderless regional temples, thus gaining control of initiates over an entire new continent. The—"

"That is enough, thank you," said Examiner.

"I know of another thirty-five," sighed Terikel. "Sometimes I wonder if there are any people anywhere who are not scheming, murdering bastards."

"Yes, but they are not the people who build etheric machines capable of turning entire kingdoms into piles of slag and char," Examiner pointed out.

"Examiner," began Terikel; then she shook her head and stared down at the floor of the cave.

"Excellent, you do appear to have reached a very important conclusion."

"Yes, thank you, I believe I have," said Terikel.

"Now, about destroying Dragonwall. We should assume our more sensitive forms for that. Please bear with us."

Examiner slowly lay out flat along the floor of the cave. First the wings began to diminish and fade, then the rest of the body dimmed and flickered out. The barrel shape of its chest collapsed with a swirl of sparkles that was sucked into a dark, dense form at its core; then a neat, elderly little woman stood before them, brushing her robes down. She bowed to her guests, then smiled broadly. Andry had the impression that she was trying to be reassuring, but he could see light spilling from her mouth, and her eyes were glowing as well. By now the other two dragons had also lain down, and were going through the same transformation.

"Judge and Teacher will be along soon," Examiner explained, taking Terikel by the arm and gesturing to a nearby wall. A door materialized in the brickwork as they approached.

Andry and Wallas followed into a small, cozy room with comfortable-looking armchairs surrounding a low table. The little woman picked up a kettle and breathed gently against the side. The water within began to bubble.

"Does everyone drink tea?" Examiner asked.

✷ ✷ ✷

Judge and Teacher arrived just as Examiner was pouring the tea, but Judge realized that they had no shortbreads, so he hurried outside again. Examiner walked over to Wallas and Andry.

"Handsome, you have been astride one hundred and thirty-seven women," she said with what might have been subtle sarcasm, but which came across as mild amusement.

"Dirty, filthy swine!" exclaimed Andry.

"Musician, you were a virgin until last night."

"A virgin!" hooted Wallas. "Princess Senterri told me you weren't man enough to roger my wife."

"One hundred and thirty-seven!" Andry shouted back. "Why so many? Would none be abed with you more than once?"

"Gentlemen, gentlemen," began Examiner.

"Once a woman has been with me, you would never dare ask her for a comparison," snorted Wallas.

"Once a woman's been with you she's put off men for months!" Andry shouted back.

"Gentlemen, please!" cried Examiner, stamping her foot. "So Andry, you first did the act last night?"

"Er, it's true," Andry mumbled.

"Pity. Why did you decide to . . . do it?"

"Because Lady Terikel said you'd eat me were I . . . uninitiated."

" 'Eat' is such a strong word," said Examiner. " 'Savor' is more accurate."

"What? Savor, as in something you do before you eat something?"

"Oh no. I might have fancied you four thousand years ago, but not now. Distractions of the flesh and all that."

"Have a shortbread, Musician?" asked Judge, coming up beside Andry with a tray.

"My thanks," said Andry, taking one.

"So, my senses tell me that you became well acquainted with Elder last night," said Judge pleasantly.

"How can you tell, sir—er, Judge Dragon? Like, with men?"

"So recently, scent alone is enough. After some days have elapsed, there are other differences. Hard to explain to humans, but any dragon can . . . savor the difference."

"Are you disappointed, sir?"

"Me? Why?"

"Because my taste has been spoiled, and it's not such a treat to eat me?"

"What sort of dragon do you take me for?" demanded Judge, his breath suddenly so hot that it singed Andry's tunic. "Eat you? A *man*?"

"I—what? I mean, what sir?" stammered Andry.

"Your only danger might have come from Examiner, but her tastes are not what they were."

"Oh. Sorry sir. No offense, sir."

"Eat a man, the very thought!" said Judge, turning away and shaking his head.

Across the room, Terikel was speaking with Teacher. He had the form of a tall, thin man with a permanent grin.

"Elder, I sense that you are troubled. Can we do anything to help?"

"Dragons want payment. I have nothing to give."

"Oh no, you have a great deal to offer, but you cannot appreciate what it is. Dragons acquire, mortals do. *You* cannot see what you offer us, because you do not appreciate it. We see you for what you are, and you are quite, quite beyond value."

"I do not understand."

"Of course not. Musician appreciates you for your kindness with him last night, and he knows that you are important and have studied a lot. But he does not understand what you *are* as a priestess, scholar, or sorceress."

"To understand a scholar, one needs to *be* a scholar."

"Precisely, Elder. And in the same way, only dragons can see what *you* are."

"I . . . do not like the meaning behind that remark," said Terikel.

"Yet is stands. Now then, would you like to help destroy Dragonwall?"

"Nothing could please me more."

"Then I shall prepare a very special casting."

"What?" exclaimed Terikel, almost laughing with incredulity. "As easily as that?"

"No, not at all. I shall be greatly weakened, and you will probably die. Your sufferings will exceed those of your wildest nightmares, and should you live, you will be changed forever."

Terikel thought about this in silence. There seemed no reply that was appropriate, but she nodded to show that she intended to face whatever was to come.

"Are there any other requests that I may help with?" asked Teacher.

"Can you mend a man's heart?" said Terikel sadly. "Can you change the past?"

"Neither, Elder."

"Then can you cure a very sick girl?"

"How sick?"

"She died some months ago. She could feed only on mortals' blood and etheric life force. Her own blood was cold, and her hearts did not beat. Now she is even more dead, more or less."

"That sounds perfectly normal to me. It's five thousand years since my own hearts last beat."

"But she does not want to be that way, she wants to be alive again," pleaded Terikel. "She starves herself rather than kill, and she has grown very weak."

"Is she the one with the worldname Velander?"

"That is her. She is my closest friend, and she is Andry's sweetheart."

"Sweetheart? He must be very tolerant. Oh! But you and Musician . . . So, she must be very tolerant, too."

"Will you see her? You may be able to help."

"I have already seen the girl. Her skyname is Enforcer."

Suddenly Terikel lost her composure, and she smashed her cup of tea to the ground.

"Will you *listen* to me, you silly old man?" she demanded. "Somebody needs help and all you do is play word games!"

Teacher snapped his fingers, and both Andry and Wallas winked out of existence.

Andry looked around, recognizing the shore, river, and general gloom of the borderland between life and death. The gleaming white boat was of a similar design to Alberin's smallest river ferries, and as it got closer he realized that the ferrygirl was different as well. This did not mean that she was unfamiliar, however.

"Madame Jilli?" called Andry, staring at the red dress and what it was not covering.

"Andry, what are you doing here?" Madame Jilli cried across the dark waters, staring with astonishment. "You're not in the Abstracts or the Register!"

"I think I'm still alive."

"Then why are you here?"

"Can't say, I was talking to a glass dragon called Examiner, then I was here. But Madame Jilli, you're alive."

"Well actually, I'm not. But I am a ferrygirl."

"You look wonderful!"

"Thank you, I designed the dress myself. It distracts the customers, like. Dying is never pleasant. I carried Porter and Hartman, they said to say hullo next time I saw you."

"Oh ta. How were they?"

"Well, dead, as one might expect. But it's so nice to see someone alive, like you."

The boat grounded on the black pebbles of the river's bank, and Andry took Madame Jilli's pole and helped her from the boat. They embraced, and Andry had the sensation of holding a live, warm woman in his arms. He suspected that it was just his mind, telling him what he should expect to feel.

"You dirty little boy," laughed Madame Jilli, taking her

pole back from him. "You would not be able to imagine me like that without rather more direct experience of girls in your life."

"Aye, that's true," Andry confessed.

Madame Jilli took her pole and minced over to a group of shadows who were standing or sitting on the riverbank.

"I shall not be long, an old and very dear friend has dropped in," she began in a manner that was studiously charming. Andry noticed that she had changed her grasp on her pole to a quarterstaff grip; then, without any warning whatsoever, Madame Jilli slammed the pole into the groin of a spirit rather more solidly shaped than the others.

"Bastard, I'll make you pay for slithering your way into my bed with your lies and courtly babbling, while I could have had Andry as my last lover!" she shouted as she chased the doubled-over Wallas into the dark waters.

An enormous head with glowing slit eyes surfaced before him and rumbled, "No swimming to the afterlife." Wallas stopped, glancing from the monster to Madame Jilli, trying to decide which was the more fearsome.

"If he tries to wade ashore, Chavarleon, eat him!" Madame Jilli shouted from the shore, her legs apart and her ferry pole held in a very businesslike manner.

Several of the dead spirits began to applaud. Madame Jilli bowed, then blew them a kiss before returning to Andry.

"My goodness, but that feels better," she announced as she linked arms with Andry and led him higher up the bank, where there were more spirits seated, and waiting with the patience of the dead.

"Er, are you sure you're allowed to hit the spirits?" asked Andry.

"It is all part of my style. As long as Lordship Change does not complain, I shall do what I like with those I do not like. He's so nice, you would like him. Besides, Wallas is not dead yet—but enough of Wallas! I heard from Hartman that Velander is your lass now."

"Aye," said Andry guardedly, "but she is very sick, that is, dead—actually more dead than usual. Soon she will be one of your clients."

"She is not in my Register or Abstracts. Do not be too despondent."

"Madame Jilli, I know I have lost her, and there was so much I wanted us to do together. The music taverns of Alberin, the dance festivals in the streets of Wharfside and Bargeyards. I wanted to play my tunes while she danced, I wanted to teach her the lyre so we could play in the band together. And—and after spending a night with Terikel—"

"Terikel! No, don't tell me, just go on."

"I, I wanted to show her what it's like to wake up in the arms of someone after a night of being so close that . . . Ah, Madame Jilli, I'm not an educated lad, I can't say the pretty words that describes it all. I want Vel to be happy, that's all."

With that Andry took the rebec from his pack and began to play a bracket of reels. Several of the souls standing near the waterside began to dance with each other, and others clapped. Andry's feeling was that he played for a very long time. He stopped when Madame Jilli laid a hand on his arm.

"Andry, here is a task for you," she said. "Return to Alberin, and wait there for Velander."

"But she is in Alpenfast, dead. I mean, not-moving dead, as opposed to walking-around dead."

"Oh, she can travel, Andry. I have it on good authority from some people who are in a position to know."

"But why Alberin?"

"Because it is your home, and because Velander has no home."

Andry and Wallas winked out of existence. Madame Jilli watched as the vast, black thing submerged itself beneath the waters of the river; then she bent over and put a hand on the shoulder of the soul sitting beside her.

"Velander, you heard everything," she said softly. "He loves you, he wants you, he has plans for a wonderful life with you, he now even knows what to do after a pleasant evening in the taverns."

"So tired," said the spirit. "All the time, so tired."

"You are on the borderland of my little realm, but you are not ready to cross yet. Do you have a reason to go back, or do you want to linger here for what might be a very long time?"

"So tired, resting here."

"You could be alive, with Andry. Is that worth a bit of effort?"

"Andry . . . failed him."

"Not so. *I* failed Andry. *You* still have a chance."

Madame Jilli straightened and strode back to her boat, where she called a name then helped a spirit aboard. Glancing up the bank as she pushed away, she noticed that there was now a space where Velander had been sitting.

Terikel stared at the space where Andry and Wallas had been.

"I am neither silly, nor a man," Teacher was explaining. "Neither am I playing word games. Your friend Enforcer is changing. You cannot see that while part of her grows ever weaker, part of her grows obscenely strong. If she decides to live again . . . any sensible dragon would reduce her body to ash while she is still helpless. She certainly frightens *me,* yet I am not sensible."

Terikel was suddenly badly unsettled and confused. Teacher not only knew Velander, he was frightened by her. Teacher, a glass dragon.

"If you are not sensible, what are you?" asked Terikel.

"I am romantic. Romantic people kill rivals in duels over lovers. Sensible people would kill millions, just because they pick up their eating knife with their right hand instead of their left. If you ask me, the romantic ones are the lesser of two evils. On the other hand, I am a romantic dragon, and that is not the same as a romantic person . . . but you would have to be a dragon to understand. I was hoping that Enforcer would fade away, but now I am not so sure. Sensible dragons annoy me almost as much as sensible people. Enforcer killed a very sensible dragon, so I rather like her."

"Teacher, you have lost me completely," Terikel admitted.

"You want Enforcer saved. I shall save her, if she wants to be saved. She will be able to eat boiled turnips, baked fish, roast rats on a stick, and whatever else you mortals eat. If and when Musician takes her in his arms, Enforcer will be warm—I mean, provided that you are willing to look the other way, morality has changed so much over the last five thousand years. Olgez V'lrau made me court her for two years before she married me, it was all very proper in those days."

Terikel took a moment to comprehend what she had been told.

"Teacher, that is wonderful," she cried, close to disbelief. "What can I do for you in return?"

"Destroy Dragonwall."

Once again, Terikel took a moment to comprehend what she had been told.

"Destroy Dragonwall?" she exclaimed. "Yes! Yes, yes, yes! That's why I'm bloody well here in the first place! If I already knew how to do that, do you think . . . All right then, tell me how. You seem to think I can do it, so I am open to suggestions."

"Fly east until you can fly no farther."

"Fly? But— "

"Do not interrupt. On the equator, you will find Ringstone Counter. Apply this to the central megalith."

Teacher held up a fist, then slowly opened his fingers. On the palm of his hand was a black sphere about the size of an apple, its surface seething and ill defined.

"Now, do be calm, Elder, I do not intend to make lewd advances upon you."

Teacher thrust the sphere into Terikel's chest, just above her breasts. The cloth of her tunic began to smoke as it passed through, and flakes of char fell away. For some moments her muscles were paralyzed, she could not breathe, and she felt as if a large bag of pins had exploded within her chest. Suddenly she was released, and she took great gasps of air as she put a hand to her chest. Beneath the burned fabric, her skin was unharmed.

"Goodness," said Teacher, looking down at his hand.

"Last time I touched a woman there . . . Palion was a fishing village of thirty souls, not counting six pigs, eleven sheep, and a cow. Got my face slapped for my trouble."

"That thing!" she whispered. "What did you do to me?"

"It was something that I can spare, but it took a thousand years to collect. Listen carefully, and I shall give you the casting words to draw on it in times of need, as well as to apply it at the end of your quest."

Terikel listened, repeating the casting words several times until Teacher was satisfied that she had them.

"Now, you must go soon," he concluded, "mainly because we have to go too. No sense being in a dragons' cave with no dragons to talk to, is there? One more thing, though."

"Yes?"

"Your skyname is Featherwings."

Teacher made a complex, fluid gesture, and both Wallas and Andry reappeared. Both of them seemed distressed, but Wallas was far more distressed than Andry. Examiner now joined them, dusting crumbs from the collar of her coat.

"Andry, you played very well for us on your rebec," she announced. "Judge and I have decided to grant you a request. Ask something, and we shall try to grant it to you."

"I would ask you to cure Velander and bring her back to life, ladyship," Andry said at once.

"I have had a message, don't ask what sort of message. Velander passed her crisis a few minutes ago, and is already improving. There is no point in that wish."

"You mean she will live?" exclaimed Andry.

"Provided you return to Alberin, yes."

"But how can you know? She is back in Alpenfast—Alberin! How did you know that? Was that dream . . . really a dream?"

"If it was the one I was in, I'd describe it as more of a nightmare," said Wallas.

"Velander is now getting weaker because she is getting stronger," said Examiner.

"I don't understand, Dragon Examiner."

"Andry, do not try. What else would you like?"

"What else? Ah, can you free Elder Terikel from her betrayal daemon?"

Terikel turned crimson, and stifled a squeak of protest. Even Wallas looked embarrassed.

"Ooooh, can't do that," said Judge.

"Already done," added Teacher.

"What?" exclaimed Terikel.

"Only she doesn't know it," concluded Examiner. "What about trying again, young man? I really do like you, you know? Two requests, and both were for other people. We could tell you the location of ancient caches of gold, raise your etheric initiation level to ten or eleven in a few weeks, or, well, do lots of very clever things for you." Examiner linked her scrawny arm in Andry's and smiled at him with glowing eyes. "Come now, try again."

Andry thought carefully. Wallas took a shortbread from his pocket and began to munch it.

"Already done?" muttered Terikel softly, scratching her head.

"Could you release Wallas from *his* daemon?" asked Andry.

Wallas dropped the remains of his shortbread. Terikel smiled slyly.

"He has several," said Examiner. "Which one did you have in mind?"

"What in all levels of all hells do you think you are doing, Andry?" demanded Wallas fearfully.

"Oh . . . the worst of them," replied Andry.

"Andry, lad, I'm very attached to my daemons," babbled Wallas. "They are a source of great comfort to me."

"His terrible ballads?" asked Examiner.

"You have heard them?" gasped Wallas.

"Oh yes, when I'm not up here, doing dragon things, I sometimes wash tankards in various taverns. Judge sweeps steps in Alpenfast, and Teacher does a bit of gardening here and there."

"Very serene," said Judge. "You sweep a step, look out over Skymirror, think about something profound, then descend to the next step and sweep it too."

Andry tried to remember the face of the elderly caretaker in the palace where he had stayed at Alpenfast. Wallas did actually remember the little old lady who collected the empty tankard in a Clovesser tavern named the Dragon's Breath. Terikel began to massage her temples yet again.

"Terikel, dear," said Examiner, "just because we are learned, deadly, immortal, and more powerful than the entire Sargolan Imperial Militia, it does not mean that we cannot be small, eccentric, and slightly peculiar."

"It gives one a more balanced approach to life in general," said Judge.

"Can you do something about Wallas's problem with women?" suggested Andry.

"What?" cried Wallas. "No! I like my problem with women, it gives me great solace—no! Get away from me!"

Judge and Teacher seized Wallas by the arms and lifted his tunic. Examiner advanced on him, slowly raising one bony, withered hand. A black sphere about the size of a pea was between her thumb and forefinger, and she flung it at Wallas. It struck him in the groin, leaving a large, smoking hole in the front of his trousers.

"You burned it off!" shrieked Wallas.

"Oh no, nothing so crude as that," said Examiner. "Look closer, I think it's rather pretty."

A small and rather frilly head with suspicious-looking beady eyes had replaced Wallas's penis. It was on a long, scaly neck, and it turned to look quizzically up at Wallas. A forked tongue flickered out.

"Get it away from me!" shouted Wallas, backing away from himself until he collided with a wall.

"But it is *you*," said Examiner.

"I think it looks a little like Judge in his early days," said Teacher.

"I always did fancy myself as a protector of public morals, I must confess," said Judge. "Perhaps it was an unconscious intent on Examiner's part."

"Goodness me," said Terikel, bending over to examine Wallas's magical prosthesis.

The little dragon opened its mouth and hissed at her. Terikel skipped back. Examiner held her hand out before it, and the dragon spat a stream of sparks at her. They were of an angry purple color.

"Were I a mortal woman, those sparks would sting rather

severely," said Examiner. "Now, what should we call him?"

Wallas had no suggestions, and was pressed against the wall, gibbering incoherently.

"Something that fits comfortably with Wallas," suggested Terikel.

"Willy!" exclaimed Examiner. "Wallas and Willy. Wallas's own little Willy. Wallas's faithful Willy."

"Willy doesn't like anyone else but you, Wallas," said Teacher to the severely distraught Wallas, "so keep him away from other people or else the consequences could be full of scope for embarrassment."

"Monsters!" screamed Wallas. "You're absolute monsters."

"Well true, we *are* glass dragons, after all," said Examiner.

"How long will, er, Willy last?" asked Andry.

"Oh there's a lifetime guarantee on all my work," Examiner assured him.

"A lifetime?" shrieked Wallas, who then fainted.

"We have a little warning for when you descend," said Teacher. "Fourteen Alpennien rangers are hiding within bowshot of your horses. They probably have orders to kill you."

"Us?" exclaimed Andry. "But I thought the princess and the castellan were, er, at peace."

"They are, but Terikel has vowed to destroy Dragonwall."

"Why should the castellan care?"

"The entire Alpennien region has been cut in half by the Dragonwall. A rebellion has taken place on the western side, and the Sargolan governors and militiamen have been overthrown. Those on the western side are frantically building castles, walls, and armies. When the Dragonwall is eventually turned off, they will storm into the eastern Alpennien region of the Capefang Mountains. Worse, Wilbar is already teaching Alpennien sorcerers how to make his inclined ringstones, and that is a real disaster."

"But what about the castellan?" asked Andry. "He's, er, in love with Princess Senterri, isn't he?"

"All the better. What had been a rebellion will now become a war of succession. The castellan will claim that he is married to the heir to the Sargolan throne. Senterri's four brothers are even now raising armies to fight each other for the throne. The castellan just has to wait until they are weakened and spent from the fighting, then send his own army out to claim the throne in the name of Senterri. Their first son will become the next emperor. If Terikel destroys the Dragonwall too quickly, the Alpennien secret army will no longer be a secret. More to the point, it will not be properly trained, fully equipped, or big enough to take on the armies of the princes."

"And the princes will not have spent enough time fighting each other," added Examiner.

"That too. Well now, we have to become dragons again and attend to dragon matters, so farewell, and may Fortune favor you."

The three mortals emerged into the mists and descended largely in silence, Andry struggling along with Wallas across his shoulders. The sun was now below the highest peaks, and less than an hour from setting.

"So what were they, then?" Andry asked Terikel as they slowly picked their way down the path. "How can lizards talk—and look like people?"

"Dragons are not lizards, they are like us," said Terikel.

"Er, ladyship?" asked Andry.

"There is a casting that only eleventh-level initiates can attempt, and even fewer can master," she said as she stopped to check whether Wallas was conscious yet. "It is called air-walking. One must generate a set of wings by imagining them while doing a casting. An initiate who can do this casting can use the wings to fly. I have done it, once. In Alberin, Learned Wensomer is famous for that casting. She once did it while visiting the Palion royal palace. She cast huge wings, two hundred feet across and nearly invisible. She gave the emperor a ride on her back as she circled the palace. The empress was not amused, but what could she do?"

Wallas groaned. Terikel took the ax from her belt and beat him over the head with the handle.

"Now what was I saying? Oh yes, airwalking is the first stage on the long road to becoming a dragon."

"Becoming a dragon?" asked Andry. "A *person* becoming a *dragon*?"

"A glass dragon, specifically, not some common dragon that is no more than a lizard that can do fire castings."

"So those dragons that sank the *Stormbird* were just common dragons?"

"Correct. Glass dragons are sorcerers and sorceresses who master airwalking far too well. Over the years they learn to enmesh themselves in more and more castings to make their bodies into better flying shapes. They begin to spend days in the castings, flying and soaring. Years of that pass, and eventually they cease to leave the castings. Some say that they get true enlightenment and serenity from flying, and that they find they never want to revert to being like us anymore. They become obsessed with the gathering of etheric and life-force energies, they worship control of energies. Their physical bodies become suspended in time and age, enmeshed in etheric structures. They can live for centuries, and longer. Attitudes change when you are a dragon. You cease to be yourself. Change attitudes, and you change people. They still retain speech and reason, but they have attitudes that might be described as smugly superior and very cold."

"So those things in the cave were people?" asked Andry.

"Yes."

"But they were fifty feet high!" he insisted. "Maybe higher. Then they became just, well, like us."

"The small bodies that you saw are their real bodies. Or perhaps 'real' is not a good word, but it will do. Teacher, Judge, and Examiner are the oldest of glass dragons, they are over five thousand years of age."

"They seemed like they were raving mad," said Andry.

"Those three are so wise and powerful that they voluntarily spend time as people, to get a better perspective on the world."

"So they became glass dragons to rise above being people, and rose so far above being people that they now spend time as people."

"Andry, I think you are trivializing their situation."

✳ ✳ ✳

Sergal was sufficiently desperate to consider the Windfire
casting by the time the hundredth inclined ringstone attached itself to Dragonwall. It was not as if there was anything special about the number one hundred; it was just a
number that was passably large, and it had the effect of un-
derlining the seriousness of the situation. Nearly three thousand sorcerers were now locked into the energies of
Dragonwall, and at any moment one of them was going to
discover that first, nobody was really in control, and second,
all of them had access to everything. *Everything* meant an
ever-increasing amount of energy.

Windfire was Sergal's single hope. All he knew was that it
was a way of draining energy from Dragonwall, and that if
enough energy drained from it, Dragonwall might lose its
form and the world-spanning casting would collapse. *Not
much time*, he kept reminding himself. *Not much time at all.*
Sergal performed the Windfire casting.

Sergal's viewpoint happened to be at Ringstone Centras
when Windfire split from Dragonwall. The sorcerers of
Dragonwall were not the only witnesses to the birth of
Windfire. Across three continents, millions saw the rainbow
that capped Dragonwall shimmering and flowing upward.
Above the rainbow a shimmering line of blue grew bright
and flickered malignantly.

The shimmering blue line of fire separated from Dragonwall with a flash that lit up thirty-four kingdoms. The line
of blue moved slowly against the stars. It was bright, but had
no thickness at all. Those citizens in the desert city of
Zalmek saw that it was hinged on the blue spike of Ringstone Centras.

✳ ✳ ✳

Terikel and Andry sat together on a narrow ledge, in the last
of the sunlight. Having grown weary of carrying Wallas,
Andry emptied part of a small waterskin over his head. Having regained consciousness, Wallas looked around, then

checked his anatomy to confirm that what was in his memory was only a bad dream. Having confirmed that it was not, he began to rave, gibber, and thrash about on the ground. Andry and Terikel had to pin him down, then bind and gag him.

With Wallas subdued, they ate, then for a while they went over what had happened in the cave; then Dragonwall became the subject of their conversation. Looming above them, the ether machine glowed and flickered in the sky as the daylight faded.

"That thing is a weapon," said Terikel, with a glance upward at Dragonwall. "A very powerful weapon, that is. It can destroy kingdoms."

"Sounds a worry," said Andry, comprehending importance, but not detail.

"Control the winds? Tame the Torean Storms? Rubbish! Dragonwall's purpose is bigger than that."

"Begging your pardon, ladyship, but the Torean Storms are very, very big."

"Precisely. That gives you an idea of how immense the threat from Dragonwall could really be. The trouble is that every monarch, sorcerer, and warlord on three continents has a different agenda for Dragonwall, and they all can have a say in its control. Inclined ringstones allow that."

"So every churl can be a god," replied Andry, who was feeling seriously out of his depth. "Bad idea, knowing some churls that I do. Just think, Wallas the God. Who would allow such a stupid thing?"

"People who want *everyone* brought low, Andry. I suspect that glass dragons have a hand . . . or a claw, in all this."

"So what do we do?" asked Andry. "Can I help?"

"It is up to me alone. I must do things. Difficult things."

"What sorts of things, ladyship?"

"Actions that will get me into a lot of trouble."

"More trouble than you're in already, ladyship?"

"Infinitely more trouble, Andry," she said, pointing up at a thin, bright line of blue moving slowly across the sky, and away from Dragonwall. "And with every sorcerer in Dragonwall. From the look of that blue thing's motion against the stars, I should think it circles our world once every day. Given that it should be a complete circle, that means part of that thing passes over every city, castle, shipyard, bridge, and garrison in existence. Every academy, as well. Destroy all that, and what is left?"

"Roads, farms, and no masters—begging your pardon, ladyship."

"Andry, Andry, this time last night we were making love, then sleeping together," said Terikel, sounding suddenly more tired and distraught. "Please do not forget that, and please call me Teri."

"Sorry ladyship—Teri, that is."

"One little addition to your answer, if it does not offend."

"No offense possible, la—Teri."

"No masters means no good masters as well as no bad masters. A half-dozen churls with weapons get together, loot and burn a farm, use the women shamefully and kill the men. Their leader is a master. More churls see them living well, and join them. Let a month go past, and you have a lot of ruined farms, a petty warlord, and fifty armed churls. He is a master too, Andry, and his word is life or death. Would you prefer him, or the crown prince of Alberin?"

Andry laughed mirthlessly, shaking his head as he tossed pebbles over the edge into the darkness.

"Aye, with no rulers there's no rules, you're right," he said at last. "Dragonwall's like that, isn't it? The sorcerer folk all can do as like, because no rules temper them. Trouble is, they've cartloads more power than a half-dozen churls."

"So lad, I'd best be smashin' the bottle and get right into them, eh?" said Terikel in quite a good parody of Andry's accent.

They were both laughing as they stood up, but Andry could not sustain a smile as he reached for her hand.

"Before we go, like, I need to say, er . . . don't take this the wrong way . . ."

"Unless you tell me, I can't take it the right way either."

"Well, like, Vel's my lass, but I love you. And I'm worried about you. You're like a lad going into a lane full of hard men because they need sorting out, and that's grand—"

Terikel's embrace squeezed the breath out of Andry for a moment, and she held him close for a lot longer.

"I can do it because a lad once did it for me, Andry," she whispered. "I am afraid I love you as I wanted to love Roval. I was never good enough for him, but you and I are of a kind."

Terikel went through her pack, removing a book, some jewelry and hairpins, and several etheric amulets. She handed them to Andry.

"The book is for you, to remember me by. Sell the rest, they're from Torea so it's rare."

"*Basic Castings and Charmshaping for Amateurs of Talent*?" read Andry.

"I've been reading it to improve my grasp of Alberinese, but it's a good primer for one as bright as you," she explained. "Soon I shall leave you, Andry. I shall have a lot on my mind, but I shall fight all the better if I know someone is, er, looking out for some friends of mine. Should you get to Alberin, could you keep an eye on Roval?"

"I swear it, Teri."

"Also, should an Alberinese lady named Wensomer find herself in trouble—again—please do what you can. She is a brilliant sorceress, and her belly dancing is, well, astonishing."

"Aye."

"And last, take Laron to Alberin with you. Wensomer and Roval are his only friends left in all the world."

"That I shall."

"You know what happens now, Andry?"

"Oh aye, you get a present from me, all my rations, like," said Andry, handing two bags to her. "I'll borrow from Wallas, he's always got plenty."

"Andry—I, I don't understand."

"Seeing as you're going to die tonight, and all. Dead people's enemies don't follow them, even I know that. I'll make a big show of sorrow, and all. I see meanings behind words, and I see yours."

"I am glad not to have you as an enemy, Andry, you are always a step ahead. And thank you for all this, there are no rations to be had where I am going."

As they stood up to leave, Andry jerked his thumb in the direction of Wallas. Although still bound and gagged, he was now lying asleep.

"I'd rather not be carrying Wallas much farther," he said. "What's to do about him?"

"I know some healers' techniques and skills with charms, I can put a glamour on his mind to cloak his memories where Willy is concerned. It is used to calm girls who have been ravished, or children who have seen terrible atrocities."

"How long will it last?"

"Until he needs to piss."

Wallas was able to walk by the time they began to descend again, even though he was not entirely sure of what had happened in the cave of the glass dragons. Thus they made much better progress, and by late evening they had reached the place where they had left the horses. Andry halted them before they began the final descent.

"The horses are still there," he said, staring down at the little patch of pasture.

"I almost wish the glass dragons had eaten them," grumbled Wallas. "Don't know what is worse, walking and being footsore, or riding and being saddlesore."

"They're been moved," said Andry.

"Don't be daft, they're still there," replied Wallas.

"The tether stakes have been moved only ten feet or so, but it's just enough to have them always in the light from the Dragonwall."

"Are you sure?"

"I'm a carpenter, Wallas! I have a good eye for measurements and lines."

"I thought you said Terikel put guard castings on the horses' tethers," Wallas suddenly recalled.

"I lied," said Andry. "The dragons were right. Someone is down there, awaiting us."

"Waiting to kill us?" asked Wallas morosely.

"Waiting to kill *me*," said Terikel.

"Aye, that's right," said Wallas, suddenly brightening. "So they are not specifically chasing me—or Andry."

Andry put his arm around Terikel, shaking his head as he did.

"Whatever the circumstances, ladyship, you spent last night with me. You're my lass now, and I'll never abandon you. Wallas, you can piss off if you want to."

"The horses are being watched, and Logiar is another ten days by foot," said Wallas.

"Aye, and the watchers are heavies who want to do painful things to our bodies," Andry pointed out.

"Don't take this the wrong way, but it really is only Lady Terikel they want," said Wallas. "I could go down, explain that the dragons are still talking to you two, then ride away. I'd fetch the reccons, and they could come back here and send the Alpenniens packing."

"Wallas, they are likely to assume that *anyone* who has been up there could have been told how to destroy Dragonwall," said Terikel. "You would be shot."

"You can't know that!" retorted Wallas.

"Very well, go," said Terikel, offering Wallas a white cloth.

"On the other hand, we all know how those crude, lower-class soldiers often jump to silly conclusions," sighed Wallas, waving the cloth away.

"They think we can go nowhere without horses," said Andry, now looking to where the road skirted the mountain. "But *we* can go where horses cannot. Wait here."

Andry crawled off, and was gone for half an hour.

"They have horses, and they have our horses, but they can only go where horses can go if they want to ride," he explained when he returned. "*We* can *climb*."

"Climb?" asked Wallas. "You mean back up to the dragons and their cave? I doubt they will be terribly helpful."

"Not up, around. As the road passes this mountain it becomes very narrow. It's a natural place for an ambush."

"Why should we be concerned with that?" asked Wallas. "We're already being ambushed *here*!"

"The important word is 'narrowing,' not 'ambushed,' " said Andry.

✳ ✳ ✳

It took four hours to skirt the mountain, and it was not far from midnight when they had reached the road on the other side. There was a rather ugly incident when Wallas decided that he needed to urinate, and Terikel had to reapply the oblivion casting to get him coherent again, but those who were stalking them were too far away to hear any of that. After the stretch where it was bounded by the mountain on one side and the sheer drop on the other, the road turned away into a small, grassy field.

"Now to even up the transport arrangements," said Andry. "Wait here."

"Why not just flee?" asked Wallas. "It will be a day or more before they realize we are not going to return."

"But then they will *ride* after us. They have horses, and horses travel four or five times faster than we can walk—or in your case, hobble. Ladyship, stay here until you hear a very loud rumble, then count to three hundred. If we do not rejoin you by then, set off for Logiar. Wallas, come with me."

"We're not going to do anything heroic, are we?" asked Wallas.

"If we were, I'd not take you."

Andry took Terikel in his arms, and she responded by squeezing him with unexpected force.

"Honored to be fancied by you, ladyship," Andry whispered.

"Honored to be your lass, reccon," she whispered back. "Goodbye."

Andry and Wallas moved away quietly, crouched over and keeping to the shadows. Andry led the way up a path so narrow that it was little more than a series of handholds. Wallas declared that he could go no farther when they reached a ledge about a hundred feet above the road.

"Then wait here," whispered Andry.

"But don't you need my help?" asked Wallas.

"Of course not, I just brought you this far because I'd not leave Ladyship alone with you."

Wallas sat quietly for a while; then he peered over the edge of the ledge. The road was a depressingly long way down, and Terikel was out of sight, within shadows. He thought about climbing back down alone and raising the subject of betraying Andry with her, but decided that trying to climb down without Andry's help was probably courting disaster. This was a high price to pay for courting Terikel, so instead he sat back and closed his eyes.

"Well, here I am, alone, in the middle of the Capefang Mountains, surrounded by giant dragons and enemy lancers, with hardly any food, no horse, and no prospects of reaching civilization this side of a ten-day walk. What else could possibly happen to me?"

Something involving the glass dragons' cave began to stir at the back of his mind, but Wallas could not quite resolve it into a memory.

"Still, you have to laugh," he added with a gusty sigh. "Who would have thought that the Master of Royal Music could have been brought to this? I'd unpack my board lyre and sing a lament . . . but it's been shot. What an irony: brought low amid the highest peaks in all Acrema. Actually, that could be a good opening line for a ballad . . ."

Wallas began to compose snatches of verse.

Terikel looked over the edge of the road. The bottom of the cliff was lost in shadows a long, long way down. She removed her trail cloak, then took off her chain mail by bending over and letting it flow off like some exotic, knitted fluid. Even though the mail shirt was worth a year's wages for a well-qualified artisan, she heaved it over the edge of the cliff. It gleamed in Dragonwall's light for a long time before falling into shadows.

Now Terikel went over her clothing, tightening every one of the lacings, and tucking everything in. With her knife she made a small cut on the back of her hand and sprinkled a few drops of blood about on the roadside. Removing her pack, she selected a few items, then ate and drank as much as felt comfortable. Working carefully, but with haste, she made a roll pack of her trail cloak for what she had decided to keep. After placing her pack and ax together on the ground, she fastened her roll pack around her shoulders.

What she really needed to do would have taken over half an hour, perhaps longer, but she only had minutes. She spent some of those minutes fashioning a harness and padding

from her rope and roll pack, then spoke the foundation of a
casting into her hands and shaped it into an outline, which
she wove about her harness.

Again Terikel spoke a foundation casting, and breathed
life force into the dimly glowing mass. A spike began to
grow out of the center. The more the spike grew, the less the
complex casting glowed. She felt herself weaken with every
breath, and was aware that anyone chancing upon her now
would find her ridiculously easy prey. A light wind worried
at the spike as it continued to grow, and she knew that any
more wind would make it impossible for her to continue. It
was sheer luck that the lull in the Torean Storms had lasted
so long in the mountains, but she reminded herself that em-
pires sometimes rose or fell through sheer luck. The spike
was just over fifty feet high before Terikel decided that she
could not gamble on trying to grow it any larger.

*Half what it should be, and the harness is cheating, but
there's no examiner here to fail me*, Terikel thought as she
paused to shake her head clear and blink her eyes into focus.

Very carefully she lifted the harness over her head, then
reached up and split the spike. As the two sides spread apart,
they broadened. When they were forty-five degrees apart,
Terikel reached back with one hand and merged the etheric
wings into the casting woven into the harness on her back.
Then she continued to spread the wings. They were just five
degrees from a straight line when she finally stopped to rest
again.

It had been a time of great vulnerability, like the minutes
between when a butterfly emerges from its cocoon and when
it has finished unfolding its wings, yet Fortune had been
kind to Terikel. All she had to do now was jump. She thought
through a mental checklist that she had been assembling
since leaving Palion. Nothing seemed forgotten, and the circumstances seemed better than she could ever have hoped
for. She would be thought to be dead once she had vanished,
so she would no longer be hunted.

Terikel stood up, feeling the almost invisible wings of woven ether catching currents of air and pulling her about. It
was time to jump, before a stray gust of wind pulled her off
balance. She jumped. An updraft caught Terikel after only a

few yards, and she was swept upward as she glided away from the cliff. She was dressed in the dark clothing, so against the night sky, the shadows of the distant peaks, and the general gloom, she was practically invisible. Below her were great splashes of black valley shadow, and all around her were peaks gleaming with snow and glaciers. Air currents buffeted her. Cold air currents. They stripped away heat from her body. Before an hour was past she would be frozen to death, but she did not need an hour in the air.

Wallas awoke to the sound of a heavy rumble in the distance. He shook his head. The ground beneath him had trembled slightly. *Earthquake*, he thought, frozen with fear for a moment. Silence returned. *Perhaps it was only a small earthquake*, he decided. His thoughts returned to his lament. He began to recite it to himself.

"Wallas, time to go," said Andry from somewhere above.

"What's to do? I heard a loud rumble."

"No more cabbage broth for you," said Andry, climbing down out of the shadows.

"What was that noise?" insisted Wallas.

"What noise?" asked Andry, picking up his pack.

"It shook the ground."

"Oh, that noise," replied Andry, as he began to slip into the pack straps.

"Could have been a dragon."

"Don't know. Do dragons fart, I wonder? Look smart."

"Talk sense!" snapped Wallas as they began climbing down. "Was that rumble you?"

"Not so, I don't fart as loud as that."

"Andry! What really happened?"

"Not to panic. I just climbed above the road, where it passes through the narrow ravine, and set off a rockslide. Quite a few boulders were ready to topple. Now there's a rockslide over the road that will take a day or two to clear."

"A rockslide? But even I can clamber over a rockslide."

"Oh aye, but not with a horse. Before they can get a horse past, they'll have to spend time clearing away rocks. They can only run after us as we run away from them, and that gives us a better chance, don't you think? Now then, I can see the road more clearly—but where's Ladyship?"

They descended to the road. There was now a green glow on the peaks where they were not lit by Dragonwall. Miral was nearly clear of the eastern horizon, and the road where Terikel had been was now lit directly by the ringed lord-world. Wallas cautiously moved in the direction of the cliff's edge. He found Terikel's pack and ax. He found nothing else.

"Elder, we must go!" he called as loudly as he dared.

His cry did not attract the Elder's attention, but Andry was quickly beside him.

"Keep your frigging voice down!" he hissed. "Where is she?"

"Her pack's here, but she's not."

Andry made a hurried check of the area.

"Pack, ax, both put neatly to one side. Nothing else around—oh no! There is too!"

"What?"

"Here, on the road, near the edge. Dark, sticky, cold."

"What? Dark, sticky, cold? Talk sense! Sounds like you in a doorway after a night on the taverns."

"It's blood!" hissed Andry.

"Blood?" gasped Wallas.

"All around, some of it smeared. Looks like someone caught her unawares and stabbed her. But she fought with him."

"Who?"

"There must have been one Alpennien left on guard this side of my rockslide. Ladyship! Where are you?"

"Do I get a prize for saying *down there*?" said Wallas, pointing over the edge.

"The bastard tried to kill her."

"The bastard did a passable good job of it, too."

"But she took whoever it was over the edge with her," said Andry, his voice starting to break, but not quite becoming sobs. "She—she died in the arms of some bloody Alpennien—"

"And *you* call *me* a hopeless poet?" cried Wallas. "Andry, snap out of it! We have to start running."

Andry peered over the edge. Wallas looked over too, then quickly pulled back and closed his eyes.

"Maybe she's alive down there, she might have had her fall broken by pine trees or something," ventured Andry.

"What? Don't be daft, boy!" said Wallas, pulling him away from the edge.

"I've got to do *something*."

"It would take hours to climb down there, and you'd need a rope a mile long."

"If only I could see!" cried Andry, crawling back to the edge. "It's so dark down there you couldn't find your own gronnic with a tracker dog."

"No tracker dog's ever going near my gronnic—" began Wallas.

"Shush! What's that?"

In the distance they could hear voices—and barking.

"The Alpenniens!" cried Wallas. "And they've got a gronnick dog—I mean a tracker dog."

"Farewell lass, and Fortune's smile be with you," said Andry, looking over the edge for a last time. "Now come on, Wallas, run!"

Wallas managed to run for three minutes. Then he jogged for another fifteen. At the end of an hour he was managing a fast walk, and by dawn he was down to a rather listless shuffle. The beauty of the mountain dawn in the east and the exquisite curtain of shimmering light that was Dragonwall in the west was lost on the pair. Wallas was fed up with exertion, and Andry was fed up with Wallas.

"Can't we just climb off the road and hide?" pleaded Wallas.

"Remember the tracker dog?" replied Andry.

"But this is hopeless! We'll not reach the border post even if we struggle on until evening."

"Aye, but we might make a farmstead with a horse. Now shuffle faster."

"No, pause a moment, I've not had a piss since I can remember."

It had to happen, thought Andry as Wallas lifted his tunic, rediscovered the hole burned in his trousers, and set the mountains echoing with his shriek of horror.

✴ ✴ ✴

For Velander, having the threads of her life force rewoven into the dragon-shape casting was nowhere nearly as painful as the trauma of brushing against the severed control channels of the casting and forming attachments at random. It was the difference between being in a really vindictive fistfight and being given a very thorough massage. Both involved pain, but one knew the massage was in one's best interests.

"You will notice that your body is growing weaker," said Teacher. "The reason for this is that we do not know what we are doing. You are the first of your kind to come here."

"Where is this?" asked Velander, her voice merely a whisper.

"You are still in Alpenfast, in the same bed. It is just that the bed has been carried up onto the roof, so that you can be treated without damaging the interiors and furnishings."

"I could not damage anything," moaned Velander. "I have barely the strength to speak."

"Oh not so, not so at all. You see, you have been dead for some time. This is nothing to worry about, however."

Velander tried to laugh.

"In a sense, all of us are a bit like you, Velander," said Teacher. "Only plants can truly claim not to be sustained by the life force of other beings. Whenever a mortal eats a nut, a turnip, a mince pie, or a chicken leg, that person is being sustained by the life force of others. You have been close to the borderlands of death, in fact you have spent an unhealthy amount of time just a little over them, so your needs are more . . . shall we say extreme?"

"The blood of live people."

"Yes, yes, and now you are starving yourself because you hate what you have become, yet another part of you is out of control and you are not even aware of it. You have absorbed the casting that turned a mortal into a dragon, my dear. It took him many years to build it, and he developed a very good control of it during those years. Suddenly *you* have it, and you have no idea of what to do. The consciousness beneath your consciousness has been controlling it, but now we must hand the reins over to you. There is, however, a very large number of reins."

"I understand details, but not the whole," Velander confessed.

"Look at me," said Teacher. "I am a glass dragon."

Velander opened her eyes, stared— and realized that she could see! She tried to sit up, but found herself unable to move. Alpenfast's beauty overwhelmed her for a time. It was early morning, and the temples and buildings gleamed against the mountain slopes like exotic crystals growing out of dark, volcanic rock. Skymirror reflected the gaudy colors of the clouds, Miral's ringed disk was pale in the brightening sky, and Dragonwall was a sheer cliff of orange towering above them. For someone who had been blind since Clovesser, the sights were utterly overwhelming, and Velander felt as if she might have swooned had she not been lying down already. The wind was freshening with an approaching storm, however, and there was an especially sharp chill on the air. Velander realized that they were on a roof.

Teacher was a tall, scrawny man standing beside her bed. He smiled down at her, and then his skin became a fine mesh of faintly glowing blue.

"I am a dragon," he said. "In Alpenfast we are all either glass dragons, dragon students, or failed dragon students. Oh, the mortals think we all are priests, but that is just to save a lot of messy explanations, and to stop heroes coming up here in search of dragons to kill. Watch now. I can expand this mesh on my skin to become a dragon with a two-hundred-foot wingspan, but I would have to swallow rocks or water for ballast to stop the wind blowing me away, because energy weighs nothing."

"Nothing?"

"Well, actually that statement would have some glass-dragon theoreticians throwing up their wings in horror, but you will need a couple of centuries of study before you can understand all that. The point is, Velander, that you have the etheric tools to be a dragon, but you also have an image problem. A very severe image problem. You are also not quite alive, which is rather a precedent for me. I am taking you back to the borderlands of death. Terikel told me that Laron took you there, and gave you your current . . . status, is about the only word I can muster to describe it. He brought you back undead, but I shall bring you back alive."

"Alive?" gasped Velander.

"Yes, yes, warm blood, pulse, eat food served in taverns instead of the patrons, all that, but only while Miral is down. When Miral is up, you will be like me."

"You—you mean, er, a part-time dragon?"

"A glass dragon, yes, but with one very important difference, and that is a very dangerous difference. I may make a few enemies in glass-dragon circles for what I am going to do for you, but then I am already rather cross with those particular dragons, so I look upon it as the World Mother's way of punishing them for being stupid."

By noon the blood from Wallas's new blisters was seeping from his boots and leaving a dark patch in the dust with every step he took. They encountered no farmsteads or travelers, and there was no sign of the reccons.

"Damn you!" hissed Wallas yet again as they walked.

"Willy was not quite what I had in mind," Andry admitted.

"What fate *did* you have in mind?"

"Oh, I thought the glass dragons might make you nicer to women, perhaps."

"I was already nice to women. Exceedingly nice."

"Or even turn you into a girl—"

"A girl?"

"To experience your style of seduction from the other side."

"Monster."

"I wonder what was really achieved back in the cave of the glass dragons?" said Andry, glancing back over his shoulder.

Wallas lifted his tunic and pointed to Willy.

"Apart from *that*," said Andry.

"*Him!*" said Wallas firmly.

"Willy might be a girl," Andry speculated.

"A female penis?"

"All right, all right, him. What I mean is, I wish I'd understood what it was Terikel learned. Then we could carry on her work."

"*You* might. *I* am going to be palace cook in Logiar. Can we stop at those rocks? I need to piss again."

Andry sat down and took a drink from his waterskin while Wallas went behind the rocks.

"Gah, I still can't bring myself to touch the wretched thing," grumbled Wallas.

"Don't ask me to help," replied Andry.

"Go on, you horror, point at that crevice—Hah! Now will you look at that?"

"No thank you," called Andry.

"Willy obeys orders, he pointed at the crevice."

"Oh aye, then he should be in the militia," suggested Andry.

"I wonder if I could teach him to juggle?"

It was midafternoon when Andry and Wallas heard the sound of barking in the distance. By now Wallas was leaning heavily on Andry for support, and as Andry pointed out, he could have got down on his knees and crawled faster.

"Tracker dog!" panted Andry.

"Maybe they're looking for your gronnic," replied Wallas.

"Least they'd have some chance of finding mine!" retorted Andry.

"Did you hear that, Willy? He's just jealous because he has a common, mundane gronnic."

"At least I can use mine to—"

"One hundred and thirty-seven, remember?" gasped Wallas. "Oh my feet! It's the end, they have us," moaned Wallas.

"No, we must find somewhere to make a stand until nightfall. Maybe then we can steal a horse from one of them."

"If I put a plan like that in one of my ballads, strong men

would roll about on the floor with laughter," replied Wallas.

"Oh aye, but at least this way you can die sitting down."

"You—you do have a point. Up there, that pile of rocks on the hill."

The rocks turned out to be an ancient shrine. It made a passable stronghold, with reasonable cover and good views all around. More practically, it was on a steep hillock that a horse could not climb easily. The Alpennien riders came into sight, and Andry counted fourteen, just as the dragon had warned. There was one tracker dog, and the dog turned off the trail and made straight for the shrine. Andry managed to hit the dog with the fourth shot from his cavalry crossbow.

"At least they can't find us by our scent anymore," said Andry.

"Who cares, they've already found us!" replied Wallas.

The Alpenniens closed in, but their longbows did not have the range of Andry's weapon, so they hung back. Another eleven shots resulted in one Alpennien with a bolt through his thigh, and one Alpennien horse with a bolt in its rump. This had caused the horse to kick, accidentally striking the Alpennien behind it and apparently breaking his leg.

"They're getting ready to rush us," said Andry, letting off another bolt.

"Save the bolts, you only have nine left," Wallas reminded him.

"Got him! I hit one in the foot."

"I'm sure that makes all the difference. I—Did you hear that?"

"What?"

"A sort of roaring."

"Distant thunder. The sky is clouding over and the wind is rising."

Seven axmen were approaching, clustered together, and with their kite shields held up and their axes above their heads. The archers were fanned out to either side of them. Andry crouched with his crossbow loaded, waiting and watching. The slope was too steep for a charge, but the enemy had portable cover. Andry bobbed up and fired, then ducked again as several arrows flew where his head had been.

"Got a look at them, Wallas. We need Plan Rock."

"Plan Rock it is," said Wallas under his breath.

They lifted a large rock between them, then stopped with it at shoulder height.

"Count of three," said Andry. "One, two, three!"

The rock weighed about eighty pounds, but between them they managed to heave it out with quite impressive speed. It struck the middle man's shield with considerable force, and because the shields had been locked together, when he fell backward he took the four men to his right with him. The three others now scrambled forward in what approximated a charge, and came over the lip of the roofless shrine.

Andry had his ax and Terikel's in either hand as he stood up and engaged the first Alpennien. An archer took a shot at him, but hit one of his own men in the buttocks, causing him to fall backward and tumble down the slope. The third man engaged Wallas, shield-ramming him, and sweeping his right foot from under him. Wallas fell on his back, the Alpennien put his foot on Wallas's groin and raised his ax—and Willy burned through Wallas's tunic, set the Alpennien's trouser leg on fire with a stream of incandescent sparkles, then sank his fangs into the man's boot. He shrieked in horror, dropped his guard—and Wallas buried his own ax in the man's neck. Getting to his feet, Wallas noticed that both Andry and the third Alpennien had stopped fighting, and were staring at Willy. Wallas swung the ax around at the Alpennien, practically severing his head from his neck.

Wearing an Alpennien helmet, Andry checked what the others were doing, and found them to be regrouping for a skirmishing assault, this time with closer archery support.

"That was for Ladyship, ye friggers!" shouted Andry defiantly. "Aye, but the next one's for free. Come on, come on, who's next?"

"Don't encourage them, you daft bastard!" was Wallas's thought on the situation.

An arrow clinged from a stone near Andry's head.

"Aye, that's great. Waste all the arrows you like."

"For the gods' sake, Andry, what did I say about encouraging them?" cried Wallas as he exchanged his burned-out tunic for that of a dead Alpennien. "Oh, look here! He's carrying a pouch full of silver."

Suddenly there was an echoing bellow from the direction in which they had come. Andry saw all the surviving Alpenniens turn to look, then freeze for a moment. Andry turned also, and saw an enormous bird hurtling along the road on legs taller than most houses in his area of Alberin. The Alpenniens began to scatter. Two of the wounded, who had been left with the horses, clambered straight up onto their mounts and rode due south, away from the road. The bird caught the first of the Alpenniens who were fleeing on foot. It seized his head, shook hard, and sent a headless body tumbling through the air. The enormous predator bit its next victim in two.

"Our lucky day," said Andry.

"What?" gasped Wallas, staring at the nightmare that was flinging the two halves of an archer in different directions.

"One of the dragons has come to rescue us."

"It looks nothing like a dragon!"

"I think it's a baby dragon."

"They don't have babies, sorcerers turn into dragons, remember?"

"Well maybe a dragon sorcerer has to learn to walk before he can fly."

"We're doomed."

"Not so, think on it, Wallas. Of all those hereabouts, we're the only ones with somewhere to hide."

The archers rallied, and poured volley after volley into the approaching bird. Every arrow hit, but unfortunately none of them had the slightest effect. It lumbered past the ruined shrine where Andry and Wallas were cowering; then there were more cries and shrieks as it reached the archers. Wallas looked away, his hands over his eyes. Andry threw up, then slowly raised his head again.

"Perhaps if we remain very, very still," said Wallas, pressing against the wall with his arms over his head.

The bird tossed its head and swallowed the next man that it caught. The head was on top of about fifteen feet of snake-like neck, and it had the body of an enormous beer barrel on twenty-foot wading-bird legs. The thing also had a rather stubby tail that featured a few scraggy feathers. A tiny pair of wings looked as if they had been stuck onto its shoulders as a decorative afterthought.

The two Alpenniens who had mounted up at the first sight of the bird had ridden in a great loop and were now retreating back east. The bird looked at them, turned back to the terrified but firmly tethered horses, seemed to stop and think for a moment, then bellowed like a prolonged thunderclap and set off after the riders.

"Once it goes around the hill where the road curves, we get down to those horses, pick two, cut the rest loose, and ride west as fast as we can," said Andry. "Any questions?"

"Gnng!" replied Wallas.

Bodies, bits of bodies, and abandoned weapons were scattered about everywhere as Andry and Wallas scrambled out of the shrine and hobbled for the horses. They selected the most placid of the horses for Wallas, and Andry took the horse that seemed to have the next most steady nerves, given the circumstances.

By evening they were at the border of the Alpennien frontier. They showed their papers at the customs post, paid a bribe, and explained that they were trying to catch up with the group of reccons. A border guard explained that the reccons had passed by the day before. Andry managed to barter two fresh palfreys for their exhausted Alpennien warhorses, forty silver vassals, and a look at Willy.

"Shouldn't we have warned them about the dragon bird?" asked Wallas as they rode off.

"Do you seriously think they'll want to see its papers before letting it past?" replied Andry, who was longing for the anonymity of being in a city as large as Logiar.

The road now turned almost due south, and they rode on through the night, by the light of Dragonwall. Early the next morning Wallas persuaded a farmer that their sweating, spent palfreys were a fair exchange for two fresh horses— while Andry trained his crossbow between the man's eyes. His wife and daughter looked on in apprehension, their arms around each other.

"My horses are all that you want, then?" asked the farmer, who was beginning to realize that the intruders only wanted a fair price without any haggling at all.

"Look, we're leaving our two horses, and they're fair exchange once they're rested," said Andry.

"So the honor of my wife and daughter are not in danger?"

"I won't, he can't," began Andry.

"Are you telling him I'm a eunuch?" demanded Wallas, who was growing sensitive on the subject. "Well I've got one, and it's far more interesting than his."

With that Wallas lifted the front of his tunic. Willy hissed at the farmer, then breathed a streamer of flame and sparkles at the man's wife and daughter, as a warning to keep their distance. The two women immediately fainted, still in each other's arms. The goggle-eyed farmer pointed at Wallas and moved his lips, but no sounds came out of his mouth.

"Oh aye, I can't take them anywhere," explained Andry, lowering his crossbow. "Come, Wallas, let's be riding."

Terikel did not fly far after leaping from the road. Her search for updrafts took her some miles from Taloncrag, but once she had gained height she turned back. Her needs were much the same as those of any dragon. A place sheltered from the wind, with a flat landing area, and convenient access to a sheer drop for takeoff. As she returned she caught sight of two figures hurrying west on foot, and noted that the road had been blocked by a rockfall that had not been there only minutes earlier. She circled Taloncrag, then dropped her legs, lost speed until she almost stalled, and landed at a run outside the cave of the glass dragons.

Nothing came out to either challenge or welcome Terikel. It was as she suspected. The dragons had traps and warning castings for those approaching on foot, but not for airborne visitors.

"Begging your pardon, but I'll not be long," said Terikel for the benefit of anyone listening. Then she released her arms from her wings and got to work.

Terikel breathed a casting from words of formation for a tangle of mesh with a slight glow to it. This she lifted, then pressed it hard onto the crown of her head. She pulled. The mesh spread down over her head and to her shoulders. She continued to pull, covering her body with the mesh, and then she pushed her arms out. The mesh formed into sleeves and gloves over her clothing. She pulled down again, and soon had herself covered in a faintly luminescent bodysuit. Even before she had finished, her body's temperature had begun to rise. The casting suit did not provide heat, but it was an extremely good insulator, and she knew that it would not be long before she began to cook with her own body's warmth.

She was wrapped in warm furs under oilcloth, and had improvised a gauze windshield over her eyes. Over all of this was the bodysuit casting, trapping her own heat. She even improvised a parchment scroll of notes, rolling it into a beaklike shape to preheat the air she would breathe with her own body heat. Without the etheric mesh she would freeze within an hour, but without the chill air she would die of heatstroke even sooner. Flying, she would be comfortable. She spread her wings, slowly and carefully, then walked to the edge of the drop in front of the cave. Ahead was a truly harrowing experience, but she knew it would have to be faced—even if she did not entirely understand why. First she had a detour to make, however.

"It will be for only a short time, Roval, but I'm coming to see you," whispered Terikel. "Yes, I left you, but . . . but Andry is decent, not like the others. You have to be told that, and I must face you with my shame and say it." She leaped.

After clearing Taloncrag, Terikel turned and flew parallel with the orange curtain of etheric energies that was Dragonwall. She covered a distance that would have taken days, even on horseback, in less than an hour. Hunting for updrafts as she glided, she was nevertheless careful not to get too close to the shimmering orange curtain.

Up ahead, a column of blue mesh intermingled with the orange glow of the wind curtain, and it stretched from the ground up to the rainbow that crowned Dragonwall. Terikel knew that it marked Ringstone Logiar, and that the site was about a mile from the coast. Glancing about, she noticed that the clouds were thickening. Soon even Dragonwall began to be obscured by the storm clouds, and the wind was strengthening alarmingly. No amount of banking and wing warping could keep Terikel from drifting east. The ringstone itself came into view, and from the apparent size of the ringstone circles, Terikel estimated that she was about four thousand feet high and two miles distant.

As Terikel glided out over the water, the full force of the westerly winds slipping through Dragonwall hit her, scouring away all thoughts except those of control. She knew she was being blown east, but Scalticar was to the south. One hundred and forty miles to the south, to be precise. Terikel took a bearing from the wind and tilted her wings to add a small southward bias to her easterly direction. Already the glow from Dragonwall was being dimmed by the storm. Rain hissed down over Terikel, and she began to feel uncomfortably cool. This was the beginnings of a problem, she knew that only too well. The wings weighed nothing, but water and ice on the wings could amount to a great deal more than her entire body weight, and that could drag her out of the sky.

✦ ✦ ✦

Terikel had completely lost track of time and distance by the time the rain had stopped and the sky began to lighten. Somewhere beyond the clouds there would be a sunrise, she thought. The question was only a matter of whether or not she was above land. She began to make out the forms of waves moving below her. They were very large, almost ponderous waves, the sort that were squeezed through the Strait of Dismay by the Torean Storms, so she knew she was still above the strait.

Away in the distance, an immense column of white appeared, and then collapsed again. Faced with the unknown, Terikel was always wary, but whatever this was it did appear to be at least two thousand feet below her. There was more than just the columns of spray, she realized presently. Something thin and dark remained after each burst of white. Seadragon Pinnacle! It was waves bursting over Seadragon Pinnacle; she had last seen it from the *Stormbird*. That meant she was close to North Scalticar, but this was also where the coast of North Scalticar turned south.

Terikel warped her wings and banked very sharply. With

her wings almost vertical and giving her no lift, she began to drop quickly, but in doing so she also gained speed. That speed took her south. Minutes passed. Seadragon Pinnacle was to her left at her closest approach. A wave over half the height of the rock's three hundred feet hammered against it, sending spray higher than the tallest tower ever built.

It was only as she looked away that Terikel noticed that the horizon was slightly jagged. *North Scalticar*, she thought, yet even as the triumph of the thought burned through her body, the chill of doubt was following. She was too low to gain much more speed by diving. No speed meant no headway. Terikel dropped again, this time to within a few feet of the wavetops. The peaks on the North Scalticar coast were closer, but by now she was being blown backward. Terikel climbed again, this time looking for a high air current in a different direction. She climbed into clouds, then above the clouds. Using the sun, she oriented herself again, then dived.

It was noon by the time Terikel gave up trying to make landfall. She was above an unrelieved expanse of water. *A boat*, she thought. *If I see a boat I can come down in the water, climb aboard, and buy my passage to North Scalticar.* She fought the wind that was driving her east for the rest of the day, but saw no boat. She admitted defeat and began to climb as the grey daylight faded into the deeper grey of evening.

"Roval! I tried!" she called to the western horizon; then she turned east and flew with the wind.

With this casting there could be no rest, Terikel knew that as well as any senior initiate. Were she to sleep, the image of wings would collapse and she would not be able to regenerate them again before hitting the water. Ahead was the open ocean, with the southern coast of the dead continent of Torea on the other side, but several days away. To the south, but much closer, was the large island of Zurlan. Another five hundred miles, she recalled from the maps. That would involve a night of staying awake and fighting to edge south through the westerly wind. Terikel stared into blackness as she was swept on, guessing at her direction only by the wind that was blowing past her.

Chapter Eight

DRAGONCHICK

 Andry and Wallas caught up with the reccons when the walls of Logiar were actually in sight. By the time they had related how Terikel had died, and how the guardsmen were going to have to cope with a fifty-foot-high chicken if they did not hurry, they had reached the city gates.

"So, what are your plans?" Wallas asked Andry when they arrived at the garrison's barracks.

"I'm with the reccons again."

"You said you deserted."

"I lied. I persuaded Marshal Essen to give me a ticket of leave to look after Terikel."

"She needed no looking after! She had me."

"Oh aye, that's why I got a ticket of leave. Now the marshal's decided we can spend two days in the city's taverns, blending in with the locals and looking for the fugitives. You're technically attached to the reccons as menial support, so you're to go with us."

"Oh. And what happens if we catch sight of them?"

"Keep your voice down, and don't tell anyone."

"I see. So, we're to have a pint at the expense of the princess?"

"All but me."

"What? You'll go to a tavern, but you'll not have a pint?"

"True."

"But it's always been a pint. Ever since I met you it's been a pint."

"I promised Velander—"

"Velander's gone. Why not have a pint in her memory?"

"She'd prefer it if I'd refused a pint in her memory."

"Go on! Swallow a pint, sing a dirty song, and pinch a wench on the bottom."

Andry laughed, then punched Wallas's shoulder.

"Strange, this. Here's me trying to polish my manners, and you trying to roughen yours. Now that I think of it, Velander does owe me one night on the taverns."

"There you are, then."

"No, no, I think I'll save it for something special."

"Something special? We just survived a journey that makes even the most exciting of the bardic epics look like a quiet day in a badly attended temple, and you don't think it's worth celebrating the fact that we're alive?"

"It's like virginity, Wallas. Don't lose it too hastily, and you might end up doing something truly special with it."

"Now *that* was uncalled for."

The reccons spent their first night in Logiar just sleeping in the garrison barracks, and they did not emerge until late the following afternoon. Essen ordered them to clean up and wear their best, as if they were genuinely on leave for a night, and looking for a good time. He broke them into pairs, and assigned Andry to himself. As they walked through the garrison compound's gates he borrowed Andry's comb.

"Thanks, lad, have to look our best when on leave," he said as they walked.

Essen glanced skyward for a moment. Towering over the city was Dragonwall, taking up half the sky.

"So how did you learn Diomedan, sir?" asked Andry.

"Lived there, lad. Five years in a border garrison, just north of Saltberry. Redstone was its name."

"Aye, did you? As what?"

"A mercenary."

"But Wallas told me Redstone was taken by the Sargolan invaders in the Senterri War. Word had it that all the Diomedan defenders were slaughtered."

"Oh aye, even though it was slavers who abducted her, not the Diomedans."

"I would have thought a mercenary in the pay of Diomeda would have been first to the chopping block."

"Quite so, lad, but I'm from Alberin. I was put in chains while the Sargolan folk decided what to do with me. Then they learned that the Diomedans had not kidnapped Senterri after all. Here's your comb back, thanks."

"You're actually Alberinese, sir?"

"Oh aye, born on Forge Hill," said Essen, switching to Alberinese. "I was a bowsmith's apprentice until one of my master's crossbows got used in an assassination. Fronted to work one morning to find the shop burning and my master's body on the street. 'Cept for his head. That was on a pole that a member of the militia was holding. The other militiamen were talking to the locals, like, and I thought that they might just be asking about anyone else who worked at Bowman's Bows."

"Bowman's Bows?" asked Andry as he began to comb out his hair. "There a song about him. Flash Borry Bowman."

"Aye, I know it. Course after a year the palace declared that they'd probably been a bit hasty in killing not just the assassin, but his family, drinking mates, tailor, bowsmith, and bolt fletcher. By then I was a mercenary drummer boy in the Lacer garrison. Thirty years on, and I've served in Sargol reccons, Alear desert patrols, Diomeda's river militia, and even with the vineyard keepers of Gladenfalle. When the emperor realized that almost the entire Redstone garrison had been slaughtered, he thought to make it up to the few as was still alive. His Royal Journey Guard got ambushed and thrashed three or four times that year, so he decided that they needed reccons to scout ahead for them. Now you know everything."

"Now you're a reccon marshal. Nice rise for a commoner."

"Aye, but I'll never be a gentleman, lad."

"Would you want to be one, sir?"

"Doesn't everyone?"

"I've been thinking on it. Being gentlemanly, now that's got a lot in its favor, but think back on the gentlemen of the Journey Guard. Apart from the captains and the marshal, did ever any one of them speak with you? Speak, as in 'How's the day with ye, lad?' Not one and not once, I'll wager. We might as well have been hounds, for all the talk that was for us. I've listened to them talking among themselves, though, 'cause they talk louder when there's commoners around as they want to impress us. Sir, they talk bollix! How many gold crowns a year their fathers are worth. What other nobles invited them to morning tea or dinner, and how many times. What their armor cost, which master axsmiths forged their blades, and how many windows in the family mansion have glass in 'em."

"Come to think of it, lad, they're not company I'd seek out, either."

"They're boring, sir. They live to impress each other. They're so obsessed with living to impress that they've forgotten to be alive."

Essen laughed, but nodded his head. "So all your work on manners over the weeks past is for nowt, lad?"

"Not so, sir. I learned about being gentlemanly, and that's different. Lots of lads are gentlemanly in their own way. You and the other reccons are gentlemanly."

"Don't know about that, Andry lad."

"Trust my word on it, sir."

Andry's hair was completely combed out and tied back by the time they neared the first tavern on Essen's list.

"The first tavern's near the sorceric academy," said the marshal. "We could do a few tunes and songs with the students, talk a bit of wisdom in good company, and drink a quiet ale. Students like to talk of distant parts that they've only read of. I've had many a drink free, all for speaking of my travels and battles."

"That must be the Logiar Academy of Etheric Studies for Gentlemen," said Andry as he and Essen stopped before a gargoyle-encrusted gate in a high wall.

The gate was closed, but there was a ladder against the wall.

"That ladder is bolted to the wall," observed Andry.

"Aye, the students don't want some churl to steal it," said Essen, walking on.

"Why lock the students in, yet leave a ladder?"

"So they may be educated."

In a narrow street nearby they located the Mug of Inspiration. Singing poured out of it, and upon entering they found that the ale was good, but that the food was merely salt sausage and cold fruit pies. The next hour passed pleasantly, and they played hornpipe and rebec while the male students danced with the local girls. Andry and Essen had taken a break for a drink when Andry heard a familiar, earnest, and very penetrating voice above the general babble.

"Brothers, friends, you may ask who I am, but you should ask who is the establishment? None but the new regent, and her soon-to-be-consort, aye, it is true, and mark these words, brothers, her road to the throne was not an honest one."

"It's that student girl from Clovesser, isn't it?" said Essen.

"Aye it's Riellen, and she's talking treason," said Andry. "Oh aye, and she's handing out pamphlets, too. You're not going to arrest her, are you sir?"

"Nay. Who gives a toss about a penniless waif, preaching treason?"

"Well, I can see a couple of tossers who might, sir. Look to the door."

"Militiamen," whispered Essen. "And there'll be more outside: two at the door and one at each window, that's standard for arrests."

"Well, sir?"

"Well what, Andry?"

"What's to do, sir?"

"By law, we ought to help with the arrest, lad."

"So what are your orders, sir?"

Essen rubbed his chin thoughtfully, staring at Andry. He seemed in search of some subtle cue in the expression on his face.

"Have you ever broken the law for a bit of fun, lad?"

"That I have, sir."

"Care to do so now?"

"That I do, sir. Permission to voice a desperate plan, sir?"

"Granted."

"Get over to Riellen, shut her up, and get her out. I'll look to the militia."

"Rendezvous at the Quill and Jar in a quarter hour, or as

soon thereafter as you can," replied Essen. "And give your rebec here, we can't have it damaged."

Andry walked over to one of the militiamen, raised his mug, and put on a very heavy Alberinese accent on his limited Sargolan.

"Brother, good see you. Drink, yes? Fortune favor Princess Regent Senterri!"

The militiaman raised his baton for a moment, then saw the star of a delegate on Andry's tunic and recognized the reccon's uniform. *Somebody important, probably a hero, definitely a foreigner, looks like a highly paid mercenary*, and *something to do with the new princess regent* flashed through his mind.

"Hail, reccon, but I'm on duty," he began.

"Duty of all loyal Sargolans, drink health, Princess Regent!"

"Yes, yes, in a moment, now why don't you just get over to the serving board and I'll join you after—"

"Drink now, else treason!" shouted Andry, taking the militiaman by the arm, swinging him around, and tripping him up.

The militiaman's backup began to draw his ax, but Andry drew his ax by the head and swung the handle around as his opponent was trying to change grip. While a sharp, expensive ax blade will kill very effectively, a piece of wood a yard long will certainly leave an opponent stunned, lying on the floor, and completely harmless for a few minutes. Andry's handle connected with the militiaman's helmet. The helmet was the cheap and very lightweight type, made of butt leather and metal bands, and more designed as a symbol of authority than to be of use in a fight. Nearly all of the momentum of Andry's ax handle was transferred through the helmet to the man's head. The man went down. By now the original militiaman was scrambling to his feet, but Andry glanced around and backhanded him in the stomach. He doubled over. Andry struck him on the back of the head for good measure.

Two more militiamen entered the front door, but by now there was a press of students trying to leave in extreme haste. The militiamen both had an ax in one hand and a baton in the other. Andry aimed for a gap between two students and thrust out with the butt of his ax handle, striking a militiaman in the midriff. He doubled over. The fourth man had by now taken in the fact that this particular drunken reccon had dropped three of the Logiar City Militia without getting so much as a bruise in return. He turned and tried to flee. Andry reached over the top of the crowd of students and struck him quite hard on the standard-issue City Militia helmet. The helmet collapsed, and so did the wearer.

A fifth militiaman was still watching through a window, but he now decided that it might be a good idea to go in search of considerably more militiamen.

Danol and Sander were at the Quill and Jar, speaking to Essen and Riellen as Andry arrived. There was a moment of tension; then they realized that he was smiling, and did not look as if he was being pursued.

"Pleased to report, one enemy put to flight, four dropped with minor wounds, and no civilian casualties," said Andry as he saluted Essen.

"Sir, what in all hells are you doing?" exclaimed Danol.

"Andry and I have resigned as mercenary reccons," replied Essen.

"What? You can't do that—sir! I was once, er, a legal clerk, I know the laws."

"Oh aye, but we *can* resign, Danolarian. It's getting the resignations *accepted* that's the hard part."

"But why resign?" insisted Danol. "You are heroes."

"I made a promise to someone to get someone else to Alberin," said Andry. "Besides, after what I heard during the verity casting, I'd rather keep distance from the princess."

"Aye, the story of that is known well enough," said Essen. "All those who were questioned went around telling everyone else's confessions to try to cover their own. The princess is not one I'd like to serve any longer. Nine out of ten in the Journey Guard died to preserve her honor, and now she's bedding the enemy's leader and making an alliance to turn on her own brothers. In a week or two we could be dying in a war with them, and in two weeks they'll be inviting each other to dinner again. Besides, I like both captains, and I'll not hunt them down just because the princess is in a temper. Dolvienne gave her good years of service too, and now even she's on the run. How long before the princess turns on us? I've had enough."

"But you're technically deserters if you don't report in tomorrow," Danol pointed out.

"Deserters!" exclaimed Sander. "Both of you."

"Oh aye," said Essen. "But only tomorrow, when we don't report back to the garrison noble of the day."

"But, but what about us reccons?" asked Sander. "That's marshal and delegate gone! Who'se to lead, who'se to speak for us?"

"There's three of you left, vote for a new delegate," said Essen.

"Er, what's to happen to me, brother?" asked Riellen, who had decided that even revolutionaries needed to be polite to military men who were showing promising signs of keeping them out of the hands of the establishment.

"We are going to find a quiet place to discuss good techniques for keeping out of sight, staying alive, and perhaps going to Alberin," replied Essen. "Provided you don't lecture about revolutions or hand out pamphlets, you are welcome to come along."

Andry, Essen, and Riellen left the tavern, but they had not gone far when both reccons let their hands fall to their axes.

"Running feet behind us, Andry," said Essen.

"Turn and fight, sir?" asked Andry.

"I would not bother, sir," said Riellen. "It's Sander and Danol."

Sander and Danol fell in with them. For a time they walked in silence.

"Can someone write out a resignation for me too, sir?" asked Sander.

"I'll do it, sir," said Danol.

"Better forget the 'sir,' lads, we're common deserters now," Essen pointed out.

"I must say I am very gratified that you men are joining the Sorceric Conspiracies and Occult Plots Exposure Collective," began Riellen.

"Wrong, lass," said Andry. "*You* are joining the Princess Regent's First Reccon Deserters. That is, if you don't want to star in a public entertainment involving a very short meeting with a very strong man with a very large ax tomorrow morning."

* * *

They found Costiger in the Pig in a Poke, but he reported that Wallas had not met him at the garrison gates. Andry and Essen explained that they had decided to desert, and invited Costiger to join them.

"Sir, granted that I'm not the sharpest tool in the workshop, like, even I'm bright enough to see that," said Costiger, removing his reccon cap and scratching his head. "But why desert?"

"Because we're meant to hunt down three fine, brave, and good folk as got on the wrong side of royalty," said Essen.

"Besides, Princess Regent Senterri is not *our* royalty," said Andry. "We're all from Alberin. The crown prince is our real monarch."

"But the crown prince is also a bit of a case," Danol pointed out. "Have you ever stopped to think why the emperor of North Scalticar refused to have him crowned king when his father died?"

"Er, no," admitted Andry, whose knowledge of and interest in politics had been nonexistent before he had arrived in Sargol.

"The man's a weirdo. Last year he held a banquet where all the meals were served up using naked lamplight girls as dishes, and all the guests had to come in cat costumes. Nobody was allowed to say anything except 'meow,' and the penalty for breaking that rule involved a bowl of cream, a feather duster, and a large bell."

They fell silent again, each forming their own mental images of the crown prince of Alberin's banquet.

"He has never started a war," said Riellen.

"Hah!" laughed Danol. "Alberin has had total peace ever since the death of his father. There's not a monarch in all of Scalticar who does not live in terror of being crossed off the guest list for his orgies."

Riellen cleared her throat. All five men turned to her. Suddenly feeling intimidated, she removed her spectacles and began to wipe them on her sleeve.

"Well, compared to the two monarchs that I've seen over the weeks past, I think the crown prince is a rather nice man," she declared.

Riellen put her spectacles on again. The five heads surrounding her were nodding.

"I suppose I'm with you," said Costiger. "Not been home for years."

"Well, that's settled, then," Essen declared quietly. "We go to Alberin."

"How?" asked Danol. "I've made inquiries, like in case the captains and Dolvienne were thinking of fleeing there too. All the big ships are sunk, or smashed up so badly that they'd only stay above water if stuck on a sandbar. All that's left is a few fishing boats, and they don't go beyond the inlet leading to Logiar's harbor."

"I'd rather cross the Strait of Dismay in a bathtub than serve in Sargol anymore," said Essen.

"I'm with you," said Andry.

"Look, I may just be a scholar, with little experience in practical matters," said Riellen, "but six of us is a bit excessive for a bathtub, even for a cruise of the harbor on a very calm day. The last calm day on the Strait of Dismay was, er, well I don't think there's *ever* been one."

Andry suddenly brought his fist down on the table. Everyone turned to him, but he just sat quite still, his mouth hanging open and his mind far away.

"You've had a thought, lad?" asked Essen.

"We *can* cross the Strait of Dismay," said Andry, almost in a whisper. "All we need is a tub."

"That was meant to be a joke, Andry," said Essen.

"And there are probably suitable tubs around," continued Andry.

"Joke, sir," called Riellen. "They are funny plays on

words, amusing little stories. You're meant to laugh at them, but not take them seriously."

"Gentlefolk, did I ever tell you about the wreck of the *Haulier*?" asked Andry.

They shook their heads, and hunched forward over the table.

"It's the reason my dad stopped going to sea as a ship's carpenter. The *Haulier* was a big deepwater trader, and it got caught in a storm off the coast of eastern Scalticar. Huge waves broke over the decks and smashed the hatch covers away. Waves kept washing over the decks, and so much water poured down below that she began to sink. Dad jumped for it as she went under, and he thought he was a drowned man until he spied a washtub floating past amid some other flotsam. He swam over and climbed in, and a bit of water splashed in with him, but he bailed it out with his hands. Do you know what?"

Five heads shook.

"He did not have to bail again until he was washed up on the Scalticarian coast, two days later. The ship was so big and heavy that it had to smash through the waves, but the washtub *rode* the same waves."

"I still maintain that a washtub would be a little crowded," began Riellen.

"No, a tub!" insisted Andry. "A tubby little boat. One small enough to rise and fall with huge waves, rather than fight them. You said it yourself, Danol. There's still a few small boats on the water."

"If it were possible, why has nobody yet done it?" asked Essen.

"Sheer terror," suggested Danol.

Suddenly Riellen waved her hands over the table, palms down. She had decided that if she was going to be part of a military unit, she would have to make a fair contribution. Spotting danger at a distance and warning those who could fight seemed more within her abilities than actually fighting, so she had appointed herself as the unofficial sentry.

"Face at the window, looking past the edge of the shutters," she said quietly. "Had a militia helmet."

"Not there now," said Andry.

"Make no sudden movements," warned Essen.

"The door is opening, one militiaman entering," said Riellen. "He's seen us, he's staring, this could be—"

"It's Wallas!" sighed Andry, almost collapsing across the table with relief.

Wallas hurried straight over to their table and squeezed onto the end of a bench. Andry pointed out that people came to taverns to drink, and that he would look suspicious without one. Wallas snatched Andry's mug, drained the contents, then held it tightly in front of him.

"I was recognized!" Wallas explained breathlessly. "I was hailed as Milvarios of Tourlossen just as soon as I shaved and trimmed my hair. Master of Royal Music and royal assassin of emperors by appointment. Pah!"

"You killed the head of the establishment?" gasped Riellen, awestruck.

"So what happened?" asked Essen.

"Oh, I had a bath, then put on fine robes to show off my newly trim and muscular body. I mean, you did tell us to dress up for a night of revelry."

"I said for a night on the taverns, not the Logiar royal court," said Essen. "Go on."

"I was scarcely out in the corridor when I met with a herald from the Palion court. He screamed like all the demons of the underworld had just come around the corner, then bolted. I bolted in the other direction, and straight back to my room. I had the shavings of my beard glued back onto my face in a thrice, and dumped my newly bought fine robes into the fire. Then I went back outside and asked a marshal what was going on. He made me help search for myself for an hour. Eventually it was decided that the herald had been muzzy with the wine he'd quaffed for dinner—but it's over for me here. My beard is already falling off, look." He wiped a hand across his cheek, and held up a palm smeared with glue and hair. "I cannot hide long enough to grow a new one."

"My mother always warned me about boys with hairy palms," said Andry.

Wallas was not familiar with whatever piece of folklore Andry was alluding to, but he correctly assumed that it was at his expense when all the other Alberinese present laughed.

"How good are you as a sailor, sir?" Andry asked Essen.

"I've served aboard galley ships as a marine, lad. There I helped with bailing, rigging, and the like."

"Better skilled at it than most, then. What about you, Wallas? Have you really been to sea?"

"I have played aboard the royal barge on the River Palion, during ceremonial occasions, and I know the eight Water Music sonatas of Elberrili by heart."

"A simple 'no' would have been enough," said Danol. "I've been a sailor, and served in the Tor— er, Diomedan marines, sir."

"Any others?" asked Essen. "No? Then that's two sailors and a ship's carpenter. A navigator would be helpful."

"We can press-gang one!" said Andry. "Good enough for me, good enough for someone else."

"Oh, but I know some astronomy," said Riellen brightly, raising her hand.

"Offer appreciated, lass, but we're unlikely to see much of the sky, what with the storms out in the strait. We need someone who also knows navigation by the way of wind, waves, swells, and the like."

"Sir, we should take a trip to the docks," said Andry to Essen. "Just you and me, I suggest. There's bound to be navigators there."

"That we will," said Essen. "The rest of you stay here, and out of trouble. And Riellen! If you try to start a revolutionary movement in here while I'm away, I'll kill you myself."

"Delegate, sir, do you still have that scroll from the princess?" asked Danol. "The one she gave you at the ball in Glasbury?"

"Oh aye, in my jacket pocket. Why do you need it?"

"Just a little whim, sir, indulge me."

Andry and Essen strolled slowly through the shipyards on the edge of Logiar's harbor, and were quite discouraged by what they saw. There were no large ships at all. A couple of smallish ships were in the early stages of construction, but little work had been done on them for quite some time. Several middling-sized vessels had struggled into Logiar after surviving the huge waves and ferocious winds beyond the harbor mouth, but none were larger than a corrak. They had all been beached, and no work had been done on their damage, except to make them sufficiently weatherproof for people to live in. Their timbers had dried out, and they would have needed extensive recaulking and soaking if they were not to sink once put back in the water.

The wind was blowing very hard, and there was thin but stinging rain on it. Nobody was much inclined to be out and about, so Andry and Essen were free to go pretty well where they pleased without challenge. Down at the piers, the swells entering the harbor from the Strait of Dismay were ponderously rising and falling by twenty feet, rather like speeded-up tides. Vertical extensions had been built on the piers to cope with the new conditions. A few fishing boats were tied up there, but nothing seemed big enough to cross the strait, even in good weather.

"There's one a little bigger, sir," said Essen, pointing to a small schooner with two lateen-rigged masts and a rather tubby profile.

It was on the water, rising and falling with the swells, but protected from the edge of the pier by knotted rope fenders. A thin streamer of smoke was rising from the galley stovepipe at the side.

"Someone's aboard, and it looks to be big enough to take ten or so souls," said Andry. "Let's board it and ask."

They jumped aboard at the top of a swell, and at the sound of their footsteps a panel slid aside under the little quarterdeck. An astonishingly elderly head appeared.

"Bugger orf!" it declared, but it did not back up the words with dangerous displays of weapons or magical castings.

"Good afternoon, sir," said Essen in Sargolan Common as he squatted down. "We'd like to hire your fine schooner for a cruise of the harbor."

"Do ye, now?"

"It's to impress some ladies."

"Well I can't do it," snapped the old man.

"May I ask why not?"

" 'Cause I don't own it!" The elderly head gave a series of hacking coughs that might have been laughter.

"Have you caught the gist of that?" asked Essen in Alberinese, turning to Andry.

"He has made a threat and a bad joke, and we now know that he is not the owner. Let's make an inspection."

The schooner turned out to be a little down-at-heel, but in reasonably seaworthy condition. The old man lived aboard during the day, then spent the nights in one of the beached ships. The boatmaster and deckswain spent the nights ashore, then slept aboard during the day. By now it was evening.

"We could wait for them to return," suggested Essen.

"Aye, but we need to leave Logiar in a hurry," replied Andry.

"If we can hire this seagoing barrel then we will first need to buy supplies for the crossing."

"True, but we'll only need food for a week and some barrels of water."

"But there's no night market in this weather."

"Well then, some innkeeper will sell us what we need from his cellar. Best to fly the coop now, while we don't have to escape the princess's militia as well as provision the boat."

"Enough, I'm convinced," said Essen. "Keeper, where is the owner to be found?"

"Norrieav's boatmaster and owner," the old man mumbled. "Black Acreman from the north. Hazlok is deckswain. He's short of an eye, nose is broke, lost a few teeth, missing a finger on . . . er, one of his hands. Find 'em drinking at the Jolly Pint."

They went back on deck, then jumped for the pier as a swell peaked. Andry looked back at the schooner.

"The *Shadowmoon*," he said, staring at the name on the bow in the fading light.

"We should have asked where the Jolly Pint is to be found," said Essen, slapping his forehead with the palm of his hand. "I'll jump back aboard."

"Oh I know where it is, sir. Best to collect the others and get there."

"Well where is it, then?" asked Essen.

"Remember the old forecastle song?

> "Jolly Pint, fight's delight,
> Best of brawlin' in old Sargolan.
> Asher Way and Down Street corner."

To avoid seeming like a large and suspicious-looking group, they decided that Andry, Essen, and Wallas would enter the Jolly Pint first. The tapman glowered sourly at them, then returned to smearing grease more evenly around a tin mug. A serving maid glared at them from a bench beside the serving board, but did not attempt to get up. She had a physique that would have seriously tempted any recruiting marshal to offer her the emperor's silver vassal and a five-year contract, and she held a splintered ax handle in one hand. Quite a large collection of men who had probably once been sailors looked up and glared at the newcomers, then exchanged a complex series of nudges, winks, whispers, nods, and gestures. Several looked back at them with slightly more appraising expressions on their faces.

"See anyone likely?" asked Andry.

"Churl as minds the boat said Norrieav was a black Acreman from the north kingdoms, and that Hazlok was rough enough to sand a ship with," replied Essen.

"I see nine black Acremans and three dozen others. All look passably rough."

"Hazlok is missing an eye."

"Seven men are missing an eye—but wait up. There's one is missing an eye who is talking to a black Acreman."

They made their way across to where the two men were sitting. The Acreman was exceedingly drunk. His companion put his head back, messily poured beer into his nostrils, then forced it out through the tear duct of his good eye in a thin stream. Beer also dribbled out from beneath his eye-patch. The Acreman clapped.

"Boatmaster Norrieav, I presume?" asked Andry brightly in Diomedan.

"Gerrout'verem'broke," managed the boatmaster, who then flopped forward, striking his head alarmingly hard on the table.

"Well then, you must be Deckswain Hazlok," said Andry.

The stream of beer from Hazlok's eye fell, became a dribble, then stopped.

"Thas me boatmaster, an' 'e owes me," managed Hazlok, a little more coherently.

"The ugly one can still talk," Wallas advised.

"Who you callin' ugly?" demanded Hazlok, trying to stand up.

"The churl who owes him money," said Andry quickly.

"Ach, thas not me then," declared Hazlok, flopping down again.

"Can we buy you a round of drinks?" asked Essen.

Hazlok's head flopped in a nodding motion. Wallas and Andry took this as an affirmative answer, and both sat down while Essen waved for the serving maid. The serving maid pointedly ignored him. Riellen entered, then cowered near the door, unwilling to move too far from an escape route. She attracted some very appraising stares, and inspired a flurry of winks, nods, and gestures.

"You have a boat for hire?" said Andry. "A schooner?"

"Besht schooner onner water," declared Hazlok. "Or under."

"That is not encouraging," said Wallas.

"I've looked over the boat, it seems sound," said Andry. "My good Hazlok, what amount would you charge to hire your excellent schooner for a short cruise?"

"Cruise of harbor, five silver vassals. Anywhere else, not enough money in all the world."

"Well, that seems quite reasonable," said Andry. "Do you speak for Boatmaster Norrieav?"

"Course I shpeaks fer Boatmasser Norrrrieaev," managed Hazlok. "He can't shpeak."

He thumped Norrieav on the shoulder. Norrieav grunted.

"I'll take that for a yes," said Andry.

Hazlok fell backward and struck the back of his head on the floor. Andry and Wallas lifted him back onto the bench and checked that he was still alive.

"Just like pay night in Bargeyards," said Andry.

"Passable resemblance to a Musicians' Guild dinner as well," said Wallas.

The door opened. Everyone looked up and glowered. Andry and Wallas looked to the door as well. Laron entered. Most looked away again. A few continued to stare, and exchanged winks, nods, and gestures. Laron caught sight of Andry and Hazlot. He gave them a stiff nod, then walked over to the serving board. Laron said something. Both the serving maid and tapman ignored him. Laron punched the tapman in the face with no warning whatsoever. The tapman glared at him, but the punch appeared to have had no other discernible effect. Laron rubbed his fist, then selected several tin mugs and a large jar of wine. He dropped a coin in front of the tapman, then walked over to where Andry, Essen, and Wallas were sitting.

"Bad to drink alone," he declared, then sat down, smashed the neck of the jar off, and poured a generous measure into each mug.

They each took a mug and they clanged them together. Andry put his mug down, untouched. Wallas took several gulps. Laron drained his mug and poured out another measure. Riellen watched. For a time there was silence.

"Well, don't just stand there, arrest me!" declared Laron. "But I'll expect a good fight. This is the best fighting tavern in all Sargol's empire."

"There's even a song about it," said Wallas. "Do you want me to sing it for you?"

"Shag off," said Andry.

"Manners!" said Wallas.

"Er, then fornicate off."

"We've just deserted," explained Essen.

Everyone in the tavern except for the tapman and serving maid gave them a particularly intense appraising stare.

"Look, er, I'm not really sure that trying to cross the Strait of Dismay is not more dangerous than staying here," Wallas said quietly.

"Cross the Strait of Dismay?" cried Laron. "Funny thing, that! I want to cross the Strait of Dismay as well. Came here to find a certain boatmaster. Fool's errand, we're sure to die, but I promised my friends . . ." Laron drained half of the contents of his mug. "Nice to have friends, real friends. No money, militia closing in, reward on my head, but I've got friends."

"You, sir, have been drinking," declared Wallas.

"We have just secured a schooner—" began Andry.

"Splendid! I was once a navigator."

"Indeed!" exclaimed Andry. "And I've been a sailor and carpenter. Wallas has been a cook, and these two are the boatmaster and the deckswain. Essen and Danol know sailor work."

Laron lifted Norrieav's head and peered at his face. He looked over the edge of the table at Hazlok.

"Know these men. Served with them. On the *Shadow-moon.*"

"But that's the schooner that stands ready in the harbor," said Essen.

"Splendid! Great little schooner. Plenty of . . ." Laron lowered his voice conspiratorially. "Special features."

The door opened again. Two men dressed as Zurlanese warriors entered. They were unarmed. A small, shabby man entered with them. He looked around, then whispered to his clients. He pointed in the direction of the reccons, then left hurriedly. The two Zurlanese walked over to the table. One produced a small, battered book, checked something, then bowed.

"Er, good evening. I am Akiro. This is my brother, Aziro. We are having, ah, tavern fight tour of Acrema. I am told, er, you are great heroes. Save princess. You are, er, interested in nice fight?"

"Er, presently," said Laron agreeably. "Maybe soon." Laron had another pull at his drink. "Do sit down. Drink?"

"Do not drink before fighting," said Akiro and Aziro together, but they both sat down.

"Look, I really think we ought to leave," said Wallas. "This place looks very dangerous."

"No, no, no, be brave, you're a master assassin, and you killed the emperor!" cried Laron genially. "There's a reward of a five hundred gold crowns for you, dead or alive . . . or is it five thousand?"

"Shut up!" hissed Wallas, hunching over and putting his hands to his face.

"But why?" cried Laron, as loudly as ever. "You should be proud to be a feared killer in a place like this. Remember when you rolled that spy lady back in Glasbury, told her all those secrets and nearly got the princess regent killed?"

"I never did!" shouted Wallas.

"Oh, and didn't you kill that Throne Guard in Palion?"

"It was over a cream cake," suggested Andry.

There was absolute silence for some seconds. Riellen was cowering so thoroughly that she was nearly doubled over. Every one of the regular patrons was now looking on in terror. One man eased the shutters of a window open, only to find it barred on the other side. The tapman and serving maid showed no reaction at all to the exchange.

"Gentlemen, ladies, please," Essen began.

"But I'm in the Special Warrior Service, we're even tougher," Laron declared.

"Ooooh!" exclaimed Akiro and Aziro.

"You know of us?"

"Greatest warriors in world!" exclaimed Akiro. "Must have fight."

"Why not? You against me, Wallas can sort out your brother."

Before Wallas could even register that a threat existed, Aziro took a step forward and kneed him in the groin—then tried to pull away, with a piercing shriek that somehow seemed too highly pitched to be from a man. Willy had its teeth buried in his kneecap, and was breathing flames from its nostrils. Willy released him and retreated under Wallas's tunic. Aziro rolled on the floor to put out the flames in his burning trousers.

"Now, there's something you don't see every day," said the tapman, and the serving maid nodded.

Essen walked across to the tapman and held out a gold crown. The tapman accepted it.

"While we were doing our business transaction in here,

my reccons were in your cellar, stealing some supplies," Essen declared. "That is payment."

The tapman flipped the gold coin high into the air. It landed in the serving maid's cleavage. She did not so much as blink.

"Must fight you, SWS man!" cried Akiro, then he rushed Laron.

Laron gave a subtle sidestep and bent his body as he snared the arms of the charging Akiro. The Zurlanese rolled over his back and flew through the air, crashing down among the terrified regular patrons of the Jolly Pint. In a blind panic, they began kicking and beating Akiro. Aziro hobbled over to help his brother, the remains of his trousers still smoking. Essen began shepherding his charges out through the front door.

Once outside the tavern, Laron left to fetch Dolvienne and Gilvray, accompanied by Andry. Over the following quarter hour twelve people boarded the *Shadowmoon*, bringing with them a barrel of wine, a barrel of water, a bag of salt sausage, and five crates of what Costiger thought were ship's biscuit. Upon seeing the size of the *Shadowmoon*, Wallas turned and attempted to flee, but he was chased and tackled by Costiger. It took all five reccons to carry him aboard. The ancient keeper who had been minding the *Shadowmoon* during the daylight hours stood waving on the pier, oblivious of the heavier rain that was now falling, and the wind that was driving it. Danol was standing on the pier beside him, waiting for the order to cast off. The reccon pressed a silver vassal and a package of papers into the keeper's bony hand.

"Take that to the duty noble at the garrison," he called above the wind.

"Danol, cast off!" called Andry, and Danol released the last rope from its bollard and jumped for the deck. As the *Shadowmoon* began to move away from the pier, Danol returned the scroll that Senterri had given Andry.

"What was that about?" asked Andry.

"I forged releases for all us reccons," replied Danol.

"Signed by the princess herself, or at least a pretty damn fine imitation of her writing and signature."

Andry steered while Essen and Danol raised a very small storm sail.

"Once through the harbor mouth we need to get a bearing from Laron," called Andry above the wind.

"Laron's asleep below deck, sir, alongside the boatmaster and the deckswain," reported Danol. "Dolvienne and Gilvray are in the master cabin. The captain's very tired with the long ride here, his head wound being so bad and all."

"Well get Costiger to drag Laron up here and dump a pail of water over his head."

"Why do we need him, sir? Can't you steer?"

"Aye, but only he can navigate. I know rigging and steering, but there's an end of it. Now get Laron up here and awake!"

Above the wind the came a distant but still impressive bellow.

"The dragon bird again!" exclaimed Andry, glancing back to Logiar. "Pray to whatever gods you believe in that it can't swim."

✦ ✦ ✦

Velander was so weak that she could hardly push aside the straw that covered her in the tray of the wagon. She flopped from the tray to the road, barely able to keep her feet beneath her. Examiner looked down from the driver's seat, where she was holding the reins. Judge was with the horse, scratching it behind the ears while Teacher fed it an apple.

"Are you sure you know what you are doing, Velander?" asked Examiner.

"Andry . . . is he close?" she panted.

"I have been making investigations," said Teacher. "I was told he is going to the Jolly Pint, to make inquiries about a boat to cross the Strait of Dismay. I suppose you want to run away to see him."

"Jolly Pint. How to reach?"

Teacher gave her directions, then she tottered away down the dark, rainswept street.

Rollaric and Shylaren shadowed Velander at a distance calculated not to cause a victim too much alarm. They were deciding what might be a good place for closing in. When she turned onto a bridge to cross the Loriaken River, they were taken by surprise. The area on the other side was dangerous even for a lone man. She stopped, put her hands on the stone railing, and stared out over the dark water.

"So what's she doin', Rol?" asked Shylaren.

"Nothin'. Might be in a mind to take her own life."

"Ach, that's bad. And us not robbed her yet, and all."

"Right you are. Should she hit the water, the river gleaners will have rights fer lootin'."

"Best make a move."

They had failed to notice that something resembling a faint casting was flickering and dancing over Velander's skin.

"Oh aye, ladyship, and a grand night for it and all!" called Shylaren as he approached.

Rollaric was hurrying over the bridge behind them as he spoke, but now he stopped and turned, blocking her escape. They began to close with her.

"Would ye be lookin' for a job o' work, then?" he called. "I got a job o' work, needs doin'."

Velander gave no sign of noticing their approach. Rollaric came around behind Velander, took her by the arm, and locked his arm, under her chin. An experienced predator of the streets who applies a headlock from behind expects many things on the strength of experience. Victims always grab for the arm and try to ease the pressure on the throat. They then try to pull away, and sometimes they try to spin around. Velander did seize Rollaric's arm, but what he did not expect was the way she pushed backward, into him. Before Shylaren could gather his wits, Rollaric had been pushed straight across the bridge until he met the opposite railing. He tumbled over, taking Velander with him.

Shylaren hurried across and looked over the railing, but it

was too dark to see anything clearly. There was an upturned boat half sunk just below the surface—or perhaps it was on the surface. No, it was rising into the air—an enormous beak, larger than a horse, and a glowing blue eye! The head came level with the petrified Shylaren, the blue eye glared at him, then more and more neck emerged from the river. The head towered over Shylaren, the beak opened, the thing bellowed. It was a roar so shatteringly loud that Shylaren only felt the sound. The beak closed around him, and he was dead before he was tossed in the air, caught, and swallowed.

Two of the night militia emerged from the darkened street at the edge of the bridge, walking in a meander that averaged into a straight line, and with their arms around each other's shoulders, on the theory that four legs are more stable than two.

"Aye, an' it could only have been thunder," slurred the one on the right.

"Well, if's case, we'd better take shelter at the Queen's Head," replied his companion.

"But it's already rainin'."

They stopped, aware that an eye in a head with a beak that was bigger than most rowboats was looking down at them. More and more neck was emerging from the river, followed by a body the size of the local watch shelter. A leg emerged from the river and a muddy, three-taloned foot came down on the stone bridge. A stonemason who had died three hundred years before would have been very, very proud, because his bridge did not collapse as the twenty tons of gigantic dragon bird heaved itself out of the river.

"Going—I—am!" thundered a voice in broken Diomedan from a neck longer than the longest organ pipe ever built in Acrema.

"Don't let us stop you," managed the militiaman on the right.

"Don't talk to it, Passor, it's can't be existin'," said his companion.

With that the bird stepped over the militiamen and into the laneway behind them. The laneway had been too narrow for it, but by the time it had passed there was plenty of room.

Rollaric and Shylaren stared with considerable apprehension at the woman wearing the red dress who was standing before the white boat. She was holding her pole like a quarterstaff.

"Attack my friend Velander, would you?" she said in a low and menacing voice. "Well now, Rollaric and Shylaren, this *will* be an entertaining trip."

Velander was dimly aware of herself within the body of her approximation of a dragon. She had never been very good at drawing dragons, and could not quite get the proportions right. Her wings were only the size of bedsheets, for example, and the fine details of a dragon's snout and head were beyond her imagination, so she just formed a bird's beak. Absolute size was a different matter, however. This incarnation had much longer legs than all the others her subconscious had fabricated, so that her eyes were fifty feet above the ground. The body was composed of pure etheric energies, carefully woven into a compressible casting by the sorcerer that she had killed in Clovesser, and thus it weighed no more than Velander's body, and could have easily been blown about in the wind. She made up for this by filling it with water. The water also had the effect of slowing any weapons or missiles that struck it.

As a result of having received some therapy from Teacher, Velander's consciousness was now in theory controlling the dragon casting, but control was still not a particularly precise matter. The dragon could eat anything, and it did require a large amount of life-force food. All that Velander could do was point it in the right direction, and try to make sure there were no innocent bystanders in the way when she released control of the head. Navigating through Logiar was quite a problem. Velander did not know the streets very well, and now she was trying to find her way about from a perspective of over forty-five feet higher up. With a sudden flash of inspiration, she lowered her head to

almost street level and walked hunched over, following
Teacher's directions. This made navigation easier, but
caused considerable consternation among those walking the
streets. Seeing a fifty-foot-high monster walking in the distance is alarming enough. Encountering such a creature's
head at street level with no warning at all definitely called
for a scream-and-run reaction.

The Jolly Pint came into view. Velander now straightened,
then looked down at the slate roof. The sounds of one of the
Jolly Pint's famous fights reached her as she cocked her head
on its side. She plunged her head through the slate roof,
opened her beak, and bellowed. By now she knew that this
had the effect of making intended victims freeze with terror.
Akiro, Aziro, and the regular drinkers certainly did freeze.
Velander cocked her head on one side and scanned the faces
staring up at her. Andry's was not there.

"Now, there's something you don't see every day," said
the tapman, and even the serving maid raised an eyebrow
and gave a slight nod in Velander's direction.

As if on cue, the patrons of the Jolly Pint burst from the
tavern. Literally. Two burly sailors ran at the door, broke it
from its hinges without so much as a fumble with the latch,
and fled between Velander's thirty-foot-high legs. A huge
docker jumped for a shuttered window and crashed through
it, taking the shutters, frame, and external bars in his stride.
Others fled for the cellar, took refuge behind the serving
maid, or even chopped and kicked their way through the
lath-and-plaster walls.

Velander noticed that two patrons remained behind. Akiro
was trapped beneath a heavy roof beam that weighed in excess of a ton, and Aziro was frantically trying to pull his
brother free. Cubic yards of air rumbled as if traveling
through an enormous organ pipe as she inhaled.

"Boring!" she bellowed, the sheer volume of the sound
shattering bottles and windowpanes in the immediate vicinity.

Somehow this gave Akiro access to reserves of strength
not normally available to mortals. He heaved the beam off
his brother, tossed it aside, picked up Aziro, and ran.

"I wouldn't have said boring," said the tapman to Velander.

"Aye, a lot livelier than usual," agreed the serving maid.

"Where—is—Andry?" demanded a very deep voice from the huge head.

"If he's one of those sailors as were here before, gone to the docks," said the tapman.

"Sailing," added the serving maid.

"To Alberin, in Scalticar," concluded the tapman.

The last of the Jolly Pint's patrons did not come out of hiding until eleven weeks later, but it was two years before anyone learned the fate of Akiro and Aziro. A precious-metals merchant reported that they were working in a gold mine, two thousand miles away in the mountains of northeast Acrema. The same merchant said that they never, never came to the surface.

Velander withdrew her head, and raised herself to her full height. While the streets were something of a problem to navigate from fifty feet high when one was looking for a specific building, finding the city's docklands was positively easy once one was above the clutter of the houses. She set off at a lumbering run, and was standing on the pier within a couple of minutes. Out on the water she could see a small boat flying a storm sail. The pier collapsed under her weight, and she waded out of the water, roaring with frustration and anguish. Standing on the shore, she looked out along the inlet where the *Shadowmoon* was receding, and bellowed Andry's name. The sound was like a peal of thunder that lasted for a full quarter minute.

"Are you quite finished, my dear?" called Teacher from behind her in the dead Larmentallian language.

Without any warning at all, Velander's dragon-bird form collapsed, releasing some twenty tons of reeking river water, along with Velander's body, and the bodies of Rollaric and Shylaren.

"My, my, you are a twisted little thing, are you not?" said Examiner, wading through the dispersing water and helping Velander to sit up.

"That why I am here," gasped Velander, shivering with cold and misery.

"It is time to finish your lessons," said Teacher.

"What am I?" asked Velander.

"You are not quite anything," replied Teacher. "Not quite

glass dragon, not really human, not entirely alive, but only a little dead."

"You are a woman," said Examiner. "More or less."

"That is a relief," responded Velander. "But I want to be alive, too."

"We explained that already, you can only be half alive," said Teacher.

"He means alive half of the time," interjected Judge. "Really, Teacher, don't you know that bad expression and grammar can start wars? Now, Velander, there is the question of your vocation. What do you wish to be? You can be partly alive, but you will have to be a dragon as well. You killed a glass dragon and drank its etheric energies. That is totally without precedent, and now you can do things that would take two hundred years of training for anyone else. Do you wish to be a dragon?"

"Yes, I do suppose it."

"You will need more commitment than that," said Judge.

"Yes, I *wish* it," responded Velander firmly. "I wish to be a glass dragon so that I may be alive for Andry."

The three of them hauled Velander into the tray of the cart, then Judge and Teacher erected the frames and rain covers. It was a quarter hour before they started out for the city gates. Judge and Teacher sat with Velander on the straw in the tray of the cart, discussing her background.

"Twenty-one years of age," said Teacher. "You passed the ninth level of initiation, then killed a glass dragon thirty days ago, by feeding upon its life essences."

"One of those stupid young political-activist dragons," said Judge. "Wind Warrior Mauler, as I recall."

"Lavolten, in your naming, Velander. Good riddance, I say."

"How could a mortal have drunk the dragon-form casting that is his life's essence?" asked Teacher. "It would kill a mortal."

"But I was not a mortal, and I was not alive," explained Velander.

"Ah, now I see a precedent," said Teacher. "The youth named Laron. He was dead, yet he could walk only when Miral was up, and he drank blood and life essence from those that were living. I first met him two centuries ago. Charming manners, even though he had a silly beard stuck on to hide his acne. But he said that he was the only one of his kind. Where did you come from?"

"Laron created me."

"Oh dear. I do hope you are not going to mate," Examiner called from the driver's bench.

"Never!" said Velander emphatically, then she began to sob, pressing her knees against her eyes. "Oh Andry, you don't even know I'm alive again."

"Andry," sighed Examiner. "Such a noble young man."

They were within sight of the city gates now, and a guardsman approached, huddled under a rain cape.

"Gates closed until further notice," he called.

"Oh dear, so you want one of those bribe things to open it, I suppose?" replied Examiner in Sargolan Common.

"All the gold in the empire would not make me open that gate," replied the guard emphatically. "There's monsters about."

"Monsters?" asked Examiner, sounding concerned rather than frightened.

"I think he means us," suggested Judge from behind her.

"But we're not monsters, we're very respectable and we only want to leave the city with our student."

The guard put his hands on his hips beneath his rain cape. "Now listen lady, just piss off to some hostelry and watch the postings board. The deputy acting regent has declared a state of siege, and until he decides to—"

Examiner stood up, opened her mouth, and poured a star-hot torrent of incandescent plasma at the gate with a sound that should not have been possible without either very advanced technology or very large natural phenomena. The shift officer hurried out in time to see the guard getting to his feet and the cart trundling through the gateway. Six crossbowmen were following him. All that remained of the great double gates were the four glowing stubs of the hinges, which were hissing in the rain.

"What in all levels of the hells just happened?" demanded the officer. "Archers, wind ratchets and load bolts."

"The little old lady in the cart—" began the guard.

"What? Are you drunk on duty, man?"

"No sir, but—"

"Go after that cart! Stop it!"

"Not for all the gold in Acrema, sir."

"Do you defy me, sir?" demanded the officer.

"No sir, I'm just not goin' near that cart."

"I'll stop them myself, sir, then have you on a charge. Archers, take aim at that cart! Ready . . ."

One of the crossbowmen noted the speed with which the guardsman leaped to one side, made an exceedingly fast decision, dropped his crossbow, and leaped also. When they looked back at where the officer and five other crossbowmen had been standing, there was a long, oval patch of liquid rock surrounded by glowing cobblestones.

"It's probably the World Mother's way of weeding out the stupid ones," whispered the guardsman.

"And the slow ones," added the crossbowman.

Aboard the cart, Velander was having the diagnosis of the glass dragons explained to her.

"You ran away in the middle of our treatment," sighed Teacher. "We had so much more to do with you."

"Yes, especially with all those life-force tendrils that you thought were attacking you," said Judge. "They were the dragon-form casting of that stupid Wind Warrior Mauler dragon."

"The political activist," called Examiner from the driver's seat.

"They were attaching themselves to your soul at random," continued Teacher. "Some were good life-force matches, others were woeful. We shall have to do it all again, properly this time, and then attach all the others as well."

"It hurt so much," complained Velander weakly.

"Ah, but it will be controlled. After that you will be a glass dragon like us."

"But not quite like us," added Judge.

"But I am sure we can still be friends," Examiner assured her.

✳ ✳ ✳

True to Andry's word, the *Shadowmoon* rose and fell on the enormous waves, and was swept along with them. The two storm sails were torn away within the first hour of clearing the inlet leading to Port Logiar, and by dawn most of the rigging had been demolished by the wind, and the occasional wave that the vessel did not quite ride.

Laron kept telling everyone that he must have been drunk to embark on such a voyage, Wallas had himself lashed to the forecastle so that he could be sick into the orlops whenever he wished, and Riellen kept asking Andry when they were going to die. They finally managed to arrange a durable rigging in the form of a ten-foot stub of mainmast, a spar lashed to the stub and the railings, and a triple thickness of sail tied to this extremely sturdy arrangement. Laron impressed on everyone the importance of keeping to a heading as close to south as possible, and to do that they merely had to keep the wind to starboard.

When Norrieav and Hazlok awoke they attempted to have all their passengers tried for mutiny and put in irons, but Laron pointed out that even with everyone working to bail, repair, and steer the *Shadowmoon*, they were barely managing to stay afloat and on course. On the second day out, Laron admitted that he had no idea whether they had gone ten miles or a hundred, but because the waves were so big, they were probably still in the Strait of Dismay. It was on the third day that Laron left Danol, Costiger, Riellen, and Hazlok trying to keep the steering pole under control, and went below deck to address those in the sick bay. By now the sick bay consisted of the entire interior of the ship. When they had sailed, Gilvray had been the sickest person aboard, but now he was the *Shadowmoon*'s medicar, and he was locked in a desperate struggle with injuries, wind chill, hysteria, exhaustion, seasickness, and blind terror as he tried to keep the company of the schooner fit to serve on deck, or to bail and pump below.

"What are your injuries, sir?" he called as Laron came down the steps, along with a generous measure of seawater.

"None to speak of," Laron shouted above the crashing water, groaning timbers, and howling wind. "How are you faring?"

"Always wanted to be a medicar, sir, but my father said the

vocation was too middle-class. I did all the medicar units at the Officer's Academy of the Imperial Militia, though, so—"

"No, I mean are you well?"

"No worse than any other, sir."

"As bad as that? Well, pass the word about. I have good news and bad news. The good news is that the sea swells and wave shapes indicate we're not far from North Scalticar."

"The bad news will need to be bad indeed to dampen that, sir," replied Gilvray.

"It is. Those gigantic waves out there are starting to break as they reach the shallower water. Sooner or later one will break over the *Shadowmoon*."

"And then we'll all die, sir?"

"And then we may have one chance in ten thousand if the pump has kept the ship as free of water as possible down here. Put everything into keeping the pump working. I'm going back up."

"You heard the man!" shouted Andry, who was currently in charge of the pump. "With all your strength, now."

"Not you, Andry," called Norricav, who was lashed to an improvised bunk. "Get up to the steering pole, they'll need another set of muscles soon. I'll command the pump crew."

All of those up on the quarterdeck were tied to the railings and any other boat's fittings that looked sturdy. With six of them working the steering pole, the *Shadowmoon* was still keeping the wind roughly to starboard. Suddenly Laron pointed ahead.

"Land!" he cried. "Mountains! North Scalticar! We're too close."

"Thought the idea was to get close enough to step ashore," called Riellen above the wind.

"No, we needed to keep to the middle of the strait until we pass Seadragon Pinnacle, then work around to the sheltered east coast of the continent. There the waves are only a tenth as big. We would be able to sail right into Alberin's harbor from the east after maybe a week."

"So what happens now, sir?" asked Andry.

"A giant wave breaks over us if we pass over water that's too shallow, and we all drown. We're too close to Northspur Peninsula, the northernmost part of Scalticar."

"Would the sort of giant wave be like that one, sir?" cried Costiger, pointing into the wind.

They all looked. In the west, the entire horizon seemed to be slowly rising, as well as arching over and turning into foam.

"Turn! Turn, three octans to port!" shouted Laron. "We must take it sternside or even Lady Fortune will think we're a bad joke."

The *Shadowmoon* came around slowly, but they could all feel themselves dropping as the schooner plunged into the trough before the enormous wave. They began to rise again.

"Don't look!" shrieked Laron after glancing back.

Everybody looked. Everybody wished that they had not looked. Within moments the *Shadowmoon* was traveling downward at an angle of about forty-five degrees, and the angle was increasing all the time.

"It we tip over we're dead!" shouted Laron.

"You mean we're not dead already, sir?" cried Riellen, clinging to the base of the steering pole and Danol's leg.

"Hold on tight, it's breaking over us!" shouted Laron.

The wavetop began to break up, but the *Shadowmoon* remained on an even keel as many thousands of tons of water thundered down upon them. Suddenly everything was muted, and they realized that they were actually under the surface. Riellen felt herself torn away from the steering pole and the others. She groped for the rope tied to her waist, fighting the voice in her mind that kept insisting that she had to be dead, given the circumstances—and then they were on the surface again, with surf boiling all around them. Danol was hauling on her tether.

"Grab the side nettings!" shouted Danol as the turbulence dashed her against the *Shadowmoon*.

As Riellen clambered over the side of the *Shadowmoon* she noticed that the schooner was beginning to drop again.

"What in all hells is going on?" called Norrieav from the open hatch.

"Close that bloody hatch!" shouted Laron; then he added, "And keep pumping!"

"We're up to our balls in water, it will take a quarter hour to clear even—"

"You have a minute or less, now seal the hatch!"

The roughly rigged sail had been torn away, so that this time they had a far better view as the *Shadowmoon* was borne upward, yet pointed almost straight down.

"Must be doing fifty knots!" shouted Laron, but nobody was listening.

The *Shadowmoon* began to slew over, and water started spilling over the middeck.

"To port, two octens," ordered Laron, but water was already thundering down onto the schooner.

They seemed to stay submerged for a much longer time, and when they again broke the surface they were riding much lower in the water. The hatch was flung open again.

"Damn you, Laron, we're up to our necks in it now," shouted Norrieav. "It's too deep to use the pump unless we move it up on deck."

"Do that and the next one will wash it away!" retorted Laron.

"Next one will sink us anyway!" Norrieav shouted back.

"Well get everyone out on deck and tie them down," replied Laron. "Then seal the bloody hatch!"

The *Shadowmoon* was already rising as those from below deck were being tethered.

"When we go under again, count to one hundred, then wait until your lungs will stand no more, then release the slipknots on your tethers," ordered Norrieav. "There's a chance some of use may survive the waves and rocks, and crawl ashore, but stay with the boat until there's no hope, and—Oh World Mother, are they all as huge as that?" he exclaimed, looking back over the quarterdeck.

"Five octans starboard!" shouted Laron. "Five, damn you all! Five!"

"Too hard, sir," shouted Costiger. "The force—"

"Five, dammit! I'm coming up to help."

"Your tether, Laron!" shouted Norrieav. "You'll be swept away."

"Five octans, starboard!" cried Laron, ignoring him.

This wave was different, and the *Shadowmoon* seemed to take a lot longer to rise. Mountains loomed to starboard, and spray burst high into the air as it slammed over the rocks on and near the shore. Andry suddenly realized that the water behind them was no longer higher than the *Shadowmoon*. The schooner was moving so fast that the wind was blowing the wet hair back from his face as he looked forward, and what he saw was a long, deep inlet where the waves had become long, rolling swells. All around Andry, the others were cheering and throwing off their tethers.

"Scalticar!" shouted Costiger. "Three cheers times three for Navigator Laron!"

* * *

The regional port of Falgat was at the head of the inlet, but it took the rest of the day for the *Shadowmoon* to limp the fifteen miles to a berth. The pump was working for the entire time, and everyone not on the pump was bailing continuously. Even so, the water level scarcely dropped. Early in the evening they reached the docks, and the *Shadowmoon* was thrown a line as it edged up to the only slipway. Ropes followed, and the schooner was hauled onto a roller trolley. Presently the *Shadowmoon* was clear of the waves, and water was pouring from the hull.

"Too many seals have burst," said Norrieav, standing with his hands on his hips and shaking his head. "The poor girl is a wreck. It will cost nearly as much to repair her as it did to build her."

"But we all got here safely," said Laron.

"I thought you were dead, Laron—and after what you did to my boat, I almost wish you were."

"We paid for passage, and you can have the remaining supplies."

"Oh aye, and that will barely cover just the mooring and slipway fees."

Norrieav walked off in the direction of the portmaster's tower. Essen and Andry joined Laron, who was still staring at the *Shadowmoon* as the water drained out.

"The boat should have sunk twice over," said Andry. "I know boats and all, yet the *Shadowmoon* just couldn't be drowned. It was almost as if Fortune had her hand underneath, keeping us up."

"Not fortune, Andry," replied Laron. "The boat is a submersible, designed to sink, and designed to bob up again. No other vessel could have beaten the strait."

"A what, Captain?"

"A submersible, a spy boat. It can be sunk to hide under water, then brought back to the surface."

"Captain, you're making this up."

Laron put a hand out to one of the strange, small, square hatches in the *Shadowmoon*'s hull. It was closed, and water was pouring out through burst seams all around it.

"Yes Andry, I'm making it up. Lady Fortune was awfully kind to us, so we had better not impose upon her in the immediate future."

Now Gilvray and Dolvienne joined them, and although shaky on their feet, they were actually smiling.

"Well, Boatmaster Norrieav will be a rich and happy man now," said Gilvray.

"Why?" asked Laron, looking puzzled.

"With all those boxes of medicar's bark in the *Shadowmoon*, below deck. It was all sealed in sheepgut, so I doubt any was ruined—apart from the little I used to treat us during the voyage."

"Medicar's bark, sir?" asked Laron. "Costiger said it was ship's biscuit."

"Costiger can't read," said Andry. "The boxes just looked a bit like ship's-biscuit crates. I'd say the Jolly Pint's landlord took them as payment in kind for some bill."

"It is grown in the far north of Acrema, in the tropics," explained Gilvray. "It's cheap enough there, but what with Scalticar being cut off by the Torean Storms it's probably priceless here by now. I took the liberty of, well, liberating a few lengths from the open case. One for each reccon, and the other passengers. The boatmaster will be so rich after this, I'm sure he will not mind."

Laron hurried away to the portmaster's office to let Norrieav know the good news, and the others gathered together to discuss where to spend the night.

"A good move would be to march to Alberin and sell our medicar's bark before Norrieav's crates arrive there and flood the market," suggested Essen.

"You're in charge, sir," replied Andry.

"No I'm not, lad. We're just unattached mercenaries here, and we're equals. You're Andry, I'm Essen. Are you for Alberin?"

"Oh aye, I've family there."

"March with us then? The others think to go there too."

"March with you I will, Essen. For now let's find hot food."

✳ ✳ ✳

Essen led then into Falgat, flanked by Laron on one side and Gilvray and Dolvienne on the other. Riellen was with the reccons, and Wallas was at the rear, walking unsteadily, but nevertheless walking. They stopped at an inn called Ocean's View, from which one could see the waters of the inlet if one stood on the roof, but none of them was the slightest bit interested in looking at water.

"Well, Alberin's sixty miles away, through passably hilly country," said Andry as they gathered around the fire in the taproom. "Three days, at a walk."

"Aye, this is a small place, with no prospects," agreed Essen.

"I say we ride," declared Wallas.

"Ride?" asked Andry. "On what? In case you've not noticed, nearly all our money went into the hire of the *Shadow-moon.*"

"Aye, and we're no longer in Sargol's militia," added Essen. "We can't just ask for a horse and get given one."

"I could sell my medicar's bark here," said Wallas. "That would buy a horse."

"Aye, but you'd be selling it for a twentieth of its value in Alberin," Essen pointed out. "Boatmaster Norrieav has just taken three cases off to the local merchants, to pay for the *Shadowmoon*'s rebuild. There's bark to burn here, but little in Alberin—yet."

"My inclination is to leave tomorrow and travel together," advised Andry.

"Well my inclination is to rest first," said Wallas. "We have enough coin to sleep under a roof and eat for a week."

"Yes, it's been a very trying voyage," agreed Gilvray.

"Andry, can I have a quiet word with you?" said Laron.

They walked over to the serving board, and asked the youth there to attend those near the fire. Once they were alone, Laron leaned closer to Andry.

"I have to visit the College of Warriors," he said softly. "It is on the way to Alberin. I shall leave you there."

"I promised someone I would take you to Alberin," replied Andry.

"Did you indeed?" said Laron. "And who was that?"

"Someone who thought you needed to be there."

"Terikel?"

"In Alberin is a lad named Roval, I was told. He's in need of a friend, just now."

"But I have important business in the college," insisted Laron. "It involves the fate of the world, believe me when I say it."

"If you've no concern for the fate of a friend, how can you speak for the world?" asked Andry, looking into Laron's eyes as if challenging him to give an honest answer.

Laron put a hand to his mouth and looked away to the others. They were relaxed and even happy, from what he could see. Several had escaped a sentence of death, two were in love, and the reccons were close to home after many years away. All would soon have money, and were probably looking forward to an unexciting life. Wallas stood up and spread his arms, taking a deep breath.

> "Upon Taloncrag's rocky slopes,
> We crouched together, lacking hopes,
> Of escaping, we all knew full well,
> Andry, Wallas and Terikel.
>
> A dragoncharmer, we would—Harrrgh!"

Costiger had decided that the contents of his tankard would be best employed down the back of Wallas's neck.

"All right, Andry, come with me to the college tomorrow,"

said Laron, applauding Costiger, who was taking a bow. "If the college decides that I am needed, there is an end to it. If not, I'll go on to Alberin with you."

As it happened, all of the others decided to come along after a discussion that lasted for most of the evening. This decision was partly due to the attraction of traveling in a large, well-armed group, as well as the prospect of arriving in Alberin before the city's market had been flooded with medicar's bark.

There was but a single trace left of the College of Warriors. This was a stone archway over a turnoff from the main road, close to the thirty-mile stone for Alberin. It bore the inscription COLLEGE OF WARRIORS, and this was underlined by a row of crossed axes. The keystone featured an immense eye. Beyond the archway was a field of complete desolation, from which wisps of smoke were curling into the evening sky in a few places. Some of the more solid stone buildings had retained something of their original shape, and the roads were the least damaged features of all.

"Dragons," said Essen as the group stood peering past the archway.

"Bloody big dragons," said Costiger.

Nothing was moving, except for the smoke. Andry walked through the archway and toward the edge of the charred area.

"Andry Tennoner, a very dangerous place, that is!" called Dolvienne after him in heavily accented Alberinese.

Andry stopped at the edge of the burned area, went down on one knee, and put his hand out.

"Warm, just warm," said Andry. "This happened some time ago."

"We should move on, Andry," called Laron. "Whatever did this may come back."

"I doubt it, lordship. Nothing to come back to." He stood up, his hands on his hips. "We should at least check over this place, and report it."

"Report it to who?" cried Wallas. "The World Mother?

'Er, excuse me, World Mother, but one of the lesser deities is being careless with his thunderbolts, you know, reducing areas the size of a largeish town to slag and the mortals to puffs of smoke, and well, they don't like it.' "

"Andry's right, we should at least learn what we can here," Laron decided, as if to annoy Wallas. "Captain Gilvray, would you lead the others a half mile down the road and set up camp for the night? Andry and I will stay here while the light lasts, and see what is to be seen."

"You will need me as well," said Riellen, following after Laron and Andry as they walked through the archway.

"What? No, it's too dangerous!" exclaimed Laron, turning and spreading his arms to stop her.

"Andry just said it was not dangerous anymore."

"It's too dangerous for a woman."

"What does my being female have to do with anything?" she demanded angrily.

"You're not as strong as us, and you can't fight."

"And you're not a scholar."

"I'm an uncommissioned sorcerer," said Laron, fumbling in his clothing, then producing a battered and somewhat water-stained scroll. "See, Madame Yvendel's Academy, in Diomeda."

"And how much have you studied of the cold sciences?" demanded Riellen. "I have specialized in the cold sciences and—"

"Let her come, Laron," called Andry.

"But she's—"

"Lordship, in my limited experience, ladies as work in men's trades are three times better than men. Fall in, lass, you can walk with me."

The surface was powdery with ash, but underlaid with crunchy, glassy material.

"Warrior sorcerers do battle castings," said Andry softly as he and Riellen walked. "Looks like they did one and got it wrong."

"Or some enemy got one right," replied Riellen.

"Yet this is like what happened in Clovesser," observed Andry. "Was it Dragonwall, I wonder? I wish there was a way of telling."

"There is, and I am doing it," said Riellen, and now Andry noticed that she was taking measured, even paces, and walking in a straight line.

There were bodies here and there, half char and half bloody flesh. They were quite undisturbed, and Andry surmised that the local scavenger birds and animals had not yet got up the nerve to go near the place. Riellen reached the other side of the burned area, picked up a charred stick and a scrap of slate, and wrote something. She then began pacing back.

"Don't you want to measure something else?" asked Andry.

"I am doing just that. If I take half as many paces back, I reach the center. If I walk out at right angles from the center, I can tell if this area is a circle or ellipse."

"Is that important?"

"Oh yes. An ellipse means the heat came from the Dragonwall, but a circle means it came from overhead."

"Er, what's an ellipse?"

"Something like an oval."

"What's an oval?"

The charred area turned out to be a perfect circle. Riellen made several more notes, then directed Andry's attention to a rock.

"Notice, it's glazed on the top, and evenly all around," she said. "All the rocks that I have seen show the same feature. The fire came from directly above, from a single point, and from very high. There was probably just a single, short burst. A long burst would have made the bodies char to ash, but they are only partly burned. The rocks are not actually melted, they just have a thin glaze."

"Then what did it?" asked Andry.

"Not Dragonwall, it would have left an elliptical shape on the ground, and glazed the rocks on the west side. Not a dragon either, because even a huge dragon would have taken more than a single blast of fire to do this."

"But how can you tell that this was done in an instant?"

"The pattern of the bodies. They look to have been going about their normal business, and not a single one had a weapon in hand. The warriors and their recruits never knew what hit them."

"So we don't know what did it, but we know what didn't do it," said Andry, as he waved to Laron and beckoned him over.

"It was Dragonwall."

"But you just said—"

"Look, a piece of stone from the top of the west wall of the Clovesser Academy," said Riellen, taking a chip of sandstone from her purse. "I picked it up as we fled, it was so hot I had to wrap it in my scarf. Now break off a chip from that sandstone block there and compare the depth of the melting."

The depth of melting was identical. Laron joined them as they stood up. Riellen made some more notes on the slate.

"Well, from the scale of the devastation, I say it was a flock of dragons that did all this," Laron suggested as they moved off.

Andry felt smugly superior yet slightly disturbed as Riellen began to explain her observations to Laron. Education, rank, wealth, power, and even manners made no difference when it came to being right or wrong. *So why bother getting an education, and why learn good manners?* The thought was almost as disturbing to Andry as the devastation all around them.

"Sorry your comrades are all dead," he said to Laron as Riellen completed her explanation.

"All gone," said Laron, sounding beyond emotion. "Apart from Roval, and even he is dead inside."

The others were camped near a farmstead that was owned by the SWS, and one of the peasants had been outside chopping wood when the college had been destroyed. He described a sizzling crackle followed by a blast like thunder, and a cloud of smoke rising straight up into the sky. It had been the day before, and although there had been some cloud about, the sky above the college complex had been clear, and no dragons had been visible. Nearly every member of the SWS on the continent had been there. A meeting of their general council had been called to discuss the situation with the Skepticals.

"So the Skepticals have been giving trouble to the SWS?" asked Laron. "That seems unlikely, they are just an order of agnostic priests dedicated to the study of the cold sciences. They are no military threat to anyone."

"Well, they aren't now, lordship," said the peasant. "Somethin' burned their temples to char and slag on a single night."

"What? But there were at least a dozen of them."

"Aye lordship, that's why the warriors of the college were meeting. Something horrible is about in the land. I say it's that Dragonwall thing."

"Andry and I will press on to Alberin tomorrow," said Laron to Riellen when the man had gone. "We need to tell the militia about this. If the others want to come, they have to keep to a forced march regimen."

Laron had expected an argument about needing to take a vote, but instead Riellen pointed upward.

"You had better tell them about that," she said.

The cloud cover was breaking up, and the stars were showing through in places. What was also showing through was a thin, sharp, and intense line of blue light.

"First noticed it back on Taloncrag, but it's been cloudy since then," said Andry. "Teri—that is, Terikel thought it was a worry."

"See, it moves slowly against the stars," said Riellen, "and by the look of its angle across the sky, I would say it intersected Dragonwall at Ringstone Centras, on the equator."

"It is attached to Dragonwall, yet it passes over the entire world," Laron suddenly realized. "It would have passed over . . ."

"The SWS grounds, and the Skepticals' temples," Riellen concluded for him. "That thing can deliver Dragonwall's fire to anywhere on the world. Nothing is safe."

The coast of Torea was at first a slight discoloration on the horizon, then it resolved itself into land as Terikel approached, riding the winds before a storm that had been sweeping her east for a full day. She slowly lost height, and tried to match what she could see with maps in her memory. The land had an odd glitter about it, and there was not a trace of green. She caught sight of a hill on the coast, then a range

of mountains farther inland. The hill was covered by a mo-
saic of lines, and several lines extended out into the sea. A
small city, with a harbor and stone piers. And a single hill.
Zantrias. The port had been her last view of Torea the previous year, just before the continent had been annihilated.

It was evening now, but it had been morning when she had
last seen Zantrias as a thriving, living town. She circled the
ruins, on the buffeting winds from the storm that was still
out to sea, gradually dropping, spiraling in on the hill where
the ruins of the Metrologan temple were still visible. She
had by now been in the air for three days, and was drowsing,
then jerking awake. *Drowse too long, and you lose the image
of your wings*, she told herself every time that it happened.
Lose the image, and you lose the wings as well. The remains
of the main Metrologan temple and the other buildings of its
complex were still recognizable, although everything that
had been supported by timber had collapsed.

Terikel felt her mind throwing off the cobwebs of exhaustion, now that she had something other than water to look
down upon. She passed over the Metrologans' ceremonial
plaza, where candidates for ordination once endured their
ordeals. The hearth in the shape of a huge stone hand was
still there, although flaked and broken in places by the extreme heat that had passed over it during the fire-circle that
destroyed Torea. Velander had been the last person to endure
an ordeal here, Terikel recalled. She soared out over the harbor, and quickly recognized the stone pier where the *Shadowmoon* had been berthed during Velander's ordination
ordeal. Fused glass glittered along its length, like some dis-
ease of the skin. The *Shadowmoon* had been tied up there
when . . . she forced herself to recall that she had been in the
arms of the *Shadowmoon*'s boatmaster, Feran, while Velander had been undergoing the ordeal. She shuddered at the
memory of the Elder ordering her to seduce the spy, and to
abandon her soulmate vigil for Velander.

"Had I my time over again, I'd tell the old bag to do her
own 'missions of softness,' " said Terikel said to herself,
hoping that it was really true.

She remembered looking out through the latticework windows of the *Shadowmoon*'s master cabin at an absolutely

clear sky on a balmy, relaxed morning. Within a half hour the port and everyone in it had been wiped away, along with the rest of the continent. Those aboard the *Shadowmoon* had survived because the vessel could be sunk and had an airtight refuge. Velander had run all the way from the temple after working out the mathematics of Silverdeath's threat. Laron had taken her warning seriously, and the *Shadowmoon* had ridden out the fire-circles on the harborbottom. Ever since then, the sight of a calm, sunny, tranquil morning had left Terikel unsettled.

The scene below was one of uniform devastation, yet she wanted to land. It was like visiting a grave. Without the people, it was no longer the same, yet there were memories to sharpen, and ghosts to lay to rest. Seals and turtlelike arcarelles were lying on the stone pier, even though waves whipped up by the rising wind were breaking over them. It was the stone pier where she had once strolled with Velander—and where she had hurried furtively late one night, hand in hand with Feran, little realizing that those were to be her last footsteps on Torea.

"Must walk on Torea again, can't have that turd sharing my last memory of the place," she said angrily. "This is as good a place as any to land, sleep, wait out the storm."

Terikel was searching for a wide, flat place to land when a movement in one of the ruin-lined streets caught her eye. As she passed overhead, a dark shape suddenly became a running figure, then vanished around a corner. Another figure hurried between shadows before being lost to sight. *Zantrias is inhabited, then*, thought Terikel. They were probably sealers, perhaps marooned when the Torean Storms made sea travel more suicidal than merely dangerous. At a distance, she knew that she resembled a small dragon. The sealers would avoid such a creature. The small ones were known to be the worst, because they were always very hungry for life force. The sorcerers at their core had ceased to be people, and some would prey on anything with life force that could be absorbed. On the other hand, if the sealers did not know about dragons, Terikel was just a lone, exhausted woman with wing castings.

Landing at the ruins suddenly seemed like a bad idea, and sleeping there was out of the question, yet she did need sleep. Sleep meant losing her wing castings, however, and so she needed somewhere secure to rest. Somewhere desolate, far inland, of no interest to people picking over the corpse of Torea. The Torean Storm was sweeping in from the sea, and already the wind was gusting too sharply for a safe landing. Terikel used the updrafts around Zantrias to gain height, then drifted inland. Staying awake had become an issue by her second day in the air, and was now a serious problem. Still, over inland Torea there would be plenty of opportunities to land, collapse her castings, and rest. She was not particularly hungry, as she had been eating from her pack while in the air. As she had done in midflight, Terikel freed an arm and reached into her pack of rations. Only half of her food was gone, but the waterskin was close to empty.

Night had fallen by the time she stopped climbing, and she was now above the clouds. Again she ate, more for distraction than from hunger. Miral's great, green, ringed disk was setting in the west, although a gibbous moonworld was higher in the sky and shining brightly. Terikel went over her plans and problems. Torea was beneath her, and with the coming of dawn she could find somewhere to land. There she would sleep for perhaps two days before setting out to cross the Infinital Ocean. Her water was running out, but there was plenty of fresh water in glass-lined pools on Torea. The problem was that there was nothing else but fresh water on Torea, and she had food for only another three days.

"Go hungry, hunger will keep you awake," she told herself, speaking her thoughts to keep herself alert.

Terikel awoke with her wings gone.

She was in the early stages of a plunge to the ground that would take two or three minutes and end in instant oblivion. Within moments she had a casting between her hands and was breathing a new etheric spike into existence. The problem was that once she split the spike it could be grown no further, and that limited the wingspan. She had perhaps five feet grown as she entered the cloud tops of the storm. Ten times that length was needed for soaring, but she would have barely half that grown before she hit the ground.

"More time, only three minutes!" shouted Terikel, pleading with Fate.

Surrounded by rushing air and total blackness, she decided that any plan, even an inferior plan, was better than blind panic. She split her spike at only fifteen feet. The wing casting opened out slowly in the rushing slipstream, and was still a shallow V shape as she struggled to attach her shoulder straps. Another minute passed, and Terikel was now flying in a shallow dive rather than falling.

Lightning was flickering around her as Terikel dropped through the base of the clouds. The flashes lit up peaks that were not far below her altitude. Making yet another quick and desperate decision, she began to search for somewhere flat. She was well below the highest of the peaks and navigating only by lightning flashes as she lined up a reasonably straight and vaguely flat sheet of whiteness, and began her approach at sixty miles per hour.

"Let there be snow, let there be lots of soft snow," prayed Terikel as she trailed her legs down and raised her stubby wings, hoping to stall, while hoping that she was not too far above whatever was beneath her.

Chapter Nine

DRAGONGIRL

It was evening as Laron led his group of refugees over the final hill that separated them from Alberin. They found themselves standing beside a ruined tower, between the city and the Ridgeback Mountains. Alberin was spread out on the dark plain beside the ocean, like a carpet covered in small, bright sparks that were slowly burning into its fabric and giving off tendrils of smoke.

"Hard to believe that's Alberin," said Andry to Essen, as they all stared out across the city. "I've never seen it like this."

"But weren't you born here too?"

"Aye, but I've only seen the place from the docks, and the river on the way to Ahrag. I've seen this tower in the distance, and thought some great duke lived here. I never knew it was a ruin. Now I'm looking at Alberin from near it, like some great lord, just home from the wars. And we *are* home! Really home!"

"*You're* home," muttered Wallas. "It's not my home, and it still seems a long way off. The cramps in my calves are up to my thighs."

"You can you smell the musken bushes and the pine trees!" said Andry, taking great breaths. "I just can't say how good that makes me feel."

"That's why we poets have a place," Wallas pointed out. "Why I—"

The five reccons drew their axes and ringed Wallas's head with the blades.

"Don't even think about it," said Andry.

Laron continued to stare out over the city. "I've been here too, and I know the distance to be a three-hour walk," he said. "Best to start."

The path was all downhill, but as Wallas knew by now, this was not all good. Uphill was hard on the leg muscles, downhill was a strain on the feet.

"So what do we do now?" asked Wallas. "What about money, food, a place to stay, a drink, nice soft bandages, and soothing ointments for my feet?"

"There's the Bureau of Coinage and Precious Materials at Riverside Gate," said Andry. "It never closes, because of barges arriving at odd times from inland. We can sell our medicar's bark there, then take a ferry along the river to Wharfside, where there's plenty of taverns and rooming houses."

"This is all sounding too good to be true," said Wallas.

"What are the girls like in Wharfside these days, Andry?" asked Costiger. "It's nine years since I, er . . ."

"Decided to follow a military vocation in foreign lands?" laughed Danol.

"There's always girls in Alberin," said Andry.

"Girls," sighed Wallas, but Willy immediately gave an outraged hiss from beneath his tunic. Wallas clapped a hand to his forehead. "There! I knew it was too good to be true."

"Why isn't that thing in its protector?" asked Andry.

"Because it chafes my legs when I walk."

Alberin was roughly six miles by seven, and built around a bay that was protected from waves, storm surges, enemy fleets, and privateer raiders by a maze of shoals and sandbars. The only shipping channel was overlooked by Trebuchet Tower, a fortress built on one of the shoals that was bristling with siege engines and hellbreath-oil projectors. It also doubled as a lighthouse. The southeast quarter of the city was on higher ground, and contained the palace, larger temples, mansions of the nobility, and houses of the merely prosperous. South of this was the reasonably respectable artisan belt; then the River Alber divided the city. North of the Alber was the teeming, industrial heart of Alberin, and there was only a single bridge between the two sections of the city. This was supplemented by dozens of ferries. Having a single bridge was a deliberate policy of the city authorities, who were not anxious for social mixing to be too easy in Alberin.

At Riverside Gate they changed what money they had for Scalticarian silver nobles, and discovered that medicar's bark was fetching a very good price. Those in the group who had no papers merely bought a set each; then they boarded a ferry. Wallas scrambled aboard first, then bent down and kissed the wooden bench before he sat down.

"What's that for then?" asked Andry as he sat down beside him.

"It takes me where I want to go without me walking," explained Wallas, closing his eyes in sheer bliss as he put his feet up on the bench opposite.

Dolvienne and Gilvray sat on Andry's left, and he pointed out the city's features as the ferryman pushed them out into the sluggish current with his pole.

"So that's the famous barge pole that people wouldn't touch things with," said Wallas, opening his eyes.

"That's actually a ferry pole," said Andry. "It's the same length, but lighter."

"And you say there is only one bridge," said Dolvienne.

"Oh aye, ladyship. There, just around the bend. It's called Bridge, because it's the only bridge."

"So everyone must cross by it?"

"Oh no, there's ferries as well. Most are tiny boats, with oars or poles. The ferrymen sleep in them, under a canvas. Wake them up, any time, give them a copper, and they row you over. See, there's a few near that landing. The nice folk live out south, the scruffies like me live north. We'll pass Bargeyards, where my home is."

"Oh. And where are we going?"

"The part where the river meets the harbor. Wharfside is the scruffy part of the respectable south, where the richer folk go for, er . . ."

"Song, drink, and a naughty time?"

"Er, aye, that's it. But it's safe. Sort of. Neverside is the other side of the river, and it's the scruffy part of the scruffy part. I suppose it's called Neverside because it's never a good idea to go there, especially after dark."

"It's rough, then?" asked Gilvray.

" 'Dangerous' is a better word. The Metrologans have set their temple up in Wharfside, but I've not been there. Where are you thinking of going, Wallas?"

"Oh, Wharfside sounds like my area. I was thinking of getting work as a cook, specializing in Sargolan dishes."

"Oh aye, wise. Try the Lamplighter, at the end of Shipyards Street. They play a lot of Sargolan music there, and they have cheap rooms. Me and the lads would take a ferry across after work, grab a pie and pint, play until the midnight bell, then take a room and flake out on the floor. One night we got fifteen into a room."

"Sounds like a scene of disgust," commented Wallas. "I shall have to raise the tone by attracting a better clientele with my cooking."

"When you've had a few ales, it all tastes the same," said Andry.

Nobody had noticed a slight change in Wallas since they had entered the city, and that change was in his confidence.

He was finally in a metropolis where he was not wanted by the authorities, indeed was not even known to them. Apart from having enough money to live comfortably for a few weeks, he even had prospects of employment. All of that meant independence from Andry and the reccons. A lot of resentments, sufferings, and insults began to emerge from his memory, and Andry had been responsible for a great many of them.

"I suppose you have some girl waiting for you," said Wallas sullenly, aware that Willy was going to be something of a social liability in his new home.

"Not a one, Velander was my one and only," said Andry wistfully.

"What about Terikel?" asked Wallas.

"Terikel?" exclaimed Laron, Gilvray, and Dolvienne together.

"She was just dragonproofing me," explained Andry sheepishly, a hand over his eyes.

"I have heard a lot of reasons for persuading people to do it," said Dolvienne, "but that one is new to me."

"She didn't offer to dragonproof *me*," muttered Wallas.

"Why am I not surprised?" said Laron.

"Well you were unfaithful to Velander!" said Wallas, with a sneer at Andry.

"If I weakened, it's from spending too much time in your company," retorted Andry. "At least Vel is dead, and will never know. The spirit of my lovely lass is gone."

"Lovely lass? She smelled like a carpet left on an alleyway rubbish heap for a year, all moldy, damp, and sort of rotting smells. And her breath! It smelled like the scraps tins outside the butchery yards, like meat gone bad, and mixed with stale blood."

"Andry, sir, is that the Wharfside ferry landing ahead of us?" asked Dolvienne, who had noticed that the exchange had moved from sarcastic banter to dangerously personal insults.

"The only reason she didn't tear your throat out and drink your blood is that she had good taste!" cried Andry, ignoring Dolvienne.

"The only reason she fancied you is that you're as dirty and smelly as she was!" retorted Wallas.

"Take that back! In my Bargeyards home it's out to the back for a wash in cold water with tar soap, every morning. We change our clothes once a week, sometimes twice."

"Lower-class aping of upper-class values. Your girls only learn good manners and habits when people like me visit them in the bawdyhouses, then they go home and tell their menfolk that—"

Andry brought the back of his fist down very hard on Wallas's groin. Willy immediately burned through Wallas's tunic and sank his little fangs into Andry's wrist. Unable to bring himself to touch Willy, Andry punched Wallas in the face with his free hand.

"Stop it!" cried Dolvienne, throwing her arms around Andry and trying to drag him back. "Both of you, stop it!"

"You listen, Willy, I'll just keep hitting him till you let go!" shouted Andry, punching Wallas again and again.

They were, by now, the center of attention on the ferry, and the onlookers included the ferryman. The ferry ran into the stone landing with just sufficient force to stave in a few bow timbers. Slowly, it began to sink. The passengers scrambled off, and were soon standing at the end of Shipyards Street.

"Now I know why my mother never let me play with rowdy, lower-class children!" said Wallas as he stood holding his roll pack over the front of his tunic with one hand and wiping the blood from his nose with the other.

"That thing better not be poisonous," said Andry, who was nursing his right wrist, which was also bleeding.

"Poison? How crass!" snorted Wallas, who then bid the group goodnight and walked into the Lamplighter.

"The Metrologan temple is at the other end of the street," said Andry. "Who's for there? You can probably stay the night if you make a contribution."

Laron raised his hand; then Gilvray and Dolvienne raised theirs as well.

"I suppose I had better go there too," said Riellen, slowly raising her hand last of all. "But I need to know where the city's sorceric academy is to be found."

"I'll see you all there, then," said Andry. "They might take a look at my wrist."

"Me and the reccons might catch a pint at the Lamplighter," said Essen.

"We'll play strangers, like, until we know whether we're wanted," explained Costiger.

"I suspect the reason why I fled has been born, brought up, been taught a trade, and got married by now," said Sander.

"I might join you there, later," said Andry. "I've not had my rebec out of its wax and leather wrapping since the voyage over, and I'm of a mind to try it out."

The Metrologan temple was a third of a mile from the river, and there was a green lamp burning above the door to show that it was a place of healing. Laron was welcomed by a priestess whose name was Justiva, and he introduced the others to her. The refugees were soon taken away to the guest rooms, but Andry remained in the foyer with Justiva. After examining the bite to his wrist, and hearing his explanation of how it had happened, she assured him that etheric castings like Willy were not poisonous.

"Look, er, before I go I want you to have this," said Andry, holding out a packet. "It's medicar's bark, we brought it over from Acrema."

"Medicar's bark?" exclaimed Justiva. "But, but, this is worth a lot of money, even such a small amount."

"About sixty nobles, I'd say."

"Andry, I can't thank you enough," responded the astounded Justiva. "This is a very generous donation."

"I knew a couple of Metrologans, ladyship. They were fine ladies, so I thought if the rest of you were as nice, you'd use the medicar's bark to help poor, deserving scruffies."

"Metrologan priestesses?" asked Justiva, her features suddenly hardening. "Was one named Learned Terikel?"

"Oh I knew her too, but my lass was Velander."

"You—Velander?" gasped Justiva, her eyes wide. "But I was told she was dead."

"Aye, she is."

"Andry, did you say she was your *lass*?"

"Aye."

"Lass, as in hold hands, kiss, and sit around looking into each other's eyes?"

"Aye. Ladyship, I know lots of folk thought Velander a bit difficult, but I saw her good side. Now I'd best be on my way."

"Andry, wait. I mean, you can stay here the night if you need a roof to sleep beneath. I have questions, lots of them."

"Well, thanks so much ladyship, but I thought I might get back to the Lamplighter, have a few tunes with the lads, then sleep on a couch until dawn. My folks will be abed by now, and they're cranky about being woken. Perhaps I can attend your questions some other time."

"Is not anyone but warriors and Skepticals dying today?" asked Madame Jilli as her boat grounded into the pebbles again.

"Died without a fight," muttered the spirit of a magnificently muscled SWS warrior.

"I don't believe in any of this," said a Skeptical as he sat down behind him.

Wallas was certainly familiar with meteoric falls from grace, but an exceedingly fast rise back up to grace was something that he had never even dreamed about, let alone hoped for. He entered the Lamplighter, to discover that the cook was sick and that the place was full of hungry patrons. He offered his services as a cook, was engaged by a pathetically grateful landlord, and with an apron covering the hole that Willy had burned in his tunic found himself in front of an ironhearth stove within five minutes of walking through the front door.

An hour later Andry and Essen were in the taproom, playing all the latest tunes from the Sargolan Empire. Word was spreading through Wharfside that the Lamplighter was a particularly good place to be on this night, swelling the crowd further. The minstrel of the crown prince happened to pass by, on his way home from a nocturnal assignation, just as the scent of some quite alluring Sargolan dishes was beginning to hang on the air outside the Lamplighter. He decided to have a meal. After eating, he asked for an introduction to the chef, and once the landlord worked out what a chef might be, Wallas was presented to the courtier, who happened to know the Master of Tables of the crown prince of Alberin. Wallas was given an invitation to attend the palace kitchens the following day.

At 10 the following morning, an hour before Wallas was due to leave for the palace, Andry was shown into the kitchen by the landlord's wife.

"The poor lad's, like, been thrown out of home," she explained to Wallas, "and after all that fine playin' last night, too. Can you see your way clear to fixing him up with a bit of bread and cheese, and a hot drink, Wallas lad?"

Wallas was too intrigued to bother recalling the unpleasantness of their trip in the ferry, and he offered Andry a stool near the stove. Andry just wanted someone to complain to about his misfortunes, and was not particular who it might be.

"I've been gone sixty days!" said Andry, beyond anger, and sounding very hurt. "My mum was, like, up packing the lunchies for the family at work, and when I walked in—well, you never saw the like."

"I won't know unless you tell me," said Wallas, warming a bread roll for him on the ironrack.

"She threw the chopping board at me, and all I'd done was say hullo."

He showed Wallas the mark where the chopping board had struck his raised forearm.

"Then she started shouting about who the hell did I think I was, walking in there after pissing off for so long, and when I tried to tell her she came after me with the bread knife. Bit of a temper, my mum. Doesn't like oceangoing sailors, and my sister Florrey reckons one rolled her and ran, back when—"

"So *you* ran?" interjected Wallas.

"Er no, I was away from the door by then. I cross-blocked her knife arm and sort of ducked, pulling it downward. She rolled over my back and came down on the serving table, and it, er . . . sort of broke."

"You threw your *mother*?" gasped Wallas.

"Aye."

"Was she hurt?"

"I'd not say so. She picked up a table leg and came after me again, so I ran for the door. By then my dad had come to see what the noise was about, and he had an ax. I dodged a chop, and sort of pushed him in the face and got away into the alley."

"*Sort of pushed him in the face?*" asked Wallas, his eyes narrowing.

"Well, I punched him pretty hard. I mean can you believe it? And I had sixteen Sargolan silver vassals and five Scalticarian silver nobles from my travels. That's more than what I could have earned for twice sixty days in the bargeyards."

"You said you were short of money when we landed at Falgat," Wallas pointed out.

"I was only out of money for buying you a horse to ride on to get here."

"I endured a two-day forced march to get here!" cried Wallas, not having to feign outrage.

"But it made you lose a lot of weight, Wallas, and you look good. The girls will like the look of you."

"Fat lot of good that will do me with Willy to preserve my chastity. Still, it will help to look good for the crown prince. I'm to see him in an hour, and there's a prospect of becoming his cook. Have to look good for that."

"So he likes Sargolan cooking, then?"

"Apparently. I wonder if he needs a Master of Music?"

"Don't try it, you might put him off his food."

"I'd expect nothing less than sarcasm from you. So, what are your plans?"

"I'm not thinking past tonight, and tonight I intend to get

filthy, legless, rolling drunk. Velander owes me one night on the town. Want to come?"

"Sorry, I may I have a very important cooking assignment, in the very palace itself, by then. Get the reccons to go with you."

The Metrologans' temple was at the base of Palace Hill, not far from the main temple of the city, the Universale. The Metrologans were on the very edge of Wharfside, however, while the Universale looked out along a long, straight avenue that cut through the city, crossed the river at Bridge, and pierced the wall at Riverside Gate. The architecture of the Metrologan temple suggested that it was several centuries old, and the words HARBOR MILITIA, faintly visible beneath a layer of whitewash, suggested that it had not been in use as a temple at the time of acquisition.

The last visitor for the seventh day of Sixmonth arrived only moments before the bell tower in the Universale began tolling midnight. The hospitality deaconess was a local recruit to the order, and had been with the Metrologans for only a few months. The visitor was a woman in her early twenties, of average height, with brown hair that had been tied back tightly. What was unusual about her was that she was not dressed like the lamplight girls, who were the only people who normally came to the Metrologans at that hour—usually after being attacked, and beaten. Beneath her rain cloak she was wearing a vaguely military-looking black coat, a black calf-length skirt, and black riding boots. There was a cloak over her arm, and a hat with a feather in her hand. The clothing seemed as if it was appropriate to somewhere warmer and drier than Alberin.

"Have need, seeing acting Elder," she said in Diomedan.

"It's midnight, Worthy Justiva is asleep," replied the deaconess. "Do you need refuge?"

"Not needing."

"Then you will have to make an appointment for tomorrow. What is your name?"

"Worthy Velander Salvaras, late of the Zantrias and He-lion temples."

Within no more than a minute, Velander was being shown into a high-ceilinged chamber where Worthy Justiva was hurriedly dusting what was apparently the Elder's throne. This was a wooden chair with a cloth draped over it. Velander cleared her throat politely. Justiva squarked, turned, dropped the dusting cloth on the throne's seat, and sat down on it.

"Worthy Velander, you took us by surprise," she said in Zantrian.

"Speak Diomedan, if you please, acting Elder," said Velander as she bowed. "I am trying to improve my grasp of it."

"But I know very little Diomedan, Worthy Velander. Best if we stay with Zantrian."

Having established the language that they were going to use, they lapsed into silence. Worthy Justiva folded her arms, then unfolded them again and placed them on the armrests of the chair. Velander stood with her hands clasped before her. The urge to unclasp her hands and clasp them behind her was almost irresistible, but she was hoping to seem relaxed, so she tried to keep still. Justiva's right hand twitched. She clasped her hands together, then returned them to the armrests and gripped the ends tightly. *Any moment now*, thought Velander.

"Learned and Worthy Terikel Arimer named me as acting Elder!" Justiva blurted out as rapidly as a drummer beating out a roll.

"I bow to your authority," said Velander, who then bowed.

This had a seriously destabilizing effect on Justiva. She had hurriedly keyed herself up for a fight. Now there was no fight. What was to be done?

"Oh. Ah . . . well, that's nice," she said in what was still quite an aggressive tone. "What can I do for you?"

"I am a Metrologan priestess. This is a Metrologan temple. You are my Elder."

"Oh. That's nice—I mean, nice that you, ah, thought to return to us Metrologans. I mean, being a Metrologan."

Aware that she was saying nothing sensible, Justiva forced herself to be silent, then considered what her visitor had said. Velander stood respectfully before her. The senior priestess had bowed to Justiva's authority, yet there was bound to be a catch.

"Well, naturally we shall look after you," Justiva declared.

"My thanks," said Velander, bowing again.

"The Learned Elder spoke of you often, before she went to Acrema," Justiva continued. "She said you had changed. You sent her several letters. You said you had, well, changed. Changed a lot, I mean."

"Changed. Yes, I have changed. I am alive again. Mostly."

Justiva swallowed. "Oh. Well then, that's all right . . . I suppose. Did you know that Learned Terikel is dead?"

"Yes."

"I was told that you were dead too!" exclaimed Justiva, who then braced herself for some devastating retort or revelation.

"Only sometimes," replied Velander quietly.

Justiva rubbed her face in her hands, then massaged her temples, a reaction to stress that she had learned from Terikel. Velander did not move.

"We must hold elections for a new Elder."

"Yes."

"Ah, so you have returned to stand."

"No."

Justiva did not believe that any reply other than yes was possible. Her powers of patience and diplomacy buckled.

"Worthy Velander, what do you want?" cried Justiva. "I mean, *really* want? We have no reserves, we have hardly enough money to feed ourselves. Learned Terikel almost bankrupted the order when she hired the *Stormbird* to go to Sargol."

"I can donate twenty Sargolan gold crowns to the Order," said Velander, taking a purse from her coat and offering it to Justiva.

"Oh, er, thank you," said Justiva, accepting the purse. She checked the contents. There were twenty coins within, and they were gold.

"I shall not be sleeping here, is that acceptable in terms of your authority?" Velander asked, bowing deeply, her hands still clasped before her.

"Er, yes, it is, yes." Justiva felt an overwhelming urge to

totter away and lie down somewhere quiet, with a damp cloth over her eyes. "Well then, you may go. This audience is at an end."

"No, Elder, it is not."

"It isn't?"

"You must ask me if there is anything further."

"Oh. Yes. Of course. Well, er, is there?"

Justiva had made the mistake of allowing her defenses to collapse too early, and now she found it impossible to rally them again.

"How did you learn that Terikel is dead?" asked Velander.

"Laron told me."

"Laron! He is in Alberin?"

"Yes, and under this very roof. He arrived an hour ago."

"Acting Elder, may I ask something personal?"

"Personal? But we hardly know each other—I mean, you hardly know anything about me."

"Personal, regarding Laron."

"Laron? Oh no, I have never had an affair with him—I mean, any affairs with him."

"I think you mean dealings."

"Yes—well, no, apart from now, that is. He is sleeping with us—I mean my priestesses—I mean, here, alone. Dragonwall! He has to see important people about it. Tomorrow."

"So do I. Was anyone with Laron?"

"Oh, yes, some quite lovely people. A medicar named Gilvray and his nurse Dolvienne are staying here—and Riellen is the other, she's a student. Nice girl, and she has more scholarship than the rest of us here put together, but some of her ideas are, er . . ."

"Liable to get her hanged for treason?"

"Yes."

Velander considered what she had been told. Laron's group had reached Alberin and was staying at the temple. Andry's had not. That was confusing. Andry was alive. Possibly. He had talked about a tavern called the Lamplighter a lot. She decided to check there later.

"Acting Elder, when is the election to be held?"

"The election? Tomorrow, I suppose. All those who can vote are currently in Alberin."

"Tell me the hour, and I shall attend. I shall vote for you, of course, I am very impressed with your leadership."

The compliment was too much for Justiva. She slumped in the throne chair, put a hand over her face, and sniffled. Velander waited to be told when the election was to take place, her hands clasped respectfully before her.

"My leadership?" Justiva finally managed to whisper between sobs. "Three years ago I was a lamplight girl on Helion Island, bedding sailors for ten coppers a time—fifteen on public holidays and when merchant fleets were in port. Now what's changed? I am not even Learned Terikel's throne cushion, and I don't have a tenth of her scholarship. I just keep the Metrologans going, I don't give them direction. Velander, in the depths of my hearts, I know that *you* should take over this throne and rule the Metrologans."

Velander shook her head. Justiva shivered, thoroughly miserable.

"They love you, they fear me," said Velander, spacing the words quite evenly. "They would die for you, but not me." Velander helped Justiva to her feet. "That is all that I have to say, Worthy Elder, and now I should let you get back to bed. I have a room at a tavern nearby, the Bargeman's Fancy. Please tell nobody that I am in Alberin."

"Yes. Anything. But, look—I, er, I'll stay on as Elder if, that is if you will advise me in matters that are, well, important matters. Please? Sort of, be the Elder to the Elder, if you see what I mean?"

"Very well," said Velander, squeezing her hand then releasing it as they set off for the door. "Here is my first advice. Begin moving your staff, archives, records, and anything valuable out of here and into safe hiding places. Establish a small clinic to treat the poor in some shop, and keep this place empty."

"Oh, I've already started people packing, and told them to do all that," said Justiva. "Everything important will be out by tomorrow, and some Metrologans are already staying elsewhere."

For the first time that night, Velander displayed surprise.

"Uh, why?" she asked as they walked.

"Because I heard the temples of the Skepticals were being annihilated. Most people are saying that it's the gods punishing the Skepticals for not believing in them. That may be true, but they do research and teaching in the cold sciences, and so do we. I decided that we too could be on the list of something powerful and deadly, something with a dislike of the cold sciences, so I began dispersing the Order throughout Alberin."

Justiva opened the door to the street for Velander, who bowed to her, stepped through, then stopped and turned back.

"At the risk of sounding disrespectful, Acting Elder, do not ever, ever again let me hear you whining that you are not a wise and brilliant leader!" said Velander very firmly, then she strode away into the darkness and windswept drizzle.

Academician Garris, the rector of the Alberin Academy of Etheric Philosophies, did have a bed, but it was a matter of debate whether he ever spent any time in it. Every night, after dinner, he would sit before the fire with his notes, books, and scrolls, and read. Eventually he would fall asleep, generally around midnight. The hearth maid would arrive at 1 A.M., drape a rug over him, put another log on the fire, then go up to his bedroom and spend the rest of the night in the academician's large and luxurious bed.

"Garris."

The word came across like a threatening hiss. Garris jerked awake, removed his reading spectacles, and looked around. Occasionally a pocket of sap in the firewood gave off a hiss as the flames touched it. Garris was no stranger to fires. Some wood popped violently as it burned, sending clouds of sparks everywhere. Other varieties sent jets of smoky steam shooting out into the room. Once a lump in a log turned out to be an iron arrowhead that had struck the tree decades ago, and been grown over. Garris had even seen a little wood sprite appear in the flames, liberated from the body of the dead tree. She had waved to him, then vanished up the chimney. Chuckling to himself, Garris began to settle down again.

"Garris, in danger, you are."

Garris thought to check behind his chair, then wished that he had not. A pale face was floating in the gloom. There was a suggestion of bath salts on the air, and essence of musken. The face floated closer, and a woman's body became distinguishable. A cloak covered a military-style black jacket with a double row of silver buttons. She was wearing a calf-length skirt and riding boots, and that was unusual for Alberin. With the cape fastened, she would have looked like a youth, because she also wore a crescent hat with a black feather. Now Garris noticed another smell on the air. An ill-defined but definite suggestion of tailors' shops, mothballs, and brand-new clothing. She had spoken in accented Diomedan.

"Er, who are you?" asked Garris.

"Have name, Enforcer," replied Velander.

"Oh. Well, a fine, strong name. What can I do for you Lady Enforcer?"

"Yesterday, passed Special Warrior Service College. All charred. Circle. Temples of Skepticals, charred circles. Academy of Sublime Etheric Vision, all charred. World Mother Temple in Ridgeback Mountains, charred circle. Seeing pattern?"

"My word, you do seem to have covered a lot of ground."

"Am thinking, teaching places, charred. This place, is teaching, for purpose of. Is like snake biting finger. Do nothing, maybe die. Chop off arm, very drastic, and maybe snake not poisonous. What is decision, of yours?"

"Ah well, yes, in such a situation perhaps I would reach for the *What Snake Is That?* chart, as a humane alternative. Humane to me, that is, ha, ha."

"Have such chart, for academies?"

"Well, no. But look here, I mean what is there to do?" asked Garris, struggling out of his chair. "These things you speak of, cutting arms off, all that sort of thing. I mean they sound serious. I mean I could declare a test of the old Catastrophe Contingency Plan, what? You know, relocate staff, students, vintage wine collection, books, records, magical amulets and apparatus, and so on."

"No. Move people, books only. No time for rest."

"But, but, I mean, look here young lady. You sneak in

here, unannounced, tell me a lot of alarming theories, try to make me disrupt the entire academy, along with all the special guests, and on what evidence?"

"Metrologans moved, yesterday. Elder Justiva, will help move, your books."

"The Metrologans have moved? Well, that is a precedent, I suppose, but . . . such a big step, invoking the Catastrophe Contingency Plan."

"Be charred. Big step?"

"Er, oh! Yes. Quite so. But seven thousand books to move!"

"Soon, perhaps, only library in Scalticar."

"But why? What is the actual source of the threat?"

"Cannot say, but evidence speaks! Academies charred, are being."

"My dear young woman, were you to come in here and say 'Hide, there's a hungry wolf in the corridor!' I would have to take you seriously, but you are merely saying 'Hide, or something horrible might happen.' Thank you for your concern, but I am afraid that the academy stays where it is. I have over ninety guests, all senior sorcerers."

"What? Who?"

"Oh, dissidents, sorcerers who would not join Dragonwall. Here for a conference, they are. Some are only alive because they came here, their temples and academies were destroyed."

"Conference?" asked Velander, hardly able to believe her ears.

"Yes, about all this Dragonwall nonsense. Dragonwall Dissidents and Objectors is the title. There are five Skepticals, two from the Academy of Sublime Etheric Vision, the deputy reverend mother of the World Mother Temple—"

"Under one roof?" demanded Velander.

"Well, in the dormitories, which have three wings, so there are three roofs, technically."

"Who is calling conference? You?"

"Oh no, I was just sitting here, thinking etheric things, and people started to turn up. They told me all about this conference that I had called, and, well, I did not have the heart to tell them that nothing was happening. Spent all today drawing up a program, and arranging catering while the dean of applied castings took them on a tour of the River Alber in a ferryboat convoy."

Velander had much to think about as she left the academy. Someone had called a conference, a conference of virtually every sorcerer of consequence who was not already officially or unofficially part of Dragonwall. They were in one small area, and that area was smaller than the grounds of the SWS College.

✳ ✳ ✳

It was not that Wharfside was totally safe so much as that its criminals tended to be more discreet than in Neverside. Through the misty drizzle, Velander noticed that three figures were following her; then she took note as the three became two. The street meandered, following the path first defined by some flock of sheep beside a tiny stockade in the wilderness, millennia ago. In the distance she could see a lone walker heading toward her. As they closed, he drew his ax and held it out before him to bar the way.

"Hie, lad, Wharfside Militia," he called. "Would thee be fleeing a crime?"

"Not so," replied Velander, stopping.

"Well then, I'm sure thou will not begrudge tarrying while I check that none be chasing thee."

"None chasing."

Indeed, nobody was following. The man glanced past her, looking vaguely annoyed; then he looked back.

"You're a girl!" he exclaimed suddenly.

"Dress as boy, Sargolan new fashion," she replied, looking about warily. Two groups of men were now visible in the dim light of the public lantern.

"Well then, who be these?" cried the militiaman. "There's four and four lads in a hurry, maybe in pursuit of a thief."

The man grasped Velander by the shoulder, but she swung her arm up and around, tearing his hand loose. The two groups were converging on her from both directions, so she ran for a lane, but the lane ended in a featureless brick wall.

"Only minutes, only damn minutes," Velander muttered to herself as she turned back and drew her ax. She swung it experimentally, but she was unused to swinging a weapon without the supernatural strength of what she had been. The nine men gathered at the entrance to the lane, filling it and blocking what little light was filtering in from a distant public lantern. "Minutes, dammit, only minutes," she whispered, holding the ax up and out in a guard-and-stand position. Someone snickered. The men closed, but cautiously. They wanted no trouble, they only wanted a victim, and now they had a girl as a bonus.

The mass of outlined heads drew closer. Velander dropped her weight and slashed across with her ax, holding it with both hands for control. She felt it cut something, then something else. There was a curse.

"Fortune, Fortune walk with me now," she said aloud in Zantrian.

"Foreigner," said a voice in Alberinese.

"They're hot, got movement."

"Cut me, get the warrior heat when I'm cut."

"Crowd her."

Velander's next swing hit a baton, and then someone rolled into her legs and brought her down. The ax was twisted out of her hands, and she heard it clatter as it was flung away down the lane. Hands grabbed her legs, hands grasped at her skirts, she screamed, then head-butted at a shape in the gloom. Something crunched; the pain in her forehead made the scene reel before her eyes. Velander screamed again, and then an arm snaked around her neck and a cloth was stuffed into her mouth. She felt wet cobblestones and slime against her legs, and the sheer weight of the shadowy figures held her down.

A bottle smashed nearby.

"Thas terrible. Summat should be done 'bout like of you."

Every member of the gang froze. Velander froze too. At the end of the lane stood a lone figure, outlined against the glow from a public lantern somewhere down the street. For a moment all eyes were upon him. He seemed unsteady on his feet.

"Dozen t' one, and one's a woman, like. You think thas good odds? Hie then, try now, wi' one more."

Velander did not understand the Alberinese. The drunk bent over to pick up Velander's ax. A broken bottle gleamed faintly in his other hand. Two of the gang walked briskly back down the lane to bracket him, but as they closed he made a weaving motion, causing one to swing his stick in an arc that swept around into the other. There was a very heavy thud as the ax handle crashed down on a head; then the other was swung by the arm and into a wall.

"Piss weak, ye friggers!" bawled the drunk. "Oh aye, compliments o' the night, miss."

Three more now advanced on the drunk, whose identity was, for Velander, suddenly beyond question. There was an exchange of clacks of wood on wood, and heavy, soft, muted thuds. Again, a single, swaying figure was outlined against the entrance of the laneway.

"Hell's levels, let's be goin'!" barked the man holding Velander's arms down. All three released her at once and began a dash for the entrance, but Velander twisted up and lunged after them, catching two trouser legs. The legs belonged to two different man, and both fell headlong. There was a loud thump as her rescuer drove the end of his ax handle into the stomach of the third, and a crack as he hit him over the head. The last two had shaken Velander off by now, but one went limp as her rescuer kicked him in the face as he tried to get up. The last of the gang actually managed to grapple with Andry, and there were several heavy thuds as bodies slammed against walls. Velander saw a head being pounded against a wall; then only one figure was outlined against the entrance, yet again. Velander finally thought to pull the cloth out of her mouth.

"Speaking some Diomedan," she said.

"Oh aye, I do too," said the very, very familiar voice in Diomedan. "Er, would ye be all right then, miss?"

Andry, thought Velander. *Andry alive*. Somehow she could not face the prospect of being wet, disheveled, and filthy when she revealed to him that she was also still alive. Besides, she was about to undergo a transformation that she was still feeling rather embarrassed about.

"Dignity gone, kept honor," she replied, hoping he would not recognize her voice.

"Ah then, best could do. Give hand here, then, and let's away."

Outside the lane, in the dim lantern light, Velander saw that her rescuer definitely was Andry. A group of lamplight girls was loitering warily nearby, sheltering from the drizzle under an awning.

"Mind lane girls, I's sorted out heavies who tried te roll Ladyship," explained Andry, who then dropped to his knees and threw up quite a large amount of dark, alcoholic-smelling fluid.

One of the women picked up his ax, then approached the entrance to the lane with two others. Andry curled up on the ground, in the drizzle, looking as if he were settling there for the night. Velander stroked his head, then looked up at the lamplight girls.

"Speaking Diomedan?" she asked. They looked to each other, some shrugging. "Looking after this one," she said, patting Andry's arm. "Good man, brave man. Myself go, finding help."

Some minutes later two members of the Wharfside night militia came past, one with a lantern on a pole. One of the lamplight women seized Andry by the foot, attempted to drag him away, realized that her companions had already fled, and decided to flee as well. Andry was left alone, in the drizzle, on the street, still curled up and asleep. Velander's ax was beside him.

"Oh aye, he's got an ax!" said the man with the lantern.

"So does every bugger in Alberin," said his companion, nudging Andry with his boot. "Let's see the type. Diomedan scalloping, three blade holes, quarter-cross weave on handle grip—oi, it's covered in blood underneath!"

The man with the lantern lowered it to near cobblestone level. "Aye, looky there, blood underside, where the rain's not touched it. Murder nearby."

The two militiamen walked to the laneway entrance,

peered around the corner, and held up the lantern. After gasps of shock that were appropriate to the sight before them, one began blowing a whistle while the other walked farther in with his lantern.

"Twilight Rangers," said the lantern bearer. "Here's Jarrin the Hawk, master of the Waylayers and Accosters Brotherhood."

"The Midnight Lamplight Sisterhood has filed more complaints against them than I've had hangovers."

"Who's the churl who sliced 'em, then?"

"Foreign surcoat. Guardsman, of sorts."

A vast shadow glided above them, and a shape settled onto a nearby roof with no more sound than some creaking of timbers and cracking of tiles. It wrapped its wings around itself, so that it superficially resembled a dark tower with two faintly glowing eyes. Nobody noticed, however. Other militiamen arrived at a cautious jog-trot, and soon the street and lane were filled with them. The two faintly glowing eyes peered down as the nine bodies were loaded onto a cart, then Andry was heaved up onto the pile of dead.

Selford was neither surprised nor alarmed when a scroll of introduction for a foreign countess arrived while he was having breakfast with Parchen, the royal accountant.

"A Torean, and a Metrologan priestess besides," Parchen observed, peering over at the scroll.

"Matter of urgency . . . earliest possible convenience . . . arriving at ten," read Selford. "Well, the Metrologans do a lot to keep the riffraff healthy, and they do a bit of free teaching besides. Best to meet this countess."

"Can she be a genuine countess?"

"I think so. Probably a surplus daughter, forced to become a priestess and sent overseas to get rid of her. Then that rogue ether machine—"

"Silverdeath."

"Yes, it melted Torea down to the bedrock, so the count and all his heirs were rendered into brownish smoke, and she's now a countess. Suppose we'd better do something vaguely

official. Round up half a dozen sober courtiers, and tell Miss
Flez to set up tea and scones for ten in the west gallery."

Justiva had advised Velander to write to the crown prince,
but was not at all surprised when they arrived at the palace
to be informed that the prince was indisposed, and that the
royal minstrel, Selford, would be meeting them to welcome
Velander to Alberin. A gaggle of bored courtiers exchanged
boring pleasantries over tea and scones for half an hour;
then Selford arrived and made a short speech of welcome
on behalf of the crown prince. The courtiers then melted
away within moments, leaving Selford alone with the two
priestesses.

"Have request," began Velander.

"Ah yes, the matter of urgency?" asked Selford, raising an
eyebrow. "I understand that the Metrologans are close to
bankruptcy, so I have a fair idea of what you are about to ask."

"Please, arrest all sorcerers in Alberin, lock in secret dungeon," said Velander earnestly.

"What?" exclaimed the astounded Selford, before he suddenly realized that a joke was probably involved. "Countess,
I—oh, I suppose you want me to ransack their homes and
academies as well?"

"Only take books, and hide," replied Velander with no
change in her expression.

"But why?"

"Danger."

"Countess, Countess," laughed the minstrel. "You will
need to give the prince better incentive for action than that.
Sorcerers can be very dangerous when roused, one does not
just antagonize them gratuitously."

"Ah. Then, have little scandal, tell you," began Velander.

"No finer place for scandals than the Alberin royal court,
Countess," he responded with a discreet wink. "We have scandals that other kingdoms have not even dreamed possible."

"Elder Justiva?" said Velander, with a gesture to the
Metrologan Elder.

"Some months ago, former Elder Terikel had an affair

with the prince," said Justiva in a disturbingly confident voice. "At least that is what she told me."

"Secrecy can be as titillating as the most blatant orgy," responded Selford.

"Perhaps so, perhaps not. In return for authorizing the last large ship in the Alberinese merchant navy to be leased to the Metrologans for a very dangerous voyage, she offered to entertain the prince in her bed for some hours."

"Ah, the currency of love, it is more often exchanged than gold and silver."

"I was asked to watch over their privacy."

"Such a thankless task, sitting vigil over the amours of other, I do it all the time for the prince."

"When he left, I followed him."

Selford's mouth opened, then his jaw froze. His eyes darted from Justiva to Velander, then back to Justiva. He remembered to close his mouth.

"I was once a lamplight girl, lordship, a harlot. I am very skilled at moving with discretion on dark streets. The prince entered Madame Featheringly's All-Night Herbal Remedies and Special Massage Parlor by the tradesman's entrance, and precisely seventeen pulse beats later you emerged through the front door. That is the time that it takes to pace the length of the building."

"Who have you told?" whispered Selford, suddenly a very different person.

"Until last night, nobody. Then Countess Velander told me that the sorcerers and academicians staying in the Alberin academy were in great danger, yet she could not convince them to heed her warnings. I told her about your adventure with Elder Terikel."

"Look, the crown prince cannot be everywhere at once," began Selford, "so people like me sometimes, ah, deputize—"

"Last night Palace Supplies and Infrastructure Committee met in Citadel Tower, in the palace," said Velander.

"That is on the palace meetings board," said Selford, with all the confidence of someone waving a wooden sword at a dragon and hoping it was nearsighted.

"Listened at window."

"At the highest window of the highest tower in the palace?"

"Have two-hundred-foot wings, neck longer than room, I do. Go check tower battlements, see claw marks. Was there. To meeting, listened. Like to hearing minutes?"

"No! No, no, no. Look, we had better have another meeting, now. This way, ladies, it will take but moments to get everyone together."

✳ ✳ ✳

It took about as long to arrange the meeting as it took to climb to the top of the citadel tower and lock themselves in a small and plainly furnished but quite cozy room. Selford looked out of the window, noted several deep scratches in the stonework of the battlements above, then pulled the shutters closed. There was a knock at the door, and the royal minstrel admitted a rather furtive-looking little man with a pointy beard and a bald head. He was carrying a large, leather-bound book. An amiable looking woman with grey hair followed, carrying a tray of scones, a teapot, and three cups. They seemed surprised to see Velander and Justiva.

"Countess, Elder, meet Parchen," said Selford, rather like a general announcing a humiliating defeat to his peers. "Parchen is the royal accountant. Miss Flcz is holding the tea tray. She is the tea lady. Parchen, Miss Flez, meet Elder Justiva, head of the Metrologan Order. Countess Velander is also a Metrologan priestess. She is also a glass dragon."

Parchen and Flez took some moments to assimilate this, then to decide that it was not all a joke.

"Should I get two more cups?" asked Miss Flez.

"Don't touch it," said Justiva.

"Trying, cut back," said Velander.

"Just one more introduction," said Selford, who then pulled a cloth cover from what Velander and Justiva had assumed to be an item of disused furniture.

The mummified body of the crown prince stared across the room at them with glass eyes. Selford pushed the prince's chair over to a circular table at the center of the room, but had to go outside to find stools for Velander and Justiva. By the time he returned Miss Flez had poured out the tea for the Palace Supplies and Infrastructure Committee. Selford barred the door, then joined the others at the table and sipped at his tea. Velander accepted a macaroon from Miss Flez. Justiva clasped her hands and stared at Selford.

"Well?" she said.

"The crown prince died five years ago, after choking on a chocolate-coated strawberry," Selford began.

"It was one of mine," added Miss Flez.

"It was during my first meeting with him after his father's death," said Parchen. "He was finding my explanation of the palace accounts too boring, so he decided to have the auditions for a new minstrel and juggler while I was speaking."

"I only brought my lute, I did not realize that I had to juggle as well," continued Selford. "Thus I took some of Miss Flez's chocolate-coated strawberries, and juggled with them. Every so often I would catch one in my mouth and eat it."

"Don't tell me, the prince told you to toss a chocolate strawberry into his mouth," said Justiva.

"Ah, essentially," said Selford, Parchen, and Miss Flez together.

"And he choked."

"Yes," said Selford.

"But it was an accident. Why did you tell nobody?"

"My meeting," said Parchen.

"My juggling," said Selford.

"My chocolate strawberry," said Miss Flez.

"You see, the commander of the Palace Guard was not a nice man," explained Selford. "The former king died after getting blind drunk, then falling down the stairs while trying to make a grand entrance down a spiral stairway during the Ambassadors' Ball. The commander had the royal butler, chef, cellarmaster, and taster executed for contributing to the king's death."

"By providing him with wine, that he then drank in excess?" asked Justiva.

"Precisely. We thought to pretend that the prince was alive for a few days, while we arranged a pretext for putting the commander to death, but that proved a little more difficult than we thought. It was five months before we managed to get him kneeling down at the chopping block. In the meantime Parchen had to do a course on taxidermy, because the prince was going off."

"And I've fed the stray cats in Wharfside alleys for years," said Miss Flez, "so nobody thought it odd that I was leaving the palace with pails of meat that was a bit smelly."

"Once we had a new commander appointed, we then had the problem of how to account for the prince being in a somewhat unusual state of preservation," said Parcher. "I'd made his joints out of cloth so that he could be set up to be seen by people lying in bed, dozing in a chair, and sitting up at meetings of the Palace Supplies and Infrastructure Committee. There's even a lever at his back so that he can wave to the crowds from the battlements on public occasions."

"I cannot believe that none of the courtiers or ambassadors noticed," said Justiva, shaking her head.

"Well, I do a pretty impressive revel," said Selford. "With five or six revels a week, the courtiers and other nobles are seldom in a fit state to notice anything. Parcher ran the kingdom's accounts so well that within a year the state debt was paid off and the North Scalticarian emperor gave the prince a medal for good economic management. Miss Flez kept a very close watch on the palace conspiracies, and we managed to exile, execute, or corrupt all conspirators before they did any damage. Months became years, and . . ."

"So, er, golden age of Alberin prosperity . . . due to minstrel, accountant, and tea lady?" asked Velander, who was sitting back with her eyes closed and massaging her forehead with her fingertips, Terikel-style.

"Essentially," said Selford. "I am the same height and build as the prince, so I grew a beard like his and made sure that all the prince's amorous assignations were in total darkness."

"I eat his meals," confessed Parcher. "But I don't drink, so Miss Flez takes care of his wine."

"I like a nice drop," added Miss Flez.

Justiva put a hand over her eyes. "Enough! Just let me recount the situation as I understand it. The crown prince of Alberin died five years ago, and for that entire period you three have run the kingdom, organized the orgies, eaten his meals, slept with his lovers, savored his fine wines, and dusted off his body from time to time."

"Well, you could put it that way," said Parcher.

"Splendid. The Palace Supplies and Infrastructure Committee, also known as the crown prince of Alberin, is about to have every sorcerer, visiting sorcerer, and student of sorcery in Alberin arrested. You will then organize for their libraries to be burgled and moved to locations on a list that I shall provide before I leave. In return, I shall preserve your secret."

"And that's all?" asked Parcher. "Don't you want gold, honors, titles, property?"

"No," replied Justiva. "Do you?"

"If please!" said Velander, raising her hand. "Small request, I have."

Andry awoke slowly, and to increasing levels of pain. His ribs ached, several teeth seemed loose, his head felt ready to split, and his mouth tasted as if something very unpleasant had been living in it for a long time. When he tried to open his eyes, he found that one was closed and swollen.

"Oh gah," he groaned softly. "Body's all hurting. . . . Oh aye, a fight, I think. Maybe I've got beaten to death."

He sat up and looked around, discovering that he was in a small and bare cell. It had a narrow oak door, and light was entering through a small, barred grille.

"Oh no, I'm in watchhouse. Again." He rapped at the door. "Hie there, Desk Marshal?"

"Aye?"

"Er, like, I'm awake now."

"So?"

"So what did I do?"

"Killed nine."

"Oh shyte!" exclaimed Andry, sliding down the cell wall to sit on the floor.

A few minutes later there was a rattle and clinking from

outside as the door was unlocked. Andry was escorted out by two guardsmen in chain mail and unfamiliar scarlet surcoats. They marched him out of the watchhouse and down the street, where another half-dozen mounted guards were waiting with a coach.

"Marshal, sir, could I, like, borrow a comb and wash my face before I face the magistrate?" Andry asked the guard marshal who had climbed into the coach with him.

"I've no comb, and you're not to face a magistrate."

No magistrate, thought Andry. Then he noticed that the coach was on the way up Palace Hill. That meant the crown prince, and that meant sentence by royal decree. That was usually reserved for important criminals, but if he had killed nine, perhaps he was important. The coach rumbled into the palace grounds through the main gates, then was driven to a side entrance. Andry was taken inside, and down three flights of stairs. He presently found himself in the palace dungeons. The marshal introduced him to a pair of large, muscular, hooded men, who turned out to be the royal torturer, Igonnier, and his apprentice. A small, thin man with a bald head and a pointed beard appeared from behind the two torturers. He was flourishing a scroll.

"Andry Tennoner of Bargeyards, it's been brought to the attention of the crown prince that you did murder nine citizens in a Wharfside alley last night."

"Lordship, I—"

"Silence! You are sentenced to death by beheading in the Wharfside marketplace during the next break in the rain."

"Oh shyte."

"However, His Royal Highness is willing to review your case on the condition that you enlist in the Palace Guard. Will you do so?"

"Is that a trick question?" exclaimed Andry.

"I shall take that as a yes. Guardsman Tennoner, here is the prince's silver noble, sign here on the scroll. Congratulations, the prince is to declare you a civic hero for ridding the city of nine notorious felons without the expense of a trial. Igonnier, Torfen, have him scrubbed, groomed, and into a guardsman's uniform and gear within ten minutes. There is to be a short ceremony to honor you, Tennoner, and we cannot have the crown prince waiting."

Deprived of the opportunity to execute Andry, Igonnier and his apprentice made the process of cleaning him up as unpleasant as possible. He was stripped naked, dropped into the water-torture trough, and scrubbed with a flagstone scour until his skin almost glowed in the dark, then compelled to dry himself and dress in guardsman's clothing while being escorted up nine flights of stairs to the east reception chamber of the palace. He arrived damp, but dressed and reasonably presentable.

About three dozen courtiers who looked as if they had severe hangovers were waiting in the chamber as Andry entered. The marshal pushed Andry in the direction of a bearded man who seemed to be in his thirties. Unlike most of the others in the room, he did not look sick. He also had the odd, subtle confidence of the members of royal families that Andry had encountered in his travels through the Sargolan Empire. Andry noticed that he was wearing a burgundy coat over a black silk shirt, and that he had wavy black hair and neatly trimmed beard. This vaguely matched the copies of portraits of the crown prince that hung in most Alberinese taverns. The others who were present showed him quite a degree of deference, yet something seemed to be wrong. *This can't be the crown prince*, thought Andry. *The man has a reputation for decadence as notorious as Wallas's ballads, but this one looks halfway normal.*

A herald stamped the floor with a ceremonial-looking thing that might have evolved out of some weapon over the past three thousand years.

"Announcing Guardsman Kavelar Andrian Tennoner, Palace Company, late Reccon Andry Tennoner, granted in Sargol of Senterri, black ax with melted blade on a powder green field, late of Sargolan Imperial Militia, Reconnoiter Service, Royal Personal."

There was a patter of measured and formal applause. The herald banged his ceremonial staff on the floor again. Most faces winced at the sound.

"Be it known that on the eighth hour past noon on day twelve of Sixmonth of this current year, Reccon Tennoner did, alone, rescue the person and honor of a lady of nobility from the attentions of a street warlord gang, known as the Twilight Rangers, killing all nine members, and thus annihilating the gang."

There was another patter of applause, as if Andry had merely played a jig on his rebec. *Oh shyte, the girl from the alleyway*, thought Andry, whose memories of the previous night were slowly floundering to the surface of his mind. *So that's why I sorted out those heavies, they were crowding her*. The herald banged the staff for a third time.

"Be it known throughout the realm that Reccon Tennoner has been granted the thanks of the crown prince, and will henceforth be entitled to bear the appellation 'Civic Hero.' "

The man in the burgundy coat now approached Andry. "The crown prince cannot attend, so he sends his regrets, too much decadence last night, ha, ha. I'm Selford, his minstrel, he asked me to thank you for ridding Alberin of the Twilight Rangers, and for rescuing the countess from them."

Andry was aware that the crown prince was "Your Highness," but although he was well acquainted with another royal musician, the matter of formal address for such a person had never been raised. The title "countess" had not registered in Andry's severely overloaded brain.

"I'm honored, sir" seemed appropriate to Andry.

"Bad times, Tennoner. Riffraff assaulting nobility, people getting ideas. The prince doesn't like people getting ideas. That Dragonwall was a very bad idea. Sorcerers running the world, indeed! Next it will be engineers trying to take over, and after that, perhaps even lawyers."

"Surely not, sir."

"Now then, should anyone ask, say that you joined the Alberin Palace Company yesterday," said Selford in a near-whisper. "I've backdated your scroll of enlistment, and you will get an extra day's pay, of course."

"Lordship?"

"Looks good for the crown prince, having one of his Palace Company save a foreign countess."

"Countess?"

"No, I'm the royal minstrel— that was a joke. Your first duty will be to guard the countess you rescued last night—

only try not to kill quite so many of the riffraff should she
find herself in danger again."

"A countess, sir?" asked the astounded Andry, finally realizing that he had again rescued someone important.

"Yes, and she only speaks Diomedan—do you speak
Diomedan?"

"Aye, that I do," said Andry, switching to Diomedan without thinking.

"Splendid, that means I'll not have to hire a translator as
well. Countess Velander Salvaras of Zantrias, you have obviously met Guardsman Kavelar Andry Tennoner already."

To Andry, Velander seemed to materialize into focus beside Selford, even though she had only walked up from behind him. She was dressed just as she had been the night
before, but now her clothes were clean and dry. On her
jacket was a double row of silver buttons, giving her a
slightly rakish look, and silver claw combs held her wavy,
brown, shoulder-length hair back from her face. She was
with Justiva, the Metrologan priestess.

"Guardsman Tennoner, gallant and gentleman," she said
as she curtsied before him. "In your hands, shall feel happy."

Terikel was the first person to see the ruins of Larmentel
from two miles above. In the near-horizontal sunlight of
dawn, vast, concentric, circular waves of glass gleamed out
of the shadows. After her plunge of several nights earlier,
she had slept in an ice cave, woken to eat, then slept again.
When she launched herself again, the sun had risen sufficiently to throw sparkles and glints off the wavelets on the
water between the rings of glass. Here and there a few
stubby protrusions broke the perfection of the vast panorama
of rings, like the stumps of petrified trees. These were the
columns of temples and palaces that had once been the pride
of Larmental.

"Alas, poor Larmentel, what have you come to?" said
Terikel softly. "Where are your beautiful university towers,
your palaces so white that they looked as if they had been
built from blocks of frozen milk?"

Terikel had lived in Larmentel for two years, and had graduated from its university with the highest honors of the entire decade before joining the Metrologans. She had spent time appreciating the beauty of the city around her, however, but now it had become quite pure and beautiful in a quite different way. It was like a beautiful seashell in a glass case: quite exquisite, but dead.

Alone in her uncomfortable refuge after crashing on the mountain, Terikel had drawn a great number of conclusions about things that she had not yet stopped to consider in detail. Teacher had obviously put a vast amount of stored energy into her with the casting to use against the supposed ringstone at the ends of the world. For all she knew, Teacher might have given her a hundred years of his stored energy; he was five thousand years old and had plenty to spare. He might even have given her his stores from a thousand years. It could be used to generate wing spikes, or perhaps to flap very large wings. She also thought about the physical structure of birds.

When the storm had finally passed, and she began preparing to fly off again, Terikel did a thermal-body-mesh casting that included a chest keel and wishbone. After some experimentation, she partially drew out Teacher's energy casting from her chest, and tied it into a dozen contraction tendrils. Last of all came the regenerated wings, and Terikel cast a spike a full hundred feet high before splitting it. She had attached the contraction tendrils to the wings, then gave a few slow, tentative beats.

One mighty contraction of etheric tendrils powered by Teacher's energy had her ten feet off the ground, and by the fifth flap of her regenerated wings Terikel was flying both high and fast enough to level out above the mountains. She turned north, and presently cleared the mountains and flew in a steady, majestic manner for Larmentel.

"I probably don't look like much of a glass dragon, but then I'm not a glass dragon," Terikel told herself as she watched her shadow traveling over the glazed surface of Torea.

Larmentel had been where Silverdeath had escaped control. The most beautiful city in Torea was now frozen, concentric waves of glass, miles across, and slowly filling with rainwater. Laron and Velander had travelled there, and Terikel wanted to somehow join their small and elite club. She had already walked the soil of Torea again, even though it had technically been snow, so both ambitions had now been satisfied. Dead Larmentel was strangely beautiful, and this in turn made it very upsetting for Terikel. The result of such evil and so much death should not have been allowed to be beautiful, as far as she was concerned, yet there were the concentric lakes between concentric rings of solid glass.

Before long she turned due east again, but this time she did not try to gain height. Instead she drove herself along with mighty, ponderous flaps of her wings, using Teacher's energy to work the contraction tendrils. The Bax River gleamed brightly in the sun, a different texture of silver sheen on the brilliantly gleaming, glassy landscape. Terikel passed over the confluence of the Bax and Dioran rivers, then saw the texture of a melted city straddling the Dioran. The *Shadowmoon* had moored there, Laron had told her. The weather was reasonably clear over that part of Torea, and she could not help but note the irony that the continent whose death had spawned the Torean Storms was actually experiencing more fine, clear weather than Alberin.

The weather remained clear over the Bay of Islands, and the islands themselves resembled nothing less than pale, polished opals laid out for display on the dark blue velvet of the sea. The westerly winds were a lot weaker here, and Terikel made slow progress. Night had fallen over the Klawlan Peninsula as she crossed the coast, although at Terikel's altitude there was still sunlight. She set her timer casting.

"Terikel."

The timer was another of her own innovations. It was an annoying but persistent casting that chirped her name regularly, reminding her that she had to stay awake.

Once she was past the peninsula, there was only the vast nothingness of the Middle Infinital Ocean, with a six-thousand-mile chasm of water to the Dacostian coast. Terikel had never visited Klawlan before Torea had been burned. It was a rural area, with no universities, and even the sorcerers were the hedgerow kind. She felt as if she should take back memories of her trip above it, but there was little to see, and even that was all shadows.

"Terikel."

The timer casting faithfully chirped her name, but Terikel was wide awake. Not only was she one of the few Toreans to survive Silverdeath's fire, she was one of even fewer who had managed to go home again. Home. She had to admit that the place really was home. A surreal, frozen home of melted glass, to be sure, but quite tranquil.

Crown Prince Dalzori was widely known for not conforming to the preconceptions of anyone, and when it came to being a decadent tyrant, he seemed to go out of his way to upset the chroniclers of the present and the historians of the future. He was said to rise with the dawn, don his first disguise of the day, then go on a tour of the palace to check that everyone was behaving or misbehaving appropriately.

Selford generally started his day in the dungeons below the palace, where he had Dalzori's political prisoners turned out of their cells so that he could lead them through an hour of aerobic exercises in a hall that had once been a vast torture chamber. In a sense it still was, as far as the prisoners were concerned. At the end of this they hurried back to their cells for a rest that they knew would not last. Dalzori was said to like his prisoners to be healthy.

Prince Dalzori was said to take a bath in a marble pool at the center of the royal dining cloisters, but nobody ever saw him doing this. Those courtiers who were either awake already or had not quite found their way to bed, breakfasted and discussed expensive foods, rare wines, interesting decadent exploits, and occasionally even matters of state.

Dalzori breakfasted alone, generally having scrambled eggs and chopped onions on whole-meal toast. Sometimes, when he was feeling particularly decadent, he would have the toast buttered. He liked to get punishments out of the way early, so he read the lists, then sent his verdicts out with his accountant, Parchen. Courtiers to be excluded from the night's orgy would be sentenced straight after breakfast. Occasionally a serious offender would be actually exiled from the palace for as long as a month, but such extreme punishments were rare. While Dalzori apparently considered himself to be a strict disciplinarian, he was not a sadist.

The crown prince had certain attributes that made him a very effective ruler, in spite of his unconventional ideas about administration. He read twice as fast as most others, totaled and compared figures in his head faster than a skilled clerk with an abacus frame, remembered names, backgrounds, political affiliations, and scandals better than the court genealogist, and needed only two or three hours of sleep per night. Above all, he had an agenda that his rather more conventional rivals and enemies had never been entirely able to work out.

On this day Dalzori was known to be away somewhere in disguise while Selford sampled a meal prepared by a Sargolan cook who had been discovered at the Lamplighter tavern a night or two earlier. The meal was truly excellent, although Selford sampled only portions of it. When he had finished, the minstrel had the new cook summoned. Presently the herald of the floor banged his staff for attention.

"Presenting former militiaman Wallas Baker, late of the Empire of Sargol," declared the herald, and a very uneasy-looking Wallas was shown to the center of the audience dais by a lackey. Wallas looked in dismay at the largely uneaten meal before Selford. The minstrel got up and began to pace slowly around Wallas.

"So, Wallas Baker, you are tall, strong, healthy, and lean," began the prince's minstrel, and the assembled courtiers ceased eating and talking, to give the audience their complete attention. "*Never trust a lean cook* is the relevant saying, as I recall."

"With permission, sir?"

"Yes?"

"That is a very silly saying."

"Indeed? Now, I have made a few discreet enquiries about you, I do like to know the prince's staff at a personal level. I have a rather long and rather interesting report about you. Firstly, I believe that your penis has been turned into a dragon named Willy, and secondly, Willy has rather high standards in matters of morality. He is also rather protective of your chastity and general well-being. Floor herald, kick him in the groin."

The herald stepped onto the dais and did as he was instructed. There was an outraged hiss and a gout of flames, sparks, and smoke from beneath Wallas's tunic. The herald screamed, tried to pull away, then fell backward from the dais, leaving a gilded kid-leather slipper burning in Willy's jaws. Willy tossed the slipper aside and withdrew beneath the hem of the tunic. The courtiers applauded politely. A guard stamped out the burning slipper, then removed it, along with the herald, who was in a state somewhere between advanced hysterics and nervous collapse.

"Splendid, the prince does like proof to go with reports of the wild and fantastical," said Selford. "Now then, reading on . . . you were formerly Milvarios of Tourlossen, the Master of Royal Music in the Sargolan imperial court. Boring. Oh, but it says here that unofficially you were the worst bard on the continent of Acrema, and quite possibly the entire world. Now that is promising."

"It is?" exclaimed Wallas.

"Fourthly, you reportedly assassinated the Sargolan emperor."

" 'Assassinated' is a rather extreme word, sir."

"He was a boring man with no vices, the sort who would start wars that laid waste cities and killed millions, merely because their rulers behaved like, well, *our* prince. Contract assassin, were you, or was it personal?"

"Sir, you don't understand."

"It wasn't *idealism*, was it?" said Selford, suddenly looking alarmingly suspicious.

"There was a team involved," said Wallas slowly, suddenly realizing that the prince and emperor might not have been on the best of terms.

"A contractor, then, excellent! The prince does so hate idealists, they get *ideas* about things. Good to see assassins joining the market economy. Going on . . . notorious lecher, liar, coward, and bore."

"They are also rather extreme words, sir."

"Yet point ten tells us that you showed extreme courage at a battle called, ah, the Battle of Racewater Bridge. Oh dear, that will never do."

"But I am a deserter, sir. I fled the personal guard of Princess Senterri herself."

"Indeed? Promising. The prince will want that verified, of course. Next, you helped rescue some people from a glass dragon in Clovesser."

"Only because a hand-crossbow was held against my ear, sir."

"What about crossing the Strait of Dismay in a small schooner?"

"I was dragged aboard kicking and screaming, sir. It took five strong men—"

"Oh splendid, I felt sure there was an explanation. Point thirteen will be hard to explain away, however. You traveled many hundreds of miles with Elder Terikel of the Metrologans without seducing her."

"I tried, sir, but she took offense and her casting nearly removed my hand. See this burn—"

"Hah, it might have been from hot cooking oil. You will have to try harder to impress me, Wallas Baker."

"Sir, at the great ball for Princess Senterri at Glasbury, I seduced both a kitchen maid *and* Countess Bellesarion within three minutes."

"Oh yes, I read an auton carrier bird report from her about that ball, but she named no specific names. Would you have been 'well hung but tasteless'?"

"That may have been her impression of me, sir."

"Splendid, splendid, you will fit in perfectly. I shall have a declaration of tenure drawn up this very hour and—oh, I almost forgot. Do you have any experience supervising teams of kitchen hands? You will have to prepare entire banquets from time to time, say two days in three."

"I have supervised bands and string orchestras, sir."

"No matter, musicians, cooks, they are all the same. Well, back to the kitchens with you, Wallas. A lackey will bring you some scrolls to sign, along with the menu for a rather special banquet tonight."

Next on the agenda of the crown prince was not so much the night of the assassins as the afternoon tea of abductions. All senior sorceric, priestly, and academic people left in the city were rounded up in a well-coordinated swoop, and put under guard in the palace hostelry and dungeons—where they found chilled snowline claret and goose-liver pâté on savory ricebread awaiting them in their rooms and cells. Those who attempted to speak dangerous castings had their teeth wired together, then they found themselves in the palace torture hall just in time for late-afternoon aerobics and weights training. An hour later the prisoners rushed off to hide in their cells, and Selford spoke with his Head of Creative Torture, Igonnier.

"I am not entirely sure why we had to arrest all these learned people, but seeing they are here, we might as well be horrible to them," decreed Selford.

"For Garris, perhaps an all-female inquisition to question him about his sex life?" suggested Igonnier.

"I did not know that he had a sex life," replied Selford. "Not one that involved anybody else, anyway."

"Precisely, lordship. Just imagine him in the grip of a verity casting, before the whole court."

"Ah yes, that should do."

"Now Learned Wensomer Callientor is quite a prize. She is the only level-thirteen initiate in the known world who refuses to be graded to level thirteen. She is a difficult subject, to be sure."

"The prince hates her," said Selford firmly. "Half of the city thinks she does better revels than him."

"Well, she has impressive credentials: overweight, lazy, unambitious, fond of tall, lean, fit warriors with a large sexual capacity, and even more fond of cream pastries and sundry other luxury foods and fortified wines. Favorite pastimes and vices include eating, belly dancing, sex, expensive silk underwear that covers roughly one part in five hundred of her body's surface area, and lying about on cushions fash-

ioned in the shape of selected parts of the anatomy, while
reading scholarly tracts on obscure sorceric castings."

"Do not trouble yourself about her, I have her fate
planned," said Selford.

"Lord Selford, of all the people arrested, she is the one
who puzzles me the most. All the others are the sorceric left-
overs, peculiar geniuses, professional dissenters, priestly
nobodies, and academic refugees from honest work. Wensomer is both powerful and brilliant, why she is even said to
have personally destroyed Silverdeath, the ancient etheric
weapon that melted Torea. She is nothing like the others."

"She is also the only senior initiate in all of Scalticar to
call the Grand Council of Supreme Ringstone Initiates a
pack of pathetic wankers. That was when they issued her
with a command to join the initiates powering Dragonwall. I
believe her message casting took the form of a pair of talking buttocks, and they want revenge for the insult, I am led to
believe."

"That seems somewhat petty, with them wielding godlike
powers and suchlike."

"No, they *fear* her. Remember, she destroyed Silverdeath,
another immensely powerful etheric machine."

After cooking, tasting, shouting at kitchen hands, and throwing hysterical tantrums all afternoon, Wallas was close to exhaustion by the time the evening's banquet got under way.
Serving lackeys bore the heavily laden dishes and bowls
away, and brought back preliminary reports of great appreci-
ation on the part of the diners. Wallas selected a jar of fine
wine, slumped on a bench, smashed the neck off the jar, and
poured the wine in the general direction of his mouth. Most
of it found the target. Wallas then tossed the empty jar aside,
and it smashed at the edge of a hearth.

Wallas had not actually planned to spy on the court, but he
did like to watch people enjoying themselves as they ate
what he had cooked and prepared. He got slowly to his feet,
reeled away to the palace laundry, called for a soaking vat to
be filled with warm water, then climbed in without bothering

to undress. During the course of the next hour, he slowly removed his clothes, then rang for a lackey and sent him to fetch the pack that had his change of clothing and a towel. When he returned, the overzealous lackey made the mistake of trying to scoop Wallas's wet clothing out of the vat. Willy's head broke the surface, breathing fire. The lackey fled screaming, which annoyed Wallas because he had left the towels out of reach.

Wallas was feeling particularly relaxed and at ease with the world by the time he had finished dressing. Suddenly he remembered a vital item of equipment, and reached into his pack. He had not been wearing the quarterstaff protector since arriving in Alberin, but given Willy's potential for social disruption, Wallas felt it was time to put it back into service. It was a vaguely heart-shaped metal bowl, padded at the edges and inside, and trailing straps. Wallas removed his trousers and showed the protector to Willy. Willy eyed it doubtfully. He had been confined to it before.

"This is to make your life easier, Willy," Wallas assured the little dragon. "Remember, this stops all those horrible people who have designs on the most intimate and tender parts of my body. It stops them long before you have to burn or bite them."

Willy was incapable of smiling, but it seemed resigned to again be covered and confined by the protector.

"This should also save a fortune in tunics and trews," muttered Wallas as he tied the straps.

As Wallas climbed the steps to the banqueting hall, he began to notice the screams above the music and background of laughing and talking. They were the screams of a woman, but also of a tortured soul, someone in a mindless extreme of torment. It also struck Wallas that it sounded like her teeth had been wired together. The liaison balcony was where the warden of the court floor watched over all feasts, orgies, and revels, looking out for signals from whoever was presiding to bring on the next course, entertainment, or novelty. The warden was flanked by four guards, just in case anyone unauthorized entered and tried to aim a projectile weapon from what was undeniably an ideal vantage point.

Wallas knocked at the door, and after some moments the warden opened it.

"Ah, my dear master of meals, welcome," said the warden. "Splendid meal, splendid. Especially the torment food."

"Torment food?" gasped Wallas.

"Yes, yes, a masterpiece. Come, see for yourself."

A woman was tied to a chair on the circular dias, so that all the courtiers could see her from their tables. She was in the costume of a belly dancer, and before her was a very large pig, its red leather leash held by the floor herald. It was in the process of scoffing down the last of a plate of ground-nut pastries that Wallas had been particularly proud of. The floor herald banged his staff on the floor.

"Honey-cream icing and shredded chocolate on coconut macaroon cake," he called, and the courtiers applauded.

Trays were brought to each table simultaneously by a team of lackeys, but a separate tray was brought for the pig, uncovered, and presented to it on the floor. The pig began to gobble the macaroons down, the woman began to squeal in tormented outrage between her wired teeth, and some of the courtiers laughed and applauded.

"Ah, that Prince Dalzori, he does excel himself sometimes," said the warden approvingly.

Dazed with shock, Wallas let his eyes wander about the tables, scanning over strangely dressed and sometimes mostly undressed bodies, all of them showing signs of excessive eating. Selford sat smiling on a throne, dressed in sober black silk, and sipping from a glass of water. Wallas looked back to the woman, who suddenly seemed familiar. She had the foundations of a good figure—upon which a little more than was probably safe had been built. A pang of sympathy almost doubled Wallas over.

"Who is she?" he head himself ask softly.

"Oh, the great sorceress Wensomer," replied the warden.

"But, but, what has she done?"

"Given too many feasts and revels that were considered better than those of the prince. Not to worry, though, in a month or so she will be told that this was all a big mistake, the pig will be turning on a spit, and Learned Wensomer will be invited to the feast."

Wallas left the balcony with his head spinning. What the minstrel had failed to deduce from his dossier was that while he was a coward and a cad, when backed into a corner he was actually capable of acts of remarkable bravery and altruism. The sight of what was happening to Wensomer had definitely forced Wallas into a corner.

It had been well after dark when Andry and Velander finally decided to get out of bed, wash, and dress. Andry noticed that she smelled of rosewater and muskenberry juice, and that she was putting on clothes so clean that the press marks were fresh and there were no creases.

"Laron saved me from death. Showed me, ah, surviving. You saved me, ah, from undead existing. Made me want life. Again. Tonight, special treat, you will have."

"More special than we've had all day?" laughed Andry. "Not possible."

"Not so. Most of day, Miral is down. I am alive."

"I am not sure that I understand."

"As you see me, am live girl. Miral rise, am dragon. Body dead, but moving, speak, be warm, all, by using of etheric energies. Make form of me, spread over skin. Dragon in Velander form. Or maybe, dragon in dragon form."

"Er, is this liable to kill me?" asked Andry, not having to try very hard to feign apprehension.

"Mentor dragons say no. For now, walk down street, hold hands, go to tavern. Love, you play rebec, I listen."

"My rebec! Essen said he'd mind it last night, when I was looking unsteady."

"Well, find Essen. Time, we have."

Chapter Ten

DRAGONBIRTH

The weather in the tropics was unstable, rather than particularly bad. Terikel crossed the coast of Torea at twenty thousand feet, following an air current that was taking her east, with a slight northerly bias. The scenario below her was scattered with cumulus clouds, which were thickening into a forest of thunderheads. Terikel began climbing slowly, aware that the thunderheads could rise higher than where she could breathe.

Flying as a dragon was like riding a horse. One controlled vastly more power than one's muscles had to offer, yet control was not hard. It was very much like being in bed. Terikel thought of the sorceress who had taught her the castings and skills for airwalking. Wensomer had a weight problem, disliked being out of bed before noon, and took the matters of eating and drinking very seriously indeed. In a sense, she seemed the last person one would expect to find studying the skills of airwalking, yet Terikel now realized that it was very easy and even relaxing. That was why Wensomer liked it. The relaxing part was also the biggest problem. Fall asleep, and those parts of the casting not bound to anything physical would collapse within half an hour. If one was flying sufficiently high, this allowed time to generate new wings, but it was a risky and harrowing sort of prompt to wake up.

"Terikel!"

The alarm casting chirped her name every quarter hour. She was wide awake, but it was not wise to allow herself the luxury of hours of serenity. They might end in another very long fall. The sky was darkening as the sun dropped to the horizon behind her. The clouds below her were lighting up with splashes of red, orange, pink, and gold, while lightning flickered white, violet, and occasionally green in the distant thunderstorm. Terikel banked lazily, to gaze at the sunset, then completed the circle and resumed her former heading.

"Terikel!"

The colors faded beneath her, but the flickering of the lightning continued. She was in the tropics, and Wensomer had told her that thunderheads could rise as high as . . . Terikel struggled to convert the figures in her mind. Sixty thousand feet. That was double the height at which she could breathe, and three times her current altitude. They were to be skirted, not overflown.

The stars and Lupan were visible now. Terikel took her bearings and adjusted her heading. Ahead of her was seven thousand miles of ocean before she reached Dacostia, even by the estimates of the most reliable maps and models she had studied. The Infinital Ocean was truly vast, stretching over twelve thousand miles if one traced a path just south of the equator. That was half the diameter of the world. Little of it had been mapped, for there was no incentive to sail there. Even before the Torean Storms, there was no record of anyone having crossed it. Flight might be relaxing, but that amount of flight would be a distinct strain.

"Terikel!"

Still, she would be the first human to fly the Middle Infinital Ocean. Someone else could have the glory of the South Infinital. The storms there lashed themselves up over thousands of miles of water broken by no land at all, roared into the Occidanic Ocean, then were slammed through the Strait of Dismay. And that was the normal storms. With the Torean Storms, the waves and weather in the strait were almost beyond comprehension, let alone measurement.

Terikel took another sighting from the stars, adjusted her course with a slight tilting of her wings, then allowed herself the first of many brief dozes that would be all of her rest for the next eight days.

"Terikel!"

She jerked awake, then thought through the image of the wings in her mind. Again she dozed.

Terikel was five days into her flight when she caught sight of Dragonwall. It was early evening, and the ocean below was completely blanketed by clouds. The sunset was making them glow like a vast forest of luminous, crimson trees, and Terikel was preparing for a cycle of brief dozes when she noticed that the entire eastern horizon was glowing.

For a moment Terikel was completely disoriented. Was she flying west instead of east? She banked sharply and looked to the sun. Half of the disk was among the clouds. She completed the circle. There was still a glow at the opposite side of the sky. It was a golden-orange glow, confused by the colors of the sunset.

"Terikel!" the timer casting chirped at her, but she certainly did not need it now.

Terikel began a much larger circle. Perhaps she was totally disoriented, and was confusing sunrise with sunset. As the minutes passed, she saw the sun sink below the clouds at the horizon. Using the stars, she resumed her former heading. The glow in the east remained. It was not the glow of sunset. She had not seen Dragonwall from so very high, yet it still looked familiar: a vast rainbow crowning an orange curtain of light. If this was indeed Dragonwall, the ether machine . . . but that did not make sense. According to the current theories of the world's circumference, she should have been almost precisely on the other side, not back over Acrema. The blue line moved slowly across the sky above her, pivoted on Dragonwall.

The Metrologan priestess in Terikel asserted herself. When in doubt, measure what can be measured. She took sightings from several of the brighter stars and two moonworlds. They put her about a dozen degrees north of the equator. That meant she was above the deserts of North Acrema, just a little north of Ringstone Wasteland. Terikel considered flying below the clouds, but there was no point. The desert looked the same as the ocean in total darkness: unrelieved black. On the other hand, a vertical column of blue energies would be stabbing skyward at Ringstone Wasteland, and would extend through the clouds right into Dragonwall. That would be her reference. She could follow Dragonwall south, land in the desert near Ringstone Centras, collapse her wings, and deliver the gift from Teacher.

Terikel banked in a wide, leisurely circle, turning south and dropping to a level where the prevailing winds were not so strong from the west. Hours passed, and Terikel monitored the stars. At ten degrees north of the equator, there was no column of blue, glowing energies from Ringstone Wasteland. That was, of course, not possible. The ringstone sites were at ten-degree intervals of latitude. On the other hand, she had never visited Ringstone Wasteland, so perhaps it had been put in the wrong place and nobody had ever noticed.

Hours passed, but Terikel did not doze at all. At dawn she was five degrees north of the equator. Dragonwall was still in the sky, and the westerly winds had driven her closer to it. Although trying to fly parallel to the other machine, she was now only a hundred miles west, by her best estimate. Below her was unbroken cloud, as far as the horizon in every direction. As the sky lightened, Dragonwall faded to just an orange curtain against the blue of day, but it never faded entirely, even at noon.

❊ ❊ ❊

Terikel made the decision to descend below the clouds once it was daylight. Sand dunes would look rather different to waves by day, and they moved a lot slower. One way or another, her location would be determined. Height was gained with effort, and was not to be discarded lightly, even though she was now so much better in the air than when she had tried to cross the Strait of Dismay. Thus Terikel took some time to make the decision.

The drop from four miles to one mile took over an hour,

and most of it was through clouds. Terikel descended into rain. That was bad, as the extra weight of water on her wings detracted seriously from her ability to get lift. Clouds swirled around her, a grey, pearly murk, and rain-laden gusts of wind buffeted her wings. If she was over mountains, and the mountains were enshrouded with cloud . . . she would never know what she hit.

When Terikel finally emerged through the cloud base, she was barely two hundred feet above the water.

Ocean. There should not have been water within seven hundred miles. The thought that it might have been a tract of flooded desert crossed her mind, but the waves looked more like huge, mid-ocean rollers than the waves on a relatively shallow, inland flood. That much she had learned from her voyages on *Shadowmoon*, *Megazoid*, and *Stormbird*. She began slowly beating her wings to gain height. Contract! There was a hiss and crackle of etheric energies as Teacher's gift contracted the tendrils to her keel casting. Relax! The wings were raised as her body dropped. Contract! Terikel gained a little more height. The weight of rain hitting and streaming off her two-hundred-foot span made flying a lot harder than in the clear, calm serenity to be found at five miles. It was late afternoon before she managed to struggle above the clouds again. A glance to the east told her that she was no more than ten miles from Dragonwall. Three hundred and fifteen flaps of her wings, she had counted. How much etheric energy had that required? What was left of Teacher's gift?

Taking stock, Terikel tried to make sense out of impossible facts. She was possibly over an ocean where no ocean had a right to be. Alternatively, she was half a world away from where she ought to have been. There had been no ringstone column at ten degrees north of the equator, where Ringstone Wasteland should have been. The only possible conclusion was that Dragonwall did not vanish into the poles, but totally encircled the world. That would not allow the energies being fed into it to be dispersed, however. If there were no ringstone control sites for half a world, it would be like a spinning wagon wheel with spokes in only half of its circumference. It would very soon develop wobbles and tear itself to pieces. Even one spoke on the opposite side would provide a great deal of stability. Was there one spoke, in the middle of the Infinital Ocean? It would have to be right on the equator, because the blue line across the sky was pivoted on it.

Almost as the thought was passing through her mind, Terikel caught sight of a blue column of light in the distance. It emerged from the clouds and stretched all the way up to the rainbow edging of Dragonwall. She knew that she was close to the equator. A ringstone site there would provide balance and stability— but stability for what? Energies would not pour into the earth or the rotation arms in the sky. Two equatorial ringstones meant that the rotation ring was anchored at two points, and was spinning between them. This meant that the ring could accumulate energies without developing the wobbles that came with higher concentrations of energies. If the energies were free to accumulate . . . there was probably no limit to the amount that could be built up by Dragonwall. She dropped into the cloud cover again.

Ringstone Counter turned out to be on an island, most of which was a volcanic cone. Its east side flattened into a ledge about the area of a small town, and this was where the actual ringstone was located. There were no ships anchored near the island, and no buildings on it. A movement almost below Terikel suddenly secured her undivided attention. A truly vast body of vaguely fish shape ponderously broke the surface, stretched a huge mouth open, then dived again. The seabirds in the area were like dots by comparison, so Terikel estimated it to be in the vicinity of two hundred feet in length. No ship would last long if attacked by something of that size, so if there were several of them on either side of Dragonwall, no ship could approach the island. That meant that only glass dragons and seabirds could reach the island. Dragon castings were highly visible to anyone who was darkwalking, that strange out-of-body trance in which the etheric view of the world could be experienced. All of those in the ringstones were actually darkwalking, so no dragon could approach unannounced. Dragons showed up strongly to darkwalking sorcerers;

they were pure etheric energy, after all. The energy level of
Terikel's wing casting was minute by comparison, but
would they notice it?

"The end will be so quick that I shall never know it," she
whispered to herself as she banked to head straight for the
island.

There was a wide beach of black sand at the base of the
west side of the volcanic cone, and Terikel began stretching
and flexing her legs as she made her approach. She was glid-
ing into a wind blowing from the south, a wind that was
slightly above her stall speed. She slowed, dropped, hovered
like a seagull above the littoral of the black beach, then
dropped gently to the sand.

"Best landing I've ever done, even if it is only my fifth
landing," she told herself as she began to collapse her wing
castings. The rain had thinned to drizzle, and even the drizzle was fading as she began to skirt the island's volcano. It
was not a particularly big island, being an oblong roughly a
mile in length with a volcanic cone at one end. There were
some bushes growing in the rich soil, but no trees. The reek
of sulfides was on the air, and the air was uncomfortably
warm and humid.

A slow walk through broken scoria for over an hour had the
ringstone in sight. From this distance, Terikel was able to
confirm what she had suspected all along. The ringstone was
formed entirely of glass dragons. There were four concentric
rings of sixteen, and instead of being on stones, the glass
dragons merely sat at the appropriate positions. Spikes of
blue light were rising out of their backs where their wings
should have been, and these spiraled upward, interweaving
into a fabric of light to form the column. The faint shimmer
of the etheric curtain that was Dragonwall stretched away to
the north and south.

Terikel pondered what to do next. There were too many
mysteries here, but there were answers in abundance too.
The location of Dragonwall's ringstones was not optimal

in terms of convenience, thought Terikel. *A few hundred miles to the east would have had it far closer to many major cities, and the comforts and conveniences that sorcerers prefer to have nearby.* It also cut through the largest roosting sites of the glass dragons in Acrema and Torea. Now there was an answer to the question of the placement. This island *had* to be precisely on the opposite side of the globe, because the counter ringstone was going to be located there.

Dragons, powering a ringstone, thought Terikel. It finally made sense. A ringstone so very far away was like a long lever under a huge, heavy rock. The rock could be moved by the touch of a mere child. Terikel felt vulnerable, yet in a sense she was quite safe. No ship or intruder dragon could reach the island, and those that had set up the ringstone clearly had not believed that there was any other way to reach the place. Her wing casting had been too faint to be noticed by the dragons of Ringstone Counter, and with her wings and thermal casting collapsed, she was now invisible in terms of magical fields. There was the casting that Teacher had given to her, but although she could bleed off enough energy to flap her wings, most of it was sealed too tightly to be detected. She had, however, been told how to release the casting, and she had also been told to bring it to this place. Now she was here. There was nothing else to do that she could think of, other than to speak the release words for the casting.

Terikel looked out over the little lava plain. There was no cover at all if she decided to approach it, but whatever was watching over the place was probably not able to see a person. *Do I believe that or hope that?* she wondered. *Big distinction.* Terikel began to walk. Nothing happened to her, and nothing moved, other than herself. She walked for the nearest gap between the dragons of the outer ring. The light around her was pale blue, and her skin began to tingle. The glass dragons towered sightlessly above her as she walked between them, yet they might as well have been glowing, translucent statues. She passed the next ring, and now she noticed a background hissing crackle, and the the scent of ozone on the

air began to overwhelm that of the sulfides from the volcano.

What happens when I release the casting? she wondered.
There was perhaps as much as a thousand years of accumu-
lated etheric energy in Teacher's casting. It would be
highly visible to the darkwalking dragons. She walked
steadily past the inner ring of glass dragons. The last ring
was not far away. Terikel knew that she would release the
casting; it was inevitable. Perhaps Teacher had taken her
determination into account, in assigning her the mission.
Teacher was over five thousand years old and his motives
were not only unknown, they were probably incomprehen-
sible. Terikel decided to trust Teacher, hoping that he
would value her life more than an archer cared for the fate
of an arrow.

She stopped before the central dragon. It wore no woven,
etheric armor, and its dragon casting was more translucent
than those of the others. The dark shape of the sorcerer at its
core was clearly discernible. *Can he see me?* wondered
Terikel. *Well, if he can't, he soon will.*

Terikel spoke a minor casting, then quickly pressed it into
her chest. When she drew her hand away, the black sphere
was on her palm. She took a deep breath, braced herself for
whatever the afterlife might hold for her, then spoke the release casting. The surface of the sphere shimmered through
rainbow colors, then blazed brilliant white.

"Press me into the central glass dragon, then leave before
it's too late," declared Teacher's voice, slowly and clearly.

Terikel slapped the sphere against the dragon's flank at
once, then pressed as hard as she could. It dissolved through
the glassy skin, like a jelly being forced through a sieve. She
stood back, staring at her hand, genuinely surprised to find it
still attached to her body. Looking back to the central
dragon, she noticed that an angry red blush was spreading
across and through its body, and it was beginning to shiver.
Terikel turned and ran on legs that were stiff and cramped
from days of inactivity.

Nothing moved but Terikel as she passed through the
rings of glass dragons, but there was an increasingly strong
red glow behind her. The light was also flickering. A flicker-

ing casting meant an unstable casting. This was a casting, and this was flickering, but then this was quite probably the largest casting that had ever been generated by sorcerers— and dragons. What would happen if it collapsed? Terikel was actually past the outer ring of dragons before she realized that she was now vulnerable to something in the sky that could melt rocks in less time than it took to blink. Still nothing happened.

The strain of running now made itself felt as agony in Terikel's legs as she floundered through the scoria at the base of the volcano. Even under the best of conditions it would have been a very difficult climb, and she knew that she would not get far before she collapsed with exhaustion. A boulder the size of a large house loomed, and she made yet another hasty decision as intense scarlet light pulsed out of the ringstone behind her. A wing casting would be very faint when compared to the etheric field of a glass dragon, but if the dragons of the ringstone were now actually looking for faint castings, she might be noticed. Her choices were to either skirt the volcano and hope that the collapse of the Dragonwall casting would not be powerful enough to destroy an entire mountain, or take a chance and try to fly. Terikel needed only one glance back at Ringstone Counter to help her make up her mind. The glass dragons were gone, and there was just a cylinder of translucent, pulsing red that reached into the clouds.

Climbing up onto the boulder, Terikel began to generate her wing casting. In spite of the state of Ringstone Counter, she held her nerve through the minutes and grew the spike until it was close to the hundred-foot optimum. As the spike began to divide, she generated a casting for a wishbone and keel. By now the ground was shuddering under her feet. There was no longer the casting from Teacher to tap for etheric energy to flap her wings, but she did have a little energy of her own. She did not bother with a thermal casting to keep herself warm, in fact she did not even pause to take a deep breath before leaping.

Terikel was only fifty feet above sea level when she launched herself. Realizing that she would hit the water within moments, she contracted her etheric tendrils with her own life force. The pain was like being rolled in a sack of needles as Terikel leveled out, and it was as if every muscle in her body had been working at the limit of its capacity for a quarter hour. *Height*, thought Terikel. If she tried to bank, she would dip a wingtip into the waves. There was only one choice for her. She beat her wings again.

Even though Terikel had thought she could endure five beats of her wings before she became exhausted, her body now felt as if she had been running at the very limit of her endurance for a half hour. She had more height, that was true, but she could not face the prospect of another beat. She was two minutes from the volcano, and had traveled over a mile. A gust of wind from the south caught Terikel and lifted her a little farther. She warped her wings, trying to get the maximum advantage from the wind. Another flap would put her at a far better height, but Terikel could not face the pain. She glided on, slowly losing height, but occasionally being boosted by the wind.

Terikel was not facing the island when Ringstone Counter collapsed, but she was still dazzled by the reflection of the light from the waves and clouds. *No sound*, thought Terikel, beginning to count. *The sound is sure to come, six, seven, eight. This is daylight, yet it seems like night after that blast of light, seventeen, eighteen, nineteen. Could there be so much light without any sound? Twenty-eight, twenty-nine, thirty.*

Terikel remembered what came next as a solid thunder-clap that she heard with her entire body. She was flung tumbling through the air, drenched in salt spray. A second blast slammed past her, somehow sucking her upward in a swirl of turbulence and salt spray, like a rainstorm in reverse. Terikel could tell the direction of the island from the heat radiating through the murk. *Heat*, she thought. *Rising air, thermals*. She did not so much turn back to the island as begin to circle a vast column of steam that was roiling up into the sky. Dust and even pebbles rained out of it, but it provided lift. She ascended rapidly, and was concentrating so hard on staying with the thermals that she hardly noticed as she rode through the layer of cloud and into the sunlight. The sun was low in the sky, and evening was not far off. Terikel now remembered that she had no thermal casting to keep her body proof against the extreme chill at this altitude. Drifting a little more distant from the mass of cloud and warm air, she released her arms and began to speak and form the thermal casting for her body.

Dragonwall was gone. She was aware that this was probably the case, otherwise she would not have been able to circle the island, but now she could actually see that the orange curtain of glow was gone. Still the cloud rose, taking Terikel with it. What finally forced her to break away from it was the fact that breathing was becoming difficult. She took a sighting on the setting sun and two of the moonworlds, then set off on a course ten degrees south of east, within a jetstream.

Terikel could not know that the explosion from the collapse of Dragonwall had opened fissures in the volcano, and that water was pouring in and encountering molten magma. It would take weeks, but there would be a second, and much larger, explosion, this one powered by steam rather than etheric energies. When the dust, smoke, and steam cleared, there would be no island left.

✦ ✦ ✦

Wallas found Andry in the Lamplighter, playing his rebec with Essen. There was a short but intense exchange of whispers and gestures between the cook and guardsman. Then Andry turned back to Essen.

"Best mind the rebec a while longer, lad," said Andry. "There's work for doing."

"Heads to kick?" asked Essen.

"Doors to open. Vel, will you stay here?"

"From dead, came back, for to sit in this place. Now, shall sit. Under protection, from Essen."

Andry had only been gone a few minutes when Riellen entered, heard Essen playing "The Dashing Young Marshal," and hurried over.

"Essen, sir, quickly, I need to find Velander!" she cried above the music.

Essen did not stop playing, but he did point to where Velander was sitting with his hornpipe. Moments later Riellen had Velander outside.

"Wilbar is here!" she cried, waving her hands in quite atypical agitation.

"Wilbar, being youth friendly with you from Clovesser?" asked Velander, her arms folded, but in fact quite impressed by Riellen's concern. "With you, came over, on *Shadowmoon*?"

"You don't understand. He was not on the boat! He just appeared, I've see him in the palace grounds, near the hostelry. When I hailed him, he ran."

"How, he has crossed strait?"

"How did *you* cross the strait?"

"Special way. Wilbar, not able to use."

"The *Shadowmoon* was the only seaworthy vessel in Logiar. How did Wilbar get over here if not on the schooner? It must have been the same way as you."

"I said, is special way—" began Velander. Then she stopped. According to Teacher, Wilbar had taught dozens of Alpenniens how to do the auger casting with the inclined ringstones, locking them into a casting statis but leaving them potentially immortal. Mysterious people had called a conference of sorcerers, concentrating all sorcerers hostile to Dragonwall in one place. Now all those sorcerers had been arrested and concentrated in the palace—and Wilbar was snooping about near where they were confined.

"How long have you known Wilbar?" asked Velander.

"Oh, just months," said Riellen. "He just appeared at the Clovesser academy this year."

"No past, maybe can fly, looking for sorcerers after moving. Er, are knowing 'second line of defense' expression?"

"Yes, and—oh no!" cried Riellen, her hands pressed against her cheeks.

"Suddenly all looking clear."

✴ ✴ ✴

Releasing Wensomer was not particularly hard for Andry and Wallas. Assisting her to escape was another matter entirely. Every so often Selford had her carried out of the feast, still tied to her chair, while dancers came on to perform. She was carried over to a room in the base of Citadel Tower, which had barred windows and a single door. A flight of stone stairs curved up one inner wall, and ended at a heavy, iron-bound door that was bolted shut and padlocked. A single lantern hanging from a wall hook was the only source of light. The guards who had brought her in checked each window in turn, insuring that the bars were secure, then one ran up the stone steps and rattled the padlock. Satisfied that the room was quite secure, they left to watch the dancing, after bolting and padlocking the door from outside.

Moments after they were gone, Wensomer heard a noise from above her. She turned her head as far as she could. A tall, handsome man came hurrying down the steps carrying a picnic basket.

"Wat ish dish?" Wensomer asked between her wired teeth as he began to untie her bindings.

"I'm Wallas, ladyship, a new palace cook," he explained, his voice close to breaking. "I just couldn't stand the way you were being tormented and tortured with my very best Sargolan creations."

"Huw dith yu git in?"

"I got in a quarter hour ago, I have a friend who is a guardsman."

"Wallas, will you hurry up?" called Andry from above them.

"That friend, specifically. The guards checked the lock of that door door up there, but not the hinges, which are missing their pins. Andry and I were holding it in place from above. There, now we start climbing. This is the base of a tower. There is no way to walk out, except through this room, but I know another way to escape. I have a pair of pincers here, I'll have your teeth unwired in a thrice."

With Wensomer's teeth unwired, they began climbing the steps. Andry pulled the upper door closed behind them.

"What's in the basket?" panted Wensomer as they reached the third flight of stairs. "A rope?"

"No, a selection of my best pastries and macaroons, a slice of warm pork pie, a jar of chilled honeywine, and—"

"Show me!" demanded Wensomer. "Give it here."

Wensomer started with a slice of pork pie, and by the time they passed a heavily padlocked door near the top bearing a plaque inscribed PALACE SUPPLIES AND INFRASTRUCTURE COMMITTEE, she had finished five macaroons and three pastries. They continued on up the last flight of stairs, through the access hatch to the top of the tower, and into the night air. As they paused for breath, Andry bolted the access hatch, and Wallas and Wensomer began sharing the bottle of honeywine.

"I was hoping that you could do the airwalker casting," panted Wallas, cautiously peering between the crenellations of the battlements.

"Oh I can and I shall, but two of you would be a strain to carry," she replied. "You can ride clinging to my back, Wallas, but what do we do with your guardsman friend?"

Andry produced a length of cord from under his surcoat.

"Leave me bound and gagged, up here," said Andry, his tone sounding almost impatient. "I'll say Wallas forced me to help you, then I was abandoned."

"It sounds unlikely," said Wensomer.

"Not as unlikely as some of the truth about Wallas."

"When we land on the roof of my villa I shall lock the place with castings that an army could not get past," said Wensomer, looking out over the courtyard below in case there were archers about. "Then, Wallas, you will find that my gratitude—"

"All in good time, ladyship," said a voice from the shadows of the crenellations. "Just now it is unsafe to return there."

A small, elderly woman with a kindly smile stood up, dusted off her skirts, and walked across to them.

"Ladyship," said Andry, bowing, though his eyes were wide with surprise.

"I do not believe we have met," said Wensomer warily.

"But *we* have," said Wallas, managing to look frightened

yet angry at the same time. "Lady Wensomer, meet Examiner."

"Examiner of what?" asked Wensomer. "No, wait a moment, do I know that name . . ."

"Just Examiner," replied Wallas. "This lady is a glass dragon."

The look on Wensomer's face said that she did not believe a word.

"It really is true," said Examiner.

"Show me evidence," demanded Wensomer.

"I am afraid I do not do tricks, my dear, I have a public image to maintain," said Examiner apologetically.

"I do," said Wallas, raising his tunic and pulling the drawstring of his trousers. They fell to the stone floor. Beneath was a quarterstaff protector. Wallas pulled at another string.

"Wallas, can't this wait until we reach my villa?" asked Wensomer, looking nervously to Examiner and Andry.

The protector fell aside. Willy uncurled, took one look at Wensomer, and hissed, bearing his fangs and pouring a stream of sparks in her direction. Wensomer shrieked and skipped back, nearly colliding with Examiner.

"All my own work," said Examiner proudly. "You can put Willy away now, Wallas."

Wensomer walked forward cautiously and bent over. "Does he bite?" she asked.

"I'm afraid he does," Examiner assured her.

Wensomer took a macaroon from Wallas's basket and tossed it in the general direction of his groin. The tiny dragon growing out of Wallas caught it with a single snap, then tossed it between the tower's crenellations. Wensomer bent over again with her hands on her knees, regarding Willy from a safe distance.

"This is exquisitely good charmshaping," she declared, "speaking from a purely professional position, of course."

"Of course," agreed Wallas.

"Thank you," said Examiner, clasping her hands and looking very pleased with herself. "Wallas's body provides the etheric energies for Willy. Willy also has about the same degree of intelligence as a dog, along with similar loyalty."

"And a lot of jealousy," added Wallas.

"Scales all individually cast, tapering fangs, functional eyes, mobility, and even—oh look, I do believe he's shy. Can't take a compliment, Willy?"

"He doesn't like women," said Wallas. "He doesn't really like anyone but me, if it comes to that."

"Well, put him back in the protector," Wensomer sighed. "Examiner, is there anything that we can do to persuade you to lift this, er, curse?"

"It is not a curse," said Examiner. "Willy gives Wallas a more . . . harmonious outlook on life. He makes him a better person."

Wensomer turned to Examiner and shook her hand.

"This does not prove that you are a glass dragon, but I am impressed by the quality of your casting. Tell me, why is it not safe to return to my villa?"

"Because scores are being settled, Lady Wensomer. You have plenty of enemies, and most of them have recently realized that they control Dragonwall, Windfire, and all of their combined energies."

"Examiner, you do not know my enemies," said Wensomer, folding her arms and with her head to one side, as if trying to deduce whether the woman was a powerful godling, or well informed but mad. "Most of them would be far more interested in killing each other before killing me. They would never cooperate."

"You do not understand, Wensomer. They *all* have control of Dragonwall. That is its flaw. Nearly five thousand people and dragons are now locked into Dragonwall, and now all of them have access to Dragonwall's power. Four thousand nine hundred and four gods, all with agendas to push and scores to settle. That is why there has been no pattern in the attacks and destruction. They have been slowly learning what powers are available to them and experimenting with randomly chosen targets. Every major city could soon be destroyed, along with every castle, fortress, army, and fleet. The sorcerers of Lemtas and Acrema have also begun to incinerate each others' masters, patrons, academies, and cities."

"Like Alpenfast?" asked Wallas.

"Alpenfast was attacked three days ago, but its defenses have held so far. Parts of Palion, Diomeda, Glasbury, Logiar and Gladenfalle are on fire, and the Alpennien armies are all charred meat and armor."

"My mother!" exclaimed Wensomer. "She has an applied-castings academy in Diomeda."

"The academy complex was annihilated," said Examiner. "I am sorry."

Wensomer sat down and leaned against the battlements. She did not weep, but she paid her companions little attention. A bell began to ring lower down in the tower. Presently someone rattled the access hatch from below, then began pounding at it and demanding that they open up.

Examiner pointed to the sky, where the line of blue that was Windfire was almost overhead.

"*That* is the weapon," she said. "The energies are fed into that thing from Dragonwall through Ringstone Centras and a ringstone at the world's end. Will anyone in control of it notice Alberin on this pass? It took only two passes to destroy nearly everything sorceric on Lemtas, and that is the largest continent in the world."

"I mean it's not as if Mother and I really got along," continued Wensomer to nobody in particular.

"We saw the ruins of the Special Warrior Service College," said Wallas.

"All but one or two of the SWS were there at a meeting, to discuss Dragonwall. The temptation to destroy the entire SWS in one swoop must have been too great for some faction with a grudge. It took us a long time to work out what the agenda of those behind all this really was, you see. A small, radical faction of the glass dragons thinks that mortals are too powerful, and that they should just be breeding stock for the occasional new dragons. What better way to destroy your civilizations than to give massive destructive powers to everyone, with no constraints? The highest priority was given to destroying books, teachers, academies, and dissident sorcerers. Wensomer is an extremely dissident sorceress, so she is in great danger."

"Mother, dead," whimpered Wensomer. "I mean, I hated her. I hated my sister, too, but they deserved better."

"All dissident sorcerers are currently in Alberin, also for a conference. Need I suggest who probably called the conference, and—"

A luridly blue-white flash lit up the city from a line that seemed to come vertically down out of the sky. The immediate area of Wensomer's mansion became an ascending, roiling fireball from which debris rained down onto the neighborhood. Moments later a wall of sound slammed into them. Wensomer looked from the mushroom-shaped cloud to Wallas.

"If I'd listened to you I'd be there by now!" she cried.

"So would I!" Wallas retorted.

Another flash and blast erupted, this time in the Wharf-side area. Fragments of the Metrologans' temple showered down over the palace, and the watchers in Citadel Tower crouched down with their hands over their heads. Andry noticed that the guardsmen below the hatch were no longer pounding on it, and had probably left hurriedly. As they looked up at the fireball that marked the destruction of the temple, there was another flash, followed by an even louder blast.

"That will be the academy," said Examiner. "They were after the library."

"Why?" asked Wensomer. "There's nothing special about the academy library, even mine was better."

"There is probably not another large library surviving in Scalticar, if not the world. Nobody wants anyone else to have an advantage. Libraries, temples, academies, armies, castles, ports, shipyards, bridges, and even the homes of prominent sorcerers are being burned to char and slag—"

Examiner was interrupted by a fourth blaze of light. This one came from directly above the tower, and was so intense that they all clamped their hands over their eyes. *I'm dead*, thought Wensomer, but as the light slowly faded it was clear that they were all still alive, and that the palace was undamaged. Examiner was looking up and pointing. From what Wensomer could see of the sky past the clouds of smoke from the first three explosions, the blue line across the sky that marked Windfire was gone.

"Did something really significant just happen?" asked Wensomer, slowly standing up.

"Windfire is part of Dragonwall," said Examiner, still looking at the sky. "If it is gone, then Dragonwall is gone too. It has a number of subtle vulnerabilities, but then political idealists seldom take an interest in what is subtle. We had several attacks in progress on Dragonwall. It seems that one has succeeded."

Down in the city there were dozens of small fires dotting the roofscape as a result of burning debris raining down. Alarm bells reached the ears of the watchers on Citadel Tower, along with the sound of whistles, bugles, and shouting people.

"Ladyship, is this the tallest tower in the palace?" asked Andry, who was looking in the opposite direction to the others.

"Well-known fact," replied Wensomer without turning.

"Then why is that one taller now?"

They all turned. The pointed roof of the northeast tower was suddenly well above Citadel Tower's summit.

"That tower is like this one," said Andry. "It should not have a pointed roof."

"But it does have a roof!" insisted Wallas.

As they watched, the roof began to unfold.

"Down, all of you!" warned Examiner as the glass dragon spread its wings.

Wensomer had expected the dragon to launch itself into the air, but instead it looked downward, then sent a puff of incandescence into the courtyard below. Everything that could burn, including a dozen guardsmen, burst into flames. The dragon dropped lightly from the tower to the courtyard, then bent over.

"It's looking at the base of our tower," said Andry.

A stream of fire blasted away the door at the base of the tower, then turned the chamber where Wensomer had been imprisoned into a space that was at roughly the temperature of white-hot steel.

"That was meant for you," Examiner told Wensomer as the flame winked out.

"You're a glass dragon, do something!" cried Wensomer.

"I would have to kill him, and that would annihilate the city."

"What do you mean?"

"That glass dragon is only young, but nevertheless has been accumulating etheric energies for centuries. Killing it would release the lot in a moment, and that would be a stunningly bad idea."

"It's turning to the hospitality wing," reported Andry. "Most of the arrested sorcery students are there."

The dragon spat a streamer of white-hot plasma into the building in a zigzag, turning it into an inferno within moments. Something seemed wrong to Wensomer, however, and evidently the dragon shared her opinion. There were no screams of agony and desperation; it was almost as if an empty building were ablaze. The glass dragon looked more closely. It was just then that a vast shadow outlined in violet tracery sailed across from the Wharfside area and slammed into it.

Both glass dragons weighed only as much as their host bodies, but both controlled vast amounts of energy, and their etheric bodies were very strong. Blue and violet streamers boiled up around the tower, along with plaster dust, fragments of masonry, and slate tiles. Wensomer looked down into a tangle of glowing wings, legs, tails, and heads thrashing and writhing in the courtyard of the palace.

"Is that dragon on our side?" asked Andry.

"That thing down there is not really a dragon, although it has a dragon form," said Examiner. "Nothing could stand against it."

"The other dragon seems to be doing a pretty good job of that," said Wallas.

"Look again," said Andry.

The violet dragon was straddling the other, its neck in its jaws, just below the head. What Wallas had taken for a fight had merely been the impotent thrashings of the doomed blue glass dragon. After about three minutes the blue dragon began to flicker and lose resolution. By then it was no longer struggling.

"The violet one is what is technically known as a

vampyre," said Examiner. "It is slowly draining the life force from the one that tried to kill Wensomer and the sorcery students."

"And me," added Wallas.

"Draining the life force," whispered Andry.

Examiner put her hand on his arm. "There, there, my dear, it was the best we could do for Velander. While Miral is down, she is now a perfectly normal girl, delightfully normal in fact. She can share a goblet of wine with you in the Lamplighter, eat mince cutlets for dinner, and lie in your arms with beating hearts and a warm body as you make love together. While Miral is up, however . . ."

"*That* is *Velander*?" demanded Wallas, pointing down into the courtyard.

"Well, only for another ten hours," replied Examiner indignantly. "And she can reconfigure her etheric image to look almost like, well, Velander. That is what I am doing at this very moment. Being a part-time glass dragon is better than being dead, you must admit. She is draining the energies from the other dragon, killing it slowly so there will be no explosion. The city is safe, and so are we."

Quite abruptly, all was silent. There was no longer any blue light coming from the courtyard, but the violet outline of a very large head began to rise out of the swirling smoke and gloom below. A crest rose up to the level of the crenellations, then two bluish-violet eyes drew level with the watchers at the top of the Citadel Tower. The head was not much smaller than the schooner *Shadowmoon*. Andry walked over, put his hands on the stones of the battlements, and sighed.

"Oh, Velander lass, what's to become of us?" he said.

The glass dragon's jaws opened slightly, and a deep voice rumbled out.

"Examiner, taking Wallas away, if please," said Velander, like a long, distant peal of thunder. "Private words for Wensomer. Very private words for Andry."

Examiner and Wallas hurried across to the hatchway at the center of the tower and descended into the darkness, which was now quite hot after the attack on Wensomer's prison at the base. Fortunately all the steps were of stone,

and while they were about as hot as the hearth of a fireplace, they had not burned away. Examiner stopped at the
door marked PALACE SUPPLIES AND INFRASTRUCTURE COM-
MITTEE, breathed on it, then stepped through the ash and
charcoal that remained. She emerged with a large but light
bundle.

"Would not want him to miss his wedding," she explained
to the perplexed Wallas.

Once they were in the courtyard outside, Wallas saw
that Velander was clinging to the tower with her feet and
wing claws. Back at the summit of the tower, Andry was
looking into her eyes, even though she was talking to Wensomer.

"Wensomer, marry prince, become princess," said Velander.

"Marry the filthy wretch?" cried Wensomer in outrage, in
spite of who and what she was addressing. "After what he
did to me?"

"Justiva will explain. In power, need one like you."

"But I despise rulers."

"Things you love, needing protecting."

"I'll not ever share a bed with him."

"Definitely, is true. Now go, marry prince."

With Wensomer gone, Andry had Velander to himself. He
was having some trouble adjusting to the fact that she was a
hundred and fifty feet long, and capable of flattening the
city if her mood soured, but he could nevertheless tell that it
was her.

"Is end for us, Andry," she rumbled sadly. "Not able to
stay, with you. Miral up, am this. Miral down, am normal
girl. Very soon, while Miral up, am hard on patience, of
yours."

"Not so, lass. We can find you a tower to perch on, or
something. There's a ruined one on the hill away to the north
of Alberin."

"Andry, cannot be. Too much power, in myself. Must live
with Teacher, Examiner, and Judge, learn control, wisdom,
all that. Dragonwall showed lesson, of when fools get too
much power. I have too much power, so . . . have much to

learn. To become dragon, takes sorcerers centuries. To become dragon, vampyre just kills dragon, drinks energies. Is what I did. Now much to learn. Take centuries."

"Can't we at least, well, visit each other?" suggested Andry.

"Is why I am here. Visit, I did. Saw you, walked street, holding hands. Kiss you, sleep with you, hear music you play in Lamplighter, was warm in your arms. Now is over, this visit."

"Maybe I could visit you?" pleaded Andry.

"You would? Looking forward to it, already I am."

"Where will you be?"

"Deep in Ridgeback Mountains, have new home. Perhaps, one year, waiting. Then visit."

"Can you stay here until you transform back into, well, a girl? Like, so we can have another day?"

"Is best not. Examiner, myself, fly away now. Is long journey, for mortal. If you cannot manage, I understand."

"I've journeyed to the edge of death, lass, and there I've asked the ferrygirl herself to spare you. What's a walk to a mountain?"

Andry reached out and ran his hand over the surface of the dragon's lips. Violet fire danced over his skin.

"Live well, my countess and my lass," he said.

"Live well, brave and gallant kavelar, of mine," rumbled softly from Velander's throat.

✳ ✳ ✳

Where the rogue glass dragon had been killed was the body of Wilbar.

"His name was Guard, and Talberan, and Wilbar, we have known about him for a long time," said Examiner. "His faction seems to have concentrated all the Scalticarian sorcerers in Alberin to destroy them as the SWS was destroyed. When he realized that the buildings that were to be annihilated were empty, he decided to go after them himself."

Wallas kicked the dead sorcerer as he walked past. "Lady Examiner, what about me?" he asked.

"What about you?"

"Can I please be made whole and normal? You know, be rid of Willy?"

"You don't like Willy?"

"No! Look, surely I have been punished enough, for, well, whatever the reason was to give me Willy?"

"It was not punishment, Wallas, it was concern for you. I have met many people of great talent over the millennia, and some have been like you. Your potential is enormous, but your drives are base. You need to be liberated from your drives, in order to reach your full potential."

"Turning me into a virtual eunuch is not liberating me!" snapped Wallas.

"You were not a nice person, you were an animal."

"I liked being an animal. I want to be whole again. Remember, without me, Wensomer would have died. Surely I am owed something for that?"

Examiner sighed, then put a hand to her throat and made a fist. As her fingers opened, Wallas noticed that a small sphere of blackness was on her palm. She held it out to him.

"Wensomer will tell you how to use this," said Examiner. "It can certainly restore you to what you were, if that is what you both want. However, Wallas, remember that I do like Wensomer, and I do not like you. I shall not have you hurting her, and if you are to be her consort I would prefer to know that your soul has changed for the better. Only she can make the choice on using this thing, but only you can apply it."

"Good enough for me," declared Wallas, accepting the sphere. "What do we do?"

"You need to press the sphere against your chest when you decide you want to change. Wensomer must read the, ah, warning label and instructions that I have included in the casting. Now I shall leave you, Wallas, and transform. I have to escort Velander away, once she finishes saying her farewells to Andry."

Examiner had gone by the time Wensomer emerged from the tower, and Wallas hurried up to her with the sphere of darkness on his palm.

"What do you make of this?" he asked, holding his hand out to her.

"An encased casting," she said at once. "I can do them too, but you would need a magnifier to see one of mine."

"Are they safe?"

"I have ways of telling," she said, speaking a minor casting that skittered over the dark surface. She held it up close to her face. *"What changes Wallas, What Wensomer wants, What restores Wallas.* Yes, this one will do the job, no trickery involved, you just speak the appropriate words and press it into your chest. Just checking the warnings . . . Goodness! Interfering old bat, but she does have a sense of humor." Suddenly Wensomer looked up at the sound of footsteps. "Ah, Justiva, I thought you were under arrest?"

Justiva was approaching with Selford, Parcher, and Miss Flez, who was holding a lantern. Selford and Parcher were carrying a large sack between them.

"Er, we just saw a little old lady transform into a dragon bigger than that one," said Parcher, pointing up at Velander, who was still entwined around the tower. "Before she transformed, she gave us this bundle."

As he was speaking, Velander slowly peeled away from the tower, twisted aside, then launched herself into the air, sending a swirl of dust and ash through the courtyard and fanning the small fires that were still burning. Moments later Examiner launched herself from behind the ruins of the hospitality wing. They vanished from sight for some moments, then reappeared together as two faintly glowing outlines flying west.

"For one horrible moment I thought they were going to apply for work permits and stay here," said Wensomer, looking to where Andry was waving from the top of the tower.

"Can we speak to you in private, ladyship?" asked Selford, glancing nervously at Wallas. "A matter of urgency, and all that?"

"Come into the throne hall, we can talk while I catch up on my share of the feast," declared Wensomer. "Wallas, wait here. When Andry comes down, send him in to see me."

"Andry?" exclaimed Wallas. "Why?"

"Well, I expect he will need some comforting tonight, now that Velander is gone. What say we have a little revel in the throne hall, when these folk are done with me? I'll practice being a princess, and Andry can play prince. That should revive his spirits."

"And what about me?" demanded Wallas indignantly. "Am I to be head eunuch?"

"Only if you're qualified," laughed Wensomer with a sly smile. "Ladies, gentlemen, shall we repair to the throne hall?"

Left by himself, Wallas quickly lost what little composure remained to him. He glared at the black sphere that rested in the palm of his hand, then glanced up at the tower's summit where Andry was still gazing after Velander.

"So, you are what changes Wallas, what Wensomer wants, and what restores Wallas," he said, holding it up to his eyes. "Why then does she not apply you straightaway?"

He looked back up at Andry.

"She wants a tumble with our pure and gallant young gentleman up there, before settling down to pure lust with me," he concluded. "Well, I'll not spend another night in Willy's company if I can help it. Casting, attend my instructions! I want what changes Wallas, what Wensomer wants, what restores Wallas."

At his words the casting shaded itself a light blue, and began to glow faintly.

"Yes!" hissed Wallas in triumph, who then looked around the firelit courtyard. There were benches where guardsmen sat while their horses were being fetched, and it was to one of these that Wallas now hurried. "Would not do if I fell down in a faint during the restoration, bloodied my nose, then had to compete for Wensomer's favors next to young, pure, and handsome Andry," he said to the casting as he sat down and removed his tunic. Without another word he slapped the casting into the center of his chest.

✳ ✳ ✳

Wensomer and her companions entered the throne hall, which was completely deserted. The lamps were burning brightly, however, and what remained of the feast was still laid out. Selecting a goblet of wine and a chicken leg, Wensomer walked up to the throne, sat down on it, and draped a leg over an armrest. She drained the goblet, then took a dainty bite from the chicken leg.

"I swear, it was Igonnier who suggested the torture with the pig—" began Selford, but he fell silent when Wensomer flung her goblet at him. Her aim was wide, and the goblet struck Parcher. He cringed, rubbing the top of his head.

"Look, er, we need to talk," said Justiva.

"Selford, I want another goblet of wine, and one of those platters of cutlets with the pine nuts and herbs," commanded Wensomer. Selford hastened to fetch them for her.

"There are certain matters of state," Justiva warned.

"I am going to have a certain pig turned into pork sausages," declared Wensomer. "Then I am going to host a revel with a very porcine theme. If the crown prince does not approve, I am going to be very, very angry."

"There should be no problem with that," said Selford. "In fact I'm sure the crown prince will be happy to agree to anything you say."

"Meet the crown prince," said Justiva, gesturing to Selford, Parcher, and Miss Flez.

Wensomer sat up and blinked. "But I met the crown prince five years ago. These are the royal minstrel, the royal accountant, and the royal tea lady."

"The crown prince choked on one of Miss Flez's chocolate strawberries, which was being juggled by Selford during one of Parcher's more boring financial briefings," said Justiva. "He has been dead five years. His embalmed and mummified body is in that sack."

Wensomer slowly stood up, descended the steps of the throne dais, selected a pitcher of wine from one of the tables, then returned to the throne. She draped her leg over the armrest again, then raised the pitcher of wine to her lips. After what seemed to be a considerable time to her audience of four, she lowered the pitcher to the other armrest.

"I think I can cope now," she announced. "Go on."

"That's all," said Justiva.

"But the prince was a well-known rake," Wensomer pointed out.

Selford cringed, raised his hand, and waggled his fingers.

"He was a master of disguise and espionage. His ears seemed to be everywhere."

"You would be surprised how many secret matters people discuss over tea," said Miss Flez, raising her hand also.

"And I suppose the mystery of how he was so dissipated, yet ran Alberin's finances so well, has been solved," said Wensomer, turning to Parcher.

"Well yes, but I do have a little glass of sherry before going to bed," Parcher admitted.

Wensomer pointed at the sack with a waggling finger. "So I have to marry that?" she asked. "The wedding night sounds like it will leave a lot to be desired."

"Oh no, you just marry him now, and we then take him to the tower and set him alight. We then claim he died defending you from the dragon—Wilbar, that is."

"He should burn well," said Miss Flez.

"I can do marriages," said Justiva.

"But why?" asked Wensomer.

"The façade is proving too hard to maintain," said Selford. "People are saying that the prince is under too much influence from his minstrel, accountant, and tea lady. Others want access to his, shall we say, real presence?"

"We can say that business with feeding delicacies to the pig was just a prenuptial prank, sort of like a stag party," added Parcher. "Were you to replace the prince, all our mutual problems would go away."

"Provided I cut back on the chocolate strawberries," concluded Wensomer. "Very well then, but keep it quick."

Parcher detached one of the prince's hands and carried it up to the throne. He held it out to Wensomer. Justiva cleared her throat.

"Wensomer Callientor, do you agree to marry the prince of Alberin?" she asked.

"Yes," said Wensomer, laying a finger on the mummified hand.

"Prince Dalzori, so you agree to marry Wensomer?"

"Yes," said Selford, Parcher, and Flez together.

"Then consider yourselves married."

Parcher and Selford hurried out of the throne hall with the sack, followed by Miss Flez with a jar of lamp oil.

"And if you see Guardsman Tennoner, tell him to come in here," called Wensomer after them before she drained the last of the wine from the terra-cotta pitcher. "Princess Wensomer," she muttered. "That sounds like some skinny, consumptive virgin who can't drink weak tea without swooning. Do you know how much I despise royalty, rank, and all that garbage that our taxes are wasted on? Is this not too absurd to contemplate?"

"No more absurd than a former harlot becoming the most senior surviving Metrologan in Scalticar," said Justiva, who was completing the paperwork for the marriage on one of the feasting tables.

A large black cat entered the throne hall by the double doors, then began the long walk down the richly patterned processional carpet leading to the throne. It caught Wensomer's attention at once, because cats very seldom walk in straight lines for any distance. It stopped at the lowest step of the throne dais and sat down, all the while with its gaze fixed on Wensomer.

"I thought you said Examiner's casting involved no trickery," said Wallas's voice.

The empty wine pitcher fell from Wensomer's fingers and smashed on the throne dais.

"Tell me that is not Wallas," said Justiva.

Wensomer got up, descended to the feasting tables again, selected another pitcher of wine and a saucer, then walked over to the throne dais and sat on the lowest step, beside the cat. After pouring a little wine into the saucer, she drank most of what was left in the pitcher.

"Once again, think I can . . . cope," said Wensomer. "Very well, Wallash, what did you do?"

"I just spoke the instructions, precisely as you said."

"How precisely?"

"I said 'I want what changes Wallas, what Wensomer wants, what restores Wallas.' "

Wensomer put the pitcher down, rested her elbows on her knees and her chin on her hands, then looked down at Wallas.

"They were three *alternativeshs*, you clown, not one inshtruction," she said very slowly and precisely. "First . . . leaves you with Willy. Second, gives you . . . functional entertainment organ, with your current—well, recent fit and muschcular body. Third, er, you become Wallash as when she cast Willy on you, originat—er, origan—I mean originally. Documentation said . . . fatter, blistered feet, burned fingers . . . can't remember rest. All three together . . . changed you, restored you, gave me . . . what I wanted."

"You wanted a cat?" exclaimed Wallas.

"My dear and beloved cat died . . . few months ago," sniffled Wensomer. "Pussington . . . Oh Pussington, how I miss you."

Tears began to run down Wensomer's cheeks.

"He died of sclerosis of the liver," said Justiva, looking back at her paperwork. "Five hundred people were invited to the wake. Each had to be dressed only in furry black underwear, and be accompanied by a cat."

Wensomer began to snore, still propped up on her elbows. Wallas shook his head, settled down, and began to lap at his saucer of wine.

As Andry descended the still warm stone stairs of the tower, he noticed a smell rather like that of burning leather and cloth. He reached the base of the tower, to find Selford, Parcher, and Miss Flez sitting around what seemed to be a pile of burning rubbish in the flame-scoured shell of Wensomer's former prison.

"Lovely night for it," said Selford awkwardly.

"Reminds me of my days in the Young Men's Warrior Association camps," said Parcher.

"You're wanted in the throne hall," said Miss Flez.

Andry walked out into the courtyard, stepped over Wilbar's body, and entered the throne hall. There he found Justiva packing up some papers and scrolls, and Wensomer asleep on the steps of the throne dais. A large black cat looked up from a saucer and belched at him.

"Kindly get Princess Wensomer up over your shoulders and carry her to the royal bedchamber," said Justiva.

"*Princess* Wensomer?" exclaimed Andry. "Already?"

"Yes. The prince married Wensomer, then the dragon killed the prince."

"The prince is dead?"

"Yes. Long live the princess."

Madame Yvendel stood on the pier beside her ship, staring at Lavenci, her hands on her hips. Before speaking she leaned forward and sniffed the academician's breath, but had to conclude that she had not been drinking.

"So Wensomer's mansion has been destroyed, but Wensomer is now princess of the city?" she said, not entirely able to comprehend what she had just heard.

"It all happened last night, while we were at sea," explained the albino academician.

"So, after all that time at sea, coming to Alberin is almost as much of a disaster as staying in Diomeda."

"But she is your daughter, she will not harm us."

"Maybe not, but she is liable to make belly dancing compulsory on my syllabus, along with advanced indulgence, basic sloth, lust at honors level, and a thesis on hangover cures. Lavenci, Madame Yvendel's Academy is about to become Madame Yvendel's Secret Academy."

Madame Jilli held her pole in one hand while beckoning to the terrified spirit with the other.

"Come to the boat, Wilbar, Talberan, Guard, or whatever you want to call yourself."

"No way, these others told me what you're liable to do."

"After what you tried to do to my friends? I shall do a lot more than they have seen me do. Come on, you can't stay there on the edge of the river of the afterlife forever."

"I can give it a pretty good try. Your contract will not last forever."

"No? That nice deity Change is very happy with my work, but suit yourself. There is only one way across, and I am the only transport. Who was next?"

Over the next few weeks the citizens and rulers went to considerable lengths to restore something resembling normality to Alberin. Reports began to arrive of cities burned or at least severely damaged, and of craters a half mile across where the ringstones had stood. Dragonwall's location was marked by a trench a hundred feet across and thirty feet deep that extended in a north-south line right across Scalticar, Alberin, and Lemtas.

The empire of North Scalticar had ceased to exist. The capital had been partly destroyed, along with the army and most of the larger fortresses. Wensomer was quite surprised when she realized that Alberin and its lands had sustained only three minor hits from Dragonwall, and were thus almost intact compared with other realms. She was even more surprised when the newly crowned or surviving rulers of much of Scalticar began to arrive in Alberin. Wensomer discovered that she was the host of the Assembly of Scalticarian Monarchs, by virtue of the fact that her city was more or less intact, and because she still had a palace in which to host the conference.

At the top of the agenda was the Treaty for the Elimination of Sorcery for the Public Good. Sorcerers were, of course, blamed for all that Dragonwall had done, and were not in favor with many people. The Sorceric Inquisition was established, with Wensomer as the inquisitor-general. People proved to be guilty of practicing sorcery were to be punished by the laws of the kingdom where they were caught, and these varied from being burned at the stake to being locked in a dungeon with one's teeth wired together. There was the small problem that two-thirds of the monarchs had sorceric training to the eighth or ninth level, however, and Wensomer was initiated to twelve and qualified for thirteen. Thus it was also decreed that senior sorceric inquisitors were required to have some background in sorceric studies, so that they could identify other sorcerers.

Next, the Cooperative Empire of Scalticar was established, encompassing those areas of Scalticar that were not under more than half a mile of polar ice. Wensomer found herself empress of the new state. After getting over the shock, she ordered a truly memorable revel for the new leaders of the continent's client kingdoms. She was quite specific that it should be organized by Selford, Parcher, and Miss Flez.

Andry was shivering with apprehension as he was shown into the presence of the empress by two guards of the inner chamber. Wensomer was lying on a cushion the size of a large bed, eating raw honeycombs and drinking some quite expensive wine from the bottle as she read a sheaf of papers. She looked up to see Andry standing rigidly to attention and staring straight ahead.

"Stop that, Andry, it's only me," she ordered, then she looked back down at her papers. "You once carried me to bed, after all."

"Your Majesty, I swear on my honor that I took no liberties with you," babbled Andry.

"I was afraid you would say that. Guardsman Tennoner, this has been the worst day of my life."

"Very good, Your Majesty," replied Andry, trying to restore some formality to his voice.

"With the possible exception of the day that I destroyed Silverdeath," continued Wensomer, "but that was at night, so it does not count. The most powerful surviving sorceress in the world, and I am put in charge of the Sorceric Inquisition."

"A sad conflict of interests, Your Majesty."

"And made empress. All I wanted was to be left alone to read interesting magical texts, refine my casting skills, eat and drink in the manner to which I am accustomed, have the occasional affair as the whim took me, and throw the occasional dinner party for which dress is optional. And that reminds me," she said, reaching behind her and lifting a large and rather overweight cat from behind the pile of smaller cushions that she was propped up against. "Down to the kitchens, you lazy wretch, and have the staff prepare a lavish dinner for one."

She dropped the cat over the edge of her cushion. It looked up at Andry, then padded over to the door.

"Would you mind opening for me, Andry?" it asked in a familiar voice with a Sargolan accent. "She refuses to have a cat flap installed."

"Tell me you're not Wallas," whispered Andry, once he had recovered his breath.

"My mother taught me never to lie to men in uniform," replied the cat. "Now about this door?"

Andry opened the door, and the cat sauntered through.

"But, but . . . how?"

"Come down to the kitchen when you're off duty, we can catch up about the months past over a saucer of ale."

Andry closed the door behind the cat. Wensomer looked up from her paperwork again.

"All my life I have despised and ridiculed people in authority," muttered Wensomer, "so what does Fate do to me? Empress of fifty million people and an entire continent. Enough of my problems, however. I am forming an elite secret constabulary, in my capacity as inquisitor-general. Examiner recommended that you be a member."

"She did—Your Majesty?"

"Yes. Your job will be to rescue sorcerers from constables of the Sorceric Inquisition."

"You are forming a squad of constables to frustrate the work of your own constables?" asked Andry, scratching his head.

"Bright boy, Tennoner, I like your style. Sorcerers are necessary, but they need to feel guilty and nervous about being sorcerers or they get ideas about running the place. I don't like sorcerers with ideas . . . except for myself, that is. You will need Special Warrior Service training, and I happen to know that the only surviving SWS instructor in the world is in Alberin. His name is Roval, he was asleep under a table in the Lamplighter when the SWS fortress was razed."

"Roval, as in Lady Terikel's Roval?" asked Andry, the pit of his stomach suddenly freezing solid.

"You know each other?"

"Yes, yes, I, er, play in the Lamplighter. He still drinks there. I have little to do with him, though."

"I'm not surprised, Wallas told me about you and Terikel—don't worry, however, your secret is safe. I put a contraction-ring casting around Wallas's testicles, keyed to that subject matter. Should he ever speak of it again, the ring will shrink to the diameter of a pinhead, with profoundly distressing consequences for Wallas."

"Er, ah, my thanks."

"Now, returning to Roval, the man is very dear to me. He was once my warrior escort, and we were even lovers for one night—although that turned into the greatest shambles since my rooftop underwear party for the midwinter solstice. Roval has been a broken man since Terikel left him, he needs to be given a sense of purpose again. Sober him up and ask if he wants to join the Secret Constables."

"Very good, Your Majesty. Any others?"

"The girl that you rescued in Clovesser, Riellen. You obviously know her."

"But she is currently under arrest for treason, Your Majesty."

" 'Arrest'-is such a strong word. More of a guest, I would say, for being a hero of the empire. After all, she stormed into the hostelry shouting revolutionary slogans and led all the sorcery students down to the dungeons to liberate the dissident sorcerers just minutes before a glass dragon flamed the place. Of course, the dungeon guards arrested them all, but the students remained alive, which was the whole point, one supposes. Arrange for her to escape. Give this bribe to the duty marshal of the dungeons, and if it costs any more send Parcher an invoice."

"Ah, how many others are in the Secret Constables, Your Majesty?"

"So far, three . . . but I suppose you will need at least double that number. Any suggestions?"

"I shall make inquiries."

"Splendid. Wallas shall be your liaison with me from now on."

"But I am a Palace Company guard. Surely face-to-face meetings are easier."

"Not in your case, Andry, you must now distance yourself from me. You are about to get drunk on duty, and bring disgrace upon the Palace Company." Wensomer tossed him her bottle of wine. "I'd like to add a charge of undue familiarity with the empress, but I suspect that you have all those silly ideals about faithfulness to Velander or Terikel, or whoever you true love might truly be. Once you are dishonorably ejected from the palace, go to the Wayfarer Constables, they have orders to recruit you. Now finish that bottle, get out of here, free Riellen, then get yourself noticed being drunk."

Once Andry was gone, Laron entered.

"That was a good plan, Laron, thank you," said Wensomer without looking up. "I like to keep competing interests competing, especially rulers and sorcerers. It weakens them very effectively. We make a good team. Are you sure you would not like to be my consort as well as my advisor?"

"I think our relationship needs to be kept professional, Your Majesty," Laron replied.

"So, snubbed again. You seem a lot happier, of late. Met some girl, have you?"

"Not so, Your Majesty."

"Then what?"

"I . . . am seven centuries old, but I look fifteen. As your advisor, I can speak as a wise old man, in fact I can *be* an old man, hiding in the shadows, helping to run quite a large empire. At last I am being allowed to live as if I am old and wise. Being young and wise is no fun at all."

"Andry is young and wise."

"No, he is young and learning. Oh he is truly remarkable, though. I mean who else has traveled to the River of the Afterlife and given a concert for the ferrygirl, just to give his sweetheart another chance at life? All the while he secretly loved someone else, too. He rescued Velander because it was the right thing to do, not because he could not go on without her. Andry sees colors, not just black and white, and he tolerates a lot from others. That is his strength, and in that way he is just like you."

"Indeed? Should I put him on my guest list, then?"

"No, I am just saying that he is good ruler material, just as you are a good empress."

The following night the reccons met with Andry in the Lamplighter to commiserate with him for being thrown out of the Palace Guard. Riellen was there also, dressed as a boy. Andry and Riellen took Essen aside to a corner table while the other reccons were joining in the singing, and the plan for the Secret Inquisition Constables was outlined.

"So we are to be paid by the inquisition to rescue sorcerers from the inquisition?" asked Essen, his hands clasped over his head.

"Aye," replied Andry.

"And sorceresses," added Riellen.

"But we are to be employed by the Wayfarer Constables."

"That we are."

"And our liaison with the inquisition is a cat that used to be Wallas?"

"I'm still Wallas," said a voice from beneath the table, "and could I have another saucer of wine? The 3138 chardonelle from Waterglen."

"Well, it seems a worthy cause, lad," said Essen. "Who is to be leader?"

"You are, sir," replied Andry.

"We should have a vote," Riellen pointed out.

"All in favor of Essen as leader?" asked Andry, raising his hand. Riellen frowned, then raised her hand as well. A meow came from beneath the table. "Those against? Essen, you are marshal of the Secret Inquisition Constables by two votes, a meow, and one abstention. Congratulations."

"What about the other reccons?" asked Riellen.

"Oh, I'll not tell them," said Essen, putting a finger to his lips.

"You don't understand, we want to recruit them as well," explained Andry.

Within a half hour the ranks of the Secret Inquisition Constables had grown to six people and one cat. In their first meeting it was decided that Danol would be Riellen's mentor and that Roval was probably not yet quite reliable enough to be a member of the squad, but that he could be employed to teach them the skills of the Special Warrior Service, while gradually being weaned away from the drink. He was then invited over to their table, bought a large tankard of amber, and given what sounded like a harmless proposal.

"So if you teach us the ways of the SWS, Roval, the service need not die out," concluded Essen.

"We're all military men," added Andry, who then kicked Riellen under the table as she began to open her mouth. "You need only refine what skills we already have."

"Mussen . . . work for wrong people," said Roval emphatically.

"Our secret sponsor is the new empress," explained Andry.

"Wensy? Lovely girl, but bites a bit hard."

Roval put a hand to his shoulder, Andry put a hand to his eyes, the reccons looked startled, and Riellen looked puzzled.

"What is your word, then?" asked Essen presently.

"Could use the silver," mumbled Roval. "Circumstances . . . reduced."

"We understand," said Essen.

"Brought low by a woman."

"Happens to the best of us," replied Andry, with a preemptive kick at Riellen's shin.

"Betrayed me, left me," said Roval.

"Have another drink," said Costiger.

"Turned me into a laughingstock."

"Better a laughingstock than a cat," said a voice beneath the table.

✵ ✵ ✵

Justiva and her Metrologans were priestesses of the cold sciences, so that they and the surviving Skepticals were now highly valued as teaching scholars in the new, post-Dragonwall world. Although they were given new premises to establish an academy, Justiva petitioned Wensomer for the Metrologan temple to be rebuilt to symbolize the revival of scholarship in the empire. Within four months the site had been cleared, the foundations dug, and the columns erected to support the roof. Justiva often spent her nights on the darkened building site, meditating. This was a personal act of defiance, because she was making sure that the temple never fell out of use, even though it had been destroyed and was now being rebuilt.

The little dragon arrived not long after midnight, dropping quietly out of a clear, dark sky and landing on the edge of the temple's roof frame. Justiva watched as it surveyed the building site. It had obviously come there in search of the Metrologans, and she was a Metrologan. She cleared her throat.

"Can I help you?" she called. "I am the Elder of the Metrologans."

The dragon looked down warily, then folded its wings back. They still towered at least a hundred feet into the air, but its body was quite surprisingly small. It was, in fact, only the size of a person.

"Can you climb the scaffolding?" asked the dragon in a muffled but velvety voice. "I am too encumbered to descend."

Justiva climbed a ladder to the stone beam that capped the columns and sat before the dragon. Now she could see that it was probably a sorcerer in a very advanced airwalking casting. It had a breastbone keel like a bird, to enable it to beat its wings. What looked like a beak from a distance was a streamlined mask and steering crest.

"So, the Metrologans survived Dragonwall?" the dragon asked after an awkward silence.

"Yes. The temple was attacked, but we lost not a person nor a book. Now we are rebuilding. Do you have business with us?"

"In a way. I was once a priestess. I have come to renounce my vows."

"Terikel?" gasped Justiva.

"I have another name now. I kept the wings too long, and now I cannot give them up."

"You mean you are trapped?"

"Not so. I discovered that I like floating five miles above the ground. I can live there happily, contemplating the patterns in the stars and the textures of the land below. I am happiest when I am up there. My teachers call me Feather-wings, and I give my wings feathery tips and trailing edges, it's vanity, really, but we dragons are very vain. Perhaps there will come a time when I need never come down."

"Terikel, about Roval," began Justiva.

"There is no excuse for what I did," declared Terikel. "I have learned that I can never be a very good person, so I am ceasing to be a person."

"I am trying to ask for forgiveness, Terikel. I betrayed you to Roval, I was disgusted by what you did, but—but it was not my place to judge you. I—I told him what you were doing on your last night in Alberin. What more can I say? It broke his spirit, it made the other Metrologans hate you, yet it achieved nothing. I am a monster."

"I am the only monster here, Justiva. Do you accept the renunciation of my vows?"

"I suppose so. Until just now, everyone thought you to be dead. Andry and Wallas said you fell over a precipice."

"Best to leave me dead. I was not a nice person, and I am best away from all those I might hurt."

"But do you not miss those things that once made you like the rest of us? Can you live without the taste of wine and fine food, the touch of a lover?"

"Yes. And when did you last experience wine, fine food, or the touch of a lover?"

The question took Justiva by surprise. Terikel was lost to her, yet Terikel was happy. Could she wish anything better for her friends than happiness, she wondered. Terikel looked up, and Justiva followed her gaze. Justiva saw nothing, but Terikel began to spread her wings.

"My mentor will be getting anxious," said Terikel. "Time to go."

"Wait, please!" exclaimed Justiva. "Will you forgive me for—for Roval, and all that?"

"You may have my forgiveness, but you need your own forgiveness even more. I could never forgive myself, so now I flee from myself. One day, you may have to do the same. Goodbye."

Terikel leaped without waiting for another word from Justiva. The elevation of the temple roof and a single beat of her wings took her banking out over Wharfside, and she was quickly lost to Justiva's view. There was a soft creak from below as someone began to climb the scaffolding ladder. Lavenci presently joined Justiva on the stone beam.

"You were with a glass dragon," said the albino uneasily, putting a hand to her shoulder.

" 'Dragon' is such a strong word," replied Justiva.

"Then what?"

"It was a ghost, come to say goodbye."

EPILOGUE

Madame Karracel's Exclusive and Intimate Services was as good a front as any for Madame Yvendel's Secret Academy of Applied Sorceric Arts. Young men and women were seen entering and leaving at odd hours, looking furtive, and many genuine customers for exclusive and intimate services were turned away at the door, with the explanation that entry was by invitation only.

Lavenci tended to stand out rather too well for a member of a secret, underground organization. She was a tall, angular albino, with hair at least as long as Wensomer's and wide lips that she insisted on painting bright crimson. Being a senior academician, she was also an important member of the selection panel for Madame Yvendel's academy, and this involved traveling outside the academy to scores of secret rendezvous houses across Acrema. Here she would assess potential students of sorcery for latent talent, before the long series of security checks for admission was begun. It was dangerous, uncertain work, as the Inquisition Constables were aware that sorcerers were not only hiding in Acrema, but teaching as well.

The night had not been a success for Lavenci. The candidate student had negligible sorceric talent, and somehow lacked a foundation of interest in the arts of castings, darkwalking, charmshaping, and arcane knowledge in general. Sensing a setup, Lavenci cut the interview short, climbed out of the rooming house through a window, negotiated a path across several rooftops, and dropped to the street. Looking back to the rooming house, she noted that armed men with torches had blockaded the entrance, and that a team of guardsmen was getting a chain-mesh castings net ready. Whoever had organized the raid knew that their quarry had sorceric powers.

The sorceress hurried away, relieved to have escaped, but alarmed that the Inquisition Constables had come so close to

catching her. Her path across the city was something of a
sawtooth pattern in the direction of Neverside. In many
ways, Neverside was the logical place for a sorceric academy. So much suspect activity went on there that it seemed
the natural place for anyone living outside the law to base
themselves. Madame Yvendel did indeed have a type of
academy there, but it was more of a largish house with some
three dozen secret entrances and bolt-holes. It was in fact a
switching station for sorcerers to evade pursuers, and little
else. Some of the passageways extended as much as a quarter of a mile from the house, through tunnels and drains, and
over roofs. The house was leased to dealers in stolen property, who ran it as a warehouse and market, ignored the sorcerers who occasionally passed through, and killed any
intruders who looked as if they worked for the guards, constables, or militias.

Lavenci's mistake was to let her near-escape panic her into
making for the nearest entrance to the house. She strode con-
fidently along a street lit only by Miral's light, turned into a
laneway, and counted thirty steps in the gloom before reaching out to the right. As she expected, the door was there, along
with the keyhole. Her key turned in the lock—but Lavenci
could not push the door open! A chain-mesh castings net was
dropped onto her from above, and she was immediately set
upon by several strong men with chain mail under their clothing. Before she could speak a fire casting, a gag was stuffed
into her mouth and tied in place as she was held down in the
darkness. Someone uncovered a lantern on a pole.

"Inquisition Constables, you are under arrest," declared a
voice from beneath a hood.

Lavenci saw that boards had been screwed to the top and
base of the door, and that nine masked figures in black were
in the lane with her.

"I believe you are a sorceric academician," said one of the
men standing over her. "That is good, there is a lot we wish
to learn from you."

He kicked her in the ribs, and a bright flash of pain con-
torted her body. Lavenci gave a muffled squeal through the
gag, and the pain of her next breath announced to her that a
rib had been broken.

"That is our form of payment, and you will find that we pay very generously."

He delivered another kick to her ribs, and Lavenci managed a squeal that trailed into a hopeless moan. From somewhere nearby there was the crash-tinkle of a bottle being smashed.

"Thas terrible, somethin' ought to be done about likes o' you!" called a voice from the entrance to the laneway.

"What in all hell's levels—" began Lavenci's tormentor, but half a brick sailed out of the darkness, encountered his head, and cut him off. He fell against the lamp on the pole, knocking it against one of those holding Lavenci down, spilling oil over him, and setting him afire. By now the drunken Alberinese had engaged the other Inquisition Constables, and in the confusion Lavenci broke free and dashed for the laneway's entrance, ripping the gag away as she ran. She crashed straight into another group of men, and again found herself surrounded.

"Are you all right, miss?" asked someone in an educated voice.

"We're friends, ladyship," rumbled a considerably larger figure in front of her.

"That man, you have to help him!" exclaimed Lavenci, ignoring the burning slash of pain in her side and hoping that they really were friends. "That scruffy drunk, he's just gone against nine Inquisition Constables with a beer bottle."

"His weapon of choice, ladyship," said the big man.

For Lavenci, the world suddenly ceased to make any sort of sense. Thuds, thumps, and rather sickening-sounding whacks came out of the lane, along with moans and cries of pain.

"What is, er . . ." she managed at last.

"He will try not to hurt them too much, miss," said the educated voice.

"But, but, but . . . one against nine?" insisted Lavenci.

"Secret Inquisition Constable, miss, he's one of our best men."

"Secret Inquisition Constable?" asked Lavenci.

"Yes, miss."

"As opposed to Inquisition Constables?"

"Oh no miss, we are nothing to do with those horrid people."

Lavenci noticed that the laneway had suddenly gone quiet. Her thin, scruffy rescuer emerged, tossed his broken beer bottle aside, removed a tuft of hair from the toe of his boot, then straightened his clothing and bowed to her.

"Had to drop a couple of bodies over the burning churl, smother the flames," he announced. "Sorry for the delay, miss."

"Told yer he was humane," said the large man. "Never killed anyone, that lad."

"We shall see you back to Madame Yvendel's," said the educated youth.

"Madame Yvendel's—no! I mean, I don't know anything about Madame Yvendel's, er, house."

"Neither do we, miss. Come along."

Lavenci suddenly noticed that her escort had dwindled to three.

"Best to hold hands with Danolarian," said the one who seemed to be in charge. "If you look to be hurried, you look suspicious. This way we're just a lad, his lass, and their tagalongs off to the tavern."

There was a shriek of pain somewhere behind them.

"Must have been another inquisition churl trailing you, miss," said Danol, giving her hand a coy squeeze.

They took a ferry across the River Alber, and were soon in the Lamplighter, where the Secret Inquisition Constables known as Essen and Andry were given their hornpipe and rebec from behind the serving board by the tapman. When they began playing a reel, the young and charming Danol bowed to Lavenci and asked if she wished to dance. There was pain like a white-hot poker being dragged across her ribs as Lavenci brought her arm up to Danol's outstretched hand, but the sorceress gritted her teeth and turned her grimace into a smile as she stood up. They began to dance. Later, as she and Danol sat resting, Lavenci pointed to Andry. He was playing a lament on his rebec.

"Just who is that young man?" she asked. "Is he some kavelar or noble in disguise? He can fight like an epic ballad's hero, play the most enchanting music, and, well, his manners are somehow so charming. He can't really be a commoner, can he?"

"He's just a lad," replied Danol. "Had two lasses, but lost them both after a single night with each. Now he keeps his heart to himself. He says that he carries a curse that hurts anyone inclined to be his sweetheart."

Andry and Essen began playing another bracket of dance tunes, and this time it was Lavenci who invited Danol to dance. *I would not give up this night, this tavern, and these gentlemen for the throne of Empress Wensomer herself*, thought Lavenci as the drinkers banged their tankards or clapped to the beat, and the musicians played the reel "Ladies of Alberin."